FOUND

Castle Coven Book One

By Hazel Hunter

FOUND
Castle Coven Book One

Though novice witch Hailey Devereaux seems to have settled into her latest coven, she knows that it can't last. Tucked against the remote Alps of northern Italy, the Angioli coven is ill at ease with their newest member. Whispers and fearful glances follow her everywhere.

But the arrival of a Magus Corps major ends all that. Kieran McCallen isn't afraid of her singular ability. Instead he's been sent to nurture and test it. Though Hailey's waif-like and delicate beauty are charming, her power is the stuff of legend.

Each loners in their own way, Kieran glimpses Hailey's fiercely protective spirit when it comes to friends. For her part, Hailey dares to hope that she's found the person and place meant for her. But their bond is put to the test by danger and by duty, forcing each of them to impossible choices.

CHAPTER ONE

THOUGH THE COMMON halls of the Angioli coven's holding were tall and vaulted, as befit the medieval monastery it had once been, most of the private rooms were dark and small. Even the abbot's quarters were dim in the midday light. Though the monastery had been wired for electricity a generation ago, Donato Angioli kept the light low.

Today, though, the coven master could wish that he had chosen differently.

In the shadows of his personal chambers, the man who stood in front of him looked primitive, almost savage. He was tall, and there was a powerful bulk to him that made the coven master think of bears and wolves, the powerful beasts that ruled the Alps and paid no attention to the dominion of this lord or that country.

Donato was seated behind his desk, and the man stood in front of it. By any measure, the man was a supplicant. He had come to ask for a favor. Donato himself held the rank of coven master. He was a powerful warlock who had survived for almost three hundred years. He had many allies and contacts from all over the world. But he knew with painstaking clarity that mattered little in this situation. The man's deferential posture was a courtesy. It rankled, and Donato frowned.

"You are being deliberately vague in your request," Donato said at last.

The shadowed man shrugged.

"I have been perfectly clear. The Magus Corps is interested in Hailey Devereaux's skills, and I am here to evaluate them."

"The Magus Corps plays the long game, and that tells me nothing," snapped Donato.

His nerves were fraying, and he knew it. The Magus Corps had a long reach and longer claws. Having a Magus Corps major in his coven made him nervous.

"It may be as you say, but my orders are clear. I am here to evaluate her. What comes next is not something I am prepared to discuss with you."

The dismissal was implied but pointed. Donato's lips sheered back from his teeth. A shower of sparks sputtered and danced around his fingertips. Though he knew what a very bad idea it was to do battle with a major of the Magus Corps, he was tempted to it anyway. He had ruled the Angioli coven for generations, and he had not done it by allowing insolence.

The man in front of him did nothing. He did not acknowledge the coven master's threat with word or motion, but suddenly, the window at Donato's elbow blew in, carrying with it a breath of alpine air that was colder than it should have been. Donato hissed at the chill and then watched as a thin blade of ice formed in front of his eyes.

It was as narrow as a pencil, but wickedly sharp at the tip. It danced through the air, weaving patterns just inches away from Donato's face. The threat was clear, and the coven master dropped his hand.

"What, pray tell, does evaluating her involve?" Donato asked stiffly. "She is under my care."

The man inclined his head, the ice blade melting to nothing.

"Nothing that will harm her. Nothing that will harm any members of your coven. I swear it on the iron pentacle that I wear. But my orders are precise and, coven master, I am the will of the Magus Corps. We will not be denied."

The words were uttered softly but with an edge of menace like distant thunder. Donato swallowed twice and nodded.

"You will have my full cooperation, of course," he said stiffly. "Shall I summon Miss Devereaux to us for this test?"

For the first time, the man hesitated. Then he shook his head.

"No. I will go find her myself."

Donato allowed himself a small smile.

"Then the best of luck to you, Major. I wish you joy of her."

• • • • •

When Hailey had first learned that she was being sent to Italy to hone her powers, her head had been full of visions of Rome, of sun-kissed vineyards and of a beautiful Mediterranean country lush with beauty. She had not pictured the snowy reaches of the Amato Valley, one of the northernmost and remote of Italy's provinces. She had not pictured seeing her breath more than twenty days out of thirty, and she had not imagined the only village being a good two hours' hike down the hill. The plains of Italy rolled straight into the foothills of the Alps, and even in the summer, there was a bite of cold to the air.

Despite the persistent chill that left her feeling eternally a little tired, there was a certain beauty to the Angioli coven's stronghold. It had been a monastery once upon a time, but the Italian coven had taken it over centuries ago.

As she walked the long road down to the village, in her hoodie, jeans and boots, Hailey looked even younger than she was. She knew that technically she should have been at her books, but that morning she had pulled down the ancient treatise she had been translating and made an important realization.

If I have to sit here and translate with the twittering of the other coven members in my ears, I do believe that I shall scream.

The thought appeared bright and fully formed in her mind. Just then, she heard a twitter of hushed giggles behind her. Turning around, she could see Letizia and Francesca watching her over their books. In that moment she had realized that she'd been completely and utterly right.

She had sighed, stretched, and leaving her books where they lay, she'd made as if she was going to go to the bathroom. Instead she'd taken a quick detour that was now turning into a hike down the mountain. She smiled to leave her coven mates behind.

The day was crisp and cool. Though the temperatures would drop like a rock when night fell, right now there was sun on her face, and she walked with a bounce in her step. With her red hair, short stature and slender build, she looked like she should have been in the Scottish highlands rather than the Italian mountains. She smiled up at the clear blue sky, and her smile got even wider when she heard her name whispered close by.

She paused, looking around, but she was unsurprised that she couldn't see anyone.

"Beatrice, come out," she said, trying and failing to hide a smile. "You know you're not supposed to leave the coven grounds without permission."

One moment, it looked like she was alone on the narrow track, and the next, there was a grinning teen with long, curling black hair hanging down her back. Even at the age of sixteen, Beatrice was taller than Hailey and curvier besides, something the teen loved to point out when they bickered.

"Who's to say that I didn't get permission? Perhaps I am out running an errand for Donato."

Hailey crossed her arms over her chest and raised an eyebrow.

"I find that fairly unlikely. Donato takes your education seriously. I doubt he would let you out of your tutoring today simply to go down to the village. What did you do to your tutor?"

Beatrice waved her hand airily.

"Nothing, nothing," she said, and when Hailey continued to look unimpressed, she rolled her eyes.

"Fine, he believes that I am studiously working on my mathematics. I asked Luca to project an image of me in the study."

"Beatrice, he's only ten!" Hailey cried, slightly scandalized.

"So it only cost me a handful of candy and my old comics to do the deed, yes? Besides, I know all of that already. He will find no fault in me when the time comes to test my knowledge."

Beatrice tossed her hair and walked down the path ahead of Hailey, all leggy grace and adolescent pride.

Hailey wondered what it would have been like to be born into the Wiccan world rather than being born a magic worker to non-magical parents. Beatrice and Luca were among the handful of children and teens studying at Angioli who had been born to witches and warlocks. They had known their entire lives that they had special powers. Unlike Hailey's, which had awakened when she lost her virginity, the powers of Wiccan-born witches and warlocks appeared when they were still children.

Still, no one could say that Wiccan children had it easy. Beatrice's parents had been killed years ago in a Templar raid. The girl sometimes still woke up screaming from the memories of that night. When she remembered that, Hailey's heart softened, and she would let Beatrice get away with far more than she should have.

Still, it was a beautiful day, and if she had been tempted to sneak out and avoid her own work, she could hardly be self-righteous about Beatrice wanting to do the same. She hurried to catch up with her friend, threading her arm through Beatrice's and walking with her.

"All right, but we're going to make this quick, okay? It's probably not good for Luca to keep up a spell like that too long. No matter how good you are at mathematics, you still need to put in the work."

"Just like you need to study the works of the ancients, yes?" asked Beatrice slyly.

Hailey shook her head.

"Latin makes my head spin, and frankly, I wasn't feeling all that welcome in the library today."

Beatrice's cheerful grin turned into a storm cloud in an instant, and she took Hailey's hand, holding it tightly.

"Who was it this time? What did they say?"

Hailey shook her head, feeling tired of the whole mess.

"They didn't say anything, Bea, they never do. They're probably too smart for that. It's loads better than when I first came here though."

Beatrice relaxed, but her look was still stormy.

"Ah, because it is so much better to be mocked and reviled than it is to be feared. I see."

"You're overstating. No one was mocking or reviling me."

Not that it hadn't almost come to that on occasion, Hailey thought. But that wasn't something Beatrice needed to know.

"It's terrible. We heard of you coming here, and right away there were people who protested. In the old days, some said, you would never have a coven to call your own. Covens would refuse to take people like you. Francesca was so frightened she told everyone she would never even let you cross her path."

The pang was an old one, but it was still there, and Hailey

shrugged.

"That's not new. They said the same thing when I went to the coven in Canada, and to the one in Buenos Aires before that."

"Oh yes, they are so wise," Beatrice scoffed. "And then you came, and look, all you wanted to do was study our books and peer at our old scrolls. What a monster!"

Hailey had to laugh at her friend's offense. Beatrice's skill was to make herself unseen. It always struck Hailey as a strange gift for a young woman who thrived on making her opinions, wishes and thoughts known in the most obvious way.

"Yes, I am a monster," Hailey agreed. "Roar, I'm coming to eat your babies and to throw your maidens off the high cliffs!"

Beatrice frowned and started to say something, but she yelped instead when Hailey lunged for her, pushing her into the soft grass at the side of the road. With an offended yowl, the teenager fought her friend off, and stood a few steps away, smoothing down her long dark skirt with a fussy catlike expression.

"You are no monster," she said sternly. "The people who laugh at you now are the same ones who were wetting themselves with terror just a few months ago. They simply do not like being reminded that they were afraid for so little reason."

Hailey laughed ruefully.

"I wish everyone saw what you did. Come on, I'm sorry I ruffled your clothing. Let's walk a little faster. It's going to get colder the longer we dawdle."

For a little while, they walked in silence, but then Beatrice glanced at her friend again.

"There is something going on, though," she said thoughtfully, and Hailey regarded her warily.

"What doors have you been listening at?" she asked. "You're lucky they haven't caught you yet."

"They will never catch me," said Beatrice with a smile. "I am far too clever. And I've not been listening at doors. I've been watching. Have you noticed how angry Donato looks? Have you noticed how the elders of the coven are rustling like old books?"

Hailey paused, biting her lip. Despite Beatrice's flair for the dramatic, the younger witch wasn't wrong. There was something going on in the Angioli coven, and though she knew that she hadn't been doing anything wrong, that had never stopped bad things from happening before.

She wondered if the coven had simply become tired or too stressed from her presence. This had happened before, and then it was only a matter of time before she was told that she had to be taken to a new place. There were excuses for it, and plenty of explanations. It was often explained as the best option for everyone concerned.

Hailey had grown up in the United States foster care system, however, and she was familiar enough with that speech that it stopped stinging. Mostly.

"No one's told me anything about it," she said firmly. "Until someone makes it my business, I don't have to worry."

Beatrice looked monumentally unsatisfied with this, but she shrugged, linking arms with Hailey again. Below them, the red roofs of the village could be seen. It was nearly as ancient as the monastery above, but Hailey knew that the village had modernized in many ways. It was a lovely place, and in the warmer months, it always hosted at least a few tourists who were charmed by its beauty. Most of the villagers simply assumed that the people who lived at the old monastery were members of a communal farm. The coven members were considered perhaps a little radical, but pleasant overall. The village had several stores, ranging from the bakery to the butcher's, but what drew Hailey was the bookshop.

It was an ancient place, and she could imagine that it had

looked exactly the same as it had for the last few centuries. It was a beautiful store, dark and dry, and the leaded windows let in gorgeous pinpoints of brightness. When the bell above the door rang, a large marmalade tom trotted out to meet them, winding first around Hailey's ankles and then Beatrice's.

The proprietor, a wizened man with only a few tufts of frail hair left on his bald head, smiled to see them. His English was quite good, which made their exchange much easier.

"Ah, signorina, what a pleasure it is to see you. I take it you are looking for the Liona di Orsini work that I promised you?"

Hailey grinned. If she could never get along with her own coven members, she could get along with ancient bookstore owners. No matter where she went or who she was with, she had always had more books than friends, and some things simply did not change.

"Yes, Mr. Vestri," she said. "I've been looking forward to it, and the day was so beautiful that I simply could not stay away."

"Ah, you are in luck then," said the older man. "Let me go and get it for you."

He hustled to the back room, and given how messy she knew it was, Hailey was prepared for him to take some time. She glanced over to see that Beatrice was already perusing the books on ancient astronomy and leaned down to pet the cat. The bell of the door tinkled, followed by a chill like an omen.

Hailey looked up and found herself staring at the man in the doorway.

He was dressed all in black, and though Hailey was a little cold in her hoodie, he looked comfortable in his button-down shirt, the sleeves folded up to reveal forearms that were corded with muscle. He was tall—tall enough to tower over her. In that moment, with the afternoon sun behind him, he looked like a god of the mysteries, something mysterious and foreign come to earth.

Then he stepped forward, and she breathed a silent sigh of relief. He was only a man, though one that was strikingly handsome. With sleek black hair and the high cheekbones that signified Slavic blood, there was not a hint of softness to him. At least, that was what she thought until he set eyes on her. His lips curled into a small smile, and startled, she smiled back.

"Are you American?" he asked, and she was startled to find out that his English was perfect, though slightly accented.

"I am," she said hesitantly. "Is it so very obvious?"

Hailey was aware that Beatrice was watching everything avidly from the cover of the shelves.

"A little. I've only been in Italy for a few days, but I already miss understanding what's going on around me."

"It's not so bad," Hailey said with a slight smile. "I find that I can get around well enough."

He started to answer, but then the shop owner came back, a green leather-bound book in his hands. The spine was quite gone, and the stitching was all that was holding the pages together, but Hailey still smiled to see it.

"Is this really it?" she asked, and Mr. Vestri smiled, passing it to her reverent hands.

"It is, and it was not so easy to get."

Liona di Orsini was a woman written about in history books. Though many historians wrote about her, very few of them knew that she was a witch of some renown. Her own work, an untitled volume distinguished only by the illustration of a stained glass rose window on the first plate, was considered a minor work of mysticism, but when it was a witch or warlock reading it, it revealed much more.

Hailey opened the book to see the signature rose window, and she knew that she was smiling broadly. She was not expecting to have the book plucked out of her hands. With a startled yelp, she looked around, only to see her precious book in the hands of the man who had come into the store. He was looking at it curiously, turning it over and over, and she stifled the urge to snatch it back from him.

"That's not yours," she said, her voice just short of a snarl.

"It's not yours either, is it?" he asked casually.

He opened the book, looking at the same page that she had been examining, and one dark eyebrow lifted.

"Liona di Orsini? What kind of work are you doing?"

"What does it matter? That's my book that you're holding, and I will thank you to give it back."

He ignored her, flipping through the pages with a carelessness that made her grit her teeth. There were very few reproductions of this volume. It was not precisely valuable, because the interest in it was so low, but it was difficult to find. She couldn't imagine what this tourist could want with it.

"It's not in amazing condition, but it's not bad," he allowed.

To the proprietor, he turned and pulled out a wad of euros. Both Hailey and the bookseller gasped to see how much it was. The tourist smiled slightly.

"I'd like to take this book off your hands," he said.

Hailey could have stomped her foot with rage.

"That's…" she started, and then she stopped.

The amount of money in his hand was far more than the book was worth, and he seemed willing to pay simply to make her angry. She bit her lip, and made her decision. If he wanted it, he would have to pay.

"Signore," she said. "I insist that you sell that book to me. I am willing to offer you four hundred euros."

"And I'll give you five," the man said.

The old man glanced between them, clearly distressed.

"Six," she offered, but the man raised her another hundred without pause.

She chewed her lip as if debating, and when she said eight hundred euros, the tourist offered a round nine hundred without hesitating. Hailey wondered if she could have pushed it further, but her nerve broke, and she only scowled.

"I don't have any more," she muttered, doing her best to look downcast and beaten. She would miss the Liona di Orsini, but there were other books anyway.

The tourist smiled at her, and she lifted her chin angrily.

There was a strange tug to his smile, something that pulled at her in a strange and yearning way. Then she remembered the book and pushed the feeling aside.

He laid down the euros on the table, making the proprietor's eyes bug out. With book in hand, he turned to Hailey.

"Thank you for an interesting afternoon," he said.

Hailey would have made a bitter retort, but then he was gone.

"Oh signorina, you waited so long for that book," the bookseller said sorrowfully. "If you had but allowed me to speak, I would have given it to you."

Hailey smiled a little. Beatrice came out from behind her shelf then, her arms full of books.

"Well, now that awful man has his book, Mr. Vestri here has nine hundred euros, and everyone's happy."

"Not you," Beatrice pointed out.

Hailey could only shrug and sigh.

CHAPTER TWO

THE WALK BACK to the coven grounds was a long one, and by the time that Hailey and Beatrice got back to the gates, Hailey was tired out. Not only was the hill steep, she had to deal with Beatrice's fascination with the stranger.

"Say what you will about his manners, Hailey, he was handsome, don't you think?"

"I don't know, I think I was a little too irritated with what an ass he was making out of himself to really see if he looked like a movie star, you know?"

"Ah, now you are joking," Beatrice insisted. "Don't you remember little boys pulling your hair to show you that they liked you?"

"No," Hailey said firmly. "What I remember is little boys pulling my hair to bully me. Beatrice, that man wasn't interested in me. That was something else."

Beatrice tilted her head, looking at Hailey curiously.

"What do you mean?"

Hailey wouldn't have put her feeling to words if she hadn't been talking to her friend, but now that she had to, she could tell that what she felt was correct.

"That wasn't flirting, and if it was, the guy's a total psychopath. No, it was something else."

She teased it apart in her head. She thought of the way that the man had confronted her, the way he had snatched the book out of her hands. With a start, she realized that the man's bright blue eyes had been on her far more than they had been on the brown pages, and it wasn't a look of lust that she had seen. There was something frankly challenging to his gaze, something that wanted to see what she was going to do.

"He was testing me," she said at last. "He wanted to see what I was made of and what it took to push me."

Beatrice stilled, and from the way her hand tightened a little on Hailey's arm, Hailey could tell that she understood.

"Why would he do that?" she asked, sounding terribly young, and Hailey shook her head. She was only a handful of years older than Beatrice, but in that moment, she felt much older.

"Because that's what predators do," Hailey said firmly. "They push, and that's why it's important not to give an inch."

"You didn't get the book," Beatrice pointed out, and Hailey grinned.

"I was a lot happier with Signore Vestri getting all of that lovely money. I couldn't give it to him, and I don't need the book as much as I think he needs the cash."

The Alpine sky was shading to violet when they made it back to the coven grounds, and Hailey was unsurprised when Luca ran out to meet them. He was a slender boy, as fair as Beatrice was dark, and like her, he had lost his family to Templars. Now he wore a tight and pinched look on his face as he waved them down.

"I'm sorry. I got distracted and your tutor was pretty mad when you disappeared."

Beatrice made a face, but ruffled his hair affectionately.

"Well, it worked for a while, and I got to run down to the village with Hailey. Don't be so worried, eh?"

Luca shook his head and looked at Hailey.

"Donato's been looking everywhere for you, and no one could find you."

Hailey blinked in surprise. She was a member of the coven like everyone else, and that meant that she had free reign of the place. She had some duties, but she wasn't really shirking them when she left to go to the village.

She remembered what Beatrice had said, and she felt a cool heavy resignation sink on her shoulders. She had expected to last longer at Angioli, she really had. She had only been there for nine months, and it really had felt like people were getting used to her. Then she remembered the whispers of the other witches in the library and realized that perhaps she was wrong.

Hailey straightened up and squared her shoulders. So it had turned out that they didn't want her. So be it. She had heard that news before, and chances seemed good that she would hear that again. She turned to Beatrice who was looking at her with concern, and she pulled the other girl into a warm hug.

"This sounds like goodbye, my friend," she said softly, and with a soft cry, Beatrice wrapped her arms around Hailey as well.

"You can't go, you just got here. This is meant to be your home," Beatrice cried, and Hailey broke away, shaking her head.

"It doesn't matter. If my presence is disturbing the coven, it's Donato's job to fix that."

Beatrice looked like she was going to protest, but Luca was nodding. There was something lost and sad and, terribly enough, something resigned on his young face.

"That's the way it happens," he said, and she remembered that he had only recently come to Angioli.

"Oh no, not for you," Hailey said, squeezing his shoulder. "It'll be different for you, I promise."

Luca didn't look convinced, and she leaned down to give him a tight hug. She couldn't tell him that he was at a place where he would be cherished and taught. It was a lesson he could only learn with time. It was one that Hailey had yet to learn herself.

The hug had to end, however, and she gave her two young friends a smile before she went off looking for Donato. The sun was just beginning its slow descent. She paused to watch the streaks of violet across the sky. It was beautiful, and she wondered when she was going to find a place she could stay permanently.

She knocked crisply on the door to Donato's office, and when she heard his greeting, she entered. The coven master, a rather lean and saturnine man, was at his accustomed place behind his desk, but the man who stood next to him was unexpected.

Hailey blinked, convinced that she was mistaken, and then she realized that she was not.

"You!" she exclaimed, forgetting to greet Donato at all. "What the hell are you doing here?"

"Hailey!"

Donato's voice was like a whip crack, and she turned to him in surprise.

Donato hadn't been happy to introduce her to his coven, but he had been fair to her. She knew that he ruled his coven with a firm hand, but no one was abused. All had the same opportunities to hone their talents. Now he looked at her with an expression that she had never seen before. When she stopped to really look at him, she could see that he was afraid.

In the pause, Donato calmed himself, and started again.

"Hailey, this is Major Kieran McCallen of the Magus Corps. He's here on Corps business and needs to speak with you."

That was all Donato said before he walked past her and out of the room. He didn't meet her eyes, and when he closed the door behind him, Hailey felt as if she was trapped with a large predator.

The silence stretched out between them longer and longer, and when Hailey lifted her eyes to meet the man's gaze, she did it with all the strength and force of will that she could bring. Her whole life, both before she knew of her skills and after, people had sat in judgment over her. One more man, no matter who he worked for, or what rank he held, was no different.

"So what do you want?" she said, meeting his gaze.

• • • • •

The first time he laid eyes on Hailey Devereaux, Kieran had been charmed. She looked like a sweet, little urchin, with her red hair caught in a loose braid and blowing around her face. If he had been on his own time, things would have gone differently, but he wasn't. He was there to test and to examine, and so he had bullied her. It was a crude tool, but an effective one, and as soon as he had seen that flash of temper in her bold green eyes, he knew that he had found the woman he had been looking for.

At the same time, watching her stand up to a man who was easily twice her size, a blush on her cheeks and an utter sense of fearlessness radiating from her small body, made something stir inside him that had not moved in a long time. It wasn't until later, when he realized that nine hundred euros could help the old bookseller a great deal, that he realized that she was compassionate as well.

Right now, she was so lovely that it took everything he had not to grin. Instead, he kept a straight face and nodded at her.

"What I need is to test you," he said bluntly. "The Magus Corps is aware of your talents, and we think that they may be of use–"

"I don't care."

Kieran blinked as Hailey stared up at him, arms crossed over her chest and an expression that could only be described as stony.

"I don't care," she repeated, when it looked like he wasn't getting the idea. "Do you understand? I don't care what you think of my talents. I'm doing work, good work here, and it is not up to you to pull me away from it."

"Good work. You mean translating old manuscripts and going over the work of Wiccans long dead?"

She bristled.

"Yes," she said. "I'm not interested in any kind of work you have for me."

"The Magus Corps–"

"Can look for its own torturers."

The words stunned him to silence, and apparently it made Hailey think that they were done. She nodded stiffly to him, and he was so surprised he almost let her get out the door.

"Hailey, wait."

Without thinking about it, he grasped her wrist as she walked past. He was startled to see how small it was. She stilled completely when she felt the touch of his bare skin on hers.

"You touched me," she said, her eyes wide with surprise.

"You were leaving," he pointed out. "Our talk isn't done."

"You *touched* me."

"I did." Kieran paused, worried. "Are you all right? I didn't intend to hurt you."

He let go of her hand, but she seemed to be so stunned that she forgot all about leaving. Instead, her bright eyes flicked between her wrist and his hand. Finally, she looked up at him.

"Did they not tell you anything about me?"

Her tone was torn between shock and pity, and perhaps there was even some rage there. Kieran realized with a sense of shock that the rage was on his behalf.

"What do you mean?"

She paused, and for a moment, it was impossible to tell what she was thinking or what she felt. Then she took a deep breath as if bracing herself for a jump into cold water.

"They didn't tell you what I am and what I can do."

"I assure you they did, Hailey."

Her glance was cutting.

"I don't think they could have. Let me explain it to you, Major. I'm a vampire. If I put my hands on a witch or a warlock, I can drain them. I don't have any magic of my own. I can't do *anything* if you put me in a room by myself. But if I touch a witch or a warlock, if I have my skin on their skin, I can steal some of their power, and then I can do anything with it."

"Anything?"

"As far as we can tell. It doesn't seem limited to what the person I stole from can do. Suddenly, I have power, and I can use it in nearly any way that I can think of. It's that simple." She shook her head. "Whoever sent you here without telling you what I can do, well. I don't think much of them."

"You're wrong," Kieran said quietly. "I knew exactly what you could do, and I need to learn more."

She stilled, and now there was doubt in her eyes.

"I'm safe," she said, and there was a new sense of urgency in her tone. "I am… Please. You have to believe me. Ask anyone. I've never lost control, not in the time that I've been living with a coven. I didn't understand my powers when I was first awakened, but I do now. I swear it. I would swear it on anything that you cared to name…"

Kieran flinched at the rising panic in her voice.

"I am not here to punish you for what you cannot help," he said, keeping his voice as gentle as he could. "I told you that I am only here to evaluate you and to learn more about what it is you can do."

"To what end?" she asked, frustrated. "Why in the world do you want to know about what I can do? Almost everyone else has been content to make sure that I wasn't lurking around trying to suck the life out of them. And I'm not."

Kieran shook his head.

"That's something that will only be revealed to you at a later point. In truth, there is a chance that I am simply going to observe you for a few days, and then leave you right where you are. It is not the intent of the Magus Corps to disrupt your life or to make things difficult for you."

"And yours?"

Her comment caught him by surprise.

"What do yo mean?"

"What are your intentions towards me?"

For a single insane moment, watching her stare him down with all the ferocity and determination of a hunted fox brought to bay, the only thing he could think of to say was *to kiss you.* That was a dangerous road, and one that would be treacherous to both of them. He shook the thought away, alarmed by his own impulses.

"My intentions towards you are the same as that of the Magus Corps"' he said stiffly. "Beyond the aims of my mission, my duty is of course to protect you, the way it is to protect all witches and warlocks that live under our rule."

She was silent, watching him with those gorgeous green eyes. He could almost hear her thoughts: *I will believe that when I see it.*

Kieran nodded, acknowledging her distrust. He knew that in some quarters, the Magus Corps was seen as a necessary evil. Some of the more militant covens, especially those in the most remote parts of Canada and Russia, didn't even think of them as necessary. He'd had to earn the regard of the people that he was trying to protect more than once. He was unsurprised that it was going to happen again.

"Will you cooperate?" he asked.

After a long pause, she nodded. There was still a proud set to her shoulders, however, and he could tell that her agreement was good only so long as she saw him worthy of it.

"Then that is all I ask from you," he said. "I will see you at dawn at the practice field tomorrow. Dress warmly."

"Yes, Major. Of course, Major."

The respect in her voice was overdone, almost syrupy, but he thought she meant it. He stepped aside to let her pass, but as she reached for the door, he couldn't help calling her name.

"Hailey."

"Yes, Major?"

Her expression was skeptical, but he couldn't prevent himself from making one more try.

"Hailey, I'm not your enemy."

For a single moment, he thought he saw something flicker across her expression. He couldn't read it; it was there and gone.

Then she nodded, and Kieran thought that there was something there, something that he could build on. Perhaps it was a place where they were not at each other's throats.

"Thank you, Major," she said softly.

She closed the door behind her gently, and Kieran sighed.

In a little while, he would have to find Donato and return the man's office to him. He would have to find sleeping quarters, and he would have to see to getting in contact with his superiors.

At the moment, however, all he felt was tired, and he wandered to the window, where the bright Alpine sky was deepening to purple. Below him, he could see a handful of Wiccan children playing in the courtyard. Beyond them was the curtain wall that surrounded the monastery, and beyond that were the mountains themselves.

As he watched, he could hear a single wolf howl, greeting the night and sending a message to those that could hear it. *Here I am,* that message said. *Here I am, and I am alone.*

Kieran smiled a little to himself and turned away. After all, there was a great deal to do.

• • • • •

That night, in the tiny room that she called her own, Hailey wasn't sure what to think. She had eaten dinner alone. When she had passed Donato, he had pulled her aside.

"Your meeting today with the major from the Magus Corps…"

"Yes, sir?" she asked warily.

Donato had treated her fairly, even if he had always made it clear that he was unhappy with her presence. Now, though, there was a thunderous expression on his face. He glared down at her from his far greater height.

"You are still a member of this coven," he said at last. "Whatever he wants you to do, if you don't want to do it, if you feel he is crossing lines, I want you to come to me."

Hailey stared up at the coven master in surprise before she found her tongue.

"Yes… yes sir, I will."

Satisfied with her answer, he walked on, leaving Hailey staring after him.

She was touched that the coven master cared to tell her that, but when she thought about it for a little bit longer, she realized what it was. Power struggles between covens and the Magus Corps were legendary. Right now, Donato was probably looking on her as the bone that was being pulled between them. Still, it was far better than he needed to do. Another man might have just turned her over to the Magus Corps without a single qualm, especially if the witch in question had a set of powers as intimidating as hers. Instead, Donato had said that he would stand with her, and that was a comfort.

In her own room, dressed only in the white nightgown she had brought with her, Hailey brushed her hair thoughtfully. It gleamed by the light of the single bare bulb, and after a moment, she opened the window.

The cold moonlight streamed into her room. After a moment, a winged creature flared outside and alighted silently on her window sill. Before she had awakened as a Wiccan, Hailey had seen pictures of snowy owls before, but pictures did not convey the real size of these animals. Merit was a young female, and a large one at that. She had a five foot wingspan that could knock the breath out of someone who was caught unawares, and in the faint light of the room, her golden eyes shone.

"Good evening, beautiful one," Hailey said softly. "Have you come for a visit?"

The owl blinked twice and inclined her head so that Hailey could ruffle her horns, the feathery tufts at the top of her crown. There was still something awe-inspiring about the fact that this wild animal had decided to be her familiar. They had been together for almost as long as Hailey had been a witch, and now, though the bird hunted the forest, she still came to see her mistress every day.

"What do you think, Merit?" Hailey whispered. "Do you think this is going to be okay?

The owl turned her honey-colored eyes to Hailey, and the sound she made was oddly gentle. She nibbled lightly on Hailey's fingers with a beak that could easily kill a full-grown rabbit. Hailey smiled. This great predator had never been anything but gentle with her.

The owl gave one last affectionate peck to Hailey's wrist and swept off into the night. Her white wings flickered against the dark, and then she was lost to sight.

"If only I could fly away with you," Hailey said quietly.

She closed the window and climbed in to bed. Dawn was coming very quickly, and she wanted some sleep before she had to face the major again.

CHAPTER THREE

MORNING CAME ALL too soon. When Hailey's feet hit the stone floor, she wanted nothing more than to climb back into bed. Red was already streaking the sky, though, so she dressed hurriedly. She found a pair of comfortably worn jeans, and she stomped into the heavy boots that had served her so well in the Alpine territory. A thick hoodie finished her outfit, and as she trotted down to the courtyard, she hastily plaited her hair. Flyaway strands escaped her braid, but that was hardly unusual. When she was done, she opened the small gate that lead to the interior courtyard. It was a walled area that in times past had served as a meditation garden for the monks. Now it was the common training area for the Angioli coven, offering them an open place to practice their craft without worrying about interference or spies from the village.

The cold air took her breath away for a moment. She wished she had thought to put on at least another layer of clothing or bring along a pair of gloves. In the dim light of dawn, she could make out the figure of Kieran McCallen standing at the far wall, pulling what looked like long sticks out of a bag.

Warily, she approached him. To her surprise, he wasn't shivering at all, despite his thin clothes. In plain black, he could have been a modern monk, but given his size and his obviously muscular build, it would have been a warlike order indeed. She let her eyes linger over how broad his shoulders were and how narrow his waist was before reminding herself of who he was and how very dangerous he could be.

Hailey had a defensive answer on her lips for why she wasn't there and waiting for him, but he seemed unconcerned.

"There you are. Let's get started, yes?"

At her wary nod, he gestured towards the bag.

"Are you familiar with quarterstaves?"

"You mean the art of hitting each other with sticks?" she blurted out.

He didn't smile, well not exactly, but his eyes crinkled with something like amusement.

"Have you ever fought with one?"

She shook her head, and he handed her a thick length of wood that was just a little taller than she was. It was rounded and smooth, and she was surprised to see how comfortable it felt in her hand.

"That one will do for today. Quarterstaves are an excellent choice for a young witch or warlock who has had no training in martial arts before. It is innocuous because it looks like a walking stick, and it can defend you from most things that aren't projectiles without the risk of carrying a sword."

Hailey wanted to ask why a highly-ranked member of the Magus Corps was stopping to give her instructions on fighting, but she bit her tongue. He had a plan here, and whatever it was, she was going to have to go along with it.

To her surprise, Kieran turned out to be a patient teacher. He showed her how to hold the staff, and patiently corrected her stance every time.

"Let me show you why it's so important," he said, standing up straight. "Drop into your stance."

She did as he said, standing with one shoulder towards him and spreading her feet to be a little wider than her shoulders.

"Do you see the difference between us right now?"

Hailey considered.

"You're up higher than I am," she said. "Your stance is narrow, and you're relaxed."

His smile was slight, and it took his face from being simply handsome to being something that could touch the heart. It shocked her, and it made her shake her head so that she could focus on what he was saying.

"That's precisely right. When I stand like this, I can be knocked over more easily. I am not centered, I am not focused, and because my stance is so narrow, I can easily be surprised. You see?"

She nodded, and they continued. She took her stance more readily, and when she didn't, he tapped her leg lightly with the butt of his own staff to remind her.

Hailey, who had never enjoyed any sport before in her life, was startled by what the instruction of a good teacher could do. Kieran seemed endlessly patient, and he was willing to explain things and demonstrate them until she got them right.

As the sun crept higher in the sky, she learned to block and parry, and soon enough, she was making small feints herself, attacking when he directed her to, and striking where she could. He looked pleased with her progress, but Hailey tried to remind herself that this had more to do with his mysterious purposes than it did with helping her.

Hailey was covered in sweat, and her fingers, unused to holding the staff, were sore, but she was oddly loath to take the break he offered. She sipped delicately from the water bottle he offered her, and she watched out of the corner of her eye as he shed his jacket.

Underneath, he wore a black tank top that showed her exactly what lifetimes of fighting would do to a body. He was as muscled as any career soldier, and the scars that criss-crossed his arms and his upper chest looked too innumerable to count.

Too late, she realized that she was staring, and he looked over at her with a wry grin.

"I'd ask if you liked what you see, but I think your expression tells me not to do that."

Hailey's eyes went wide. She could hear the faint note of self-deprecation in his voice. The thought that she had made him ashamed of his body, which was beautiful, and his scars, which after all were earned fairly, made her blush with shame.

"No, no, I do like what I see! I mean, I like all of it."

She heard what she said and stammered to a stop, and instead of laughing at her, Kieran looked surprised.

"The scars bother many people," he said with a shrug. "They used to bother me, but if you live long enough, I think you learn to be grateful for them."

Almost without thinking about it, Hailey stepped a little closer. His skin was as pale as her own, and the scars were vivid against it. When she got close enough, she could see that they were raised as well. Some of them were as thin as the blade of a knife, and others were thick and knotted. She shivered to think what could have made them. She raised her hand to touch one that trailed over his bare shoulder, but she stopped short when he cleared his throat.

"Oh! Oh my god, I'm sorry. I wasn't thinking at all."

There was that slight smile again, the one that made her go warm to the depths of her belly, and he shook his head.

"Let's put it this way. Any other time, I would be happy to have as lovely a woman as you touch me while making that face, but right now we have other things to do."

What face? she wondered, but he was picking up his staff again.

"You've learned very well for someone who has never picked up a staff before," he commented. "Now let's see what you can do with it."

She was barely in the guard position before he was on top of her. When the first blow stung her upper arm, she couldn't help but cry out. The blow had been lightning fast, far faster than she could defend against. She skittered backwards in shock.

Hailey looked up at Kieran wide-eyed, but he was coming again. She blocked the first blow, but not the second, and it caught her hard on the thigh.

"Kieran!"

"That's battle, little fox. Defend yourself or suffer the consequences."

She was nearly in tears with another few blows, and then he was driving her around and around the courtyard. She was able to fend off some of his blows, but most of them caught her. They fell like rain, and though few of them were as heavy as the blows he had struck at first, they all shocked her.

"Come on, is this all you have?" Kieran called, circling her.

He reminded her of a wolf watching its prey. She panted, doing her best to remain facing him while catching her breath.

"Yes it is," she snarled, horrified to feel tears lumping in the back of her throat. "It is. I haven't picked up a staff before in my life, so yes, this is all I have!"

Kieran snorted.

"The Templars won't care. I don't either."

He darted towards her again, catching her hard against the side, and again she was standing under a flurry of blows. She was losing strength, her arms stung from holding up the staff, and her hands were almost numb from the grasp she had to take on it.

More than once he got close enough for her to touch, and

more than once, her clenched knuckles brushed against his skin. Her power clamored to be used, but she fought it off.

He can't kill me, Hailey reminded herself. *He can't even hurt me, and if he does, Anjelica in the infirmary will patch me up right away.*

She hung on to the thought like grim death, but as he continued herding her to and fro across the interior courtyard, she began to wonder whether he knew that he couldn't hurt her. Her entire body was shrieking with pain and panic, and she knew tears of pain and frustration were running down her face.

Hailey stayed on her feet, she kept fighting. It was all she knew how to do.

Suddenly she found there was nowhere to run. He had backed her against the wall, and with a blow that almost seemed careless, he knocked the staff out of her numb hands.

He was standing close enough to touch, and a distant part of her buried somewhere under a bone-deep layer of pain and nerves thought about how beautiful he was. He was a predator, and now he had brought her to bay.

"I expected more than this," he said, and he raised his staff.

Hailey stared up at him, and then a scream rent the cold morning air. They both turned, and where before the courtyard had been empty, now there was an enraged teenager a mere few yards away.

Beatrice's face was twisted with fury, and she lunged at Kieran with a feline quickness that shocked Hailey.

Kieran turned, and all Hailey saw was that staff coming up, the one that she knew could deliver such painful blows. A flash of that weapon striking Beatrice seared through her mind, and with an enraged snarl all her own, she threw herself at the far bigger man.

The moment her palm hit his bare scarred shoulder, she could feel her power twisting over his, pulling at it and wrenching it away. It was a terrible pleasure, it was heat driving through her and giving her exactly what she needed to defend the girl who had welcomed her with open arms.

There was a flash of copper light, and Kieran was flung back several feet. Hailey's hands were in the air and between her hands and Kieran was a round, transparent copper shield. Through its haze, she could see his shocked face, and behind her, she could feel Beatrice trembling.

"Hailey, oh Hailey," Beatrice whispered.

At first, Hailey thought that the teenager was afraid of what she had done, and her spirit shrunk in shame.

"Beatrice…"

"You must run away," the teen whispered. "You should not have struck a major of the Magus Corps like that. You shouldn't have!"

It took Hailey a few moments to realize that her friend was not horrified by her actions, and then she shook her head.

"He shouldn't have struck you," Hailey said firmly. "You're a member of the Angioli coven. He has no right to raise a hand against you."

"Actually, I have no right to raise a hand against either of you."

They turned to see that Kieran was standing on the other side of the shield, gazing at it with frank curiosity. To Hailey's surprise, he looked completely unperturbed by the blow she had dealt him.

"What the hell was that?" she demanded.

"I needed to see what your power could do," he explained. "Do you think you could drop the shield?"

"I can, but I won't," she snapped, and he nodded, looking faintly chagrined at himself.

"That was completely unfair, and it was meant to be. Even with a little bit of training, you wouldn't have been able to hold out against someone who has actually trained with a staff. I needed to see what you would do with your power if you were pressed." He shook his head. "You wouldn't turn it against me. We were at that perhaps three times as long as I thought we would be, and you never chose to use your power on your own behalf."

He looked like he was going to continue, but Hailey dropped the shield, and stared at him with anger.

"It was another test," she said. "It was another test, just like the book from earlier, wasn't it?"

He nodded, and the rage and frustration that she felt boiled over. She could feel tears spilling down her cheeks.

"How dare you," she choked. "How dare you. You could simply have *asked*."

He opened his mouth to speak, and she couldn't take another moment. It was a quick step to where he stood, and she could still feel the remnants of his power boiling under her skin. This time she used it to throw him back further.

Kieran fell back, barely keeping his feet, but Hailey didn't bother to stay to see it. She stormed across the field, giving her fallen staff a vicious kick, and she slammed the door to the courtyard behind her.

• • • • •

Her blow was as powerful as it was unexpected. It was like some giant hand had appeared invisibly between the two of them and shoved Kieran back quickly and violently. He had seldom felt something so powerful in his long life, and when he righted himself, Hailey was disappearing back into the monastery.

Kieran shook his head, and as he bent to pick up his fallen staff, he remembered that he was not alone. The teenager who had interrupted their practice had murder in her eyes, and he frowned.

"You shouldn't interfere with the affairs of adults," he growled, and she narrowed her eyes.

"You should treat others the way you wish to be treated," she retorted. "That did not need to go the way it did."

"You know very little about the world, young lady, and I don't have the time to teach you."

"Oh yes? Well perhaps I have the time to teach you. I know very little about the world, but I know plenty about Hailey."

Kieran paused, eying her warily.

"You were trembling in her shadow just a few minutes ago," he commented. "What's changed?"

The teen tossed her hair as if everything he said was beneath her.

"I was afraid for her, not myself. She has reasons to be afraid of you, but I do not."

"I would say that she has no reason to be afraid of me anyway, but go ahead. What do I need to know?"

The girl met his gaze coolly and steadily. He realized that she was quite a beauty, and when she grew into her looks, there would be no saving the Wiccans of Italy.

"Go apologize to her," she said, "because you have done her a great wrong. Speak to her frankly, and tell her what you can tell her. Apologize for not being able to tell her more. Treat her the way that you would treat a man in this regard."

Kieran nodded slowly, forced to think about her words.

"You…may be right." He paused. "I thank you. It is difficult sometimes–"

The girl cut him off with a sharp motion.

"You owe me nothing, except for perhaps an apology for attempting to stave my head in. Tell it to Hailey."

"I wouldn't have struck you."

"I didn't know that. Hailey didn't know that."

"My apologies for acting unwisely towards both of you. I'm sorry that my actions were such that you could think that."

She studied him for a long moment, and then she nodded slowly.

"You are not used to being trusted, are you?"

"Perceptive of you. No, the Magus Corps does a lot of field work, and most of what we do has nothing to do with the covens. We technically have authority over them, but it's a precarious prospect."

The girl's smile was small but genuine.

"Well, if you see troubled waters, you should build bridges, as my teachers always tell me. Go and build a bridge with Hailey."

Before he could respond, she disappeared, and he was alone. He shook his head.

"I'd wager that your teachers adore that trick," he muttered, and he was answered with a light laugh.

"Do not tell them I am going to the village. It would only worry them."

Then Kieran was alone, or at least, he could pretend he was. He thought of Hailey and how he might have bungled it. He wasn't really a man who was made for diplomacy. Though he had been chosen for this mission with his strengths in mind, there was very little he could do about the tasks in front of him beyond blunder through. He shrugged his jacket back on and picked up the staves, but paused. He considered the girl's words yet again.

"All right," he said softly.

CHAPTER FOUR

EVER SINCE SHE was a small child, Hailey had always been clever at finding the best hiding places wherever she was living. It had served her well when she was a child bouncing from indifferent home to indifferent home, and somehow, she had never lost the habit as an adult. Sometimes, she felt a little embarrassed about her childish habit, but at the moment, she was too upset to worry about it much.

The sanctuary of the monastery had a choir loft built into it. In centuries past, skilled singers would ascend to the hidden area, and the people below would be enchanted by the ethereal sounds that seemed to drift down. In the days of the Angioli coven, the choir loft was mostly a place to store extra supplies, and most people only ventured into it once or twice a year.

Hailey had discovered it when she was exploring her new home. She had found a perfect little nook between two upended old pews that fit her perfectly. She was seated below one of the open areas that looked over the sanctuary, and it let enough light in for her to avoid feeling like she was trapped.

She sat and tried to calm her breathing, but for the longest time, every thought and every breath only brought more tears. She realized distantly that she hadn't cried in ages, and then there was no stopping her tears. She cried until she was drained and tired, and then she simply sat. She felt like a child, and she knew that eventually, she would have to go downstairs to face Kieran and the coven. She knew it, but she couldn't, and soon enough, she heard the door to the choir loft open.

Hailey was only a little surprised to see Kieran crossing the floor to come sit by her side. If she had had more pride, perhaps she would have tried to hide the fact that she was crying. She was so tired, however, that she only looked at him.

"Is this where I apologize for running out on you?" she asked. To her surprise, he shook his head.

"No, actually, this is where I apologize to you. I acted inappropriately when I tried to force you to do something that you didn't want to do, and I certainly should not have tried to trick you into it. I had a plan, and I put it into action without ever thinking about what it could mean. I was wrong, and I am very sorry."

Hailey froze, hardly able to believe her ears. She thought that at the very least, she would have been dressed down thoroughly. The Magus Corps could exercise some discipline over Wiccans who disobeyed them. At worst, she might have been removed from the coven, and who knows what might have happened to her then. This humble apology caught her completely off guard. She was silent for so long that Kieran must have taken that as continuing fury.

"I understand that what I have done might have destroyed any possibility of trust between us, and if that is the case, I will speak to my commandant. I can have myself removed from this affair entirely. However, I will warn you that just because I am gone does not mean that the Magus Corps's interest in you is gone. Someone else will be sent–"

"I don't want you to leave," Hailey said at last. Kieran looked at her with surprise. "I don't. I just need to know what's going on.

Can you tell me that at least? Please?"

For the first time, Hailey saw Kieran look uncertain. It made him look younger, and she wondered what his past was like. Once they had been initiated by an act of unprotected sex with another Wiccan, witches and warlocks were effectively immortal. Members of the Magus Corps, known for their strength, their power and their wisdom, were all initiated warlocks. There was no telling how old Kieran was. He could have been thirty years old, or he could have been eight hundred years old.

"I will tell you what I can," he said at last. "It isn't much, but I swear to you it is simply because I do not know much."

He settled down beside her, and suddenly it made her think of the calmer periods of her childhood, when she and another foster child would rest next to each other, at peace for once. Her life had been too fractured for anything like real friendship, but this peace was the next best thing.

"You must know that witches like you are quite rare. Warlocks don't seem to develop this power at all. We have records of witches with your power dating back to the Renaissance, and, well. It was a different time."

"You mean they were shunned," Hailey said bitterly, and he nodded.

"They were forced out. Some of them survived, and some of them didn't. I and many others of the Magus Corps consider it a great shame that that happened, and Hailey, I swear that is not what is going to happen to you." She looked up, startled, but Kieran continued. "There is a certain coven in the United States, in Wyoming. It's dedicated to study, and as far as I and the rest of the Magus Corps are concerned, it does some of the most important work in the world when it comes to protecting us."

"From Templars?"

"From anyone who would hurt us. They call it the Castle, and recently, they learned of your existence."

Hailey shivered.

"You know, that sounds pretty terrifying," she said. "When people say things like that, it means that they want to experiment on you."

Kieran flinched, and she could tell that he had read some of the same books that she had. If he was old enough, he would have known some of the writers. Humans didn't have a monopoly on terrible deeds. Some of the covens from the dark days of Wiccan history had created nightmares.

"That is not going to happen to you."

"Why not?" she asked, and then Kieran looked at her fully.

She was shocked by how blue his eyes were, and when he looked at her like that, it was as if he was allowing her to look inside him.

"I won't let them," he said simply, and that was all it took. In that moment, she believed him with everything inside her.

She found that her hand had crept across the space to rest on his. Now she could feel how warm he was, and self-consciously she pulled away.

"If they don't want to perform strange experiments on me, what is it they want, then?"

"It wasn't entirely clear to me, but the coven master in Wyoming believes that you can use your power to do something amazing. It was told to me that he thinks this could be a turning point in the way the Wiccan world operates—if you are strong enough. If you are willing."

Hailey shivered. There had never been a time in her life when she wanted attention. It brought danger, and she knew that it was far safer to be quiet.

"But you must be willing." Kieran sighed. "I had forgotten that. I was focused on your strength, which already looks formidable, and I am sorry."

"I accept your apology," Hailey said, but her mind was whirling. "But I can't be that important."

Kieran's smile was rueful.

"I promise you, you are. The coven master heard about you from the master of your old coven in Canada, and he ripped that old man up one side and down the other for failing to see your potential."

Hailey choked back a giggle at that. The Canadian coven master had been a terror, and he had shoved her off as soon as he could. It pleased her to think of him having to take a tongue lashing on her account, even if she hadn't gotten to see it.

"So now I have to ask you. Will you let me test your strength? I can't tell you what kind of use the coven master in Wyoming has for you, but I will promise you that you will come to no harm through it. I'll be with you every step of the way. This has to be your choice, and if you commit yourself, there will be no more tricks."

"And what if I say no?"

The silence stretched between them, and Kieran shook his head.

"Then I will leave and you will never need to set eyes on me again. I will report to the Magus Corps that you are unsuited for the work they have in mind, and they will have to search for someone else."

"But they will send someone else?"

Kieran looked torn.

"I cannot promise that they wouldn't, but I would do everything in my power to stop them."

Hailey was not someone who could read the future. She had met a few Wiccans who could, and on the whole, they tended to be a closed-mouth lot. However, there had been a young woman in Canada who was strong in the gift, and she believed that everyone had a little.

"You can't always tell what can happen," the girl had said, "but lots of times, you can tell when something's *about* to happen."

Hailey didn't understand what that had meant at the time, but she certainly understood it now. Life as she knew it split two ways in front of her. On one path was her life the way it had been. She could stay at the Angioli coven until she was tired of whispers or until someone made a strong case to get her placed elsewhere. The cycle would then repeat, over and over again, with no end in sight.

Or she could walk down the path that Kieran was leading her towards. There was no guarantee that it would be better, and from what he said, it sounded far more dangerous.

She thought about it, but already knew her decision.

"All right," she said softly. "Let's give it a shot."

Kieran didn't smile at her. Instead he nodded in a way that seemed almost like a bow, a gesture of respect for what she was offering him.

"Thank you," he said, and climbing to his feet, he offered her his hand so that she could do the same.

She took it, marveling at how warm he was and how gently he held her hand, and then she didn't want to let go. She realized with a start that since she had discovered her power and her heritage, the people willing to touch her had been very few. Yet here was Kieran, offering his hand. Her thoughts were full of what it might mean.

But as she rose with his help, her sore body protested. After the punishing test and then sitting, she hadn't realized how stiff she'd gotten. She took an awkward step and caught her foot on the uneven floorboards. A tiny yelp was all the warning Kieran got before she pitched forward into him.

He spun and half caught her, but the surprise and her momentum pushed him back into the wall. For a long moment, they only stared at each other in the dusky space. Hailey's eyes were full of him, and, as large as he was, he seemed to take up the world. She remembered that seer again. Hailey knew for sure that something was about to happen.

Kieran's large hands around her body were warm, and very slowly, he brought his face down to hers. He was giving her time to back out, and realized that she had no intention of doing that. The warmth of their bodies together made her feel slow and languid. In the choir loft, there was a certain timelessness to the moment. Nothing they did here mattered. Nothing they did here meant something else.

Instead of kissing her the way that Hailey thought he would, Kieran leaned down to rub his face against hers. She could feel the slight prickle of his stubble and his warm breath against her neck. Something in it made a shiver race through her body. It was like wolves meeting in the wild. Kieran brushed his lips against her throat, and she lifted her chin to give him better access. His breath was so warm, and when he passed his lips over the point of her pulse, she whimpered a little. It had been so long since she had been touched like this that she was nearly drunk with it.

"Hailey… Hailey, are you sure?"

His urgent whisper cut through the haze, but she nodded her head.

"I am," she murmured. "Bolt the door."

When she looked up, his face was unreadable in the dim light. Then she lifted her hand and laid it against the side of his neck. She laughed softly.

"Don't try to fool me. Your pulse is racing."

"You have a singular effect on me," he retorted, but he turned to bolt the door.

There was not much room in the choir loft, but she found a dim space that was open enough for what she wanted. Hailey spared a thought for the people who had sang in that loft in centuries past. Had any of those men sneaked their lovers into this quiet space? Had they removed their clothes in this sacred darkness? Held each other, kissed? More?

Kieran's arms came around her from behind, stilling her thoughts. This close, his scent filled her nose. There was something spicy about it, sharp and masculine. She turned and buried her face in his chest. He was a big man, a giant compared to her diminutive height, but for once, she didn't care at all. All she wanted was to be close to him.

"I want you, but…" His voice trailed off.

"There's nothing that stands in our way," Hailey said forcefully. "When we go down those stairs, we are back in the world. There are Templars to fight, orders to follow and tests to complete. Not now."

He looked like he would argue, but after a moment, he nodded. There was no need for words.

Hailey's hands went to her clothing, but with a gentle touch, he warded her away. Instead, he knelt on one knee like a supplicant, and his strong hands, swept over her body. At first, they only touched her gently. He ran his hands over her arms, down her legs, up her back and down her sides. She was fully clothed, but still she was learning his touch and feeling everything that he was offering. There was no sense of urgency, nothing dangerous about this. He was learning about her, and it was infinitely patient and kind.

His fingers eventually landed on the zipper of her hoodie, and the sound of it opening was loud in the quiet place. She stood in her camisole, and in a moment, he lifted that over her head as well. For a moment, Hailey wanted to cover her breasts. She was small on top, small enough that she hadn't bothered with a bra that morning.

Now she stood exposed, and he could see her tender pink nipples crinkling in the slight chill.

"I…I'm…"

"You're perfect, utterly perfect," Kieran said firmly.

He leaned forward to set his mouth against the pebbled bud, and his lips were so tender that she sighed. Her nipples were almost achingly sensitive, but he made no move to pinch or nip. Instead, his mouth traveled languorously from one to the other, and then he leaned up to tangle his hand in her hair. He held her still, pulling her lower, and slowly ravished her mouth with his. She slid her tongue into his mouth, and he groaned as she teasingly slid it in and out.

She could feel the moment the tension changed. There was a shift in the atmosphere between them. He was kissing her with more ferocity, and she could feel the tug of excitement as he pulled her close to him. Even on his knee he was a powerful man.

Just as she was ready to give in to that energy entirely, he reined himself in, smiling up at her ruefully.

"That's not how I want things to go."

"What do you mean?"

"Let me show you."

He kissed a path from her chin, down her throat to her navel, and when he got to the waistband of her jeans, he started moving up again. His movements would have been maddening, but his hands were wrapped around her hips, holding her still.

Hailey gave in to the sensations, until she couldn't resist any longer. She twined her fingers through his hair, and pulled him close, wanting more of him.

She started to get down on the ground with him, but he shook his head.

"This old room will give you splinters. Here, let me."

Kieran's strong hands made quick work of her jeans, her underwear, her socks and her shoes. Now she was naked in front of him, and he was still entirely dressed. Instead of making her feel nervous, it sent a spike of hot arousal through her. It made her think of good men of the church, tempted in their sleep by the women in their dreams. They woke hard and wanting, their supposedly pure minds defiled by a sly smile, a beckoning finger.

He sat down on an old pew, his long legs stretched in front of him. When she gave him her hand, he pulled her down so that she straddled his hips. Through his trousers, she could feel how hard he was. Without thinking about it, she rocked herself on the length of his cock, drawing a moan from his lips.

She liked the sound so much she did it again. He put his hands on her hips, grinding lightly up against her tender body. She could feel the strength in him and the power in his frame; she could also feel the restraint under which he held himself. Hailey wondered what it would take to break that restraint.

Kieran kissed her over and over again, holding her steady on his lap. She was helpless to move closer for more contact. In a matter of moments, she was crying out. She could tell how aroused he was, but he seemed immune to her wriggling, her soft moans for more.

"Please," she said finally. "Please, I need you. I need more than this."

There was perhaps a hint of triumph in his laugh, but all he did was shift her backwards. He freed his cock, and almost immediately she reached for it, measuring the hot length in her hand. It was thick enough to make her swallow hard.

Hailey watched as he smoothed a condom down over his erection, and she looked up to meet his eyes.

"Yes?" he asked hoarsely, and she nodded.

She shifted up so that for a moment, his cock was pressed between their bodies, and that was a kind of heaven as well. The length of him was nudged up between her inner lips, parting them slightly, making them even wetter. He could feel her arousal now, and for a moment, he rested his forehead against her shoulder, pulling her close as if he couldn't bear to be parted from her.

It was sudden, but she couldn't wait any more. She reached down to take his cock in her hand, and holding him still, she pressed him against her, letting his shaft part her folds. There was a moment where it stung a little as she slid down on him, but at his inquisitive noise, she only shook her head and whimpered in pleasure.

The thought of fitting his entire length inside her body made her feel faint with pleasure. With his hands supporting her and holding her firmly by the hips, she slid down until their bodies were flush. The feeling of being joined was incredible, and Hailey opened her eyes to look at him.

Kieran's lips were slightly parted, and his eyes were nearly black with desire. He could still stop if she told him to, she knew it, but it would be a close thing. The thought made her smile, and in response, he leaned up to press his mouth to hers.

As he did so, he started pushing up into her. Now she felt like she was riding him in earnest, and she pressed herself down even as he pushed himself up.

"Oh god," she heard herself whimper. "Oh god, I want you…"

Somehow, he had his hand between their bodies, and he was stroking her clit. The combined sensation of his hard cock filling her and his skillful fingers on her clit made her buck wildly, but there was no where she could go to escape the sensations. They were driving through her with the force of lightning, and all she could do was hang on while the sensations played out.

She felt like she was being wound tighter and tighter. Hailey's nails dug into Kieran's shoulders, his clothed shoulders, and she remembered all over again how naked she was, and how clothed he was. Her errant thought before, of a wanton demoness seducing a pure man, returned in full force. The thought brought her an extra burst of pleasure.

Kieran was pushing up into her, she was holding him tight, and suddenly, she spilled over the edge. Her thighs went rigid, and she shook so hard, she had to squeeze her eyes shut. Her body was rocked with a maelstrom of sensations. She couldn't help it if she tried. Her climax exploded, making her bury her face in Kieran's shoulder so that she could stay quiet.

She was still shuddering when he thrust up into her one last time, and for a very long moment, all she could think was how perfect it was.

"Hailey?"

"Hmm?"

"Are you well?"

She smiled a little at the concern in his voice, and she leaned up to kiss him. They were still joined intimately. Now she could feel a certain soreness between her legs, but still she had no urge to move or to do much of anything beyond revel in the closeness they shared.

"Very well, Major," she said softly. "And you?"

His laugh was slightly self-conscious.

"I think after something like that, there aren't many questions on my account, but thank you for asking. Hailey…"

There was something in his voice that made her stiffen. She wondered if he was going to tell her that it didn't mean anything. She wasn't quite sure she could take it if she had to hear it. Instead, she gently pulled away, staggering to her feet.

Kieran made a noise of concern and reached to steady her, but she stepped aside neatly. She turned her back when she went to dress herself. After a moment, she heard him sigh and do the same.

"Don't worry, I don't think that anything has changed between us," she said, trying to keep her voice low and easy. "This isn't going to make me ask for favors or make me think that it gets me off the hook."

"Hailey."

"I'm not someone who's going to go chasing after you, either. I know that as a Magus Corps agent, you need to be free to go wherever your duty takes you. Don't worry."

She was mostly dressed now, and she moved over to one of the openings that looked down over the sanctuary. She was faintly surprised to see by the light that it was likely only a little while past noon. Her morning sparring with Kieran felt distant now. She was tired, she realized.

"Hailey, stop."

She turned to look at him. Kieran was dressed now, but the act that they had shared had left his hair tousled and a faint blush on his fair skin. It made him look boyish, and she surprised herself with an unexpected longing for him.

"What?"

"This," he gestured between the two of them. "This is not nothing. I don't do this lightly, and correct me if I'm wrong, but I don't think you do it lightly either."

"Maybe I do," she said, lifting her chin up defiantly. "Maybe this is something I do with all of the men who decide that they want to beat me into the ground with sticks."

Kieran blinked several times.

"I would be very surprised."

"Well, I don't, but you didn't know that, did you?"

Kieran looked like he was going to contradict her, and she cut him off with a sharp gesture of her hand.

"What we did here, it doesn't matter right now, okay? It doesn't. It can't. We barely know each other." Kieran's face set in a stubborn fashion that she was beginning to know. "Even if there is something between us, there's a lot going on."

Kieran arched an eyebrow. The man could look bloody sardonic when he wanted to.

"So what you're saying is that there *might* be something between us?"

Hailey chewed her lip and nodded.

"What my heart is telling me and what my head is telling me are two very different things. You're a member of the Magus Corps, and you were sent to investigate me for some top secret thing. You're also an amazing lover who spoke to me as if I were a human being, who made me feel as if…"

She bit down on the words, but Kieran didn't look inclined to let her get away so easily.

"As if what, Hailey?"

"As if I was yours."

The words were nearly breathed, and Kieran covered the space between them in a matter of seconds. For such a big man, he could move very quickly. He went to put his arms around her, but she halted him with a single hand against his chest.

"But I'm not," she whispered, though she didn't push him away.

"But perhaps you'll allow yourself to be courted?"

Hailey laughed a little at the antiquated word, but then she surprised herself by nodding.

"I'm not in a place to offer you anything right this minute. Let me think. Let me sit with the idea for a little."

Kieran thought for a moment, and then he nodded.

He took her hand gently in his, and he brought it up to his lips. Hailey found that she was mesmerized by his mouth. It was finely shaped and soft from the kissing that they had been doing. She thought he was going to kiss the back of her hand, but then he turned it over and kissed the palm instead. The soft touch of his mouth to the tender skin there sent a shiver up her spine, and from the sly look on his face, she could see that he knew it.

"As you like. Think. Sit. Do what you need. I will be here when you are done."

Hailey realized that she was staring, but then she shook herself.

"All right. Um. All right. Let's get on with things. I mean, I can't imagine there's much you can do to test my abilities while we're up in the choir loft."

Kieran laughed.

"Well, there are things that I would like to do up here, but we should return to the courtyard, yes."

Hailey groaned.

"Not more sticks?"

"No, I had something different in mind."

CHAPTER FIVE

AFTER MAKING SURE that she had some food and some water, Kieran took Hailey back to the courtyard. She marveled at how different things were now than just a little while ago. She listened to him, and she was ready to show him what she could do.

At least, she was until he started explaining what he needed her to do.

"From the reports that we had from your previous covens, no one has ever tested to see how far your powers could go."

"Well, no. No one was lining up to have their powers drained away even temporarily so that I could practice, especially not after the rumor went around that people who I drained would never get it back."

Kieran snorted.

"Pure foolishness, of course. We have records on witches like you, though there have never been many with your gifts. They have never drained someone to the point where their powers never came back. Usually all it takes is a meal and some sleep, and soon enough, things are right back where they should be."

"You can tell people that all you like, but I had remarkably few volunteers. As far as I can tell though, there's not much limit to what I can do if I have, um, someone willing to lend me their power. I've thrown fire, I've managed to read minds for a while, and I've gone invisible as well."

"And you can throw ill-behaved Magus Corps majors back on their asses," Kieran added with a grin. "We know that." He paused and became serious. "Now what I want to do is to see how far your powers might go if you had the right volunteer. I'm fairly strong as far as these things are reckoned, so I'm going to give you the power you need."

Hailey hesitated, and Kieran could read the doubt on her face.

"Remember. No one has ever been permanently injured in these experiences. A few were knocked out, but that is because the witches in question were deliberately trying to hurt them. I know that you are not deliberately trying to hurt me at all."

Hailey warmed at his words, and then she nodded. She had agreed to do this. There was literally no other way to get the kind of power that she needed to test it.

"All right," she said. "What do you want me to do?"

"Let's start with what you know. Go easy, and try to send fire into the air."

He rolled up his sleeve and offered his bare forearm to her. Hailey laid her hand on his wrist, marveling at how warm and muscular he felt for a moment before she started concentrating.

She had done this a few times before, but never with someone with whom she had been intimate. The difference between touching Kieran now and draining him of power a few hours before was vast. Now she could sense his power, his energy. His reserve was vast. In her head, the image that appeared was of gazing out over a vast ocean. She could reach down and scoop some of that water up without ever running out.

Hailey pulled some of that power from him, and in the space of a moment, she sent it straight up into the air in a burst of fire. It was a geyser of red and gold, and she could feel it crisp the ends of her hair slightly. The exhalation of all of that power made her lightheaded, and by the time the flame died down, she found herself laughing.

To her surprise, Kieran was laughing as well, and his eyes lit up like a boy's.

"That was amazing!" he exclaimed. "Have you ever done anything like that before?"

"I lit a candle flame," she said between laughs. "I lit a bonfire!"

She sobered suddenly when she thought of how much power it took to send that much fire into the sky.

"Oh, Kieran, are you all right?"

He tilted his head, looking at her quizzically.

"You can see very well that I am, can't you?"

"I didn't take too much?"

Kieran frowned, and he held out his own hand. Hailey shivered as the temperature dropped and ice crystals started dancing above his palm. They were beautiful, formed from the moisture in the air. They spun faster and faster, and grew larger and larger. With a sudden movement, almost too fast for her to see, he flung the ice out, embedding them with pinpoint accuracy into the wooden door a hundred paces away.

"I feel fine," he said after considering it for a moment. "Maybe a little tired? Other than that, just fine. Let's try it again."

Hailey eyed him suspiciously.

"Is this some kind of macho thing? I don't want to do something like that and have you keel over."

Kieran held up his hands placatingly.

"I'm not much interested in keeling over either. Let's try it again, and if I feel like I'm about to get knocked over, we'll give it a rest. This time, let's try something that you've never tried before. Something a little more difficult."

Hailey thought for a moment.

"What about weather witching?"

"Sounds fantastic. Looks like there's some clouds over there for you to play with, so try it."

He offered her his hand again, and this time she took it more readily.

Weather witching was a much more precise form of magic. Some of the members of the Magus Corps would use it for offensive attacks, but other witches who had the power to influence the weather used it for more practical and benevolent purposes. Some of them brought an end to droughts, others quelled floods. It was a type of magic that was very dissimilar from simply shooting fire into the sky. Hailey had never tried it.

Once again, she drew power from Kieran, and once again, she had a dizzying impression of a power supply so vast she could never reach its end. She saw the clouds and thought about what she had read of weather witching. It was all about coaxing the world into the shape that she wanted to see it in. It was about pulling water from the air, like Kieran had done with his ice and about creating a change in the sky.

Hailey was beginning to feel a headache forming between her temples, but then she heard it.

There was a patter of rain that started as soft as cat's feet, and then it sped up. She didn't feel any droplets however, and in confusion she opened her eyes.

"That's the kind of thing that used to get you burned," Kieran remarked.

It was raining, and the rest of the courtyard was getting soundly soaked. However, the spot where Kieran and Hailey stood was dry as a bone. When she reached her hand out into the rain, she shivered at how cold it was and drew back immediately.

"Kieran…"

"This is the work of a powerful and trained weather witch. You said that you've never done this kind of work before?"

"No, never in my life."

Kieran's look was thoughtful.

"Hmm. Are you up for one more trial?"

"I am. But this time, can I choose?"

There was something immediately gratifying about the way he nodded and offered her his arm again. This time, she had a different idea. She remembered the electric touch of his lips against her palm. Now she did it to him, and the results were immediate and electric.

He pulled his breath in at the sensation, but Hailey couldn't concentrate on it. That power was there. She didn't need tools. She was the tool, and it was all there for her. The feeling of that much power coursing through her, vibrating through her, becoming a part of her, was intoxicating. Though she'd had vague ideas of what she could do with it, now there was only one thing in her mind. She grabbed hold of Kieran's hand, and in a moment, they were airborne. She lofted them into the air with a thought, and with dizzying speed, the monastery fell away beneath them.

Kieran shouted with excitement, and they were spiraling up into the sky. From their vantage point, they could see the snow-capped mountains laid out around them, see the dark and craggy faces that were turned to the world.

"This is incredible!" Kieran shouted, and Hailey could only laugh with agreement.

The air was frigid, but that mattered so much less to her than what they were doing. At first she only took them straight up, but when that palled, she began to fly them both in earnest. There was no fear in what she was doing, no worry or pain. All that she could feel was the excitement of flight and of the way the world stretched below them.

She pulled them up through the cloud cover and then down below it again. Then she could see the village at the foot of the hills, and on impulse, she darted closer, tugging Kieran behind.

"Don't do anything foolish," Kieran called.

"Wouldn't dream of it!"

However, there was a tall church steeple on the edge of the village, straight and iron, and she alighted them next to it. There was a ledge that was just wide enough for both of them to stand, and below, the people walking by looked small and far away.

"I certainly hope you have the power to get us down," Kieran said.

Instead of replying, she wrapped her arms around him and leaned up.

This kiss was different from the ones that they had shared before. It was electric, deep and sustaining. She could feel him so intimately like this. It was almost as intimate as being joined with him physically. She was tapped into him.

When she reached for his power, this time it came rushing up to meet her. She meant to fly them back to the monastery, but then something else occurred, and they both disappeared.

• • • • •

One moment, Kieran had been high above the village and looking down. The next, they were back in the main hall of the monastery, and people around them were shouting with surprise. Kieran, who had had centuries of battle preparation and trial by combat, was only a bit surprised, and looked down at Hailey, grinning like a fool.

To his shock, however, she was looking around her in dismay.

"Hailey? What's the matter?"

"I… that wasn't what I was… I meant to *fly* us back."

"Hailey, love, there's nothing to be concerned about. Nothing! I'm fine, you're well, you're better than well. You're amazing. Please, look at me."

Instead of doing that, Hailey stumbled backwards, her eyes as wide as dinner plates.

"Kieran, don't you understand? I completely lost control. I could have drained you dry. I could have seriously hurt you!"

Kieran made an impatient gesture.

"The mountains could rise up and dance. The sky could fall on our heads. Neither of those things happened, Hailey, and you didn't hurt me either. Come, come and look, just look for yourself."

He tried to offer her his arm again, but to his shock and his pain, she recoiled from him.

"Hailey?"

"Oh god, Kieran, I can't! I can't. You don't understand. I wasn't *in control*. I could have done anything."

"I trust you. I wasn't afraid at all."

"*I am!*"

The words were torn from her, and seeing the look of pain on her face, Kieran fell silent, completely stunned. Hailey had just accomplished some of the most amazing feats he had ever seen in his long life, and instead of being proud of herself, instead of being exhilarated, she looked horrified.

"Hailey, please, just look?"

She shook her head wildly, backing away from him so quickly she almost fell. When he tried to right her, she jerked away.

"No! No, don't!"

Hailey turned and fled, leaving Kieran to gaze after her.

His first instinct was to go after her, but rationally, he knew that all that would happen would be the same thing all over again. Instead, he restrained himself, shaking his head. He looked up to see that there were people in the main hall staring at him, and even worse, he could see Donato at the back. Though he wanted nothing better than to go to Hailey and to make sure that she was all right, he grit his teeth and walked up to the coven master instead.

"So you've awakened the dragon," Donato said. Kieran could have struck him.

"I am performing my function as a major in the Magus Corps, coven master," Kieran said stiffly. "I would thank you to remember that."

"I don't question your resolve or your function. I only want to know what you have done to a member of my coven."

Kieran's temper boiled at the man's tone.

"Member of your coven? What it looks like to me is that Hailey is kept wrapped in cotton. You know what her powers are, how amazing she could be, and you keep her locked away from her ability to use it. In times past, that would border on torture."

Donato's eyes sharpened, and he stood up straight. He was nowhere near as tall as Kieran, but he had a commanding presence that reminded the major that Donato had ruled the coven for generations.

"Are you truly so naive? Do you think that you can bring a woman with that set of powers here and allow her to merely use them as she saw fit? I would have had a justifiable panic on my hands. If she had looked like she was stepping the least bit out of line. Well. People are afraid of her, Major. There are stories about her kind."

"Oh yes, those tales of warlocks and witches drained dry? Learn a new story. That's just a myth. Look at me, for the love of all that's holy."

Donato eyed Kieran up and down as the major gestured.

"In a single day, she has used me to throw fire into the sky, to make it rain, to fly and to teleport. Before that, when I menaced a woman—one of your precious coven members—she struck me back. Do I look drawn? Do I look like I'm on the verge of losing what I am?"

Donato snorted inelegantly.

"Why should you? You're bonded to her."

Kieran halted, struck to the core. Donato raked Kieran over with disdainful eyes.

"To be perfectly honest, perhaps you could have been a little more subtle than to claim each other in the choir loft, but that is something that I'm willing to overlook. What surprises me, Major, is how you could avoid recognizing what happened."

Kieran finally found words.

"We're not bonded. I haven't initiated her. We used protection."

Donato's glance was almost pitying.

"Some bonds don't need initiation, but I can see it with my own eyes. You're bonded. You will enhance each other's powers whether you know it or not. Just don't expect anyone else to offer themselves up, Major." Donato shook his head. "Work it out for yourself, and leave the rest of my coven out of it. Things are difficult enough with Beatrice going missing."

The name seemed to ring a bell, but he nodded icily at Donato, and the two men parted ways.

Now that he had time away to think, he could reflect on Donato's words, and slowly, he recognized them for nothing but the honest truth. Witches and warlocks that had a special bond could do far more together than they could do apart.

What Hailey had done was impressive, and when he thought about it, it should have been impossible. The amount of power it took to send two Wiccans flying through the air was one thing, but to teleport them back over any sort of distance at all was phenomenal. That was something that would likely leave most witches or warlocks tired—if they were doing it under their own power.

When Kieran assessed himself, he realized that he felt less tired than excited. He and Hailey were on the brink of something new. He had a role in this, and there was no part of him that did not want to be in that space with her.

He needed to think, so he walked down to the kitchen. The monastery had a kitchen of course, with an enormous fireplace that stretched from wall to wall. However, the Angioli coven was under no vow of poverty, and the kitchen held all of the modern conveniences that might be necessary. There were some people there, chatting and joking, but when they saw the Magus Corps major and his thunderous expression, they cleared out quickly. Kieran felt a little guilty for their reaction, but he couldn't worry about it too much when there was so much on the line.

There was fresh-baked bread sprinkled with rosemary on the cutting board, and investigation into one of the refrigerators yielded a soft white cheese and a hard salami. Kieran cut generous slices of both for himself. Now that he was no longer flying through the air, he realized he was hungry, and for at least a little while, he could concern himself only with eating. The food was simple but hearty, and he ate until he could no longer feel the rumblings of hunger in his belly.

He was just getting up to go when he realized that he was being watched. The young boy couldn't have been older than ten, with a shock of fair hair and wide dark eyes that looked like they had already seen too much. If he was part of the Angioli coven at this age, that meant he was Wiccan-born.

Most Wiccan children were raised with loving care, but life was unpredictable. Kieran could tell it had been so for this boy, and so he gentled his tone when he spoke.

"What are you looking for, hm? Are you afraid that I'm a draugen who's going to eat you?"

The young boy looked nervous, but was caught by the foreign word.

"What's a draugen?"

"It's a man from the sea. A man drowns, and a monster comes back out, enormous, dripping with seawater and seaweed, hungry to eat the flesh of those who were luckier."

The boy considered.

"I've never seen the sea."

"Well, then I must not be a draugen, and I must be safe to know. Are you hungry, to be staring at my food with eyes like that?"

The boy's face cracked into a shy grin, and he nodded.

There was a certain kind of safety and security in being able to do a task as simple as looking after a small child. Kieran cut some bread, cheese and meat for the boy, and from the boy's quiet direction, he found a pitcher of lemonade and a bag of apples as well. He took an apple for himself and sat down beside the boy.

"Beatrice said that you were pushing Hailey too hard today," the boy said without preamble.

Kieran winced.

"So the story has spread so far?" he asked. "Does Beatrice think that I'm a monster?"

The boy's grin was lopsided.

"Beatrice thinks that everyone's a monster or a Templar until she decides otherwise," he told Kieran confidently. "She used to be even worse before she came here though, so it's all right."

Kieran thought of the beautiful young witch who had interrupted the sparring session he had had with Hailey that morning. That already felt like it was a hundred years ago, and looking back on it now, he could see where he had gone all wrong. He realized that she would never have lashed out to defend herself. Instead it had taken a danger to her friend to bring her out.

A cold part of his mind told him that it was a lever that could be used, either by the Magus Corps or by the coven that was so interested in Hailey's talents. He shuddered when he realized that after gaining her trust, he would be the tool to manipulate her.

Kieran shook his head, and he glanced back at where the boy was watching him with solemn eyes.

"What about you? Do you think I pushed her too hard?"

The boy scowled, and he gave the question serious consideration before he answered. It was incredible in some ways to think that this child held within himself a seed for great power and long life, but there it was. There was no real natural end to a Wiccan lifespan after they had been initiated, and this boy could live out the new millennium if he was lucky.

"I don't think you should push anyone," the boy said finally. "I think that you should tell them what you need, and if they have the generosity and the spirit to help you, they will give it to you."

Kieran chuckled in surprise.

"Well, that was certainly a wise thing to hear out of you. I believe I will take your advice, little master…?"

"Luca. They call me Luca here. I don't remember what my name was before."

Kieran frowned a little. The potential for a long life was no guarantee of a safe one after all, and many children born into Wiccan families found themselves orphaned. He himself had been one of them.

Luca finished his meal and dutifully washed his plate and Kieran's as well. Before leaving, the boy glanced over his shoulder at the major, and Kieran felt as if he was being judged by quite an old soul.

"Hailey can hide even better than Beatrice or me if she wants to," the young boy said at last. "If you're going to go ask her instead of pushing her, I can tell you where she probably went."

"I would be very grateful. I know that I acted poorly earlier, and I am in no hurry to repeat my mistake. Tell me where to find her, and neither you nor she will regret it."

It seemed like that was enough for Luca, who nodded.

"If she is not in her room, she's probably in the west tower. Donato says that it used to be a place for rich people to look out over the land while they were trapped at the monastery, but it became so old that none of us care to go up there."

"Thank you, Luca."

The boy grinned and left, and Kieran was once again left to his own thoughts.

In some ways, he thought, he wasn't all that different from Hailey. Members of the Magus Corps served an extremely vital function when it came to protecting the Wiccan world from the predations of Templars and other enemies. However their combative powers and, in many cases, their combative natures made them a poor fit for the people they protected. His clashes with Donato were just the most recent example of the kind of welcome most Magus Corps agents expected when they had to deal closely with covens.

With a sigh, Kieran rose up. He still wasn't quite ready to face Hailey yet. If he had to guess, there was a chance that she was still too upset to deal with him. The inner courtyard waited, and he had gone a few days without the training and conditioning that he preferred to do regularly. He would wear himself out and then go to find her.

CHAPTER SIX

THE WEST TOWER was like much of the monastery that was not frequently used by the Angioli coven. It was dusty and rundown, but underneath the grime, there were remnants of a truly fine tradition of craftsmen. Hailey didn't know anything about the monks who had once walked through the hallways where Wiccans now lived, but she wondered about them from time to time.

The west tower had an enormous leaded glass window with a few utterly clear panes that must have cost a fortune when they were first installed. Through them, she could look out over the land, away from the mountains, towards the village.

She had been told that the tower was a favored haunt for exiles when she first arrived, a place for them to look out over the hills and to imagine the world they had left behind. The Angioli coven was a bustling place, full of people who knew what they wanted and what they were looking for, but it was also a place for people who treasured their solitude.

Hailey was someone who had become used to being alone, but she was unsure if she would ever treasure it. Unbidden, the thought of Kieran's hands sliding all over her body came to her. She shivered to think of his eyes gazing deeply into hers, at how much he could see of her, at how much he wanted to see.

She carefully pulled away from the thought of their flight and her use of the teleportation ability to bring them back. She had felt power beyond imagining when she touched the major, and something told her that if she fell into its depths, she would never come back up again. She might light up the sky like a Roman candle, but she had no confidence that Kieran would survive it.

She was so lost in her thoughts that she didn't notice the knock at first. It was only when it came again and more insistently that she looked up.

When she opened the door, she was unsurprised to find Kieran. He had bathed sometime since she had last seen him, and his dark hair was slicked down. Even in the dim light, she could make out a pink scar along his temple. Without thinking about it, she reached out to touch him, and it wasn't until her fingers were on that tender skin that she realized how rude it was.

Blushing, she jerked her hand away, and Kieran chuckled.

"I think that after everything that we did today, that wouldn't be a problem," he rumbled, closing the door behind him.

The west tower should have felt tight and cramped with him in it, but instead it only felt right. After a moment, she simply took his hand and tugged him over to the window. There was a deep stone bench that was set directly beneath the glass. They sat close for a very long moment, and Hailey rested her head lightly on his shoulder.

"I'm afraid of what all of this means," she whispered, and his large hand came up to stroke her cheek.

"It means that you are a very powerful witch who could do a world of good."

Hailey laughed a little sadly.

"Do you understand how new that feels? Before you came here, they called me a vampire. I was something that was meant to be carefully housed, but I was always meant to be watched. Of course there would always come the day when my lust for power overcame whatever feeble bonds I could form. Then I would attack everyone around me and have to be put down like a mad dog. I've read the histories, Kieran. Sometimes it was the Magus Corps that was called in to deal with witches like me."

Kieran held her a little closer.

"Times have a way of changing, especially when you're willing to make them change. That would not happen today. I would not allow it to happen."

"Am I really such an asset that I cannot be risked?" Hailey asked bitterly. She felt the way that Kieran stiffened against her, and she immediately felt ashamed.

"I will not allow it to happen because it is not right, and because regardless of what others fear, you do not deserve that kind of abuse. You have done nothing wrong. Instead what I have seen over the past day is a woman who would do anything to save the people that she cares about, who only has to hear that she could do good before she throws herself into it. Also…"

"Also?"

"There are also my feelings for you," he said quietly. "They are not important at the moment, and they cannot be important, not for the work that lies in front of you."

"What if I say that they're more important?" Hailey demanded, but even as she asked, she knew the answer.

"It wouldn't last," Kieran responded promptly. "You could be happy by my side for a few months, perhaps even a few years, but then the need to attend to something greater would eat at you. It is what lies at the core of you. It is what makes you so uniquely yourself."

Hailey buried her face in his shoulder.

"You believe me to be much better than I am," she muttered,

and he chuckled softly.

"I believe you to be exactly as you are, sweetheart."

Hailey shook her head. Here, cuddled up against Kieran's bulk and without the stares of the rest of the coven around her, she could be honest.

"You didn't feel what I felt," she whispered. "You didn't feel how…how deep things are. I could see what you were offering me, and it was endless. It was intoxicating. It was so much power that I could do anything I wanted. What if the need for it became overwhelming? What if I took too much? You're not invulnerable."

"Sweetheart, I have lived for centuries, and despite it, one thing that I have always known is that I was meant to die someday. I have the scars to prove it, too. I do not fear you, and I wish you wouldn't fear yourself."

His blunt and utterly calm words loosened a great knot in the back of her throat. Hailey fought back tears for what felt like a long while. When she looked up, at least her eyes were dry.

"You say some pretty incredible things, Major," she said, keeping her voice deliberately light. "Let's see if you still believe them after I've taken over the world."

"Well, please let me be the first to swear loyalty to our new queen."

Hailey smiled a little at his grave pronouncement.

"How much more testing do we have to do? Is there going to be a lot the coven or the Magus Corps needs to know before they decide if they want to front me a ticket across the world?"

"I'd like to do some more tomorrow, after we're both rested."

Kieran offered her his hand and pulled her off of the bench, leading her towards the door.

"I think we should both eat, sleep and rest up for tomorrow. Perhaps if you can find your friend Beatrice, you can sit and tell her that I'm not a monster after all."

Hailey frowned.

"What do you mean, find Beatrice?"

Kieran shrugged.

"Donato mentioned that she was missing, but she told me she was going down to the village. I imagine she'll be back at any time now."

The feeling of unease that had been budding in the back of her mind grew large, and frantic. Hailey glanced behind her. Outside the window, night was falling with the typical Alpine speed. There were still a few streaks of scarlet in the sky, but in a very small amount of time, it was going to be pitch black.

Kieran seemed to pick up on her panic.

"What? What is it?"

Hailey threw the door open, and nearly started running down the hall. After a shocked moment, Kieran was on her heels, and she explained to him.

"Beatrice's parents were killed by Templars, and the only reason that the Templars didn't kill her too is because her mother shut her in a wooden chest. She nearly suffocated in there, but it was better than what the Templars had in store for her. She had to stay in that chest for hours, and ever since then, she can't stand to be in the dark. There's no way she would be out in the woods in the pitch black. Something's wrong."

"Stay calm," Kieran cautioned. "Perhaps she's come back."

Hailey hoped that Kieran's words were true, but after checking in with an increasingly worried Donato, she learned that they were not. With the dark setting in fast and the chill growing even deeper, the coven mobilized to find the missing teen.

Through it all, Kieran was silent, watching the proceedings unfold. He only spoke up when Donato asked him to search as well, and he nodded quickly.

"I'll take Hailey with me. With her teleportation, we can start from the village and work our way back towards this location."

Donato paused, but then he nodded. Hailey was relieved. If this had happened and Kieran wasn't present, there was a good chance that she would have been left to simmer at the monastery. Instead, she grabbed a long, black coat from her room and a pair of thick gloves as well. She found Kieran outfitting himself similarly, and when she arrived, he offered her his arm.

This time she simply took the power that he offered. It was still deep and strong and strange, but even with a little experience, she was learning to make the most of it. She saw the apprehensive looks of the coven as they blinked out, but when they appeared again on the outskirts of the village, she was only focused on searching. She was just turning to Kieran to see where he wanted to start when there was a puff of air and a heavy weight alighted on her shoulder.

"Merit!"

The owl blinked at her, and in the light of the nearly full moon, she was completely alert and aware. The owl looked past her to Kieran and to Hailey's surprise, made a soft crooning noise.

"This is Merit. She's never made that noise to anyone who wasn't me."

Despite the dire situation, Kieran smiled.

"She's a beauty, and she'll be a great deal of help in our search. That likely means that it's time to introduce you to Cavanaugh."

Hailey watched with curiosity as Kieran stepped further into the treeline, and then he tilted his head back and howled. It was full-throated and powerful, ringing through the trees and up into the mountains. It made Hailey think less of a human imitating a wolf than what a human would sound like if he howled to communicate with his pack.

The answering howl was immediate, and in just a few minutes, an enormous wolf bounded down the hill towards them. Hailey gasped. She had known Wiccans with wolf familiars before, but few of them had wolves as large as the one that approached Kieran.

On her shoulder, Merit fluttered nervously, but Hailey reached up and calmed her. For his part, Kieran reached down and seized the wolf's head squarely in his hands. Instead of rubbing and petting the wolf as if he were a dog, he gripped the wolf's fur firmly, resting his own forehead on the wolf's broad head.

When he stood, he turned to Hailey with a grin.

"This is Cavanaugh. I met him when I was doing a mission in Canada for the Magus Corps, and I've had him with me for two years."

"He's handsome," Hailey murmured, and to her surprise, the wolf came over to examine her. She stood very still. Familiars weren't pets, not really. Wild familiars especially could be unpredictable with people who were not theirs, and she had heard of more than one unwise encounter in the past.

Cavanaugh approached her with his ears and tail up, and he sniffed at her curiously. She felt as if she was being evaluated by a keen and alien eye, but whatever the wolf was looking for, he found it. He trotted closer, and pressed companionably against her hip with his large head before turning back to Kieran. He looked for all the world like a soldier awaiting orders. Hailey thought that there was some wisdom in the saying that familiars picked their owners, rather than the other way around.

"Nothing in the village could hold Beatrice if she didn't want to be held," Hailey said. "She must be somewhere between here and the monastery."

Kieran nodded.

"We can walk the path slowly, looking for any sign of her, but I bet we can also convince Cavanaugh and Merit to criss-cross to either side of it. They have better eyes than we do."

It took a little bit of time to explain what was necessary to the two animals, but soon enough, Merit winged silently into the woods, Cavanaugh loped off in the opposite direction, and Hailey and Kieran started up the trail.

They walked in silence, halting every time one of the animals crossed in front of them, but finally, Hailey had to ask what had been on her mind ever since she heard that Beatrice was missing.

"Is it possible that it could be Templars?" she asked quietly, and to her dismay, Kieran didn't immediately say no.

"There are many things it could be," he said slowly. "Unfortunately, Templars are not out of the question."

Hailey shivered.

"I didn't think that they were active in this part of the world."

"They usually aren't. The problem is that we're seeing more Templar activity all over the world. They're showing up throughout North and South America, and there have been reports throughout South Asia and the Middle East as well. They've always been their strongest in Europe, but they're growing even worse. Something's got them stirred up, and well. The last time they got rattled, they lead a secret witch burning crusade that stormed across Northern Europe."

"Is that why you were sent to find me?"

Kieran didn't bother hiding it.

"It was. With more Templars on the move, it is becoming even more important that we weaponize whatever resources we have."

His words clunked like a stone on her chest, but she also remembered how warm his eyes had been when they had spoken before, how gentle he had been with her. There was more to her than a weapon, and she knew he understood that.

They walked in silence for a moment, the moon lighting their way. Just when Hailey was beginning to despair, she heard a loud scream that she recognized as Merit's.

"Kieran, this way!"

Without thinking about it, she reached for his power. Touching his cheek with her fingers, she found it and took what she needed.

A greenish ball of light formed in her palm, throwing the woods around them into relief. In the starkness of her light, they could see well enough to leave the path. After Kieran uttered a short sharp howl, he turned to follow her, and she knew that Cavanaugh wouldn't be far behind.

In a clearing less than a quarter mile from the trail, Merit was circling above a cloth that was crumpled on the ground. When she picked it up and examined it, Hailey nodded.

"This is Beatrice's, there's no doubt in my mind."

"Excellent, let me have it."

Kieran took the scrap of fabric and held it up to Cavanaugh, who had come bounding up behind them. The wolf's reaction was strange. With his ears up, he took in the scent, and then suddenly, he laid his ears back and the fur on the back of his neck stood up. The growl that he uttered was the stuff of nightmares, and Kieran pulled the cloth away.

"Templars," he said grimly. "We've dealt with them before."

He looked at Cavanaugh directly, and Hailey wondered at the communion that passed between man and wolf. Merit alighted on her shoulder again, careful of her talons, and absently, Hailey stroked the back of Merit's head and back.

After a long moment, Cavanaugh put his nose to the ground and started casting around for the scent while Kieran stepped back to rejoin Hailey.

"He'll search out the scent, and now we can follow him. Make sure that you don't get between him and a Templar. It won't be safe for you."

"There's no doubt about it, then? This is the work of a Templar?"

Kieran nodded soberly.

"They didn't kill her out of hand. They took her somewhere. That means that they have an interest in keeping her alive. That works in our favor."

"There's something you're not telling me," Hailey said, and Kieran shook his head.

"There's nothing that I'm going to tell you," he corrected. "I've rescued people who were captured by Templars before. Some were fine afterward. Some weren't."

There was a world of pain, suffering and torture in that final word, and Hailey almost let the panic overwhelm her before she stuffed it back down. She had to believe that Beatrice was still alive. She had to believe that Beatrice was going to be fine. Afterward, she could collapse if she needed to, but she certainly wasn't going to do that now.

After a few moments, Cavanaugh howled again and raced off into the woods, Kieran and Hailey hot on his heels. It would have been impossible for Hailey to keep up at all if the way hadn't been narrow and tangled. More than once, man and wolf got caught up by briars, while she used Merit for guidance.

They were going deeper into the mountains, and every moment they climbed, she was getting colder. She prayed that Beatrice was out of the chill, that no matter what was happening, that she was somewhere warm.

They walked for more than an hour, and then Kieran stopped abruptly. Hailey almost crashed into his back, and then she pulled back. They were in a clear spot in the woods. She dimmed her witch light, wrapping her fingers around the glow. Green light leaked through her fingers, but it quelled the brightness a great deal.

"There's a cabin up ahead, and Cavanaugh thinks that's where Beatrice is. Hailey, I need you to stay quiet, and to stay hidden."

Hailey stared at him.

"Are you crazy? That's my friend in there."

Kieran wrapped his hands around her shoulders, and he made her look him in the eye.

"And I am a major of the Magus Corps. I've performed dozens of extractions, and I need to pull rank."

Hailey opened her mouth to argue, and he shook his head.

"You've helped me get here, and you're going to help me more later, I know that. Right now, though, you need to understand that there are things that I can't control in there. I need you to let me do the thing that I know best how to do. Do you understand?"

Biting her lip, she nodded, and in return, he gave her a tender kiss.

"Beatrice is going to be fine. We'll be going back to the monastery soon."

With nothing more than that, he slipped away into the shadows. Hailey blinked, startled by how invisible he could make himself, and she leaned back against a tree to wait. From her vantage point, she could see the cabin quite clearly. She could see a brief moment where Cavanaugh was lit up by the moonlight, but she couldn't see Kieran.

The windows of the cabin were bright. A man's silhouette paced back and forth in front of the window, and Hailey could see him gesturing wildly. From the distance, she could tell that he was shouting.

It made her stomach flip over in terror to think of Beatrice tied up, hurt or even worse on the floor of that cabin, but she kept herself calm. She trusted Kieran with every fiber of her being, and if he said that he was going to bring Beatrice out, then he would.

She could see some activity near the rear of the cabin. She waited.

Suddenly there was a shout, and one of the windows broke. She could see two men fighting, and she heard Cavanaugh howling like a demon let out of hell.

Hailey forced herself to stand still. She knew that if she charged into a battle with no clue what was going on, she would be just as much of a liability for Kieran as she would be a help.

She managed to maintain that stasis until she saw another figure, one she did not recognize running through the clearing towards the cabin. It was not Kieran, it was no one she recognized, and she realized that Kieran and Cavanaugh were going to have some very unwanted company.

She froze for a moment, and then without thinking about it further, she surged toward the cabin.

CHAPTER SEVEN

KIERAN HAD MANAGED to get a look at the cabin after he made his way to the rear. There was a window that had the blind rolled up just a little bit extra, and what he saw made his blood boil.

The teen who had confronted him in the courtyard less than twenty four hours ago was on the ground. She lay terribly still, and there was a man standing over her. He was nearly as big as Kieran himself, but there was something jerky and uncoordinated about his motions. He looked like he was talking to himself, and from time to time, he would look down on Beatrice and spit.

The man's fury was rising to what Kieran feared was a crescendo, and there was a large knife beside the man as well. When he reached for that knife, his dark eyes focused on Beatrice's helpless form, Kieran knew that he couldn't wait to act. He gestured for Cavanaugh to enter through the other window, and with a flicker of his will, he used his powers over the cold to freeze and then shatter the glass.

In a matter of seconds, he heaved himself over the edge of the window. The man in front of him whirled around to face him. His hands were up, the knife driving straight for Kieran's face. Kieran fell back enough for Cavanaugh to swarm the man, a whirlwind of fur and teeth. When the man was distracted, Kieran struck him from behind.

The Templar was powerful, but he went down under the onslaught swiftly. He was biting, swearing and trying his best to heave them both off of his body, but it was only a matter of time. He moved at the wrong moment, baring his neck, and with absolutely no hesitation, Cavanaugh ripped his throat out.

Kieran felt no pity for the dying man who had made a teenager's day into a lifelong nightmare. After he was sure that the man was dead, he moved over to where Beatrice lay. She was frightfully still, but her chest rose and fell. Her hands were tied in front of her, and he winced to see how deeply the cords bit into her tender wrists.

"Okay, honey, we've got you."

She stirred a little at his words, which was promising, and he lifted her gently in his arms.

That was the vulnerable position he was in when the door burst open, and another man stood there. This one bore a sword, and he took the scene in at a glance. He raised his weapon, and all Kieran could think was that he was too slow, too slow by far. He heard Cavanaugh roaring with anger, he tried to reach for his own power, but Beatrice was there, weighing him down.

Suddenly a shock of light filled the cabin. It was so brilliant that it was all he could see, and even after the light died away, everything was a blur for him. Kieran stumbled up to defend himself, somehow putting Beatrice down and behind him, and then he felt a light touch across his cheek, and a soft murmured 'sorry.'

It was agony not being able to see what was happening, but he heard a single shout from the man who had entered and the clatter of a sword against the ground. Then all was silent except for Cavanaugh's confused whimper, and Hailey's shocked cry.

• • • • •

Hailey knew that Kieran considered her a very powerful witch, but now, in the darkness and only with a light that she had fueled with his power, Hailey felt useless. No matter how ineffectual she felt, however, that didn't change what she had to do. When she saw the mysterious figure approach the cabin, she knew she had to act.

The light was all she had, so that was what she used. She trailed the man into the cabin, and it was child's play to follow him through the door. She could see a confusion of people in front of her. There was a man on the ground, and Cavanaugh was tearing his flesh. More importantly, however, there was Kieran, and there would be nothing between him and the man that had entered.

That was when she held the light in her hand high and forced the rest of the power she had taken through it. Her eyes were shut tight in anticipation of the blast, but she knew that no one else had that luxury. Instead, she heard shouts of dismay and fright, and when she opened her eyes, everyone else was blinking and blind.

She crossed the space between her and Kieran as quickly as she could, and without thinking about it, she touched his face. It was a strangely intimate moment in the middle of all of the carnage. All she could think to say was a murmured apology as she passed by.

It was the same as it had been before. She could feel the depth of his power and the strength of what they shared. This time, however, instead of doing something for pleasure or to test her abilities, it was deadly serious.

The power thrummed through her like a river of fire. She was lit up with it when she turned to face the Templar. His sword was still in his hand. Blinded, he was warding with it, keeping it close to his body so that he could fend off anyone who came at him. He was blinking his eyes rapidly to try to make them adjust, but she could have told him that it was already too late.

She knew that Kieran was a master of cold and ice, and she wondered distantly if that had something to do with her comfort now. She looked at the man in front of her, and in that timeless moment, she could see many details. She could see that he was older than she was, grizzled with a beard that went down his chest. She saw that his eyes were a pale, pale blue and that there was a scar on his face that pulled the side of his mouth down.

Hailey saw the details as indifferently as she would note the features of a rock face. It didn't change what she needed to do to someone who had threatened Kieran and Beatrice.

She imagined the veins in his body, the veins that ran with blood. Blood was liquid and was as susceptible to cold as water, and so she concentrated on his blood chilling and slowing.

She imagined it freezing.

There was one moment of horror where the man knew exactly what it was she was doing. There was nothing in his face but anger and hate. He made a choked sound, and then the sword fell out of his hand. She watched it hit the ground, and his heavy body followed just a moment later.

The enormity of what she had done struck Hailey with the force of a blow, and with a soft cry, she stumbled back. It had only taken her a few moments to kill a man who had been living, and the reality of it suffocated her. She couldn't get enough air into her body. Her heart was beating so fast it felt like it could burst out of her chest. Her knees felt weak, and her stomach rebelled. If she had eaten anything in the last few hours she would have lost it, but instead, she only retched piteously.

She was reeling through a world that she no longer recognized, and when powerful arms wrapped around her, she could have sobbed with relief.

"Hailey, Hailey, darling it's all right."

His words were like cool water on a burn, but she couldn't let herself give in to them, not yet. She jerked away, and in doing so, she managed to reclaim some of the calm that had been taken over the last few minutes.

"Can you see?" she asked urgently.

He nodded slowly.

"It's coming back to me. I can make out shapes now, and I can almost see your face. It'll come. Hailey, what did you–"

He was interrupted by a soft and frightened cry from Beatrice. Hailey knelt by the girl's side, crooning softly to her. Beatrice recognized Hailey in an instant and clung to the older woman, burying her face in Hailey's neck.

Hailey felt a relief that was so great she nearly fell over. It was Beatrice, and she was safe, and as she held her, Beatrice babbled out what had happened.

She had been on the path, heading back hours ago, and she had heard a voice calling for help. She didn't know what she could do, but she knew that she simply couldn't leave someone helpless and alone on the mountainside. She had walked carefully into the woods, but then she had been struck down from behind.

"And you haven't woken up since?"

Beatrice shook her head, and Hailey thanked the gods for that small mercy. Beatrice had never seen the men who had taken her, and though there would likely be repercussions for this night, they would hopefully not be as bad as what she suffered after her experiences as a child.

"Hailey, Hailey, what happened?"

Beatrice started to sit up and turn, but Hailey firmly kept her turned away from the two dead men in the cottage. Instead, she guided her to the table, set with three mugs and three bowls that she pushed aside, and seated her down.

"Okay, look at me, honey."

Beatrice did as she was told, and Hailey was relieved to see that her pupils were the same size.

"I don't think that you have a concussion, but we'll have someone in the infirmary take a look at you when we get back."

"Can you teleport us back?"

That was Kieran, standing up from his study of the man she had killed, and his face was so blank that it made her shiver.

She nodded without thinking about it, and she recoiled a little when he offered her his arm.

"Kieran, I can't, not when I just took it from you without asking before."

"Hailey, you're not thinking clearly. If you had asked, I would have given it to you. Right now, we need to get Beatrice home."

He was right, and she knew it. She rested her hand on his bare arm, and she sought that power that he gave her so willingly. With her hands tight on both of them, she sent the three of them jumping through space, back to the safety of the monastery.

As they faded out, the door to the cabin creaked open.

CHAPTER EIGHT

PEOPLE WERE STILL out searching when Hailey, Kieran, and Beatrice returned to the Angioli coven's monastery, but there were enough coven members around to help them when they appeared in the courtyard. A man and a woman caught Beatrice in their arms and hurried her to medical aid. Donato strode up to confront them.

Hailey had always thought that the coven master was cool towards her. She was shocked to her core when he swept her up in his arms.

"Thank you," he whispered in her ear. "Thank you for what you have done."

His words dissolved the last of the control that had been holding her up, and she dissolved into tears. It was a deep well of grief that came up out of nowhere, but it reached to the core of her. She wept for the pain that Beatrice had suffered that night. She wept for the sorrow and panic she had felt since she realized her friend was missing. The shade of the man that she had killed lingered there too. When she could find words, they were garbled and panicked.

"I killed him, Donato, sir, I killed him, oh gods, I reached for the power, and I–"

She subsided into sobs, and to her shock, Donato didn't let her go in disgust and fear. Instead, she felt him turn to Kieran.

"She killed a Templar?"

"To protect Beatrice, yes."

"Good."

That emphatic pronouncement was too much for her. It was all too much, and her knees sagged underneath her. Her vision dimmed, and the last thing she heard was Kieran's frantic voice calling her name.

• • • • •

"This really isn't the way I wanted to see your bedroom," Kieran joked, but it was a poor one, and he was glad Hailey couldn't hear it. He sat by her narrow bed in a straight-backed chair that was only growing more uncomfortable by the hour.

In her bed, Hailey was nearly as white as the sheets, her red hair the only color to be seen. He had brushed it earlier, and so it lay prettily enough, but she was so still that it reminded him uncomfortably of a deathbed memorial.

The woman who ran the infirmary had come by a few hours ago. She was a lovely witch, tall with a streak of silver in her dark hair. She had not spoken, but instead she had passed her hands lightly over Hailey's body, a pale golden glow radiating in the space between her palms and Hailey's skin.

She nodded when she was done, and turned to go.

"Well, what's wrong?"

The woman shrugged, and Kieran realized that she must be mute. She pointed to Hailey's head, and she spread her hands out. She shook her head.

"She's stressed, but she'll heal?"

The medic nodded.

"When?"

She shrugged, and with that, Kieran had to be content.

Luca came and brought him food. He ate it without tasting it. The boy's company was welcome, but at some point, he had gone off to sleep.

It was a lonely vigil, and eventually Kieran dozed off in the night. He was seated on the chair, but he had leaned his body across her bed.

When he awakened. The first thing that he realized was that someone was holding his hand. The second was that someone was petting his hair. He raised his head, and looked up into a pair of beautiful green eyes.

"You're awake," he said softly, and her answering smile was narrow and strange.

"I am. I think I'm glad of it."

Kieran sat up, straightening the kink out of his back.

"Why would you say that? Of course you should be glad that you're up."

"I killed a man, Kieran. He died because of me."

"Hailey, you killed a man who was going to kill me and Beatrice. If you hadn't acted, the gods alone know what would have happened. You saved us."

She shook her head as if she didn't want to hear it.

"I took his life, and I took that power from you. I didn't even think about it. I didn't even care."

Kieran took a tighter grip on her hand. Somehow, he felt as if she was drifting away, as if he were losing her. It was a foolish thought. She was sitting right there, and he knew that she was fine, but it didn't quell the panic that was rising up in him.

"Do you know how many people I've killed, Hailey? I don't. Every person who I've killed has been trying to kill me, and that was exactly what happened last night." She made a sound of protest, but he kept talking. "If you can't excuse yourself, you can't excuse me, and there is no excuse that is necessary at all. We all do what we have to do to survive. Nothing changes that, and that man who came in the door would have killed me and Beatrice. He would have killed you as well. These men were Templars. They want us all dead."

Hailey's brilliant green eyes welled up with tears again. When she pulled away, he forced himself to open his hand.

"I can't think of it that way. It's all mushed up in my head. I took power from you, and I killed him. I didn't weigh my options. I didn't try to strike him down from behind, and I didn't try to make Merit attack him. I acted like an animal."

Kieran felt something inside him wrench. She was beautiful and fragile sitting up in her narrow bed. She was tearing herself up over something that he did on a semi-regular basis, but he could see that she didn't think of it that way.

"You took a life to protect Beatrice and me. You did nothing wrong."

Hailey was silent for a long moment, and she turned her face to the wall.

"Will you leave me please?"

"Hailey?"

"Please. I have to think, and I can't do so while you're here. I'm sorry. Please."

Her voice was so small and soft that he wished he could raise that Templar from the dead and kill him again. Instead, he kept his temper, and he nodded. He reached for her to stroke her hair, but he stopped himself at the last moment.

He left, and there was something final in it.

CHAPTER NINE

HAILEY THOUGHT THAT she could think while Kieran was gone, but four days proved her wrong. Her memories of that brutal night were jumbled. She could remember the feeling of power she held in her hands, she could remember the sound of the man's body striking the ground. She could remember Kieran holding her, and she remembered holding Beatrice. When she concentrated on those events too closely, she felt sick. But try as she might, she couldn't bring them into focus.

Beatrice came by, and the two of them climbed into Hailey's bed together, simply holding each other. It was painful to see Beatrice so worn and drawn, but there was already a glimmer of her old humor around the edges of it. Hailey knew that her friend would bounce back, even if it took a while.

Donato came by as well, and for the first time, he sat and spoke with Hailey at length. The gratitude for her rescue of Beatrice was real, and the coven master apologized for the way she had been treated in her time at the Angioli coven. He swore that she would always have a home there, and that no matter what the Magus Corps wanted, if she didn't want to go, then she wouldn't. It had made her tear up again. Once she had dreamed of a welcome like this, and now that she had it, she didn't know what to do.

Kieran didn't come by at all.

She ate sparingly at first, but by the second day, her appetite was recovered. Her mind went back to that night, over and over, and no matter what she did, she couldn't get it clear. On the morning of her fourth day in bed, she gave up.

She bathed, relishing the feel of the ice cold water more than she had anything in the last few days. Hailey dressed herself warmly, and she walked out into the forest. She had wondered if she would find the trees frightening after everything that had happened, but instead, she found a comfort in them and in the rise of the hills around her.

Hailey wandered for almost an hour. There was a thin skim of snow on the ground, but the sun was shining bright. When she came to a little trickle of water running through the trees, too small to properly be called a creek, she bent to scoop some of it on her face.

When she looked up, there was an enormous wolf watching her curiously from the other side, and she smiled.

"Hello, Cavanaugh. Is your master about?"

"I am."

The man appeared as swiftly and silently as the wolf, and seeing them next to each other in good light for the first time, she could see how similar they really were. They were both tall and broad, and they both gazed at her with eyes that were completely without judgment.

I love him.

The thought rose up idly in her mind, and she knew that it was true as much as she knew the sky was blue.

"You look beautiful."

The words were so unexpected that Hailey laughed. It was a bright surprised sound, startling birds out of the trees. Cavanaugh looked affronted by her noise, and with a snort, he turned tail and loped off into the forest.

"I don't think your wolf agrees. Why would you say such a thing?"

"I've been thinking for the last few days. I've not spent that much time with the coven. Instead, I've been roughing it out here with Cavanaugh, and even with Merit for a little while. I thought about everything that I wanted to say to you, and that was the sum of it. You're beautiful, every inch of you. Your personality, your spirit and your soul. All of it shines. All of it draws me to you. I don't think that will ever change."

His words were calm and measured, and Hailey wanted nothing more than to reach for him.

"Hailey, only you can decide how you feel about what happened. I'm a major in the Magus Corps. That means I walk with death as my companion. I have for many years, and I am used to it in a way that I think few people in the world can be. It was wrong of me to ask you to brush it aside."

"Kieran, I don't know if I can ever see things the way that you do."

"You don't need to."

Kieran's face was a mask, but she knew him too well by now to think that he was emotionless.

"You have a choice," he continued. "No matter what, you will always have a choice. You can stay here. If you choose to do that, I will support your decision to the utmost of my ability. If they try to force you out, I will put in my resignation as a member of the Magus Corps and then they will have me to contend with."

"Kieran!"

His smile was lopsided.

"There's an old quote that goes 'My country right or wrong. If right to be maintained, and if wrong to be set right.' If the Magus Corps would force you to do something like this that you don't want to do, they are not an organization that I wish to serve. It is as simple as that. If you want to come to Wyoming, you could do a great deal of good. You could save lives. You could change the world. But it must be your choice. No matter what you do, I will of course try to protect you. I will do everything that I can to make sure that you have what you need."

"And you?"

He looked startled.

"What do you mean?"

"What do you need?"

Kieran let out a long breath, and Hailey wondered how long it had been since he had been asked that.

"I need you," he said simply. "No matter what, I need you safe, and I want you happy."

It was everything that she wanted to hear, or nearly so. She wondered why it didn't make her happy.

"I'm sorry," she forced herself to say. "I just don't know."

And she didn't. The choices were simply too great.

"What can I give you that will help?"

There was no blame in his voice, only an endless readiness to be of service, to aid, to help, to give her what she needed.

"Time," she said finally. "Give me time."

"All I can give you," he swore, and he reached for her hand over the water.

She took it, and though every instinct in her body told her to leap across and to be with him, she didn't.

"Thank you."

Her words hung in the air. After a long moment, they let go, and Kieran turned away. She watched him go, and it felt like a loss.

She didn't know what to do with her emotions then, so she walked into the forest. Perhaps she would find where Merit was nesting that day, or perhaps she would see Cavanaugh. She knew the woods well enough, she didn't fear getting lost.

It turned out that getting lost wasn't what she had to fear. She was aware of a blur of motion to her right and a rustle of brambles that told her that someone didn't care about being hidden anymore. That was all she knew before a rag soaked in strong chemicals was pressed against her face. Her vision went dark, and all she could think of was Kieran.

CHAPTER TEN

WHEN HAILEY'S VISION returned, she was first aware of a smoky scent. Something was on fire, and there was a rankness to it that made her twitch.

"So sleeping beauty awakens."

She turned to see an older man dressed in rugged outdoor clothing watching her from a chair. She was laid on a bed, comfortable enough except that her hands and feet were bound. She could tell she was in a cabin, and with a sickening plummet of her stomach, she realized it was the same one where she and Kieran had killed the Templars. She remembered the three bowls on the table—this was the third man. Outside the broken window, she could see that it was nearly pitch black. She had been unconscious for a while.

"What manner of woman are you?" he asked politely enough. "See, I've known my share of witches. None of them are like you. Are you some kind of new thing?"

"I'm not a witch at all," she said, and the man moved so fast that she could barely believe it.

He stepped close and slapped her. As pain lanced through her jaw, her head snapped sideways. Rough fingers grabbed her chin, bringing her face back to him. Stars flitted at the periphery of her narrowing vision. His face was twisted with fury and, when he shouted, it was with the voice of a demon.

"Liar!" he screamed, letting her go with a shove. "I know you're a liar. I saw what you did that night! You looked at a man, and he fell dead! You and your warlock, you killed them with your powers!"

Hailey watched in terror as the man visibly regained his composure. In a split second, he was calm again. He looked like a friendly old man, the type she might meet at any small store in the world, and that made his outburst even more frightening.

"All right. We both want things. I want the truth, and that's a small enough thing to want in these dark times, don't you think? What do you want?"

"I want you to let me go," Hailey said urgently.

If he was calm, perhaps he would listen to reason.

"No, you don't want to be let go," he said patiently, unbuttoning her coat.

Her heart leapt into her throat as she watched each button come undone. Delicately, he lifted the bottom of her sweater. As he laid her midriff bare, Hailey sucked in a shaky breath. When his rough fingers grazed her skin, she shuddered.

"What you want," he said calmly, sliding his fingers back the other way, "is to stay whole."

Hailey's eyes widened as he crossed the cabin to the fire. It was bright and crackling cheerfully. When he pulled a poker from its coals, the end gleamed a dull, ashy orange.

"Yes, you want to stay whole. Now, what manner of thing are you?"

"I…I'm a witch, but I'm a bad one. There's nothing that I can do. Nothing!"

"Liar."

This time the accusation was punctuated with a quick stab of the poker. Though she writhed desperately, it managed to graze her side. To her horror she heard the sizzle and then felt the blistering pain. Hailey screamed, emptying her lungs.

"Now try again. What manner of thing are you?"

For all the pain, Hailey felt a numbing calm. She realized in a distant kind of way that she was in shock. When her answer failed to come, he brought the poker to her again. It was slower this time. The searing heat moved over the first burn and touched down beside it. She jerked convulsively in the restraints.

"I'm a witch!" she screamed, and he took the poker away. She gasped for air. "But I can't do magic." Pain radiated from her side, flooding through her. She'd have doubled over if she could. "I can't do magic." She gulped for air. "Not without another witch or warlock."

The man looked thoughtful, and he nodded. Through the haze of pain, Hailey stared at his face, waiting for his reaction, knowing her life depended on it.

"What happens if you have another witch present?"

She opened her mouth to answer, but she realized that the chill in the cabin was growing worse. It had gone from cold to bone-chilling, making her teeth chatter. She looked up just in time to see blades of ice form out of nowhere, and just as the old man noticed them, they spun towards him.

His shriek was terrible. The blades of ice had flown to his body as if drawn there. He was still wailing when Kieran rushed through the door.

Hailey had never seen anyone so angry. His face was a mask of fury, and now she had an idea why the Magus Corps was so feared. For what they needed to protect, they had to be utterly ruthless, completely without mercy.

A larger blade of ice appeared out of the air, and though Hailey couldn't see its descent, she heard the old man's final groan when it struck home. Only then did Kieran turn to her, the fury melting into something else. His face blanched.

"Hailey, gods above, he hurt you."

Kieran conjured more ice and cupped it carefully against her wounds. She hissed at the contact, but then relaxed when the cool relieved some of the pain.

"Get me out of here, Kieran, please," she whispered, and he nodded.

• • • • •

Kieran knew how lucky he was. He knew it was a miracle that Merit had come looking for him when Hailey was taken. He knew that it was against all odds that Cavanaugh had tracked Hailey to the cabin. He knew it was almost beyond belief that Hailey had had the strength to teleport them back, this time directly to the infirmary. But then she'd gone frighteningly limp, and he'd laid her gently on the table. The silent witch had taken one look at her, and bustled about for a salve. The wounds weren't life-threatening. They would heal well after magical intervention, for which he was very grateful.

They had both been very lucky.

So why did he feel like he had lost everything?

He knew what she had seen when he had killed that Templar. She had seen the full force of his fury and his ability to do whatever he had to do. Few people could live with it, and Hailey was very young. She had every right to be frightened.

And she'd been tortured.

Even now he could picture her ashen face, and his hands bunched into fists.

But it had been three days since he had rescued her from that cabin, and still she was nowhere to be seen. Kieran had taken one of the rooms that Donato had offered him just to be close, but his only visitors were the boy Luca, and Beatrice who told him to be hopeful. She spoke quietly of Hailey's nightmares lessening.

Hailey needed time to recover, and to think on what she really wanted, but Kieran realized with a pang that he didn't have that time. There was work he needed to get back to. He had to realize that this was a closed chapter in their time together, and with a heart that felt like it was turned to lead, he sent a message to Hailey telling her he was leaving the next day.

He was at the gates of the monastery just a little after dawn. He had said farewell to Beatrice and Luca and exchanged courtesies with Donato. Now all that was left was Hailey.

He waited, and after a few moments, he heard her familiar steps. Kieran turned, and to his shock, he saw that she had a suitcase with her.

"Hailey?"

"You gave me time, and I made a decision," she said softly. "I choose this. I choose you."

He couldn't resist her. He never could. Careful of her side, Kieran pulled her into his arms for a deep kiss.

"I love you," he whispered. "I love you in this moment and for every one that comes after."

"No matter where we go?"

"I will love you everywhere in the world and every moment that passes on it."

Her smile lit up like fireworks, and she kissed him hard on the mouth.

CHAPTER ELEVEN

THREE DAYS LATER, they were seated in the private first class cabin of a jet headed from Rome to New York. Hailey couldn't believe how fast life had changed, and though a part of her shied away from the challenges ahead, another part of her felt calm and ready.

Instead of her normal jeans and sweaters, she wore a light sleeveless green dress. It made Kieran smile and he'd told her she looked like a huldra, one of the enchanting forest women from his homeland.

"Do I really enchant you?" she said, trying to sound sultry.

It sounded ridiculous, and she made a face, but he laughed.

"Never doubt it," he promised. "It doesn't matter what you wear, but I'll admit I have a taste for you in green."

Something about the way his voice dropped on the word *taste* made her blush, and to hide her fluster, she pulled the scratchy blanket up to her chin defiantly. Something about that motion only made him eye her more avidly, and she could feel the familiar heat that he could invoke so easily rise in her body. They had barely been able to keep their hands off of each other since she had agreed to come with him.

She bit her lip, and glanced around. They were in the seats closest to the pilot's cockpit, and the man seated across the aisle from them had been drinking since takeoff. He was nodding off now, and she turned back to find Kieran watching her.

"I think I'm going to get some sleep," she said primly, and from under the blanket, she took his hand.

"That's a very good idea," Kieran agreed pleasantly. "It's going to be another eight hours before we land in New York."

Hailey blushed when she felt him tug the hem of her dress up, and then it was just the warmth of his hand gliding over her knee. She shivered, and his hand grazed against the tender skin of her thigh. There was something deliciously illicit about pretending to be drowsing when he was touching her so intimately. She kept herself perfectly still as he touched her thighs, encouraging them to spread for his hand.

He stilled, the only indication that he had discovered that Hailey hadn't bothered with panties that morning.

"Beautiful little witch."

It was uttered so softly that she could have imagined it, but she knew she hadn't.

Slowly, his fingertips traced her slit, brushing the light dusting of hair there. She kept her breathing as even as she could, when his fingers became firmer. He was avoiding her clit, instead choosing to tease her over and over again until her folds parted easily for him.

His fingers were moving more smoothly against her flesh as she grew more aroused, and for a brief moment, she knew for sure that she wouldn't be satisfied with his fingers, skilled though they were. Images of sneaking into the bathroom, of finding the pleasure that they both needed, filled her mind, but before she could do that, he ghosted his fingertip over her clit.

It was all she could do not to arch against his touch and whimper for more. She wondered if she would always crave his touch like this, if they would always hunger for each other. There was a day soon in the future, she knew, when he would ask to initiate her. Sex without barriers of any kind would make her effectively immortal the way that he was. It symbolized an eternity together, and when he asked, she knew she would say yes.

He toyed with her, all the while playing with the tumbler of whiskey in his free hand. For all the world, he looked like a man lost in his thoughts when his companion slumbered. No one would know from looking at him that he had his hand nestled in her most tender parts, driving her insane.

The strain of keeping still and silent made her even more aware of her body, and she knew that he was playing with her. Every time he brushed her clitoris, he pulled back and returned to stroking her, getting her wetter and even more frantic.

"Please," she breathed. "More please."

Languidly, his fingers found her clit and began stroking it with the rhythm that he knew she craved. Under the blanket, her hand landed on his wrist to make sure that he had no thoughts of pulling away or teasing her more.

Her body stiffened, and she ground her teeth together. She was used to being able to move, to twist, to rock against him, and right now, she could do none of that. Instead, all she could do was lie as still as she could and keep her eyes shut.

His fingers continued their relentless rhythm, stroking her until her whole body was trembling. She felt her climax start to roar through her, and the way she was tensed made it even more intense. It was inevitable that she would orgasm, and she let the sensations overtake her.

She was trembling and shaking, and she was so needy she could have cried. Instead, she bit the inside of her cheek to hold herself together. When the full force of the climax struck her, all she did was breathe a little faster and a little harder.

Kieran's hand stilled on her body, holding her together, and when she shifted, he pulled it back.

"I think I need a nap," she whispered, and she heard Kieran laugh.

• • • • •

Kieran smiled at Hailey's sleeping face. She was still a little flushed, and her mouth was a delicate shade of pink that made him ache to kiss it, but she needed her rest. He could have watched her for the rest of the flight, but then his phone beeped at him insistently.

He frowned, flicking it open. He read the message, and then he read it again. He could feel something breaking inside himself, but he put it away. He could deal with it later, if there was a later. Kieran put his phone away, and he gave into his temptation. He leaned over and gave Hailey a soft, full kiss on the lips. She stirred a little, smiling at him.

"What's the matter?" she whispered.

"Nothing at all," he lied. "I just wanted to kiss you."

CHAPTER TWELVE

FROM NEW YORK, they took a flight to Casper Airport in central Wyoming, and when they made landfall, it was almost evening.

Hailey had to take the time to collect a very irritated Merit from the baggage handlers, and when she returned to Kieran, she linked her arm through his, smiling up at him.

"Are you ready?" he asked.

"Are you?" Hailey teased. "You look like death."

He didn't smile at her jibe. Instead, he looked more distant than ever, and he shook his head.

"Hailey, you'll be going to the coven alone."

Hailey felt her stomach sink. Surely she had misheard, or somehow misunderstood.

"What?"

Kieran took a deep breath. "You'll be going to the coven alone."

Hearing it again didn't help. In fact, it had the opposite effect. She swallowed hard against a rising tide of panic.

"I don't understand. So you'll be following me?"

"No."

Merit picked up on her distress and ruffled her wings nervously in the cage. Hailey took the distraction to calm her familiar, hoping it would calm her nerves, but it didn't. Her heart fluttered uncontrollably.

"Kieran, what are you talking about?"

He shook his head. When she laid her hand on his forearm, she was shocked to realize he was shaking.

"I can't go on with you. You'll be going on to the coven alone."

"But…but you told me–"

"That can't happen."

She gasped. His voice was like a slap. She took a step back, staring up at him with dismay.

"Kieran…"

"Hailey, this is the way things have to be. I'll stay with you until the coven's representative comes to find you, and then I'm leaving on a different transport."

Hailey tried to make sense of his words, but she couldn't. There was no way that the man who had treated her so tenderly, so lovingly over the last few days could abandon her like this. She shook her head. How did this make sense?

"What are you doing? Why are you doing this?"

He was silent, but she grasped his arm, desperate to understand.

"Did you lie to me all this time?" she whispered. "Did you do all this to get me to Wyoming?"

He was still and silent. Numbly she let go of his arm.

"Hailey–"

"Don't," she said, her voice soft but broken. Her stomach flip-flopped, and she clutched the fabric there. "Please, don't. Whatever games you wanted to play, they're over now, aren't they? I'm here now."

Kieran sucked in a sharp breath at her words. They wounded him, and she knew that they weren't true, but he didn't do anything to contradict them.

"I am sorry."

She waited but there was nothing else.

"So is that all you have to say to me?"

"It's all I can say to you, yes. Hailey, I wish I could go on with you, but I can't."

"And you can't tell me why."

His silence was all the answer she got.

Hailey let the reality of the situation sink into her body, let it chill her bones and numb her. It was shock of a kind, not so dissimilar from when the old Templar had burned her. The wound was healing well, but the medic from the Angioli coven told her that there would always be a scar. There would always be a scar from this as well.

"Do we have anything else to say to each other?" she asked.

She sounded formal even to her own ears.

As she stared at the ground, unable to meet his gaze, the silence stretched between them.

"We don't," Kieran finally said. "Goodbye, Hailey."

She didn't have anything to say to him. She couldn't find words at all. What did you say to a man who, only minutes ago, you loved? Who you were convinced loved you?

After a moment, he turned and left.

By the time she looked up, her vision blurred by tears, he was lost in the crowd. For several long seconds, Hailey was convinced he was coming back. She knew the explanation would come spilling out. He would tell her what was wrong. He would at least come back to kiss her. He would tell her that he loved her. And though she waited, none of those things happened.

She pressed a hand to her mouth and closed her eyes, tears slipping down her cheeks.

Then the crowd jostled her, and Merit nibbled on her fingers from inside the cage. She opened her eyes. The world was still standing. The only thing that was different was that Kieran was gone—and she was hollow.

She found her way to one of the benches, suddenly aware that she had no idea what came next. She didn't know how to recognize someone from the Wyoming coven; she didn't even know where they were going exactly. She had the number to get in contact with the Angioli coven again, but she couldn't even muster up the energy to do that.

Hailey might have sat on that bench for hours if someone hadn't coughed delicately.

She turned her head, and looked up and up.

The woman who stood by her side was tall and rangy. She looked big-boned and as strong as a mare, her smile bright and warm. She was dressed in a flannel shirt and jeans. She tilted her head at Hailey inquisitively.

"Are you Hailey Devereaux?" she asked, and when Hailey nodded, the woman smiled even more broadly.

"I'm Julie Ashbrook, and I'm from the Castle. I'm here to take you on the last leg of your round the world trip."

Hailey regarded the woman warily. She wanted to trust her, but she felt so raw that she wasn't sure she could trust much of anything.

"I'm sorry, no one told me who I was meeting…"

"And you'd rather not wander off with someone who's going to hand you over to the newest Templar in town. I got you. Here, let me show you."

Julie looked around cautiously, and showed Hailey the three clear glass marbles she held in her hand. As Hailey watched, they lifted from the woman's palm and wove an intricate dance before dropping down again.

"Once we get out of town, I can show you something really special, but that'll do for now. Is that good enough?"

Hailey nodded, and picked up Merit's cage, allowing Julie to grab her bag.

"How did you know who I was?"

"Owl. Not everyone coming through Casper is going to be carrying a snowy owl, you know? Though I was also looking for a big guy from the Magus Corps too. Did he get lost or something?"

Hailey flinched.

"I don't know. He said he had to leave."

If Julie thought that was strange, she didn't mention it. Instead, she got Hailey into the tiny plane on the private runway while maintaining a stream of chatter that was all about Wyoming and her flight experience.

Hailey's grief over the loss of Kieran didn't diminish, but she did try to set it aside to concentrate on what the woman was saying.

"I've lived with a few covens before," Hailey offered. "The last one was even in the mountains."

"Oh sweetie, you might have lived in the mountains, but there's no place like the Castle. You'll see."

The plane was small enough that they could easily converse as Julie flew it, and Hailey watched in awe as the woman handled the talk with the tower and got them into the air.

It was sunset, and even in the midst of her anger and her sorrow, Hailey's breath was taken away by the scope of the Wyoming sky. The blue was being overtaken by orange and scarlet, and it painted the mountains with gold. She held her breath as the little plane lofted easily over the peaks. They had left the scanty towns behind, and there was nothing beneath them but wilderness. Then she put the plane in a steep bank. She pointed out Hailey's window.

"There it is."

Nestled firmly on the slope of one peak, and sheltered by another, was what looked like a French castle. It was low and sprawling, larger by far than the Angioli monastery, and the setting sun gilded it, giving it a fairytale air.

"That's the Castle," Julie said with obvious pride. "Welcome home."

The words hurt in a way that Hailey had never felt before, and amidst the grief she felt at Kieran's absence, something else was waking up.

"Welcome home," she echoed, and wondered what came next.

• • • • •

Hailey's story continues in ABANDONED: Castle Coven Book Two, available now.

For a sneak peek, turn the page.

Excerpt:

ABANDONED

Castle Coven Book Two

"Hailey?" Piers said quietly.

She looked at him, still thinking of Kieran, but also her new place in the world. Piers seemed to sense that she was making a decision. He was as still as a statue, and she knew that he had centuries of practice with patience. He could not have been an impatient man and built the Castle. He knew that some things must never be rushed if they were to happen appropriately at all.

Moving as slowly as a glacier, she reached her hand out, letting it graze his cheekbone. He did not flinch. Instead, he only leaned slightly into her hand, encouraging her to touch him even more. Slowly, she smoothed the ball of her thumb across his cheek, sliding it down to his generous mouth.

She was unsurprised when his tongue flicked out and lapped at it. She shivered at the warmth and the wetness of it. After a moment, she slid her thumb into his mouth, a hot, velvet heaven. When she pulled back, he took her hand in his and kissed it gallantly and chastely on her fingertips.

"I want to know what you're thinking," he said.

"I should think it was obvious," Hailey replied, feeling slightly crushed.

Her experience with men wasn't extensive, but she thought

she had made her intentions very clear.

"I need to know that this isn't some kind of thank you," he said bluntly. "Regardless of what you feel about the Castle, I need you to understand that you have a place here. You don't have to 'earn' it with me."

Hailey blushed hotly.

"No, that's not what I think!"

"Good." Piers's smile was bright. "I also need to know what you want from me. I'm attracted to you. I'm sure you've noticed by now. You're a lovely woman. I want to know what you need from me."

That caught Hailey by surprise. She felt awkward speaking of such things. But he gazed earnestly at her, and waited for an answer.

"I want pleasure," she said, her voice barely above a whisper. "This place, this night with you. Inside these walls, I want whatever you can give me."

Piers made a noise that was somewhere between a groan and a hiss. She watched his hands fist and then loosen again.

"Do you know what you do to me when you say things like that?" he asked her softly.

There was a naked yearning in his voice. Hailey felt a heat kindle inside her to know that she had been the one to cause it.

"I can guess."

"It makes me want you. It makes me want you bare and squirming. It makes me want to lay you down and give you all the pleasure that you can take. After that, I want to give you even more."

Hailey was caught up in the rhythm of his words. She

knew her mouth was open, that she was staring wide-eyed at him.

"Yes," was all she could think to say. "Yes, Piers, yes."

It was the last bit of permission he needed. He cupped her face in his hands and held her still as he rained kisses on her upturned face. Her eyes fluttered closed as he kissed her eyelids, her cheeks, and her chin. Then he passed his lips over hers, once, twice and again. The tender touch woke her body like a storm passing over the prairie. She opened her mouth and drew his tongue into it, sucking on it gently before letting go. In a perfect, wild moment, she wondered what it would be like to suck on his cock the same way, to feel it jump in her mouth and to know that she was bringing him so much pleasure.

"I don't think you need this anymore."

Piers's fingers had found the pull of her hoodie zipper.

• • • • •

MORE BOOKS BY HAZEL HUNTER

THE HOLLOW CITY COVEN SERIES

A daring quest. A deadly enemy. A protector who won't quit. Although Wiccan Gillian Granger's life's work is finding a legendary city, her research in musty libraries hasn't prepared her for the field, let alone a gorgeous escort. Shayne Savatier knows he's on a milk run, especially after he meets his beautiful charge. But when enemies attack her, everything changes. Passion intertwines with protection, and duty bonds hard with desire.

Possessed (Hollow City Coven Book One)

Shadowed (Hollow City Coven Book Two)

Trapped (Hollow City Coven Book Three)

Sign up for my newsletter to be notified of new releases!

THE SILVER WOOD COVEN SERIES

Though she's taken the name given her by a kind stranger, Summer can no more explain waking up homeless and covered in blood, than she can the extreme attraction drawing people to her. Amnesiac, confused, and frightened, she's not even aware that she's a witch. But help arrives in two very different forms: the cool and restrained Templar Michael Charbon and his centuries-long friend Wiccan Major Troy Atwater.

Rescued (Silver Wood Coven Book One)

Stolen (Silver Wood Coven Book Two)

United (Silver Wood Coven Book Three)

Betrayed (Silver Wood Coven Book Four)

Revealed (Silver Wood Coven Book Five)

THE CASTLE COVEN SERIES

Novice witch Hailey Devereaux had resolved to live life as an outsider. Possessed of a unique Wiccan ability, her own people shun her. But that all ends when two very different men enter her life: the brooding Major Kieran McCallen and Coven Master Piers Dayton. But their training and tests are only the beginning. As she struggles to fulfill her destiny and find her place in the world, Hailey also discovers love.

Found (Castle Coven Book One)

Abandoned (Castle Coven Book Two)

Healed (Castle Coven Book Three)

Claimed (Castle Coven Book Four)

Imprisoned (Castle Coven Book Five)

Sacrificed (Castle Coven Book Six)

Castle Coven Box Set (Books 1 - 6)

THE MAGUS CORPS SERIES

Meet the warlocks of the Magus Corps, sworn to protect Wiccans at all costs. As they find and track fledgling witches, it's a race against an ancient enemy that would rather see all Wiccans dead. But where danger and intimacy come together, passion is never far behind.

Dominic (Her Warlock Protector Book 1)

Sebastian (Her Warlock Protector Book 2)

Logan (Her Warlock Protector Book 3)

Colin (Her Warlock Protector Book 4)

Vincent (Her Warlock Protector Book 5)

Jackson (Her Warlock Protector Book 6)

Trent (Her Warlock Protector Book 7)

Her Warlock Protector Box Set (Books 1 - 7)

THE SECOND SIGHT SERIES

Join psychic Isabelle de Grey and FBI profiler Mac MacMillan as they hunt a serial killer in the streets of Los Angeles. Even as their search closes in on the kidnapper, they discover not only clues, but a fiery passion that quickly consumes them.

Touched (Second Sight Book 1)

Torn (Second Sight Book 2)

Taken (Second Sight Book 3)

Chosen (Second Sight Book 4)

Charmed (Second Sight Book 5)

Changed (Second Sight Book 6)

Second Sight Box Set (Books 1 - 6)

THE EROTIC EXPEDITION SERIES

Travel the world in these breathless tales of erotic romance. Each features a different couple in fast-paced tales of fiery passion.

Arctic Exposure

A young couple is stranded in an Alaskan storm.

Desert Thirst

In the Sahara, a master tracker has the scent of his fiery client.

Jungle Fever

A forensic accountant blossoms under the care of a plantation owner in Thailand.

Mountain Wilds
A beautiful doctor on the rebound crashes with her pilot in British Columbia.

Island Magic
Two treasure-hunting scuba divers are kidnapped in the Caribbean.

THE ROMANCE IN THE RUINS NOVELS

Explore the ancient world and the new in these standalone novels of erotic romance. Each features a hero and heroine who come together against all odds, in exotic and remote settings where danger and love are found in equal measure.

Words of Love
Set in the heartland of the ancient Maya.

Labyrinth of Love
Set on the ancient Greek island of Crete.

Stars of Love
Set in the rugged Pueblo Southwest.

Sign up for my newsletter to be notified of new releases!

NOTE FROM THE AUTHOR

Dear Wonderful Reader,

Thank you so much for spending time with me. I can't tell you how much I appreciate it! My newsletter will let you know about new releases and *only* new releases. Don't miss the next sizzling, hot romance! Visit HazelHunter.com/books to find more great stories available *today*.

XOXO,
Hazel

Version 8.0

ABANDONED

Castle Coven Book Two

By Hazel Hunter

ABANDONED
Castle Coven Book Two

On the verge of starting a new life with the man she loves, novice witch Hailey Deveraux's world is yanked from underneath her. Without explanation, Major Kieran McCallen has abandoned her at the doorstep of a new coven. Though her heart and soul tell Hailey that he loved her too, it doesn't change the shattered spirit he leaves behind.

Though Hailey must restart her life yet again, the remote Castle coven of Wyoming is different. From the smallest child to the most experienced Wiccan, they seem to embrace the strange gift that she brings, especially the enigmatic coven master, Piers Dayton.

Though Piers already knew that Hailey would fit into his future plans for the coven, he had no idea how perfectly she would fill the jagged hole in his life. Though he begins slowly with the elfin and fragile Hailey, his need to dominate her unleashes desire in them both. But before she can truly learn the extent of her power, a vile evil breaches the coven's border.

CHAPTER THIRTEEN

THE TINY PLANE banked alarmingly, and Hailey yelped in dismay, clutching the armrests of her seat. From the pilot's cockpit, Julie laughed, a sound that rolled like barrels of root beer.

"Don't worry, sweetie," Julie said. "I've made this descent hundreds of times."

"You've never had a problem with it before?" Hailey asked hopefully.

"I'm still here, ain't I?"

Hailey could have said that was less than comforting, but then the plane started losing altitude quickly. Though it made her belly a little queasy, she couldn't take her eyes off of the view through the passenger window. Stretched below her and nestled between two sheltering peaks was the last thing that someone would have expected to see in the remote Wyoming wilds. The Castle looked like a French palace, spread out low and sprawling across what had to be a protected valley. Whether it was nature or Wiccan magic that had carved out the perfect space for the Castle, Hailey couldn't say, but she could tell that unless one knew exactly where it was, it would be practically invisible.

Hailey jumped as the radio buzzed. Julie was calling in. Her guide was a big bluff woman in denim and flannel who had met

Hailey at the airport in Casper. Hailey liked Julie right away, and she began to entertain the tremulous thought that her welcome at the Castle would be a warm one.

Her awakening as a magic user had at first been a revelation. The realization that she belonged to a group of ancient magic users had at first made her feel as if she had found a family, one that had been denied to her since her parents died. Then when the full scope and nature of her powers became known, she realized it was all just a bitter dream.

That had all changed with the arrival of Kieran McCallen. Even the thought of his name made her flinch. It was Kieran who had been unafraid, who had convinced her to find her true potential, to see how deep her powers could go. He had maddened her, encouraged her, supported her, challenged her, and finally, he had loved her.

Hailey believed that he loved her with all her heart and soul. That was what had made his abandonment even harsher. If she thought about their stilted goodbye in the Wyoming airport, she would start to cry, so instead she focused on the Castle below.

Kieran had told her that it was an elite coven dedicated to study. It was a place for powerful witches and warlocks to hone their talents for the betterment of their kind. It was a place where he had promised that she would find a home. He had also promised that they would go there together. A suspicious, ungracious part of her wondered if it was all a trick. Perhaps Kieran had seduced her to bring her away from the Angioli coven in Italy, meaning to dump her in Wyoming all the while. Hailey shuddered. That would mean that he had essentially prostituted himself to bring her to the Castle. She couldn't tarnish their time together with that. Nor did she really think it was true.

The aircraft landed with the gentlest bump on a long, grass runway. Julie slowed the plane, then turned and taxied back nearly to the beginning. She let it roll into longer grass off to the side, then into a small hanger the size of a barn. She cut the engine, bringing them to a stop.

"Welcome to the Castle, honey," she said comfortably, opening her door. Then she paused. "It's a great place, but can I give you a piece of advice?"

Hailey nodded curiously.

"Just about everyone here is the best at something. Maybe they're top-notch firecrackers, or maybe they've been fighting Templars since the flood. Most of them are great people, but when you get together too many people who are the best, well, it can make them kinda act like assholes."

Hailey giggled a little.

"So take no crap?" she asked, and Julie grinned.

"You got it in one, sweetie. Now, I know you have some real special skills in your toolbox."

Hailey blinked.

"You know about what I can do?"

"I don't let anyone on my plane unless I know what they can do or they're in a world of hurt." Julie winked. "Piers filled me in."

Hailey felt her world slightly tip sideways. As long as she had been a witch, her power had been met with incredulity and fear. Julie's calm acceptance was unheard of.

"What we respect at the Castle is strength and cleverness. You wouldn't be here if you didn't have plenty of both. Don't be afraid to show it, okay?"

Mystified, Hailey nodded. On the back seat, her snow owl familiar Merit hooted in irritation from her large cage. When Hailey reached her fingers between the bars, Merit responded by grumpily nipping at them.

"Brave new world, Merit," she murmured as Julie hopped out.

Hailey did the same, folded her seat forward, and took Merit's cage.

"I've got to do the post flight check," Julie said, clipboard in hand. "So go ahead and walk up to the gate. Can't miss it. There ought to be folks there to meet you."

Suddenly Hailey felt as shy as a kindergartener on her first day at school. She didn't want to leave Julie behind. She had found comfort in the bigger woman's assurance and friendliness. Stepping away from that felt risky. She took a deep breath and told herself not to be a child. With her small pack slung over her back and her owl's cage dangling from one hand, she stepped out of the hanger.

A blast of cold air made her regret her thin green dress immediately. She held the cage a little more securely in her hand. It was still summer, but at this high altitude, the chill was a permanent thing. She hustled for the barred gate that Julie had indicated. There was a tall wall that surrounded the Castle, and from her perspective, it looked impregnable.

When she came to the gate of iron bars twisted to form an intricate and dizzying pattern, she was surprised to find that it was open. There was no one to guard it, and she slipped inside. She felt like she was getting away with something that she shouldn't have. A certain part of her delighted in that, while another part wanted her to wait for Julie.

It was foolishness. Julie had said that she was welcome, and she had no reason to think that the woman was lying to her. Taking a tighter grip on her owl cage, she walked down the stone tunnel that she knew from overhead observation would lead to a courtyard.

Before she had cleared the entryway, she heard a shout, and her blood went cold with fear. It was followed by what sounded like cries of anger and fear. In the space of a heartbeat, she made her decision. She threw Merit's cage open, letting the owl flutter free. Perhaps Merit could make a difference in what was to come, and perhaps she couldn't. Either way, her beloved white owl wouldn't be vulnerable and stuck in a cage if the worse was to happen.

Merit cleared her cage door with a whoosh of wings, but Hailey didn't stay to see it. Instead, she sprinted the last yards of the tunnel, running full speed at the cries which only seemed to become louder and angrier.

For a moment she was dazzled by the late afternoon light. Then when her vision cleared, she was appalled by what she saw.

There were perhaps five young children in front of her, and as she watched, one of them was lifted into the air and thrown hard by a tall man. The other children danced around him, trying to protect their friend, and a little girl with her hair in Bantu knots only narrowly escaped being grabbed next.

Hailey didn't think. She couldn't think. Instead, her body was pumped full of fear and nerves, and she darted for the man who was attacking these small children. She swept the little girl with Bantu knots behind her, and she hip-checked another little boy out of the way. Then she was in front of a man who looked so tall that he practically blotted out the sun. With her teeth bared, she reached for him and grabbed his wrist. Her power opened a channel between them. In a space that was shorter than a second, she saw an ocean of light, heat and warmth that went on forever. This was his power, and though her own was not nearly so vast, she reached for his with everything she had.

She felt it flow into her, giving her the ability to do whatever she needed. It wasn't her power, but she could use it. This was what made her so frightening to most Wiccans, but right now she didn't mind. Right now, Hailey was grateful for the fear that she instilled.

She stepped back, teeth bared and her hands full of fire.

"All right," she shouted. "Back the hell off."

Instead of lunging for her the way he had for the children, the man actually stepped back and looked at her with surprise. The moment of silence drew out further and further, and slowly Hailey became aware of a few things.

Instead of using her distraction to run away, the children were staring at her with varying levels of curiosity and confusion. One little girl even looked a bit vexed, as if she had been denied a treat. The second thing Hailey realized was that there were people watching from the walls. Some had quarterstaves and some were merely sitting in workout clothing, watching with curiosity. None of them seemed upset or frightened by what they had seen.

She gazed around herself, her nerves wound up tight and nearly hurting. She had an inkling that she was making a fool of herself. Her hands were still bright with fire, however, and she did not put it out.

"Why did you do that?" said a little voice.

To her surprise, it was the smallest child who said it. Though many Wiccans were born among the normal human population, there were a fair number who were born to Wiccan parents and grew up aware of their powers. This young girl was seven at most, and the ends of her pigtails were coated in ice, a sure sign of her mastery over cold.

"Do what?" Hailey asked, her voice shaking slightly.

"Stop our practice," the girl said as if it were evident, and a nearby boy nodded.

"It was just getting good, too! We were going to get him down that time."

"He threw one of you!"

A slight cough made her look behind her to see the boy who had been thrown so savagely floating in the air behind her. He waved, a slight blush on his cheeks.

"I'm fine," he said anxiously. "I really am, miss."

Her own face turned red with humiliation when she heard a few muffled snickers from the people watching by the walls. Self-consciously, she allowed the fire to go out and turned to the big man who she had attacked.

"I'm so, so sorry," she said, unable to meet his eyes.

Now that the first shock had worn off, she found a tide of cold fear coming over her. She had taken power from someone who had not permitted it. She had tapped into him in a way that was utterly unacceptable.

The covens she had lived at before would have considered that a cause for immediate ejection, if not worse. The fear of her powers was old and ingrained. In the past, it had been punished ruthlessly. Her own fear welled up and threatened to choke her. Had she forfeited her place with the coven so easily? Had she come all this way and lost everything before she had even entered the Castle itself?

The man was striding towards her, and Hailey flinched. She didn't think he would strike her in front of all these people, but her first instinct told her to be wary and afraid. The first words out of the man's mouth were not the ones that she was expecting at all.

"That was amazing! Can you do that whenever you want?"

Instead of glaring at her, the man's face was lit up with curiosity. He stopped short of touching her, but she could see that he wanted to know everything about her. It wasn't the beating and expulsion she had been afraid of, but it was still startling.

"Can you do that again?" he asked expectantly.

Hailey gave a tiny nod.

"Could you do it again right now?"

Before Hailey could babble something in response, someone's

low laugh echoed through the courtyard. Everybody turned to see Julie striding out of the entryway, an amused smile on her face.

"I think you're terrifying the poor girl, Piers. Did you forget your manners again?"

The man shook his head in chagrin.

"You know, I did. I'm sorry." The last was offered to Hailey, along with a large hand in greeting.

Tentatively, she shook it, still aware that everyone was watching.

"Still, you must be Hailey Devereaux."

"I suppose I must be," Hailey said, a small smile tugging at her mouth.

There was something about this man that she instinctively trusted, much as she had trusted Julie. He was lean but built, more a runner than a wrestler. He was tall with blond hair that was tied back in a small ponytail. In the bright summer light, his eyes were a deep and chocolatey brown. His face was perhaps a hair too severe for traditional good looks, but his smile made up for it.

"I should let you go to your rooms so you can decompress and rest up, but I confess I'm curious."

"Are you? Was the sample of my powers not enough?"

Hailey was surprised that a bantering tone had come into her voice. She wondered if it was just the adrenaline wearing off.

The man Julie had called Piers shook his head.

"Not even a little. So far, all I know is that you can surprise me when I'm playing with little children. I want to see what you can really do."

Hailey bit her lip. She knew that she should go find the coven master and present herself, but the confinement on the long flight and her hurt heart needed a little bit of recklessness.

"All right," she said. "What do you want to see?"

"Well, I've seen your fire, what about the opposite? Can you do ice?"

Ice and cold had been Kieran's power, but she didn't have time to flinch. She didn't allow herself to think about it at all. Instead, Hailey reached out her hand. Without a single moment of mistrust, he rested his hand in hers. Once again, she could feel his power pulsing like a world of light, and this time, she could feel that it was freely given.

She had done this with Kieran as well, but she had to shut that pang away.

Hailey pulled the power from him as easily as scooping a cup of cold water from a pool, and she let it fill her. She concentrated on the opposite of heat, the way warmth could be pulled from a space. She spread her hands a foot apart, and between them, ice crystals started to form. She wasn't interested in showing off sheer power at that moment. She wanted precision, and the crystals formed layer by layer. Soon there were a dozen glittering pieces of ice dancing between her hands, melting slightly in the bright sunlight.

"Beautiful," Piers murmured, and she could see that he had stepped close to watch.

Hailey could not say whether it was an imp of the perverse that whispered in her ear at that point or not, but she couldn't resist. With just a flick of her finger, she sent one of the ice chips darting down the neck of Piers's loose shirt, making the man yelp with surprise.

"That was a dirty trick," he said with a grin, and she shrugged.

"I think you'll find that I'm full of them. Now have I sated your curiosity enough?"

He shook his head, an amused glint in those dark eyes.

"Never. But I suppose I should offer you something in return. What would you like?"

Hailey wondered if there was a shade of flirtation in his tone.

"I need to find the coven master of the Castle," she said reluctantly. "I should let him know that I've arrived."

"Easily done," said Piers. "I'll take you to his library."

Hailey nodded. "My bags…"

"Someone else will see to that. Come here."

To Hailey's shock, she found herself clasped tightly to the man's chest. Distractedly, she realized that he smelled of juniper soap.

"What are you–"

"Hang on!"

Piers leapt into the air, and in a matter of seconds, they were high above the courtyard. She was looking down at the people far below, watching them watch her. She should have been afraid or upset, but instead, all she felt was a reckless glee.

"Ha, I should have known you were a flyer," she said to him.

"Oh? And why's that?"

"Everyone knows that witches and warlocks gifted with flight are unpredictable and wild," she retorted. "All the old books say so."

"Hmm, and what do the old books say about mouthing off before you're back on solid ground?"

"On that they are silent," she responded with affected dignity. "But you better take good care of me. You can't rough me up too much before I see the coven master."

"Rough you up. You know that doesn't sound like *exactly* what I want to do with you."

There was a definite flirtatiousness to his voice this time, and Hailey found herself blushing. She was saved from having to respond, however, when they found themselves at a window in one of the Castle's many towers. Piers entered, and easily set her down on her feet inside.

The room was small, but incredibly luxurious. The tower's round walls were lined with books of all kinds, and the floor was covered with a thick, plush carpet that looked like it had been knotted by hand. Off to the side was a large traditional wooden desk, and on top of that, unexpected amidst the traditional furnishings, was a sleek, little laptop.

Hailey wondered what kind of man kept this library. She wondered if he was kind or stern, if he would see her as a person or as a tool. She turned around and to her shock realized that Piers was perched on the edge of the coven master's desk.

"Um, should you really be doing that?"

"Why shouldn't I?" he asked, tilting his head slightly.

"Because you're…because the coven master will…"

Under his patient eyes, she stuttered to a stop, and then she frowned.

"You're the coven master, aren't you?"

He grinned, and she realized that he didn't need to be classically handsome. When he really smiled, he was gorgeous.

"I am. I'm sorry, I couldn't resist. It was simply too good a chance to get to know you."

Hailey was torn between feeling incredibly angry or amused about the situation. On one hand, he had taken advantage of the fact that she was new in order to play a prank on her. On the other hand, she wasn't sure that she would have been able to be as open and as easy with a man who she knew immediately as the coven master of one of the most beautiful places she had ever been. She decided that since she had tried to drain him and set him on fire when she first laid eyes on him that she would settle on amused.

"I'll call it even if you forget about me thinking that you were going to harm those kids. You weren't, right?"

He shook his head.

"No, that was me just doing my part for training the children. Eventually, they would all have latched on to me and I would take them for a little flight."

"And what does that train them to do, exactly?"

"I don't know, to hang on, perhaps? You did quite well yourself."

She flushed a little, thinking of their brief flight.

"Well, I can fly too. I've done it before."

"And it takes more to impress you than that, I'm sure. Hopefully, you'll find things at the Castle that intrigue you and encourage you to stay, even if you were unimpressed with me."

Hailey started to protest that she wasn't unimpressed. Then she saw the laugh lurking at the corner of Piers's mouth and gave in.

"All right then, impress me," she said challengingly. "Show me what makes this place so very special.

Something new lit up Piers's face, and she realized that it was an immense sense of pride and pleasure that he took in his home.

"We strive to please. I'll show you around the Castle, and at the end, you can decide for yourself. Come along. We can just take the stairs down this time."

Hailey followed behind him as he led the way, and she wondered what in the world she was getting into.

CHAPTER FOURTEEN

BEFORE SHE HAD come to the Castle, Hailey had previously lived with the Angioli coven in the cold reaches of the Amato Valley in Italy. The Angioli coven had made its home in a monastery, and though it was quite beautiful in a stark kind of way, it was also foreboding. It was a severe place for ascetic men who wished to spend their lives in prayer and repentance.

Where the Angioli monastery had had a certain solemnity, the Castle was entirely different. It was built using local stone, Piers proclaimed proudly, and it was designed to be a mixture of Renaissance French castle and modern wonder. There were tall windows everywhere, and the light gave the Castle an air of graciousness that enchanted Hailey.

"How beautiful it is," she murmured wonderingly, looking up at one of the windows. It was perfectly clear leaded glass, and the design was cut to resemble a compass rose. "The designer must have been very proud to see their efforts come out so fine."

"Thank you, I am," Piers said promptly, and she turned to look at him.

"You're teasing me again," she said dubiously. He shook his head.

"No, not this time. I like a good joke, but the Castle, well, it's one thing that I don't joke about. It's my dream made real, and every aspect of this building, from the floors to the ceilings to the wireless satellite connection to the kitchens, I decided on. It took me ten years, give or take a few, to see it grow to what it is today."

Looking at Piers and seeing the laser sharp focus in those dark eyes, Hailey could easily believe that he was the man behind all of this.

"What is this place for?" she asked quietly. "No one was quite able to tell me that. All I know is that the coven master of the Castle heard of my talents and then sent a member of the Magus Corps looking for me. You went to some trouble to make sure that I arrived here, but I still don't understand why."

Piers looked at her thoughtfully, and it occurred to her that this man was much more dangerous when he stopped joking. There was an intense focus to him. She looked at where he stood, underneath an arch of stone that rose a dozen feet above his head. In an odd way, he matched the space. It reflected him. In some ways, they were standing inside his soul, his spirit.

"I think it would be easier to show you. Come with me."

He offered his arm, and she was too startled to refuse. It should have felt showy and old-fashioned, but the courtliness of the gesture felt right. Underneath her fingers, she could feel how muscled his arm was.

The first place they stopped was a door that was marked with a mysterious symbol. Piers pointed at it.

"It's the alchemical symbol for iron," he said. "We're not exactly dealing with iron here, but it's close."

He opened the door, and Hailey blinked. It was like she had gone from a fairytale French castle to an ultramodern machine shop. There were three women and a man working at various machine stations, and as she watched, the man straightened up and waved at them.

"Hey, Piers, perfect timing. Want to come over and check this baby out?"

Piers sauntered over to the warlock's side, bringing Hailey. The lanky warlock who had called them over had a small device in his hands. It was a small cube that rested easily in his palm, and it was completely black. It was perfect, with no joins that she could see, and after a moment, a brilliant orange sheen crossed the surface.

"Pretty, Stephan," drawled Piers. "Are you looking at getting into interior design?"

Stephan snorted.

"Teach your grandmother to suck eggs, Dayton. What I have here is a reservoir for firecrackers. That's witches and warlocks that use fire, sorry." He addressed the last to Hailey, who felt a little startled for being noticed at all. "See, when it comes to fire users, they tend to blow themselves out quickly. Big bonfires, and suddenly they're done for the night. As you can imagine, that might be risky when there's danger around and when things are tough. It's one of the reasons why you don't see many firecrackers in the Magus Corps. Anyway, when things are going well, they can use this little gadget to pull away some of their power and to store it. When they need it, like in an emergency, they can set it off and send the fire flying."

Piers picked up the little cube, weighing it speculatively in his hand before handing it to Hailey. It seemed to her that it was far heavier than it looked, and warm as well.

"The offer stands you know," Piers said to Stephan. "I can give you all the workspace that you need and the best tools as well."

Stephan grinned, but shook his head. It had the feel of an old argument between them.

"Sorry, Dayton. I'm a company man, and there I will stay until they bury me."

Piers shook his head regretfully, and handed the cube back to Stephan's protective hands.

"He may not look it, but he's a major in the Magus Corps," Piers told her. "He had some leave, and I invited him out here to work with our team. That cube's just the tip of the iceberg of what he could do if he had everything he needs, but he just won't see it."

As Piers led her on, Hailey thought again about Kieran. He was a member of the Magus Corps as well, and she knew it was Magus Corps business that called him away from her. She knew that the members of the Wiccan's paramilitary force were notorious loners, and she wondered if she would spend more time missing Kieran than she did knowing him.

The next door that they stopped by did not have an alchemical symbol on it. Instead, it had a sword.

"Swordsmanship?" she asked as they entered.

"Not exactly."

The room was enormous, and there were obstacles placed all over it. As Hailey looked on curiously, she heard a loud bell, and suddenly, a young woman who had been standing unobtrusively in a corner burst into motion. She leapt over some of the obstacles and ducked low to slide under other ones. She never stopped running, she never stopped moving forward. Entranced, Hailey watched as the young woman came to a halt just a few feet away.

"How's it going?" asked Piers.

The girl shook her head.

"Not bad, but not great either. Can't seem to beat my best time."

"Well, it's your best time for a reason." He turned to Hailey. "This is Erin. She's putting herself through a course on parkour and free running. Erin, this is Hailey."

Hailey shook hands with this decisive young woman, who eyed her up and down.

"Are you interested in getting started with either? You're small. You'd probably do terrific."

At just a hair over five feet and skinny as a teen boy, Hailey had never heard of her size being an asset before.

"You think?"

"Oh yeah. I can't always slide under things so easily because my shoulders are so broad. I have to go under on my back or my stomach when I can at all. You could just slide under, I bet."

"Is it related to your power?" Hailey asked in curiosity, and Erin shrugged.

"I'm a weather witch. I'm pretty good at that, but I'm sure I'm better at this."

"Parkour and free running keep you safe when you're out in the world," Piers explained after they left. "You can't always fight back, but if you're on your feet, and even sometimes if you're not, you can get away."

The next place that they stopped was a bay window that overlooked a deep natural spring. Hailey realized that it must have been where the Castle met the cliff face of the mountain. The spring was bordered by natural rock, and its depths were black.

As she watched, a young witch, the girl with Bantu knots from before, stood on one of the rocks on the shore and lifted an enormous geyser of water into the sky. Her small face intense with concentration, she lifted the geyser higher and higher, letting it thin to a thread.

Hailey watched, enchanted, as the girl made the thin rope of water dance at her gesture, letting it switch back and forth. The little girl kept it up until her thin limbs were shaking. Then with a shout, she let the water fall back into the pond with an enormous splash. A tall black man clapped wildly for her, and she turned to him with an enormous grin.

The small scene made Hailey's heart swell with happiness even as it hurt a little. She had never thought about children before, but she very much remembered her own childhood. To have her gifts nurtured as that girl's were, to be raised as part of a community that cared about her, it was like a fairytale.

They passed by a window that looked out over a snowy cliff face. Across the hall from the window, there was a bench seat cut into the wall. Hailey and Piers sat down.

"You're giving people tools," she said softly. "That's what this place is about. Everything I've seen since I've come here, you're trying to give people the tools that they need to survive and thrive."

Piers nodded, his face serious.

"I am. Do you know what the biggest cause of death for Wiccans is?"

Hailey shook her head.

"It's other people. Templars specifically, but I'm old enough to remember when some of the witch mania spread through Scandinavia. Wiccans who had never done a bit of harm in their entire lives were hunted and killed in the most brutal ways possible. Many people died, but some of those that survived became monsters. They lost the people that they cared about. They had no place to release their grief, so they turned it to rage. That led to more killing and more pain. We are safe if we are quiet. That's what I was taught, and for many years, I felt the same way. I taught others that the best thing we could do was hide. Then I learned that no matter how well you hide, it's not always good enough."

There was something about the way that he said the last part that made Hailey shiver. There was an old pain, an old hurt there. It went deep, she could tell. Impulsively, she reached out and took his hand. He looked surprised, but after a moment, he relaxed and continued.

"That's when I realized that a place like the Castle needed to exist. I wanted a place where people can learn to defend themselves, and a place where we can work towards protecting each other. That's what the Castle is a part of, and that's why I wanted you."

"Me?" Hailey blinked.

"You look surprised."

"Well, to be perfectly honest, my skill isn't often considered one of the ones that people think will protect others. In fact, I would say that when you get right down to it, it's one of the most selfish skills out there. I literally take energy from other people and use it for myself."

Piers laughed.

"I suppose I could see how you might think that, but that's not what I've seen."

"What do you mean?"

"The first time I saw you use your power, you were doing exactly what I wanted you for. You were taking power from a willing person and using it to protect the Wiccan community. The most vulnerable among us, I might add."

Hailey frowned.

"I wasn't doing anything that anyone else couldn't have done."

"You're wrong. What if you were just a mindreader or someone who could read auras? What if you were someone who turned into a small animal like a ferret or a cat? Mindreaders and shapechangers are amazing for espionage work and information gathering, but their offensive and defensive capabilities are very poor. No, you're something special."

"Tell me what you have in mind," Hailey said.

Even she could tell that he was right, but there was a missing piece here. There was something he wanted from her. She didn't know what it was, and that made her nervous.

"I've always been someone who dreamed big. I always wanted more, and a temporary solution never pleases me as much as a permanent one. What I think we need, both at the Castle and at the other covens worldwide, is the ability to protect ourselves. We need to be able to hide. That means more than just one person becoming invisible. That means that I want to find a way to shield an entire coven from Templars and non-magical humans."

Hailey blinked. She had known many other Wiccans, and for the most part, the effects of their spells could only affect themselves. A witch might be able to turn herself invisible, but she could not make someone else invisible as well. She could read minds, but she could not give the skill to someone else.

"You're thinking of something entirely new," she said hesitantly.

Piers nodded.

"What I believe it comes down to, and many other people agree with me, is power. Our capabilities are nearly limitless, but where they start to run into problems is power. Each person, witch or warlock, only has so much power to work with. We do what we can, but our sphere of influence remains small. I believe that you're different."

Hailey frowned at Piers.

"So what are you suggesting? That you run a lot of power through me and see if you can perform enormous spells?"

Piers nodded.

"I'm not saying it's entirely without risk. I couldn't lie to you like that. However, no matter what the risks are, I believe that the rewards could be immense as well."

Hailey was silent. She could see what Piers meant. Back at the Angioli convent, she had been close with a young boy named

Luca and a lively teenager named Beatrice. Both had been orphaned by Templar attacks, and Beatrice still woke up some nights screaming in fear and pain. She realized that Piers wanted to give her the opportunity to do something about that, to make sure that it never happened again. No more crying children. No more broken families.

Piers must have interpreted her silence as reluctance.

"This isn't something that you have to decide now. Even if you should decide that the risk is too great, you would have a place here. There are ways to hone your abilities and to learn more about what you can do. Perhaps you'll change your mind, or perhaps you won't, but at the end, you would absolutely know more about yourself."

Hailey shook her head, brushing his words off.

"I'm definitely going to do it, that's not a question. I'm just thinking. I don't know how it will turn out, but yes. Yes, it is something that I want."

Piers's smile was small, but it still pleased her. With a start, she realized she'd been staring at his lips.

What are you thinking? Kieran left you less than a day ago. Are you so very shallow?

The thought of Kieran brought a stab of pain and sorrow to her heart. No matter how fickle she was, the grief was still there, and she flinched.

"Are you all right?"

Hailey looked up blankly.

"What do you mean?"

"You looked a little lost there for a second."

Piers brought up his hand and smoothed the ball of his thumb over the point of her cheek. Hailey was too entranced by his butterfly-gentle touch to mind, but then she realized how intimate it was.

"I think I'm tired," she lied clumsily. "It's been a little bit of a long day, I guess."

Piers looked chagrined.

"Of course. It was foolish of me to want to give you the grand tour while you were still fresh off your flight. Someone's likely taken your bags to your room. Do you want food first or would you like simply to rest?"

She started to open her mouth, but then her stomach growled, answering for her.

"There's my answer," he said teasingly. "Let's go."

CHAPTER FIFTEEN

PIERS WATCHED IN amusement as Hailey ate the vegetable quiche that he had found for her. The egg pie was stuffed full of peas, carrots and potatoes, and it was enormous. He doubted very much that Hailey was going to be able to finish it, but it looked like she was going to give it a determined try.

He had to admit that she wasn't what he had been expecting. He had read the histories, probably the same ones that she had. They had painted a dismal picture of the lives of witches like her. Her skills or ones very much like hers had cropped up throughout the ages. There would be one or two or even a group of young witches born with that power, but invariably, the result was the same. Their covens first became wary of them. Then in most cases, they would turn the young girls out. In some very dark cases, those young witches were persecuted as harshly by their own community as they were by the frightened, powerless humans around them. In the matter of a few cases that still made Piers shudder, their persecutors had been as bad as Templars.

Witches with Hailey's powers were still uncharitably called vampires, and from what he knew from her records, she had been bounced from one coven to the other, each one wary of her skills and her abilities.

None of that seemed to affect the young woman who was

sitting across from him. He had been expecting someone jaded, someone who had to be cajoled and perhaps even bribed to display her talents. He hadn't expected a rather elfin young woman with long red hair and green eyes that he suspected could melt through stone. He hadn't been expecting someone who would throw herself into what she thought was a fight, eager to defend children who couldn't defend themselves.

"You're looking at me."

She had given up on the quiche, and instead sat watching him, her chin propped on her hand and her eyes wide and curious. She looked like nothing so much as a curious cat then. He had to stifle a small laugh.

"Well, there's plenty to look at," he responded in amusement. "There's plenty to like."

A faint blush stole up her fair cheeks, and she toyed with her fork. There was a charming artlessness to her. It made him want to reach over and tousle that gorgeous red hair. It made him want to sweep her up for a kiss.

Piers was not a man who was used to denying his impulses. He had come of age when England ruled the seas. He was used to following his inclinations

"You don't look like you believe me," he said softly.

Hailey shrugged.

"I don't know how to answer that," she mumbled. "I like you."

The words must have slipped out, because she clapped her hand over her mouth in shock.

Piers was so delighted by her answer, he laughed out loud.

"Now that's more than I deserve," he said. "And I think you're tired, so perhaps I should show you to your room?"

She only nodded. Even the tips of her ears were turning red. He took pity on her, offering her his arm again. She was quiet, but she took it willingly, and he led her to the living quarters of the Castle. When he opened the door, he had been expecting surprise, but not the reaction he got.

"Oh…Oh is this all for me?"

Hailey stared about her wide eyed. She was standing in a roomy chamber, a sitting room that was appointed with fairly tasteful, if subdued furniture. There was a desk off to one side, and plenty of shelves for books.

She darted inside and started opening doors, revealing a bathroom, closets, a kitchen and finally her new bedroom. At the last, she stared at the large bed and turned to Piers.

"This can't all be for me," she said a little nervously. "Did you kick someone else out or something?"

"Not at all," Piers retorted. "This is a room we had open, and I had it furnished yesterday when we knew for sure that you were coming."

"You mean that all of the rooms look like this?"

"Some larger and some smaller, of course, and some people trade when they need a new space. Some of the witches and warlocks who live on the mountain proper never bother coming in at all."

Hailey turned around and around, touching the bed with a gentle hand.

"I never thought I would have a space like this all to myself," she said softly.

"I had the fortune to build as I pleased, and after you spend enough time marching through mud and trying to decipher Latin while sitting on a bench cushioned with rotting straw, you develop a love for comfort." Piers paused. "This is all yours, Hailey," he said quietly. "Use it, don't use it, leave it as it is, decorate it, sleep in that bed alone or choose to bring someone in with you. It really is yours as long as you choose to honor us with your presence."

"Bring someone in?"

Piers felt a curl of desire move through his belly when she eyed the broad expanse of the bed, and then glanced at him. She must have realized what she did, because she looked away quickly, hand coming up to hide a blush.

"Well, I suppose that is something I could do," she said quietly.

As quickly as her excitement over the room had started, it fell away again. He was no mind or aura reader, but he could tell that a veil of sadness had dropped over her. Even her eyes looked a little duller.

"Hailey, this is a lot to take in, I do understand that. That's why I want to make sure that you don't feel pressured to do this or that. This room is yours, and as long as you live at the Castle, it can be the place that you call home."

"Thank you."

Her voice was soft and subdued. Piers had to fight the urge to go over to her and take her into his arms. He wanted to take care of her and give her some of his energy. He knew that it was far too intimate a thing, however. To make sure that he behaved himself, he took a step back. Was that surprise or regret that crossed her face? He wasn't sure.

"Take all the time you want. Sleep, and when you wake up tomorrow, come find me. You want to get to know more about the Castle, and I can guarantee you that there is no one else around who can show you more than I can. I want to give you all the opportunities you require to find out if this is the right place for you."

For some reason he could not fathom, jewel-bright tears welled up in her green eyes.

Piers acted without thinking. He swept her into his arms and cuddled her against his chest. She was stiff at first, but then she dissolved into him with a cry. He sat back on the bed, pulling her into his lap. She tucked her head under his chin, wrapping her arms around his neck. For one quick, guilty moment, he realized how soft she was and how right she felt there. He ran his hand up and down her narrow back, massaging gently and willing her to relax. She sobbed quietly, like a child afraid of being found out. After a timeless span, she finally sat up, and pushed her hair out of her face.

"I'm so sorry, I didn't mean for that to happen," she murmured, and he shook his head.

"I don't mind at all," Piers said firmly. "I promise. But just tell me why it happened. Perhaps I can fix it."

She gave him a watery smile and shook her head.

"There's nothing to fix. It's just when Julie brought me here, she flew me overhead so that I could see the Castle. It's amazing, Piers. It's breathtaking when you see it for the first time that way. I was thinking that I didn't know what was coming or what this place could mean to me, and then Julie just told me 'welcome home.'"

"She was right to tell you that," Piers said urgently. "This place can be yours if you want it, Hailey. I will not allow anyone to deny you."

That nearly made her start crying again. Her body tensed up, and he could see the tears gathering in her eyes. Before they could spill however, she took a deep breath and quelled them.

"I believe you," she said, her voice only cracking a little. "I heard her, and I wondered at it, but now in this room? For the first time, I think it might be true. This might be my home."

Piers wrapped his arms around her again, wondering at how much pain this girl might have known in her life. It made him want to destroy the people who had refused to offer her a home. It made him want to wrap around her and to offer her all of the reassurances that she needed.

"No matter what, you will always have a place here."

She nodded, and she looked nearly normal when she looked up. An alarmed look crossed her face, and she hopped out of his lap, straightening her dress nervously.

"There's nothing to be afraid of," Piers offered gently. "I'm not going to hurt you."

Her laugh was bright and false.

"I…I never thought you did. It's just, I guess I'm tired, and I think I need some time to rest."

Piers could see that wasn't the only thing on his newest coven member's mind, but at the moment, he was willing to let it go. He stood and only barely resisted the urge to embrace her again.

"Come find me whenever you like. Take all the time you want. Wander around the Castle. Talk to the other people who live here so you can reassure yourself that I'm not just a crazy visionary with no idea what's going on. Then when you're ready, come find me and we can talk more about what you can do."

A shadow flitted across her face, but then it was gone again. She smiled at him. He thought it was a real smile, which pleased him.

She reached out and squeezed his hand gently. If she felt the slight jolt of electricity that passed between them, she didn't reveal it.

"Thank you," she said. "For everything."

"There's nothing to thank me for," he said firmly. "If anything, I should be thanking you for coming here at all."

Her face lit up at that, and as Piers shut the door behind him, a premonition came over him. He had known many seers in his time, some of whom could describe the future with an almost terrifying amount of accuracy. Others could only get a vague sense of what was going on, but it was always right.

He knew he had found the person he was looking for when it

came to protecting the Castle and perhaps all covens. He hadn't anticipated he might find someone who might complete a jagged empty place in him as well.

Piers pushed the thought away. He had learned early on that there was no use in planning for an uncertain future, even if—and perhaps especially if—it was something that made him feel whole. He shook his head. He had been prepared to adore Hailey ever since she stepped between him and those children. He wasn't sure if it was a good idea to pursue more. All that he knew was that every part of him wanted it.

• • • • •

When Piers left her alone in a space that was surely too large and too grand to be just hers, Hailey felt overwhelmed. It was simply too much. Her room with the Angioli coven had perhaps been a quarter of this size, though that was mostly because all of the rooms were monk's cells and quite small. Before that, she had been shuttled around from spare room to spare room, forced to put up with conditions that were small and mean. It had reminded her of being a foster child, shunted from place to place. At the time, she told herself that she was used to it, but now she wasn't so sure. Now she could see that a part of her had always longed for enough space to stretch out. Her bag was set up in a corner. In a little while, she would go and unpack her clothes, but at the moment, all she wanted was to stretch out.

Hailey stripped off her dress and her bra, pausing for a moment. It felt like so long ago when Kieran had eased his hand under her skirt and brought her to climax. He had done it slyly and smoothly, wanting nothing but her pleasure. She remembered looking at the sweet smile on his face and thinking she wanted nothing more than to see it forever. Now she wasn't sure if she would ever see him again, and the thought choked her.

If she let it overwhelm her, she knew that she would only break down into sobs. She didn't want to do that. Perhaps sometime in the next few days she would collapse, but right now, more than anything else after this remarkable day, she wanted rest.

She crawled naked into the bed. It had been freshly aired out, and the mattress sunk decadently beneath her. She thought drowsily of how it might feel to look at Piers across the wide expanse of the bed. She wondered what it might be like to pull his hair loose and to comb her fingers through it. The thought should have shocked her, but she decided that it was simply because of how tired she was, and drifted to sleep.

Sometime in the night, she heard a tapping at her window. Groggily, she got up and opened it, letting Merit glide in. The owl looked around, was satisfied with her mistress's living conditions, and drifted out again. That was the last thing she remembered before deep sleep finally claimed her.

CHAPTER SIXTEEN

FROM THE LIGHT, Hailey could tell it was already late in the day, and she groaned. She had been dealing with both jet lag and heartache the day before, and it had dropped her. She'd slept like the dead. Now that she was up, the day seemed to be nearly over. Piers was going to think she was lazy or indifferent, and she didn't want that.

In the shower, Hailey frowned at the thought. Piers was the coven master, it was true, but she was startled at how much she wanted him to think well of her. Most of the coven masters of her experience wanted little to do with her as long as she kept to herself. Piers was the first who had seen value in her talents.

Then she thought of his smile, his broad frame, his height and the way her heart fluttered when she saw him. She realized with chagrin that it was more than simply wanting him to be impressed with her.

"I am too old to have a crush," Hailey muttered.

Thinking about Kieran only made her heart ache, and it was more gratifying by far to think of the handsome master of the Castle. Hailey reasoned that it was simply a rebound. That explained it. She resolved to be professional and kind to the coven master, but nothing more.

She dressed quickly. The dress had honestly been an unusual

choice for her. She sighed with relief when she slid into a pair of jeans and a green sweater. They were warm, comfortable clothes, and thus armored, she ventured out.

She knew that there were plenty of people who lived in the Castle, but at the moment, they all seemed to be staying out of her way. She wandered the halls instead, doing what Piers had recommended. She was learning more about the building and its courtyards. The more she saw, the more she loved it.

Every line of the Castle was gracefully quiet. It had a sense of history without feeling old-fashioned. The tall windows caught every available bit of sunlight. It was a place of peace. Hailey could feel it in her bones. The fact that she would be allowed to stay, to work and to study within its halls, was still difficult for her to believe. She was part of a community now, and if Julie and Erin were any indication, she would be welcomed.

She walked through the halls, gazing out the tall windows and peeking into the practice rooms. There was something nibbling at the back of her mind, a foreign feeling that was strange but not uncomfortable. Eventually Hailey realized that it was safety.

She had never been at a place where she felt safe before. She had never thought that she had a place to stay on a permanent basis or people who would watch out for her. The Castle felt too good to be true. Perhaps there was something darker there, something she couldn't see. It almost made her cry all over again, but she stopped herself. Food would help her feel more grounded, and she found her way back to the kitchen where she had eaten the evening before.

It was dinner time, and though she guessed that all of the Wiccans of the Castle had kitchens like hers, it looked like they were a community that believed in group dining. The four long tables in the dining hall were full of people lounging around, chatting and enjoying a last little bit of dessert. She seemed to have come in at the end of the dinner hour, and she wondered if there was anything left for her.

Hailey was just sidling her way towards the kitchen when the muscular girl who was learning parkour caught sight of her. Erin trotted over, waving her down with a cheerful hello.

"Hey, where have you been hiding yourself? Thought we'd be seeing more of you today."

"Jet lag." Hailey shook her head. "My body's pretty convinced that it's late morning right now."

"Ouch, that sucks. Well, we don't have breakfast food, but let's see what we can find for you."

Erin was a young woman obviously given to command. She led Hailey straight to the food that had been prepared for the evening. There was plenty left, and Hailey put together a salad sprinkled with nuts and a thick juicy sandwich that contained a soft white cheese and a slab of grilled beef.

"You'll probably get added to the clean up roster in the next few days if you want to eat in the public kitchen regularly, but for now, don't worry about it."

Hailey thought that Erin would leave her when she had her food, but instead, the witch sat down across from her at the table. She chatted about the Castle, about parkour and free running, about how strange it was to be so far above sea level as Hailey ate her food. It was completely delicious, and that was why it took Hailey a little longer to realize that the other woman was watching her expectantly.

"Okay, what are you looking at? Do I have something on my face?"

Hailey touched her face gently with her fingertips. She hadn't ever had much opportunity to speak with other Wiccans so casually, and she realized how out of practice she was.

"Well, I guess I do have a question at that."

Hailey braced herself. She knew it was too good to be true. People always wanted to know about her power, and when they found out what it was she was capable of and what it meant, they backed off very quickly. She had enjoyed getting to sit with Erin and speak to her so warmly. The fact that it was over gave her a pang, but it was an old wound.

"Go on."

Erin's dark eyes were bright and curious.

"So what's going on with you and Piers?"

Of all the things that Hailey had expected, this was certainly not one. She must have let her surprise show, because Erin lifted her hands placatingly.

"I totally understand if that's not something that you want to share or that you don't want to discuss it with me. That's totally fine, and I'll back off, just give me the word."

"I'd tell you that you'd crossed a line if I had any idea where the line was," Hailey said in confusion. "What are you talking about?"

"So you and Piers never saw each other before yesterday?"

"No, not at all."

"Wow, most people were guessing that you were some secret lover of his from before any of us knew him. Guess that blows that theory out of the water."

Hailey felt even more at sea. Secret lover?

"Yeah, none of us have ever seen the bossman light up like that. You stopped by my training session yesterday, and I barely recognized the man."

"So he's not always so…?"

"Happy? No. This is a whole new ball game, and the busybodies of the Castle want details." Erin smiled. "It's no big deal, I promise. Folks at the Castle tend to be the devoted and dedicated type, and most of us choose to make this place home, work and entertainment all rolled up into one. I guess it makes us pretty prone to gossip and speculation. So you're not Piers's secret girlfriend come out of hiding. That's cool."

"So he looks different when he's around me?"

"Mostly he's just…really serious, you know? Quiet. Kinda stern. You've shaken things up a little bit, I can tell you that for nothing."

Hailey considered the other witch's words in surprise. She had never gotten an idea that Piers was anything but open and honest. The way he had treated her felt perfectly genuine, perfectly truthful. The fact that he had another face, one that the rest of the Castle seemed to take as a matter of course, startled her.

Erin looked as if she was going to say something, when they were interrupted by Piers himself.

"Good evening, you two. I thought I would stop by and see how you were doing."

"Just getting up, I'm afraid," said Hailey with a grimace. "Thanks to the jet lag, I've managed to sleep the day away, and now I'm ready to do things."

Piers looked startled and then speculative.

"Ready to do things? How would you feel about going on patrol?"

"Patrol?"

"Oh, that." Erin rolled her eyes, but there was no real disdain in it. "Every adult in the Castle takes a turn keeping an eye on things for a half-night shift. Some of us stay close to the walls because there's nothing to be gained from sending a weather witch into the forest in the middle of the night. Flyers like Piers here and the shapechangers tend to roam a little further afield."

"It's just a precaution to make sure that we know what's going on. Technically, I own this property, but lines between what belongs to the Castle and what is national forest start to get pretty blurry. I did my best when I was picking this place out, but its still simple enough for someone who knows their way around the woods to come onto our grounds."

Hailey shivered. He didn't have to say who had the skills and the interest to come looking for a group of Wiccans living peacefully away from the world. Templars were witch hunters, and they were relentless. They were powerful warriors who would use any means necessary to destroy the witches of the world. The Magus Corps battled them officially, but in effect, every coven had to be ready to mount a defense against the Templar forces.

"I would like to come," she said shyly. "I mean, I can even fly if you're willing?"

"More than willing," Piers said with a warm smile. "Come on, we'll get you outfitted."

As Piers turned to go, Erin met Hailey's gaze and quirked an eyebrow at the coven master. Hailey could only shrug helplessly and follow Piers. It took him a little bit of time to find a suit of all-weather clothing for her. Most of them were too big, and he had to dig until he found something that worked.

"Sorry, this was the best I could do."

Hailey made a face.

"Don't worry about it. I've been dressing out of the teen boy's section of the store my entire life."

The suit fit and felt a great deal like a ski suit, but she could feel the difference right away. It was light and flexible, and though she knew it would keep her warm, it was easy to forget it was there.

When she stepped out into the courtyard, she could see why such gear was necessary. The setting sun dyed the Castle in shades of gold and orange, but there was a nasty bite to the air. The temperatures were dropping, and they would continue to do so deep into the night.

Once they were out of the Castle, Piers turned, offering her his arm.

"I want you to take as much as you need, okay? The last thing I want is you to be sparing and then to fall right out of the sky."

"I don't think that's the way it works," Hailey said. "Usually, I just feel the energy ebb a little, and then I know it's time to land."

"Better safe than sorry. The last thing you need is to fall down the mountain."

She grinned, and then the grin faded when she saw him rolling up his sleeve. She knew that it was necessary for skin to skin contact for her to pull off some of his energy. However, now that the moment had come, she felt unexpectedly shy.

"Would it help for you to imagine that I was throwing a small child?" he asked teasingly.

"No! I mean. Well, I've only really done this with one person."

Thinking of Kieran stung, but she would have to deal with that hurt later. Right now, she wanted to learn about going on patrol around the Castle. Thankfully, Piers didn't ask her about who she had done this with. He only waited patiently as she set her hand on his bare wrist. His tanned skin was almost shockingly warm. She could feel his power again.

Just like before, it was like an ocean of light, a place of inexhaustible energy. She felt him willing it to her, offering her whatever she needed. She could become drunk on it, but she shook herself and put herself to the task at hand. She started to pull his power from him, working quickly and carefully. Through her concentration, she heard him sigh. There was something almost blissful about it, but then she was done. He stepped back briskly and nodded at her.

"So you said the flyers were unpredictable and wild. Let's see what you can do with it now, hmm?"

Hailey made a face at him, but she leaped into the air quickly and easily. She hovered a few meters above the ground for a moment. Piers raised an eyebrow at her.

"If that's all you can do, perhaps you don't need to come on patrol with me."

Hailey grinned. In response, she simply zoomed straight up into the air, spiraling away until the Castle was far beneath her. She was exhilarated by her flight, but then she quickly realized that she may have made a mistake. High up in the mountains, the air was already thinner than she was used to, even though she had lived in mountains previously. Now the air was thinner yet. She gasped, and the distraction was enough that she started to fall.

Suddenly, she felt a strong arm loop around her waist, bearing her weight easily.

"So those rumors about flyers being flighty and unpredictable. I see where they were coming from," Piers said gravely.

Hailey got enough of her breath back to laugh, but when she made to vault out of his arms, Piers held her firmly.

"Get your breath back completely, and then launch off. We're going to stay together. We're not going to go bat chasing. By all the gods if I have to put you on a leash, I will."

The image of him firmly clasping a collar and lead around her shouldn't have made her blush, but it did. Suddenly she was all too aware of the way his body felt against hers. He was lean but well-muscled, firm against her. He held her with a careless ease that told her how much power he had. She thought of that ocean of light. She wanted more.

After another few moments, she took a deep breath and nodded. Cautiously he let her go. She could tell that he was waiting to see if she was going to dart off again. The light was fading fast, the temperature was dropping rapidly.

"All right, coven master, how do you want to do this?"

Piers thought for a moment.

"I usually do a few circuits of the Castle spiraling further and further out until I come back. I want you to fly to my right and behind me. That way, you'll stay out of my way if we find something nasty out there."

"And if we do?"

Piers grinned. There was a touch of grimness to it.

"Then you come straight back to the Castle, and alert everyone that there was something I consider a threat."

She followed along behind him as he began his rounds. The first circuit was closest to the wall. It gave her an opportunity to marvel at the design of the Castle. It had seemed impressive when seen from above and when she was viewing it from inside. From her low flight now, she could see how perfect the walls were, how completely defensible. The man who had designed it had obviously had a great deal of experience fighting off concentrated attacks. She sneaked a look at Piers, who was visible by the last light of day.

His face was serene, and when he caught her looking, he smiled.

"Welcome home," he said, and she felt that shaky emotion that she had before. She had a place here. It was still a new and enchanting thing.

Another circuit and a half took them further out into the forests that covered the mountainside. Now it was full dark. Hailey had been a city child for most of her life. The deep velvety blackness of the night in the mountains made the hair on the back of her neck stand up on end, but soon, very soon, the stars came out.

She watched Piers, but she also watched the sky. As soon as the sun sank beneath the horizon, the light faded to reveal thousands upon thousands of stars. Hailey smiled up at them, enthralled to see her old friends again. The Angioli coven had had a beautiful starscape as well, but here the constellations were shifted, strange from what she knew.

She realized she had stopped flying to gaze up at them. She turned to see Piers hovering a small distance away, watching her closely.

"They're beautiful," she said.

"So are you."

The words were uttered so simply and so easily that at first she thought she had misheard them. Surely he was saying that the stars were beautiful or that the mountains around them were beautiful. Then she realized that she had not misheard. She blushed, grateful he could not see it.

"Shouldn't we be patrolling?"

"It's a quiet night. As long as we are back in reasonable order, we can take our time. Half the reason I like to have people do this is so that they can get comfortable with the countryside."

"You have a very beautiful home," Hailey responded, gazing up at the stars. "I can see why you would do everything that you can to protect it, to preserve it."

"Everyone deserves a place where they can be safe."

There was a strangeness to the way he said it. Then he flew on, and Hailey had no choice except to follow.

They swept down close to the canopy of the pine trees. Hailey was flying along, watching the sky above and the pines below, when Piers laughed. He hovered in the air, his eyes focused on the space behind her. She turned and had to laugh too. Following along behind them at a distance was Merit. The snowy owl's broad wings were completely silent. She looked a little miffed that they had spotted her and dove down into the cover of the trees.

"That's Merit," Hailey said with a grin. "She's a bit protective."

"That's wonderful. My own Grosvenor usually just leaves me to my folly."

They flew on, and Hailey made a note to ask what Piers's familiar was. Most witches and warlocks had them, though most didn't keep them with them on a permanent basis. They served as pets, as aids for focus and as protection. They had once been vital to the survival of Wiccans who needed to cross hostile territory on a regular basis, but they were less necessary these days.

Despite the protection of the cold weather gear, the chilly temperatures were beginning to take their toll on Hailey. She could feel herself lagging behind Piers's relentless speed. Though she could catch up at the moment, she realized she was flagging.

"Piers?"

He spun in the air with the grace of a born acrobat. He was by her side in an instant, wrapping his arm around her waist.

"It's fine!" she yelped in surprise. "I'm really fine!"

He looked dubious.

"Let's just say I'd rather not take the chance when the option is between me catching you, and you dropping down hundreds of feet to the forest floor, okay?"

Hailey grimaced at his blunt words.

"Okay, that's a good point. This isn't an emergency. I'm just really, really not used to flying much, and I think I'm getting tired."

"How often have you flown?"

Hailey thought.

"Counting this time? Two, maybe three?"

If anything, Piers's grip on her grew even tighter.

"And you didn't think to tell me?"

"Well, I guess I would have, but…"

"But what?"

"But you were being all challenging." Hailey paused. "I know it sounds bad when I say it like that."

"To say the least. All right, we're putting down somewhere so that you can get some serious rest."

Hailey would have protested that she didn't need much beyond a breather, but then Piers was flying with her in his arms, skimming low over the pine trees. His pace was smooth, far smoother than her own, making Hailey relax into his embrace.

She watched with interest as he circled and then slid between the slight opening in the trees. Hailey thought that he was just going to put them on the forest floor, but instead he wove through the forest. Hailey blinked when they came to what looked like an enormous round basket hanging from an ancient evergreen.

"What in the world is that?"

Piers grinned.

"The Castle has many secrets, but this is one of my favorites. Let me show you."

CHAPTER SEVENTEEN

HAILEY HAD NO idea what to expect, but Piers was obviously proud of the giant basket.

"Can you hover on your own for a moment?" he asked. "I can do this with you in my arms, but it would be clumsy."

Mystified, Hailey did as he asked.

Piers turned and pulled open a hatch, climbing inside. After a moment, a warm light appeared from inside the structure. Piers poked his head back out.

"Come in. The sooner we get inside with the door closed behind us, the warmer we'll be."

Hailey approached the structure cautiously, climbing inside as she had seen Piers do. He closed the hatch behind her as she stared around in wonder.

What had looked like an enormous round mass of twigs and branches from the outside was revealed inside to be a small room with a sturdy wooden floor and smooth wooden walls. There was a chest set against one wall, and the light radiated from a small crystal embedded in the ceiling. When Hailey shifted her weight, she was aware of a very slight sway, but other than that, she might have been in a tiny room in a cabin on the ground.

"What is this place?" she asked, looking around in wonder.

"It's one of our safe bases. Sometimes, because of the work or research we need to do, the Wiccans of the Castle need to spend their time in the forests. When that happens, they can use these safe bases as places to stay. They are self-contained, warm, and have food and water as well as bedding. This one just happens to be high in the air. There are others that are low to the ground and some that are in the ground."

"It's beautiful."

She looked around, already warm enough that she could remove her hat and gloves. Piers was stripping down as well. He didn't stop until he was down to a black T-shirt and jeans. Hailey giggled.

"What are you laughing at?" Piers's voice was amused. She pointed at his shirt.

"I would not have pegged you for a Metallica fan."

"Finest music in the past five hundred years," he said with a grin. "I've been keeping track."

"Really?"

"Nah, not quite. I like music, but keeping up on it can be a bit tiring. Usually I find a band I like, I stick with it until it is no longer fashionable, and then I drop it when everyone's ready to bury me if I don't find some new songs. I figure I've got another ten or fifteen years or so with this band before the coven threatens to revolt."

Hailey grinned.

"Have you truly lived so long?"

"I have." Piers smiled easily, but there was a shadow over his face. "I was born in England in 1597. You would not believe some of the strange music that I've listened to."

Hailey didn't necessarily want to hear about the music, but she knew a deflection when she heard one.

"This is very beautiful, the safe base. I mean, it's so cozy and warm."

Piers was checking the time on his smartphone.

"The next shift should be getting ready to come on. I can let them know that we're safe and accounted for, and then we won't have to hurry home."

As Piers messaged their relief, Hailey picked her way through the contents of the large chest. It was large enough to contain two tightly packed foam mattresses, plenty of bedding, and a small supply of food. She touched the chocolate wistfully, but she put it back, knowing that it was only for emergencies.

She looked up to find Piers watching her.

"You approve?"

"I do," she agreed. "Both of the safe bases and of you."

Piers raised an eyebrow.

"Of me?"

"Yes." Hailey hesitated for a moment before sitting on the floor. "I've been all over the world after I awakened as a witch, but it wasn't because I wanted to travel. Once the covens knew what I was, it was like they were suddenly playing a huge game of hot potato, and I was the potato. No one let me stay anywhere, and no one really wanted me around. The best they wanted was for me to be someone else's problem. You haven't done that."

"They shouldn't have done it either. Your former coven masters were short-sighted at best and plain cruel at worst. If they rejected you so easily, they will have done other things as well that are just as bad, though perhaps not as visible. Hailey, you need to understand that I didn't do anything special."

Hailey thought about that for a moment. Then she shook her head.

"Maybe you're right, and no one should have been treated the way that I was. Right now, though, this reality is pretty special."

Piers came and settled next to her on the floor. She could feel the safe base sway just a little. Instead of disturbing her, however, it made her feel protected. So high in the air and so shielded from view, there was nothing that could hurt them. There was no world outside, nothing dark or ugly. She was safe. For perhaps the first time since her parents died, she was safe in the world. She thought briefly of Kieran, who had fought so hard to protect her and then disappeared. That memory was still fiery, still painful.

"Hailey?"

She looked at him, still thinking of Kieran, but also her new place in the world. Piers seemed to sense that she was making a decision. He was as still as a statue, and she knew that he had centuries of practice with patience. He could not have been an impatient man and built the Castle. He knew that some things must never be rushed if they were to happen appropriately at all.

Moving as slowly as a glacier, she reached her hand out, letting it graze his cheekbone. He did not flinch. Instead, he only leaned slightly into her hand, encouraging her to touch him even more. Slowly, she smoothed the ball of her thumb across his cheek, sliding it down to his generous mouth.

She was unsurprised when his tongue flicked out and lapped at it. She shivered at the warmth and the wetness of it. After a moment, she slid her thumb into his mouth, a hot velvet heaven. When she pulled back, he took her hand in his and kissed it gallantly and chastely on her fingertips.

"I want to know what you're thinking," he said.

"I should think it was obvious," Hailey replied, feeling slightly crushed.

Her experience with men wasn't extensive, but she thought she had made her intentions very clear.

"I need to know that this isn't some kind of thank you," he said bluntly. "Regardless of what you feel about the Castle, I need you to understand that you have a place here. You don't have to 'earn' it with me."

Hailey blushed hotly.

"No, that's not what I think!"

"Good." Piers's smile was bright. "I also need to know what you want from me. I'm attracted to you. I'm sure you've noticed by now. You're a lovely woman. I want to know what you need from me."

That caught Hailey by surprise. She felt awkward speaking of such things. But he gazed earnestly at her, and waited for an answer.

"I want pleasure," she said, her voice barely above a whisper. "This place, this night with you. Inside these walls, I want whatever you can give me."

Piers made a noise that was somewhere between a groan and a hiss. She watched his hands fist and then loosen again.

"Do you know what you do to me when you say things like that?" he asked her softly.

There was a naked yearning in his voice. Hailey felt a heat kindle inside her to know that she had been the one to cause it.

"I can guess."

"It makes me want you. It makes me want you bare and squirming. It makes me want to lay you down and give you all the pleasure that you can take. After that, I want to give you even more."

Hailey was caught up in the rhythm of his words. She knew her mouth was open, that she was staring wide-eyed at him.

"Yes," was all she could think to say. "Yes, Piers, yes."

It was the last bit of permission he needed. He cupped her face in his hands and held her still as he rained kisses on her upturned face. Her eyes fluttered closed as he kissed her eyelids, her cheeks, and her chin. Then he passed his lips over hers, once, twice and again. The tender touch woke her body like a storm passing over the prairie. She opened her mouth and drew his tongue into it, sucking on it gently before letting go. In a perfect, wild moment, she wondered what it would be like to suck on his cock the same way, to feel it jump in her mouth and to know that she was bringing him so much pleasure.

"I don't think you need this anymore."

Piers's fingers had found the pull of her hoodie zipper. He pulled it down to reveal the thin camisole that she wore underneath. For a moment, she felt insecure. She was built slender, without much curve to chest or hip. Next to women like Julie and her friend Beatrice, she felt plain and flat.

However, Piers's expression was one of curiosity and delight, and he passed a hand up her side from hips to ribs. She could feel goosebumps rise on her skin as his hands passed over her body. She tugged at the hem of the camisole, and he pulled it over her head, revealing her narrow frame, her soft pink nipples and the slight curve of her belly.

"What a beautiful woman," he said admiringly.

Before she could protest, he put his mouth on her collarbone, licking and nuzzling. The area was almost startlingly sensitive. She whimpered when he lapped at it, and then his mouth traveled lower. It took him an achingly long time to cross the short distance to her nipple. The pink peak was deliciously sensitive, and as he lapped at one, he plucked at the other with his hand.

Hailey lay back on the floor and rolled her body up to him. He played with her nipples, caressing the scanty curve of her breasts and running his fingertips up and down her sensitive thighs. It was like being tickled, but a thousand times more sensitive. She could feel the sparks of sensation rolling up and down her body, making her arch and ache.

"I want more," she whimpered plaintively.

"I want to give it to you," he whispered.

He removed her shoes and socks before sliding her jeans and

panties down her legs. Then he simply sat up and looked at her for a long moment. Hailey wanted to cover herself, but his open admiration made her bold. Instead, she lay flat on the floor, opening her legs slightly. She was inviting his looks and his touch, and his sigh told her that he knew that.

Piers stood to strip himself, and now it was her turn to look. He was lean and golden, more a panther than a bear. His cock was thick and half-hard. When he noticed her looking so hungrily at him, it twitched, making her smile. She could see a few scars, and when he knelt close above her, she could see a smattering of freckles on his bare shoulders.

He sat with his back against the wall, and he drew her up to sit in front of him. Her back was to his chest, making her feel enveloped when his arms came around her waist. She wasn't sure what he was going to do until his hands covered her breasts, cupping them with gentle care. She could feel his cock against the base of her back, stirring against her and making her groan deep in her throat.

Skillfully, his hands played up and down her body, skirting every sensitive spot, but every now and then using just enough pressure to make her groan. She felt him explore her belly, her thighs, her breasts, her throat and her shoulders. A strange languid haze fell over her. She felt as if she wanted his ministrations to go on forever, but at the same time, she was growing desperate for more. She didn't notice that her legs were spreading wide until she heard him chuckle.

"Are you ready for more, sweetheart?" he whispered. "Do you want more of this?"

She nodded, bumping her head against his chest. She was already starting to get wet, but when he brushed his fingertip across the top of her slit, she groaned outright. She was afraid he was going to tease her more. Her hand landed on top of his, trying to push his lower, and his only response was to laugh.

"You're so beautiful, love. I want you so much."

Both of his hands pressed between her legs, one spreading her open, and the other touching her most tender bits. She should have felt exposed, perhaps even frightened, but the pleasure was building inside her. It felt so good and so intense that she tilted her hips so that he could open her more thoroughly.

She felt him stroke her clit over and over again, deliberately, almost roughly. It made her even wetter, and he drew her natural liquid up to bathe her clit. His fingers slid against her soft flesh even more readily, and in a matter of minutes, she was writhing up against him.

"Oh, oh gods, please, I need more than this. Please, I need you, Piers."

Something about her saying his name seemed to break him. Before, he had been exquisitely in control, ready and willing to take care of her pleasure as long as she wished. When she called his name, he groaned, nipping at her ear.

It made her think of a wolf claiming its mate. She rose up on her knees while dropping to her elbows. In another time, she might have blushed to think about how she was baring herself to Piers. He could see every inch of her, from the slickness of her sex to the tight pucker of her ass. She hid her face in her hands, not because she was embarrassed, but because of the intensity of doing something so intimate.

Piers's breath came hard and fast, and he shifted as well. She gasped when she felt his hands circling her hips, and he was lifting her slightly, squirming down himself until his mouth was level with her sex.

He laid one swipe of his broad tongue along her slit, and then another. Then he was lapping hard enough to make her squirm and squeal, rocking on her elbows, and desperate for more. Her juices were running down her thigh, and by the time he let her down, she was sobbing with the sensations he had given her.

"Hailey? Hailey, do you want more?"

It was an unfair question to ask when his hands were brushing against her sex, when the tip of one finger was parting her so delicately.

"Yes, yes please. I want more."

"There's a condom in the chest in front of you. I want you to go get it."

It was only a couple of feet in front of her. She didn't stand up. Instead she crawled to it, feeling decadently sexual, exhilarated to be following his orders. When she returned with the condom, he stroked her face in approval, making her purr.

"Put it on me."

Piers was the master of the Castle. She could hear the command in his voice, and it thrilled her. This was the man who had created a fortress for her, something that was meant to keep her safe. She felt a tide of feeling wash over her. She wanted him, was half crazy with it.

She tore the foil package and carefully extracted the condom. Pinching the tip, she drew the slippery skin down his cock. It gave her a chance to feel that hard flesh leap in her hands. When she smoothed the condom all the way down, she squeezed the shaft briefly. It made Piers groan before catching up her hand.

"Tell me that you want this," he murmured, his dark eyes fierce.

"I do."

Her voice was soft and needy. She did want him. She thought she might die of wanting him.

"All right then. I want you as you were before. Down in front of me, facing away."

She leaped to comply, assuming the position he had described.

Once again, she felt exposed, more naked than she had a moment before, but then his hands were between her legs again. Instead of lapping at her as he had, he slowly slid one finger into her sex, pumping it back and forth until she thought she would go mad.

Hailey mewled with need, rocking back against his fingers.

"Impatient sweetheart," he muttered. Nothing would make him speed up.

When she felt his cock brush against the back of her bare thigh, she whined. She didn't understand why he was denying her, why he was waiting.

His hands smoothed down her sides and her back again, and this time, he grasped her hips firmly with his hands. Hailey held her breath when he brushed the length of his cock along her slit. It was hard and blunt. Even with the condom in place, she could feel how hot his skin was.

"Please," she whimpered brokenly. "I need more."

His hiss was gratifying. It told her that despite his iron control, he was as aroused as she was, and he took one hand from her hip to wrap it around his cock. Slowly, she felt the large head part her sex. It was broad enough that she felt a momentary sting, but even that sensation was wrapped with the pleasure he was giving her. He moved slowly, and by the time he was fully seated inside her, she was arching and mewling for more. When he filled her, there was something right about it.

"You're awfully loud," he said teasingly. "Do you want more?"

"Yes…yes, I do, give it to me!"

"You didn't say please, sweetheart. Do you know what happens to pretty women who don't say please?"

She gasped as he thrust into her.

"I don't know," she responded when she found her voice.

"A lot of different things," was the response. "Sometimes, they get scolded. Sometimes I stop because its obvious they're being ungrateful. Sometimes they get spanked."

Hailey's whine was immediate and insistent, but he stroked her back comfortingly.

"I wouldn't do that without talking to you about it."

"About the spanking?"

Something about the position, about being so exposed, about having her ass up so that anyone could see, turned her on. Even simply talking about it with someone like Piers felt electric. She rolled her hips, making Piers hiss.

"Well, you know, good girls and bad girls get spankings. If you want, I could show you."

Hailey bit her lip, and then nodded.

"I… Will it hurt?"

"No, I promise. If you want it to stop, simply say the word no. Otherwise, I will continue to do exactly as I please. Remember that whimpering and sobbing won't stop me; only saying no will."

Hailey nodded into her forearms. She couldn't help lifting her rear a little higher. Being this open and ready for him was amazing. Knowing she was going to get her first spanking was even more incredible.

The first blow was nearly a pat on her rear. There was no strength to it, and Hailey realized that Piers was simply warming up and testing her. She spread her legs a little more widely, something that made her a little more stable.

The second strike was harder, and the third one was harder yet. He was right. When the blows were still as light as they were and with Piers's restraint, there was absolutely no pain at all. Instead her rear got warmer as he peppered it with soft spanks.

He paused, and when she turned to look over her shoulder, there was a fierce grin on his face.

"This is making you wetter," he told her, and she clenched his cock with her inner muscles.

He had stayed hard throughout her spanking. Now he started to move again. The long strokes took her breath away. They rocked back and forth against each other.

Hailey felt the slow sinking in her belly that told her an orgasm was building inside her. She didn't want this experience to be over, but with a soft sigh, she gave up the last bit of her control. She felt her thighs tremble and the pit of her belly grow warm and tense.

"I want you to come," Piers murmured, low and urgent, and that was it.

Her orgasm rolled through her body like a wave through the ocean. There was something inevitable about it. She knew that her body and her pleasure had been worked beyond her control, and that was what it took for her to a reach a kind of pleasure she had never felt before. The power of her climax left her shaking and clenching. Distantly, she was aware that Piers was thrusting into her harder and harder, his hands tight on her slender hips.

He's holding me in place, she thought dreamily, and her body convulsed again.

Her climax left her replete, drained. She sank down on the floor, the only things holding her up were his hands. She realized he was talking. He was telling her how beautiful she was, how good she felt around his cock.

Her climax was done but there was a certain intense kind of pleasure to this as well. There was something amazing about the way he slid inside her, the way he filled her completely. She concentrated on squeezing her inner muscles around his cock, gratified to hear him moan.

Piers's thrusts picked up in intensity until he was nearly shoving her forward, and then with a deep groan, he thrust into her one last time. It was primal, and in a way, it was a kind of sex that some part of her had always craved.

Slowly, he drew back from her, settling her on her side on the floor as she did so. Hailey murmured with pleasure when he stroked her back soothingly, long slow touches that made her smile. She could hear him disposing of the condom before he came back to her side.

"Sweetheart, will you come here? It's a bit softer."

He had pulled a thin foam mattress from the depths of the chest, and spread it out. It was just large enough for the two of them if they cuddled close. Making a soft, pleased sound, Hailey burrowed close to Piers's chest.

"How are you doing? Do you need some water?"

Hailey laughed softly.

"What funny questions to ask."

"Not funny at all. That got a little intense there, and I wanted to make sure that you were comfortable with all of it."

Hailey looked up at him, squinting just a little.

"You're really worried."

"Hmm, maybe a little bit. A lot of what we did usually requires at least a quick talk before."

Hailey grinned smugly.

"Well, consider me a quick study then."

Piers's laugh was soft, but it had a slight degree of menace that made her shiver.

"What happens when you've got a gag in your mouth? What happens if I want you to service me?"

"Then I guess we talk about it," she murmured, burying her burning face in Piers's chest.

"What a very good idea."

Hailey yawned, so much more tired than she had been after a simple flight. Piers cupped the back of her head with his broad hand.

"You need to get some sleep. If you bed down now, perhaps you'll catch up with the rest of us."

Hailey nodded her agreement, and before she knew it, she was nodding off.

CHAPTER EIGHTEEN

IN THE FOREST far below, the thing paced with trackless, barbed feet. It could smell prey above, but it could not catch it, not today. They were nested high above, and it was on foot. Perhaps it would not always be such. Perhaps it would not always be confined as it was.

The thing reared up anyway, and the ancient weight of the pine tree shook under its bulk. It sniffed delicately. There was fear in the pine. Something distant and old. The animals had long since fled the immediate area, dreading the thing's smell and its power. All that was left were the trees, which were rooted in place. Plants communicated with each other however, releasing simple pheromones that translated to even simpler messages.

The thing was an expert at fear, and these woods were afraid.

The thing dropped to the ground again. There were other scents in the forest. There were other things that could be found. Could be taken, could be eaten. The thing's head came up to sniff the night air.

The body that it inhabited was that of a bear, a large and shaggy grizzly that had recently been delivered of a pair of pink naked cubs. The cubs were dead. Though the bear's heart still beat, the warm memories of those cubs, of milk, of the darkness of the den, were only shadows haunting the domed skull.

There was a fresh scent on the air, and the thing cataloged the information that the bear brain gave it. There was fire and metal. There was the smell of meat being cooked. There was the smell of a man's body. There was something else that the bear had no name and no use for, but the thing knew it quite well indeed.

It was hate.

The bear's face could not grin, but the thing made it do so anyway.

Perhaps there would be better quarry than the bear today. Perhaps not all the prey would be so clever to hide in tall nests.

Dropping down to four rotting paws, the thing lumbered into the night, each step cursing the ground as it went.

CHAPTER NINETEEN

IT WASN'T A natural darkness. Hailey knew that right away. If it were natural, her eyes would eventually have adjusted, eventually sought out the barest bits of light in order to see. As it was, her sight never adjusted. She had to wander through the endless night with her hands in front of her.

There was something in the darkness with her. She knew it was there. Sometimes she could hear it breathing, and sometimes, she swore she heard it *burning*. It was somewhere behind her, then somewhere in front of her, and she knew that it was searching for her.

She could feel that old panic rise up in the back of her throat. She had been afraid before. She had been taken by a Templar that wanted nothing more than her pain and her destruction. Her hand went to her side. She knew what it was like to be afraid, but this felt like more than that. This felt like a world-ending terror. This felt like the last moments of a prey animal's life.

She couldn't even turn to face the thing that was hunting her. It had no name, and it had no face. There was just that sense of fury and rage. Hailey knew she had to get away from it. She was running now, terrified she would trip. She did stumble, but every time she managed to catch herself. But every time she slowed, she could feel the thing chasing her get closer.

Suddenly, her grasping hand found a door handle. When she turned it, Hailey fell forward through the open door. She slammed the door just in time to halt the slavering, burning thing behind her. Now she could breathe. For several long minutes, she knelt at the doorway, grateful to have its thickness between her and the thing pursuing her.

When she had caught her breath, she could look around at her surroundings. She realized that she was in a stone room. Behind her was the flickering of a torch. She turned around, letting her eyes adjust to the light, and then she gasped.

The room was barely larger than a cell, and directly behind her was a man chained to the wall. He was naked, and from the bruises and welts that covered his body, it was obvious that he had been badly beaten. He was an enormous man with a thatch of midnight black hair. When he lifted his face to look at her, he had the bluest eyes she had ever seen.

"Oh Kieran," she whispered, and she fell down by his side.

To her grief, he turned his head from her. When she tentatively laid her hand against his cheek, he flinched.

"Kieran, look at me please?" Finally, moving so slowly and crookedly that she was afraid that something was broken, he turned. She cradled his face. "What are you doing here, love?"

"You…forgot me."

Hailey sat up straight, the covers falling down around her. She couldn't tell how long she had slept. She couldn't tell where she was, but the words from her dream followed her into the waking world. Like a ghostly hitchhiker, they clung to her, rolling around in her head until she thought she was going to scream.

You forgot me.

You forgot me.

You forgot me.

She was only aware that she was crying when tears started

running down her cheeks. She was breathing hard, her breath coming in silent gasps. She knew that if she continued like this that she was going to hyperventilate, so she slowed herself as much as she could.

Hailey told herself that she hadn't forgotten Kieran. She hadn't. How could she forget someone who was so important to her? How could she forget the man who had seen her for what she was? More than anyone else in the world, he had changed her mind about what she could do, what she was capable of. He had touched her without fear. He had been the first to do so while completely aware of her powers.

She shifted, and felt the Castle's master next to her. Her gut clenched.

Was it a betrayal to be with him when Kieran had turned from her? Was it a betrayal when she might not see him again?

The questions tore at Hailey's mind. She swiped furiously at the tears that would not stop. Feelings of guilt and rage twined through her spirit, threatening to tear her apart. Was she traitorous? Was she a fool? Was she heartless? Was she being used?

Her stirring woke Piers, who seemed to take in her distress immediately. He wrapped warm arms around her, murmuring soft words. For a moment, she allowed herself the comfort of his arms, but then she pushed him away.

"Hailey? Can you tell me what's wrong?"

She opened her mouth to speak, but instead she only sobbed again. Instead of taking her in his arms again, Piers took her by the hand, staying silent and watchful.

Finally, she shook her head.

"We…we shouldn't have done what we did."

Piers breathed out a long sigh, and his hand tightened slightly on hers before relaxing a little.

"We rushed things. We moved very quickly. I understand, I–"

"You don't!"

Hailey's words broke the air like a piece of glass. She pushed Piers's hand away even though there was nothing she wanted more than to throw herself into his arms.

"You don't," she continued. "It doesn't matter how fast I did it. I shouldn't have done it at all."

"Hailey?"

Hailey shook her head hard.

"He was the one who took me out of that dark place. He was the one who refused to let me accept less for myself. He saw me for who I am. You can't understand that, Piers. I betrayed him."

Piers's words were careful.

"Someone you promised yourself to? Is this someone from your old coven?"

Hailey shook her head.

"I promised myself to him, but no, it wasn't someone from my own coven. Hell, most of them wouldn't have spat on me if I were on fire before he showed up. No. It was Kieran, the Magus Corps major who came to bring me here."

She felt Piers stiffen.

"Hailey, you've done nothing wrong. The members of the Magus Corps don't make promises, and if they do, they certainly don't keep them."

The venomous tone in Piers's voice made her forget her torrent of emotions for a moment. Hailey looked up, startled.

"There are no promises that can exist between those in covens and those who have sworn to uphold the tenets of the Magus Corps. You have made no promises because he never accepted them in good faith. He brought you here, for which I owe him a debt of gratitude, but there is no way that you can promise yourself to him anyway. There were no promises broken."

Hailey stared at him in horror.

"What are you saying? You don't understand what we did together. You don't understand what we had. You don't even know him."

"I don't have to," retorted Piers. "I know the Magus Corps, and I know how they operate. Hailey, there are many reasons that I am building the Castle, but one of them is that our dependence on the Magus Corps to protect all Wiccans everywhere is not acceptable. They are an antiquated paramilitary force that was given too much power to oversee Wiccans as a whole. We didn't consent to their rule, and if I have anything to say about it, they won't hold it for much longer."

"You have no idea what our time together was like! You know nothing about what I felt then or what we did together!"

In her anger, she threw the covers off, uncaring that she was naked. She stood and struggled for her clothes.

"Hailey, I don't need to know what you did together to know that he acted inappropriately. He was never in a position to make promises to you. He would never have stayed."

The quiet words were like dark birds pecking at her spirit. For a moment, she could not understand what he had said. Then she felt a rage boil up inside her.

"That is not something you can tell me," she hissed. "This conversation is over. This is not under discussion."

Piers started to say something, and then he shook his head.

"You're right."

He turned and dressed as well. The silence between them stretched out, tense with electricity and fraught with what lay between them.

Hailey's thoughts were a tumble of fractured images and conflicting feelings. Her body could still feel the warmth of Piers's hands on her. One moment, they evoked all the care the man had, for her, for his coven, for all of the witches and warlocks in the world. The next, they made her remember with anguish Kieran's hands. The thought of Kieran being hurt, of him being forgotten tore at her heart until she could barely stand it.

"Hailey?"

She looked up, feeling as fragile as a china dish. Piers was holding out his arm for her as if he were an old-fashioned gentleman come to call on her. She had no idea what he wanted at first. Then she realized that he was offering her his power again.

"Take it," he said softly. "What's passed between us is no matter. I am still who I am, and you are still who you are. You are a brave and passionate woman who has shown me that she can be trusted and who I very badly want as part of my coven."

"And you?"

The words came out before Hailey could stop them. For a moment, there was a riot of emotions on Piers's face before he shrugged.

"I am a fool," he said softly. "Please."

She touched his arm, closing her eyes and reaching for that power again. It was a sea of light, and this time, it was as if it lapped against her. It wanted her, responded to her. She wondered if something in their joining last night had affected the way this transfer occurred. There was something terribly familiar about it, both pleasurable and deep, but that didn't make any sense. It was not quite like the times she had pulled power from him before.

"Are you ready?"

She nodded. He pulled the door of the safe base open and gestured her through it. There was something terribly final about the way he did it. A part of her didn't want to leave the quiet, private world that they had shared in the safe base, when it had just been the two of them.

It was never just the two of them, she realized. Kieran was always there, waiting in her mind, waiting for her.

Outside, the Wyoming morning was just beginning to break over the horizon. The air was crystal cold, and for a few moments, it hurt to breathe. Then she acclimated and stepped out over thin air, floating before rising a bit above the treeline.

"Can you follow me?" Piers's words were quiet, but to her relief he sounded normal.

There was no recrimination in his voice, no anger. She wasn't sure if she could have taken any harshness in that moment. She felt like she wanted to shatter into a million pieces and let those pieces be scattered all over the world.

"I can," she said instead.

He sped towards the Castle. Hailey fell into place behind him. As she flew, she heard a sleepy call from an owl. It was likely Merit, telling her that all was well. She wished she could tell her beloved familiar the same thing.

CHAPTER TWENTY

THE FLIGHT RETURNING to the Castle was quiet, but a part of Hailey still rejoiced when she saw the golden walls of her new home again. It was a foreign concept, but it was one that felt more comfortable with every passing moment. She could tell that if she were given the time, she would grow to love it just as Piers did.

The other covens she lived in had been good places, she supposed, but they weren't the Castle. They had been communities, but they had lacked the focus of what the Castle offered. They had not had the tight bonds that the Castle gave her without reservation.

Hailey and Piers landed in the practice yard where people were exercising their bodies as well as their powers. Hailey hesitated. She wanted to say something to Piers, but she couldn't think of what. She wanted to comfort him, and she wanted to push him away.

Piers looked like he could sense her confusion, and he nodded.

"Things are difficult now," he said gently. "I understand. I'll make myself as scarce as I can for a little while. In some ways, it's likely what I should have done in the first place to let you really see that the Castle is yours as much as it is anyone's. When you are ready, come find me. I will always be happy to speak with you."

For one breathless moment, she thought that he was going to kiss her. Instead, he nodded at her, smiled a little wryly, and walked away.

Hailey went to the communal kitchen to find food. There was a large pot of barley on the stove. The round-faced man stirring it smiled at her, telling her that it could be eaten just like oatmeal. She gratefully took a bowl and added a handful of berries and nuts to it before making her way to the dining hall.

Her schedule was slowly matching up to the rest of the witches and warlocks of the Castle. There was a steady stream of people trickling in, but it was still early yet. She kept an eye out for Julie or Erin, but neither of the women seemed to be around. She was resigned to eating by herself when she noticed a lone figure sitting on the far end of one of the tables. Though people were clustering two or three or more to eat, no one approached him.

It reminded Hailey painfully of being the foster child at the table when she was younger. It stung of the rejection of the covens that she had lived in. A small, insidious voice asked her if she wanted to ally herself with someone who looked like an outsider right away. But if Piers's new world order couldn't deal with her sitting with someone less popular, that would tell her something as well.

Feeling defiant, she pushed her shoulders back and strode over to where the lone man was seated. As she drew close, he looked up. She was startled to see that it was Stephan, the Magus Corps major that she had met in the machine shop the night before.

She had met a few Magus Corps officers before Kieran, but Stephan didn't look like any of them. He was lanky with a mop of curly brown hair and steel-rimmed glasses that gave him a rather bookish air. The smatter of freckles across his nose made him look like a college student. It was hard to imagine this man killing Templars or swinging a sword.

"Do you mind if I sit?"

His smile was slightly wry but genuine.

"I'll have to make sure to clear out my copious fan club, but I'm sure I can find the space. Thank you, I'd like the company."

She settled across the table from him, glancing down at the papers that were scattered around.

"What are you working on?"

"More of my toys," he said cheerfully. "I got the little firecracker gadget you saw finished enough that someone else can handle the testing. Right now, I'm working on a kind of cloaking technology."

Hailey examined the plans more closely, intrigued.

"Do you mean like the way that some witches and warlocks can make themselves invisible?"

Stephan laughed a little.

"Yes, that combined with technology that I saw when I watched Star Trek as a kid."

Hailey grinned.

"I watched a few episodes on and off, but I know enough to ask who your favorite captain was."

"Kirk," he said firmly. "You never forget your first."

Hailey blinked.

"You were watching the original series when you were a kid? That was back in the seventies, wasn't it?"

"Sixties as a matter of fact. It's a little weird. I'm never as old as some people think I am, but I'm far older than what others think." He shrugged. "I'm one of the youngest members of the Magus Corps, and it makes for some interesting days."

"It must. The Magus Corps is, um, I'm not sure how to put it."

"Not an organization that likes to change?" Stephan's laugh was real, but there was definitely a little bitterness to it.

"I wasn't going to say it if you weren't."

"It's fine. I know what the Magus Corps' reputation is, especially here. I think you're the first person who's come to sit down next to me since I've been here."

"This must be very different from where you usually are," Hailey murmured, and he shook his head.

"Honestly, not really. I'm not exactly Magus Corps material at the bottom of it, but the Commandant I serve under, he realized that the organization needs to change or die. I'm sort of a mascot in some ways, you know? A whole new breed of Magus Corps officer, dedicated to fighting evil in brand new ways."

There was enough bitterness in his voice that he shook himself, looking faintly embarrassed.

"That was probably a lot more honest than I thought it was going to be. Look, that's all true, but that's not the whole story, okay?"

Hailey shook her head dubiously.

"I think that any organization that would treat you like a mascot isn't one that you want to be a part of."

"I'm not saying I don't have my days," Stephan admitted. "I mean, there's a reason I'm here for my break. In another world, I'd probably be living here and turning the machine shop into my own snug little berth."

"But in this world?"

He shrugged.

"In this world, I was a guy who was pulled out of a really bad place. It was a Magus Corps officer that found me after I was awakened. I didn't even know it. All I knew was that the guns I touched worked better, that the grenades I was using did more. It was an incredibly dark time, and I was lucky to get pulled out of it when I was."

He was silent for a moment, long enough to let Hailey do a

little bit of math in her head. If he had been watching the original Star Trek series, he had also likely been drafted into the Vietnam War. The idea of this mild young man in a combat situation was unnerving.

"The Magus Corps gave me what it felt like the whole world had been denying me, you know? I had a place for the first time. They wanted to see what I could do, and by God and all the saints, I wanted to give it to them. The Commandant says that my gadgets have saved lives. I was the one who insisted on getting cellphones and smartphones in the field as soon as they became available. I like to think I've done a lot of good."

"You seem very devoted," Hailey observed.

"Well, you got me on a good day. I have bad ones too, don't get me wrong. It can get pretty nasty out there, but even when it feels like one big military circle jerk, I know there are Magus Corps officers who have my back." He shrugged. "Nothing's perfect."

Hailey hesitated for a moment, and then she finally blurted out the question that had been lurking in the back of her mind ever since she sat down.

"Do you know Kieran McCallen?"

"Major McCallen? A bit, I guess. He's older, so he doesn't like my toys all that much, but he'll use 'em. Never met him before. Why do you ask?"

"Oh." Hailey couldn't help feeling a little disappointed. "I... He was the officer who got me here. That is, his mission was to find and evaluate me for a trial with the Castle."

Stephan nodded.

"We don't always play nice with the covens, but we do our best. Are you doing okay settling in?"

Hailey nodded a little shyly.

"I think so. It's a lot like what you were saying. They're giving me a place."

"I'm glad to hear it. We should all be so lucky as to find a place where we're welcome and not just tolerated."

Stephan rose, gathering up his papers and his dishes.

"I'm due for bed soon, I think. I was working all night, and I want a quick nap before I jump back in. It was a pleasure meeting you, Miss…?"

"Hailey Devereaux," she said. "Thank you for chatting."

"You're new, so can I give you some advice?"

She hesitated, and then nodded.

"God knows I'm grateful for the Magus Corps. They gave me everything I have. They made me what I am today. Most days, I like that just fine. It's just that every now and then, especially on days when I get to spend all my time in the machine shop here, I wonder what other options I might have had, you know?" He laughed a little self-consciously. "I don't regret it, but I do wonder. Before you settle down, do some exploring. Don't let the first people who offer you the barest bit of tolerance be the master you swear yourself to."

She nodded, and he walked off, leaving her to contemplate the remnants of her barley and berries.

But the Castle wasn't the first to offer me a home, she realized.

Kieran was.

She couldn't explain it, not in any kind of way that made sense. Kieran had appeared like water after a drought. He was a man who embodied most of what the people of the Castle were afraid of. He was powerful, and he wielded his authority with the ease of long practice. He did not obey the laws of any covens. He had the right to uphold the laws set in place by the Magus Corps if he so chose.

He had given her a home, however. That was something she could not escape. He was her home. Even if it was only for a little while, it was still real. It still hurt when she lost him. She wondered what it meant, but she couldn't stand another whirl of the emotions that had taken her that morning. Talking with Stephan had proven to be a respite from her own overwrought emotions at least.

Piers had told her to get to know the Castle, and she decided to do exactly that. There were more people who called the Castle home than just Piers, and she resolved to meet them.

CHAPTER TWENTY-ONE

FOR THE NEXT two weeks, Hailey threw herself into life at the Castle. The feelings she had for Kieran and the new feelings that were emerging for Piers were put aside as she found her feet in her new home. She reached out, exploring and putting down tentative roots, things that had seemed impossible just a few short weeks ago.

She had a few rough nights. There were times when she was convinced that the stability and the safety and the welcome she had found must have been figments of her imagination. Soon it would surely all be taken away from her. She would be sent away, and it would hurt all the worse for having been so wonderful for a short time.

Most days however were full of learning and exploration. She had herself put on the cleanup roster in the kitchen. Every meal time brought someone new. All of the people of the Castle were passionate about their talents. She met a young woman who could see things happening in other places, so long as she had been there before. She made the acquaintance of an older man, gruff as a bear and battered as a cliff face pine, who communed with the herds of bighorn sheep that roamed the area.

Slowly, she realized that all of the people of the Castle, no matter their Wiccan talents, were all devoted to the idea of independence. They treasured their contact with the human world, and in many ways, they were dependent on it. Supplies were regularly brought in, and a young warlock who had a real skill with teleportation made it quite easy to get what they needed from the human world.

Hailey did a few sessions with Erin, taking the other young woman up on her parkour and free running lessons. They left her aching and tired, but exuberant. She knew that she would enjoy making it a part of her routine.

Some of the witches and warlocks were even curious about her own ability. It took more than a week before the first was brave enough to submit herself for a trial run. She had set her face grimly as if expecting it to hurt, but she had still offered Hailey her arm. In many ways, it was the moment of truth. Hailey could feel the other Wiccans in the training ground watching them, not even pretending to be discreet. If she did something wrong, if she took too much or harmed this brave girl, her time at the Castle might come to a screeching halt.

Hailey should have been nervous, and the girl certainly was. However, there was a voice at the back of her head telling her that it was fine. She had skill. She had control. She wasn't going to hurt this girl.

She touched the girl lightly. There was an impression of a green and healing energy. As she removed her hand, she looked at the witch.

"Does your power have something to do with plants, with growing, maybe?"

The girl was examining her hand in surprise.

"That didn't hurt at all. And you're right, I can make plants grow quickly and produce food more readily. I feel fine!"

"You should feel fine," Hailey said firmly. "No one I've ever used this skill on has ever been harmed in the least."

"All right." The girl grinned eagerly. "Now let's see what you can do with it."

In response, Hailey spread her hands to light a flame the size of a cannon ball between them. The ball of flame hovered for a moment before flying high up into the air before dissipating. It was a maneuver that she had seen the more military minded of the Angioli coven's protectors do. It was satisfyingly showy, causing the people around her to break into applause. She turned to the crowd grinning and caught a glimpse of Piers as she did. When she looked closer, however, she couldn't find him.

After that display, warlocks and witches were calmer around Hailey. Several more offered themselves up for her work, and finally one day, Julie came looking for her.

Hailey was sitting in the kitchen with a book on the Scandinavian witch trials in front of her. She was so absorbed that she didn't notice that Julie had come up with bread and a slice of honeycomb to share.

"A lot of the folks are talking," Julie began without preamble, "and I wanted to talk to you."

Instantly, Hailey lost interest in the honeycomb, her guard up and bristling.

"Why, what are they saying?" she asked warily.

Had she been wrong? Had she overstepped herself and the place she had in the coven?

"Well, to be blunt, they're wondering why you don't ask them for a bit of their power more often. As a matter of fact, you never do."

"That sounds like…asking for trouble," Hailey said finally. "I mean, I know how personal it is. I know that people think that I'm some kind of vampire. I don't want anyone to think that I'm just being nice to them because I need some of their energy."

"No one's going to think that," Julie said. "They've seen it with their own eyes. I don't know what to think about your coven masters before, but everyone here, absolutely everyone knows that Piers wouldn't let someone dangerous live among us. They also know that he never brings in anyone who isn't some kind of genius at what it is they do. They want to see that."

"But…"

Hailey's voice trailed off. She knew that Piers had brought her to the Castle for a reason. Kieran had told her a few things about it, but his information had been vague. She thought back to what Piers had told her about a shield spell, something that could hide an entire community from Templar depredations. It would be impossible for any one witch to perform the hiding. It was impossible unless that witch was holding more power than a witch could have on her own.

For the first time, Hailey truly understood what Piers wanted and how she fit in. He had dreams that could only be fulfilled if she consented. With a start, she realized that they had become her dreams as well. The Castle was the first place that had given her a welcome, it was true, but it was more than that. She had seen a community that was worth protecting. She wanted to do her part.

"All right," she said softly. "I think I will start asking."

"Good girl," said Julie.

She showed Hailey how to break off the sticky, waxy comb and smear the whole lot onto a sturdy slice of bread. The flavor was intense and the texture exotic. It was another small gift that the Castle had given her, and Hailey was determined to be worthy of it all.

"Julie, I have a request," she began.

She worked with Julie and Erin at first, women she knew and trusted. She realized soon that Piers's hopes had been right. She could pull power from them both. It increased her own strength.

It allowed her to do far more than she had thought possible.

Other witches and warlocks came to her, curious about her experiments. She worked on different spells. Some came naturally to her, like fire and flying. To her dismay, however, hiding herself required an immense amount of effort, as did hiding something else.

"Don't worry much about it," Julie told her firmly. "Hiding is a rare skill, a lot like your own. It'll come with time."

As she continued her work, however, Hailey realized with a pang how rarely she had seen Piers. He was present on the edges of her vision and her awareness, talking with other Wiccans, arranging this or deciding that. He greeted her with a polite nod, but he never seemed to have the time to stop and talk with her.

She realized slowly that she would need to take him at his word. He was giving her all the space that she needed. He wanted her to feel ready. Her heart warmed when she realized that he wanted her to feel completely safe and secure.

Hailey knew that she was ready to speak more with him about putting her abilities to work. She understood that there were risks. If she pulled power from a number of people and then used it, the final outcome often left her feeling drained and tired. Her vision had swam once. She knew that it could get worse if the spell was truly powerful.

She wasn't worried about the spell, however. Their time apart had done nothing to dull her confusion about her feelings. She still thought of Kieran. She missed him with a passion, his eyes, his hands, his quiet humor and his power. She thought of Piers as well. He was passionate but so caring and gentle. There was a fiery spark to him that she could sense lay under the surface. She was called to both of them, and to put the conflict out of her mind, she had simply not thought about it. Thoughts too far in one direction or the other only made her heart hurt. She reasoned it had nothing to do with her powers and what she could do for the coven. That was when she decided to seek out Piers.

CHAPTER TWENTY-TWO

HAILEY KNEW THAT Piers sometimes greeted the morning on the slate roof of the west wing, the highest point of the Castle. It was a slick and unreliable perch, inaccessible except to flyers, but fortunately Hailey could be counted among their ranks. She was learning to hold power better and to learn how to judge how much of it was necessary.

Early in the morning, when the golden rays were just beginning to creep up the walls of the Castle, Hailey dressed herself warmly. Nearly silently, she stepped into the air and ascended to the slate roof.

Piers sat on the slate, long legs sprawled, watching the sky lighten above. There was something calm and peaceful about him in this moment. He was unguarded. He didn't have to have the answers to every problem the coven presented. He was merely himself.

Hailey softly landed on the roof next to him, careful of her footing. It was a little wet thanks to the mountain dew. The last thing that she wanted was to start off with a tumble.

"You're up early," he observed.

"So are you," she retorted. "Or is it late?"

Piers grinned. His habit of keeping late hours and taking naps to refresh himself was well-known, if not particularly well-liked in the Castle.

"Early, I promise. I actually got sleep last night."

Hailey paused. The talk between them was comfortable. The silence that stretched out now was too. Piers looked patient, as if he would wait as long as he needed for her to speak. She felt that warmth for him that she always had wrapping around her like a blanket.

"Have you been avoiding me?"

She expected him to deny it, but he nodded.

"A little bit. I wanted to make sure that you could judge the Castle on its own merits. It's a fine place, but it's not for everyone. I understand that better than most, and I'm the one who built it. If you go through with the work that I am interested in having you do, it means that you'll have to be about as committed as I am."

"You could have had that anyway, you know," Hailey said softly. "When I came here, I was so overwhelmed by how kind you were and how sweet everyone was, I likely would have jumped right in without a second thought."

"I really couldn't have done that, and anyone who would have is a kind of monster. I'm asking you to risk your life to do something for people who have never done you much good at all. I know about your previous coven placements, and I know that they have not been overly kind or considerate of you. I couldn't take you from a bad situation and then use your gratitude against you."

"No, you couldn't, could you?" Hailey said, smiling. "That's why I'm saying yes."

"Yes?"

"Yes. I want to help you. If you had done that, pulled me in while I was still bright-eyed and bushy-tailed about all of it, I would have helped you. Now, however, I know the Castle. I know how much fighting can happen, and I know what a pain it is sometimes to have such a small community aware of every aspect of your business. I know that I need to do this. Mere gratitude couldn't make me this eager, Piers. I swear that to you. You don't have my gratitude. You have me wanting to do this more than I've ever wanted anything in my life."

Piers's grin was enormous. In a single moment, he was on his feet, catching her up in his arms. He did it with such enthusiasm that their feet left the slick tiles of the roof. There was one stomach dropping moment where Hailey forgot about their powers and was convinced that they were going to fall. Then she remembered and started giggling.

"What a good thing it is that we are both flyers," she teased. "That would have been an unfortunate way to end your legacy as the master of the Castle."

"I would have died happy though," Piers retorted.

He started to say something else, but then they both realized how closely they were holding each other. Her hands were wrapped around his waist. They were snuggled so close that Hailey could feel the heat from Piers's body surrounding her.

Piers dropped them back to the roof of the Castle, but he didn't let her go.

"Thank you," he said softly. "This is something that I've wanted for a very long time, and I promise that I will do whatever it takes to make it worth your while. I know there are dangers to you, and I will always do my utmost to keep it safe for you."

"Don't be too careful," Hailey said with a shrug. "Nothing is ever accomplished without a risk, and I know that this project is worth a certain amount of risk. You're talking about something that can help a lot of people."

Piers's face was unexpectedly stern.

"I think you need to remember who is running this project. If

I say that something is not safe, if I say that the risks are too high, you are going to listen to me. I am the coven master of the Castle, and you are under my authority, no matter how lovely you are."

Something about the commanding tone in Piers's voice made Hailey blush, but she tossed her head.

"So you think I'm lovely?"

"Of course I do. I have since you tried to set me on fire all those weeks ago. You're changing the subject. I need to make sure that you are going to listen to me when we talk about risks. Otherwise, this is not something that I will do with you. We should get this settled right now."

Piers was serious, but there was something hot in his gaze that made Hailey lick her lips. All of a sudden, she couldn't get the thought of that mouth out of her mind. She knew how skilled it was and the utterly filthy things it could say and do to her.

She shook herself firmly, meeting his gaze.

"I will obey you," she said solemnly. "I understand that I am under your authority, and that I will submit myself to the measures that you deem appropriate and only those measures."

Piers eyed her suspiciously.

"I really do wonder, but I suppose that will have to be enough for now."

Hailey thought again about truly submitting to Piers. The idea of it made her want nothing more than to be pressed against him again. It was as if he could read her thoughts.

"Because I'm sure you're so obedient, I know I could tell you to do something and you would."

"I would," Hailey murmured, her voice coming out soft and breathy. "I would take…great…pleasure in doing exactly what you said."

Piers's eyes darkened.

"And what orders would you delight in following, little witch?"

Hailey felt her heart beat a little faster. She wanted this man, and the wanting awoke a deep ache inside her. Her body seemed to feel that she had gone long enough without his touch.

"If your hands were cold, I would be happy to warm them," she offered.

After a moment, Piers offered her his hands. She rubbed them between her own hands. They were quite cold, but when they had warmed up a little, she pressed them under her coat. Piers made a brief surprised noise when he felt the curve of her pale rounded belly. The skin there was extremely warm, and Piers smiled.

"That can't be comfortable for you," he whispered, and she shrugged.

"It's a little chilly, but I like your hands there. You know. It makes me feel submissive to your whims."

"If you're feeling submissive to my whims, I think that I wouldn't just want my hands warmed."

"Oh?" Hailey's voice was high and breathy. She coughed a little to hide it, but Piers only grinned.

"I might decide that you didn't need to wear that hoodie at all."

"But it's so cold up here! I would freeze!"

"Maybe you don't listen that well," Piers said, his voice silky with menace. "I thought I told you that I needed to make my authority very, very clear."

Hailey could feel the heat rise to her face. She fiddled with the hem of her hoodie as his hands withdrew from underneath her clothing. They had been cold, but she already missed being that close to him.

"I want you to imagine what that would be like," he murmured, standing even closer to her. "I want you to think about what it would be like to lift that hem that you're playing with. I want you to think about how the cold wind would feel on all of that tender, bare, beautiful skin. You're shivering, and I haven't even done it yet."

Hailey could imagine all too clearly what it would be like to strip out of her shirt for this man. With his eyes on her, she would pull her layers over her head, letting them fall to the slick roof beside her. The dawn sun would glint over her pale, pale skin. Her rosy nipples would stand out, inviting Piers's touch. She could imagine his hands and then his mouth brushing over them. She would be exposed for anyone who glanced up.

The feeling of being stripped in so open a space made her squirm, but it wasn't shame. There was arousal, but there was pride there as well. She wanted to be the one with Piers, the one he chose to strip and expose as he chose.

She glanced up at him. His dark eyes were nearly black. When he reached out a hand to trail tenderly down her face, she didn't push him away. Instead, she leaned into his touch, letting it send tremors down her still clothed body.

"You want to submit to me."

His words were soft, but they rang with a truth that Hailey could not deny.

"I do."

Her voice was scarcely louder than a whisper, but it was enough. He took her chin in his hand and tilted her head up. She thought he would kiss her then, but instead he turned her face from side to side. He was inspecting her. The thought sent another shiver through her body.

"So beautiful," he murmured. "I don't know if you truly know how beautiful you are. There's a light that shines inside you. When I have my hands on you, it shines brighter still."

He spoke calmly, like he was discussing the weather or a new idea for a spell that he had.

Casually, as if he had every right in the world, Piers pulled her hair elastic out, running his fingers through her red hair until it whipped in the wind. She would have protested, but then his fingers found her scalp, massaging firmly until she felt like butter warming in his hands.

At some point, she had stepped even closer to him. She leaned forward until her forehead was resting on his chest. She could smell him. She wanted to wrap herself around him and never let go. He massaged her scalp for timeless moments before letting his hands drift down to the nape of her neck and then her back. They spanned her waist, making her giggle a little.

Then they drifted lower, down her hips and cupped her rear. For a moment he squeezed her soft flesh there, almost too deliberate to be a grope.

Hailey yelped when he lifted her up by her thighs, hoisting her high enough that they could see each other eye to eye. His gaze was so intense that she almost wanted to look away, but she couldn't. His gaze demanded her attention, everything.

"Wrap your legs around my waist," he commanded, and she hastened to obey.

With her legs around his strong hips, she was brought even closer to his body. She felt his erection through their clothes. It drew a response from her immediately, something that he could see right away.

"What are you thinking of, sweet Hailey?" She tried to shake her head, but he refused to allow her to slip away. "You thought of something when you pressed yourself so close to me," he murmured. "I want to know what that was."

"Or what?" she was brave enough to ask. Piers's answering laugh was dark.

"Or I'll put you down," he said simply. "Or I'll leave you here in the cold and let you think of everything I could be doing to you."

The noise she made at being denied his heat and his warmth was soft but real. She gave in.

"I thought about undoing your clothes," she murmured. "I thought about undoing mine. I thought about letting you back me up against something, slamming me there, and pinning me." She felt his immediate reaction and wrapped her legs around his hips more tightly. "I thought about you telling me to hold still, to make sure that I hold tight to you. I thought about you filling me. I thought about the sounds that you would make."

This time he kissed her. She opened her mouth and welcomed it. She wanted every bit of what he gave her. He tasted sweet, like coming home, and more than just the passion between them, there was something right as well. It was something that she couldn't deny, not even if she wanted to. She would let this man do exactly what he liked because every time he did, it was what she liked too.

She could feel his hard body moving next to hers, feel the way he held her steady even as he kissed her, as if their lives depended on it.

This time, however, he was the one who called a halt to things.

He broke their kiss, setting her down on the roof with care. When she would have protested, he held up a hand.

"What's wrong?" she asked, hurt.

Piers shook his head.

"I'm sorry, that was…amazing, but we're really not there yet, are we?"

She wanted to ask what he meant, but she knew. When she was carried away with passion, there was Piers. He was what her body craved, what it felt like she had wanted her whole life. There too, however, was Kieran. Her heart was just as fickle as her body. She craved both men. Hailey wrapped her arms around her body as if that would hold her together.

"No, I don't think we are," she whispered.

Piers nodded, understanding even if she could still see the hurt it caused him.

"You're amazing, there's no question of that in my heart," he said bluntly. "The things I feel with you are like nothing I've felt for a very, very long time. I want you in every way that matters. However, I am also willing to wait. There is nothing so urgent about what we are doing that it needs to be rushed."

"You are a patient man," Hailey said wryly.

She did not feel the same kind of patience. Her heart and her body craved what Piers was offering. She stepped back as well. It took more willpower than she thought to do it, but she managed it somehow.

"Well, living for upwards of five hundred years does help," Piers responded.

Hailey started to say something about that when a bearded warlock that she didn't know appeared over the edge of the roof. He hovered in thin air, waving them both down. As she and Piers flew closer, Hailey was relieved the man hadn't shown up a little earlier.

"Noel, what's the matter?"

"The last patrol never came in last night."

Piers frowned.

"Who was on it?"

"Julie and Miles. They should have been back an hour ago. We can't raise them on their phones, and there's no GPS signal at all to track them."

"That's not like them at all. All right, get every available adult assembled in the courtyard. Make sure that everyone has their cold weather gear."

Noel dove back down to do as Piers said. Hailey bit her lip. Julie was her friend, and she could already feel the beginnings of a panic lapping at the edge of her mind.

"Julie and Miles are extremely capable, but the mountains are still dangerous. There might have been some kind of accident in the night. Neither of them have transport capabilities, but Julie controls fire. At the very least, they won't die of exposure before they are found."

Hailey hesitated. She thought of the fact that Kieran had been called from her side so quickly and some of the dark rumors she had heard around the Angioli coven before she left.

"Could…could it be Templars?"

Piers's face was grim.

"Likely not. However, we're going to assume that's a possibility."

"I don't know what I can do, but I want to help."

"I expected no less from you. Come on, we need to get down there."

CHAPTER TWENTY-THREE

HAILEY HAD NEVER really seen how many people lived in and around the Castle. In an hour, they were marshaling in the courtyard, dressed for cold and ready to move. She stood in their ranks, waiting for her assignment, looking around anxiously every few minutes.

Somewhere in the cold, Julie was in trouble. She had not forgotten the older woman's kindness the first days she had been at the Castle. Julie had welcomed her with the same quiet humor and kindness that she gave to everyone.

"Everybody, give me your attention, please."

Piers floated above the milling crowd, dressed warmly for the weather. To Hailey's shock, there were a pair of short swords strapped across his back. She remembered what he said about assuming Templars, even if it was unlikely.

"Julie Ashbrook and Miles Canniff never came back from their patrol last night, and as of this moment, are not reachable by phone or GPS. None of the mind readers we have spoken to can locate them either, leading us to believe that they are at the very least unconscious. That means that they are lost somewhere on the mountain and that they are in some kind of trouble." He paused, letting them silently absorb that. "We're splitting into groups of two and three to find them, with a relief staying here to coordinate reports and to cross off search areas. If you find them, send up a flare, and stay with them. If you find them and there are Templars involved, do not engage unless you are confident that you can finish the fight. If you cannot deal with the situation yourself, get away and come back quietly. If Templars are present, unfortunately, Julie and Miles' safety cannot be prioritized over that of the coven. It's likely not Templars, but the chance is never something we take lightly. Remember that at this moment, the clock is ticking. The sooner we find them, the more likely it is that they are going to be able to come home to us safe and sound. Search quickly but be careful. All right, go to the people standing at the gates for your assignments. Good luck, everyone."

Hailey started to turn to one of the people handing out assignments when Piers alighted next to her.

"You're with me. We're heading to the southern edge of where we patrol and working our way around that area."

She took his proffered arm, closing her eyes as she sank into the golden sea of his power. She could never see the end of it. It lapped over her, warming her and comforting her even in this frightening situation. Again it was familiar, but she didn't understand how.

"I thought that you would be working with people that you knew better," she said curiously.

They cleared the wall and were sailing south through the air. The morning was beautiful. Hailey tried to tell herself that it was far too beautiful a time for her friend to die. She knew, however, that beauty was no surety against danger.

"I wanted you with me for many reasons," Piers said as they flew. The wind carried his words back to her. "You're strong, quick, and listen to orders, which is something that I tend to look for. More than that, however, I know your skills and you know mine. I figured that made us a better fit than sending you with someone who didn't know your capabilities as well."

Hailey nodded, and they flew on.

"Do you really think it's Templars?"

"Think, no. Fear? Always." Piers hovered in the air for a moment, pointing out a ridge that rose as white as a bone out of the forest below them. "That's Elissa's Spine. This is the general boundary of where we patrol. I figure we start behind it and move forward."

They fell into a rhythm fairly quickly. One would stay on the ground while the other soared above. Hailey hoped that the differences in perspective would produce some results, but as time wore on, her hope began to flag. Piers insisted that she take energy from him very regularly, something she at first agreed to. The third time he came down and offered her his arm, however, she hesitated.

"I don't need it right away," she said. "I have plenty. I'm beginning to worry that you will not be able to access what you need if something terrible happens."

Piers thought before shaking his head.

"I don't think that's going to be a problem. Believe me when I say that I've been watching for signs of drain, and there's just none of that yet. I feel healthy. I feel just fine. I could keep going for hours."

Piers blinked at Hailey's wide eyes.

"What?"

"Nothing. It's nothing right now."

He looked suspicious, but he allowed her silence. As she lofted into the air above him, she could feel her heart beating faster.

She remembered what it was like to take power from Kieran. She had been drunk on it at first, amazed at what she could do and how willingly he gave it to her. After a time, they noted that the process didn't drain him, didn't seem to hurt him at all. It was the creation of a bond, something symbiotic and rare. Donato, the master of the Angioli coven, had said that they were bonded.

Other people always felt drained or a little tired after she took their energy. They recovered fairly quickly, some only needing a few moments, but there was always at least a few moments of disorientation.

Both Kieran and Piers shrugged off the effects. They even looked recharged by what they experienced with her. There was some kind of deep magic going on. Unfortunately, there were no Wiccans with her experiences that could help her. As far as she knew, she was the only witch of her generation to possess this unique skill. The witches and warlocks that had come before her had disappeared or been destroyed centuries ago.

The day wore on, and though she peered anxiously at every odd bush, every outcropping, anything that looked like it could be shelter, they were no closer to finding the two lost Wiccans.

At noon, Piers called a halt, and forced her to take some soup and some dried meat from her pack. The food tasted like newspaper in her mouth, but at Piers's insistence, she nibbled on it.

"If we can't find them by tonight, what happens next?"

"We keep on looking," Piers said firmly. "We'll continue for some time." He paused. "The mountains are a harsh place, and even some experienced and powerful Wiccans can fall prey to slippery slopes and dark nights. Julie and Miles are very well trained and strong, but bad luck can sometimes overwhelm that."

Hailey shook her head hard.

"I refuse to believe that. Believe me, I am prepared to mourn them if I have to, but I'm not going to yet. Not when we've not heard from anyone else, and not when the sun is still up on the first day of the search."

Piers started to respond to her, but his phone rang. He got up to answer it, walking away a few steps. From the tone of his voice, it wasn't good news, but it didn't sound like bad news, either. Not yet.

To distract herself, Hailey gazed around the small clearing where they rested. It was sheltered from the wind by a large stone outcropping. There was a blanket of dried pine needles on the floor, giving it a soothing, brisk smell. She wandered around the edge, beef jerky in hand, thinking about nothing in particular, but then she stopped in her tracks.

There was a small gray fox looking up at her, eyes wide, showing the white all around the edges. She backed away slowly, but the small animal still opened its mouth and growled at her, a sound that was both frightened and desperate.

"It's okay. It's okay, honey. I'm going to let you be."

That was apparently enough for the fox, which sprinted across the clearing. Piers, having hung up the phone, frowned as it went.

"That was strange," Hailey mused. "Foxes are active at dawn and dusk. They usually want to stay away from people, not menace them."

"Unless there's something they want enough," Piers said, his voice grim.

They walked to the edge of the clearing together. Now that Hailey was listening for something strange, she could hear it. The woods were utterly silent. The last time that they had stopped, the air was full of bird song. This area felt oddly muted. It was as if the woodland was holding its breath, as if it was waiting to see what would happen. Perhaps others would have found it peaceful. Hailey felt as if she was standing in a haunted house. She wanted to cover her ears and return to a place where there was sound. Instead, she stayed right where she was, determined to investigate the strange occurrence.

Suddenly she jerked, her nose crinkling up as if the tip were on a string.

"Can you smell that?" she asked.

Piers looked a little dubious, but when he sniffed the air, he startled. She could tell he could smell it now. It was a rank odor, something unhealthy and sour. She cooked with her father often as a child, and one of the memories that stuck with her was her father opening a small package that was enclosed in no fewer than three bags. The crumbled blackish-green spice on the inside had made her wrinkle her nose immediately. Her father had told her it was called devil's garlic. A tiny pinch gave many foods a singular savor, but on its own, it smelled amazingly foul.

That was what she thought of. Devil's garlic only grew in India and the countries nearby. There was no accounting for what she was smelling now.

Piers turned to her.

"Hailey, I'm being completely serious now. I need you to stay behind me. We're heading in that direction. If anything, anything at all happens to me, I want you to head straight for the Castle and sound the alarm. Do you know the way?"

Hailey nodded, biting her lip.

"What about you?"

He drew one sword, leaving the other hand free.

"I can take care of myself, but I can't do that as easily if I'm also worried about you. Please, Hailey. You can keep us both safest by doing as I say. Unless you can agree to that right now, I am going to send you back."

Hailey hesitated before nodding.

"I understand. I'll do as you ask."

Together, they set off on foot, following the foul odor. After just a few dozen paces, however, they realized that they needn't have worried about finding the source. The trunks of the trees nearby were covered with a coating of something black and unhealthy. The grass beneath their feet crumpled as if it had been rendered fragile.

Hailey could see that Piers was considering sending her back already. The only reason he didn't was because she needed to know more if she was going to prepare people at the Castle.

Soon, they started to hear a strange noise. It reminded Hailey most clearly of someone smacking their lips, but the sound was far too loud for that and it went on and on. They drew closer, and it became clear that it was a kind of speech, uttered low and in a bestial fashion.

Piers held up a hand, making Hailey halt in her tracks. Peeking around his broad form, she could see an opening in the trees in front of them, and in that clearing was someone walking.

"Which-which-which shall I choose. This one is no good, no good at all, even if he was convenient."

The voice raised goosebumps on Hailey's skin. It was a human voice certainly, but it was like a human voice that had been pushed through some other animal's voice box. There was a dead flat hum to it. Whatever it was could never have passed for human.

Piers shifted, drawing his second sword. Now Hailey could see more clearly into the clearing. When the tableau became clear, her blood ran cold.

Lying on the ground, tied up and quiet, were Julie and the man she assumed was Miles. Pacing around a small smokeless fire was a man, or what was left of a man.

He looked incredibly out of place in the forest. He wore a sharply tailored jacket over a bare chest. His sharp gray trousers were shredded below the knee, and he was barefoot. If he were any kind of a natural thing, he wouldn't have been able to walk on his bloody and lacerated feet. As it was, he ignored the blood, the shredded flesh, even the white bone that protruded from one heel.

"Which shall I choose. Human vessels are so flimsy, so flimsy these days. Once they lasted years, I believe it, I do. Once I could walk and walk forever, and they would not tatter and tear."

Demon, Hailey thought with fear. They were not unknown to Wiccans, but so rare that a century or more might go before they would be sighted.

Of course, that was if there was anyone left to report the sightings.

Demons walked outside the world, but when they chose to enter it, they brought with them nothing but despair and suffering. She could feel Piers tensing for an attack when it all went wrong.

The demon looked up, and in that moment, both Piers and Hailey were captured by its gaze. There was no telling what the man's eyes had been like before. Now they were a burning terrible yellow. The demon's gaze pinned them where they stood. Hailey could no more move her arms than she could move one of the ancient pines.

The demon shambled towards them, wagging its head back and forth as it looked over one and then the other.

"Oh, very fine, very fine, very fine indeed. A fool who believes that he knows the way out of the forest and a vampire. How very fine, indeed. We shall see, yes, we shall see what kind of pleasure they might provide. Let us crack them open."

Hailey saw the thing's hands reaching for her, for her eyes, and she knew no more.

CHAPTER TWENTY-FOUR

THE RAIN PATTERED against the window, making a steady rhythm that comforted her. Young Hailey listened to the rain instead of the man behind the desk.

"Are you listening to me, Hailey?"

On a whim, she had shaved half her head. She was underweight, which made her look even younger than her fifteen years. She dragged her eyes away from the window, and stared at him. From long practice, she kept her gaze sullen and empty. Before he could hide it, she saw the look of distaste and disgust that crossed the man's face. He took in her skirt that was far too short, the tank top that was far too tight, and the tattered boots she had gotten at the swap meet.

Do you think I'm trash? Are you thanking your lucky stars that your daughters aren't going to turn out like me?

Hailey kept her eyes turned carefully away from the pictures on the man's desk. It was a happy family life that she couldn't even dream of anymore, but the memories still cut like glass.

"Yeah," she said finally. "I'm listening."

He leaned over the desk and shoved her hard in the forehead with one bony finger.

"I don't think you are. This is your third placement this year, and it's the same goddamn story."

It always was, Hailey could have told him. Sleeping on screened porches instead of real rooms, food that was expired or far too scanty, being hungry so often, and the roving hands of her foster brothers. It was all the same story—one she had given up on telling.

"If we can't find another place that's willing to overlook all this crap, we're going to have to send you to the juvenile detention hall."

She had heard of Parkhill. The other foster kids talked about it like it was prison. The lights never went off. They could strap you to the bed if they thought you were going to be disruptive. They could put you in solitary. Hailey thought that she should have been scared, but the fear just wasn't there anymore. She wondered if she would ever feel anything again.

The sound she made must have sounded like a laugh. Whatever it was, it made her caseworker's face turn red. Moving faster than Hailey ever thought he could, he leaned over the desk and landed a hard slap to her small face.

She stared at him, he stared at her. Now that his fit of rage was over, he looked startled, almost terrified of what he had done.

Hailey had been struck before, and she would be struck again, but there was something about it this time that hurt—inside.

"If you're not careful, you are going to end up getting yourself funneled straight into the prison system after you graduate. Girls like you don't last long on the street. We are trying to find solutions for you, and you just keep ruining them. Look at how infuriating you are. Does it not occur to you to try a little harder?" The man's voice droned on and on. Finally, he stood, shaking his head in disgust. "Stay there. I have to pick up the files from downstairs, and we'll start over. Maybe this time you'll find a family that's willing to put up with your shit."

He walked out of the room, slamming the door behind him.

Her face still flaming from his blow, Hailey sat numbly in the plastic chair.

Finally she slumped over, wrapping her hands around her stomach and curling in on herself. She had been in the system for six years already. It would be another three before she could get out. Eighteen looked so far away, so impossibly far away, but it terrified her as well. After eighteen, there would be no one looking after her, no one who remembered her, who knew she was alive.

All she owned in the world was in a battered duffel by her side. She knew where her pocket knife was. It had slyly been honed to razor sharpness on the bottom of one her last foster family's bowls. She knew how easy it would be. No more foster homes. No more fear. Before she knew what was happening, her fingers were wrapped around the knife's handle. The blade was wickedly sharp. It probably wouldn't hurt at all.

Behind her, she could feel eyes watching her. She knew they were yellow, and they were watching with approval.

Yes, yes, this was what she needed to do.

She brushed the sharp blade over the white skin of her wrist, and she paused.

The thing behind her hissed in anger, but she sat still.

She looked at her wrist.

She could remember a hand on it. The hand was larger than her own, holding it tenderly. Almost in a daze, she watched as an enormous man with bright blue eyes lifted her wrist and turned it so that he could kiss the palm.

He looked around, as if saddened by what he saw, and then he looked at her again.

"You know I'm waiting, little fox. Come find me."

She rose from the chair slowly. In the past, her case worker had come back in and hurried her to his car. Now Hailey knew she wasn't in the past. She turned to see the demon.

Stripped of its human form, it was foul. It had the shape of a primitive ape, enormous and hairy, but its head was that of a warthog. It snarled at her, full of hate, but she didn't hesitate.

She moved fast and without doubt, driving the sharp knife into its eye. The thing howled with pain before disappearing.

She didn't care. She walked quickly towards the door, certain that she would not see the dull and dreary hallway of the Child Services building.

Hailey had someone she needed to find.

• • • • •

The rain was bucketing down hard, obscuring the fine details. It still wasn't enough. Piers could still hear the cries of the dying Wiccans around him. He could still smell the smoldering fires that had only recently been drenched by rain.

Piers hadn't slept for almost four days. Everything had taken on an unreal quality. His vision felt dim, and whenever he needed to turn over another body, it got dimmer. He thought that there must be an end of bodies. There must be a time when it was over.

He wondered if this was Hell, if the Templars were right after all.

He entered a timber house, and found a pair of young girls curled on the hearth, dead. At least it had been quick. They were small. He could carry them both to rest under the hastily-erected shelter outside. The shelter was still miserable and wet, but it offered a little dignity for the rows of figures that lay underneath it, covered in whatever shrouds could be found.

There were others like him moving among the dead. They looked as dazed as he was. Sometimes they fell down in the mud.

Then they had to be hauled away to rest themselves. Piers wondered if rest would ever come. He wondered if he would ever close his eyes without seeing the wreck of Costain again.

He settled the two girls on the ground, drawing a single blanket over their still faces.

He wanted to cry. He knew that there were tears inside him somewhere, but if he started, he would never stop. Instead he staggered to his feet, because there was still work to be done. This is work that would always need doing. Wiccans would never hide well enough.

He frowned when he saw a young woman with flaming red hair looking around. If he'd had more rest, he would have seen that her clothes marked her as an outlander. At the moment, he could only see that she was on her feet and unhurt. Something inside him warmed at the sight of her. Though he knew there was still work to be done, he stumbled towards her.

"Mistress, mistress, are you well? Did you survive the attack?"

She spun towards the sound of his voice. With no reserve at all, she wrapped her arms around him tightly.

"Oh Piers, oh my darling. I am so sorry. I am so sorry."

For a long moment, he stood as still as a post. Something about this woman, barely more than a girl, soothed him. She took away the distant howl of battle and vengeance.

"Mistress, if you're not well, we can take you to a healer."

She stepped back, wiping tears out of her eyes.

"No, I swear to you, Piers, I'm fine. I am. I just…I suspected… well, I didn't expect this."

Piers shook his head.

"No one did, mistress. Costain was perhaps the best defended and best hidden community in the Isles. No one expected this."

The woman nodded as if she understood something. She took his hand again. When she met his gaze, Piers realized that she had the brightest green eyes he had ever seen.

"It will get better than this, all right? You are going to survive this, and you will live a very long time. This is a dark day, but every one after this will get better."

He wanted to pull his hand from hers and spit. He wanted to drag her to the shelter to see the bodies laid out. Some of the slain were only a few years old. He wanted to rage at her words. The Templar attack on Costain was more than a dark day.

Instead, he only stood there and drew from the strength that seemed to come from this woman. He wasn't better. He wasn't stronger. But he could go on. He glanced at the surrounding devastation. Every day would get better? How?

When Piers looked up, he wasn't surprised to find she was gone.

When he turned around, he almost expected to see the pig-ape monster behind him. Almost casually, he drew his sword and struck off its head.

CHAPTER TWENTY-FIVE

A SHRILL HOWL filled the air. Hailey's first instinct was to hold her hand over her ears, but then she realized where she was. She was in the forest. Beside her, Piers was stumbling, obviously still disoriented. Though her first instinct was to rush to him, she didn't.

The man possessed by the demon was crouched down low, black blood flowing through his stained hands. She saw where one eye had been. She saw where his neck had been brutally slashed. The demon fumbled and faltered, but then it raised itself up again. It opened its mouth as if to speak, but then it roared again instead, something that made Hailey's skin crawl.

It moved toward Julie and Miles.

In an instant, Hailey understood what it wanted. Its current vessel was injured, so it needed a new one. For some reason, neither she nor Piers would do.

Hailey acted without thinking. She laid her hand against Piers's cheek, drawing power from him faster than she ever had before. But she didn't need fire. She needed cold this time. Cold had been Kieran's power. Now she called it up.

She threw herself towards the thing and wrapped her arms around it.

It turned to her, but before it could strike, she froze it. She pictured bands of ice appearing out of thin air, wrapping around the thing's chest and holding it immobile. She imagined those bands of ice tightening further and further until the thing screamed. She was touching it, and even through the thing's clothes, it made her palms burn.

But she couldn't stop. She couldn't let it hurt anyone. She knew that she had to hold on.

Help would come.

She knew that, and despite her own cries of pain, despite the howls of the trapped demon in front of her, a strange feeling descended over her. To her shock, she realized it was peace. A deep tranquility filled her, something she had been searching for her entire life without knowing.

With a roar that threatened to drown out even the demon's howls, Piers rose up with his sword bared. He struck the demon's head from its body just as she let go. With his second sword, he pinned the writhing, twitching body to the ground.

Hailey stumbled away from the monster. Her palms burned. She glanced down. They were black with the demon's blood. She felt light-headed, but she still managed to get to Julie's side. To her relief, both of the missing Wiccans were still breathing. They seemed miraculously unharmed. She turned with a smile to Piers.

He wasn't smiling, his eyes wide and focused on her.

"Hailey, Hailey are you all right?"

She started to reply that of course she was. She was fine. She was exhausted, but they had won. They had defeated a demon. They had saved Julie and Miles. Nothing else mattered.

She thought she was going to say that.

Instead, brilliant colors danced in her vision. She became aware of a burning heat that started in her hands and swept through the rest of her body. Hailey cried out and fell hard to the ground.

Piers was by her side instantly, calling her name. But when she looked up at him, he looked like he was at the top of a well. The light behind him was bright and blinding. As she fell, it began to dim. Before the darkness claimed her, she wondered if she would ever see the light again.

CHAPTER TWENTY-SIX

PIERS KNEW THAT the coven needed him. He knew that people were terrified about the approach of a demon so close to the Castle. Further research had shown that the man the demon possessed was a Templar. Fear ran high. People were restless and uneasy. They had banded together in the two weeks since the attacks, but there was still very much a sense of unease throughout.

But Piers couldn't bring himself to care.

The only time he had ever felt this defeated was when he and his friends had arrived at Costain. This time there was just one casualty, but it was Hailey.

The door to the infirmary opened. Julie came in with a tray of soup and sandwiches for him.

"I know you're not feeling too fond of the stuff right now, but you need to eat. No questions. Mathias says that he's going to kick you out if you don't."

Mechanically, Piers bit into the food, tasting none of it.

In her narrow bed, Hailey breathed softly and far too lightly. Sometimes, panicked, he was convinced she had stopped breathing entirely. They had cleaned the demon's blood off of her as soon as they had gotten her back to the coven. Mathias, the head healer, had taken him aside.

"Demon's blood is corrosive and deadly. It might take her years to heal from it. She might never heal at all."

Piers had thanked the man for his frankness. But there was no way that Hailey was going to be a thin ghost in a bed. There was no way she would leave him.

The healers managed to sustain her, but little more. Sometimes he paced in the hall, but more often than not, he sat by her bed, holding her small hand.

Julie hesitated before leaving.

"She's a brilliant girl. If anyone's going to pull through this, it's her."

"I know."

Piers tried to offer her a smile. The coven members who knew Hailey came in and out to wish her well. He was happy to see them, happy to see that there were so many who were concerned for her.

Julie squeezed his shoulder on her way out the door.

"They're doing everything they can for her. There's nothing more you can do."

Julie couldn't see it, but her words made Piers flinch.

He had been hiding from the truth for two weeks now, but he couldn't keep it up. He had put it off, but the truth stared at him like that demon. He knew what he needed to do, even if the heart he thought he had buried at Costain cried out against it.

He swallowed hard, pulling out the phone in his pocket.

Stephan had returned to the Magus Corps a week ago, carrying a full report about the demon and the unexpected Templar activity in the area. He answered on the second ring.

"Hey Piers, how's the girl?"

"Unchanged. Look, I need you to do me a favor." There was a long silence on the other end of the line. "For Hailey."

Stephan grunted a little. "All right, let's hear it."

"Who was the Magus Corps officer who escorted Hailey from Italy?"

"That was Major Kieran McCallen. Why?"

"We need him here—as soon as possible."

"It's not exactly a great time to pull officers from the field." Stephan said, but then paused. "I'll see what I can do."

Piers hung up, dropping the phone on the night stand. As he had so many times, he gently stroked the side of Hailey's soft but pallid cheek. If she wouldn't wake up for him, maybe she would for this Kieran.

• • • • •

Hailey's story continues in HEALED: Castle Coven Book Three, available now.

For a sneak peek, turn the page.

Excerpt:

HEALED

Castle Coven Book Three

Hailey let out a long breath that she hadn't been aware that she was holding. Despite the fact that she lay in the crook of Liona's arm, a leg protectively thrown over the older woman's, she had been afraid for her. Even in her short life, she knew that there were wounds that you could carry forward without showing. She thought of the scars at her side from the Templar's hot poker.

"How strong you must be," she whispered, clinging to Liona, resting her head on her shoulder. As the twilight chill had seeped into the room, they had gotten under the blanket.

"I didn't feel strong at the time," Liona said.

Her voice was light. More than a thousand years stood between this woman now and the girl who had been tortured by monsters wearing human faces.

Hailey sighed a little, drawing the blanket up over them a little more snugly.

"I don't know if I could have been as brave if it were me."

Liona's laugh was soft as she encircled her in her arms.

"We are more alike than you think. We are survivors, you and I." She paused, as though considering. "Wiccans yes, but also women. We share the same spirit, and perhaps even the same desires."

There was something about the way that Liona said the last word that brought warmth to Hailey's cheeks.

"I understood what you meant, I think," she murmured. "When you loved two men, I can see why you would love both. I am grateful that you never had to choose."

"One thing that I have learned over the course of my long life is that anyone who would force me to choose may be a fine friend, but they will never be my lover. I have had many friends and lovers over the course of my life. Both are a pleasure. Some cross the line back and forth."

"Cross the line…?"

"Mmm, yes. From friend to lover and back again over the course of the years."

Liona's voice was almost dreamy. Hailey could find it in her to be envious of the other woman's obvious good memories. She realized, however, that at some point, she would be able to make her own.

"You're blushing," Liona whispered. "Why is that, Hailey?"

"I don't know," Hailey mumbled. "You've lived such a long time. You're in my bed. You're telling me about… about…"

"About all the fun I've had as well as the pain? The pain passes, dear one, as does the pleasure. Nothing really lasts. I have come to learn that we must take pleasure where we find it."

Hailey became aware of the way that Liona was rubbing her back. Relaxed and unhurried, her hand moved up Hailey's spine and then back down. Her fingers gently kneaded the flesh at its base. Though Hailey didn't know the moment that Liona's touch had gone from comfort to something more, she definitely knew that it had passed. The barest pressure of Liona's hand nudged her hips from behind, and Hailey let them move forward. She pressed herself into Liona's side, the connection almost electric. Hailey's heart fluttered uncontrollably.

"Do you…want to find pleasure with me?" Hailey asked, her voice breathless.

•••••

MORE BOOKS BY HAZEL HUNTER

THE HOLLOW CITY COVEN SERIES

A daring quest. A deadly enemy. A protector who won't quit. Although Wiccan Gillian Granger's life's work is finding a legendary city, her research in musty libraries hasn't prepared her for the field, let alone a gorgeous escort. Shayne Savatier knows he's on a milk run, especially after he meets his beautiful charge. But when enemies attack her, everything changes. Passion intertwines with protection, and duty bonds hard with desire.

Possessed (Hollow City Coven Book One)

Shadowed (Hollow City Coven Book Two)

Trapped (Hollow City Coven Book Three)

Sign up for my newsletter to be notified of new releases!

THE SILVER WOOD COVEN SERIES

Though she's taken the name given her by a kind stranger, Summer can no more explain waking up homeless and covered in blood, than she can the extreme attraction drawing people to her. Amnesiac, confused, and frightened, she's not even aware that she's a witch. But help arrives in two very different forms: the cool and restrained Templar Michael Charbon and his centuries-long friend Wiccan Major Troy Atwater.

Rescued (Silver Wood Coven Book One)

Stolen (Silver Wood Coven Book Two)

United (Silver Wood Coven Book Three)

Betrayed (Silver Wood Coven Book Four)

Revealed (Silver Wood Coven Book Five)

THE CASTLE COVEN SERIES

Novice witch Hailey Devereaux had resolved to live life as an outsider. Possessed of a unique Wiccan ability, her own people shun her. But that all ends when two very different men enter her life: the brooding Major Kieran McCallen and Coven Master Piers Dayton. But their training and tests are only the beginning. As she struggles to fulfill her destiny and find her place in the world, Hailey also discovers love.

Found (Castle Coven Book One)

Abandoned (Castle Coven Book Two)

Healed (Castle Coven Book Three)

Claimed (Castle Coven Book Four)

Imprisoned (Castle Coven Book Five)

Sacrificed (Castle Coven Book Six)

Castle Coven Box Set (Books 1 - 6)

THE MAGUS CORPS SERIES

Meet the warlocks of the Magus Corps, sworn to protect Wiccans at all costs. As they find and track fledgling witches, it's a race against an ancient enemy that would rather see all Wiccans dead. But where danger and intimacy come together, passion is never far behind.

Dominic (Her Warlock Protector Book 1)

Sebastian (Her Warlock Protector Book 2)

Logan (Her Warlock Protector Book 3)

Colin (Her Warlock Protector Book 4)

Vincent (Her Warlock Protector Book 5)

Jackson (Her Warlock Protector Book 6)

Trent (Her Warlock Protector Book 7)

Her Warlock Protector Box Set (Books 1 - 7)

THE SECOND SIGHT SERIES

Join psychic Isabelle de Grey and FBI profiler Mac MacMillan as they hunt a serial killer in the streets of Los Angeles. Even as their search closes in on the kidnapper, they discover not only clues, but a fiery passion that quickly consumes them.

THE EROTIC EXPEDITION SERIES

Travel the world in these breathless tales of erotic romance. Each features a different couple in fast-paced tales of fiery passion.

Arctic Exposure

A young couple is stranded in an Alaskan storm.

Desert Thirst

In the Sahara, a master tracker has the scent of his fiery client.

Jungle Fever

A forensic accountant blossoms under the care of a plantation owner in Thailand.

Mountain Wilds
A beautiful doctor on the rebound crashes with her pilot in British Columbia.

Island Magic
Two treasure-hunting scuba divers are kidnapped in the Caribbean.

THE ROMANCE IN THE RUINS NOVELS

Explore the ancient world and the new in these standalone novels of erotic romance. Each features a hero and heroine who come together against all odds, in exotic and remote settings where danger and love are found in equal measure.

Words of Love
Set in the heartland of the ancient Maya.

Labyrinth of Love
Set on the ancient Greek island of Crete.

Stars of Love
Set in the rugged Pueblo Southwest.

Sign up for my newsletter to be notified of new releases!

NOTE FROM THE AUTHOR

Dear Wonderful Reader,

Thank you so much for spending time with me. I can't tell you how much I appreciate it! My newsletter will let you know about new releases and *only* new releases. Don't miss the next sizzling, hot romance! Visit HazelHunter.com/books to find more great stories available *today*.

XOXO,
Hazel

Version 6.0

HEALED

Castle Coven Book Three

By Hazel Hunter

HEALED
Castle Coven Book Three

As coven master Piers Dayton sits vigil, novice witch Hailey Deveraux lies still as death. Lost to him after being tainted with demon's blood, her spirit wanders in a nether world she can't escape. To Hailey her existence has become a solitary wander through an empty Castle coven. Memories tease her but never return. Doors open but lead nowhere.

Though Piers refuses to give up hope and tries in vain to bring Major Kieran McCallen to Hailey's side, a different aid arrives. Stepping out of legend and time, Liona di Orsini appears at the Castle. With an elegant beauty and distant gaze that Piers has only seen in the oldest of Wiccans, Liona has come to witness the turning of history. Her prophetic visions have led her to the Castle, and now to Hailey's bed.

As Liona weaves the telling of her tale with Hailey's own, she finds that she and the guileless, young beauty may share more than just great power. Brought together at a nexus beyond which Liona can't see, the pair forge a bond drawn from love, passion, and pleasure.

CHAPTER TWENTY-SEVEN

IN A SMALL white room at the heart of the Wiccan fortress called the Castle, a young woman lay as quiet as death in her bed. She was nearly as pale as the walls around her. The only color in the room was her vivid red hair, lying over her shoulder. Sometimes, her bluish lips moved as if she was whispering, but no matter how hard the man sitting by her side listened, he could never understand what she was saying.

"Hailey, please wake up," Piers murmured. "Please. I promise I'll give you anything, anything at all."

Sometimes Castle business called him away, but it could not keep him away for long. Sometimes Mathias, the infirmary master, would send him to bed, but he found he could not sleep. Sometimes he had to check Hailey's hands again to ensure that the blackness staining them had been washed away. The image of her standing up after their battle, her hands dark with the thing's blood and dirt, was something that would be seared forever into his mind. For one brief shining moment, he had thought that they had won. Then she fell, and coven master Piers Dayton was reminded that there was no victory in the world that came without a cost.

The smartphone by his side chirped, and without taking his hand from hers, he turned it on.

"Stephan, give me some good news."

"Sorry, can't do that, Dayton. I just promised you a check-in today. I wanted to get it to you before it got too late out there. Major Kieran McCallen is still on assignment, and is not available."

Piers ground his teeth.

"That is unacceptable."

"That's the truth," Stephan replied, unperturbed. "Magus Corps business. And you know what that means. Like it or not, Dayton, we don't answer to you, or to any coven."

"I know that, and right now, I don't care. If he's who I think he is, if he finds that you've kept this information from him, you and your Commandant are going to be in a world of pain."

"That's something we'll deal with when it happens," Stephan said coolly. "But I take it from your tone there's no change in Hailey?"

"No, not yet. She's been like this for two weeks now. Mathias says she's stable, but there's…there's just nothing going on."

"Frankly, Dayton, McCallen's not going to be able to help her. I hope you know that. The man's a master of snow and ice. He's not a healer or a dream-walker. You know that."

Piers didn't care. "Find him. Get him here."

Stephan sounded like he wanted to say something else, but Piers ended the call, turning his gaze back to Hailey's painfully young face.

Stephan was wrong. It didn't matter that Kieran McCallen wasn't a healer. He was the man that Hailey loved. If he was a man worthy of her love, he would be here.

The thought of her with another man tore at his heart with an eagle's talons. If he allowed himself to think about it for too long, it could take the soul out of him. There would be time later to think about what she would look like in another man's arms, to think about the idea that even if McCallen went and Hailey stayed, there would always be a part of her that went with him.

Piers couldn't think about that now. Instead, he held Hailey's pale and unmoving hand, and asked her to wake up.

He must have fallen asleep for a while. He sat up with a crick in his back, stretching and unsure what had woken him up. There was a chill to the room that told him that night had fallen. He was reaching for a second blanket for Hailey when there was a knock at the door. When he opened it, Julie walked in, followed by a woman Piers had never seen before. She was slender and had the ageless quality that he associated with the very oldest of Wiccans. Someone might have guessed that she was perhaps in her early twenties. But after a moment, they would start to wonder. There was a distant gaze in her dark eyes, as though she were only here for the time being. But perhaps most extraordinary was the fall of shimmering silver hair that drifted down her back. It was thick and heavy, moving as she did. It made Piers think of moonlight on water. She was beautiful, but there was a terrible sternness to her as well.

"Piers," Julie said, "this woman just appeared at the gate. She asked for you by name."

"That would be difficult for most people," Piers said, arching an eyebrow. "The peaks are treacherous unless you come by plane."

"Some of us have no use for planes," the woman said.

She offered him her hand. When he shook it, he could feel how cool her skin was.

"I've come here because this place is a nexus, something quite out of the ordinary."

She glanced behind him at Hailey.

Piers consciously tamped down the urge to step between them. Instead, he only nodded.

"Out of the ordinary is a mild way to put it," he said. "Perhaps if you told me your business, I could help you."

She turned her bright gaze to him. "Of course, coven master. I am Liona di Orsini, of the Lepus coven in Rome." Behind the silver-haired woman, Julie's eyes widened.

Piers blinked. "The Lepus coven disappeared more than two hundred years ago," he said carefully.

She shrugged as if it were no matter. "We have never stood close to our sister covens, and of late, we have found it safer by far to keep our distance. Still, as I said, events are turning in the world, and it is upon us once again to see and to explore. This woman, she lies at the heart of it."

"Hailey?"

She cocked her head a bit. "Is that her name?" But she didn't wait for an answer. "She has been demon-touched, and now she wanders. Unless she can find her way back, she will wither away and perish."

Piers clenched his teeth so hard they hurt. He already knew that. "I asked you if you could help her."

"I can," Liona di Orsini responded calmly. "If you allow me to stay at your coven and observe the turning of events, I will bring her back."

Piers wavered, but there was a ring of truth to the woman's words. Though Hailey still breathed, she did not live. The mindreaders and healers of the Castle could do nothing to help her.

"You may stay at the Castle as long as you wish and all doors shall be open to you, if you can help her," Piers said finally.

She nodded, circling around Piers to take his seat by Hailey's side. For a moment, her dark eyes grew unfocused, and then she shook herself, turning her attention back to the two behind her.

"I will need privacy for this. Do not enter until I call for you."

Julie looked like she was going to protest, but Piers cut her off.
"As you say."

Piers ushered Julie through the door. When it closed behind them, Julie turned to him.

"Do you really think that's Liona di Orsini?" she asked, awe in her voice.

Piers thought of the cool-water feel of the woman's hand and the shining fall of silver hair. He thought of the weight of centuries in the woman's eyes.

"I know it is," he replied.

• • • • •

Hailey had been walking around the Castle for what felt like years. It was a place that felt as familiar to her as the spread of freckles over her nose, but every now and then, when she turned a corner, there would be a dead end or a room she didn't expect.

Once or twice, she had opened a door only to be blinded by sunlight. Only when her eyes adjusted did she see that she'd just barely escaped a straight drop down the mountainside. She closed those doors and marked them by tearing a scrap of fabric from her green dress and tying it around the handle. She never saw the doors she marked again.

The Castle felt like it went on forever. Sometimes, she wondered if she had died. This wasn't her idea of an afterlife, but did she really know what to expect?

She remembered that there must have been people in the Castle with her, but their faces and names escaped her. Sometimes, she thought of a strong man, but surely he was a phantasm as well. She couldn't remember if he had short black hair or honey-blond. She couldn't remember if he was broad or lean, if he laughed or was stern.

If she thought about it too long, her head started to ache. She couldn't hold the man's face or his touch in her mind. When she tried, her head ached as if it was being split apart. She would crouch by the side of the stone halls, covering her face and sobbing until the feeling passed. She could have gone to rest or hide in one of the many bedrooms, but there was something terrifying about lying down in those cold, unspoiled sheets, something that made her skin crawl.

She never got hungry; she never got sleepy; and so she walked. She was aware of time passing. Sometimes she had to chant her own name over and over again, just to reassure herself that she still knew it. She wandered, murmuring it like a talisman. But at the back of her mind, nipping at her heels like a terrier, was the thought that it would not be enough. One day she would lose it all. She would be a ghost, nothing more than a memory of a woman trapped in endless gray halls.

"My name is Hailey," she said for what felt like the millionth time, but this time, she got a response.

"My name is Liona. What a very fine pleasure it is to meet you."

She spun around to find a woman dressed all in red, framed by the archway behind her. If someone had asked Hailey if there had been an arch behind her, she would have said no, but the geography of this terrible place was no more stable or predictable than the sea.

The newcomer had long silver hair and dark eyes. At first Hailey thought she was old, but when she took a few steps closer, she could see the woman in red was only a few years older than herself. Still there was something about her that made Hailey feel safe—for the first time since awaking in this lost place.

"How long have you been here? Are you trapped here too?"

Liona's smile was sad.

"I have only been here for a short time, but I may leave when I like. I am not trapped as you are."

"Can you show me the way out?" Hailey's voice was hoarse and ragged from disuse.

Liona thought for a moment before shaking her head regretfully.

"Only you can do that."

Hailey felt a surge of anger rise up, but in a moment the rage subsided. This place had its own twisted logic, and she knew what Liona said was right. She had been searching for a way out for what felt like years, but the way out didn't feel like an impossibility. It felt like something she had simply not found yet. Sometimes that thought was the only thing that kept her going.

"I'm so tired," Hailey said, voice trembling, trying to keep the tears back.

To her shock, Liona wrapped her arms around her, holding her close.

"My poor, brave girl. I know you are. I cannot show you the way out, but perhaps I can make this a little less difficult on you, yes?"

Before Hailey could ask how she meant to do that, Liona turned around and surveyed the hallway. She found a door apparently to her liking, and walked up to it briskly, pulling Hailey with her.

Hailey was braced for a steep fall or another room shrouded with sheets and dust. Instead, they stepped into a bright chamber, round like a tower, and lined with books on all sides. High above, the ceiling was leaded with glass. There were two wing chairs pushed close to a table laden with food. When Hailey took the seat that Liona indicated, she could smell the savory scents. For the first time in what felt like an age, she was hungry.

"That's good," Liona said encouragingly, piling slivers of ham and salami on her plate. "You remember how to be hungry."

She handed it to Hailey, who didn't hesitate to dig in.

"You're not part of this, are you?" Hailey asked between bites.

"I'm not, no. This chamber is mine. It truly exists in Rome. Perhaps some day you will see it."

They ate in silence for a while, and as they did, Hailey started to feel more than just the numbness that had seemed to fill her for so long. Eventually she stopped eating and set the plate down. Soon, there were tears flowing down her face. Not even her hands over her mouth could stop the sob that escaped her.

In a flash, Liona was at her side, holding her, rubbing her back, and crooning comforting things in her ear.

"There, there, dear one. It'll be fine. It will. All you need to do is to remember."

"I can't," Hailey cried. "I can't. I don't even know what I am trying to remember. Everything shifts. Everything moves. I can't remember…I can't remember him. I can't."

"What do you see when you reach for him?"

"So much. Sometimes he's laughing, and sometimes he's grieving. Sometimes he's fair, and sometimes he's dark. I don't understand."

Liona nodded slowly, still embracing her.

"I think I might. You need an anchor, dear one, and that is what is going to help you escape. Look, will you let me help you? I promise, there is a way out of this for you."

Hailey nodded. Relieved, she leaned into the woman's shoulder, taking in the faint honey scent of her. She felt exhausted and excited. She wanted to rest. She wanted to leave.

"Don't concentrate on the men," Liona said, separating from her. "Don't look for faces, or bodies or hands. What I want you to concentrate on is the feelings that they give you."

Hailey wiped her eyes with the palms of her hands, nodding.

She tried not to think of the confusing images that fluttered around her. She concentrated instead on the feelings that those images brought up. Instantly, she felt as if she was on firmer ground. She could feel her heart—which had felt as closed as a locked fortress—open up. What she found inside was love and safety. When she thought of those two men, and now she realized there were two, she felt treasured. There was nothing that could harm her as long as they were by her side. Warmth spread from the center of her. Something liquid and gold filled her, lighting her. When she opened her eyes, everything looked faded and far away. She could still feel Liona's hands on her shoulders, but her voice came from a great distance.

"Do you feel it now?" Liona asked. "Do you understand how it will lead you out?"

"I do," Hailey murmured, and she stood up.

She left the room behind, entering the dark Castle again. It was dim, but now she could see that it was just a fake. It was no more like the Castle than a painted backdrop. It looked shoddy. Above all, it looked weak. She glanced at the doors that she passed, but none of them were quite right.

She was remembering more now, and with the warmth inside to guide her, she understood what she was feeling: not one man, but two. She had been blessed to have the love of two powerful men who had saved her life, who would stand beside her to the end of the world. She was nothing more than herself, and yet that was all they wanted from her. It was something amazing and humbling. It made her move forward.

Finally, she came to one of the doors that she had marked previously with a scrap of green fabric. With a sense of finality, she opened the door and looked out over the steep drop. There was nothing below, nothing to catch her, but she realized that was wrong. This place was nothing but a trap, crafted of her own fears, but now she was too much for it. She thought of Kieran. She thought of Piers.

She stepped out over the darkness.

• • • • •

Hailey woke covered in sweat and flailing. The room echoed with her cry, and she twisted around, trying to figure out where she was. She was in a white room that she had never seen before. The silver-haired woman from her dream was sitting in the chair by her bed. She looked tired, and she was wearing sturdy traveling clothes rather than the splendid red dress, but Hailey still recognized her.

The woman smiled at her.

"Welcome back to the land of the living," she said warmly. "Someone's been waiting to speak to you."

Before Hailey could ask who, Liona went to open the door. Instantly, Piers was through it. He gathered Hailey up in his arms, and held her tight.

"Hailey," he breathed into her hair. "I'd almost given up. But you're back. By the gods, you've come back to me."

Hailey let herself be swallowed up in his embrace. Yes, this was the safety she had thrown herself into the void to find. She could smell him, she could touch him again, and that was all that mattered. For this, she would throw herself into the darkness a million times. She felt his cheek pressed against the top of her head. There was a dampness there that told her he was crying.

She hugged him with a ferocity that bordered on mania. She didn't want to lose him for even an instant, but then he pulled back.

"Darling, I need to get Mathias up here to look you over, all right? After that, we can look into getting you fed."

"I don't want to see Mathias and I don't want food," she growled. "I want you. I want you and–"

Kieran.

The name was on her tongue. She bit down on it in surprise, but Piers had already pulled back. His face was still joyful, but perhaps there was a sadness there, something lonely and lost.

"First Mathias, then food if he'll allow it."

He walked to the door, but before he left, he turned back to her.

"When you fell into your sleep, I did everything I could to bring Major McCallen here. I swear that to you. I am still trying."

Before she could even think to answer that, he was gone, closing the door behind him. She was left staring.

Liona, who had sat forgotten by her side, shook her head.

"Now there's one who will never hear a thing until it strikes him upside the head, make no mistake about it."

Hailey started to ask Liona what she meant, but the graceful woman rose and left before Hailey could speak.

CHAPTER TWENTY-EIGHT

FOUR DAYS LATER, Hailey was heartily sick of the infirmary room, of the kind visits of her friends, of bland soup and fruit puree, and of promises that she would be allowed out soon.

"I'm hardly an invalid," she had tried to argue.

Piers had shaken his head. He had been neglecting his duties as much as he could while she was unconscious, but now that she was back, he had to attend to them again. He could manage a few visits a day, perhaps even a meal, but otherwise, she was left to her own devices.

"You're recovering. You need to build up your strength, and that means taking things slowly. The last thing you want is to push yourself harder and find you've relapsed."

"Piers…"

"Hailey. That's enough."

There was a tone of quiet command in his voice. Though the twinkle in his eye told her that he knew exactly what it did to her, it was still serious. When he used that tone, it made her want to bend and obey him. It brought a blush to her cheeks. She glanced down at her twisting hands.

"And somehow, despite all this rest, you don't think I'm well enough yet for that."

"Oh there will be plenty of time for that soon enough, don't worry. Just rest now, darling. More than anything else, I need you healthy."

Hailey bit down on another protestation. Instead, she let him plant a kiss on her forehead before leaving the room.

She was just beginning to wonder what she was going to do for another long day bed-bound when there was a crisp knock at her door. When she gave permission to enter, the door opened, and Liona came in bearing a thick savory stew. The smell of it made Hailey's mouth water. She started eating as soon as Liona set it in front of her. It wasn't the hamburger she'd been craving, but it was far better than the bland foods she had been allowed before.

"So I'm allowed to eat like an adult now?"

"Mathias couldn't see the harm any longer, and sent me up with it. I thought I would keep you company."

Liona chatted with her about the weather, about finding her way around the Castle, and about other minor things until Hailey was done. When Hailey set the food aside, she took a good, long look at Liona before speaking again.

"You really are her, aren't you? Liona di Orsini, I mean."

Liona raised a pale eyebrow. "I've never pretended to be anyone else."

"It's just…strange I suppose. They say many things about you."

"I'm sure." Liona's smile was sly. "Do you mean the things where they speak about me drinking the blood of babies, or the things where all of the founding members of the Magus Corps are my illegitimate children?"

A laugh burst out of Hailey's mouth before she could stop herself. She shook her head.

"Neither, though I've heard those. You…you were there. You saw the future and you made it happen. It's like having King Arthur bring you stew in bed."

"Ah Artos. He had a bent for service. I will tell you that stew wasn't all that that man would bring you in bed."

For a moment, Hailey only stared.

"I…wait, you and King Arthur?"

Liona laughed, a soft and warm thing. She might have lived for centuries, but right then, she looked like a girl who had played a prank on a friend.

"You mustn't be so gullible, Hailey. When you live as long as I have, you become fond of playing tricks."

Hailey thought for a moment.

"You didn't say you *didn't* know King Arthur."

"That I didn't," Liona said smoothly.

Hailey stared at her hands for a few moments before turning back to Liona again.

"Something important is happening, isn't it? That's why you're here."

Liona's look was opaque, but Hailey knew the stories. Liona was a seer, one of the most talented and powerful clairvoyants that the Wiccan world had ever produced. What she said would happen, happened. No matter what twists or turns the story took, she was right. She had stood on the edge of history, watching with her famous black eyes. Empires rose and fell, just as she had predicted.

The fact that she had appeared from a centuries-long absence to come to Hailey's bedside in Wyoming meant something. Hailey could feel the cold wind of history against her face—and it frightened her.

"My gift is a strange and capricious thing, even after all these years," Liona said finally. "It is not a window to the future but a mirror. And what I see is often clouded. Still, there were only a few times in my history when I could see as little as I do now. I woke up one morning a month or more ago, and found that I was next to blind to the future."

"Like the rest of us."

"Exactly so. I don't know how you stand it," Liona said teasingly. Then she sobered. "The number of times my vision has been clouded can be counted on one hand. I concentrated, I worked, I researched, and from what I can tell, the key to this uncertainty came from the Castle. Namely, it came from you."

Hailey shook her head.

"I don't want to be something that changes the future," she said, and Liona took her hand with a kind smile.

"I'm sorry to tell you that you do not have a choice. If I am wrong, I would be very surprised."

Hailey could feel the weight of a thousand years hanging on her shoulders. If she thought about it for too long, she was convinced she might go mad.

As if sensing her dismay, Liona came to a decision.

"Move over, Hailey."

Surprised, Hailey moved over in the bed, allowing Liona to climb in with her. They were both slender and fit easily.

"Lay down," Liona said, her tone light, and yet the word something between a request and a command.

But if Liona di Orsini said to lay down, then you laid down. Though Hailey didn't know what to expect, Liona laying down next to her had not been it. But the easy way Liona nestled close, and the way they fit together made it feel natural. Liona draped her arm companionably over Hailey's hip. In only moments, Hailey felt safe and warm, even a little drowsy.

"The world can wait until you heal," Liona said quietly. "You looked like you were ready to fall over."

They rested in comfortable silence for a few moments. A thought drifted through Hailey's head.

"Liona?"

"Hmm?"

"When your vision has been clouded, has it always been a disaster? Is there ever a place where it turns out well?"

Liona sighed, her breath ticklish against the back of Hailey's ear.

"The future is an uncertain thing, even to me. However, what might begin as tragedy and pain may lead to wonderful places. Sometimes the pain is better than the lack of it would be." She paused and shifted. "Shall I tell you of the first time my vision was clouded and what happened after? It's your story, just as it is the story of every coven in the world and every branch of the Magus."

Hailey nodded.

Liona's voice, soft and husky, carried her back to another time and another land, where a young woman prepared for her evening engagement.

CHAPTER TWENTY-NINE

OUTSIDE OF HER window, Liona could hear the sounds of the daylight life of Rome shutting down. The baker was closing his stall. The pot-seller was gathering her unsold wares back into her cart. People were calling good-night to one another, ready for a well-deserved sleep, before starting the exact same routine the next day.

With a catlike smile, Liona combed her fingers—lightly slicked with perfumed oil—through her long black hair. It made it shine like polished jet. She called through the curtain for Augusta to come and braid it for her.

"If you're doing so well with the nobles, perhaps you can hire yourself a hairdresser, hmm?" her younger sister said. "Maybe someone who doesn't have things of her own to be doing?"

Liona playfully pinched Augusta's thigh.

"But I can't find anyone so gentle as my darling sister, and besides, you do it best."

"I do," sighed Augusta. "Now sit still before I take a pair of scissors to your head and sell it to the wig makers."

Liona examined her features carefully in the tiny disc of polished bronze she used as a mirror. She had a round face that was hardly the style for Rome's severe looks, but her large, liquid black eyes made up for the softness of her features. Her mouth was wide and generous, and highlighted with red carmine from the east. They were easily her best feature. A shimmer of powdered green malachite gave her eyes a smoky languidness. Her fingertips had been dyed deep orange with henna. Two flashing pieces of polished glass, imported from Egypt, hung from her pierced ears.

She was no Roman beauty, but in her saffron robe belted with a green silk sash, she was an exotic offering. Her skin had an olive tint to it; she could have been from almost anywhere in the Empire.

Liona watched Augusta purse her lips in concentration, coiling the tiny braids she had created becomingly on top of Liona's head, securing them with small copper pins. She was taller than her older sister, and by some trick of birth, despite being born of the same parents, she looked as pale as a Gaul, with sky blue eyes and fair hair that were cooed over whenever she went out.

"There, now you're done."

Augusta paused long enough for Liona to raise an eyebrow.

"What's the matter, rabbit?" Liona asked. "What are you worried about now?"

"Nothing…nothing, it's just that I wish you wouldn't go out tonight."

Liona laughed.

"Now you're the one who can read the future. I better be careful or you'll steal all of my clients!"

Augusta made a face.

"Oh Liona, do be serious. It's just a feeling I have."

"Well I don't have a single one except for the feeling that I'm going to make a lot of lovely money tonight. It's fine. Before you know it, it'll be dawn, and I'll be back with my robes stuffed full of silver."

Augusta smiled, but she was still troubled.

"Will you hire a man to walk you home? It has been so dangerous in the street lately."

And give up a fourth of my earnings just to walk two miles next to some bully? Not likely.

Liona nodded, throwing her gray woven wrap over her head and draping it around her shoulders loosely.

"If I think it will be a risk, I will do just that," she promised. "Now give me a kiss and get some sleep. I'll be back before you know it."

Augusta dutifully gave her sister a kiss. Liona waited until Augusta had bolted the door to their tiny apartment before she made her way to the street. They lived in one of the many apartment blocks that housed the poorer citizens of Rome, but they were lucky. Their apartment had a small window, so she needn't worry that Augusta would suffocate.

In the dim light of dusk, the daytime life of Rome had mostly disappeared, and the nighttime life was beginning to come out. It was too early yet for the young merchant's sons and nobles to come down to the gambling houses and the brothels, but the people who ran those establishments were getting ready.

A pair of women sat on a balcony, letting their bare legs dangle down, tapping prospective customers on the head and shoulders with their long toes. A young boy trotted by, arms laden with fat hares for one of the larger gambling houses on the street.

This was the life that Liona was used to. Her father had been a Roman centurion, and when he returned from the edges of the empire, he had brought her mother back with him. He didn't have a fortune or a name to protect, and so they had married. Liona remembered her father as a thin man who was always laughing, tickling her or Augusta before presenting them with a new toy from the market.

He had reenlisted, hoping for the chance to advance before he grew too old to make the attempt, but they had never heard from him again. Her mother, a stern, spare woman with Augusta's fair coloration, had taken in sewing to get by. Before she died, she had given them enough so they wouldn't have to sell themselves. Then, Liona had discovered her gift.

She had been just past eighteen, and besotted by the baker's boy. A number of hurried trysts had led to an awkward and fumbling awakening behind a cowshed, something she hadn't found particularly pleasurable, but far from traumatic either. As she lay in the itchy straw, with the young man panting beside her, a vision had slid over her eyes. She could see the baker boy with the curly-haired candle maker's girl, a pair of twins on his knees and an enormous smile on his face.

"Liona, why are you laughing?" he had asked in confusion.

"No, no reason at all," she had said, kissing him.

Then she had refused to see him again, found her mother's finest clothes, and set herself up as a fortuneteller.

When Augusta had sneaked home late one night, and the next day shot fire from her fingertips, scorching their breakfast bread, Liona had hugged her. She explained her theory to her sister.

"When we lie down with men for the first time, it opens something in us. You control fire, and I can see into the future. They're gifts from the gods. Remember how Mother seemed to make the water at the beach obey her, the day you almost drowned? I think she had it too."

"I wonder if others have it as well," Augusta wondered.

Time would prove that they were not alone. Once at an inn, Liona saw a pot boy surreptitiously light a fire with just a snap of his fingers. In the square, there had been a red-haired foreign girl who had used the wind to lift a man's cloak, just enough so she could swipe his purse.

There were other people with power in the world. If they were content to leave her and her sister alone, Liona was happy enough to let them be.

As she walked on in the fading evening light, the neighborhood grew finer. Soon the clay bricks of her own quarter gave way to the marble pillars of the better houses. When she found her way to the one she was looking for, she addressed herself to the doorman and his huge dog. The burly man grudgingly sent her though the back courtyard.

The other entertainers were already there. A pair of acrobats were stripped to the skin and applying handfuls of oil to each other's bodies. A beautiful girl with hair as pale as Augusta's tuned her cithara carefully.

Liona took a bit of the warm bread that was set aside for the performers and dipped it in a dish of oil, eating while she had the chance. She was glad of this when the matron of the house came out to shoo them to their places.

It was one of the finest houses that she had ever worked in, high on the hill, clad in marble and beautiful. As the night darkened and the torches were lit, she saw some of Rome's most powerful men and women come to enjoy the party.

In her corner, rattling a bowl full of polished tortoiseshell fragments that were inscribed with her idea of sacred runes, Liona watched the party climb higher and higher in intensity. Rome sat at the top of the world, and the people who ruled it wanted to enjoy every bit of it.

The thick wine, undiluted with water, was being drunk more and more freely. A well-dressed young man, barely more than a boy, stumbled over to her corner, a wide smile on his face.

"Hail pretty seer, do you have a fortune for me?"

She did. It was one that would leave him cold and friendless on the slopes of an Anatolian river, his corpse pecked by birds.

"A farm in the lands of Hispania await you, a Roman matron

to be your wife, a lovely local girl to be your mistress and both to bear you children."

He wanted to hear more about it, and by the end, he was so giddy he insisted on giving her silver on top of what she was already going to be paid by the mistress of the house. She demurred when he came in for a kiss however.

"I am sworn to the gods, and surely I would lose my gifts if I betrayed them," she said piously, and with a sad sound, he moved off.

The night wore on, and for several hours, she was telling fortunes as fast as she could. Most of them were true. Rich people who could attend parties like this one tended to end up better than the average baker or slave. Plenty of them threw her a bit of silver and, tossed into the bag stitched to the inside of her skirts, it added up. She and Augusta would eat well.

There was only one thing that marred the event for her. The young cithara player next to her was quite skilled. With the guild badge she wore, it should have marked her as off-limits for the guests. One of the men, however, saw no difference between that girl and the slaves that were meant to warm the beds. The young girl's piteous cries roused Liona from her reading. Her head snapped up in time to see the man pinning the girl to the wall. Perhaps her position had made her overbold of late, or perhaps that girl looked a little too much like Augusta. No matter what it was, Liona excused herself from her corner and stalked over to the man.

He was drunk, as were most of the guests. He leered down at her when Liona caught his arm, but her look was thunderous.

"Let her go, and perhaps you won't meet your end stabbed in an alley behind a house of ill-repute. Perhaps they won't bring your ring back to your crying daughter. Perhaps if you change your ways, more than just your illegitimate daughter will mourn you."

The man paled. That future was closer than some of the ones that Liona had told that night. The man seemed to know it as well. He stumbled back, cursing at both of them, and Liona turned to the girl, helping her straighten her clothes.

"It's fine, love. See, he's gone."

The girl nodded miserably.

"There will always be more like that one, but thank you." The girl paused. "Aren't you worried you are going to get in trouble?"

Liona smiled at her with more bravado than she felt.

"Oh, me, I'm fine. I've got the second sight, you see."

She turned back to her corner, to the drunken matron who was waiting to hear about how many children she would have. As she went, however, she caught the gaze of a man standing close. In the darkness, she could only make out that he was well-built and dark-haired. He wore the fine, linen robes of a well-off man. As she eyed him warily, he nodded at her. She caught a flash of a grin, and he moved off again. There was something about him that made her shiver. Though she went back to her work, the incident stayed with her.

On her way home, keeping to the quieter streets, she had time to think about that man. An army man, she figured, given that build. She didn't hold much truck with the gods, but she wondered, half-fancifully if he was one, come to watch the mortals at their sport. He was too old and too sturdy to be beautiful Bacchus, too tall to be Vulcan, the god of the forge.

She thought of the curve of his lips. It made her remember that Mars, though the god of war, was supposed to be a fine lover. She shook her head at her fanciful imaginings. It had been more than a year since she had thought of love and lovers. She should leave well enough alone.

Perhaps it was her imaginings about Mars that made her blind.

One moment she was walking through the dark streets, unafraid and secure. The next, a strong hand grabbed her by the hair while another wrapped over her mouth. The man who held her pulled her into the alleyway, moving her as if she only weighed as much as a struggling chicken.

"Bitch," he whined in her ear. "Bitch, cursing me, giving me that fate."

She recognized the man, her heart sinking. He was drunk and much stronger than she was. Panic gave her a surge of strength. Though she lashed out with feet and elbows, he seemed insensible to her struggles.

Instead, he started dragging her away, making her mind go white with terror. In the alley, someone might see them and drive him off. In a secret place with no one to see or hear, she might never be heard from again.

She braced herself to break free, but then the man stopped in his tracks. He was pulled away from her as easily as someone might pick up a puppy.

Liona twisted around just in time to see a cloaked figure turn her attacker around, and drive his head into the stone wall. The man groaned and slumped to the ground. Her rescuer took her by the arm.

"We should move on before his guards catch up. That is a rather wealthy man I have just assaulted."

Liona nodded. "Shall we run?"

"Let's."

• • • • •

Hailey's eyes widened in indignation

"Wasn't there anyone you could report that to? He attacked you!"

Liona laughed softly, stroking Hailey's hair. Though she looked as if she could have been the same age as Hailey, in that moment, Hailey felt quite young.

"No, dear one," Liona said. "He was the son of a consul, a man that you did not interfere with, if you knew what was good for you. Later on, Lucius told me–"

"Lucius?"

"The man who rescued me. He was a legatus at that point, an important role in the legion to be sure, but still he had earned that by killing a lot of men at the right time and the right place. He would win a political position in a few years, but just then, he was a little more interested in keeping a mouthy little fortuneteller alive." She paused, a little smile curving her full lips. "We ended up in a private room above a dicing parlor, where we shared a bit of wine, and…"

"And?" Hailey grinned. Her heart beat a little faster. "Was he interested in a little bit more?"

"Well, let us just say he tried."

• • • • •

With his cloak draped carelessly over the hook on the door and his powerful body sprawled on the low couch, Liona's mind danced with thoughts of Mars come to rest on Venus's couch. He was strong with a face that would have been severe except for his wide and generous mouth. That mouth was currently curled into a sly smile that Liona felt down to her toes.

"Surely you don't have to leave yet. I have this room for hours, and I'm sure that there are plenty of uses we could put it to."

The urge to say yes was surprisingly keen. She had barely known him for a few hours, but the attraction was real, that much she knew. A part of her whispered how easy it would be to climb into bed with him, to see whether the promise of that clever mouth and those long, lovely fingers held up.

She shook her head.

"As a matter of fact, my sister is likely worried sick about me. I thank you for your intervention, and I also thank you for the company, but I should be on my way."

She watched him closely to see if he would try to prevent her from leaving, but though he looked regretful, he made no move to stop her.

"Perhaps you would tell me my future. It would help me figure out if I were ever going to see you again."

"That costs silver," Liona said teasingly. "Do you have some?"

He thought for a moment, and he held up a single ivory die instead. He rolled it between his fingers speculatively, glancing up at her. Liona stood at the foot of the low bed. For a moment, she wondered if this was what a man felt, looking down at a beautiful woman he wanted to bed but couldn't.

"Odds say that you tell me my future, evens say you don't have to, how is that?"

Liona pretended to think.

"Odds I tell you your future. Evens I kiss you."

Lucius's laugh sent a shiver up her spine.

"That's beyond fair. You throw."

The die came up with a two, and she looked at him speculatively.

"Now where shall I kiss you?"

He grinned, folding his hands behind his head.

"Anywhere you like. You've won."

She leaned over his body for a long moment, smelling the clean scent of soap and the slightly sour fragrance of wine. She thought about teasing him with a kiss on his nose or his forehead, but in the end, her appetites were too much to resist.

Liona leaned down and kissed him on the mouth, dancing her tongue over his lips. His mouth was hot and wet underneath hers. It was intoxicating to take what she wanted, to thread her fingers through his short curly hair and to hold him still as she kissed him on and on.

When she finally broke away, she knew her face looked flushed. He looked like a cat who had gotten in the cream.

He held up the dice again.

"I'll try again if you will."

Liona wavered. She knew that she should go home to Augusta, but he was so handsome, temptation incarnate.

"Odds I tell your fortune, evens…evens I want you naked."

He laughed out loud.

"So long as you won't claim my clothes for a forfeit, I agree."

This time he threw the die, and it rolled up a six.

She looked at him expectantly.

"This is why they tell you not to gamble in the legion."

As she watched, he slipped off his sandals. Then his hands went to the belt that kept his robes closed and the silver medallions that fastened them at the shoulder. In a matter of seconds, his clothes were draped over the back of the chair. Lucius sat on the edge of the bed, naked, and unashamed, dark green eyes watching her intently.

Liona felt her mouth go dry. She had flirted with the idea of him being Mars, the god of warfare, but this was something different. He was muscled from a lifetime of soldiering, sleek and strong. His body was a tool for war. Every part of him below the eyebrows was shaved clean, as was the custom for the legions.

Her eyes dropped to his cock, half-hard and heavy against his thigh. It twitched as if it could feel her gaze. For a moment, she wanted nothing more than to touch it. She had friends among the girls who sold themselves. Her experience with the art of love might have been brief, but she knew what she thought about late at night.

She also knew that in the nights to come, she would think about this man and his body. She would think about sliding down to take his cock in her mouth, to hear the stifled sounds he would make.

Liona realized she was staring when he coughed slightly. A rare blush on her cheeks, she jerked her gaze up.

"Well, well, you've quite stolen my luck," he said softly. "Shall one last time pay for all?"

"I think not," she said finally. "I like to quit while I'm ahead."

He laughed. Almost indolently, he ran a hand along his shaft, bringing it fully erect. She had to shake herself. She took a step back.

"I must be off, legatus. Think fondly of me. I know I will think fondly of you."

"Your name. May I have it?"

Liona grinned.

"I should make you dice for it, but instead, I think I shall offer it to you as a gift. It's Liona."

"Liona." He rolled the name around his mouth like a delicious piece of candy, never taking his eyes from hers. "Beautiful little lioness. Thank you."

If she stayed another moment, she thought she might burst into flames or fall into bed with him. The light was coming up in the plaza, however. She knew it was best if she went home.

"You're welcome," she murmured, and slipped out the door.

• • • • •

"You left him?" Hailey asked, the dismay in her voice so evident that she had to pause and clear her throat. "I mean, that must have been a difficult thing to do."

She had cuddled against Liona's side, head resting on her shoulder, but now she looked up.

Liona laughed a little, drawing her closer. Her delicate fingers smoothed back an errant lock of hair from Hailey's forehead.

"Not to worry, dear one. There would be more opportunities." She tucked the lock of hair behind Hailey's ear. "Many more."

• • • • •

After that evening, things continued much as they ever had. Liona had made enough money that she and Augusta ate well. She walked in the plaza; she spoke with her friends. She came home at night, and she dreamed of Lucius.

She wondered what kind of spell he had placed on her. Augusta, after she got through scolding her for all the risks she had taken, teased her relentlessly about it. She called Lucius the mysterious legatus, Liona's phantom suitor. Liona, usually ready to give her sister as good as she got, found that she was oddly tongue-tied in the face of the teasing. Instead, she ducked her head, muttering something about being far too grown up for such things.

"He's a legatus, Augusta. He likely has no use for the likes of me beyond what he can get from any girl on the docks."

Augusta pulled a wise face, stroking her chin judiciously.

"Perhaps, perhaps. However, how many of those girls would have made him club a consul's son to the ground for her? How many of them would have played dice for her favors?"

"I truly wish that I had never told you about any of that," Liona groaned.

Still, though, that insidious little voice whispered that her sister was right. She kept her eyes open for him when she wandered the city. Once or twice, she had seen a man of his height, build and coloration in the market or down by the fishmongers. Her heart had beaten faster, but it was never him.

She began to think that damn sly grin of his was just meant to haunt her in her sleep. She was beginning to forget, or at least that's what she told herself.

Then Augusta disappeared.

CHAPTER THIRTY

LIONA WRAPPED A dark scarf around her head, covering her flyaway hair neatly. She put on Augusta's dark cloak, making sure that she was covered from shoulder to ankle. It was still the darkest part of the night when she set out, but the dawn was coming.

As she made her way down the street, the nightlife was finally giving up, crawling or limping or swaggering home to sleep. No one took any notice of her. She did her best to keep it that way by sticking close to the shadows, avoiding people when she could.

Augusta had been missing for almost two days. Every time Liona thought of what might have happened to her sister, her stomach twisted like a wrung cloth. She talked with her friends who worked the brothels. They shook their heads sadly at her.

"Old story, darling," one of them had said. "Girls without protectors get kidnapped, and it doesn't matter whether they're citizens or not. They're gone."

Liona clenched her teeth. Augusta did have a protector. It was her. Whenever she found out who had taken her sister, she had every intention of gutting them and leaving them for the crows. Those grim and gory thoughts at least kept her mind off what might have become of Augusta, who had simply gone out for cooking oil two days ago and never returned.

Another girl, taking pity on Liona's despair, had given her a piece of information.

"Ignacio, who keeps the big warehouse close to the docks, the one with the green tile roof, he's a slaver. I know that he's got a big lot that he's planning on sending to the markets in Thessaly. You might look there. Perhaps she got mixed in."

There was no way that a slaver of any renown was going to deal with a landless girl. Instead, Liona cloaked herself as best she could, making her way down to the docks. She had a large knife with her. If it was just one guardsman, perhaps she could threaten him into releasing Augusta.

She had just come to the dark warehouse when she realized that she was not alone. Padding silently by her side, eyes large and yellow, was one of the feral dogs that roamed the streets. It was huge, standing almost as high as her ribs. For a moment, Liona was startled, but when it opened its mouth in a large, doggy grin, she was comforted and went on her way.

She moved closer to the warehouse. From inside, she could hear the sounds of people grumbling and snoring. She knew it was the place. Liona circled it a few times, wondering what she intended to do.

Even as she had that thought, the door creaked open and a man stepped out, striding down the street and away. The door had been left open, and she slipped in quickly and quietly. The interior of the building was lit with a few lamps, and she could see a single man sitting at the table, rolling a pair of dice in his hands.

"Come back with my winnings so soon, Flavius?"

As quickly as she could, she bolted the door behind her. When she turned back to the man, the dog stood at her side, loyal as a pet.

"I am not Flavius, and you are going to tell me what I need to know."

The man sprang to his feet. He might have been willing to take his chances with a single girl, no matter how large her knife was, but the dog by her side was another matter.

"Here now, you've got no business here."

"We'll see about that. Answer my questions and I'll be done. I'm looking for a girl, about seventeen and fair. Round face, blue eyes. Do you have her here?"

The man tensed, shaking his head, but something about it made Liona suspicious. She took a step closer, knife up. The dog by her side growled, a guttural, threatening sound. She couldn't have planned the animal's reaction any better. It quickly made the man change his tune.

"We did…that is, we did for a little while. Kind of small, cursed up a storm?"

Liona nodded, eyes never leaving the man's frightened face.

"Yeah, we had her for a few days. She…she was bought along with a tall black man with scars on his face. It looked like the people who took them were looking for them."

Looking for them? Who would be looking for Augusta?

"These people, what did they look like?"

"Like people, I don't know. They all wore pendants with a hand reaching out of a flame. They had money." He glanced from the knife to the dog. "Look, that's all I know."

Though Liona might have asked him more, the dog leapt at him. To her horror it seized him by the throat before he could get his hands up. As the pair landed on the floor, Liona couldn't avert her eyes quick enough. The massive jaws ripped the man's throat out.

She stifled the urge to scream, skirted the horrific scene as best she could, and ran to a door at the back of the close room. She unbolted it, and what she saw inside made her sick.

There were possibly dozens of people packed in like sardines. The reek of the place gave her a headache. They were all collared and a chain ran from collar to collar. Some of the slaves had to be less than five years old. She found the key hanging on the wall and tossed it to one of the men, who watched her with avid eyes.

"Get out of here," she whispered urgently. She went back into the main room as the slaves started freeing themselves.

Instead of a dog with bloody jowls, she saw a man standing over the dead slaver. She was shocked, but received an even greater surprise when she recognized him.

"Lucius!"

"I'm sorry we had to meet again like this, Liona, but really. We should be running now."

• • • • •

Restless, Hailey had fidgeted. Now she and Liona lay with their foreheads snugged up to each other, close enough that she could look into the other woman's eyes.

"Him again?"

"Oh yes. That was one of Lucius's charms, turning up like a bad penny. Now do you want to hear this story or not?"

Hailey nodded quickly.

Liona chuckled.

They lay so close that the low laugh tingled in Hailey's chest.

"So nice when the younger generation remembers to listen." She caressed the side of Hailey's face so softly that Hailey barely felt it. For a moment, she thought of covering Liona's hand with her own, but then the older woman continued. "Well we ran, and we were nearly caught by the guard, but we escaped them. This time, we wound up back at my own home."

• • • • •

"So they have one of your soldiers as well?"

"Yes, his name is Titus. He's more than just another legionnaire. We've soldiered together for most of our lives. He was the man that they took with your sister." Lucius glanced at Liona inquisitively. "I honestly thought you would have more questions about the wolf."

"I'm a daughter of Rome. Our founder was suckled by a she-wolf, and old King Lykos was cursed to become a wolf at night. I've seen worse than you at a consul's party."

Lucius's grin was toothy.

"Now that I'm not so sure about, little lioness. But that brings me to my next question. Was your sister–"

"Is."

"I beg your pardon?"

"Is. Is my sister, is what you meant. She's not dead."

Lucius nodded.

"In which case, is your sister a woman of power? I can guess given your profession that you are."

"She is. She commands fire just as I see the future. And your friend Titus?"

"A man who brings the rain."

Lucius shook his head.

"There are dark things in Rome, and our families seem to have been caught up in them. Liona, I will do my best to find your sister, but perhaps you are best off out of it."

Liona looked at him levelly.

"You'll have to tear out my throat too if you want to keep me away from this, legatus. You will not keep me from my sister."

He looked chagrined, and then he nodded reluctantly.

"Tomorrow, I am going to speak to someone who may know

the symbol of a hand emerging from flame. If you wish to come with me…"

"I do."

He sighed.

"Then you can come with me. They won't be available tomorrow until afternoon, I can come find you then."

Liona hesitated.

"Stay?"

Lucius raised an eyebrow, casting a significant glance at the only bed in the place. She had shared it with Augusta, so it was at least fairly wide, but still, it was only one bed. Liona lifted her chin up defiantly.

"I'm not asking you to do anything in it. This…this may be naive of me, but I just don't want to sleep alone. Is that so hard to understand?"

Lucius's expression softened. He nodded.

"While I would perhaps suggest that you avoid making this suggestion to other men that you've only known for a short while, I do understand."

Her face burning a little, Liona turned away from him to remove her robe and to slip into her sleeveless sleeping shift. She wasn't sure that what she was doing was altogether wise. She wasn't sure that she should be lying down with a man she knew so little, and trusting him as she did. However, she hadn't been sure about anything for what felt like a long time.

What she did know was that she wanted this.

Liona climbed into the narrow bed and pulled herself against the wall, giving him as much space as she could. Behind her, she heard him remove his clothes. After a moment, he blew out the lantern. Then he slid into the bed behind her, tugging the blanket over himself as if they had been sleeping together for years.

"Yes?" he murmured, sliding an arm over her hip.

Liona nodded, relaxing against his muscular chest. He smelled of salt and of juniper, the common scrub at the bathhouses. The heat of his body against hers was wonderful. Liona's eyelids fluttered closed.

"Thank you," she whispered, before she fell asleep.

In the darkness, she felt the soft brush of his lips across the back of her neck.

How kind he is, was her last thought before the darkness claimed her.

CHAPTER THIRTY-ONE

WHEN SHE AWOKE, Liona was startled by how late it was. For a moment, she thought that everything was normal, that it was Augusta snugged up to her back. Then she realized that Augusta was never so large or warm, and she remembered what had happened.

The late morning light slanted through the window shutters, but the room was comfortingly dim. It would be hours yet before she and Lucius could go find the information that they were looking for. There would be no harm in sleeping a little longer.

Liona squirmed in order to face the legatus. Abruptly, looking over his frame, she decided that sleep was the last thing on her mind. He was quite a beautiful man, she realized. The dark crop of his hair was soft to the touch. Asleep, his mouth was soft and wet, begging for a kiss. He looked more like a wild god than Mars.

Carefully, giving in to a desire that she realized had sprung to life as soon as she had seen him, Liona kissed his collar bone lightly. The faintly salty taste of his skin was delicious on her tongue, making her lap at it a little. She wished she could bite, but that would have awakened him for sure.

Squirming a little, she kissed a soft line down his chest to his erect nipple. She teased it with her tongue, holding her breath when it made him stir. The flat, toned muscles of his stomach called to her hand, causing her to stroke him gently. When she drifted a little lower, she found the sharp curve of his hip.

His breath stuttered, but when Liona glanced up, she could see that his eyes were still shut, though his lips were parted.

Giving in to temptation, she peeked under the blanket. What she saw made her smile. His cock was almost fully hard. It made her long to wrap her hand around it. How much would it take to make him spill? How would he like to be handled? She remembered what one of her friends had said, that men were mad for mouths on their members. The thought made her blush.

She glanced up at his face, her eyes narrowing.

"How long have you been awake?" she asked.

Lucius's laugh was a deep velvety rumble.

"A little longer than you," he confessed. "I wanted to see what you would do."

"And what do you think?"

"I think that you are a lovely woman, and that I would give you all the pay the Empire owes me if you would continue."

Liona bit her lip.

"It's not so easy for me," she said finally. "I have no protections, not if there is a child. I…I want to, but I can't."

She tensed to see what his reaction would be. For all of his genial good humor, she had always thought that you saw a man's true nature when you told him 'no.'

Lucius sighed and nodded.

"As you will, beautiful lioness. Though…"

"Yes?"

"Have you any objection to me finishing what you started?"

Liona felt her face turn red. She tried to cover it by looking away.

"Why…no, not at all."

"Good."

She meant to turn away, but somehow she forgot to do so as Lucius took his cock in his large hand. She glanced up at his face to see him watching her with a glint in his eye.

"I believe it's customary to charge at least some silver if you want to watch," he murmured teasingly.

"I'll owe you," Liona whispered, unable to take her eyes away.

On his back, completely naked and with his cock in his hand, Lucius was beautiful. The muscles of his body stood out in gorgeous relief, and as he pumped himself to a full climax, Liona felt a heat grow between her own legs as well. She found herself breathing in time with him, wondering if he would make the same noises if he was burying himself to the hilt in her body.

When he came, Liona shivered as well. She averted her eyes as he rose to clean himself.

"What's the matter?" he asked over his shoulder. "Have you changed your mind about owing me?"

"No… You're just beautiful." The words were hastily blurted out, a virgin's shy compliment. She would have been embarrassed, but Lucius only laughed.

"So are you, little lioness."

She lay back in bed, watching him cleanse himself with the urn of water and the bowl on the shelf. There was something lovely about it, something safe and warm. She wondered if there would be other days like this. She wondered what Augusta would think of him.

Then she shook her head. She had to find her sister. He had to find his friend. There was no time for wooly-headed romantic nonsense, and she rose to dress herself for the day.

• • • • •

"You watched him," Hailey whispered.

The thought had never occurred to her. Unbidden and uncontrolled, images of Kieran and Piers came to her as her breath quickened. What would it be like to watch them, each gorgeous in his own way?

But she and Liona still lay face to face, and when she realized that Liona was eying her with a wry smile, Hailey tried to banish the thoughts from her mind. The struggle must have been apparent.

"I take it you've never done that," Liona said lowly, "watched your lover pleasure themselves."

Hailey shook her head a little, not trusting her voice.

"Not every delight comes from touch, dear one."

• • • • •

Liona stared at the sheer handful of fabric that Lucius offered her.

"I… You must be joking."

"You said you wished to come. This is the price of entry."

She recognized the robe, of course. It was sheerest, softest silk. It was a valuable material, brought all the way from the distant east. It was common enough among the finer women of Rome, but only a certain class of woman would wear it outside of the home or a very special, very private party with her husband.

"We're going to the Golden Bough to find information. You can't go as a fortuneteller, I'm afraid. You can come along as my companion, or you can wait here until I return with what I have found out."

Liona bit her lip. She needed to go with him. She needed to know that she was doing everything that she could to make her sister safe.

Imperiously, she gestured for him to turn around as she took the robe in hand. Liona could see him hiding a smile as he did so, but she ignored it.

The silk was slippery smooth and sleek against her skin. It was as light as a breath, and her every movement caused it to flutter. To her dismay, instead of being long and flowing as most women's gowns were, it fluttered around her thighs. It looked like what an athletic young boy might have worn. Her dark nipples were faintly visible through the fabric, causing her to cross her arms over her chest.

"Well?"

Lucius inspected her carefully from head to toe. Liona could feel her nipples tighten under his gaze, but she held herself proudly erect. She wanted his eyes on her, wanted the way his breath quickened slightly.

"Almost perfect, but may I?"

Without thinking about it, she nodded.

Less than a second later, she was pinned against the wall of her apartment, Lucius's weight pressing against her and making no secret of his arousal. His lips crashed down on hers, and his tongue pressed between her lips, the insistent rhythm a hint of what he was thinking. His hands were buried in her hair, holding her still as he kissed her breath away.

When he pulled back, there was a sharp grin on his face that reminded her that yes, his soul was twined with that of a wolf.

"Shall we go?"

Though she was a moment recovering, she could give as good as she got.

"A moment, let me fix your robe."

She stepped close and tugged on a fold, making him lean towards her. It gave her exactly the clearance she needed to wrap her arms around his shoulders and latch her teeth into the flesh at the base of his neck. After a soft cry, Lucius was still as she nipped and sucked at the space, bringing the blood to the surface.

She stepped back, grinning at the dark mark on his skin and licking her red lips.

"There, now we're a match."

Lucius looked down at her with eyes that were more yellow than brown. His grin was fierce.

"So we are, beautiful lioness. Come, let us go before we decide to really prove what kind of match we are."

They set off with hurried steps, down one street, then another. But eventually they wound their way to the old center of an already ancient city. The Golden Bough was one of the richest and most luxurious brothels in Rome, which likely meant it was one of the richest and most luxurious brothels in the world. There were armed guards at the doors. The inscription above the lintel, "Peace and Pleasure for All Within," was as much a threat as it was a promise.

Liona had worn a long, hooded cloak to carry her safely through the city, but now she could cast it aside. Everywhere she looked, there were beautiful men and women serving the most powerful men of the Senate. Most barely gave her a glance. The ones who did seemed appreciative, something that made her walk a little more closely to Lucius.

He walked through the halls of the Golden Bough as if he had been born to it, though she knew that was not the case. If he had not proven himself at war, he would never have been allowed to darken the door of the Golden Bough.

He spoke briefly with a guard carrying an enormous spear, who nodded and guided them to a secure door at the back of the house. To Liona's surprise, instead of being a palatial room clad in marble and silk, as was the rest of the house, the room that they entered was quite plain. There were shelves full of bound records and scrolls on all the walls, and a tray of simple fruit and cheese set close to a tall, narrow window. Behind a tidy desk sat an attractive woman with sleek, dark hair and olive skin, her eyes shadowed with powdered pearl.

When she saw Lucius, she stood immediately, coming to him with her arms open.

"Oh, it has been too long, Lucius," she purred.

Liona bristled a little at this woman's warm embrace, but stayed silent. Lucius greeted the woman warmly enough, but then he shook his head.

"It's business, not pleasure today, Sophia. I need information that I believe that you can give me."

Sophia's laugh was rueful, and she pulled away with a sigh.

"So stern you are. I remember when you were not so focused on your business as all that."

She must have been watching Liona out of the corner of her eye, because she laughed outright when Liona gasped.

"Forgive me, little beauty," she said warmly. "Lucius and I are a thing of the past, but could you forgive me for wanting to play a little?"

"I will forgive you because you are a thing of the past," Liona said firmly, making both Lucius and Sophia laugh. It made her feel young. They were both at least ten years older than she was, but there was no malice in their laugh.

"So I will stop playing with you now, and you will tell me what you need. Perhaps I can satisfy you, and perhaps I can't, but I shall try."

Lucius shook his head.

"I'm not going to tell you too much. If trouble comes to your door, the less you know, the better it will go for you. What we are looking for is a sect of men who are represented by a hand rising from the flames. These men are dangerous, and there may be many of them. Do you recognize the symbol at all?"

Sophia's face immediately became guarded. She sat behind the desk, distancing herself from them. Liona also realized that, though she hid it well, the woman was afraid.

"Now that is something that you don't want to get mixed up in," she said quietly.

Lucius shook his head.

"I'm afraid there's no getting around it," he said. "We need to know who these people are. We need to know where they are and what they do."

Sophia looked lost in thought for a moment, and reluctantly, she nodded her head.

"The men you are looking for are part of a mystery cult that has been circulating for a few years. You know me, I respect the gods as much as any rational person does, but these people, they're insane. They have a god that they follow, one that is not recognized by the city."

"Are they looking to have their god become one of the city gods?" asked Liona.

Sophia laughed a little bitterly.

"That would make sense if they thought that it meant anything. No, they're trying to create their god anew. They want to bring their god up to rule, and they want to do it through sacrifice."

A chill of terror ran up Liona's spine.

"Sacrifice. You mean of humans."

"You hear things in this business. You hear people talk. We hear confessions, and we hear boasts. It's a terrible thing, but yes. Humans."

Lucius's face was thunderous.

"The highest officials in the Senate must be told. This is far beyond anything any mystery cult should be allowed."

Sophia's laugh was tired. But Liona, who had been to parties with entitled Senators, had to agree with her.

"They probably are members of the cult itself," she murmured, and Sophia nodded.

"That's right. And that's all I can tell you. I'm sorry, Lucius, for I can be of no more help to you. I'm sorry that you have found yourself wrapped in something terrible."

Lucius's smile was narrow and grim.

"Truthfully, so am I. Thank you, Sophia. We won't trouble you further."

Liona opened the door to leave, startling a young girl who was going by carrying water. She paused to let the girl past, doing her best not to watch Lucius's farewell kiss to Sophia. It was too easy to imagine the two of them wrapped up in each other, touching, caressing, doing more. It didn't bother her, exactly. She couldn't tell what emotions it roused except for a guilty excitement.

He is such a very handsome man, she thought.

Lucius emerged, but as they walked down the hall, a vision struck Liona with the force of a blow. She actually gasped. Even as Lucius asked her what was wrong, she was sprinting back down the hallway, throwing open the door to Sophia's room.

"Sophia, you must leave."

Sophia raised a curious eyebrow.

"And why is that, little one? Surely you wouldn't accuse a casual friend of stealing your lover's heart away."

"I don't care about that," Liona said hotly, "but you must leave Rome. As soon as you can. Tonight if possible."

Lucius was behind her, and he put a steadying hand on her shoulder.

"What is it? What do you see, Liona?"

She shivered.

"I see fire," she whispered. "I see burning paper, burning people. I see this place on fire, Sophia, and you must get out."

Sophia regarded her with narrowed eyes.

"You have a gift for fortunetelling, then?"

"She has power, Sophia."

Sophia turned to Lucius.

"What would you do in my position?"

To Liona's relief, the other woman was asking calmly and inquisitively. At least she wasn't dismissing the warning out of hand.

"I would do what she said," Lucius said promptly. "You know me. I'm an old soldier. I follow orders, but I know when fate has a hand in things. With this one, fate whispers in her ear. I wouldn't take the chance."

Sophia nodded. "Be on your way," she said. "I imagine you both have dangerous things to do."

"But what are you–"

Lucius firmly took Liona's hand and guided her out.

"She'll do exactly what she is going to do. You've said your piece. Now we need to get started on finding the people who have taken our family."

As the sun set and as the night people of Rome started to come out, their investigation continued. Lucius's informants were spread across the city, in other brothels, in gambling dens and in the homes of moneylenders.

Most had not heard of the mystery cult represented by a hand and a flame. The few who had knew no more than Sophia had. One man, the owner of a gaming house on the edge of the city, had immediately ejected them from the premises.

Liona was dejected by their lack of progress, but Lucius only shrugged when she mentioned it.

"Every hunt must start somewhere, and no one lives in this world without leaving some trace. The men of this mystery cult, they eat, they have families and they have names. Sometime soon we will find people who know them."

Liona chewed her lip.

"But by then Augusta and Titus may be dead, sacrificed to some dark god."

Lucius's face was grim.

"Then we avenge them," he said simply. She remembered the wolf who had torn out the throat of a slaver. It was that simple for him.

"I would rather have a living sister," she murmured.

"I would rather have a living friend."

They walked in silence for a moment. Liona's feet ached, and her belly was empty. Lucius, hardened by years of warring for Rome, may have been accustomed to going without, but she was not. Still she tried to keep up with him, following him from boarding house to gambling den, until finally she stumbled.

His strong arm was there to catch her when she fell. She struggled to her feet.

"I can keep going," she protested, but he shook his head, chagrined.

"No, I don't think that's wise," he said, looking around. "You're falling asleep on your feet. There's nothing to be done this night anyway. We can pick up again in the morning."

She would have fought longer, but he was right. She was so tired that she was only staring at the pavement in front of her. She would be useless if anything happened; she'd be worse than useless because in a fight, Lucius would have to worry about her.

He found them a small boarding house that was on the slightly safer side of shabby, and after settling her on the bed, he went down to the kitchen to find them a plate of olives, bread and grilled lamb.

"Oh, that smells delicious," Liona said, sitting up.

Lucius came to sit down next to her, letting her pick what she liked from the plate.

"The woman in the kitchen is worried about you," he said teasingly. "She thinks we're up to all sorts of improper things up here."

Liona swallowed her olive and laughed.

"And what did you tell her?"

"I told her that I would guard you with my life."

Liona watched him for a moment, studying the way he seemed alert even when doing something as simple as eating, the way he had casually left himself between her and the door.

"You mean that," she said. It wasn't a question. It was a statement, one that she knew was true.

"I do." He sighed, shaking his head. "Do you want to talk about this now?"

"I think I do, yes."

"You're not the only fortuneteller in the world," he said softly. "I met a woman while I was in Hispania, and she offered me my fortune in exchange for some food."

"What did she say?"

"She told me that the worth of my life was to be found in a small lioness and a fierce eagle. If I let them go, if I allowed them to come to harm, my life would be worth no more than the ashes blowing over a ruined village."

"Evocative," Liona murmured.

She didn't know what to make of his frank words, but there was a ring of truth to it. She had heard of other fortunetellers, but never met one. Still, hearing the words in Lucius's mouth, she could feel something chill her, something like fate brushing them with the hem of her skirt.

Lucius's next words startled her.

"What do you see for us?"

She had been so set on the goal of finding Augusta that it had never occurred to her to look forward. She had always used her gift to entertain or, as she had done with Sophia, to warn.

"I… Let me see."

She reached for Lucius's hand, holding it tightly. She let her eyes drift closed. Sometimes she could see the future very plainly, but now she had to go looking for it. She concentrated on their hands, on the feel of him. She thought of Augusta. She thought of a soldier she had never met named Titus.

Images came to her, things from the past. She had a feeling that she was moving quickly, that she was flying high over water. She could feel heat. She could hear people shouting, no, they were screaming. The images were coming faster and faster. She couldn't see them. She couldn't focus on one and bring it into sharp relief. They were overwhelming her. They were swarming her. If she lost her footing, she thought she would fall and drown. She could hear her own voice crying out. Her voice became Augusta's, high and terrified. Then it turned into Lucius's voice calling her name over and over again. He sounded frightened, even terrified. A sense of terror grasped her heart. She was afraid that she would never rise out of these images, this chaos, she was going to drown. They were all going to die.

A sharp pain pierced her visionary haze. She yelped, twisting on the ground where she had fallen. Lucius was crouched by her side, his face a mask of concern and fear.

"What is it? What happened to you, Liona?"

"It was terrible. I couldn't see. I couldn't see at all, and what I could, oh Lucius, it was all fire, all terror."

"Do we fail?" There was no fear in his voice, only a calm acceptance.

She shook her head. "I can't see. I can't see at all."

Lucius looked thoughtful.

"Yet you could see Sophia's fate. Unless that was an attempt to get an old lover out of Rome?"

Despite her terror, Liona's gaze was withering.

"Don't flatter yourself, legatus. That was true. I saw what would happen very clearly."

Instead of replying, Lucius went to the door, stepping out briefly. When he returned, it was with a small boy who had his hand bandaged. Given the burns on his arms, Liona guessed that he was the pot boy, the one who turned the spits and scrubbed the dishes. He was to be a test of her ability.

"Here you are, lad, a true fortuneteller."

The boy peered at Liona shyly, making her smile.

"Here, don't be afraid, my boy, let me see what's in store for you."

She reached for his unhurt hand and held it gently. Her gift, gentle this time, lapped at the edges of her vision, giving her a picture that was far more solid, far more concrete than what she had seen before.

"I see… I see a small house in a green place. I see a young woman with her hair tied back, and she waves at you. There you are, and my, you grow up to be a fine man. You are carrying a bag. Look, it's full of chickens…"

The vision broke off. Liona smiled at the boy.

"You have a future in a green place. There's a woman who's happy to see you, so watch out for a girl with bright blue eyes, all right? It looks like she's going to do you a good turn."

The boy smiled tentatively at her. He glanced up at Lucius, who nodded, giving him permission to leave.

"He looks terrified," Liona noted.

"You should see the way you look," said Lucius, coming to sit beside her on the bed.

"The way I look?"

"You're as pale as marble, and your eyes look haunted. They

likely think I've been having my way round and round with you. That yelling you did earlier probably didn't help."

"Shame that wasn't what we were doing," she said with a half-hearted grin. "I could see that boy's fate. I still have my gift. I just can't seem to see what will become of us."

"Has that ever happened before?"

"Never."

They finished their food in silence. When they lay down to sleep, Liona stripped to her skin.

"You do like to tempt a man," Lucius observed.

Despite his calm words, there was a hunger lurking in his expression. If she were a warier woman, it would have made her nervous. She was herself, however. It only made her bold.

"I do, but this is what I want. Is this what you want as well?"

"That and more, but your wishes are more powerful than mine, little lioness."

He came to lie behind her again, his large body cupping her smaller one. This time, one large hand came to cradle her round breast. She shivered from the contact. She thought she would be aware of his body, his cock hard against her thigh, his breath, all night, but between the space of one breath and the next, she fell asleep.

CHAPTER THIRTY-TWO

THE NEXT MORNING, Liona awoke, blinking at her strange surroundings before remembering what had happened the night before. Lucius slept on next to her. She was tempted to kiss him, but her full bladder prevented that. She squirmed out from under his arm.

Dressing quickly in the scandalous silk garment, she wrapped herself in her cloak, and ventured out to find the water closet. After that, she headed to the kitchen to find them some food.

The cook was an older woman, white-haired and short. When she saw Liona, whole and apparently unharmed, she beamed. As she made up a plate of cold lamb and fruit for them, she shook her head.

"Nasty doings in the city last night, my dear. If you have a home to go back to, you should do it." Liona smiled a little ruefully, something the old cook thought she recognized. "It doesn't matter what the likes of that man did to you, you know. Your parents will forgive and take you back. You're their blood after all."

"It's not like that at all," she murmured. She couldn't change the old woman's mind, so she changed the topic instead. "What nasty doings are you talking about? Has something happened at the Senate?"

"No, dear. It's fires, fires set in the southern part of the city and the west. The brothel, the Golden Bough was struck first, and they are still pulling the bodies out."

Liona was rooted to the spot with terror, remembering what she had told Sophia the night before. She prayed the woman had at least gotten out. The apartment that she shared with Augusta was in the southern part of the city, and some of the places they had visited were in the west.

She started to thank the cook for her news, but then the old woman continued.

"At least they have an idea who has done it. They are looking for a legatus by the name of Lucius Magnus, who was found to have treasonous intent against the empire. Pray they catch him soon. We'll all sleep safer in our beds."

Liona forced the lump of fear down her throat. She had to act naturally. She thanked the old woman for passing on, what to her, should have been a piece of gossip, albeit tragic and terrible. She picked up the tray. She even waved to the pot boy who was drowsily turning the spit. She walked sedately back to their room. Once she was inside, she bolted the door.

Lucius woke up when the door closed. He smiled at her sleepily and started to reach for her, but he came to his feet when he saw the look on her face.

"What's the matter?"

"Parts of the city that we've visited were torched. The Golden Bough is destroyed, and it sounds like my place is gone as well. They… they say that a legatus named Magnus is behind it. They speak of treason."

Lucius was as still as a statue. His eyes were unfocused. He shook his head.

"This is foolishness. They cannot believe that a legatus would–"

Liona seized his hand, staring up at him fiercely.

"They do. Lucius, they do. They believe that you did it, and they are hunting you now."

He pulled his hand away from her.

"I have been a legatus for two years. I was awarded honors by the Senate itself. I will go, and I will explain this to them."

Liona felt a panic flutter in her chest, something that terrified her more than fire did.

"Lucius, you cannot afford to be blind about this. The people you are going to see, the ones that you think will defend you and set things right? Lucius, some of those people wear pendants. Those pendants have a hand rising out of flame on them. They are going to catch you, and then they are going to kill you."

Lucius looked at her coldly. "The honor of a legatus is unquestioned. They will hear me."

Liona shook her head fiercely. She grabbed his hand again and squeezed it with all of her strength. She was afraid that if she let him go, he would walk straight to the forum. Then he would be killed.

"Oh, yes, legatus. They will hear you. They will hear you, and then they will bring forward testimony that will swear up and down that you were the one who set the blazes. They will swear that you have a hundred men working for you, that you want nothing more than the downfall of the city and the empire. Before dawn, they will–"

"Damn you, it isn't true!"

"Before dawn, they will have words from people who will swear before all the gods that you are plotting to hand the city over to barbarians and foreign kings. Then, by noon, they will offer you the honorable choice of whether you wish to be killed or whether you will fall on your own sword."

In the silence after her outburst, there was a deadly stillness in the air between them. The space crackled with fear and anger. For a moment, Liona was terrified that, against all sense, he would do exactly what she was afraid of. He would march himself to the Senate and turn himself in. He would believe that his honor and his truth would protect him. Then he would die. She could see it clearly enough that she was afraid it was a vision.

Finally, he nodded.

"You're right," he said, his voice clipped and short.

"Lucius?"

"We need to leave immediately. Rome is no longer our friend, and if we want to have any hope of finding them, we will leave now."

"Lucius…"

He turned to her, and there was more yellow than brown in his eyes now.

"You are right. Gods damn you to the nine hells, but you are right. Now we must flee. Come on."

The coldness of his words pierced Liona to her core. Silently, she fell into step behind him, pulling her cloak over her head so that no one would recognize her face.

• • • • •

Hailey didn't realize that her hands were clenched into fists until Liona put her own hands over them. Still face to face, Liona stroked them until Hailey relaxed, humming a little until the younger woman sighed.

"You were right, weren't you?" Hailey said softly. "If he had gone back to the Senate, they would have killed him."

Liona nodded. There was always the ghost of a smirk on the woman's face, but now she seemed serious, even sad.

"My poor man. He was a soldier's soldier, a warrior through

and through. All his life, he had served the Empire. I'm someone who has always lived on the outside. I was the daughter of a legionnaire and a foreign woman, and there would always be those who called me foul names, a barbarian, a freak. He was different."

Hailey thought of her own life, so long an outsider that any kind of acceptance felt temporary. Any love that she could have was as easily taken away as given. She thought with a pang of Kieran, who had turned away from her.

"It must be worse for them," she mused. "The ones who have always had a place. They always knew where they fit in, and suddenly, on the day that they don't, it all comes crashing down."

Liona laughed.

"You are more generous than I would be by far. I was upset that he was so cold. Truly, it was a terrifying thing to see. He was a man who made killing his business, and when one of them looks like that, it's frightening. Don't misunderstand, though, I was furious as well. I was angry at the people who had put us on the run, and harmed all of those innocent people of course. However, I couldn't wring their necks, and well, my temper has always burned a little hot. I couldn't reach them, but I could reach him."

Liona chuckled, even if there was something sad about it.

"You exploded at him?" Hailey guessed.

"Not right away. We knew we had to get out of Rome immediately. We needed to go somewhere where they couldn't reach us. What might seem strange to someone so young as yourself is that while news traveled slowly, it would always catch up with you in the end. We couldn't go to Hispania, and we couldn't go south towards Sardinia. There were too many who would find us and betray us for a pat on the head and a letter of recognition from Rome. Instead, we found a captain who was indifferent to Rome and willing to take us to the edge of the world."

"Where was that?"

Liona smiled.

"To Gaul. It was the land of my mother's people, but to me, it was only a place of barbarism and painted savages. I was very young, after all."

For a long moment, Liona was silent, stroking Hailey's hair. Hailey closed her eyes, trying to take it all in. To someone who had not yet had the immortality of the Wiccan people awakened in her, Liona's life was unbelievable. This woman had watched empires fall. She had seen the end of cities. She had spoken to people that history only remembered as myths. Still there was something so fragile and human about her. History seemed very large, and in her convalescent bed, the two of them seemed very small.

Hailey ducked her head under Liona's chin. Her honey-scented perfume was warm and real, surrounding her like a haven. History could wait.

"You don't have to tell me more if you don't want to," Hailey murmured.

Liona shifted, drawing her close, entwining her arms around her. Hailey relaxed into her tender embrace.

"You should hear the rest. As I said before, it is your story, just as it is the story of everyone who chooses to live in a coven. Will you listen?"

Hailey nodded, aware of what an honor she had been offered. Liona di Orsini was a woman out of time. She hid in the cracks of the centuries, and once she disappeared, there was no telling when she would resurface again.

"The journey to Gaul was terrible. It was just on the end of the season where such a crossing would be possible. We were cutting things close indeed. We had a small cabin to ourselves, thank all the gods, but there was nothing in it but a bed. Lucius did not speak to me for a solid two weeks of our journey. After he made arrangements with the captain for our board, he didn't speak at all."

CHAPTER THIRTY-THREE

THE DAY WAS dark and gray, but still Liona made her way to the deck. At least the air up there was fresh, and if she was quiet, she could stay out of the way of the harried crew. There were mutters of it being foul luck to bring a woman on the ship. She hid as much as she could, but she couldn't stay for days below the decks.

At the very least, she had to go to the galley for the food that had been promised them. The fare was a little bit better that day. They had been able to put in at a nameless little port. Now there was at least some relief from the mealy bread and the salt fish that they had been eating before.

The cook grumbled at her when she came for their fair share, but she got it readily enough. It was a skewer of lamb, tough and gray, but better than that were the four oranges that were part of their portion. They were a dash of color in a world gone dim.

She took the food to the small cabin that she shared with Lucius. She was unsurprised to see him sitting in the bed, staring out the tiny window like a man obsessed. She set the food down next to him. She watched as he wordlessly ate from it. He didn't look at her. He didn't speak.

Liona ate the lamb, chewing until her jaws ached because the meat was so tough. The oranges were what she wanted, however, and she made them last. They were old, but still full of juice. The sweetness stung her mouth even as it made her body feel alive again. She chewed on one of the rinds before putting them on the plate to be borne up and dumped again.

"You cannot continue like this," she said.

The words surprised her. He had been silent. For weeks now, she had been silent as well. There was something in the air between them, something cruel and crackling.

They had bartered the fine dress she had worn in Rome for something warmer. In her dull red wool dress and in bare feet, she faced him across the tiny room.

"You know that we needed to leave Rome. You would have accomplished nothing by standing in front of the Senate. You would have been executed."

He glanced at her. She wasn't sure, but she thought she could see a spark there. It might have been anger. It might become rage. Liona didn't care. She only cared that it was more than what she had seen in the last few weeks.

"Is that what you are angry about?" she asked cuttingly. "Are you angry that you must live as a fugitive rather than dying as a legatus of the legion? Are you that foolish?"

His lips skimmed back from his teeth briefly, revealing sharp white teeth. Liona felt a dull satisfaction at seeing that. It was better than nothing. It was far better than the apathy she had seen. It was so much better than the dark day when she thought he might actually fling himself into the choppy waves.

"There is a whole world of people out there who didn't march in the legion, Lucius. There are many, many people even in Rome who never had a family name and who don't care how great the Empire grows. Do you hear me? So just because you are now one of them doesn't mean that it's some great tragedy. You don't get to be ashamed because you are simply just like me now!"

Her voice raised up to a shout on the final word, and she stilled. It had always been between them, she realized. A half-barbarian girl and a legatus of the legion. There was always that gap. Now it didn't exist. Lucius acted like it was the end of his world. For her, it was just another day.

"I never thought there would come a day when a man who had been a legatus would be so afraid of the world."

The words were diamond-sharp. The wound that they left might have been mortal. Liona didn't pause to look. She reached for the dish with the food leavings, prepared to leave for a while.

An iron hard hand shot out and grasped her wrist. She stared up into eyes that were as black as the pits of hell. There was one single moment where she was afraid. There was one moment where she thought that she had gone too far, that her words had broken something inside him, that elemental part that held the wolf at bay.

Then he pulled her hard against his body. His lips came crashing down on hers, hard enough that she tasted blood.

Thank you, thank you, thank you, her mind chanted, over and over again.

He was like a man maddened. She was reaching desperately for the hem of her dress, but he simply took two great handfuls of the fabric and tore it from her. Her body called for his, for the desperate wild mating that he demanded.

Lucius threw her down on the bed, pinning her by sheer virtue of superior weight. His hands roamed her curves, squeezing and caressing by turn. There was something savage about him, something wild and uncontrolled. He had lost some weight on their voyage. She could feel his hip bones grind cruelly against her body. It didn't matter. To have a feast of sensation when she had spent time feeling nothing was a fierce kind of bliss.

"Give it to me," she whispered. "Give me all of it, now,

please…"

He buried his head in her neck, lapping and kissing the sensitive skin until she was squirming underneath him. She could feel his erection hard against her hip. She could feel how much he needed her, how much he wanted her. She tried to spread her legs, to bring him closer, but she couldn't move enough to do it.

She felt the flash of his teeth against her skin, and then she shouted as he bit her. This was no gentle nip. It was a biting and sucking that was meant to leave a dark mark, something that claimed her as his. She welcomed the possession, could feel herself grow wet for it.

He moved over her body, kissing a path down to her breasts and then down to her hips. His breath stirred the fine, dark hair on her mound. She held her breath as he pushed her legs apart. He swiped his tongue hard against her slit, making her moan with the assault on her senses. He wasn't preparing her, she realized, but tasting her.

The beast was close to the surface in him. She welcomed it. It belonged to her as much as it belonged to him, and this ravaging was what she needed as well. She reached down and clenched her hand in his hair, giving it a hard tug. He looked up at her, and his green eyes were nearly black, though she wouldn't have been surprised to see that they were tinged with yellow.

"Take me now," she commanded, her voice hoarse with desire.

That was all he needed to hear. With a strength that took her breath away, he twisted her over on her stomach. She barely propped her elbows up before he lifted her hips high. She groaned, knowing what she must look like to him. Her body was pale in the darkness of the room, and her hindquarters were lifted as if she was an animal ready for mating.

She felt his cock against her thigh, demanding and waiting. With one hand, he guided the blunt head into her slit, and the other knotted in her hair, pulling her back towards him. It was more pleasure than pain, and she cried out as she was pulled back.

He filled her with one swift thrust, and then she did cry out, panicked and hurt. It stilled him, and he froze. For a long moment, all that she could hear in that tiny room was the sound of her own roughened breath as she tried to calm herself. It hurt. It had been too long. She was nearly as tight as she had been when she was a virgin. Their play, though it had awakened her blood and made her yearn for him, hadn't been enough.

"Liona?"

His voice was hoarse with disuse. Tentatively, he brushed a hand across her back.

"No, don't stop, please, don't stop…"

Lucius was still for a long moment. Slowly, still joined intimately, they waited for her body to relax. He stroked her back, slick with sweat. Distantly, she was aware that they were breathing in time with one another.

She took several deep breaths, and she pulled forward a little before easing herself back on his cock. That stroke was smooth, and the one after that was smoother yet. She felt him tremble behind her.

"Beast," she whispered, and it was full of love. "Beautiful monster."

He groaned, his hands tightening on her hips before he gentled himself.

"I'm sorry," he whispered.

Liona drove herself back on him more firmly, wringing another cry from him.

"I don't want sorry," she growled raggedly. "I want… I need you. I still need you."

He thrust into her this time, slowly but fully. When she cried out this time, it was with pleasure. Lucius gave her two long thrusts, and she shook her head.

"No," she murmured. "I need all of you. I love the beast, and I love the man."

With a growl that was surely a match for any wolf, he thrust into her harder, and harder still. The sensation was powerful, greater than that of a storm at sea. She cried out and rode it. As he thrust into her savagely, she reached down between her legs to touch her clit, bathing it with her own juices and stroking it in time to the rhythm Lucius set.

Her climax had no more mercy than he did. She tensed and shook like a building under siege. She could feel herself tighten around his cock. She was crying out his name over and over again, and when she fell over the edge, she saw stars.

He was still slamming into her. He was doing it so hard that she was nearly flat on the mattress. Liona's climax left her drained and floating, but she came back to herself when Lucius's thrusts became faster and more erratic. Finally, with a deep groan, he spilled inside her. She gloried in the warmth of it, the way that they were so connected.

He collapsed on top of her, but remembering himself, he pulled out of her and rolled to one side. His rough hand stroked along her back. The gentleness of his hand touched something inside her that all of the fierce lovemaking had not.

Liona tried to keep the tears back, but they came anyway, running down her face. They were silent at first, but when she sobbed, Lucius froze. He gathered her into his arms, apologizing over and over until she finally got enough control to shake her head.

"Lucius, no, stop. It's fine."

"I hurt you," he said tensely. "You're... You're in pain."

She shook her head.

"That pain, the kind you're talking about, I don't care. I asked for all of it, and I would ask again. It's just…oh Lucius, we're so far from home."

He held her as she cried out the stress and pain of the last few weeks. She was finally able to let some of that tension go. When it did, she was left limp and tired on the bed.

She was aware of him rising and leaving briefly. He returned with a small pitcher of water and cloth. She lay quietly as he stroked the damped cloth along her limbs, leaving her with a feeling of cleanliness and care. She made a noise of protest when he reached between her legs. Lucius laughed, leaning down to kiss her, stroking the fabric over her thighs again and again.

Finally, she surrendered with a sigh, letting him clean her there as well. The sensations were at once soft and arousing. She shifted her hips against his touch, making him laugh.

"Aren't you too sore?" he murmured. She thought it was rather unfair that he could ask when he was stroking her so gently.

"No," Liona whimpered, her voice just a breath of sound. "Please, Lucius?"

She could see the hesitation on his face. Then she grabbed his wrist and made him look at her.

"Can't you see how much I want you?"

Instead of entering her again, however, he lay down by her side. He ran the damp cloth over her body, making her sigh with pleasure. Then he replaced it with his bare hands. There was something beautiful about it. This man who had fought and ended lives, he was being so soft and gentle with her. There was nothing of the savagery from before. This was nothing but endless care and sweetness.

His fingers parted her slick folds gently. Her eyes fluttered closed as he soothed the slightly swollen flesh there.

"You're gorgeous," he whispered. "So sweet and pink and

soft."

She murmured as he slipped first one finger inside her and then another. His thumb came up to circle her clit. It was just the right amount of pressure, firm enough to avoid maddening her, light enough that he brought her no pain.

This time, her climax built up gently. She could feel it coming. She was open to it, and longing. The trembles started low in her body. Almost by accident, she opened her eyes and locked gazes with him. As her climax overcame her, she looked deep into his eyes and saw love there. She shuddered in his arms, burying her face into his chest.

"Are you crying, little lioness?"

"A little," she whispered. "Hold me?"

"As long as you like."

She rested in his arms for some timeless space. She could have lain there forever, but she knew that they needed to speak.

"I still see no future for us," she said finally, pulling back. "I have searched since we left Rome. I can see every detail I care to see about the captain's bad end, or the ship boy's good one, but for us, there is nothing."

Lucius breath was even and steady. He held her a little closer.

"All I know is that we must find our family, and that I want to do it together. Beyond that, the world can take care of itself."

She sighed softly against him. Her hand drifted down to her belly. She frowned as she calculated the weeks. She should be safe, according to what the midwife had told her, but she did not have access to silphium, a tincture of which could prevent birth.

"Are you worried about a baby?" Lucius asked her.

"Women always are," she said wryly. "It is not so simple for us as it is for you."

"There may be more to concern us than a child."

Liona stiffened.

"What do you mean?"

"I have heard rumors, only rumors, mind you. It was told to me by a traveler from the east that when two people of power lie together fully as we have done, that strange things can happen."

"Are our children to be born with horns or hooves?" asked Liona scornfully. "I've heard those stories too, and I don't believe them."

"No, even stranger. It is said that when two people of power lie together that they lose their way to the underworld."

Liona stared. "You mean we can't die?"

"Yes. The man who told it to me, he could move the earth with only a stomp of his foot. He looked a bare handful of years older than me, but he claimed to have been alive for a full two centuries."

Liona wanted to be scornful, but instead her question came out in a small voice. "Do you believe him?"

"I don't disbelieve him," Lucius said hesitantly. "The way he spoke, the things he knew, they could very well come from a man who had lived for two hundred years."

She shook her head.

"So what we did, here, together… It could mean that we're going to live forever?"

"Who's to know? I'm certainly not going to fall on my sword to test it."

Liona felt a welter of hysteria bubble up inside her. Living forever sounded absurd. It sounded unbelievable, like a story told to keep children quiet.

"I'll make you a deal," she said, a sharp edge in her voice. "In one hundred years time, if we are indeed still alive, I'll meet you in Rome. Those who wanted us dead will be long gone, and we can drink wine in the boarding house where we hid that last night."

Lucius's laugh was light.

"Of course, assuming we're not still together and don't make the trip in the same boat. Liona, it may be a myth. It may be a skilled con artist selling me a goose and telling me its a phoenix. It changes very little."

He thought for a moment, and then he smiled, so sunny that Liona was momentarily shocked by how handsome he really was.

"What?" she asked when she finally recovered herself.

"A hundred years with you, and then a hundred and another hundred after that. I just like the sound of it."

• • • • •

Hailey's eyes widened, as she pushed back from Liona.

"You didn't know?" Hailey sat up. "You didn't know that if you slept with another Wiccan that it would make you immortal?"

Liona's laugh was dry.

"Who was there to tell me? Augusta was younger than I was. My mother never spoke of it at all. I had seen a few others with magic, but then it was just me. There was much that I didn't know, so much that could have hurt me. I relied on my luck, as most of us did at that time."

Luck? When it came to magic? If it had been left to luck, Hailey could imagine where she'd be—especially with the particular power she possessed.

"The covens prevent that now," Hailey said slowly. "Without them, I would have gone on as just another girl, without understanding that I had any power at all."

Liona nodded and drew her back down to the bed. As Hailey settled on her back, their heads shared the pillow, and Liona draped her arm across Hailey's waist.

"You're a little like me," Liona whispered in her ear. Her warm, moist breath made Hailey sigh. "You have a knack for getting into trouble, but you also have a knack for getting out of it as well. It is a fortunate thing."

"I hope so," Hailey mumbled.

"The role of the covens has always been to protect people. Your Piers has made the Castle into a place of learning as well as peace. If I have a legacy, I hope it is this. There is power in being able to protect people and to guide them."

Liona lay quietly for a moment. Hailey wondered if she had gone to sleep, but then she started speaking again.

"The idea of a life that never ended. It terrified me at that point, but it wasn't like my fear for Augusta, or my fear of our ship being boarded by pirates. I couldn't imagine what the next few weeks were going to hold. How could I imagine what the next few centuries would bring? I put it out of my mind. A long life, well, it's mostly a good thing. You haven't made the choice yourself, yet."

Hailey shook her head.

"It is not a decision to make lightly, but I will tell you this. The longer you live, for the most part, the longer you want to live. That's how it was with me. Of course that was far from my mind when our journey finally came to an end. We hadn't chosen Gaul by accident. Lucius hoped to find some of his friends there, ones who had retired from service but never wearied of the frontier. They had gone native, so to speak, and they certainly bore Rome no love. We hoped to find them, but when the captain put to shore, our luck ran out. They had moved on, and we were left in that port town with nothing."

Hailey, who had been a foster child even before she became someone that most covens wouldn't touch, shivered. It was all too real to her, the idea of being shunted far away from home with no one to care if she lived or died. Her hands clung to

Liona's arm, but she was careful not to hold too tight. As if sensing her need, Liona hugged her close, the curves of their bodies matching.

"Finally," Liona said quietly, "in desperation, I heard word of the Altanii, a tribe that lived north of the wall. They were untamed by Rome, uncivilized, but they were friendly enough in these times. Once there had been war, but now there was a kind of peace. It was a peace very much like the one that had allowed my father to bring my mother to Rome. They were her people, my kinsmen. We were out of options, so we went to find them."

CHAPTER THIRTY-FOUR

THE COLD WAS unlike anything that Liona had ever known. Rome cooled in the winter, but there was never this soul-killing cold. She wrapped herself in the thick wool cloak, and Lucius showed her how to stuff her boots with duck feathers to keep in the warmth. The tiny, hide tent that they used was frigid at night, but when they rose in the morning, they could feel how much colder it was outside.

Lucius had awakened from his gray depression, but there was something dark and driven about him now. They spoke infrequently, and at night, they clung to each other. Sometimes they made love, and sometimes they were silent.

To Liona, Rome was like a distant memory, something far away and dreamlike. She had never felt further from Augusta. Sometimes, she imagined a silvery gray and tenuous cord between the two of them. Some days, it felt strong enough that she could follow it to her sister, but other days, it felt like it was so frail that it must break.

They were exhausted, running out of food, and high in the northern parts of Gaul when the eagle appeared. Liona spotted it first. It lofted high above them, its wingspan enormous.

"Is it a seabird?" she asked uncertainly. "I've not seen its like before."

Lucius squinted up at it.

"No, it's a raptor of some sort. I've never seen one so large."

It circled above them, and Liona got the uncomfortable idea it was watching them. She tried to take it as a good omen. Night was falling. They had a fire built up, small, secretive and smokeless. Lucius sighed.

"I should hunt," he said reluctantly.

He didn't like leaving her for the hours it took him to track prey in his wolf form. But it was the fastest and most efficient way to make sure that they both stayed fed. She had reassured him countless times that she would be fine.

Despite her weariness and the cold, she never got tired of watching his form change to that of a wolf's. It was less like a transformation than a revelation. It was as if a part of him was always the wolf. When he changed shapes, it was simply an easier thing to see.

He nuzzled her hand, dog-like, with his cold nose, making her laugh. Then he leaped over the fire, bounding into the forest. If he was lucky, in a short time, he would have a brace of fat rabbits for the fire. Though some nights he came back with nothing at all.

Liona tended the fire, watching the stars come out slowly. To her curiosity, the eagle was still circling above. She knew that raptors hunted by sight. Soon it would be flying blind. Just as she was wondering if it was ill or maddened somehow, it fell to earth like a stone. At the very last minute, however, it flared its wings, opening them wide to display their real width. Liona stumbled back. The bird was enormous, but it still landed on the opposite side of the fire with an unnatural delicacy and grace.

Now that it was grounded, a shiver of apprehension ran up Liona's spine. Standing on its enormous talons, the eagle's head was even with her ribs. The curved beak clacked at her, making her imagine it rending through tender flesh. She held her ground, keeping the fire between them. There were no stones close to hand that she could throw. There were no weapons beyond Lucius's spear and sword, things she did not know how to use.

Liona licked her dry lips.

"So what shall we do now, Master Eagle?" she murmured.

To her surprise, the eagle threw back its head, making a coughing sound that was a great deal like a human laugh. As she watched, the eagle mantled its wings, seeming to grow bigger. No, it wasn't just that the eagle seemed larger. It grew taller and broader, twisting out of the eagle shape. At the end of the transformation, there was a man standing where the eagle had landed.

He was easily of a size with Lucius, broad shouldered, and if anything, even more muscular. Instead of Roman cotton and leather armor, however, he wore a plain wool tunic and leggings, most of which was covered by what looked like an entire bear pelt. She could see the shine of a golden torque around his neck. When he smiled, she could see the glint of white teeth through his close-cropped golden beard.

"You have been looking for the Altanii," he said, his voice husky and amused. "Now you have found us."

Liona nodded slowly.

"You're a sorcerer," she said softly. "Like my mother was. It runs in the blood, then."

"It can," he said, as easily as if they spoke every day of their lives. "May I come around the fire? May I come closer to my kinswoman?"

"Swear on your gods that you will do me and mine no harm, and I will allow it."

Liona spoke with a dignity and confidence she did not really feel. It was all too obvious that this man was in his own home, in woods that he knew as well as he knew his own face. If she had dignity and confidence, it was because he had not chosen to take them away from her.

"By Brigandu, loved of war, and Cernunnos who hunts, I do so swear."

He waited for her nod. Then he came around the fire for her, his frame dwarfing hers. He smelled of something wild, smoke and burning herbs. His hand, when it came to touch her face, was surprisingly gentle.

"You have the look of a Roman," he said. "Did she claim descent from the Altanii?"

"My mother was Gaelic, and it was my sister who inherited her looks, not me. She…"

On an impulse that she could never later explain, she took his hand, making them both still. She hadn't been looking for the future this time. This time, she had only been leaving herself as open as she could be, searching for kinship, searching for a scrap of anything that might help her.

"You were a boy," she said slowly. "Just a young boy on the dock. Times were good, and you had a little sword from Rome to call your own."

"When I was young, there was a lull between our warring with Rome. We have pockets of peace now and then."

"You went down to the dock to see a woman off, one who was going to marry Rome." Liona's eyes were distant as the past unfolded in front of her like a ribbon. "There has been so much talk, because she is a woman of power, and yet she chooses to leave. Your father, the chief of the Altanii, does not wish it, but she is his foster sister, raised with him and loved as if she were blood. He can't deny her, but he…he will be angry with her for the rest of his life for what she has decided to do. He will not see her off, but you will." She smiled. "You wore a blue tunic and your sword. When your foster aunt turned, she smiled, and you've never forgotten it." Liona's eyes cleared, and she grinned at him. "That was my mother. I have never seen her so young or so happy before. Even if you turn me away now, thank you for that."

The man in fur stared at her for a long moment, nodding slowly.

"Anawyn was a gifted woman in many ways. She commanded the waters, and it was said she could sing the fish to the nets sometimes. You are her daughter then, with the ability to read the past."

"No, not usually," Liona admitted. "I usually see the strands of fate. I look forward, not back. This was the first time that happened."

The man's grin grew sly. "Perhaps that is my doing?"

"What do you mean?"

"A sorceress's powers may be enhanced by contact with the right sorcerer."

"You think that I did that because you touched my face?" Liona scoffed. "That sounds unlikely."

"We could experiment, if you like," he offered generously. "We could find out for sure."

Liona took a step back, laughing at him. Perhaps she should have felt nervous being propositioned by a strange man, but something in her gut told her that there was no harm in him, nothing that would threaten her.

"I'm sorry, I am spoken for." There was a maddened growl from close by. "And there he is."

Lucius in his wolf form bounded out of the forest, dropping a dead rabbit from his enormous jaws as he did so. He would have sprung straight for the man's throat, but Liona caught him, wrapping her arms around his neck.

"Lucius, Lucius, no, this man does not mean us harm…"

The dark wolf's eyes still glowed with a battle light. Though he stood still, he was still vibrating with tension.

"He is Altanii, one of my mother's people," she said urgently. "He can help us." When that still didn't make Lucius calm, she tried again. "He is a man of power. He is the eagle that has been watching over us."

She could feel Lucius's hesitation. Then with a barely audible sigh, he changed back into his man form, rising to offer the stranger his hand. The man grasped it in the Roman style, though his slight grin told them that he found their customs strange.

"Well then, kinswoman, I hope you will allow me to offer you a welcome suitable for the daughter of my father's foster sister. You and your bondsman are welcome in our lands and at my own hearth."

"I will feel your welcome more strongly if we know each other's names," Liona said pointedly.

The man's smile was frankly sensual. By her side, she could feel Lucius tense again.

Liona shook her head sternly.

"Will you treat us like guests, or will you persist in treating me like a girl you can buy with a bouquet of flowers and a satisfied smile?" she demanded.

Her sternness made the man raise his hands in surrender.

"Forgive, kinswoman," he said in repentance. "I am carried away by your presence and your beauty. I am Gaius, the first sorcerer of the Altanii, the speaker with the dead, and the brother of the Chieftain Artos. You are welcome among the Altanii, and you will walk without fear among us so long as I draw breath."

Liona nodded at him with the cool aloofness that she had seen the Roman matrons display.

"I am Liona of Rome, daughter of Anawyn of the Altanii and

her husband Octavian of the Forty-eighth Legion. This is–"

"Lucius. Liona's husband and guardian."

Liona blinked. Lucius held a military title. It was strange to hear him introduce himself as if his only worth was relevant to her.

If Gaius saw any confusion in it, he did not show it. He bowed to them, one hand fisted and the other wrapped over it in the Gallic style.

"It is not such a very long walk to the stronghold of the Altanii. Follow me, and we shall have you both warm and fed."

He helped them pack their gear and put out the fire. When they were ready, he led them into the forest.

• • • • •

Hailey blinked, turning to Liona, their faces so close that their noses nearly touched.

"You read his past," she said slowly. "I thought that you were only a fortuneteller."

"Only a fortuneteller. Why not spare my ego a little, hmm?" Hailey blushed and started to apologize, but Liona laughed. "Only a fortuneteller indeed! It was an odd moment for me, and even years after, I can remember how strange it was. All I knew was that I had a need to prove myself to Gaius. I sought, and I found. It was as simple as that."

"I always thought that witches and warlocks only had one power, one thing that they could do."

"If that were true, you couldn't do everything that you do, could you?"

It was as if someone had poured cold water over Hailey's head. Her power had always made her the odd one. It allowed her to pull power from others, but when she did, she was not limited to what their power allowed them to do. She could do what she liked.

"Do you mean this is something that all witches and warlocks can do?"

Liona looked thoughtful.

"Perhaps. If you live as long as I have, you will find that you are reluctant to make sweeping statements about anyone. My own powers have grown every year. If you make the choice to embrace the years as I have, perhaps yours will as well."

"That means…" Hailey swallowed hard. If her already potent magic could also grow year by year…

Liona nodded. "It would make you one of the most powerful witches history has ever seen."

She said it as casually as she might comment on the pattern of the weather or on the flight of a bird. It was too much for Hailey. She couldn't take it in. How could anyone comprehend being as Liona suggested she might be? Liona watched her, waiting, all traces of her soft laugh gone. But Hailey didn't know what to think, let alone say.

"I would like to hear more about your time among the Altanii," she murmured

CHAPTER THIRTY-FIVE

THE ALTANII LIVED in an enormous earthwork, a fortress made of packed clay so strong that it had resisted Roman rule for generations. Gaius was greeted with a kind of fearful and loving respect that put Liona in mind of the high priests of Rome. When they were brought before the chieftain, she was startled to see the other man embrace Gaius like a brother.

"I have returned a kinswoman to our midst, brother," Gaius said. "She who stands before us is the daughter of Anawyn, sister in all but blood to my father."

The man who sat on the high seat in the main hall turned to greet them both with a broad smile on his face. He was large, though not so large as Gaius. A terrible scar crossed his face, but the impression that Liona received was of an enormous and friendly bear.

"Welcome, little kinswoman, and your man as well. You are home, and after our welcome feast, I will hear the reason for your journey."

Liona was startled to realize that she was being addressed instead of Lucius, but he seemed unsurprised.

"The women of the northern clans enjoy more privileges than their sisters in Rome," he told her softly. "They own property, they have equal standing in the government. Some of them even fight."

That type of freedom was bewitching to Liona, and she watched in fascination as the feast halls filled up. There were an equal number of men and women at the high table. They were women like her mother and her sister. Her heart gave another pang for Augusta.

She should be here as well, she thought sadly.

The food was far different than what could be acquired in Rome, but it was still delicious. There was boar, chicken and something she thought might have been seal at the table. The enormous haunches of meat were roasted and dripping with fat. The only vegetables were pallid things, onions and leeks predominant among them. She was uncertain about the flavors, but Lucius tucked in with a will. She remembered that he had spent most of his life in the north.

The feast wore on for hours, with one toast to her return after another. There were many older nobles who remembered her mother fondly. She could feel the bonds of family tug at her in a way that she had never felt before. The moon was on its way to setting before the nobles drifted off to their bed. Gaius, who had been seated next to the chieftain, appeared by their side.

"If you are ready for bed, I can bring you to the baths. You can cleanse yourselves, and then I can show you to your chamber."

"You make an unlikely house steward," Lucius said. His words were mild, but there was an undercurrent there that made Liona look up in concern.

Whatever the bait might have been, Gaius only smiled.

"Whatever else I am, I am one who serves. Come with me. I think you will enjoy our baths."

The city of Rome was known for its luxurious baths. In the past, she and Augusta always spent a bit of copper at their favorite one every few days. She had no idea what to expect from the baths of barbarians.

Gaius led them outdoors again, into the biting cold. Instead of taking them to one of the buildings, however, he took them to a cave entrance within the walls of the earthwork. There were rough stairs cut into the rock. In the flickering light of the torch, she could see deep grooves where thousands of feet had worn away the stone. This was an ancient place.

As they descended, the air grew warmer and moister. When they came to level ground, Gaius walked ahead, lighting the sconces that lined the walls.

"Oh, Lucius…"

The cavern stretched out farther than the light could reach. To the right, there was a deep and still lake, terrifying in its darkness. To the left were a series of round pools that steamed in the flickering light.

"This is one of the great treasures of the Altanii," Gaius said proudly. "The breath of the Great Mother comes up to warm us, and this place has been her gift to us."

Lucius looked as impressed as Liona felt.

"This is an amazing place. When I was last in Gaul, I believe I would have given my weight in salt to be this warm."

Gaius laughed.

"Don't let me stop you. There are cloths to dry yourselves here. The pools should be enjoyed."

Liona was so eager for the water that she stripped on the spot. Then she remembered that she was around a stranger, dropping her hands to cover the curly triangle of hair between her legs.

To her surprise, Gaius was stripping as well and walking towards the largest pool.

She glanced at Lucius, who shrugged. Soon they were both stripped to the skin, and hand in hand, they approached the pool that Gaius had chosen.

There was a stone ledge carved into the walls of the pool. Gaius's eyes, a warm and living gray, watched her as she climbed in. The dark water hid her. She scooted a little closer to Lucius, leaning against his bulk.

For quite a long time, all three of them were still. There was a kind of peace in the springs that Liona had almost forgotten. It reminded her that there were such things as safety and comfort. There might have been an entire world hunting them outside, but here in the earth, there was nothing but her own heartbeat and that of the two men with her.

A deep languor overtook her body. She wasn't sleepy, exactly, but she was completely relaxed and open. The hot water warmed her in a way that she wasn't sure she had experienced since she left home. She turned to Gaius with a smile, soft and easy.

"Thank you," she said softly. "Thank you for everything."

"You have come home." He shrugged. "Perhaps soon you and your legatus will tell me why you have done so."

For a moment, Liona didn't understand why Lucius stiffened by her side. Then she realized that Gaius had called Lucius a legatus. Rome and the northern tribes were technically at peace, but such things often counted for nothing when old spilled blood was remembered so well.

"Did you think it was so well hidden?" Gaius asked idly. "I was old enough to fight when skirmishes with Rome rose up about ten years ago. I remember how a Roman looks and how a legatus carries himself."

"It wasn't just my bearing," Lucius said warily.

"No. I don't see so well as the daughter of Anawyn, perhaps, but I do see some things. I see the banner of the legion above your head. I can see your armor as clearly as if you were wearing it."

Liona stopped herself from reaching out to Gaius.

"What will you do with this knowledge?"

"Precisely nothing." The Gallic sorcerer shrugged. "Rome is at peace, and you are family, of a kind. I have no need to offer you hurt so long as you offer me and mine none."

Lucius still looked dubious. Gaius shook his head a little ruefully.

"Perhaps you won't be happy until the Empire's banner flies over all the lands of the world, legatus, but I care very little."

He rose from the spring, shedding sheets of water off of his body. Liona realized that he was well-muscled, though perhaps a little softer than Lucius. It made sense, she figured. Lucius was a soldier by trade. Gaius was a warrior because war had been thrust upon him. She watched curiously as he picked up a bundle of what looked like dry twigs lying nearby. To her surprise, he started hitting himself along the back and shoulders with them. She watched as the skin of his back got redder. She listened as the dry rattle of the branches struck his muscular back. She realized that she wasn't just turning red because of the water.

"What are you doing there?" Lucius asked after Gaius was done.

"It's an Altanii tradition," the sorcerer explained. "The dry birch branches wake up the skin. The ancients tell us that it makes the blood run faster."

It was true, there was a bright gleam in Gaius's eyes. Liona found that she could not take her eyes away from his mouth, curved into a mischievous grin.

"In Rome, some of the baths offer skilled workers who will beat your back with their fists," Lucius said thoughtfully.

"That sounds good, too. Do you want to try?"

Gaius picked up another bunch of birch twigs, tilting his head in curiosity. Something about it made Liona hold her breath. After a long moment, Lucius nodded, stepping out of the warm bath. Liona felt like a fly on the wall, a sort of female spy sent to watch what was inherently a male ritual. She stayed as quiet as she could, afraid that they would notice and send her out, or worse, stop.

Instead of giving the birch twigs to Lucius, Gaius motioned for the Roman man to stand where he had stood.

"It's better if someone else does it for you," he explained.

The first blows were stroking, far lighter than the ones that Gaius had been using on himself. Lucius's skin was darker than Gaius's. It took longer for his skin to redden. By then Gaius was striking him firmly, rocking Lucius slightly on his feet.

"How is it?" the sorcerer asked, pausing.

"I'm wondering if you can hit me any harder," Lucius said, throwing a grin over his shoulder. "Otherwise, perhaps I'll ask Liona to take a turn."

"Oh, well, I wouldn't want my poor kinswoman to tire herself out."

The next blow was loud enough to startle Liona. It made Lucius reach out a hand to steady himself against the rock wall. He groaned, but to Liona, it was as much a sound of pleasure as it was of pain.

"That's close to what I think a man can do," Lucius jibed, and there was a smokiness to Gaius's laugh that made Liona blush even harder.

The rain of blows that he laid on Lucius's back was intense, turning the other man's skin brick red. He never broke the skin. Instead, he worked the switches up and down, striking hard enough that bits of twigs flew in every direction.

Finally, he paused, inspecting the bundle.

"That's all for this bundle, I'm afraid."

The only sound in the stone chamber was Lucius's heavy breathing. It seemed to take him a moment to recover himself, but when he did, he was smiling. He was more at ease than Liona had seen him since they left Rome. Now he looked like the cocky legatus who had rescued her from her attacker. Her heart thrilled for it, singing like a bird in spring.

"I think I'm done anyway. Thank you. That's a tradition someone needs to bring back to the Empire."

"Well, all of your good ideas were initially ours anyway," said Gaius with a smile. "But aren't we forgetting someone?"

Both men turned bright eyes to Liona. She thought that if she were truly a clever woman, seeing two men look at her like that would have made her duck underneath the water. Instead, she felt her heart skip a beat. Without thinking about it, she rose from the pool. There was a new tension in the room. She could feel her heart beat in her chest. She saw their eyes roam her body. When she glanced down, she could see that they were both half-aroused. It made her smile. She stepped closer, looking at them both.

"Lucius, do you think you can do for me what Gaius did for you?"

Lucius, to his credit, glanced at the Gaelic sorcerer.

"Be careful of the small of her back," Gaius said. "Stay below the line of her shoulder. That's all. After that, she'll tell you herself what she likes."

Lucius's grin woke a fire deep in Liona's body. With an exaggerated casualness, he picked up a fresh bundle of twigs, swinging them through the air so that they made a swishing noise.

Silently, she took Lucius's place, resting her hands lightly on the rock wall.

"Remember that I'm not some war-toughened Roman legionnaire," she said sternly. "You're not meant to beat me bloody."

"I won't," Lucius promised.

He ran the bundle of twigs down her back. They were scratchy in a way that made her purr. They were quite limber. From how red Lucius's back had become, she knew that they could render quite a sting, but right now, this was only pleasure.

The first few strokes were light and gentle, searching. She could tell that Lucius was gauging her reaction. She murmured in approval, telling him that she could take more. Slowly, the blows built up in intensity, striking her shoulders, her back, her buttocks and her thighs. He was being far gentler with her than Gaius had been with him.

She gloried in the way her skin seemed to come alive. There was a snapping sting to each strike. Just as the sting began to fade, he struck her again. Soon she was leaning against the rock wall in earnest, squirming and sighing. She couldn't call it a beating, not when it was so pleasurable. The pleasure had just the finest sliver of pain to it. The combination took her breath away.

Liona was in some timeless wonderful place, barely aware of it when Lucius stopped. She felt like she was floating, borne up by the smell of the fresh birch twigs and the faint metallic scent of the springs. She was aware that Gaius and Lucius were behind her, speaking quietly. Surely she was supposed to be worried about that?

She felt a pair of strong hands ease her down onto the ground. Instead of the rock floor, there was a straw mat there. She hissed as her tender back landed on the mat, but after a moment, she settled in. Lucius was standing above her, the bundle of switches still in his hand. She smiled at him, aware of how open and vulnerable she was, but it didn't matter. She trusted him completely.

He ran the bundle of twigs over her breasts and belly. Then to her shock, he ran them over her thighs and between them.

"It will be so gentle," he promised.

She nodded.

She whimpered at the first strike. The skin of her inner thighs was so sensitive that it did not take much at all to make her squirm. He didn't make the next blow harder. Instead, he struck her gently and steadily. The beat was close to that of her heart. She gave herself up to the rhythm. She whimpered and squirmed and never wanted it to stop.

She didn't realize how she was thrusting her hips up to meet his every blow until he stopped.

In the silence after Lucius halted, Gaius's laugh was soft and sweet.

"Welcome home, kinswoman. I think you'll enjoy our barbaric ways. I believe I will take myself outside. The next part calls for bathing oneself in snow, though I think you delicate southerners might take offense. Come find me when you are done. Don't worry about keeping me waiting. I rather like the cold."

She heard his steps retreating up the stairs. She met Lucius's eyes, as hot and hungry as hers. Like a beast breaking free of its leash, he was on top of her. She knew how strong he was, but now she was reminded again. He lifted her legs easily, throwing them over his shoulders. It bent her back and lifted her rear from the mat.

With his hands cupped beneath her buttocks, he brought her up to his erection, stroking its length along her slick slit. Liona was mildly shocked when she realized how wet she was. The birching had woken her in more ways than one.

"Yes, right now, please, don't make me wait," she whispered.

Lucius obeyed her as if she were his commanding officer. He pushed into her in one sleek, smooth motion. It made them both groan. She wrapped her legs around his waist, hoping to pull him even closer.

"Touch yourself," he growled. "I won't be alone in this."

She let one hand fall on her clit, exposed and wanting with her legs so spread. It wasn't until she started squirming that he started to thrust, pushing inside her with the force of the ocean. Her entire body was sensitized to his touch. The more she received from him, the more she wanted. She felt the familiar tension take over her body. She felt herself start to shake. When she flew to pieces, her cry echoed through the chamber. She dug her nails into Lucius's wrists, urging him to finish as well. When he spilled inside her, he roared, shaking with the strength of his release.

They lay still together for a long moment. Eventually, he pulled out of her, and came to lie on the mat next to her. There was an ease to them that had been missing for what felt like a long time. It made sense, after all, Liona thought. They had come together when they were on the run. Their first joining had been a desperate, hidden thing, more a mating than something that had love or joy in it. This felt like the way their first time should have been. It was for pleasure alone. She could feel the love that flowed between them easily. He leaned over and planted a warm kiss on her mouth.

Liona lay back and enjoyed it for a while, but when his hand roamed from her belly down to her thigh, she laughed, putting her hand over his.

"While I would like nothing more than to hide from Gaul's winter here, I believe that we should likely go find Gaius. No matter how cold-blooded he is, he can't want to be in the snow all that long."

They both rinsed themselves off one more time in the pools before drying off and dressing once again. Ascending the staircase, Liona felt warm and whole. Not even the bitter chill of the Gallic night could cool her spirits.

They found Gaius, dressed and his bear skin draped over his shoulders, standing at the cave's mouth. He wore a satyr's smile on his lips. Though it made Liona blush, Lucius nodded at him as if they had been friends for years. Gaius nodded in return.

"I think we have much to speak about in the morning." Gaius said. "Come. I've promised you the welcome of my hearth, and it lies this way."

Gaius's home was a fairly spacious cottage. There was a low table covered with glass bottles and a chest underneath it. Gaius's own bed was close to the hearth, but there was also a loft above that was filled with sweet hay. Liona and Lucius climbed up the ladder to the warm bed it offered.

Lucius fell asleep as soon as they were resting in the hay. Settled in his arms, warmer than she had been in weeks, Liona found that she could not go to sleep right away. Instead, she found herself listening to Gaius moving below. She heard the gentle rattle of glass combined with the sound of liquid being poured. He was the sorcerer of the Altanii clan. He likely often had responsibilities that saw him awake through the night.

She thought of his fine bare body in the springs. She thought of the smile on his face when she had risen out of the water. She wasn't sure if it was the same smile as when he had seen Lucius's naked form, but she was willing to bet some silver on it, if not some gold.

As she finally drifted off to sleep, she imagined another body in the hay with them, another pair of arms wrapped around them both.

• • • • •

A birch bundle? The thought of it made Hailey's upper back twitch. But then she thought of Piers, how he had held her still, and the way he'd spanked her. That had begun slowly too. But then he'd peppered her rear until it was suffused in warmth. To her dismay, Hailey felt that same warmth now.

"Dear one," Liona whispered in her ear. "You're squirming."

Hailey lay on her back, Liona's arm draped across her belly.

"Sorry," Hailey said, her voice even higher than normal. Her cheeks were on fire, and she knew they had to be glowing. Trying to hide her distress, she turned her face from Liona.

"No," Liona said softly. Her fingers went to Hailey's chin and gently, but firmly, turned her face to her. "Never be rueful of that."

Though her voice was more tender than Hailey had ever heard it, she couldn't bring herself to meet Liona's eyes.

"Now," Liona said, releasing her chin to settle her am around her waist again. "Where was I?"

• • • • •

Gaius greeted them with a breakfast of cracked oats scattered with dried berries. They sat at his hearth, and as they ate, they talked. Gaius lost his smile as soon as he heard them mention a hand rising from a flame. He listened with an intent look on his face when they spoke of the disappearances.

"And then you were driven from your home and came here instead, looking for help and refuge."

"Looking for information," Lucius corrected. "We have every intention of rescuing Titus and Augusta. If you could help us with that, we would forever be in your debt."

Gaius's smile was thin.

"If you are going to rescue Titus and Augusta, who will rescue Olaf Snorrison, Athelwulf of Umbria and Berys of the Umaii tribe?"

Liona blinked.

"Other people of power," she murmured. "Our family is not

the only one that has gone missing."

Gaius nodded grimly.

"Whoever these evil men are, they are powerful, and they are looking for people just like us. I know that other clans have lost their sorcerers and sorceresses. I know that when I ventured out to Londinium a few months past, I had to fight off a pair of armed men. I thought they were after my purse, but now I see that there might have been far more sinister implications."

Though Lucius shook his head, he looked resolute. "Then we are at war."

Liona and Gaius looked at him with surprise. There was a fire in his eyes that Liona had never seen before. With a shiver, she thought it must be the look of a man who too often had to kill or be killed.

"War occurs between tribes and nations," Gaius began, but Lucius cut him off.

"No, this is a war between those like us and those who would see us destroyed. I am certain of it. We are being taken, perhaps killed. It is time we fought back."

The words he spoke brought a flicker of Liona's power. She gasped, touching her head. For a split second, her mind was crowded with the vision of snapping banners and high walls. She could hear footsteps in the dark. She could see assassins striking people down. She could see men and women of power, some with fire in their hands, others in the form of wild animals, fighting and dying.

She came to herself with Gaius on one side and Lucius on the other. For a moment, she only rested, not caring whose hands were whose.

"You are going to change the world," she said to Lucius. There was dread in her voice.

He shook his head, his face stone.

"They came after our family. If we do not show them that there are consequences to this, they will never stop. People like that don't stop."

Liona let out a slow breath.

"First we find our family. Without them, all else is pointless anyway. Then you can start your war."

Lucius's hand was warm on hers, but there was something distant about him. She wondered with a deep pit opening in her stomach if she had lost him already to some dark future she did not understand.

"We should start in Londinium," Gaius said finally. "That is the largest city in the region. It is only a few days ride away, and it is still early enough to make the crossing. We can find the answers we seek there. But make no mistake. We are at war."

• • • • •

Hailey abruptly realized that she was in her bed at the infirmary, rather than in the small cottage in Gaul. But the realization didn't lessen the pang in her chest.

"I think I've heard that before," she said softly.

Somehow they had changed positions. Now Liona lay on her back, gazing at the ceiling, and Hailey curled into her side. There was something distant and hard about the woman, Hailey realized. There was something terrible about living so long. People changed, and sometimes, the way that they changed hurt.

"I'm sure you have," Liona said. "I would wager that every member of the Magus Corps has it tattooed over their hearts."

Hailey thought of Kieran, of duty that could call him like a wolf's howl. She wondered if he had ever known of Lucius, the man who had so early on determined a need for the Magus Corps, or something like it.

Shyly, as if afraid she would spook the other woman, Hailey reached over to touch her shoulder. Liona stiffened for a moment, but then she relaxed under Hailey's touch. When she unwound, when those dark eyes fluttered closed, she looked like a girl again.

"Think very carefully before you decide to walk the long road," she said quietly. "Think very carefully upon it indeed, Hailey."

Liona lay still for such a long time that Hailey wondered if she would ever hear more. When Liona began to speak again, she did it without opening her eyes.

"Artos, the chieftain of the Altanii did not want to lose us. He considered me kin already, and of course a sorcerer such as Gaius cannot be found so easily. We swore we would return, and we did mean it, though of course Lucius made no such promise. His eyes were fixed north in Londinium. In some ways, he felt lost to me, though I would have done anything to get him back."

CHAPTER THIRTY-SIX

"RIDING LOOKED SO easy when I saw people do it in the streets," Liona whimpered, falling into the bed that Lucius had made up for her. The sturdy northern horse that she had ridden snorted as if it had heard her words. She would have made a rude gesture at it if she had the strength.

She caught her breath as she rolled on her sides. The insides of her thighs were red and sore. She felt as if she would never be able to walk correctly again.

"It's not easy, but it will get easier," Gaius promised. "Can I see?"

"If you could make me feel better, I would strip off my skin for you."

Gaius laughed.

"That won't be necessary, but I may be a little more intimate than you expect."

He glanced at Lucius, who smiled.

"If you can help her ride without making those sad little sounds, I would thank you as well."

Gaius rolled Liona slowly on her back. With a gentle hand, he pushed the hem of her wool dress up to her waist. The stone ridge that they were camped underneath kept off the worst of the wind, but still she shivered.

"Shush, shush, beautiful lioness." Somewhere along the way, he had picked up Lucius's name for her. "Let me see… Ah, poor thing. You're so raw."

He spoke with the same absent kindness he would have given a hurt bird or kitten. Liona relaxed to his touch, flinching only a little as he inspected her thighs.

"Fortunately, I have just the thing. Stay still for me, darling, and I can make this better."

Liona heard him rummaging in his bag, and then she smelled something bright, almost summery. She watched as he scooped a pat of white balm out of an unstoppered jar. She trembled when he started to sleek it against her sore flesh. His long fingers were gentle, however. Slowly, she relaxed. The tingle of the balm soothed the dull roaring ache of her skin. Soon she was stretched out on her bedding. The tenseness of her muscles had been causing her more pain than she thought. When she relaxed, the ache faded.

Gaius massaged every trace of the salve into her skin. When he took his hands away, she whimpered piteously.

"I thought you were going to make her feel better," Lucius said, a teasing lilt in his voice.

Gaius laughed, but he didn't reply to Lucius's words.

"There, that should help you sleep well. Tomorrow will still hurt, but hopefully it will hurt less. If you'll excuse me, I think I'll take a look around. I don't know the area, and I'm curious to see what I can before we lose the light entirely."

"I can tell you," Liona said. "It will be trees, trees, trees, a rock, and more trees. I think after this is all over, I'll never want to see a tree again."

Gaius smiled at that, but he slipped away, a strange expression on his face.

Once he had the fire built up, Lucius came to stretch out by her side. She turned to bury her face in his chest. With his arm around her, she felt safer than she had ever felt.

"Gaius is strange sometimes," she mumbled.

Lucius's laugh rumbled through his frame.

"I take it you didn't realize what he's off to do?"

"What do you mean?"

"He had your skirts up and his hands on your thighs. He looked like a man who liked what he saw, and would have liked even more to touch."

For a moment, Liona had no idea what Lucius was talking about. Then she figured it out, blushing fiercely.

"Does it bother you?" she whispered. "Do…do you get angry because of this?"

"Do I look angry? No," he shook his head. "I would have thought I would, but I like Gaius. He has kept us safe, and he obviously cares about you. I don't think I can find it in me to be angry at someone who cares about you as well as he does."

There was a kind of peace to Lucius's words. Years later, Liona would look back on that moment with a flinch. Now, however, she merely burrowed deeper into Lucius's chest, relishing his warmth.

"I…I like him a great deal," she muttered.

She wasn't sure if it was the truth. If it was, it wasn't all of it. The power of her emotions frightened her. Now that she was rested and safe, she could look at them more closely. What she saw startled her. The feelings she was developing for Gaius, they weren't so far off from what she felt for Lucius. It didn't matter who she had met first. It made her wonder if her affections weren't so very powerful. It felt strong to her, the presence that they had in her heart. It was like looking at the sun. She couldn't think about it for too long without flinching. Instead she fell into a light doze. At some point, Gaius returned. They had been sleeping three together for the past few nights simply because it was so cold. He slid against her back, enveloping her in warmth.

Liona dreamed of the future, but it always outpaced her. Her vision was clouded and troubled. When she awoke from a fitful sleep, someone kissed her hair, and someone else stroked her shoulder until she quieted.

• • • • •

Though Hailey had turned on her side, away from Liona, the older woman never broke their connection. She spooned Hailey's smaller frame easily from behind. Though Hailey had listened intently to Liona's tale, so many questions burned inside her. What would it be like to be immortal, or to even have that choice? What kind of power would be unleashed in her? And though Liona was a seer of legendary ability, Hailey couldn't bring herself to ask her own future.

"I know it is much to take in, dear one," Liona whispered, her breath warm against the side of Hailey's neck. "Perhaps it is best we stop."

"No!" Hailey blurted out, turning her head.

To her surprise, Liona had been trying to glimpse her face. With the barest, glancing brush, their lips touched. Before she could stop herself, Hailey gasped. As her nostrils filled with the honeyed scent of Liona's perfume, Hailey's head swam. Liona's dark eyes seemed lit from within, a brilliant sparkle gleaming from an untold depth.

"Be at ease, dear one," she crooned, nuzzling the side of Hailey's neck. The weight of her brow gently moved Hailey's head back to the pillow. "There," Liona said quietly. "Just so."

The older woman slid her hand around Hailey's waist, then slowly up her tummy. Hailey's mind blanked as Liona's deft touch left a trail of muted warmth. Her hand slipped between Hailey's breasts, pressing down gently on the breastbone.

"Your heart beats like a captured bird," Liona whispered. Hailey swallowed hard as her nipples tightened and beaded. "What troubles you?"

Hailey could hardly think straight. What was her body doing? Was it the tale she had heard of Liona's love for her two men? Was it Hailey's desire for Kieran and Piers? Did her body sense Liona's great power, and the way she seemed to know what Hailey was thinking? But as the quiet stretched on, she sensed Liona waiting.

"Please," Hailey said in a quaking voice. "Please tell me that Gaius, Lucius and you…that…that it wasn't just a dream. That the three of you…"

"Hush, dear one," Liona whispered. "Let me tell you what you need to know."

• • • • •

The crossing to Londinium was easier than the journey from Rome. Even so, Liona didn't begin to feel herself until they had found a room in one of Londinium's many inns. Within city walls, she felt herself grow stronger.

"It's not Rome," she had said to Gaius after a few mornings there. "I mean, I doubt any city is like Rome, but this isn't a bad place."

The earthwork was in the middle of the forest.

"I didn't realize that Rome smelled so foul," Gaius said drily.

But as they became used to the city, they also settled into their tasks, each seeking information in their own ways. Lucius thought the answer lay with warriors, fighters from all nations who had come to sell their swords in Londinium. Gaius sought the scholars, the ones who came looking for the future in the past.

For her part, Liona cultivated a reputation as a gossip, a young girl who read fortunes and who was always happy to chatter for a little while. She made a little bit of coin here and there, but she heard more. She talked with women at the well, with well-to-do women who went shopping in the market every day, with little girls who carried enormous bundles of wood between the houses.

One young girl, her face smudged with charcoal, looked startled when she mentioned the emblem. She looked down and around, but Liona was patient, and finally the girl spoke.

"There's a girl like you, who tells fortunes at the house with the green door on the docks. She treats with the men with that symbol. She can help you."

"Is she always there?"

"No, ma'am. I think she sails with the ships. The last of them is leaving in the next day or so. She's sure to be on it."

Liona cursed before she remembered herself. She handed the girl a few copper pieces and sent her on her way. She thought furiously. Lucius was north of the city that day, trying to find old Roman veterans who might speak with him. She didn't even know where Gaius was. There was no help for it. She would need to find this fortuneteller herself.

The girl's instructions led her to a shabby area of the docks. She kept her eyes down and walked as if she knew where she was going. After a little bit of fumbling, she found the green door the girl had promised. Biting her lip, she knocked on the door twice. A muffled voice told her to enter. When she did, she froze.

The small space was lit only with a lantern, but she could see well enough. A large man closed the door behind her. In front of her, seated at a bare table, was an ascetic-looking man, rail thin and with his hair cropped close in the Roman fashion. In his hand, he held a sharp dagger. Around his neck was a gold pendant bearing the sigil of a hand reaching out of the flame.

"Well," he said, his voice as dry as the slither of scales over rock. "We have been looking for you for quite some time."

"Who are you?" she whispered. "What did you do with my sister?"

"That is information that you will learn in time. For the moment, we have business with you."

Liona swallowed hard. She wished fiercely for the ability to turn into a wolf or an eagle, for the power to spit fire from her fingertips.

"What business could you have with me?"

"You are very lovely, aren't you?" the man spoke carelessly, as if he were praising the worth of a gem or a tool. "It does not matter, not really. Still, I have an offer to make to you."

"An offer?" Liona's voice shook. She couldn't take her eyes off the man. He was as hypnotic as a snake.

"Yes, a simple one. You can come with us tomorrow morning, willingly and on your own two feet. If you do that, your men will not be harmed."

"And what happens if I refuse?"

"Then we take you now, and when they come looking for you, they will be killed. It is as simple as that." She started to open her mouth, but he stopped her. "We have agents in every part of this town. We are deadlier and stronger than you could ever imagine. Fortunately, right now, what we want is you. If we do not get you, your sister will be killed."

Spoken as a plain fact, the last was what decided her. Something inside her died.

"You will not harm them?"

The man's lip curled as if the thought sickened him.

"We have no interest in mad dogs that we cannot control," he told her bluntly. "We have learned that men like that are not worth the time it takes to bring them in. We will leave them, or we will kill them." He shook his head. "There will be a man by the door of your inn tomorrow. Before dawn, you will come down to him, and he will take you to our ship. If you know what is best for them, you will keep them well away. Do you understand?" She nodded mutely. "We do not wish any trouble. You can make things much easier on yourself, on them, and on your sister. Do you understand?'

She nodded again. His eyes grew narrow. In that moment, she could see how much he hated her, how much he despised the fact that she shared the world with him.

"Fine. Get out of my sight."

She stumbled back into the light, feeling a thousand years older than she had a few moments before. She didn't doubt the power the man held. They had likely been waiting for weeks to find her without Gaius or Lucius.

She understood their fear well. Both Gaius and Lucius were powerful men. If they fought, they would fight to the death. If she went missing today, they would find her before the ship could sail. She had to make it easy on them. Only she could facilitate her own kidnapping.

She returned to the inn where they were lodging. She spent some of the silver she had on a roast chicken, asking that it be sent up. Her mind was a haze. She bathed herself in the basin in the room. It made her think of the safety of the hot springs cavern of the Altanii. When Gaius and Lucius returned together, it was almost dark. They were grim from their work, tired of finding nothing, but they both smiled at her when they saw her clean and waiting with food.

"Eat," she said, taking a small portion for herself. "We don't know when it will come again."

It was strange but everything seemed much clearer to her now. As if she was on the other side of a clear sheet of ice, she saw herself laugh with them, touch them both gently. It was love that bound them both together. When the light outside was gone entirely and the chicken was done, the three prepared for bed. Lucius and Liona had been taking the wide bed while Gaius contented himself with the trundle underneath. Instead of letting him pull it out, however, Liona stopped him with a hand on his arm.

"Do you wish to stay up longer, little lioness?" he asked, or at least he started to.

With her hand at the back of his neck, she pulled him down for a long, deep kiss.

"I do," she said when she released him.

She turned to Lucius, who was watching them with hooded eyes. It was hard to tell what he felt, whether it was rage or resignation, lust or joy.

"I want this," she said, nakedly and honestly.

"I would never deny you anything," he said, his voice a soft, velvet rumble.

"And me?" Gaius stayed where he was, watching Lucius carefully.

"You," Lucius said, "well, I might make you beg first."

There was a slight quirk of humor to Lucius's mouth, so lovely that Liona wanted to kiss it too. She leaned up to press her lips to his. Behind her, she felt Gaius's hand sleek down her back before coming up to tangle in her dark hair.

Somehow, all three of them tumbled into the bed together. She found herself pressed between their powerful bodies, all heat, all pleasure, and all for her. For now, this was all she wanted. She did not want to think about the ship that waited to sail, one of the last of the year. She did not want to think of what came after.

Instead, she had these two men that she loved. She had the hours of the night. That was all she needed.

She twisted so that she could kiss Gaius. Their first real kiss was surprisingly gentle. His mouth was light on hers, lapping at her lips until she moaned with the sensation. His clever fingers unbuttoned her dress before pulling it over her head. Underneath, she was bare and clean. For a moment, she felt shy, though she had certainly been naked in front of him before.

"So beautiful," Gaius murmured, leaning down to plant a soft kiss on her collar bone.

She would have replied, but there was Lucius's mouth, hot and wet against the back of her neck. He had parted the thicket of her hair to reveal her tender nape. She squirmed as he nibbled the skin there lightly.

Gaius was stripping his clothes off. Now she couldn't keep her hands off him. She couldn't stop touching his warm skin, his powerful frame. She ruffled her fingers through the light hair on his chest before leaning in to suck gently on one of his pale nipples. He tensed at the contact before cradling her head in his hands.

From behind her, Lucius wrapped his arms around her body, cradling her breasts gently. She could feel his arousal pressed against her hip. It called forth her own response. Over the months that they had been together, their bodies were in tune, like two parts of the same song. Now she found that there was room for a third part as well.

She stroked her hand down Gaius's body, pausing just short of his cock. After a moment of hesitation, she wrapped her hand around it, making him groan. She watched in fascination as he wrapped his hand over hers, showing her how he liked to be touched. She could feel the droplet of moisture at the tip of his cock, silky and warm. When he let go, she bent her head to it, lapping at it with her tongue.

She heard a soft sound from Lucius when she took Gaius in her mouth. At first she was startled, worried that it had been too much for him after all. Then she felt his hand on the back of her neck, and his mouth inches from her ear.

"You have no idea how beautiful you are when you do that, beloved."

His soft words made her groan. Though she never raised her head, she pushed her hips against Lucius, trying to show him what she needed.

"Don't let her go unsatisfied, legatus." Gaius's tone was teasing, but also breathless.

"I think you have other things to be worried about, sorcerer."

She glanced up in time to see Lucius thrust his fingers into Gaius's mouth, making the other man's eyes widen in surprise before he began to lap at them. When Lucius thought they were wet enough, he pulled them away, grinning like a demon.

"Come here, love."

Still lapping at Gaius's cock, Liona raised up on her knees as Lucius directed. He spread her legs slightly, purring at how beautiful and perfect she was. When he pressed his slicked fingers between her legs, she thought she was going to die of pleasure. He stroked her folds tenderly, finishing each stroke with a light circle around her clit.

Gaius pulled her away from his cock, making her moan slightly with disappointment. Instead, he pulled her up to kiss him. When she looked into his eyes, his pupils were so wide that there was only a scrim of gray around the edges.

"I think I've wanted you since before we spoke two words," he murmured.

She leaned in to kiss his mouth, an oddly tender and slow thing. Behind her, Lucius dropped another kiss on her shoulder while working first one, then two fingers inside. She kept on kissing Gaius, still aware that her hips were rocking towards Lucius.

"Do you want this?" Lucius asked, his voice as dark as night. "Hmm? Is this what you like, little lioness?"

She moaned into Gaius's mouth. It must have sounded like a yes because Lucius took a firm grip on her hips. She groaned as he entered her, something that made Gaius wrap his arms around her tightly.

Lucius didn't stop until he was lodged inside her fully. She whimpered, arching her back so that he would start moving, but he only laughed.

"I want to look at you like this," he murmured. "I want to see myself inside you as you kiss this man."

His words brought a hot flush of heat to her body, making her press back against him.

"Give me more, harder," she pleaded.

She felt his hands tighten on her hips. He thrust into her hard enough to push her into Gaius, who held her even more tightly. The position was awkward and cramped, but she still managed to slide her hand around Gaius's cock.

She was consumed by the noises that they made. She could hear Gaius moaning in her ear. From behind her, Lucius murmured a litany of praise to how good she felt, how beautiful she was, and how much he wanted her.

Liona could feel Lucius shake as his climax began. She quickened her hand on Gaius's erection, making him cling to her. They spilled almost in the same moment, both crying her name, both pushing as close to her as they could.

She had never been so close to other people before. She never wanted to leave them. Liona listened to their breathing slow. Against her will, tears slipped down her face. She buried her face in Gaius's chest, desperate to hide them.

She must have been successful because Lucius chuckled.

"Poor little darling. You look quite exhausted and you've not even climaxed yourself. Let us take care of that for you."

Liona found herself spread out on the bed while both men lay on either side of her.

"So very beautiful," Gaius murmured.

Perhaps another man might have thought this was a single night's pleasure. She could tell that for him, this was something real. His heart was there if she wanted it, if Lucius wanted it.

Four hands sleeked over her body, cupping her breasts, stroking her hips, carding through her long hair. Two mouths found the sensitive points at her neck, her shoulders, the sides of her breasts, her fingers and the dip of her waist.

Experimentally, she turned from kissing Gaius to kissing Lucius. Lucius was more urgent, she thought hazily, while Gaius's mouth was so soft. The sorcerer would kiss her forever if she wished. She could feel a low heat deep in her belly. She would have been pleased to let it go at that, with that pleasure, but apparently neither man agreed.

"Show me what she likes," Gaius murmured. Lucius laughed, taking the other man's hand.

"She's brilliant," Lucius promised. "Stay with us, sorcerer, and you'll see."

Liona's eyes drifted closed as Lucius guided Gaius's hand between her legs, showing him how to glide his fingers along her slit before spreading her swollen folds. She was slippery from Lucius's entry, but that didn't seem to bother Gaius at all. Soon he was pumping two fingers inside her channel, drawing the wet up to her clit to rub it as well.

His touch was gentler, a little slower than what she shared with her warrior, but soon the pleasure started to spread through her.

It was a gradual build, soothing and sweet.

"Relax and enjoy, darling. You've worked so hard today."

That was Lucius's voice tickling her ear. She turned her head to him, and obligingly, he kissed her. This was a kind of paradise, a night she could live in for a million years if the gods were kind.

The soft cries that Gaius wrung from her throat grew louder and louder. Her hips bucked up against his touch. Soon she was squirming, wanting more, but paradoxically not wanting it to end. She fought off the pleasure, but it was too much. Lucius kissed her just as she tipped over the edge. The sounds of her pleasure were muffled by his mouth. With one hand, she clung to his shoulder, with her other, she held Gaius's hand. They were three, they were one. In a strange way, she could see the pleasure spill between all three of them. She lay shaking for several long minutes. She came to herself as they were kissing her softly and soothingly.

"I love you," she said to Lucius.

"I love you," she said to Gaius.

Lucius grinned, planting a kiss on her forehead. She could see that the wound left by being ousted from Rome was healing. He would never be what he was before, but then, no one ever was.

"I love you well," he murmured, nuzzling her ear.

Gaius looked solemn, thoughtful. She had come to know him nearly as well as Lucius over the last few weeks. She had never met a man as gentle or as kind. He could be roused to a vicious temper by cruelty, but in bed with her, he was so achingly tender and sweet.

"I love you," he whispered. "Thank you for having me."

They drifted in silence. There were no gods who would consecrate their union. There was no marriage, no house, and no peace for them. There would never be another night like this, even if she was the only one who knew it.

She heard their breathing smooth and even out as they drifted to sleep. But she didn't dare. She tried to memorize the feel of their bodies instead, the weight of Lucius's arm thrown over her hip, the way Gaius felt pressed against her back.

Though Liona wished the night could last forever, at last she could see the gray light of the pre-dawn between the shutter slats. Using every trick of stealth she had ever learned, she slipped from between them and dressed herself. She smiled to see them slumbering still. It was the image she would carry with her on the perilous journey.

There was an enormous man in a heavy cloak waiting for her outside the inn. She offered no resistance when he took her by the wrist.

As the sky lightened, she knew that Lucius and Gaius would wake up to find her gone. The scene broke her heart, but even that was a lost and distant thing.

• • • • •

Liona was silent for a long time. They sat facing each other on the bed. Liona had talked the sun down. The light in the infirmary had dimmed.

"You still feel it, don't you?" Hailey whispered.

"That morning? It lives inside me, as so many memories do. I had suffered heartbreak before, and I do not think you live for centuries without experiencing it over and over again. That one, though. That one was the worst. I think it always will be."

Liona's eyes were dark and unfocused, seeing a different time. Hailey wondered what it would be like to survive leaving two people she had grown to love so well. It didn't shock her to think of Liona growing to love two men. It was not the same love, no more than you could love two parents or two children in the same way. Instead it was a natural thing that grew up between them. It made her own heart ache for Kieran and Piers. Her love for them was like a knot that had no end. She would never come to the end of what she felt for those two, no matter where they were or what they did.

Though Liona sniffed and her eyes gleamed with unshed tears, she smiled sardonically at herself.

"It's honestly ridiculous. I know what's going to happen."

"Does…does it have a happy ending?"

Even to herself, Hailey sounded so young and nervous. But it made Liona laugh. She wrapped Hailey in a warm embrace, planting a soft kiss on her forehead.

"How should I know?" Liona said, her voice light and sweet. "It hasn't ended yet."

CHAPTER THIRTY-SEVEN

THEY PUT LIONA below decks in a cell where she could touch both walls with her arms outstretched. Once a day, they came to empty her bucket and to bring her food. It was never better than hard bread, and a fingers' width of old cheese. She had no one to speak to, and the only light came from a window that she couldn't have pushed a rabbit through.

When she thought of Lucius and Gaius, it was like a hand clamped around her heart. Instead, she tried to think ahead, to a time when she could be with her sister. She would be able to find Augusta. They would escape.

She tried to access her power regularly, but everything she tried only left her with a splitting headache. Whether her power had been mangled by her kidnapping or whether the future was still so uncertain that she could not see it, she was unsure. There was nothing there that she could see, so she stopped looking.

Her hair was the worst, for some reason. She could keep it braided and behind her, but when it was loose, she couldn't stand it. She could only remember the times her lovers had touched it so sweetly. One day, she begged the man who came with her food for his knife, and as he watched, wide-eyed, she hacked it off at the nape.

At first she spent all of her time shivering under the meager blankets they gave her, but slowly she realized that the air was warming. They were sailing south again.

She thought the voyage would go on forever, but finally one day, the sounds changed. She sprang to the window, staring out. Instead of blue water, she could see the outline of a city in the early morning light. It was enormous, stretching out along the coast, but she could tell that it was not Rome. Liona did not have long to look at the coast. There was the pounding of footsteps in the hallway, and then two men came in. Before she could start to ask where the ship had arrived, a bag was placed over her head, and she was forced out. She concentrated on keeping her feet, listening for what she could. There were a mash of languages all around her. She could smell the salt of the sea, fish, grilling meat, and the smell of what must have been thousands of people living and working together.

She winced as she was pushed and shoved like a cow. She knew that she looked like one of the many slaves that were brought in and out of the major cities. No one would remember her passing. Soon enough, though, she went from the packed dirt roads to stone steps, and then she was descending down a twisting staircase. The air grew cool and damp; she was underground.

Finally, with a muffled curse, her captors shoved her forward, and a steel gate clanged shut behind her. Her hands reached for the hood that she wore, and when she pulled it off, she had to blink a few times before she could see clearly.

"Liona?"

Her eyes still needed to adjust to the dimness, but that voice, she would know that voice anywhere. She stumbled forward into her sister's arms. Augusta had lost weight, and there was an iron to her that had never been there before, but oh it was her sister. The moment she could feel those arms around her, Liona's eyes filled with tears.

"Oh Augusta, gods above, it's you!"

The sisters held each other tightly, rocking back and forth in wordless joy and relief.

Liona pulled back to inspect her sister closely. In the dim torchlight, she was gaunt and her long blond hair was stringy and matted, but she looked whole.

"Have they hurt you?"

Augusta's face twisted.

"They do terrible things here," was all Augusta would say. "They want to know more about our powers, and what we can do."

Liona felt a red tide of rage rise up in her, something that brought her closer to life than she had been in weeks. Touching her sister, she could see some of what she had experienced. There were blows across the face, a man with an iron bar. There was a funnel of cold water, which could be poured ceaselessly over a trembling body. There were men who laughed, but worse, there were men who took notes, who planned, who saw people of power as aberrations to be judged and found wanting.

"I will get us out of here," Liona swore. "I will."

Augusta looked as if she very much doubted that, but instead of saying it, she touched Liona's temple.

"What have they done to you? Your hair's growing in white."

Liona blinked, touching her temple in surprise. She had not thought of her hair in what felt like years.

"Nothing's happened to it except shock I suppose. Augusta, you must tell me about this place."

Augusta sat down with her sister on the hard wooden bench that was the cell's only furniture. Now that her eyes had adjusted, Liona could see that there was a long line of cells, separated from each other by the same steel bars.

"This is the stronghold of the Sacred Order of the Dragon,"

Augusta said in soft tones. "They are seeking to bring about the awakening of their god, a being of fire and wealth. They believe that they can do this through the blood of those with power."

"They're killing us?"

Augusta's laugh was hollow.

"They bleed us. Sometimes they kill us."

She brought Liona's hand to the many small cuts along her arms. Liona received a flash of brass tubes that caught the blood, that funneled it down over the head of a huge grimacing stone idol. Something occurred to Liona.

"They've taken a man named Titus, a legionnaire…"

To Liona's surprise, Augusta's manner changed. She rolled her eyes, looking again like a girl in the marketplace asked about a man she found annoying.

"Oh that old bag of bones? Who cares about him?"

"Keep a civil tongue in your head, you arrogant little mare," said a man nearby. "Who needs you to talk anyway?"

The voice was thin and ragged, but there was an affection there that made Liona blink. She turned to the man in the next cell, who had been sleeping when she was brought in. Now that he sat up, she could see that he was a black man with narrow features. She could see that his right cheek was terribly scarred.

"Are you Titus, of the Roman legion?"

"That I am, madame, though I cannot really render you any Imperial assistance at the moment."

"A man named Lucius Magnus is looking for you."

Titus's eyes widened.

"Still after all this time? I would have thought he would have given me up for dead long since."

Liona grinned.

"If you have soldiered together since you were boys, I believe you know how stubborn he can be."

Anything else she wanted to say was cut off by a clash of metal. Two men came down the stairs again, this time accompanied by the man she had met in Londinium.

"So here we have the seer," he said quietly.

Liona glanced at Augusta and Titus. They both sat quietly with their heads bowed. By her side, her sister was shivering a little. In this position, she could see the fresh wounds at the nape of her sister's neck.

"Yes," Liona said angrily. "By what right do you hold me here?"

"By the right of a god who will walk again. You will not speak to me like that. When you address me, you will refer to me as 'priest' and nothing else."

Liona started to say that she would do nothing of the sort, but Augusta's hand squeezed hers tight. To her shock, tears were falling down Augusta's face. The expression her sister wore was one of pure, abject misery. It curbed her tongue the way nothing else could.

"Yes, priest," she whispered.

The priest considered her for a moment, then he nodded.

"It will serve, or at least we say it will. Bring her."

They pulled her out of the cell and dragged her to a door at the end of the row of cages. As she went by, she could see that there were at least a dozen people in the cells. They all looked at her with pity and a certain relief that it was not them.

The room was simple enough. There was a table at the center of it with a drain in the floor. On the wall were a series of tools that could be found in any blacksmith's shop. But here, they created a panic in her that she had to swallow. A wide hearth across the far edge of the room lit it with an uneasy light. Most oddly of all, there was a fine writing desk in the corner. This is where the priest sat himself.

As Liona watched, he slowly sharpened his quill with a small knife and removed a bottle of ink from his robes. He did this with a calm deliberation that frightened her as much as the iron tools did.

"We are seekers of the truth here, young woman. Right now, your talents are more useful to us than your blood. In your own best interests it is best if you give us the truth, because rest assured, we will find it."

"Yes, priest."

Liona's voice was small and strained. The large man beside her was completely immobile, still as stone.

"Now, then. Your name."

"Liona."

"What is your power?"

"I see the future."

"Very well. How far can you see?"

"A person's life. Sometimes that is a very long way, and sometimes it is very short."

"Do you know who the golden god is?"

"No, priest."

"He is the one who will rise and walk. He is the one who will rule his followers and rain fire on the undeserving."

The priest gestured at the carved face above him, which Liona had not noticed. The face was narrow and fanged, and where the eyes were, the stone was carved to represent flames. Liona knew the gods and goddesses of Rome, who wore human faces and had very human appetites. This god frightened her.

"Look into his future."

"Right now?"

The priest didn't look up. He only gestured at the man who stood by her side.

A meaty hand slapped her to the ground. Her ears rang with it, and a sharp cry was forced between her lips.

"Of course right now," said the priest patiently.

She climbed to her feet, wiping away the blood at her lip. It took her a few moments to calm herself. She closed her eyes, seeking outwards for the truth. She focused on the sharp face, the flaming eyes. She had never sought after the fate of a god before.

Liona opened herself to the future, and it streamed forward with a vengeance. There were images of swords, of fire. She saw the face being smashed under a huge hammer, a figure rising above it to spit down on the broken image. She saw people dragged from a temple. She saw flames. She saw people dying.

Without knowing it, she fell to her knees. The man behind her hauled her up again as if she was as light as a kitten.

"Speak, seer."

She took a shaky breath and relayed what she could of her visions to the priest. Instead of being angry or frustrated, he wrote down her words with care and accuracy, stopping often to ask for clarification.

"And that is what you see?"

"Yes."

"Change it."

Liona looked at him in confusion.

"I cannot change what I see…"

The priest gestured to the man again. The blow knocked her down, but at least this time, she was ready for it.

"Look again."

She did as he said, her head swimming. The vision was the same, and she gasped it out to him. The priest watched her with eyes that were as colorless as water.

"Let's see if we can make you change what you see."

The man heaved her up on the table, strapping her down so that she lay flat. She could not move at all. To her terror, he pulled her shoes from her feet, leaving them bare and completely vulnerable. He reached for what looked like a very thin rod from the wall. She flinched when he tapped it against her bare soles.

"Now, let us see if there is another vision in you."

• • • • •

"Gods above," Hailey muttered through clenched teeth. They had both curled on their sides, Hailey behind Liona, her arm encircling her midriff, and her grip on the other woman fierce. "How did you stand it?"

Hailey recalled her time with the Templar and couldn't suppress a long shudder. Liona covered Hailey's cold hand with her own, rubbing it gently.

"I did what I had to do, dear one," she said. But Hailey heard the strain in her voice. "We all do."

• • • • •

The man dragged her back to the cell because she could not walk. Her voice was hoarse with screaming, but despite it, she had not changed her story. Something about the visions were too powerful. When she was in pain, they were all she could spit out. She didn't have the presence of mind to lie. They had never changed, no matter how hard the man had struck her feet, no matter how much she cried out. It always ended with the broken face of the god on the ground and with people being slain.

The man dumped her in the cell with Augusta, who came forward to hold her.

"We need to get out of here," was the first thing that Liona said, when she could speak without whimpering.

Augusta's laugh was hollow.

"That sounds very familiar."

The days fell into a certain pattern. Liona learned to cringe when the door opened, for she was never sure if it would bring food or a new onslaught of terror. To her shamed relief, they hadn't come for her again. Instead, they would take one of the others, either to the room at the back or up the stairs. She learned to shut her ears to the terrible screams from the back. Sometimes, people who went up the stairs never came back.

She and Augusta shared the food that they were given. Though she had longed to see her sister again, there was nothing for them to say. Instead, they sat in the dark. Liona was waiting for her chance, but Augusta was merely sitting, glad of any moment that did not bring pain.

They were in the dark for what felt like years, but from the meals that were brought, irregularly and often rotten, she knew it had only been a few weeks. As time wore on, she could feel the darkness gnawing away at her. It was harder to think of escape plans, easier to simply hope that whoever they were coming for that day, it wasn't her. She realized that all of the people in the cells had powers that could not be used to harm. They could bring rain, they could heal wounds, they could read minds, but none of them could be considered warriors.

Augusta, who could control fire, explained why she had stopped fighting.

"They killed a man for every wound I inflicted." She said it flatly, but the horror was with her still.

Liona was quiet. She thought, she pondered, and she discarded idea after idea. The prison was taking away her ability to think and to plan, to do anything beyond survive. She hung on to the idea that it was not permanent. It could not be.

Then they came for her and Augusta.

CHAPTER THIRTY-EIGHT

LIONA KNEW THERE was nothing to do but follow their captors up the spiral staircase. When they gained the top, she and Augusta both flinched from the light that was streaming through the glass window high above. It had been a long time since they had seen it.

There were perhaps twenty worshipers around her, all hooded, all wearing the sigil of the golden god. The alter was situated high above the carved face of the god, a sculpture which was at least three times as tall as Liona herself. To Liona's terror, the face was streaked dark with dried blood.

The man tore Augusta from her, dragging her up a short flight of stairs to the altar. She watched with fear as they tied her down. She could see the funnel her sister had spoken of which would gather the blood and spill it over the face of the god.

The priest stood up by her sister, a knife in his hands.

"Fellow brothers of the golden god, we are well met under the spirit of the dragon. Today we have before us a seer of power, a woman who will tell us the future. She will offer us a future of glory and victory, or she will offer us a sacrifice of pain and blood."

"No, please," Liona whispered, unable to take her eyes off Augusta.

The man turned her around so she could face the crowd. She saw eyes that were cold and brutal. She wasn't a person to them. She was a tool, something to offer up in sacrifice.

"Speak, seer," said the priest. "Tell us the future that you see."

At his words, the vision came forward again, the same death, the same battle, the same terror. She nearly threw up trying to hold it back, but she did.

"I see…" her voice broke and she had to try again. "I see a great victory. I see the face of the golden god on every temple in Rome. I see streets lined with cheering people, terrified and joyous. I see the Senate of Rome cleared out, making way for the face of the god…"

She spat forth as much of the false prophecy as she could. Whenever she faltered, Augusta was pricked with a knife. Terrified, she continued until finally, drained, she fell to her knees. Her voice was gone.

"The seer speaks the truth. We dedicate this death to the golden god."

From above, Augusta started screaming, and Liona's mouth opened in horror.

Then there was a terrible crash, and the assembly was littered with shattered glass. People where shouting and screaming. The man by her abandoned his post to go to the aid of the priest above.

Amidst the robed people trying to flee, she could see the dark form of a maddened wolf. It landed all four paws solid on the ground, but that was all the pause it took before leaping at a man close by. It ripped out his throat as casually as a woman would wring the neck of a chicken, and then it was on to the next. Liona heard a heavy flapping that whooshed by, but she was too frantic to pay it any heed.

As soon as she realized what was happening, she raced up the stairs towards her sister. The priest was clutching his heart as if struck by a bolt of lightning, his man trying to carry him away. Augusta was bleeding from a wound above her collar bone, but besides being terrified, she looked whole enough. Liona worked on unbuckling the straps that held her in place, cursing the fingers that were shaky with starvation and fear.

"What's happening? What is that wolf doing here?"

"He's saving us," Liona promised.

One wolf against a crowd of men, it still would have been too much if the gates below hadn't clanged open. A mass of filthy furious people boiled out, and though they might have been mind readers and weather witches, there was no reason they couldn't take the metal implements from the room of torture and use them to deadly efficiency.

Liona had just gotten Augusta free, when a hand lashed out, striking a vicious blow across Augusta's head and snatching Liona up by the nape.

"Halt!" the priest screamed. "Halt unless you want to see this one die!"

To Liona's horror, the battle did stutter to a halt. Gaius, covered in blood, stared up at her with terror. Lucius in his wolf form growled but stilled. The others paused, confused.

No, this cannot be, Liona thought with despair. *It cannot end like this. It cannot.*

The priest was speaking, talking about failure and the just cause of the god. She couldn't take it. Her powers for seeing into the future were great, but useless when she was simply being held. She couldn't take it.

She thought of Augusta, lying so quiet and limp. If only she had Augusta's power. If only she had that fire, that heat. Her hate could have fueled it, she would devour them all.

There was a great noise that sounded like ripping silk. The air around her heated. For a moment, she was blinded by the flash of light, but amidst the cries, she opened her eyes and could see clearly.

The entire platform above the god's head was on fire. The priest and the man who had been holding her burned, their skins blackening in the space of an instant. Augusta had fallen clear, and Liona burned with a white hot flame. Through the heat, she could see Gaius and Lucius, a man now. Her flame dwindled to embers and then went out all together. Liona fell to the ground, every part of her exhausted. She could hear two voices calling her name, but then it all went dark.

• • • • •

Hailey let out a long breath that she hadn't been aware that she was holding. Despite the fact that she lay in the crook of Liona's arm, a leg protectively thrown over the other woman's, she had been afraid for her. Even in her short life, she knew that there were wounds that you could carry forward without showing. She thought of the scars at her side from the Templar's hot poker.

"How strong you must be," she whispered, clinging to Liona, resting her head on her shoulder. As the twilight chill had seeped into the room, they had gotten under the blanket.

"I didn't feel strong at the time," Liona said.

Her voice was light. More than a thousand years stood between this woman now and the girl who had been tortured by monsters wearing human faces.

Hailey sighed a little, drawing the blanket up over them a little more snugly.

"I don't know if I could have been as brave if it were me."

Liona's laugh was soft as she encircled Hailey in her arms.

"We are more alike than you think. We are survivors, you and

I." She paused, as though considering. "Wiccans yes, but also women. We share the same spirit, and perhaps even the same desires."

There was something about the way that Liona said the last word that brought warmth to Hailey's cheeks.

"I understood what you meant, I think," she murmured. "When you loved two men, I can see why you would love both. I am grateful that you never had to choose."

"One thing that I have learned over the course of my long life is that anyone who would force me to choose may be a fine friend, but they will never be my lover. I have had many friends and lovers in my time. Both are a pleasure. Some cross the line back and forth."

"Cross the line…?"

"Mmm, yes. From friend to lover and back again, over the course of the years."

Liona's voice was almost dreamy. Hailey could find it in her to be envious of the other woman's obvious good memories. She realized, however, that at some point, she would be able to make her own.

"You're blushing," Liona whispered. "Why is that, Hailey?"

"I don't know," Hailey mumbled. "You've lived such a long time. You're in my bed. You're telling me about…about…"

"About all the pleasure I've had, as well as the pain? The pain passes, dear one, as does the pleasure. Nothing really lasts. I have come to learn that we must take pleasure where we find it."

Hailey became aware of the way that Liona was rubbing her back. Relaxed and unhurried, her hand moved up Hailey's spine and then back down. Her fingers gently kneaded the flesh at its base. Had Liona's touch gone from one of comfort to something more? Hailey's heart jumped a little at the thought, not quite sure. But then the barest pressure of Liona's hand nudged her hips from behind. Tentatively, Hailey let them move forward. She pressed herself into Liona's side, the connection electric. Hailey's heart fluttered uncontrollably.

"Do you…want to find pleasure with me?" Hailey asked, her voice breathless.

In response, Liona drew her close and kissed her. Her soft mouth enveloped Hailey's, gentle beyond belief. Hailey had never felt the like. Liona's lips caressed hers, clinging and then stroking in equal, rhythmic measure. It was as though Hailey had never been kissed before. She tilted her face up, yearning for more. But when Liona's tongue finally tested her, it wouldn't breach her parted lips. Instead, it danced in the space between them. They had already been lying so close, but now Hailey could feel the luxurious warmth of Liona's body along her own.

"Oh please," Hailey murmured, and Liona laughed a little.

"I won't wear you out, because the infirmary master would be quite cross with me, but my story has been so sad. Let me give you something else to think about. Lie back, dear one."

Hailey did as Liona said, feeling shockingly young and inexperienced under her guidance. She knew that Piers and Kieran were centuries older than her, but it was different with Liona. She was a powerful witch with a thousand years behind her, but she was also beautiful and tough, with a ready smirk and an open laugh. In that moment, Hailey wanted nothing more than to do exactly what Liona said.

As she pleasured Hailey's mouth, her delicate fingertips traced a line down her jaw, then her neck, dipping lightly into the hollow between her collar bones. Moving under the blanket, her light touch skimmed Hailey's breasts, her belly, and slowly circled the dip of her navel. The tender touch was just short of teasing, and way past maddening. Hailey gasped when Liona nipped her lower lip firmly.

"You were made for many things. I hope you understand that," Liona said softly. "You were made for love, and passion, and for pleasure as well. If I give you anything, let me give you the last, for I can see that you have the rest in abundance."

Liona's hand reached down and flipped up the hem of Hailey's nightgown. She sleeked her palm up the curve of Hailey's hip and then down between her thighs. Hailey's breath caught when Liona paused. Then with a soft sigh that Liona drank into her own mouth, Hailey parted her legs.

"So beautiful," Liona murmured. "Have you been with a woman before?"

Hailey blushed.

"No, I–"

Liona silenced her with another kiss, even as those clever fingertips played along Hailey's slit. She was already a little wet. She could no longer deny that the more sensual aspects of Liona's story had aroused her. She wondered if that was what Liona had intended, but she put the thought away. It was unworthy of Liona, and unworthy of her own desire to think so.

Liona's fingers found her clit with startling swiftness, but she didn't rub it. Instead, she ran the pads of her fingers around the already pulsing nub, stroking the flesh surrounding it as much as the sensitive part itself.

Hailey found herself pushing her hips towards the other woman's touch, begging for it with little squeaks and moans. When Liona's fingertips grew dry, she dipped them down further into Hailey's channel, bringing the liquid up to bathe her flesh.

"Close your legs around my hand. Close them tight."

Hailey did as Liona said. In a matter of moments she was riding the other woman's hand, her body trembling and shaking with desire.

"I think I'm going to..."

"Do it." Liona's voice was a whip crack of command.

The ecstasy, bright as the sun, ripped through Hailey's body. She shook hard, crowding against Liona, who never stopped the movement of her hand.

"Keep your legs tight," Liona murmured harshly. "Give me more."

When she kept her legs closed instead of relaxing them, the tremors of her climax died down, but they never finished. To Hailey's shock, they started rising again, faster this time. She was helpless at Liona's touch. She moaned with the need for release, her belly clenching and her channel pulsing.

"Please…" Hailey gasped. But Liona only twisted her hand, coiling even more tendrils of pleasure in Hailey's mound. "Oh gods, Liona, please…"

Her harsh whisper was like a godsend. "Now."

Hailey's back arched and her entire body quaked with her second orgasm. Liona cupped her mound, squeezing her pounding clit. Hailey could hardly get a breath. Her hips were no longer under her control. They obeyed Liona—and she wasn't done.

Hailey's mound pushed into Liona's hand as the woman's fingers cupped her harder, then relaxed, then cupped her again. Tremors of ecstasy rose and fell in time, as she rocked Hailey in her arms. Only when Hailey whimpered into her chest, did the hand that controlled her finally begin to slow. With steadily lessening pressure, Liona's gentle clasp guided Hailey's hips in small, languorous circles. The rhythmic gyration helped the last waves of pleasure to dim. Finally Liona's hand came to a rest.

Hailey collapsed back to the bed as she gasped. She was spent, her belly warm and her limbs wonderfully languid. For several moments, there was only the sound of her panting breaths. When she could finally glance at Liona, the other woman was lapping

Hailey's juices off her hand, a look of pure satisfaction on her face.

"What a little beauty you are," Liona purred. "If I had more time, and I thought you could take it, I would do so many things to you."

Something new in Liona's tone cut through the haze of lingering pleasure.

"Things?" Hailey breathed. Though she tried to stop herself from asking, she couldn't. "Like…like what?"

"Oh, so many things. I would love to see if you could make me climax the way that I made you. I would love to see that adorable rear of yours pink and sore. I might like to see if you could take my fist inside you."

Hailey grew redder and redder with every word, but she couldn't deny the rush of heat that suffused her face and other parts.

"You are a dangerous woman to know," she whispered.

"So I've been told. Sometime, you should come to Rome and see where I live. I'm not so blind that I think you are a single woman, but you could bring your coven master as well."

"It…might not just be Piers."

Liona's laugh was rich and lovely.

"More like me than I thought! Well then, after all of this is over, you'll come to Rome to see me. Bring your lovers. I have so many lovely things to show you."

Hailey almost couldn't think of a future so bright: when she was healed, when she might have Kieran and Piers together. A whole other life waited for her, one that was almost beyond her ability to imagine. She curled up at Liona's side as if to protect herself. It was too much to hope for. She couldn't think of it.

Instead, as the tremors of pleasure Liona had given her dulled to an abiding warmth, her mind drifted back to Liona's story.

"You were telling me of your rescue," she said. "Gaius and Lucius had come for you."

"You asked before if this story had a happy ending. I am willing to call it happy. For the rest, well, as I know very well, and I think you will too, life is very long."

• • • • •

Liona never remembered the time after their rescue very clearly. She knew that they had looted the temple before leaving it. The treasure that they had found allowed them to rent a villa on the edge of what she now realized was Alexandria. The other rescued people stayed with them. She could hear them sometimes, talking, laughing, crying and sometimes shouting.

The villa smelled of roses, and when she could rise from her bed, Liona found out why. There were rose bushes everywhere, small, and left to grow weedy and wild. There was a wrought iron symbol that represented a rose above the villa's gate.

She and Augusta slept in the same bed, eating slowly and healing. Gaius was by their side constantly. He fed them; he allowed them up for walks when he thought they were strong enough; he kept them abed when they were not. Slowly, they gained their strength. Liona saw the shadow in Augusta's eyes, however, and some part of her still feared for the sister she once knew.

Lucius came to see them often, but there was something dark about him. There was something that kept him restless, even when he was sitting beside her. She thought she knew what it was. She clung to his hand, trying not to think about it.

Liona slowly got her voice back. First she could speak only in whispers. After that it was almost a week before she could make a sound. Two weeks after that, Gaius judged that she was healed well enough to do as she pleased, a moment that she had been waiting for.

That night, for the first time since they had found each other again, she left Augusta's bed. She found the room that Lucius and Gaius were sharing. When she joined them there, she raised an eyebrow at them.

"Are you ready for me?" she asked, her tone throaty and nervous at the same time.

Gaius smiled as if the sun would never set. Lucius's grin was pure wickedness.

Almost as one, they lifted her and carried her to the bed, their mouths ravenous on her mouth, her cheeks, her shoulders. They stripped her clothes from her as though they were parchment, leaving her bare and needy.

"Come see what we have learned while you left us," Gaius muttered hotly against her skin.

"I never want to leave you again," she said.

When Lucius paused, she leaned up to wrap her hand around his neck, bringing him down to kiss her.

CHAPTER THIRTY-NINE

LIONA HAD A month of the life that she never knew she wanted. The villa was isolated, an old property from when Rome ruled over the entire region. Now it was left empty, though refugees from the golden god, other people of power, were finding and making it their home.

She and Gaius created a list of work that needed to be done, allocating tasks to those best suited for them. She was delighted to see the way that people healed and rallied. The going was slow, but the villa was turning into a place of safety and warmth.

Lucius was not a part of that. Liona watched as he closeted himself with Titus and increasingly with Augusta too. She knew what was going on.

One evening, Lucius asked Gaius and her to take dinner with him. They followed him to the beach where Titus and Augusta waited for them. There was a feast of cheese, bread, fruit and lamb waiting for them. The sun was setting over the water. Liona ate the food, but it tasted like ashes in her mouth.

"They're still out there," Lucius said finally. "The servers of the golden god. They called themselves the Order of the Dragon, but that is not the only name that they use. They hunt us, and this cannot be allowed to stand."

"Oh?" Gaius said. "And what do you propose to do about it?"

Liona glanced at Gaius, who seemed genuinely startled.

"They're going to go hunting," she said sadly.

Lucius watched her warily.

"This is something that needs to be done," he said. "As long as they are hunting people like us, there will never be any kind of peace."

"And so you will chase them like a hound on the scent, across the world, across the water, far away." She couldn't keep the bitterness out of her voice.

"He's right," Titus said. "They will never stop, and that means that we can't either, not while they live."

She had gotten to know him over the past weeks. He was a gentle man, amused at the aridity of the region and how hard it was for him to summon the clouds that could bring rain. She could see why Lucius loved him so well.

"That doesn't mean we have to go looking for them," Gaius said, his jaw set. "That doesn't mean we have to go looking for a war."

"We can find it or it can find us," Augusta spoke with calm determination. She had healed well after her ordeal, but the scars she bore from the sacrifice table would be with her for years if they ever faded at all.

"All three of you are fighters," Liona said. "You will go with all the love and all the luck I can give you."

Gaius stared at her. "You can't be happy that they are doing this."

Liona's laugh was dark.

"If I thought it would help, I would chain them down until they came to their senses. Gaius, they cannot be swayed from this. In a fashion, they are right."

"In a fashion?" asked Lucius.

He still looked wary. It occurred to Liona that he thought she could change his mind. She knew she could, but it would never stick. He might stay for a month, a half dozen months, or a year, but after that, the call to battle would be too strong for him.

"Gaius and I are building a place for people of power. In a little while, when people are working for pay, we can purchase this villa outright, and it will be truly ours. All who have power will be welcome here. We can help each other, support each other." She paused. "We will be a home for you to come back to."

Lucius came to kneel beside her. Gaius pressed against her other side.

"I love you both," she whispered. "We will have our lives together. We must."

• • • • •

Liona's words faded away. It was full dark now, and Hailey released the breath she had been holding.

"That was it," she whispered, awed. "That was the birth of the coven system. That was the beginning of the Magus Corps."

Liona laughed. Her voice was slightly rusty from having spoken for so long. She sat up to drink a glass of water.

"Yes. Lucius would chase the worshipers of the golden god for decades. Soon he realized that they called themselves something else, and centuries later, they became Templars. Gaius and I stayed at the villa in Alexandria, and we made it into a place for them to come back to. We found healers and mindreaders, flyers and more. We gave them a home after they had been shunned all their lives. Lucius, Augusta, and Titus sent word to us. Sometimes, they hunted together, and sometimes their travels scattered them across the globe. Augusta and Titus came home to us to be married, but they wouldn't stay."

"Did Lucius ever want to come home to you?" Hailey asked,

wanting the answer but also dreading it.

"I don't know. I like to think he would have, but I am likely wrong. He disappeared during the days of the First Crusade."

Hailey could feel tears pricking at her eyes. She threw herself across the bed to wrap herself around Liona.

"Thank you," Hailey murmured. "Thank you for everything you did, everything you endured."

Liona hugged her back just as fiercely. For a long moment, they rocked in each other's arms, each taking comfort for the other.

A crisp knock at the door startled them apart. When Piers opened it, Liona looked as composed as she had before she began telling the story.

"Hello, coven master," Liona said cordially. "Afraid I am keeping your patient up at all hours?"

Piers's smile was slight.

"As you keep reminding me, you will do as you please, and she looks well enough to me. However, I will ask for a moment with her alone. I have news that she needs to hear."

Liona nodded. She turned to give Hailey a last hug.

"The future is what it is," she said. "It will come whether we like it or not, but I will tell you this. If I had to bet, my money is going to be on you."

She left, closing the door behind her.

"She's amazing," Hailey said.

Piers nodded. "I'm trying to ask her to talk to our historian. This is something of a once in a lifetime opportunity." He came to sit on the edge of Hailey's bed, looking startled when she took his hand. "I wanted to tell you that I love you. I…I know things haven't been easy. But I do love you. This is a true thing, and I need to tell you. I love you."

She had been about to say the same words to him, when something else in his voice rang in her ears. There was something more than the words there, something tinged with grief and pain. She couldn't understand it.

"Piers?"

He took a deep breath.

"Major Kieran McCallen is on his way. He should be here in three days time."

Hailey felt her heart leap at the mention of Kieran's name.

"Piers…"

"I understand," he said softly.

The kiss he gave her was gentle. Then he rose to his feet and walked to the door.

"No matter what happens, I love you," he said.

Alone in her room, her thoughts whirled like a carousel.

Kieran is coming back. And Piers loves me.

• • • • •

Hailey's story continues in CLAIMED: Castle Coven Book Four, available now.

For a sneak peek, turn the page.

Excerpt:

CLAIMED

Castle Coven Book Four

An hour later, Hailey knocked gently at the door to Piers's room, holding her long bathrobe tightly around her body.

Piers opened it immediately, sweeping her in his arms. Her damp hair clung to his face, making her giggle a little when he pulled back to spit it out. He carried her to his bed, where he sat down with his back against the headboard and settled her on his lap.

"Is all well? Did he hurt you?"

Hailey shook her head.

"I am going with him tomorrow, Piers," she said softly. "That is not something you can talk me out of. However, I am here tonight, and I want you."

Piers sat very still for a long moment. He was dressed only in a pair of old pajama bottoms, and seated on top of him, she could feel his cock stir.

"Are you sure? I understand that with McCallen here…"

"Are you going to question what I want too?" Hailey snapped, her temper flaring up. "Why is it that when I express something that I clearly want that two of the most important men in my world keep asking me if I'm sure?"

Piers's laugh was soft. He nuzzled her behind the ear, making her purr with pleasure.

"Well, when you put it that way, it makes me sound like an ass," he murmured. "Still, I think I'm allowed to have questions, don't you?"

Hailey started to answer, but she jumped when his hand slid underneath her robe. She was completely naked underneath it. She squirmed as his warm hand crept from her knee up to her thigh.

"What…what questions do you have?" she gasped.

"Well, for example, I'm curious that after you left the room of a man with whom you have a history, you felt the need to shower before you came to see me. Why would you do that?"

His hand stroked over the curve of her hip. The edge of his thumb traced the curling hair of her mound, making her whimper.

"I…I've been in bed for weeks. I wanted the chance to get clean, to just be on my own for a little while…"

"Hmm. It's a good thing that I'm not a more suspicious man. I might have thought you needed to wash something away."

Hailey flushed when she thought of what he was implying. The blush was partially out of embarrassment, but there was something erotic about it as well.

She tumbled out of his lap to lie on her back on his bed. She looped her arm around his neck to bring him close to her.

"Are you worried I slept with him?" she whispered. "Are you worried that I stretched out on his bed, just like I'm doing for you right now?"

She teased the hem of her robe open, showing him her pale, slender body. His breath caught looking at her. He slid his palm inside her robe, running it from hip to ribs. In the cool air, her nipples hardened, but he didn't touch them.

"I know that you didn't," he murmured. "I know that you are a woman of honor, and if you had, you wouldn't have hidden it. Still…would you hate me if some part of me enjoys the idea of you coming from another lover before you came to me?"

Hailey laughed softly, pressing her forehead against Piers's shoulder.

"I have spent the day listening to an amazing story of a woman with two loves. When she told me of the lovers who shared her and who she enjoyed…well, we might have gotten a little carried away."

Piers blinked, the sensual haze halted momentarily as he pieced her words together.

"You…got carried away with Liona di Orsini?"

Hailey nodded, a slight apprehensive flutter in her chest. Playful talk with no basis in reality was one thing. Admitting to an erotic encounter with another person was something quite different, and she understood that.

"Tell me what you did."

Hailey talked about how the other witch had told her about her two lovers, how Hailey's innocent curiosity had led to a deep kiss that had led to more.

"She told me it was just for the pleasure of it, and I don't disagree. It felt…it was wonderful though, for what it was." She paused. "Are you angry with me?"

Piers kissed her comfortingly on her forehead.

"You can do whatever you please, Hailey. You are your

own person, and that is one thing that I have always admired and respected about you. All you ever need to do is to tell me." Piers grinned suddenly, more than a little bit of mischief in his eyes. "On top of that, you managed to bed a living legend. There is really only so angry that I am going to be."

"In all fairness, it was more like she bedded me. Still, I am happy you are not angry at me."

She burrowed into his arms, relieved by his open-mindedness. She wondered if the sensual moment had passed, but when his leg pushed between hers, she could feel that it most definitely had not.

"I like the thought of you with several lovers," he murmured, his voice falling back into that soft, hypnotic register that made her heart beat faster.

She briefly thought of Liona's lost Lucius, who was born to command. Then Piers's mouth was on the tender skin of her neck. She stopped thinking of anything except the man who was holding her then.

"You're such a beautiful and sensual thing, I imagine that it must take a lot to satisfy you."

"I'm not some kind of monster," Hailey protested.

Even as she said it, she could feel herself grow wetter at the thought of it. The idea of being passed from person to person, of having hands of all shapes and sizes on her made her shiver.

"I never said you were a monster. Far from it." Piers paused to suckle gently on first one nipple and then another. "You are a gorgeously sensual, responsive woman. I like the idea of people who are so dedicated to pleasuring you that you fall into a satisfied heap. I want you to be that overwhelmed, that exhausted with your own sensations."

"Would you tell me to satisfy them as well?"

• • • • •

Buy CLAIMED (Castle Coven Book 4) Now

Version 5.0

CLAIMED

Castle Coven Book Four

By Hazel Hunter

CLAIMED
Castle Coven Book Four

With the return of Major Kieran McCallen of the Magus Corps, life becomes complicated for novice witch Hailey Deveraux. Though she's still in love with the dark and brooding man, she's also in love with Piers Dayton, who couldn't be more different. As the coven master of the Castle coven, Piers has given her the protection, space, and love to become her own person.

To her shock and dismay, Hailey learns that Kieran's return isn't just about her. He's on a mission, a dangerous one, for which her talents would be ideal. Though she can't deny him her help, his closed emotions and gruff manner hurt her more deeply than she can admit.

But as the mission unfolds, her love for both Piers and Kieran can't be denied. Though coven master and Corps officer may not like one another, the one thing on which they can agree is Hailey. Emboldened by her time with Liona di Orsini, Hailey makes a request of her two lovers that takes even her breath away.

CHAPTER FORTY

IN HER INFIRMARY bed, Hailey sat bolt upright. She had been abed for what felt like weeks as she recovered from her encounter with the demon. She couldn't take another moment of bed rest, not with the news she had just received.

Kieran is here, and Piers loves me.

Her thoughts spun. It was not so long ago that she had been an outcast in the Wiccan world. She'd been shuttled from coven to coven for her ability to drain power from others to then use as her own. Major Kieran McCallen had been the one to change that. He had fought with her, trained her, believed in her, and finally loved her. He'd drawn her to a place where her life might have some purpose. Then he had abandoned her.

She didn't know what she would have done if Piers Dayton, the coven master of the Castle, hadn't stepped in. In the wake of Kieran's abrupt departure, he had shown her a whole new world. He had opened his amazing coven to her, where learning and the pursuit of the art of magic was held in the highest regard. Though it hadn't been for her sake, he had created what was perhaps the only environment where she could grow and thrive.

Hailey shook her head, trying to straighten her thoughts. They swam around her, making her feel as shaky as a windblown leaf. For weeks now, there had been no word from Kieran. As a member of the Magus Corps, he was a man who went where his commanding officer told him. Some part of her, she now realized, had never expected to see him again.

But he had returned. Her heart clenched with anticipation, but even that did not allow her to forget Piers. Piers was fair where Kieran was dark, a man who flew high above the peaks while Kieran commanded ice and snow. Like most coven masters, he was often at odds with the Magus Corps. He had made no secret of his attraction to Hailey. Their battle with the demon-infested man had driven them even closer together. She had never felt more intimate with another person.

Hailey dressed herself with trembling fingers. She didn't know what was about to happen. Her clothes from the fight with the demon had been destroyed, but she found her favorite green dress in the pile of things that had been brought for her. It hung on her a little, and she made a face. She had lost weight while she had been ill. She was already petite, with little enough fat to spare, but she couldn't think of that now.

She braided her unruly red hair and glanced at herself in the mirror above the bathroom sink. In some ways, she looked like a famished child. Her green eyes were wide and staring, a little too large for her face, which was paler than it had been. She splashed some cold water on it before shrugging. It would have to serve.

Hailey assumed Kieran would be in Piers's study, waiting for her. She stepped into the corridor and almost bumped into a woman who was only a little taller than herself.

Liona di Orsini was one of the oldest Wiccans known. Gifted with the ability to see the future, she had sensed a time of great turmoil and strife for their people. She believed it would begin with the Castle, and so she had come to observe. She was old beyond measure, though her face was that of a girl barely out of her teens. Now she looked at Hailey with a quirked eyebrow.

"Just where do you think you're going, looking like a ragged little urchin-child?" she asked.

Hailey blinked at her. "Piers told me that Kieran was here, that Kieran was here to see *me*."

"And that's how you want to meet him?"

Hailey bristled a bit. "Our romance was conducted while fighting Templars. I doubt he's expecting anything particularly pretty from me."

"It doesn't matter what he expects. Come. You'll thank me for this."

Though Hailey protested, she didn't have it in her to oppose the woman who had shaped the very world she lived in. Liona, along with her lovers Gaius and Lucius, had between them crafted the coven system. It was a world where Wiccans could rally and defend themselves, while the Magus Corps sought out their enemies and destroyed them.

But apparently despite her place in history, all Liona wanted to do now was steer Hailey to her room. Though Hailey protested, Liona shushed her and ran a brush through her hair, braiding it neatly before applying just a touch of makeup.

"There, that's pretty. Get some shoes on, and you'll be fit for a ball."

"I don't want to be fit for a ball," Hailey objected. "I want to be fit for Kieran."

"Oh, well, if that's the case…"

Hailey was turning for the door when Liona swung her around. She found herself pressed against Liona's lithe body. The other woman's hand curled around the nape of her neck, holding her still, while her mouth covered Hailey's. Her warm lips worked sensually, soft but urgent. They enveloped Hailey's, pressing down, kissing her so thoroughly and so deeply that a shocked Hailey thought she might drown. Hailey had barely summoned the presence of mind to respond when Liona let her go, stepping back with a sly grin.

Hailey blushed furiously. The memory of the story that Liona had told her, and what they had done in her bed was fresh in her mind.

"That…that's not…"

"Calm yourself, dear one," said Liona with a smirk. "I'm not laying a claim. I'm just making sure that you're properly warmed for your lover."

Hailey glanced in the mirror. Liona was right. Her eyes were brighter, her lips a vivid red, and there was a natural blush on her high cheeks.

"Maybe you could ask first, next time," Hailey said in exasperation.

But she remembered the pleasure Liona had given her too well to be truly upset.

Liona might have said something in response, but Hailey was out the door. She walked as fast as she could without breaking into a full run. At the door to Piers's study, she paused and took a deep breath. Then she opened the door.

At first, the tableau confused her. She didn't understand why Piers's hand was fisted in Kieran's shirt. She didn't understand why Kieran had his teeth bared.

"You look like you want to kill each other," she blurted out.

They froze, both staring at her for a long moment. Then Piers straightened, released his grip on Kieran's shirt, and stepped back. His brown eyes were as cold as she had ever seen them.

"Forgive us, Hailey. The major and I were having a disagreement, and I…acted rashly."

Kieran straightened out his shirt, taking longer than he had to—much longer. To Hailey's dismay, he didn't look at her. He looked down at his hands. He glanced at Piers. He seemed to be doing everything in his power to avoid looking at her.

"As Coven Master Dayton says, we were having a disagreement. It is nothing for you to concern yourself with."

"Kieran?"

When he had left her in the airport all those weeks ago, she had felt as if she had been destroyed. Kieran was the first person who had seen value in her and what she could do. When he had turned his back on her, she hadn't been able to stand it. It had taken Piers and the entire world that he had built with the Castle to begin healing from that loss. But now she realized she hadn't healed. The wound was still there, waiting for her.

"I am here in my capacity as a major of the Magus Corps," he said. There was something dead in his voice that made her shiver.

"I see." Hailey swallowed hard. "I… What does the Magus Corps want?"

"To test your capabilities."

Hailey had a moment of déjà vu.

"You already did that," she said.

When they had first met, she had been unwilling in the extreme to show anyone her powers. They were a source of fear to many other Wiccans.

"Things have changed," Kieran said.

He moved to the window, turning his back to both Piers and Hailey. When Hailey glanced at Piers, she was shocked to see that his face was a mask of anger. Piers was the coven master of the Castle, but he ruled through pointed negotiation and diplomacy. She remembered that according to Liona's story of the first coven, covens were designed to protect. With a start, she realized that Piers thought that she needed to be protected.

"I came back from my most recent assignment to find another one waiting for me. For this, I was told that I needed the right tool, and…I was told the right tool was you."

"Gods above, but you're a bastard," snarled Piers. "Hailey is a member of my coven. She is no tool, and if you try to treat her like one, I will show you that I am the one who rules here."

Kieran turned to Piers with an expression not unlike the one worn by his wolf, Cavanaugh. Hailey noted with a kind of numb sadness that while Kieran wouldn't look at her, he seemed to have no problem glaring at Piers.

"I am here doing my job, Coven Master. By my commission as a major of the Magus Corps, I have the right to demand what I need."

Piers's smile was hard.

"Not here. Never here. This is not some defenseless hamlet where you can ride in and impress the young girls with those swords that you wear, *Major*. This is the Castle. We never asked for your protection. We never needed it."

Kieran was going to snarl something in response, but Hailey decided that she'd had enough.

"Stop it!"

Startled, both men looked at her.

"You forgot I was standing here, didn't you?" she asked, her own voice crackling with anger. "I am not a tool, but neither am I a damsel that needs to be protected by my coven master. Kieran, you have business with me?"

For the first time, Kieran met her gaze. His blue eyes were unreadable, but for a moment she saw something flicker. She had seen it when they made love, and she had seen it when he walked away from her. It made her heart ache but she bit back the pain.

"Yes, I do," he said. "I and the Magus Corps do not call lightly."

Hailey nodded tightly.

"All right then. I will meet you in the courtyard in half an hour. I need to change."

Kieran looked down with something that might have been shame. Piers started to speak. But Hailey had had enough. She exited, closed the door silently behind her, and ran for her room. When she got there, she locked the door behind her. With short, vicious movements, she took off the dress and threw it as if it were made of fire. The last time she had worn it, Kieran had said goodbye to her. Their reunion had been no better.

She put on her jeans and a thick black sweater instead, stomping her feet into the heavy boots. She went to the bathroom and scrubbed away the makeup that Liona had applied so carefully. It washed away, and with it the hope she hadn't realized she'd held—not until a few moments ago. She looked at herself in the mirror. Her eyes burned with a different glow. Her skin was blotchy red and white. She didn't care. If Kieran wanted to test her ability to wage battle, he had done exactly right.

CHAPTER FORTY-ONE

THE WYOMING SUNSET threw shades of pink, coral, gold and deep blue on the mountains around them. The Castle was an enormous series of buildings nestled in the shelter of space between two peaks. Those peaks offered some shelter from the winds, but the chill still bit deep, particularly as the sun went down.

The practice yard was a broad courtyard that would have seen a few people practicing their gifts even this late. But today, it was empty. Hailey wondered briefly if Piers had cleared it out before their demonstration. Then she decided that she didn't quite care.

Kieran stood at the center of the space, dressed in black and watching the sky. There was something terribly lonely about him just then. He looked as if he was only being held up by his own will, his own power. When he turned to her, however, he was completely professional, as distant and cool as most of the Magus Corps members she had ever met.

"Thank you for coming," he said softly.

Is that all you can say? Hailey wanted to scream. *The things we did to each other, the things we said to each other, and now you simply thank me for appearing?*

Hailey was a woman who burned, not one who froze, but for now, she would give him as good as she got. Later on, there would be space to cry, to weep, to question everything that they were to each other. Now she only nodded.

"The Magus Corps performs an important service for the covens," she said, her voice soft. "There is a debt there."

Kieran flinched a little at the mention of a debt, but he nodded.

"It is not my intention to bring you pain or to drag you along on a task for which you are ill-suited," he said. "I will make this as quick as possible."

He crossed the space to her. She had forgotten how fast he was, how smoothly he could move. Somewhere in the distance, she heard a lonely wolf's howl. She wondered if it was Cavanaugh, trying to make sure that he knew where his master was at all times.

She stared for a long moment as he pulled off his black leather gloves and offered her his bare hand.

"Take what you need, and we will begin."

Her power allowed her to take strength from other Wiccans when she touched their skin. She did not need to use their particular gift, but she could instead turn it towards any task she cared to name. She had flown in the air, channeled fire through her body, and even moved herself from place to place with only a thought. To do all of that, however, she needed to touch another Wiccan's skin.

"You can't be serious," she said.

"Hailey?"

She took two steps back, fast.

"I…I don't want to. Not like…"

Her words spilled out like stones tumbling one after another. She kept shaking her head. She couldn't stand to touch Kieran, not when his blue eyes were so dark and so empty.

"Here, take my hand instead."

To her relief, Liona had appeared behind her. From Kieran's startled glance, she knew that it was more than just a matter of the other witch walking quietly. Liona also had more powers than any other witch she had ever met. She turned to her gratefully.

"This won't hurt you," Hailey promised. "You may be a little tired, but I promise, it won't hurt."

Liona raised an eyebrow at Hailey.

"I very much doubt you could hurt me, no matter how much you took."

Liona turned to Kieran.

"I don't know what your game is, Major, but I do know that you have chosen to play it with someone you don't deserve. Remember that, and remember that a witch's curse is a very long thing."

If Kieran had any feelings about Liona's words, he didn't show it. Instead, he took several steps back, nodding.

"As you please."

Hailey took a deep breath. Liona offered her hand, letting Hailey wrap her cold fingers around it. Liona's hand was warm, and at first, Hailey clutched it for comfort as much as for anything else. Then she remembered that she needed to demonstrate her skills yet again. She steeled herself, closing her eyes.

Taking power was always different from person to person. With Piers, it was like falling into a sea of light. With Kieran, it was like pulling from a vast ocean, deeper than she could imagine. With either of them, she could draw from their supply and feel as if it would never run out.

When she closed her eyes and reached for Liona's power, what she felt was a forest of shadows. Things shifted, creating a gradient in the darkness, but it was so dim. There was something dark and primitive about it. She could feel small yellow eyes on the back of her neck, she could feel the small hairs on her arms rise defensively. Liona's power was as tangled as the roots of a great tree. When she pulled from Liona, she was touching something old and terrifying.

She stumbled back with a soft cry, hugging herself. To her shock, she fell straight into Kieran's arms. Even in that brief contact, there was something achingly familiar about the way he touched her. Her body was more foolish than her heart or her mind. It didn't understand why she couldn't linger, taking in the fresh and oddly cool smell of him, listening to his breath and feeling his arms around her. She pulled away from him.

"Are you all right?" asked Kieran.

If she didn't know better, she would have said that there was something hopeful about his voice. It made her bristle.

"I am, yes." Hailey turned to Liona. "Are *you* all right? That can be draining for some."

Liona's dark eyes were thoughtful.

"Yes…yes, I am. That does tell me something though. Come speak with me later. I have some information that might interest you."

She turned and walked away, leaving Hailey alone with Kieran.

"So, Major," she said, her voice breaking a little on his title. "What do you want to see?"

Kieran's eyes followed Liona for a moment before turning back to her.

"I remember what you could do while we…"

"While we were together?" she asked.

He nodded.

"I would like to see what you can summon up in the way of fire. You were able to summon up flames when last we spoke, but I need to know whether you can make them burn hotter."

There was that strange hope again, but Hailey pushed it out of her mind. If he wanted to pretend that they had never touched each other, so be it.

She nodded icily, stepping back from him.

It did not matter that Liona was skilled in far seeing. She had the power that Liona carried within her. Now she could wield it exactly how she chose.

She thought of flame. She thought of the hearts of volcanoes, and the way the world split to reveal a core of magma underneath. She thought of heat that could melt through steel, through rock, through things far stronger than human flesh and bone.

She heard a deep roar, like the sound of an oncoming train, followed by a snapping in the air.

When she opened her eyes, she realized that she was standing in a column of flame that was so hot it was a bluish white. Beyond the sheet of fire, she could see Kieran, staring at her with wide eyes.

She reached through the flame in wonder. She knew that it would not hurt her. Instead, licks of the white flame danced on her fingertips. There was a faint ticklish sensation where the flame kissed her. When she walked forward or back, the flame walked with her. It was a good thing that the ground of the practice field was nothing but packed dirt. Beneath her feet, it singed to black, but it did not catch.

Without thinking about how she could do such a thing, she brought a lick of the flame to dance on her fingertips before sending it flying from her. That narrow and deadly point of heat flew from her fingertips to embed itself on the stone wall on the far side of the courtyard.

The fire felt pure and beautiful. It was only with a sigh that she let it go. She was shocked by how cold she felt immediately after.

"That was more than you could do all those weeks ago,"

Kieran observed.

"It has felt like a very long time for me," she said. Her words came out softer than she thought they would. She thought that they would be recriminating, but instead, they were nearly a plea.

"I will need to see more," Kieran said, looking away.

He offered her his hand again, but this time it was Piers, falling out of the sky.

He was a flyer, given to the high cold air. Flyers were known for their whimsical and fickle nature, but now she wondered if they should be known for their tempers as well.

"That looked like it could singe the clouds," Piers observed. "What more do you need to see?"

"I was sent to do a job, Coven Master," said Kieran, and now he sounded more tired than anything else.

Hailey stepped between them to prevent another fight.

"Piers, will you give me your hand?"

Piers didn't hesitate before rolling up his sleeve. Taking a deep breath, she touched her fingertips to the inside of his wrist. Even that gentle touch was enough to feel his strength, his energy. Where Liona was a primeval power rooted in the earth and reaching towards the sky, Piers was a sea of light. Sometimes, she felt as if she could drink it all in, and then see to the end of the universe.

She pulled her power from him, feeling the warmth settle in her bones like a kind of embrace from the man himself. She knew that taking power from him would not harm him or even overly drain him. When she shared power with someone she was close with, it left both of them stronger than they were before.

"What would you like to see now?" she asked, her tone measured.

"I would like to see you fly." Kieran's voice was quiet. She wondered if she heard a kind of defeat there.

Without a word, she pushed off from the ground, leaving the two men far below her. There was some remnant of the flames with her still. The thin mountain air should have brought a chill to her exposed skin, but the coolness was almost welcome this time. She moved through the air like a fish, completely confident of her ability to go where she pleased. She knew how to use her body to steer herself, to fall and to let the wind catch her, and to power her way even higher.

Piers was a skilled flyer with a lifetime of experience, but her own ability was raw power. She knew that she could stay aloft for hours. Instead, she spun nimbly head over heels before showing Kieran how fast she could go by looping around the towers of the Castle.

When she lighted back on her feet, she risked a smile at Piers. There was a kind of fierce pride in his gaze, something that told her that he would always be there and ready to defend her, but that he was more than happy to let her defend herself as well.

Kieran's expression was a little more difficult to decipher. There was pleasure there, pride like there had been in Piers's face, but there was a kind of defeat as well. She couldn't read it, couldn't even begin to do so.

"Kieran?"

He nodded, distant and cool as a glacier.

"I want to see if you can change your shape next," he said. Now they could both hear a desperate tone in his voice, something that scrabbled at the edges of his face for purchase. "It's fairly difficult. Shapechangers tend to bloom later. It can take them years before they have complete control of what they can do."

Kieran sounded like he was warning her off.

Hailey tossed her head in disregard.

"I'll try anything once," she said, forcing an edge of bravado into her tone. “Piers, if you don’t mind?”

“No. I need you to pull that power from me this time. Otherwise, there’s no reason to do this at all.”

Hailey bit her lip, nodding. Piers looked furious. If he had any kind of reason to step in, she knew that he would have.

“All right. I… All right.”

She didn’t realize she was holding her breath until she stepped a little closer to Kieran. Her body still recognized his. Even if he was as distant as a glimmering star, some part of her simply didn’t understand why she didn’t embrace him, or why he didn’t reach for her.

He offered her his hand. Closing her eyes, she touched his bare skin with just her fingertips. His power rolled and tossed like the sea in a storm. It turned over and over. When she went to draw it from him, she had a sensation of being drowned, of being carried under. It was still so deep and so powerful, but unlike the calm that he had always had before, now there was something deeper and crueler about it.

She broke away from him with a cry, staring at him with wide eyes. Piers started for her, but she shook her head.

“What happened to you?” she whispered.

Kieran paused. Then he shook his head.

“Nothing that I can speak of,” he said finally. “Can you pull power from me or not?”

“I can.”

She thought about her shapechanging transformation for a moment. The first candidate that came to mind was the shape of an owl, like her own familiar, Merit. Merit lived in the forests outside the keep. She brought death on beautifully silent wings. While she knew Merit’s form well enough, Hailey decided that the prospect of needing to fly was too intimidating.

Instead, she thought of Cavanaugh, Kieran’s wolf. Cavanaugh

was a Mackenzie Valley wolf, one of the largest species in the world. He was powerful and unforgiving in a way that prey animals never were. It was clear that he only recognized Kieran as his pack, though by the end he had allowed Hailey to touch him as well.

She closed her eyes, reaching for the power that she had pulled from Kieran. She imagined her body twisting and changing, losing fat, gaining muscle. She imagined dark hair sprouting all over her form, she thought of a nose that was far keener than hers and eyes that could see through the dark.

She was aware of a faint pain, of popping noises that would have disturbed her if she had thought of them. She wasn't sure how long it had gone on, but when she looked up, the world looked very different. She turned in a circle to see herself before glancing up at Piers and Kieran.

They both stared at her. Piers moved first.

"Though I have to admit I prefer you as a woman, you make a very fine wolf, Hailey."

He offered his hand. To Hailey's intense irritation, her first instinct was to sniff it. Instead, she took his hand between her powerful jaws, closing her teeth on his skin with the utmost gentleness. Her senses—sensitive and marvelous—could detect the fact that his heart started beating faster, that the pupils of his eyes were dilated black. He was fascinated, but he was afraid too. Some wolfish part of her liked that a great deal.

"That is amazing."

She turned to Kieran, cocking her head curiously. There was something rueful in his face too. Without thinking about it, she approached him, thrusting her nose in his direction. Even as a human, she could sense something was off about him. Even when she had a poor human nose, she knew something was wrong. Now that she was a wolf, she could sense even more. The scent that rolled off him was one that her human brain labeled with the word 'sorrow,' though her wolf brain was more inclined to call it a sickness, albeit one of the soul.

She whined deep in her throat, flicking her ears back.

Kieran's laugh was hollow.

"In just a few short weeks, you have fulfilled the promise that both Piers and the Magus Corps saw in you."

"The Magus Corps?" Piers's voice was sharp. "And what exactly does the Magus Corps have to say about Hailey's *promise*?"

Kieran glanced at him.

"The Magus Corps is more than just a club for bullies and time wasters, no matter what you seem to think of it, Coven Master. We need resources just as your precious Castle does, and we also understand that we must grow them up carefully." He sighed. "Hailey, will you please return to your human form? I have something I must tell you."

Hailey almost wanted to deny him. The wolf form was so sensitive and so wonderful. She wondered what it would be like to go wandering through the forest. She wondered what it would be like to go running in the night. She wondered what it would be like to chase down prey. The idea of killing something in this form, of feeling the red gush of blood and life over her tongue woke her up. She was repulsed by it and at once fascinated and excited. It jarred her so thoroughly that she gave up her wolf form entirely, rising up to stand on her own two feet again.

Kieran was there, steadying her with a hand on her shoulder.

"Are you well? I should not have asked you to do that without any preparation."

"Leave me be, Kieran," she said, something in her snapping. "I can't take this. If I meant so little to you that you were willing to avoid me until the Magus Corps sent you my way again, don't pretend that you care when I'm just shaky on my feet!"

He stepped back as if stung. For a moment, it was like she had ripped him open. She could see the shock and the hurt on his face. She could no longer believe that their parting was pain only for her. There was grief in him as well. He covered it up again quickly, but she could never deny that she had seen it.

"Rightly so. My apologies."

For a moment, he couldn't even look at her. When he spoke again, there was a deadness to his voice.

"Hailey, I am on a mission for the Magus Corps. At the moment, the scope of the mission is unknown, but my commandant believes, and I agree with him, that this is going to be more than what we usually deal with."

"I fail to see how that is an issue for anyone here," Piers said icily.

Kieran ignored him.

"What this means is that I need you to come with me. You have shown yourself fully capable and fully in use of powers that are commanded by no one in the Magus Corps."

"The Magus Corps has no authority at the Castle," snapped Piers. "There is absolutely nothing that you can do to take Hailey out of here, nothing that you can do to drag her out against her will."

Kieran turned to Piers. He looked almost relieved to be talking to the coven master instead of to Hailey.

"What you say and want means very little to me, Dayton. I am here on a mission, and I owe my loyalty to a higher power than you."

Piers's eyes narrowed.

"How fascinating. What you need to understand, Major, is that I owe my loyalty to Hailey. Does that make any sense to you at all? Do you understand what that means? That means that it is my life's work keeping her and the other members of my coven safe. That goes far beyond your mandate and far deeper."

Kieran's face was split in a snarl. At that moment, he looked more like Cavanaugh than Hailey would have thought possible.

"My business here is not with you–"

"Stop it!"

Hailey's voice echoed across the practice yard. She could hear the way the sound reverberated through the thin mountain air.

Both men froze, staring at her. She was nearly trembling with rage and with emotion.

"I need to understand this very clearly," she said at last. It occurred to her that her voice was strung as tight as piano wire.

"I will of course answer any questions that I can," Kieran said. His voice was soft and subdued, as if she were a wild animal that he did not want to harm or startle.

"You came here to recruit me for a mission that the Magus Corps thinks is dangerous. Is that correct?"

"It is."

"You came here because…someone decided that I was the best tool to use for the job. Who was that?" Kieran's pause was long enough that her nerves frayed. "You need to tell me, Kieran," she said, her voice growing louder. "I need to know if it was your commandant or…or Stephan or you that decided that I had the right skill set to be brought in for whatever it is that you are planning."

"It was my commandant," Kieran said at last. "Hailey, you must believe me. When I submitted my report on the mission that…on the mission, I related what we accomplished together. I had no idea that it would be used to count you among the resources that the Magus Corps commands."

Hailey flinched. There had been a part of her that hoped, that prayed, that Kieran had used this opportunity to come see her. She wanted him to want her the way he had, the way that she still wanted him. That hope died a hard death in her heart. She struggled to keep her voice level.

"This mission. What is happening?"

"Over the last seven months, we have lost nearly as many Magus Corps officers. None of them were in situations that we consider normal, and we were able to recover none of the bodies. This has taken place in the Alps, mountainous cold territory that makes me a good fit for the mission. This region has long been known for its Templar activity, something that makes many of the Magus Corps nervous. We have considered sending in an entire strike team, but the concern is that they would be too obvious."

"So they want to send you and me in instead?"

Kieran nodded.

"Throughout the history of the Magus Corps, smaller teams tend to have a greater level of success than larger ones. They saw the file that I created. They saw your powers."

A sudden thought occurred to Hailey, one so terrible that it momentarily made her head swim. She stared at Kieran.

"What else was in that report?" she asked. It felt as if her entire body had gone numb.

"Hailey?"

"Kieran, tell me what else was in that report. Did you tell them everything that we did together? Did you tell them that I was…I am in love with you?"

Kieran's face had gone white.

"Hailey…"

"You're not saying no," she whispered. "Dear gods above, you filed me in your report like your swords or your gear. That's why they sent you."

Kieran started to deny it, but there was nothing he said that would have convinced her otherwise. It was too clear. The Magus

Corps saw her as a tool to be used. When they made that decision, it only made the most sense to send the person who could use it in the most able fashion.

She couldn't take any more.

She shook her head, turned and walked away.

CHAPTER FORTY-TWO

IN TIMES OF trouble, Hailey had a habit of seeking the highest ground she could. When she was staying with the Angioli coven in Italy, she often took refuge in the choir loft. Though the Castle was short on choir lofts, there were still many odd corners and closets where she could hide.

She found an unused bedroom in one of the towers, a place where someone had stored a small library's worth of books before abandoning them. She sat on the window seat, gazing out over the dark mountainside. She had been so happy to come to the Castle. It had been an island both in time and in space. It marked the first place where she had felt truly safe, truly cared for. It was a community that was for her. She gave back to it with every bit of will and power that she could. Now she was being asked to leave it again.

The only light in the room was from a small lamp. She sat in the dimness thinking about what it would be like to pull back from this place, to leave it. Even in such a short time, the Castle had become her home. The idea of leaving it made her feel hollow and empty.

There was a knock on the door behind her. Hailey's first impulse was to hide, to pretend that there was no one in the small room. Then she was disgusted with her own cowardice.

"Come in," she said.

It only took her a moment to recognize Piers's silhouette in the door. He entered, closing the door behind him, but in deference to her sensibilities, he didn't turn on the light. She felt a surge of the love that she had for him. It was warm and lovely. She remembered that she could trust him.

In the light of the lamp, he looked uncertain, almost nervous. She held her hand out to him.

"Come sit with me," she said softly. "I need you close."

Obediently, he came to sit at her side on the window seat. She only hesitated a moment before she leaned against him, burrowing into his side. His arm around her felt like the warmth that she had been seeking her entire life.

"You have a decision to make," he said finally.

When she tried to sit up, he held her closer. Giving in, she snuggled closer against him. In the dimness of the room, it felt like everything outside was a story, a fairytale that was designed to frighten her. This was real.

"He cannot take you from here unless you wish to go. That is not something that I will permit. Unless you say that you are willing to go with him, you will remain right where you are, and he will leave empty-handed." Piers paused. "I understand that you have a history together."

"Piers…"

"It is one that I respect. Hailey, if you want something, I think I would move heaven and earth to get it for you. I understand that he has been someone very important to you. The fact that he had a hand in making you who you are, that alone would be enough."

"Piers, I do love you. Please, you must understand that as well."

Piers's smile was crooked.

"And if I thought that love was enough to make the world

work the way that I wish it to, I would be a far happier man, I think. I love you as well. However, I'm not so great a fool as to think that you don't love Kieran McCallen."

Hailey bit her lip.

"But we're not talking about love right this moment," Piers said. "What we are talking about is a choice that you have to make. It is up to you whether you want to aid Kieran McCallen on his mission. However, that is your choice. You do not need to fear him or the Magus Corps. They may stamp and bluster. Let them. There is no way on earth they can pull you from these walls if you do not wish to go."

"But...but they help Wiccans. They protect us."

Piers shook his head.

"They may do that for other covens. I would even guess that they do it very well and very willingly. However the Castle has always been different. We have always been a place that is self-sufficient. We protect our own, and we do it without needing to resort to the services of the Magus Corps. Things are different for other covens. I understand that. However, they have no authority here."

Hailey thought for a moment.

"Thank you," she said at last. "I need to learn more to decide what I want to do. But Piers, what if I decide to go with him?"

Piers was silent for a long moment.

"Then you will. That is your decision, and just like Kieran cannot force you to go, I will not force you to stay. What I want for you, what I want for every Wiccan, is freedom of choice. You are not my prisoner, and you are not his tool. You are a person who has been asked to help someone who needs your skills—or thinks he needs them."

Hailey's smile was faint, but it was real.

Slowly, she leaned up to kiss him. The kiss that they shared was almost chaste. They had only recently begun to learn each other's bodies. She could feel the spark there, lying under the surface and ready to get fanned into flames at a moment's notice. She warmed herself against it for a moment before turning away.

"I want to come to you tonight," she said huskily. "That is one thing I want. However, before I do that, I need to talk to him."

Piers's face was very still, betraying nothing.

"Go and be quick, then," he said softly. There was a certain heat to his voice that made Hailey blush. "I'll be in my quarters, come looking for me when you are done."

Feeling more calm, if not more in control, Hailey hopped off the window seat and followed Piers to the door. When she stepped into the brighter light of the corridor, her eyes widened.

"Piers, what happened to your chin?"

There was a dark bruise on Piers's face. It was a vivid purple. He had definitely not had it when she'd been with him earlier.

"Some understandings are created through fair words and considered speech. Some…are not. Let's leave it at that."

Hailey decided to let it go. With another gentle kiss, she walked down to the guest quarters where she knew Kieran was going to be sleeping.

• • • • •

When she knocked on the door, she could hear a stirring inside. Kieran opened the door, and immediately she presented him with a piece of cold steak from the kitchen.

"I figured you would need this."

Kieran frowned, but then he shrugged, a rueful look on his face. It would have been useless to protest given the black eye that he bore.

"Can I come in?"

He nodded, gesturing her in. The guest quarters were quite bare, but it struck her suddenly and with a forceful blow how little he traveled with. She understood in a vague way that the life of a Magus Corps officer must be a rather barren one, but it had never quite occurred to her how barren it might be. Kieran's effects seemed to consist of a small duffel bag and a larger bag that she knew contained his weapons.

She seated herself on the arm of the couch, watching him as he sat down on the other end. He pressed the cold cut of meat against his bruise and picked up the tumbler of alcohol that he had obviously put down to answer the door.

The quiet stretched between them, but Hailey was patient. She had become strong in the face of silence. Finally, Kieran spoke.

"I didn't want to come here," he said.

Hailey felt a brief pang at that, but she kept her face calm.

"Why is that?"

"Because I didn't want you mixed up in this. You… You already have more experience in killing Templars than most recruits do in their first year. You've done enough. You've found your place."

"Have I?"

Kieran quirked an eyebrow at her.

"You fit here the way a hand fits in a glove. You've grown here even in the short time you've been here. You deserve to be here, Hailey. I didn't want to be the one who took that away from you."

Did you intend to leave me at the airport the way you did? Is it only your humanity that twinges when you think of me? Do you think of me at all?

"I need to know more about what you want me to do," she said instead. "I need to know what is at stake."

Kieran shook his head.

"I've already told you most of what I know. There is a place in the Alps that seems to be sucking in Magus Corps officers. They go missing, and they're never heard from again. We believe that there's Templar activity in the area. We need to find out what's going on. The last person to disappear there was of an equal rank with mine. This is not a simple mission, and I did not want to involve you."

"Simply because of your conscience?"

She was watching him closely. Kieran was a master of ice and cold. He could be as still as a frozen pond if he wished. She saw him stiffen as if someone had taken a whip to his shoulders.

"I can't… I don't want you to make a decision based just on…"

"I'm going," Hailey said, her voice crisp. She hadn't known it before she said it, but when she said it, she knew that it was the truth. "It's more than just the Magus Corps having done me a good turn. If there are people out there in trouble and I can help them, I can't stay safe behind Piers's walls." She paused. "What I need to know is why you were so reluctant to come. You are devoted to your work and to your brothers in arms. You believe in what the Magus Corps does and stands for. Why would you hesitate when you have a tool like me here? Why would you even pause before–"

Hailey's words were cut off when Kieran jumped to his feet. He laid his alcohol and the cut of meat aside. He crossed the space between them to loom above her.

"Gods above Hailey, don't!"

That cry stopped her the way that even a slap wouldn't have. His voice was hoarse, as if he had been running for a long time. It occurred to her somehow that he was exhausted, that he had been even before she ever met him.

She started to say something, but then she was interrupted by his mouth on hers. She nearly tipped off of the arm of the couch. Instead, she had to cling to him for stability.

She should have been terrified. Perhaps she should have been furious. But this was Kieran, and there was something about him that was so right. Perhaps it would always seem right to her, no matter what was between them.

Hailey clung to his straining body, kissing him back with all of the passion that she felt for him. When his tongue pushed between her lips, she whimpered, pulling it in and wanting more. She could no more stop her hands from roaming his body than she could stop the string of broken sounds she was making.

His body was shaking when he pushed her down to the couch. She could feel the weight of his body on top of hers. She could feel how much he wanted her. The pleasure was overwhelming. She was ready to give herself up to it.

Then she pulled her mouth from his. Her hand came up and settled over his lips.

"No, Kieran, let me up."

He moved as if he had been shocked. He stumbled back from her. His face was pale, and his blue eyes were nearly black from the way his pupils were blown wide.

"Hailey, gods, forgive me, I didn't mean…I wouldn't do anything against your will…"

Hailey sat up, her head swimming. If she stayed on the couch, if she stayed on her back with that beloved body looming over her, she didn't think that she would be able to resist him. The pull between them was powerful, but she couldn't give in to it, not right now.

"I never thought you would do anything against my will," she said. "I swear it. I know that much about you." She stood up, straightening her clothes and stepping wide around him. "There may be people in trouble, and I can help them. If I'm realistic about it, that is really all that I need to know."

There was a moment where Kieran could have taken her in his

arms, explained what he felt to her. That would have been all that it took for her defenses to fall.

The moment passed.

"Hailey…" Her name was a whisper on his lips.

"I'll see you in the morning, Kieran. I'll be ready to leave no later than noon tomorrow."

She wanted a hand to wrap around her wrist, she wanted him to ask her to stay. Instead, she walked out of the room, shutting the door gently behind her.

• • • • •

An hour later, she knocked gently at the door to Piers's room, holding her long bathrobe tightly around her body.

Piers opened it immediately, sweeping her in his arms. Her damp hair clung to his face, making her giggle a little when he pulled back to spit it out. He carried her to his bed, where he sat down with his back against the headboard and settled her on his lap.

"Is all well? Did he hurt you?"

Hailey shook her head.

"I am going with him tomorrow, Piers," she said softly. "That is not something you can talk me out of. However, I am here tonight, and I want you."

Piers sat very still for a long moment. He was dressed only in a pair of old pajama bottoms, and seated on top of him, she could feel his cock stir.

"Are you sure? I understand that with McCallen here…"

"Are you going to question what I want too?" Hailey snapped, her temper flaring up. "Why is it that when I express something that I clearly want that two of the most important men in my world keep asking me if I'm sure?"

Piers's laugh was soft. He nuzzled her behind the ear, making her purr with pleasure.

"Well, when you put it that way, it makes me sound like an ass," he murmured. "Still, I think I'm allowed to have questions, don't you?"

Hailey started to answer, but she jumped when his hand slid underneath her robe. She was completely naked underneath it. She squirmed as his warm hand crept from her knee up to her thigh.

"What...what questions do you have?" she gasped.

"Well, for example, I'm curious that after you left the room of a man with whom you have a history, you felt the need to shower before you came to see me. Why would you do that?"

His hand stroked over the curve of her hip. The edge of his thumb traced the curling hair of her mound, making her whimper.

"I...I've been in bed for weeks. I wanted the chance to get clean, to just be on my own for a little while..."

"Hmm. It's a good thing that I'm not a more suspicious man. I might have thought you needed to wash something away."

Hailey flushed when she thought of what he was implying. The blush was partially out of embarrassment, but there was something erotic about it as well.

She tumbled out of his lap to lie on her back on his bed. She looped her arm around his neck to bring him close to her.

"Are you worried I slept with him?" she whispered. "Are you worried that I stretched out on his bed, just like I'm doing for you right now?"

She teased the hem of her robe open, showing him her pale, slender body. His breath caught looking at her. He slid his palm inside her robe, running it from hip to ribs. In the cool air, her nipples hardened, but he didn't touch them.

"I know that you didn't," he murmured. "I know that you are a woman of honor, and if you had, you wouldn't have hidden it. Still…would you hate me if some part of me enjoys the idea of you coming from another lover before you came to me?"

Hailey laughed softly, pressing her forehead against Piers's shoulder.

"I have spent the day listening to an amazing story of a woman with two loves. When she told me of the lovers who shared her and who she enjoyed…well, we might have gotten a little carried away."

Piers blinked, the sensual haze halted momentarily as he pieced her words together.

"You…got carried away with Liona di Orsini?"

Hailey nodded, a slight apprehensive flutter in her chest. Playful talk with no basis in reality was one thing. Admitting to an erotic encounter with another person was something quite different, and she understood that.

"Tell me what you did."

Hailey talked about how the other witch had told her about her two lovers, how Hailey's innocent curiosity had led to a deep kiss that had led to more.

"She told me it was just for the pleasure of it, and I don't disagree. It felt…it was wonderful though, for what it was." She paused. "Are you angry with me?"

Piers kissed her comfortingly on her forehead.

"You can do whatever you please, Hailey. You are your own person, and that is one thing that I have always admired and respected about you. All you ever need to do is to tell me." Piers grinned suddenly, more than a little bit of mischief in his eyes. "On top of that, you managed to bed a living legend. There is really only so angry that I am going to be."

"In all fairness, it was more like she bedded me. Still, I am happy you are not angry at me."

She burrowed into his arms, relieved by his open-mindedness. She wondered if the sensual moment had passed, but when his leg pushed between hers, she could feel that it most definitely had not.

"I like the thought of you with several lovers," he murmured, his voice falling back into that soft, hypnotic register that made her heart beat faster.

She briefly thought of Liona's lost Lucius, who was born to command. Then Piers's mouth was on the tender skin of her neck. She stopped thinking of anything except the man who was holding her then.

"You're such a beautiful and sensual thing, I imagine that it must take a lot to satisfy you."

"I'm not some kind of monster," Hailey protested.

Even as she said it, she could feel herself grow wetter at the thought of it. The idea of being passed from person to person, of having hands of all shapes and sizes on her made her shiver.

"I never said you were a monster. Far from it." Piers paused to suckle gently on first one nipple and then another. "You are a gorgeously sensual, responsive woman. I like the idea of people who are so dedicated to pleasuring you that you fall into a satisfied heap. I want you to be that overwhelmed, that exhausted with your own sensations."

"Would you tell me to satisfy them as well?"

Hailey didn't know where the thought had come from, or perhaps she did. At the heart of her, there were sensual daydreams and fantasies that had always flitted in and out of focus. Some of them were simple enough, but others were strange things—things that she never thought could be true. Then she had met Kieran and then Piers. She had flown over Italian mountains and battled a demon. She had fought with men who wanted nothing more than to end her life. She had been bedded by a woman who had seen countries rise and fall.

When she could do six impossible things before nightfall, it made what she did after nightfall seem commonplace.

"Make you satisfy them… How exactly do you propose to do that?"

Piers's voice was so soft it was nearly a purr. There was a certain knowledge to his tone that told her that he knew exactly what she was asking, but he was still going to make her say it.

"I…with my hands? My mouth?"

"Is that all, beautiful Hailey? Do you think I would let you stop there?"

His hand drifted down between her legs. She found herself opening for him without a single protest. She had allowed him a measure of control over their lovemaking before. This felt natural, a little bit of pretend that she could enjoy in the darkness with him.

"You wouldn't let me stop there?" she asked softly. His answering laugh was slightly menacing.

"Perhaps I would be possessive and keep some parts of you to myself, but you truly are such a beautiful woman. I can see why others would want to touch you, hold you, explore you."

On the last two words, his fingers slid along her slit, parting her folds easily to find her wet and waiting. She whimpered, clinging to his hand, but she spread her legs wider still. She wanted him to have all of her. She could feel his love thrumming through his body, through the words that he said to her, even through the gentle touch of his hands.

"Would you watch?" she asked, her voice high and soft. She moaned when he slid a single finger into her depths. "Would you want to see what they did to me?"

"Of course," he responded, his voice oddly tender for the

sentiment. "You are completely precious to me, and I always want to make sure that you are well taken care of. That is all I have ever wanted."

She ended up on her side with her back to Piers's chest. She whimpered as he whispered into her ear what all of those people would do to her, how he would take such good care of her. Wrapped in his arms, she felt completely safe. It was a strange sort of freedom to be able to explore this part of herself.

Soon she was arching and moaning, pushing herself on to his fingers while he ground his erection against her rear. She cried out when he nipped at her earlobe, but all she knew was that she wanted more and more.

She could feel the heat between them rising further and further, higher and hotter. She knew she was going to climax soon, but that wasn't what she wanted.

"I want you inside me," she moaned. "I want you to be inside me, please!"

Piers's laugh was ragged. He planted another kiss on her shoulder.

"I could never deny you anything," he whispered. He moved briefly to slide a condom over his erection, but then he was back again, totally nude. Hailey thought that he was going to move her, either to her back or up to her knees, but instead he left her lying on her side.

She watched wide eyed as he straddled her lower leg while throwing her upper leg over his shoulder. The position stretched her legs nearly as wide as they would go. When she felt the blunt tip of his cock slide against her wet slit, she moaned.

"Do you like this position?" he asked softly. "Try and close your legs."

Hailey did as he asked, realizing that she couldn't. She was so open to him, so very vulnerable. In that moment, however, she still knew that he would never harm her, never hurt her.

"I want you so much," she said, and he pressed forward.

He entered her with one long thrust. Then he started moving like a man possessed, forcing wave after wave of sensation on her. She could feel the rising tide of pleasure come up over her, but though she squirmed and begged, it wouldn't crest. To have her pleasure right there but to feel it denied to her was impossible. Her gasping sobs took on a pleading note.

"Here, show me," he said.

Piers paused his thrusts to take her hand. To her shock, he slid it down to her mound.

"Show me what you like," he whispered. "I want you to climax for me, darling."

Hailey's first thought was that she had been pushed too far. She had of course pleasured herself, but it was a secret and furtive thing. She had never done so with anyone watching, let alone the man who was now loving her so well.

Then she was filled with a surge of love and confidence. She knew that Piers would like what he saw. She knew that he would enjoy it. That was all the encouragement that she needed to do as he said, touching herself the way she did when she was alone. The familiar sensations flowed with the feel of him inside her and above her.

The tension built up low in her body, rising like smoke from a fire. When her climax hit her, she cried out, digging the nails of her free hand into Piers's arm. She could feel his muscles tense and flex as he thrust into her before he went still and shaking.

Through the haze of her own pleasure, she wondered what it would be like to do this without the condom, to feel him spill inside her, hot and liquid.

He disentangled their limbs and removed the condom before coming back to hold her. Her eyes were drifting shut when he planted a kiss behind her ear.

"Did you enjoy that?"

Hailey's laugh was tired and drowsy.

"I have absolutely no complaints, Coven Master. I enjoyed it a great deal. I would direct you to how loud I was, but you know. You kind of had your own thing going on there."

"My own thing?" Piers laughed.

It made him sound surprisingly boyish. She knew that he was hundreds of years old and charged with the running of a large community, but just then, he only seemed a handful of years older than she was.

"You need to tell me what you like and what you don't like," he said more soberly. "In the heat of the moment, it is very easy to get carried away."

Hailey opened one eye to look up at him.

"I don't mind if you carry me away," she said softly. "And trust me to say no if something really hurts, or even if I don't like it, all right? I'm fine."

Piers sighed and nodded, even if he didn't exactly look convinced.

"Sleep well, love. We have a long day in front of us tomorrow."

Hailey would have wondered what he meant by that 'we,' but she was so exhausted by her day, and what had gone before, that sleep claimed her before she could get the words out.

CHAPTER FORTY-THREE

TO HAILEY'S DISAPPOINTMENT, Piers was not there when she woke up the next morning. She had been hoping to speak with him, to let him know what he meant to her. In her heart of hearts, she had been looking forward to some morning play as well.

Well, I suppose I will see him at some point before Kieran and I leave.

She went to her own chambers, and then to the supply rooms where the cold weather gear was kept. She could figure out what she needed well enough. The Alps were presumably not so different from the cold of the Wyoming mountains, and the Castle's gear was among the best.

Back in her room, fitting everything into a small pack that she could carry easily, she wondered what the next few weeks would bring. She wondered how it would feel traveling with Kieran, and what would become of them. Somewhere in the Alps was a group of men who were dedicated to wiping her and her people out of existence. From what Kieran was telling her, they were going to walk right up to those men.

A knock at the door made her turn.

"Come in," she said, hoping that it was Piers.

Instead it was Liona, who registered the disappointment on Hailey's face with a quirked eyebrow.

"I'm aware that I am not the most impressive thousand year old witch that you know, but have I done something to disappoint you lately?"

Hailey laughed at the other woman's jibe.

"No, I'm sorry. I was just hoping to see Piers before I left."

"Hmm. So I understand that you are leaving with that man from the Magus Corps."

"He told you about that?"

"Something like that."

Liona paused, as uncertain as Hailey had ever seen her.

"Hailey, are you sure that you want to go?"

Hailey blinked at Liona's question.

"Kieran tells me that I could save someone's life. There's really no question after that. If I can help someone, I need to do it."

Liona's gaze was distant.

"There is something about what is going to happen out there. Every time I try to see, I come up blind and wanting. I see flickers, dark things. Nothing ever stays the same, but I think that if you go out there, there is a good chance that you will come back changed."

Hailey tried to laugh off her friend's words.

"You sound like a state fair fortuneteller warning me of my dark fate."

Liona smiled a little at that.

"Well, I've done fortuneteller tricks more than once in my life, so I suppose I deserve that. I wish I had more to tell you and more useful things at that, but it is what I have. I also wanted you to join me on the wall for a few moments if you have the time."

Hailey looked over her bags. She was as packed as she would be, and soon enough, it would be noon, when she would meet Kieran. Honestly, she was a little hurt that Piers had never appeared, but perhaps it was too difficult for him to say goodbye.

He had mentioned having a busy day last night, so she put the sting out of her mind.

Liona took them first to the armory, where there were a number of weapons to choose from. She bypassed the guns, and in the back, she found what she was looking for. She pulled a primitive-looking longbow, plucking the string a few times to ensure that it was sound. Instead of taking the quiver of arrows that sat to the side, she pulled out only one to take with her.

"All right, let's get up to the wall."

The day outside was misty and cool. Liona led her up the twisting staircase to the eastern wall, which faced out to the forest.

"What are we doing out here?"

"Something I want to do," was the only answer. "Give me your hand."

Hailey did as Liona said, only to yelp with shock when the other woman pulled out a small pocketknife to prick her finger. She watched in confusion as Liona dabbed some of her blood on the arrow's point.

"First, that hurt," Hailey said, "and second, you still haven't told me what this is for."

"This arrow represents you now," Liona explained.

There was a faintly foreign cadence to her speech. When they usually spoke, Liona did not have an accent. She could have been a woman from the Midwest, from the east coast or from the mountains of the west. Now though, distracted with what she was doing, Hailey could hear another language shadowing her speech, perhaps several of them. She realized that if Liona had been born in ancient Rome, her first language was likely Latin. It made her feel faintly dizzy to realize all of the languages that Liona had seen live and die over the course of her lifetime.

"So flies this arrow, so will you fly. So the arrow finds its mark, so will you find yours. So the arrow fulfills its purpose, so will you. So the arrow travels safely, so will you."

Hailey watched as Liona nocked the bloody arrow, stretching the bowstring to its full extension. She was faintly surprised to see the muscles of Liona's arm. It was obviously not a new art to her.

When she let go of the string, the air rustled with a sound like tearing silk. The arrow arched over the trees, disappearing into the forest below.

"What do you think it hit?" Hailey asked after a moment.

"I don't know," Liona said. "All we know is that its path was straight and true."

Liona put down the bow and turned to Hailey, taking her in her arms. The kiss that she planted on Hailey's mouth was firm and sweet at the same time. For a moment, Hailey could simply relax into the other woman's embrace. Older than many countries, she was a fixed point that Hailey could trust.

"Are you truly afraid for me?" Hailey asked softly.

Liona sighed.

"Sometimes. Other times, I see the strength you have in you. Not just your powers, but the strength of your heart. Then I know that whatever happens, you will be just fine."

Hailey nodded, tears prickling her eyes. Liona's comfort could be strange at times, but she knew it was real.

"Thank you for everything. In the future though, I would prefer a warning before you steal my blood."

"I'll keep that in mind. Here's something that you should think about, however. Do you know what happens when you pull power from others?"

Hailey blinked.

"They call me a vampire," she said cautiously. "They say that I remove energy from others to make it my own."

Liona shook her head.

"Perhaps that's what it seems like to people who are unused to their power. No. When you drew power from me, you were also giving it back."

Hailey blinked.

"I don't think I understand."

"Power is a strange thing in Wiccans, Hailey. It isn't like a jar of sugar that you can scoop from, it doesn't empty out over time. I have found that when I practice my own powers, it is a great deal more like the rising of a tide, something that beats in time with my own heartbeat. There is no end to it, not really. Not for people like you, and I suspect, for your men."

"My…my men?"

Liona's smile was sly.

"Oh, yes, both of them. And if you don't see it now, well, I think there is a good chance that you will see it sooner rather than later. What I need to say, however, is that when you are taking power from others, you are also trying to give them what you have."

Hailey frowned.

"I'm not sure I understand."

"When you reached for me, I was ready to feel my power being drained. I did feel that, but more than that, I felt you trying to give me your power as well. When that happens, I think that it is more than an exchange. I could feel that between the two of us, we were creating more than had been there before."

"Like…like a pump of some kind. Two components come together to make something greater."

"Or an explosion, perhaps," said Liona with some degree of satisfaction. "Regardless of what happens with it, it is something that you should be aware of."

"I will be, thank you. Thank you for everything that you have give me, as well."

Hailey hugged Liona, wondering if this would be the last time she would be able to do so. If the mission to the Alps was as dangerous as Kieran was telling her it was, there was a possibility that she would not return at all.

"You're very welcome. I hope you return whole of heart and stronger than ever."

CHAPTER FORTY-FOUR

HAILEY CARRIED HER things down to the courtyard at noon. She had said goodbye to the other friends she had made at the Castle. She was as ready as she thought she was going to be. Kieran was waiting for her with an unreadable expression on his face. There was no trace of the desperate man who had kissed her the night before. Even in the cloudy light of the day, the bruise on his face was dark and obvious.

"Well, here I am," she said. "Shall we go?"

"We're still waiting for one more," was his answer.

"What, what are you talking about?"

Kieran grimaced and pointed behind her. Confused, Hailey turned to see Piers approaching, dressed to travel and with a bag much like hers over his shoulder.

"Piers?"

"I'm sorry I missed you this morning. There was a lot of delegating and organization that I needed to do to make sure that the Castle would run well in my absence, whether that absence was one that lasted a few weeks or whether it was one that proved to be permanent."

"You...you can't do that!" Hailey cried in astonishment. "You *are* the Castle! The people here need you."

"I created the Castle to give Wiccans the protections that they needed as well as to offer them all of the choices that they deserved. In this way, this is my choice, not yours, Hailey."

Piers's voice was calm. There was nothing that she could do to dissuade him, so she turned to Kieran.

"Are you going to let him come along?"

Kieran's smile was twisted.

"I'm not actually sure that I can stop him. Also, I'm going to point out that if this mission was serious enough that I was willing to endanger you, I'm certainly not going to say no to more firepower, no matter what form it takes."

There were no further arguments that Hailey could make, so she followed the two of them out of the Castle. A short ways into the forest was a small plane ably hidden underneath a camouflage tarp. When Kieran stripped it away, she and Piers got on board. As Kieran started his pre-flight checks, she leaned closer to Piers.

"Why are you here?" she asked softly. "The Castle means the world to you."

Piers's laugh was soft. He reached out to touch her face gently, just once.

"The Castle might be my world, but I have found that you are my heart. I can't be in two places at once, but I know where I need to be most. I created the Castle to be a defense in its own right. I might be the coven master here, but I have always looked ahead to a time when I might be out of the picture. The Castle will survive even if I do not."

The idea of Piers dying was a sobering one to her. Her heart clenched with fear. When she glanced at Kieran's broad back in the cockpit in front of them, she felt the same way. She wondered if Piers felt the same thing when he looked at her, if Kieran did as well.

We will come back from this, she thought firmly to herself. *We will fly as Liona's arrow did, we will find our targets, and then we will find our way home.*

The plane began its slow ascent into the sky. Hailey looked out the small window just in time to see the Castle fall away. It was the first home that she had ever known. She wondered briefly whether she would ever be able to see it again.

Next to her, Piers took her hand gently, bringing it to his lips for a kiss.

"It'll be fine, and so will we."

Settling in for the flight, she tried to believe him.

CHAPTER FORTY-FIVE

LESS THAN A day later, Hailey was on the other side of the world. They had taken a commercial flight from the United States to Italy, but from there, they had found a taciturn man with a small plane to take them further.

"There's a Magus Corps safe house that we can use to find our feet," Kieran said. "It's as close as you can get to the place we are heading. From there, we can strike into their territory on foot."

"Will we see Cavanaugh there?" Hailey had wondered. Cavanaugh was Kieran's wolf familiar. It felt almost strange to see Kieran without his companion.

Kieran had shaken his head.

"As a matter of fact, I left him at the Castle. It's a place that's close enough to his home, and if I don't come back, I know he'll thrive."

That was all that Kieran had had to say about the matter, but Hailey could read a world there. She had left Merit in Wyoming for much the same reason.

There was very much a sense that they might not come back from their mission, though if Piers or Kieran's thoughts ran along the same lines that hers did, they did not reveal it.

The safe house that Kieran led them to was only a simple cabin in the forest. The plane had dropped them off with supplies for a few days, but when they entered the cabin, it hardly seemed warmer than the winds outside.

"I'll get the generator started," Kieran volunteered, heading outside again.

While he was gone, Hailey looked around the cabin with her flashlight. It was a surprisingly cozy place, with a few colorful quilts thrown over the couch and a shelf of paperback books in a variety of languages.

"Do you regret coming with me?" she asked softly.

Piers chuckled.

"If you think I'm going to be driven from your side by a few mildewed books and a cold cabin, you don't think enough of me. I have faith that things will be fine. I also don't disagree with you on why you are here."

Hailey looked at him with curiosity before posing her question.

"You've…had very little good to say about the Magus Corps since I've known you. Why the change of heart?"

"The Magus Corps as an institution makes me nervous. They have had a lot of unquestioned power for a long time, and they have not always used it wisely. On the other hand, there have been a number of Magus Corps officers that I have cared for a great deal, even loved. You met Stephan when you first came to the Castle, the inventor? He is a fine person, one that I wish would leave the Corps and come to the Castle. If it were him that was lost, I would want to come find him. No one deserves to be lost to the Templars, not when there is a chance that I can help win them free."

"You sound a little like Liona when you speak of such things. She told me that the covens were designed to protect people, and so was the Magus Corps. Two different organizations with the exact same goals."

Piers smiled wryly at her.

"That being said, I would like to point out that I would far rather enjoy your company in your quarters or mine back at the Castle. This place feels a little like a set from a horror movie."

"Oh? Are you worried that some masked killer is going to come chase us around?"

Hailey sidled up to Piers, wrapping her arm around his waist. To her delight, he scooped her up in his arms, holding her close. She was light in his arms, but she still wrapped her legs around his waist for stability.

"Fear is an amazing aphrodisiac," she whispered. "Perhaps I wouldn't mind being chased around if that meant that I could collapse in your arms, hmm?"

Piers was going to reply when two things happened at once. The generator kicked on, bringing the lights up, and the door behind them opened to reveal Kieran in the doorway.

Hailey had a moment to remember how large he was, how he could fill up the room. After a frozen moment, however, he merely closed the door behind him.

"Lights on," he said gruffly. "Heat should follow soon. I want to leave at first light, so we should likely eat and rest."

He walked past them to pick up his bag, and then he walked up the stairs, where there was a bathroom and a bedroom.

Hailey blushed guiltily, turning to Piers, who had a strange expression on his face.

"That was awkward to say the least," she muttered.

"You know, I don't know about that."

"What do you mean, Piers?"

"Nothing right this moment, but I do wonder what an aura reader or a mind reader would have made of your major just then."

Dinner consisted of tins hastily heated up over the stove. It was poor fare, but all three of them ate like they weren't sure when they were next going to see food at all. Hailey watched Piers and Kieran. Piers was at his ease, though perhaps uncharacteristically quiet. Kieran was as silent as a stone. There was something lost and hurt about him. Despite what lay between them, it hurt her to see it. Whoever he was, no matter how tangled his loyalties, she didn't think she could stand to see him look like that.

"Tomorrow we are going to head north into the forest," Kieran said after they had cleaned up. "Within half a day, perhaps a little more, we will be in the territory where the last officer was lost. He had heard talk of strange happenings out in this region, and he went to investigate."

"Strange happenings, what does that mean?" asked Piers with a frown.

"According to his report, lights above the trees, things that were like elk walking on their hind legs, shadows that were not cast by anything people could see. He came to investigate, wondering if there was a renegade witch or warlock in the region, or perhaps even a lost coven. He never came back."

Hailey shivered, making Kieran glance at her.

"If you want to leave, that is still possible. You are not sworn to the Magus Corps, and you have no reason to follow orders from me."

Hailey tilted her chin up defiantly.

"I have no intention of leaving this mission. Unless you can look me in the eye and tell me that you think I will hamper you or that I will hurt your chances for success, then I am staying."

Kieran looked at her for a long moment. Finally, he smiled, a slightly rueful thing.

"If I thought that you would slow me down, either of you, I would never have brought you. Our chances for success go up if you are both here. Even I know that. I just…"

"Don't want to see her harmed."

Hailey jumped a little when Piers spoke. There was an understanding there that eluded her. For a long moment, both men looked at each other across the simple wooden table. There was no anger or animosity there. Instead, there was the beginning of something that she couldn't quite name.

Kieran nodded.

"The last thing in the world I want is to see her harmed. It…it is something I will prevent at all costs, but I know what is needed and what might happen out there. I can offer no guarantees, and for that I apologize to you both."

"Life offers no guarantees," Hailey said firmly. "All I need to know is that I am here, and here is where I want to be. With you. With both of you."

Kieran looked a little startled at the emphasis of her words. There was something shuttered about him again. He stood and clear the table settings away.

"I want to be moving at first light. There is one bedroom upstairs, and the bed should suit the pair of you."

Did she imagine the faint twitch at his temple? The black eye that Piers had presumably given him was still bright, still livid.

"What about you?" she asked. Her voice came out a little huskier than she thought it would.

"I can make a perfectly serviceable bed for myself down here. Good night."

Kieran spoke with a finality that was meant to end the discussion. Feeling somewhat defeated, Hailey washed up and followed Piers to the small bedroom above.

The bed was startlingly large. There were sheets and blankets in the chest at the foot of the bed. As they made up the bed together, Hailey caught Piers watching her speculatively.

"What are you looking at?" she asked warily.

Piers shook his head.

"Just thinking about the things that you can learn during the course of a life as long as mine. That's all."

"And what do you think that would be?"

"That sometimes, the things that we want can be ours if only we ask for them."

She watched him with suspicion.

"So I should ask?"

"It's usually the best course. Otherwise, no one will know what it is you want."

Hailey bit her lip. It was right there, waiting for her to speak it, but still she hesitated.

"Who won the fight that the two of you had?" she asked instead.

Piers shrugged.

"It wasn't a fight, really," he said, temporizing. "It was much closer to being a discussion that was punctuated by blows."

"Uh-huh. And who punctuated the hardest?"

"I would have to say that it was him. I did get in a few good ones though."

"Yes, I saw his eye." Hailey hesitated, and then she finally said what they both had been thinking the entire time.

"I don't want Kieran to sleep alone tonight," she said finally. "I want him to come to our bed. Is that possible?"

Piers's face betrayed not a moment of anger or upset. Instead, he seemed calm, as if he fielded such requests all the time.

"What would you want him to do in this great big bed of ours, Hailey?"

Hailey blushed at the pictures that danced through her mind for a moment. Then she straightened, shaking her head.

"I don't care. I want to do what he wants. If all he wants to do is to sleep, that's fine. If he wants to…to make love with us, I want that too. Is that what you want?"

Piers thought for a moment. Then he nodded.

"He has a piece of you, Hailey. That is something that I have known for quite some time. It doesn't bother me, exactly, but I would prefer you whole and happy. He has your best interests, your safety and your care as his first priority, and that is what I needed to know. If you want to bring him to our bed, I would welcome him."

Hailey thought for a moment, and then she nodded.

"That's what I want. I want to bring him up here with us."

"Then you should go get him before it gets too late, shouldn't you?"

Her heart pounding, Hailey turned towards the door.

"You don't need clothes to go get him, do you, Hailey?"

Hailey shivered. It was Piers's secret voice, the one that he used to command her when they were intimate. It immediately sent a bolt of subtle lightning through her body, making her quiver with desire.

Without saying a word, she slid out of her clothes, folding them and setting them aside. When she stood naked, she presented herself to Piers, who nodded thoughtfully.

She thought he would kiss her, but instead, he only ran his hands over her shoulders and her arms, cupping her breasts momentarily before releasing her.

"You are a difficult woman to resist at any point, my love. Like this, you are completely compelling. Go. Bring your prize to bed."

He dropped a kiss on the delicate shell of her ear.

Shaking just a little, she walked out of their bedroom and down the stairs. It was almost completely dark in the house, but her memory was good. She managed to make it down the stairs without bumping into anything.

The fire in the seating area was banked low. By its rather sullen light, she could see Kieran's frame curled up on the couch. Some part of her absently thought that it was just as well she and Piers were inviting him to bed; otherwise, he would have woken up quite cramped.

Kieran looked up at her approach. His eyes went wide when he realized that she was naked. He seemed frozen in place as she crossed the floor to his side.

She thought he would speak, that he might protest or send her away. Instead, he only watched her as she knelt on the floor beside him. He flinched a little when she raised her hand to stroke his hair. He didn't move as she kissed his forehead, his cheek and the bruise under his eye. When she dropped her mouth to his, however, he wrapped his hand around her wrist to hold her still.

"Hailey," he rasped, "what in the name of the nine hells do you think you're doing?"

"Exactly what I want to do," she said softly. "I want you. I love you, and I always will. Will you come back to bed with me?"

He sat up, the blankets sliding down around his hips. His chest was bare. She had forgotten how thickly muscled he was, how dense he felt when she was close to him. He had the body of a warrior. She longed to touch it the way that she had all those weeks ago.

"What does this mean?" he said softly.

She wondered if there was a little bit of fear in his voice. It occurred to her that ever since he had realized that she and Piers were together, it must have felt as if he had been looking at something he could never have.

"It means whatever you make of it," she said. "I'm with Piers, and I love him. I love you too. I want to give you what I can give and to have you in the way that feels right to me. Will you come?"

She could tell that there were a thousand questions in his mind, on his tongue. Instead, he leaned down to kiss her with a softness and a reverence that made her want him forever. She could kiss this man until the stars fell down into the sea. It still wouldn't be enough.

She took his hand in hers, pulling on it so that he stood. When he did, she realized that he was as naked as she was. Silently, she led him up the stairs. Together, they entered the bedroom.

Inside the door, Piers had dimmed the lights. He was stretched out on the bed, the blanket thrown across his hips the only concession to modesty. He was leaner than Kieran though still quite muscled. Hailey realized that it was fairly impressive that he had tried to stand against the bigger man at all.

"I was beginning to get worried," he commented.

"That I would stay gone?" she teased.

"That you would freeze," Piers retorted. "Are you both ready to come to bed?"

In response, Hailey slid in beside Piers. Then she turned and offered her hand to Kieran, who stood at the edge of the bed. He wasn't a man given to embarrassment or shyness, but now he couldn't seem to meet their gazes.

"Come here," Hailey said, her voice nearly a whisper. "You're wanted, you're loved."

Piers nodded behind her.

"Come to bed. There's nothing keeping you out but your own fears"

Hailey wasn't sure whose words it was that convinced him. With a breath that was almost too soft to be a sigh, he slid underneath the covers with them. He reached for her. She rewarded him by moving closer to his body. It was at once familiar and new to her. She pressed her face against his chest, simply taking in the scent of him and the feel of him.

"Oh I have missed you, love," she murmured.

She felt him shift against her before he ran his hand from the point of her shoulder down her arm to her hip.

Piers chuckled softly as he came to press against her back.

"I like this," he said, his voice just a hair off from a growl. "I like having people around who want to please Hailey."

"That's what I want to do. I am not as interested in pleasing you," Kieran said with a hint of heat.

"Oh? That's a shame." Piers's voice was innocence itself. "I don't mind the idea of pleasing you at all."

Hailey didn't know what Kieran's response to that was going to be. She decided she didn't much care. She squirmed up to place a deep kiss on Kieran's mouth. At the same time, she reached behind her to slide her hand down between Piers's legs, wrapping her hand around his half-hard erection.

Both men gasped and were wordless, which was what she had intended. She drew back from Kieran and pulled her hand away, smiling even though she knew that they couldn't see it.

"We do have to be up early in the morning," she commented. "I think that it would serve all of our best interests if we started doing what it is we want to do right now."

The words were barely out of her mouth when Kieran's hands ended up in her hair, holding her still while he kissed her mouth hard. There was a barely restrained savagery to his motions. He had been without her for a long time. She could feel his erection against her thigh. She moved her leg enticingly against him. She wanted to let him know that she wanted him, that there was nothing that was barred from his touch and his want.

With Piers's hands running up and down her body, she put her focus into kissing Kieran. It felt as if it had been years since they last touched like this, since they had drowned in each other's bodies. He was dense and powerful in a way that Piers wasn't. He could be overwhelming.

After the first onslaught, his mouth gentled against hers. He kissed her with care, but there was still an urgency to it. He wanted her, but he wanted to please her more. There was something almost beseeching about the way he touched her.

Encouraged by Piers's touches, she pushed herself over him, straddling his hips. His cock was trapped against her belly. She ground down on him, forcing a groan from his lips. There was something wild about riding him like this. She held his satisfaction in her hands, but she didn't have to give it to him, not yet.

She felt Piers move behind her. He wrapped her wild red hair in his fist, pulling it away so that he could kiss the back of her neck. She shivered when his wet lips touched her sensitive skin. She was so taken with Piers's mouth on her that she flinched when she felt Kieran's hands come up to cup her small breasts. He ran his calloused thumbs over the erect peak of her nipples, making her writhe and press down on him.

"I can feel how wet you are," Kieran murmured. "I can smell how much you want this."

"I want both of you," Hailey found herself whimpering. "I want both of you so much..."

Piers's laugh was dark and full of promise.

"Then that's what you'll have, little darling. We want to give it all to you."

She could feel Piers's cock pressed against her back just as she could feel Kieran's on her belly. She blushed furiously at the sensations, but they were far too intense to deny.

"I...I want to use my mouth," she stuttered. "While one of you takes me from behind."

She felt as much as heard Kieran's breath go shallow and fast. Piers's cock grew even harder.

"Well, well, I do like a woman who knows what she wants,"

Piers said, a laugh in his voice.
"Come on, let's get set up for that."

"You speak as if we're setting up camp," Kieran said, his voice barely above a growl. Piers seemed unperturbed.

"Sex is an activity, and like any other, when you make the right preparations and do the right setup, things can go very well. For example, come here."

Hailey watched, eyes wide and mouth slightly wet as Piers reached for a condom in the night stand. Instead of handing it to Kieran, however, he opened it himself. Kieran was as still as a statue as Piers smoothed it down Kieran's cock. When it was on, Piers ran gentle fingers down Kieran's erection, a slight smile on his face.

"Come here, Hailey…"

It wasn't quite Piers's command tone, but it was close enough that Hailey came to attention. Piers settled himself against the headboard of the bed, his legs sprawled so that Hailey could crawl between them. He took her hand and wrapped it around the base of his erection.

"I'm going to put my hand on the back of your head. I'm not going to push you, so just do whatever you like, all right, love?"

She purred at the touch of his hands in her hair, and she lapped at the tip of his cock. She relished the taste of him. When she was ready, she suckled on the tip, making him stiffen and moan.

Just when she was wondering what Kieran thought of all of this, Piers gestured to him.

"Are you waiting for a formal invitation, Major?"

The bed shifted as Kieran moved closer, kneeling between Hailey's legs. She felt his hands on her hips lightly, almost tentatively. When he brushed the tip of his cock against her wet slit, she nearly moaned with it.

She needed him, she wanted this, why was he denying her? She pressed her hips back against him as if doing that would encourage him forward. It made him hiss with arousal. She felt him take his cock in hand and guide it into her.

She was so open and wet for him that he slid in easily, drawing a cry from both of them.

"I…don't want to hurt you," Kieran said through gritted teeth.

Hailey raised her head long enough to twist her head around to look at him.

"You won't, love, I promise you won't. I just need you now, please…"

Something in Kieran unleashed. He withdrew from her almost completely before sliding back in. He did it with such force that she was pushed onto Piers's cock, taking him deeper than she had before.

As he had promised, Piers's hands never forced her down or caused her to choke, but he did clench his fingers in her hair.

"You feel amazing, Hailey," he whispered. "Gods above, you feel like heaven."

Hailey was pinned between the two men that she loved most, giving them pleasure with her body. She twisted and moaned, wanting to tell them how good it felt, but Piers apparently thought it meant something different.

"Use your hand on her," he said to Kieran. There was a command in his tone that Kieran snapped to obey. In less than a second, Hailey felt Kieran's skilled fingers at her slit, pulling her open. At the first touch, her whole body twisted with pleasure, making both men groan.

How connected we are, she thought. *We are feeling all of this together.*

She had enjoyed bringing both of them pleasure, but now she could not concentrate on it at all. Instead, her body was a channel for her own pleasure. The feel of both of them inside her drove her mad. She loved the idea of being so filled, of having them both take their pleasure with her. Kieran's fingers on her own body made her arch. She couldn't control the way that she was moving and bucking. However, with her body pinned between the two of them, there was no where she could go.

Being helpless between two of the most powerful men that she knew was intoxicating. She could feel her own arousal soar higher and higher. Soon her whole body was shaking. Her climax pushed her over the edge in a blinding flash of sensation. The pleasure was so intense that she nearly lost consciousness for a moment.

Behind her, Kieran thrust into her one last time, his hands gripping her hips with a nearly bruising intensity. He was saying her name over and over again, telling her he loved her, that he wanted her.

She pulled away from Piers's still hard cock to rest her forehead against his hip. His hands were in her hair, stroking and comforting her. Distantly, she was aware that Kieran had pulled out of her. She rolled over to her side, simply trying to catch her breath.

"Let me…let me take care of you," she tried to say to Piers. Now that her body was cooling slightly, she felt guilty that she had not brought him to a climax as well.

Piers's laugh was soft.

"I would like to spill inside you, love. May I?"

She nodded, almost sleepy in how satisfied she was. She felt Piers shift as he sheathed his own cock in a condom. He climbed over her, carrying most of his bulk on his arms when he rolled her to her back.

She felt exhausted but so satisfied as he pressed inside her.

"I wish I could come again," she murmured. He leaned down to kiss her.

"Another night, we'll keep you up and make sure that you feel every bit of pleasure that your body can tolerate. That's what I want you to have."

Hailey draped her arms around Piers's neck, drawing him close.

"I want you to come now," she said, her voice as soft as velvet. "I want you to spill. I want to think of there being nothing between us so I can feel how hot it would be."

Piers tensed at her words, thrusting into her harder and faster. His movements became frenzied. At the last, he planted his mouth over hers when he thrust one more time. She could feel the deep groan he made and the way his body shook as if he were under a lash.

He pulled away from her to lie on his side, though his hand stayed knotted in her hair.

Hailey turned to look at Kieran, who sat on the edge of the bed, watching them.

"I don't know what to do now," he said.

Hailey smiled.

"It's easy," she said with a yawn. "Come to bed. Sleep with us. That is all you have to think about right now."

Kieran looked like he was prepared to resist for a moment, but then he nodded. He crawled into the bed, resting next to her. After Piers had cleaned himself up, he came to lie down on her other side.

As she drifted off to sleep, she thought of how lucky she was, and how loved. She thought of the nervous way that Kieran had looked at her at the last, and she found herself wondering if he would respond to Piers's pleasure at directing things the way she did.

When she finally fell asleep, her arm was draped over Kieran's chest, and Piers was spooned against her back. She had spent most of her life without a home; now she wondered if she had found it between these two men.

CHAPTER FORTY-SIX

HAILEY WOKE WHEN Piers got out of bed. The light was still dim, and when she slid out from under the covers, she shivered at how cold it was. She dressed warmly, and when she came down to the kitchen, she found that Kieran had already eaten.

"There's eggs and oatmeal in the oven. Eat up. That will probably be the best food we'll get all day."

His manner was brusque to the point of being rude, a far cry from the passionate lover he had been the night before. Hailey ate her food quietly, unsure of how to take this change. Piers seemed unperturbed, eating his meal quickly and giving her a brief kiss as he went to wash his plates.

When they went outside, Kieran turned to them both.

"I want to make our way into the mountains as quickly and as subtly as possible. Piers, I want you above, keeping an eye on things, and I'll move forward on foot. Hailey, it would be safest if you stayed in animal forms if you can, wolf when you're with me and eagle when you're with Piers. With three pairs of eyes, hopefully we'll be able to see something, whether it's a sign of Templars or a sign of the man who went missing. If we haven't seen anything by dusk, we'll break off and camp. Do you have any questions?"

Both Piers and Hailey shook their heads. Kieran nodded.

"All right, Piers up in the air, Hailey, go ahead and start with your wolf form."

Piers launched himself up into the sky. Hailey watched him for a moment before turning to Kieran.

"Kieran…"

"There is a mission that we need to accomplish, Hailey. That comes first."

He could see that she was stung by his words. He sighed, started to reach for her, and then drew his hand back.

"There is…too much to deal with right now. I promise, though, when we return, I will give you the answers that you are looking for. I swear."

Hailey nodded, knowing even in her disappointment that he was right. She took his hand, pulling from the dark sea that represented his power. She remembered what Liona had said, about how she wasn't just taking energy from him. Instead she thought about sharing it. The ocean she could see was dark and choppy, but as she pulled power from Kieran, she tried to think about it as bringing light to him as well.

She wasn't sure if what she had tried to do had worked at all, but when she pulled back, there was a slightly confused look on his face. He looked like he wanted to speak, but instead shook his head.

"Are you ready?"

She nodded, not trusting herself to speak. Instead, she closed her eyes and concentrated on her transformation. In a matter of seconds, her body had twisted and changed. She saw the world through eyes that were much sharper, but it was the scents that truly changed how she experienced things. It was all she could do not to run off into the forest to see what was going on.

Kieran seemed to sense her excitement. She won a grin out of him, something that made him into a man that she recognized again. She thought in that moment that she would do anything for him. Any amount of fighting and risk was worth it, if he would stay at her side.

"Come, Hailey. We have a long road ahead of us and a great deal of ground to cover. Stay close by my side, but remember to use that nose of yours. If something seems out of place, dangerous or odd, let me know at once."

She would have saluted teasingly if she could. Instead she barked briskly and fell into place by his side. She loved her new body. It felt tireless, as if she could keep up her steady trot forever and a day. Hailey forced herself to remember that she wasn't out in the woods for a stroll. There was a man's life at stake. There might be Templars in the area.

The sky grew lighter and dawn finally appeared. Hailey was fascinated by the fact that she could sense a great deal of what had passed the night before. She could sense where a badger had crossed their path, and she was more interested than she felt comfortable with in a spot where a fox had made a meal of a rabbit.

She kept her mind on the task at hand, however, looking for the scent that would tell her that that something strange had occurred.

It was a few hours past dawn when Piers came down to rest in the tree above them.

"There's smoke coming up from something that's slightly to the west of us. Is it possible that there's an old mountaineer or hermit in these parts?"

Kieran shook his head.

"No, this area of the mountains is typically a little too dangerous for people to simply want to live here. We should definitely have a peek. Here, while you're down, feed your face."

He tossed a protein bar at Piers, who caught it. Kieran turned to Hailey.

"Change up, and have some food as well. After that, you can join Dayton in the sky."

It almost hurt to leave her wolf form, to feel her sharp senses being exchanged for senses that were not half so fine. She sighed. At least in her human form, she could touch Piers when he leaped down from the tree.

After she finished her protein bar, she took Piers's arm, pulling his golden energy from him and trying to make it more than it was, as she had done with Kieran. He definitely looked startled, but then he shook his head, as if not quite certain what he had felt.

Hailey took a deep breath and concentrated. She wished for a moment that she could have changed into an owl, as she knew her own familiar's body well. However, a man who lived at the first coven she had lived at had turned into an eagle. Once she had asked him what it was like. He fixed her with an eye that was far keener than a human's.

"It's like being sharpened," he said at last. "It's like all of your focus, all of your will and your power is focused in your eyes. You can see farther than any other animal in the world. You can see as clearly under water as you can in dry air. It's like being a king."

She focused on his words, and she imagined what it would be like to soar into the air on wings that were broad and strong. She imagined what it would be like to have heavy talons that could bring down small deer. She barely noticed when she started shrinking and twisting.

When Hailey opened her eyes, she almost cried out. The forest that they had been walking through had been beautiful in its own right, but now it was lit from within, showing her a panoply of gem-like colors all in a vivid degree of sharpness that she had never imagined existed. Her sense of smell was not too different from what she had as a human, but it palled in comparison to what her eyes could see.

Piers grinned down at her.

"All right, darling, ready to fly?"

"Be careful." Kieran's voice was sharp. "If you get tired, come down at once."

Hailey barely listened to either of them as she pumped her wings twice, hard. Then with a loud cry, she launched herself from the ground. It was clumsier than she thought it would be. Her first flaps were slow and lumbering, but as she put more distance between herself and the ground, she felt herself grow lighter and lighter. Soon she was hundreds of feet above where Kieran stood. Piers shot up next to her, nudging her slightly as he rose. She glanced up to see a sharp, proud grin on his face.

"Come on, Hailey, try and keep up," he shouted, and with an inward grin, she shot after him.

Quickly, they fell into a search pattern that would maximize their range. They flew from side to side, crossing paths close to where Kieran still walked. Using him as a center, they could cover a great deal of ground.

She couldn't get over how much she could see. If she cared to look, every rock and every rustle in the branches was obvious to her. She did quickly realize that the instincts of the eagle were more powerful than those of the wolf, however. More than once, she stopped herself from going into a dive. Seeing a fish in a stream or a rabbit in a bare patch of land made her talons itch.

More than an hour later, her sharp eyes caught sight of a strange shape in a clearing in her path. Letting out a loud scream, she spiraled over the spot, making sure that Piers saw her go down. When she landed, she returned to her human form, Piers lighting down beside her.

"Is that...what I think it is?" she asked, her voice soft and scared.

In the clearing were the remnants of a tent. It had been caved in from the top, and there were supplies scattered around the dead campfire. The light dusting of snow did nothing to cover the destroyed site. Instead, it only added to the air of desolation and fear.

Kieran appeared as if materializing out of the forest, his face grim.

"I saw you both drop down and came to look. Stand back, I want to get closer."

Piers and Hailey hung back while Kieran carefully turned over the site. For a full twenty minutes, he went over the goods, occasionally nodding to himself. Finally, he stood and walked over to where they stood.

"It's definitely a Magus Corps officer's campsite. Those are the same supplies as the ones that I've used and we're using right now. I don't know what could take him out of it like this; he wouldn't have left it this way on his own."

"Something large," mused Piers, looking over the destruction. "But it didn't kill him, did it?"

"No, or at least, there's no sign of blood or anything else. As far as I can tell, something came down and dragged him off."

Hailey shivered to think about what could be powerful enough to remove a Magus Corps officer from his tent. All of them were trained in the armed and unarmed forms of combat. Some of them, like Kieran himself, had had centuries to hone themselves in the arts of war.

"I was looking for incendiary devices," Kieran continued. "Templars and the Magus Corps have been at this war for some time, and they will leave bombs in places that they have attacked. There's nothing like that here. It makes me think that they were in a hurry or simply did not have the mind to leave something behind."

He turned to Hailey.

"We're taking a break to refuel on water and food. After that, I want you down here in your wolf form. We're going to start moving slowly to prevent ourselves from missing anything."

"And me?" asked Piers.

"I still want you in the air. If something happens to me, I want you ready to take Hailey out of here."

Piers nodded. The three of them sat down to eat, by silent consensus staying away from the wrecked campsite. After they were done, Kieran went to clean it up, taking what supplies survived and piling the rest together so that the site would not be so obvious.

This time, when Hailey took Kieran's hand, she could access his power with even more speed than she normally did. It was almost a heady feeling, having it right there. There was something powerful happening. She had never taken power from anyone as often as she had taken it from Kieran.

In her wolf form, she cast around the area carefully. Now she could tell that there had been a man at the site. His scent was the strongest, but the other scent that she found confused her badly. Her wolf brain tried to put it in a way that her human mind could understand, but it was at a loss.

Water. Blood. Bad. Old. Rot.

Hailey shook her head as if to get the scent out of her nose. For a moment, all she could think to do was to sit up and howl in a panic. Whatever had taken the man, it was not human. It was not right, and her body twisted, trying to pull away from it.

She shook her head and twisted into her human form.

"There is something very wrong with whatever took this man," she told Kieran. Piers was already far above, watching them closely.

"What do you mean?"

"Templars are men. I know they are because I've seen them die. This…I don't know what this is. The wolf is telling me that it is bad and, more than that, wrong."

Kieran frowned.

"Do you mean something like a mountain lion or a bear?"

Hailey shook her head in frustration, wishing she could explain.

"No. I mean something *wrong*. A mountain lion or a bear is not a good thing, but it makes sense. They're just other predators who want the same thing that the wolf does. This…thing…is something else."

Kieran nodded soberly.

"All right. Follow the scent, but stay close to me. I don't want to lose sight of you."

She took his arm again, and when she felt strong, she returned to her wolf form. She forced herself to be calm, and so she set off after the scent of the man who had been carried away.

There was a brief moment where she could smell another wolf, a scent which confused her. Wolves were actually a rarity in the mountains of Europe. In many regions, they had been hunted to extinction. She knew this was true. Some of the men she had known in the Angioli coven in Italy even spoke of the old wolf hunts.

All of that was true, but she could definitely smell the scent of another wolf here. The scent was fresh. She supposed that there must be long holdouts, wolves that hid so well that they bred in secret populations throughout the mountains.

She put the thought to one side. Instead, she put her nose to the ground and started casting about for the scent. As she had feared, the *wrong* scent that she had detected was wrapped with the scent of the man who had been taken away. The two scents twined around each other, telling her that they were moving in the same direction.

There was one comforting thought that occurred to her as she followed the trail at least. As time wore on, she became more convinced that the man was alive. He might have been unconscious or otherwise immobile, but he was definitely alive.

The trail was not a direct one. It wove through the forests, following a path that she couldn't discern. Sometimes it doubled back on itself. She wondered if the thing was afraid of being tracked or caught. As she followed the trail, Kieran followed her closely, though he stood back whenever she needed to sort out the trail. He knew that she needed him not to foul the track with his own scent, but he was always right behind her.

Then, suddenly and without warning, he was not.

She looked up from a strange twist in the trail only to realize that she was alone. At first, Hailey thought that she must be wrong. Surely Kieran was right behind her. Perhaps he was hanging back to let her work out the trail. At worst, he had walked to one side or the other to see if there were any other traces worth following.

She stood stock still for a few long moments. Then she had to come to the dark conclusion that he was not behind her. Hailey took a deep breath. The wolf brain was not one that was inclined to panic, so she used it to her advantage. She followed her own track back patiently. She couldn't have lost him all that long ago, she knew that.

Less than twenty minutes after she started following her own back trail, she found Kieran's scent again. The fur of her back started to rise, and without even thinking of it, she uttered a deep and ferocious growl. That *wrong* scent was back again, fresher than ever. It mingled with Kieran's scent, tumbled with it. She could see no blood on the ground, but neither could she see any tracks leading away. To her shock and fear, she realized that whatever had taken him had carried him straight up.

She didn't bother thinking about what she did next. Instead, her body started shrinking. Instead of a human form twisting out of the wolf's, an eagle's feathered body emerged instead. The expenditure of power was large, but she didn't care. As soon as she had wings that were great enough to bear her upwards, she sprang into the air. She lofted herself well above the trees, circling the area where she and Kieran had been. She sought desperately for Piers, but even the power of her sharp eyes did not reveal his presence.

Hailey circled the area for what felt like hours, but what she knew was only minutes. They were simply not there to be found. If she was a human, there would have been some doubt. However, there was no fooling her eagle eyes or her wolf nose. Something had taken both men, plucked them away as if they had never existed.

With a final cry, she circled back down to the forest floor. After a moment of thought, she came out of her eagle form. Though the eagle's body was useful, there was too much distraction for her in it. There was simply too much animal instinct within it for her to think clearly.

Hailey's mind was in a panic. She knew what she should do. Kieran had not predicted that both he and Piers would disappear. If he had, though, he would have told her to stay in her eagle form and to make her way back to civilization. From there, she could contact the Magus Corps and the Castle, letting them know what had happened.

Hailey understood this, but she couldn't make herself do it. She couldn't leave the last place she had seen Piers and Kieran. She couldn't leave them to whatever fates were waiting for them.

She took a deep breath. She had to find them. She still had power to spare, she realized, something that should have been impossible. She should have at least been flagging a little. Instead, buoyed by panic and worry, she was as strong now as when she had begun. She started concentrating on her wolf form, thinking about the power and the speed it could give her.

A deep, thunderous growl halted her in her tracks.

In front of her was the wolf that she had smelled. It was no shy animal, hiding away from men and guns. Instead, it was a giant. If it stood on its hind legs, it would have been as tall as Piers. Its fur was long and shaggy, speaking of its ability to survive the mountain winters. Its eyes were yellow, possessed of a deep fire that spoke of an uncanny intelligence.

It lowered its head and growled at her again.

• • • • •

Hailey froze. She couldn't transform into a wolf or an eagle. Her transformations were fast, but they weren't fast enough to catch a huge wolf in mid-lunge. She could neither fight nor fly away from the beast.

Instead, she stood frozen as it approached her, head down and tail up.

When she started to edge away, it uttered another ferocious growl, making her freeze. She had power to spare, but something kept her from summoning fire. She knew that she could set the beast alight, but she couldn't bring herself to do it, not to something that had not yet offered her any harm.

Still she kept the idea of a bright white-hot flame in her mind as it stalked closer and closer.

It seemed confused by her the closer it got. Several times, it drew its head back, once or twice uttering a plaintive whine that sounded positively bewildered. It circled her several times. Though it made the hair at the back of her neck prickle to have it behind her, she allowed it to look.

It was examining her, she realized. It wanted to know what she was and why she was in its territory. She took a deep breath. She submitted to its curiosity, reminding herself over and over again that she was not helpless. She could fight, but she didn't wish to, not when her opponent was only an animal that had done her no wrong.

Finally, the wolf made a deep whuffing sound, sitting down a few feet in front of her. Instead of regarding her as a threat, now it only looked curious, as if it wanted to see what she was going to do next.

"Well, are you done?" she asked softly.

To her surprise, the wolf barked. Wolves in the wild didn't vocalize the same way that dogs did, she knew that. Wolves were mostly silent, though of course they howled and they vocalized to communicate with their cubs. It was dogs that barked, or so she had been told. Dogs barked because they wanted to talk with their human companions. This was obviously a wolf and not a dog, but the bark that it had uttered made her think of a golden retriever at one of her foster homes. It was a bright and cheerful sound, something that was utterly out of place in the dark forest.

"Are you used to living with people?" she wondered out loud. "Did you once live in a zoo or a circus or something?"

The wolf offered no further answers. Instead, it only looked at her expectantly. Never taking her eyes off the animal, she edged away from it. Though it followed her, she could not detect any harm or ill intent coming from it.

Hailey realized that she was starting to lose the light. If she was going to have any chance of finding Kieran and Piers she had to get back on the trail she had been following. Still keeping an eye on the wolf, she reached for the power inside her again. To her surprise, the wolf did not growl or snap when she started to change. Instead, when she emerged in her wolf form, it trotted up and licked her face companionably.

When she sought after the trail, the wolf followed her.

Soon, Hailey had no time to keep an eye on the wolf at all. The trail twisted and turned a few more times, but soon enough, it led on a straight track through the woods. As she had guessed, it was leading her towards the smoke that Piers had seen earlier. She stuck with the twisting scent trail until dark had truly fallen. Even in her wolf form, she shivered a little bit from the cold.

As if sensing her discomfort, the wolf shouldered up against her, guiding her towards a well-concealed den underneath a fallen tree. The scraped earth burrow there was tight for two, but it was a cozy berth nonetheless. The wolf, far bigger than her own form, lay closer to the opening, shielding her from the cold.

Hailey thought that she wouldn't sleep at all, that there was far too much to occupy her mind. Before she knew it, however, she was drifting off, her cold nose buried in the wolf's ruff.

CHAPTER FORTY-SEVEN

WHEN HAILEY WOKE up, she was slightly startled to realize that she had reverted to her human form in the night. The burrow had been tight when she was a wolf. Now she realized that she was cramped and sore from curling her human limbs into it.

With a staggering step, she rose out of the hollow, shaking out her legs and arms as best she could in the predawn light. Her mouth tasted foul, and she spat a few times. Her rations had disappeared along with Kieran.

She still had power enough to transform. She was just getting ready to do so when there was a rustling in the bushes close to her. She looked up, expecting it be her mysterious wolf friend again, but instead, it was a man.

She barely stifled a cry of surprise, causing the man to look at her curiously.

He was dressed in a strange mix of modern clothing and things that could have come out of a Renaissance Faire trash heap. His dark hair was tied back with a leather thong, giving him a rather Viking appearance. He wore ragged black tactical gear, but over it was a coat of roughly tanned leather. It took her a moment to realize that he was holding a skewer of meat in his hand.

"I brought breakfast," he said mildly. "Eat up. It's good."

Hailey stared at him in confusion, making him push the meat towards her again.

"I…I don't know who you are," she said. "I try not to take food from people I don't know."

He grinned, his teeth sharp and white.

"We spent the night together. Usually that means that we're doing all right."

"The wolf was you? You're a shapechanger?'

He thought about it.

"I guess that's a word for me. Do you want the hare or no? It's getting cold."

She took the skewer of meat that he offered her, nibbling at the charred bits and never taking her eyes off of him as they stood there.

"It's good, thank you. Who are you? What are you doing far out here?"

"I've been here as long as I can remember," he shrugged. "Might as well ask you and your men what you're doing out here."

Hailey was glad her mouth was filled with food. It gave her a brief moment to review her options and to figure out how much she wanted to tell this stranger.

"We're looking for another man who came here. He was taken by something with a strange smell, not killed, though."

The man made a disgusted face.

"The dead-walkers," he growled, more than a touch of the wolf in his voice. "They've been showing up off and on for the last year, but now there are more of them than ever."

"Dead-walkers… You've run into them before?"

The grin that he gave her this time was honestly a little terrifying. There was death in that smile.

"I've killed them before, miss. They fight hard, but they die like anyone."

Hailey took a gamble.

"Are you a member of the Magus Corps?"

A faint shadow passed over his face. He frowned at her as if uncertain what she asked.

"That...they're hunters, yes? Men of power who hunt killers?"

Hailey nodded, encouraged. "Yes. They protect people who live in covens, like me."

He shook his head.

"They come through from time to time. I see them. I stay out of their way unless they need help."

"The man who was on the ground with me, he's part of that group. The man in the sky is a coven master. They were both taken, and I need to find them."

"And then what?"

"Find them, free them, hurt the ones who took them," Hailey said promptly.

The man stared at her uncertainly.

"Are you a killer?" he asked. "You don't look like one."

Hailey took a deep breath. In the mountains of northern Italy, a Templar had caught Kieran and her own friend Beatrice unawares. There was nothing standing between them and an enraged Templar but her. She had reached for the power that Kieran had given her, freezing the man's blood in his veins and killing him.

"I am," she said. "I would do it again if my loved ones were in danger."

The man nodded to himself.

"I can guide you to where they have been taken. I can even get you in. But I will warn you, the closer we come to that place, the more likely it is that I will lose myself."

Hailey shook her head.

"I don't understand what that means."

"I don't either," the man said helplessly.

• • • • •

In the end, she had no choice. She could have kept following the twisted trail that she had been on, but those scents were already fading. This man offered her a direct path that she needed to find the most important people in the world to her.

In her wolf form, she could keep up with him. As she ran, she observed her strange new companion. He was far more skilled in his wolf form than she was in hers. After a certain point, she began to suspect that it was due to long use. She was a human wearing a wolf's skin, but he was someone who seemed to inhabit both bodies equally. Something about it tickled the back of her brain, but then it was gone.

They ran for most of the day, pausing only briefly to hunt and kill food. Hailey found herself eating half of a rabbit that he had killed for her before she even thought of it. The idea of eating raw steaming meat in her human form sickened her, but in her wolf form, nothing could be more natural.

As they ran, she did her best to keep her thoughts focused. She couldn't afford to think too deeply on what was happening to Piers and to Kieran. She could only pray that they had not been harmed, and that she could rescue them.

The shadows grew longer, the light dimming steadily. The first sign that something was wrong with her companion was when he sat down, pointing his nose at the sky with a whine. She came up to him, offering wordless comfort by pressing her flank against his. That time, he got up and started running as he had before, but it grew worse. He seemed confused and distressed, whining and panting with his great red mouth open. Once she prevented him from running off their path. Another time, he nearly bit her in the face. Finally, she changed back into her human form, speaking quiet words of comfort as he leaned against the tree and panted. He whined several times, high and sad in a way that hurt her heart.

"It's all right," she murmured. "It's fine, I swear it's fine. You're taking me right where I need to go."

His form flowed until it was a man who knelt in the pine needles, his face pressed against her belly and his large hands clasped around her hips. She would have been startled and even frightened to suddenly be so close to a strange man, but he shook just like the wolf did.

"They came for me and broke me, and they did it all here," he muttered, his teeth chattering. "Years and years. They forgot me. They left me. They broke me."

"Who?" Hailey whispered, her voice intent. She thought she knew the answer, but she needed to be certain. "Who hurt you so?"

He shuddered.

"They've been called so many names. So have I. They—the Templars—hurt me. They broke me. I can have thoughts now. I can think. I don't always have to be the wolf."

She wondered if the simpler mind of the wolf protected him from whatever they had done to him.

"You smell right," he said, his voice barely more than a whimper. "I know you. I know you. Why do I know you?"

"I don't know," she murmured. "I wish I did."

When his panic had begun to grow, in her wolf form, she could smell more of that dead cold scent. It was unnatural. It made the hair on the back of her neck stand up. However bad it was for her, however, it seemed ten times worse for this man. She sat on the ground with him and tried to think. It was growing darker. She would reach the center of the disturbances soon. She looked at the shaking man, wondering if she should bring him.

"I don't want to bring you into the heart of that madness, but I'm not sure I can go on my own, either. Do you think you can help me? I wouldn't ask, but there are lives on the line. At the very least, Kieran and Piers are at risk. I don't know, but there might be more. Can you help me?"

For a long moment, she thought the man would refuse. She couldn't have blamed him. She could sense that she was asking him to risk his sanity and his safety to go further with her.

Slowly, however, he nodded, standing up straight. He was not a tall man, but like Piers and Kieran, he was a man who had presence. Hailey sensed that whatever he used to be, she was seeing a shade of it now.

"I will help you," he said, though his voice was soft and uncertain. "I must, and I will. Only let me stay a wolf. If I am a wolf, I am less likely to be turned. I will not harm you if I am a wolf." Hailey nodded her agreement. "Best you stay as a woman now," he said. "There are tasks ahead that call for hands and fingers."

She watched as he flowed back into his wolf form. He still shook slightly, but when she laid her tentative hand on his shoulder, he started walking. Their progress was slower now, but it mattered very little. Just as the last streaks of light disappeared from the sky, they came to a canyon's mouth.

The canyon was guarded on three sides by rock, but from where they stood, Hailey could see an unlikely thing. It was a stone fortress, an edifice so large it fell just short of being a castle. In the dim light, there were a few windows that were lit up, but overall, there was a sense of gloom and abandonment about it. Next to her, the wolf shivered, touching her hip.

"It'll be fine, I promise," she whispered, though she knew that it could be the worst lie she had ever told.

She had power, though it was less than it had been this morning. She could feel the edges of exhaustion lap against her. But she had enough strength to threaten someone, to kill them if need be. It would do. It had to.

The wolf led her close to the canyon wall. It was so dark that she had to navigate by feel, trusting her own slow feet and the wolf's patient guidance to steer her. Not willing to risk being seen, she left her small flashlight in her pocket. It seemed to take an eternity, but the wolf led her to what looked like an iron gate set into the building.

To her dismay, it looked like it had been blocked with rubble and scree from the inside. However, the wolf pawed at the gate itself, whining until she opened it. It wasn't locked; likely whoever lived in the fortress now figured the rubble would hold back any invaders. Hailey was inclined to believe the same, but then she saw what the wolf was trying to show her.

Near the top of the pile of rubble, there seemed to be a narrow tunnel, a channel where the scree and stone had been pushed and pulled away. It was painfully narrow, however. The way forward led only into darkness.

She bit her lip, hesitating. As she paused, however, the wolf scrabbled into the tunnel, squirming forward into it.

Well, when there's only one way forward, you need to take it, Hailey thought to herself.

She clambered up the wall of rubble, easing herself into the tunnel as quietly as she could. It was barely wide enough to pass through. More than once, she had to scrape her shoulders or her elbows to push her way through. She was uncomfortably aware that there would be no way for Piers or Kieran to pass this way. If they were going to escape, they would have to do it in some other fashion.

The tunnel was dark and close. Hailey had never been afraid of enclosed places, but now she saw how she could be. It seemed to go on forever with no place to turn around, no place to stretch out. She might have been buried under miles of rock and stone for all she knew. Just when she thought that the darkness would drive her mad, she felt air instead of the tunnel floor in front of her. A moment later, a cold wet nose was pushed into her seeking hand and a warm tongue licked at her fingers.

The opening was located three feet from the ground. She had to slither out of the hole, head first. Though she was careful, she still managed to scrape herself on the way down. She sat on the floor breathing hard, wrapping her arms around the wolf for comfort.

"All right then," she whispered, when she had her breath back. "What are we looking at?"

She carefully pointed her flashlight to the ground before turning it on. To her surprise, she wasn't in a deep, dark dungeon. Instead, it seemed like she had come out in what had once been a larder. There were crates that held desiccated vegetables, and not far from where she sat, there was an ancient bag of what looked like moldy potatoes. The place was frigid.

She realized that the tunnel she had crawled through must have been an escape hatch long ago. The people who had lived here had wanted a way to get out if things went wrong. People must have come along later and realized that the exit was a liability that they didn't need, filling it up with stone.

Hailey climbed to her feet, heading to the wooden door across the room. As she had hoped, it opened at her touch, though it did make a creak that sounded like it would wake the dead. Beside her, the wolf winced, as if sharing her opinion.

They ventured into the dark corridors beyond the little cellar. The wolf slowly gained confidence as they walked through.

Perhaps he was becoming more accustomed to the darkness of the place. Perhaps he was simply as resolute as she was.

The way through the halls was dark and twisted. Through the passageways, however, there was something oddly familiar to Hailey about all of it. Something about this dark place made her think of her beloved Castle, the place that Piers had created to be a sanctuary of safety and peace. Like the Castle, this place had been built with a purpose in mind, and that thought chilled her.

Once, they heard a voice singing. She recognized the language as French, though she could not understand a word of it. For a moment, she was panicked, as the voices got closer. The wolf tensed as if to attack. Hailey realized that she could not allow that. Instead, she twisted her fingers through the wolf's ruff, pulling him into an alcove nearby. It was dark and shadowed, but to be sure, she closed her eyes and covered the wolf's eyes with her hands. It would prevent any errant light from shining in their faces and betraying them.

It was harrowing to wait as the man passed, stumping by on some errand or another. Templars were just normal men. She knew that. They're sole purpose in life was to wipe out Wiccans as a whole. They were terribly strong, as skilled in the arts of war as the Magus Corps. Despite all that, they were just men. However, there was a strange taint that followed the ones that she had met. It was as if they had promised themselves to something dark and cruel. In turn, that cruelty had marked them.

She let the man pass by and counted to a hundred. When she was sure he was gone, she released her death grip on the wolf and stepped back into the corridor.

She thought that the path would never end. The building was dark and cold, terrible in its quiet. Then she started hearing noises. It started out subtly at first. She wondered if it was just the sounds of the wind blowing through the old stone. However, the longer they walked, the clearer the sounds became. It was not the wind. Instead, they were cries of pain, echoing against stone. Sometimes, if the corridors bent right, she could hear words in it. Many of the words were in languages that she simply did not understand. The words she could understand made her blood run cold.

Kill me.

Let me go.

Please.

I will die down here.

There is no light.

She kept walking because there was nothing else that she could do. The wolf by her side was patient, trembling from time to time, but he led her straight through the dark maze. She realized after a while that the ground was sloping. They were walking underground. The stone floor underneath grew rough and uneven before it finally became packed dirt. The air, already frigid, took on a clammy feel.

Just as Hailey was starting to worry that there was no end to the darkness, they rounded a corner and were confronted with a wooden door. It was massive, stained and old, but when she touched it gingerly, it swung open.

She faced a large stone room, the floor marked with runes. Lining the edge of the rooms were a series of cells, barred and small. The keys were hung on the wall by the door. It struck her as careless until she remembered that as long as the prisoners couldn't reach it, it might as well be in plain sight. Her heart beating faster, she started to walk around the room, peering into the dim depths.

The cells were filthy and foul. In one of them, she could see what looked like a skeleton. In another, she saw a pile of rags that perhaps once had been human. She continued, forcing herself to look and to mark what she saw. Close to the end of the circuit, she stifled a cry of pain. In cells side-by-side were Piers and Kieran. They looked whole, but they both lay on their backs, arms and legs flung at strange angles as if they had been dropped their by some strange hand.

She unlocked the door to Piers's cell. She would have rushed in if the wolf had not blocked her body with his. She looked down, confused, only to see him scrabbling at a chalk figure on the floor in front of her.

Hailey felt the hair at the back of her neck rise. She had spent some time researching runes and ancient magics back before she had been allowed to use her real powers. This was a rune, and though she did not know much about it, she knew that it was meant to work on anything in its path.

Gingerly, she wiped the rune out of existence with her foot, making Piers blink and groan.

"Hailey… Hailey, where are you?"

"Right here," she murmured.

She squeezed his hand so that he would know that it was truly her. He clung to her hand when she offered it. He was shaking. She thought of the rune that she had erased and winced. Runes that were meant to bind were seldom pleasant things. It had likely kept him from harming his captors by plunging him into some nightmare realm.

She didn't want to leave his side, but she knew that she had to. "Come on, we have to get Kieran."

He nodded jerkily, rising to follow her from his cell. She wiped the rune away from the floor of Kieran's cell, leading him to spring to his feet.

He was moving so quickly that there was no way for Hailey to have prepared herself. In the space of a moment, he had her pinned against the wall with his forearm across her throat.

"Demon, you will not trick me again," he snarled.

There was murder in his eyes. For a moment, Hailey thought that he would kill her where she stood.

The wolf's growl was loud and vicious. Before it could spring, however, Piers stepped forward. He put both of his hands on Kieran's shoulders, not pulling but simply letting him know that there was someone else there.

"Peace, Major. She's no demon. You love her, and you shall not hurt her."

Kieran's body stayed as tensed as a coiled spring. Then slowly, inch by inch, he relaxed, letting her away from the wall.

"Kieran?" she whispered.

He shook his head as if it was fogged. When he met her eyes, he swept her up in his arms.

"Gods above, Hailey, I'm so sorry. I didn't know who you were. I didn't know what was happening, and I hurt you."

"No, no Kieran, you didn't hurt me. You didn't, I swear. I'm fine. Now we just need to get out of here."

"We can't." Kieran stood a little straighter. "Or at least, I can't. This is where we need to be. I need to find out what happened to the other Magus Corps officers, and I know this is where I am going to find my answers."

Hailey turned to Piers pleadingly.

"Please, tell him that we need to get out of here. Now that we know the location, we can send for help, we can find others who can fight their way in."

As Piers shook his head slowly, she realized why they couldn't leave.

"There may be more alive here," she whispered.

Kieran nodded. "Hailey, if you want to leave, please, that's what I want you to do."

Hailey shook her head.

"No. Either we're leaving together, all three of us or we're not leaving at all."

Piers looked like he was going to argue with her, but then the wolf started to growl. His fur stood up high on the back of his neck, and he stalked stiff-legged in the direction of the door.

Kieran swore. With a single motion he thrust Hailey behind him. She could feel his skin grow several degrees colder as in front of him thin blades of ice started to form out of the condensation from the air. In a matter of moments, they were longer than her forearm, moving in a deadly glittering dance.

Beside her, Piers offered her his arm, a dark look on his face. She started to protest, but he shook his head.

"I want to make sure that you have every chance of surviving what comes next, Hailey. Please."

Nodding, she took a deep breath and pulled the power that she could from him. In return, she tried to feed it back to him as well. This time, she was certain of it. They were more together than they ever could be apart. When he pulled back from her, she could sense the power radiating from him.

The door swung open, revealing five figures behind it. At first Hailey thought that they were enormous men, but then she realized how wrong she was.

The first man through the door was normal enough, though she could tell by the sword he wore that he must have been a Templar. The four figures behind him, however, had only once been men.

Hailey had barely survived a demon attack before. At that point, the demon had only possessed the man for a short time, but even then, the damage was profound. The man had been a shambling wreck, and it had been clear that the demon needed a new body very quickly.

These things were something else. From the stench that rose

from their bodies and the way the faces were damaged and twisted, she could tell that there were demons inside. The demons had made the men grow monstrous, however, and these things showed no signs of hurt or harm.

The man who led them swore. With a single gesture of his hand, he commanded his hellish troops forward. To Hailey's surprise, they were slow and sluggish, moving towards them with a lumbering stride.

The wolf dove at them as Kieran sent his ice blades whirling through the air. Piers had taken flight, and she gave thanks to all the gods that the ceiling was so tall. He whirled above them, coming down to plant all of his weight behind one of the demon's necks. It should have snapped the thing's spine, but instead it only screamed, reaching around clumsily to grab at him.

Hailey thought frantically, trying to think of a skill that she could use to help fight. In her panic, her mind was maddeningly blank. Suddenly, a piece of inspiration came to her. She closed her eyes, summoning up her power.

When she opened her eyes, she could see auras of color around the figures in the room. Both Piers and Kieran were a blazing scarlet, their auras showing their full battle frenzy. The demons to her surprise, were a dirty yellow, a color that she sensed meant despair. When she turned to the Templar who controlled them, however, she found what she had been looking for.

He was a big man, and his aura was a flickering, liver red. Her eyes focused not on his aura, however, but on the white-gold outline of something on his chest.

Kieran, Piers and the wolf were holding their own against the four demons, but she could see that no matter what they did, they weren't hurting them. The demons continued to come for them, ignoring any injuries that they received. They were slow and clumsy, but they were still powerful. Eventually, it would be a matter of endurance. Her lovers would lose.

Moving as stealthily as she could, Hailey clung to the wall and made her way to the Templar. This close, she could see that he was an older man, his face twisted in a parody of pleasure. He didn't notice her sidle up to him until it was far too late.

Her hand scrabbled at his chest. When he reached for her, ice blades of her own came up to dance in front of his eyes.

Behind her, she could suddenly hear a deafening silence, but she didn't dare turn her eyes to look. Instead, she grasped the thing with the bright white aura on his chest. It was a tarnished silver medallion, something inscribed with a twisted face that it hurt her to look at. She pulled it away from him with enough force that she was sent skittering backwards. She almost caught herself, but then she fell flat on her back.

For a moment, Hailey was sure that it was over. She was going to have her throat slit by the Templar or she would simply be crushed by the demons he commanded.

As one the demons moved. They pulled away from the battle, heedless of the ice slivers buried in their ruined skin or the blood that was flowing down their backs.

"No! No, goddamn you! You belong to me! I am the one who controls you!"

His cries went unheard as the demons converged upon him. They moved with a deliberate, stone-like determination that filled Hailey with a kind of terror. Almost delicately, each one took one of the Templar's limbs in their hands.

Oh no, they can't, Hailey thought blankly.

The Templar started to scream. Piers landed by Hailey's side, his face dead white. Kieran came to stand with them.

The demons pulled the Templar to pieces with a terrible wet sound that Hailey was sure she would hear in nightmares the rest of her life. She looked away, but she couldn't get the image out of her head. She felt sick, more than a little dizzy, but when she could bring herself to look, she realized that it wasn't over yet.

The demons stood over the mangled body for a long moment. In that instant, they looked like nothing more than broken dolls whose springs had worn out. Hailey dared to believe that it was over for a single moment, but then they turned.

Piers and Kieran tensed as the demons focused their attention on Hailey. They were getting ready to attack them again when Hailey took a deep breath.

"Stop!"

As if they had walked into a wall, the demons stopped. She had an insane moment where she realized that she could tell them to go again and they would. It would be like the world's most dangerous game of Simon Says.

"Hailey, what's going on?" whispered Piers, never taking his eyes from the demons.

"This medallion controls them, I think. I think it's safe now."

"Yes, because it was so safe for that Templar," said Kieran darkly. "We need to figure out where these things came from."

"I think I know," said Hailey softly.

She could feel grief rise up in her chest. She would have given anything to be wrong. Instead, she took a step closer to the tallest demon. The scars running over his bare torso should not have been survivable. Some of them still bled sluggishly, soaking into the stone beneath him with an ugly, pattering sound.

"Can you speak?"

There was a pause where she was sure the answer would be 'no.'

"I can speak, mistress."

The demon's voice sounded like it came from deep underground, as if it burrowed up with worms and moles.

"Are there any others in this place?"

"No, mistress. The one who held the medallion before was the only one who brought us here, who created us."

Hailey thought for a moment.

"Piers and Kieran were snatched from the ground and the air. There was no scent left behind. Did you do that?"

Silently, the monster pointed at one of the demons beside him. This one unlimbered wings that looked broken and tattered. Hailey wondered if such a thing could even get into the air, but when she saw the enormous twitching muscles across the demon's chest, she realized that it could do so easily. That was another mystery solved.

"Who are you?"

There was a long silence. Then to Hailey's horror, the demon raised a slow hand and started tearing at its own face. She cried out in shock as the blood flowed down, but when the demon spoke next, it was with a voice that was almost painfully human.

"I am Colonel Thomas Wyecomb of the Magus Corps," he rasped. "I was captured by that Templar and infected with a demon."

Kieran stepped forward, reaching for the colonel with one hand. Wyecomb waved him back with a swipe and a growl.

"No, don't touch me. I'm possessed by this demon, and it has put its roots down deep in me. The Templar bound it to me, and now we are one."

Kieran looked sickened.

"What can we do to heal you? What can be done to pull the demon away?"

Wyecomb made a dark and gurgling sound that Hailey had to strain to recognize as a laugh.

"There's nothing you can do for us. All you can do is to destroy us. We are all members of the Magus Corps, and we have all fallen. Better to be remembered as a fallen Corps man rather than a monster."

"I can't do that," Kieran protested. "I was sent to find you, to find all of you."

Wyecomb's eye, a vivid hazel, peered out of the wreck of his face.

"Then you're a member of the Magus Corps as well?"

"Yes. I am Major Kieran McCallen."

"This will be easy then. As a member of your brotherhood, I charge you with the final mercy that you can visit upon us. There is a room just outside this chamber with weapons in it. Find something that will take off our heads and give us peace."

"I can't! Don't ask me to do that."

"I am not asking you, I am ordering you, Major!" Wyecomb's voice came out as a roar. He lunged at Kieran, arms out to crush him.

"Stop!" Hailey cried. As before, he stumbled to a halt.

Wyecomb turned his eye to Hailey. Under that maddened, pained gaze, she felt a hot spike of pity and grief.

"You could keep us as we are, ma'am," Wyecomb said, his voice almost pleasant. "You could do it with that little toy that you've got in your hands. You could keep us still until the Magus Corps sends more men out here. What I will tell you is that they will find nothing more than what I have told you. We are dead, and if we continue as we are, we are damned."

Hailey found herself nodding. She turned to Kieran, her eyes wide and beseeching. For a moment, she thought that he wouldn't relent. Finally, he nodded, his face like a granite mask. There was something deadened about him in that moment, something so defeated.

"Yes. I'll do it."

He started for the room, but then Piers stepped forward.

"Wait. Before we let these men go to their last rest, we can take their names. They will not be forgotten. They will be remembered as the heroes that they were."

This caused a stir in the beings in front of them.

Wyecomb stood up straight.

"Colonel Thomas Wyecomb of the Magus Corps. Born 1709. No last words."

Almost as if by clockwork, the second stood forward.

"Second Lieutenant James Orris of the Magus Corps. Born 1890. No last words."

"Captain Royce Martel of the Magus Corps. Born 1534. Tell my brother Stephan that he is a fine man and excellent officer."

The last stood up, but though he moved his mouth, he could not speak. He tried, making several deep groaning noises. When he realized that he would not be able to speak, he stood with his head hanging and his sides heaving. Finally, he reached somewhere into his tattered ragged clothing and withdrew something small and dark. He pressed it into Hailey's hand.

She stared at it in confusion. Though it was battered and bent, she could see that it was a pin featuring a pair of interlocked iron pentacles.

"It's the insignia of a lieutenant commander," Kieran said. "It's enough."

But it would never be enough, Hailey realized with a pang. These were four men who had their lives taken from them. Then those lives were used to harm others. If she thought about it for too long, she would break down and weep. Instead she tucked the insignia into one of the inner pockets of her cold weather gear for safekeeping. When Kieran returned with an enormous ax, she kept her face immobile.

Wyecomb knelt first. As Kieran lifted the ax, Wyecomb whispered *thank you.* Kieran was strong and fast. It was over in a heartbeat.

Hailey could feel hot tears streaming down her face. When Piers took her hand in his, she squeezed it as tight as she could, but she didn't look away.

Orris was next, followed by Martel. Kieran was flecked with dark blood, but he was impassive as he did his cruel, merciful work.

Slowly, the last knelt, the nameless, the man who couldn't even die with his past respected.

As Kieran raised the ax one last time, Hailey realized that there was something wrong. She couldn't explain what it was. It was a nameless dread that rose up from the core of her being. This last man was different, the one who couldn't speak. She put out her hand to stop Kieran, but it was too late. The ax came down, the head hit the floor, but the body did not fall.

Three humans and a wolf stood frozen as the headless body rose up from the ground. They couldn't speak as a strange and sibilant laughter filled the room.

"Oh, but I am dead, and I am dead, what a terrible day this is!"

The voice seemed to come from everywhere and nowhere, ringing through the chamber and echoing until Hailey thought that she would go mad. The thing's mocking tone was shrill and unnatural, like aluminum being torn apart.

"What are you?" Hailey said from between numb lips.

"Oh did I not tell you, child? I am dead, I am dead, your man has killed me. But just because I am passed on does not mean that I lack power. Just because I am dead does not mean that I will leave you in peace, yes?"

The body's misshapen legs raised up one after the other, stomping in the pooled blood on the floor. After a moment, Hailey realized that it was dancing.

"Oh, but I have so little, so little time left, so what shall I do with it? Shall I make you kill each other? Shall I force you on each other?"

Hailey felt her stomach turn as she realized that this thing, even though it was dying, could do that.

"No! No. Do what you want to me, please, but let these two go," she said.

The thing turned to her, or at least it turned its body to her.

"Let them go? Why what a good idea. I will find a lovely place, a safe place for them, and then I will let them go. Clever girl, smart girl, strong girl, I will let them go."

The demon's final words rose up into a shriek. It was a demon's death curse, its final breath of malevolence before it was forced to exit the world. Hailey's hands were finally free so she could plant them over her ears. The sound whipped around the room as if it were a sandstorm. Somewhere, the wolf was howling. Piers and Kieran were screaming.

Then, mercifully and terribly, everything was quiet. Hailey had fallen on the ground, curled up to protect herself from the demon's cries. Now she could stand up and look around.

The wolf was staggering to his feet, shaking his head and whining, but both Piers and Kieran were laid out on their backs. She dashed to Kieran first. He had stood the closest to the demon. To her relief, he still breathed, but his skin was waxen. A dull, dark liquid dripped out of his nose and his ears. When she tried to rouse him, screaming and finally slapping his face, he lay as still as a cast-off doll. Piers was the same, blood coming from his nose and his ears, and the same dead feeling.

Hailey slumped to the floor between them, numbed and afraid. She had lost the ability to think or move.

The wolf approached her, but then he flowed into his man shape. She didn't protest when he lifted her in his arms as tenderly as he would a child. She closed her eyes and let the darkness take her.

CHAPTER FORTY-EIGHT

HAILEY WOKE UP feeling as though she had been beaten with a sack of rocks. Every part of her hurt. Everything in her felt broken. Then she remembered the past twenty-four hours. She thought that her head would break apart.

When she looked to her left, she saw a stone window beyond which was deep forest. She could see the ruined iron gate that she'd passed through with the wolf. The wall under the window was lined with glass cabinets. To her right was a long row of beds. Directly next to her was Piers. Beyond him was Kieran. To her grief, they lay as the dead, pale and still. She realized that she was in some kind of infirmary. She staggered out of bed to stand between them, resting her hands on their chests. She didn't know what she was going to do.

The door behind her opened, and the man who had been a wolf came in. He bore a tray with roasted meat on it. The scent of it turned her stomach. He must have seen the look on her face.

"You have to eat," he said.

Already lightheaded, she knew he was right. But she could hardly take her eyes from Piers and Kieran. It didn't feel right eating, when they couldn't, when they–

"You can't help them by starving," the man said. He sat on the bed beyond Kieran, and laid the platter on it. "Come."

Mechanically, she did as he said. She sat, took a drumstick of the roasted rabbit, and ate. As she did, she realized he was watching her intently.

"What is it?" she asked, her voice dull.

"There's something about you," he said quietly. "There's a scent on you. One that I know but I can't remember."

Something about the way he spoke finally turned a key in her memory. She remembered lying in bed, curled up with Liona. Liona had had two lovers. One, Gaius, had stood beside her when she built up the covens. The other had gone to start the organization that would become the Magus Corps. He had been lost to time. He had disappeared centuries ago.

"Lucius?" she whispered, her eyes wide.

Saying the name wrought an immediate change in the man. His dark eyes went wide. He shuddered as if he was in pain. Suddenly he stood to loom over her, his face dark and confused. His hands clenched and unclenched at his sides.

"What is that name?" he said, his voice dropped down to a wolfish growl. "What does that name mean?"

"It's an old name," she said softly, trying to keep her voice low and level.

This was a man who the Templars had broken, and when he'd escaped, little remained of the man that Liona knew. Hailey knew that there was as much beast in him as man, but the beast had helped her. She had to remember that.

"What does it mean? Why…why does it hurt?"

"It was your name," she continued. "You are Lucius Magnus, a legatus of Rome."

He growled at her, lashing out blindly with one arm. The plate of meat clattered to the floor as Hailey stood. Some very ancient and primal part of her wanted to run and hide, to put something between herself and what this man was. But she held her ground. This was what he needed to hear, whether he knew it or not.

"You fell in love with a girl named Liona, and when your family was kidnapped, you both went looking for them."

"You're lying," he snarled.

He put up an arm as if he would fend off the words that she was saying. She was relentless.

"You were both banished from Rome, and in Gaul, you met a sorcerer named Gaius. He joined your quest, and then you lost her."

"Liona…we lost her. She was taken." His voice was wondering. "We tore that town apart looking for her."

"But you found her again…"

"Yes, in Alexandria." A shadow passed over his face. "They hurt her."

"And she healed. And you found your family."

"I…I…"

He jerked as if he had been struck with a whip. To Hailey's shock, he fell to his knees with a wolf-like howl. He curled in on himself, trembling on the floor. Hailey knelt beside him even though she knew it was foolish. He was a powerful man, either in his wolf form or as he was. He could have killed her without thinking. But she wrapped her arms around his body just as she had when he was a wolf.

"She healed," she whispered. "Her and her sister and your friend, all of them did. You stayed with them for a while, but there were other things you wanted. You are Lucius Magnus, and you are remembered. You founded an organization that would protect people for a thousand years and still does. You are Lucius."

He shook until finally he went still. Hailey waited, her mind oddly calm. Minutes may have passed, but when he finally rose, there was a strength in him that hadn't been there before. He stood up straight, and his eyes were sharper. She could see the legatus now, the officer who had commanded men, Liona's lover, and the warlock who had helped to create the world she lived in.

"I am Lucius Magnus," he said, his voice calm and strong. "I owe you a great debt of service, Hailey."

Hailey smiled and stood up from the ground with him.

"You smelled Liona on me. She has missed you."

"And I her. I'll go to her as soon as I can, but first we must deal with your men."

"What can be done?" she asked. "I lay abed for a long time when I was just wounded by a demon. This is worse."

"The first and most obvious thing is to kill them."

Hailey snarled at him before she knew what she was doing. He looked at her with a perfectly serious face.

"You need someone who can enter the world the demon cast them in to. You need someone who can bring them back out of it. Do you understand what that world is like?"

Hailey shivered, hugging herself tightly. She did. When she had been wounded by a demon herself, she had walked through endless halls in an empty castle. It felt like she had walked there forever, and she might have if Liona hadn't appeared to bring her out.

"That was a powerful demon," Lucius said. "It died laying a curse on these two. It would have sent them far deeper than what an average witch could do. It would have taken them to some place that was truly hellish."

"Will they stay there forever?" she whispered.

"Until they die or until someone comes for them." There was a subtle shake to Lucius' voice. He was not as unaffected as he looked. There was something wolf-like about his impassivity, but she wondered if it was from all his long years at war as well.

"Liona could go for them."

"She could. They are dying quickly though. You can see it if you look. They are dying with the demon's taint on them."

Hailey felt hopelessness yawn underneath her like a chasm. She could feel the weight of Lucius's words. Then her mind latched on to one brief hope.

"Could I do it?"

Lucius frowned at her.

"You are not a dream walker," he said. "I saw you change forms."

"I'm many things," she said, confidence reasserting itself in her voice. "All I know is that I will do anything to save them. I need them."

Lucius nodded slowly, his eyes narrowed.

"It was a skill of Liona's. Others might have it as well. You must be asleep to follow them. You must be able to find them in your dreams."

"If all it takes is will and dreams to find them, I will."

Lucius hesitated.

"This is not without risks," he said finally. "Simply because you fall asleep to enter this world does not mean that you can leave it simply by waking up. If you venture too far into the realm that the demons call their own, you may become stuck there. You may become as trapped as they are."

Hailey could remember the endless tunnels she had been lost in before Liona had found her. Her mind and spirit had been fading, even as her body died.

"I am willing to take that risk," she said firmly.

Lucius looked at her and nodded.

"They have medicine here. I will go and see if there is anything that can help you sleep."

As he went to rummage in the cabinets, she came to stand

between Piers and Kieran. She touched their faces tenderly. She kissed their hands.

"Hold on," she whispered. "Please hold on. That's all you have to do, until I get there. We'll win free of this. I love you. I love you so much."

Lucius returned with a vial of clear liquid and a fresh syringe.

"Morphine," he said. "It will send you off to a deep slumber. Are you sure you want to do this?"

Hailey lay back on her bed. Outside, dawn was breaking, filling the sky with light.

"I am," she said, her voice thin but strong. "Please, help me."

He came to stand over her, swabbing her arm with alcohol. She felt the sharp prick of the needle, and then the slow, milky languor that came over her body.

As she was overwhelmed by the drug, she thought of the arrow that Liona had shot for her before she left the Castle.

May I fly straight and true, and may I find what I seek. Piers, Kieran, please wait for me. I need you. I love you.

• • • • •

Hailey's story continues in IMPRISONED: Castle Coven Book Five, available now.

For a sneak peek, turn the page.

Excerpt:

IMPRISONED

Castle Coven Book Five

Kieran started to say something, but then Piers squeezed him between the legs through his trousers. Kieran gasped, his hips bucking a little.

"You were already hard," Piers commented. "I don't think it would take that much before I got you to beg."

Kieran swore helplessly at Piers, who only laughed. Hailey felt a hot blush on her cheeks as Piers deftly unfastened Kieran's trouser, drawing his erection out fully. He pumped the other man's cock almost lazily, in absolutely no hurry at all.

When Piers stepped back, Kieran was fully hard and panting slightly. To Hailey's shock, Piers slapped the other man's hard flesh lightly, making Kieran groan.

"That's good for you right now. I have some other things I want to do."

Hailey realized that Piers was looking straight at her. She stood her ground as he walked over to her. The idea of being held and aroused helplessly made her want to whimper, but instead he only looked her over.

"Strip for me," he said finally. "Down to the skin. I've never thought that you should wear clothes."

Hailey gulped and nodded. Her boots and outer garments went quickly enough, but when she got down to her underthings, she paused. The hall was cold, and not only were Piers's avid eyes on her, but so were Kieran's. The suits of armor she knew were insensible, but they were a presence as well.

Taking a deep breath, she stripped the last of her clothing off to stand naked in front of Piers. She resisted the instinctive urge to cover herself. He had seen her naked before, but never in this cool and calculated way.

Piers examined her much as he had examined Kieran. When he reached for her, she expected a gentle caress or even a passionate one, but instead his hands ran down her shoulders and her arms, along her flanks and down her thighs. When he swept his fingers through the length of her red hair, she shivered at how close he was to her and everything that she could feel.

She felt like an object he was examining, perhaps deciding if he wished to purchase her or use her. When he tweaked first one nipple and then the other, she squeaked a little, making him smile.

"You're perfect for me," he said casually. "I've always thought so, but I love you like this."

She started to ask what he meant, but instead, she gasped when he lifted her in his arms as if she was as light as a feather. She clung to him for a moment, but they weren't going far. He was only depositing her on his desk, heedless of the papers that lay on it. She tried to close her legs, but he held them open, letting them dangle over the edge of the desk. She blinked when she realized that she was able to look straight at Kieran, who was still held by the suit of armor.

He looked absolutely starved. His eyes were wide and glassy, and his gaze flickered between her naked body and the way Piers stood to one side, watching her closely.

Almost casually, much as he had done with Kieran, his hand closed over the space between her legs. She held her breath as he cupped that tender flesh before running his fingertip along her slit. Her lower lips were full and warm, but when he traced his finger along the seam between, she grew wet.

"Do you like being displayed, Hailey? Do you like me showing Kieran how wet you get for me? Would you like me to show you to an army of men, just like this?"

Hailey shook her head to clear it. She had to try twice before she could find her voice.

"I like being displayed," she said softly. "But I just want you and Kieran to see me. I…trust your eyes. I love you both."

She wondered if Piers would be displeased, but he only chuckled.

"My perfect, beautiful, little pet."

As if to reward her for speaking, he ghosted a fingertip over her clit, smearing some of the wetness from below over it. She purred, turning her face to rest it against his side, but he didn't do that for very long.

"Let's see how you like this."

She focused on a chain between his hands. She realized there were small clamps on either end, making her gasp.

"Do you know where these are going to go?"

Hailey gulped.

"I have an idea."

• • • • •

MORE BOOKS BY HAZEL HUNTER

THE HOLLOW CITY COVEN SERIES

A daring quest. A deadly enemy. A protector who won't quit. Although Wiccan Gillian Granger's life's work is finding a legendary city, her research in musty libraries hasn't prepared her for the field, let alone a gorgeous escort. Shayne Savatier knows he's on a milk run, especially after he meets his beautiful charge. But when enemies attack her, everything changes. Passion intertwines with protection, and duty bonds hard with desire.

Possessed (Hollow City Coven Book One)

Shadowed (Hollow City Coven Book Two)

Trapped (Hollow City Coven Book Three)

Sign up for my newsletter to be notified of new releases!

THE SILVER WOOD COVEN SERIES

Though she's taken the name given her by a kind stranger, Summer can no more explain waking up homeless and covered in blood, than she can the extreme attraction drawing people to her. Amnesiac, confused, and frightened, she's not even aware that she's a witch. But help arrives in two very different forms: the cool and restrained Templar Michael Charbon and his centuries-long friend Wiccan Major Troy Atwater.

Rescued (Silver Wood Coven Book One)

Stolen (Silver Wood Coven Book Two)

United (Silver Wood Coven Book Three)

Betrayed (Silver Wood Coven Book Four)

Revealed (Silver Wood Coven Book Five)

THE CASTLE COVEN SERIES

Novice witch Hailey Devereaux had resolved to live life as an outsider. Possessed of a unique Wiccan ability, her own people shun her. But that all ends when two very different men enter her life: the brooding Major Kieran McCallen and Coven Master Piers Dayton. But their training and tests are only the beginning. As she struggles to fulfill her destiny and find her place in the world, Hailey also discovers love.

Found (Castle Coven Book One)

Abandoned (Castle Coven Book Two)

Healed (Castle Coven Book Three)

Claimed (Castle Coven Book Four)

Imprisoned (Castle Coven Book Five)

Sacrificed (Castle Coven Book Six)

Castle Coven Box Set (Books 1 - 6)

THE MAGUS CORPS SERIES

Meet the warlocks of the Magus Corps, sworn to protect Wiccans at all costs. As they find and track fledgling witches, it's a race against an ancient enemy that would rather see all Wiccans dead. But where danger and intimacy come together, passion is never far behind.

Dominic (Her Warlock Protector Book 1)

Sebastian (Her Warlock Protector Book 2)

Logan (Her Warlock Protector Book 3)

Colin (Her Warlock Protector Book 4)

Vincent (Her Warlock Protector Book 5)

Jackson (Her Warlock Protector Book 6)

Trent (Her Warlock Protector Book 7)

Her Warlock Protector Box Set (Books 1 - 7)

THE SECOND SIGHT SERIES

Join psychic Isabelle de Grey and FBI profiler Mac MacMillan as they hunt a serial killer in the streets of Los Angeles. Even as their search closes in on the kidnapper, they discover not only clues, but a fiery passion that quickly consumes them.

Touched (Second Sight Book 1)

Torn (Second Sight Book 2)

Taken (Second Sight Book 3)

Chosen (Second Sight Book 4)

Charmed (Second Sight Book 5)

Changed (Second Sight Book 6)

Second Sight Box Set (Books 1 - 6)

THE EROTIC EXPEDITION SERIES

Travel the world in these breathless tales of erotic romance. Each features a different couple in fast-paced tales of fiery passion.

Arctic Exposure

A young couple is stranded in an Alaskan storm.

Desert Thirst

In the Sahara, a master tracker has the scent of his fiery client.

Jungle Fever

A forensic accountant blossoms under the care of a plantation owner in Thailand.

Mountain Wilds
A beautiful doctor on the rebound crashes with her pilot in British Columbia.

Island Magic
Two treasure-hunting scuba divers are kidnapped in the Caribbean.

THE ROMANCE IN THE RUINS NOVELS

Explore the ancient world and the new in these standalone novels of erotic romance. Each features a hero and heroine who come together against all odds, in exotic and remote settings where danger and love are found in equal measure.

Words of Love
Set in the heartland of the ancient Maya.

Labyrinth of Love
Set on the ancient Greek island of Crete.

Stars of Love
Set in the rugged Pueblo Southwest.

Sign up for my newsletter to be notified of new releases!

NOTE FROM THE AUTHOR

Dear Wonderful Reader,

Thank you so much for spending time with me. I can't tell you how much I appreciate it! My newsletter will let you know about new releases and *only* new releases. Don't miss the next sizzling, hot romance! Visit HazelHunter.com/books to find more great stories available *today*.

XOXO,
Hazel

Version 5.0

• • • • •

IMPRISONED

Castle Coven Book Five

By Hazel Hunter

IMPRISONED
Castle Coven Book Five

In the hellish world of the Shadow Walk Prison, novice witch Hailey Deveraux is running out of time. As her body languishes in the real world, her spirit searches a bizarre and changing landscape. Though she'd dearly like to leave, she won't without her two lovers.

The dark and brooding Kieran McCallen and coven master Piers Dayton are missing. Cursed by a demon, they have been banished to endlessly wander the horrible realm. Using only her feelings to guide her, Hailey navigates the Shadow Walk Prison to find them. But what she discovers are two men caught up in terrors of the past.

As Hailey is swept into their nightmares, her only fixed point is the love she feels for them. But as fears and demons assault them, the trio comes together and fractures apart. As time slips away, Hailey must ask herself one question: Is her love strong enough to bring them home?

CHAPTER FORTY-NINE

HAILEY OPENED HER eyes, aware of a dull throbbing cloud of pain in her head. For a long moment, it distracted her from thinking about anything else beyond getting out of bed and getting some water. The light in her apartment was faint, telling her that it was just past dawn.

Dressed only in her nightgown, she padded the short distance to the tiny kitchen where last night's take-out was still sitting on the edge of the counter. A drink of water helped the headache ease a little bit, but she could tell that it was already going to be a bad day.

Her waitress uniform was draped over a chair. She regarded it with animosity. Some day soon, she was going to get another job, one that actually suited her, but for now, she guessed it was fine. It was too late for her to go back to bed so she supposed that she might as well get ready for work. A peek out the window showed a dull gray alley where rain was spitting down.

She felt a bone-deep dissatisfaction that slowly faded away to resignation. It was fine. It was life. It was as it always had been. Maybe she could look into going to school or moving out of the city for a while.

Even those thoughts were normal. What wasn't normal was the man in the Roman centurion costume who opened the door to her apartment. For a long moment, Hailey just stared at him. Things like this didn't happen in her dull, uninteresting world. Who the hell was he?

"Hailey? Where are you?"

"How the hell do you know my name?" she asked, unnerved. "How did you unlock my door?"

He stared at her. He was handsome enough, she supposed, with dark curly hair and a muscular frame. However, he would have been a lot more attractive if he hadn't been wearing what looked like a very real sword and invading her personal space.

"It's not important. I can't stay long. You need to get a move on–"

"Damn straight you can't stay long," she said loudly, trying to forget the fact that she was only wearing a long flannel nightgown. "You're leaving right the hell now, before I call the cops."

Not sure how I can do that on a disconnected land-line, but whatever.

"Hailey, stop this. This place isn't real. You're not really wherever this is."

Hailey snorted. Great, not only did she have to wake up and go to work, she had to deal with a costumed druggie who had wandered into her home.

"Yeah, right, I'll bet it's all Alice in Wonderland for you, Centurion. Now get the hell out of here. I mean it, I don't want to hurt you but I will."

The man sighed with anger, something that Hailey found quite unkind for someone who had definitely not been invited to her home.

"Stop this at once. You have a task to do, and this illusion does not become you."

"Become this," she snapped.

The closest thing to hand was an old lamp that she had never liked anyway. It flew through the air in a perfect arc. If he hadn't dodged so nimbly, it would have smashed him right in the face.

"Gods below, Hailey!"

"There's more where that came from, asshole. I can do this all day!"

The man looked like he was going to say something else, but then he shrugged.

"As you will then, Hailey. Defend yourself."

She knew that she must have fallen into some terrible nightmare world because the man blurred. When she could focus on him again, she didn't see a costumed Roman, but instead an enormous black wolf.

It snarled at her, stalking towards her stiff-legged and bristling.

"Nice doggy," she said, and its growl only grew louder.

There was nothing close to hand. She started backing away, wondering if she could get on the fire escape, and if the fire escape would even support her weight.

She saw the wolf tensed to spring on her. She tried to step out of the way, but the next thing she knew it was on top of her, the blunt nails digging into her thigh as those enormous teeth snapped just inches away from her face.

Her hands flailed on the ground, desperate to find something, anything that was going to help her. Instead, there was nothing, but something pinged in her mind when her hand brushed the wolf's sturdy body. Somehow, she could feel an endless source of heat and light, like lava flowing under the earth. Somehow, she could tell that it represented the wolf's power, his life force.

Fire. Wolves are afraid of fire, right?

Suddenly, her hands were full of fire. She shoved the flames into the wolf's face, making it leap backwards off her with a loud yelp. She climbed to her feet, wary of another attack. Then she realized that she held fire in her hands, and everything went a little funny. Her mind seemed like it was trying to hold two realities. In one, she was a graduate of the foster kid program, sent out into the world and making her way as a waitress in some gray little town. In the other, she was a witch, a woman who held power, who had two lovers, who triumphed over the evil that had been set in her path.

The two realities fought with one another, bringing back her headache with a vengeance. She shouted with the pain. In the edge of her vision, the wolf turned into the Roman again. It had finally happened. She was going crazy.

She looked at her hands, which were still burning without hurting her at all. She could remember other things, ice as well as fire, the power of flight, how amazing it was to fly on wings with an eagle's vision.

The images were coming faster and faster now, drowning out the images of her little apartment, of the quiet gray life she had been living for years. There was a real version of her, and it didn't live alone. Finally, the names *Piers* and *Kieran* rang in her mind like a bell. She could remember everything, and she raised her eyes to Lucius.

"I remember who I am," she whispered. "I know what I am, and what I must do."

He nodded, and just as he did so, the walls started melting around them. She yelped with fear, but Lucius only made a face. He turned around, opening the oozing door to her apartment.

"Come along. This place can't feed on your fear any longer, and so it is falling to nothing."

She hurried after him, casting a nervous glance behind her. Just as the door closed, she could see an image of a slender, red-haired woman in the melting mass. The idea that there was still a version of herself trapped in those fears made her shudder.

Outside the door was a dark and twisted wasteland. The sky

above was an ugly, bruised color, occasionally lit with green. The ground beneath was brown and crackling as if it had been dead for quite some time. Here and there were twisted black trees. When she passed close to one, she heard a deep groan that nearly modulated itself into words.

"Where are we?" she whispered, hurrying to catch up with Lucius.

She remembered him now. He had been a legatus in the days of ancient Rome. With Liona di Orsini, he had started the organization that would turn into the Magus Corps, a group of officers who were sworn to protect Wiccans at all costs. He had been lost for hundreds of years, tortured and broken by Templars. Now that she was looking at him closely, she could see that he looked far healthier than when she last saw him. He was fully fleshed and well muscled, with no hint of hesitation in his stride.

"You look well," she said cautiously. He turned to throw a sharp smile her way.

"This is a strange place, Hailey, and what you feel and what you believe help shape it. Do you remember what brought you here?"

Hailey's memories were coming back to her. She nodded slowly.

"In the battle against the Templar's demons, Piers and Kieran were hurt. They were affected by a demon's death curse. It brought them here. You helped me come and find them."

Lucius nodded.

"Where we are right now is a place called the Shadow Walk Prison. Some Wiccans have made it their life work to understand it, and most of those were lost or driven mad by it. Liona did some research into it, but the more she learned, the less she wanted to do with it."

Hailey looked around, shivering.

"This place feels wrong."

"It is a wrong place. Humans, even Wiccans like us, can only access it while we are unconscious. However, though we can enter easily enough, we cannot so easily leave. If you, Piers and Kieran stay too long, your bodies will suffer and eventually die."

"I have been here before," Hailey said slowly. "I remember… I remember endless hallways and closed doors, one after another. Liona came to find me."

Lucius's smile was brief.

"She'd always had more guts than sense. It's dangerous, even for a witch like her, and I think that where you are going, it will be more dangerous still."

"What do you mean?"

"This is where demons come from, or at least, that's what many people think. They come from this place, and they feed on humans. They especially love people of power, and when your two lovers were thrust into this place, well, I can only imagine that it was something that drew many of those monsters."

"How will I free them?"

"I cannot tell you, and to my sorrow, I don't believe that I can help you any longer either."

To Hailey's dismay, Lucius was already fading, his form becoming less substantial and his voice flat and tinny, as if it was being relayed over an old-fashioned telephone.

"I could only stay for a little while to ensure that you went on your way. I cannot send myself into a deeper sleep to guide you without the use of a drug, not and keep your bodies safe as well. Good luck, Hailey. Be wary, and be strong. Will is everything in this world, and you have more of it than most."

By the end he was completely transparent, a ghost in all but name. Hailey reached for him, but he slipped through her fingers. In a split second, it was like he had never been there at all. He was lost entirely.

She was alone.

For a moment, she wanted to curl in on herself. The landscape that she was in was disturbingly alien. She knew she was not up to the task of facing demons, of finding Kieran and Piers. The despair swept through her, numbing her from the toes up. She felt frozen in place, wooden.

The final thought snapped something in her, making her look down. To her shock, her toes were disappearing into the ground beneath her, small dark rootlets burrowing into the soil. She instinctively leaped away, shaking her bare feet hard. The roots disappeared, but she could still see the disturbed place in the dirt.

She looked around at the twisted trees scattered across the plain. Suddenly the noises that they made took on a fresh horror.

Lucius said this place was all about will, but I think it's more than that.

Hailey wondered if the place fed off of fear. She made a face. She had never felt like a very brave woman. She did what she had to do, but most of the time, she did it while she was terrified out of her wits. It did give her hope for Kieran and Piers, however, for they were two of the bravest men that she had ever seen. She knew that she wouldn't find them as trees.

She shook her head. Regardless of how well she could cope with the alien landscape, she needed to learn to navigate it. She was a witch who other Wiccans called a vampire, someone would drain power from others and use it herself. This place only seemed limited by her imagination and her fears.

To test out the theory, she looked down at her clothes. She was still wearing the flannel gown from her dreary apartment vision. A moment of concentration changed that. Now she was wearing her normal jeans and hoodie. On her feet were a sturdy pair of boots. She paused to tie back her wavy red hair. She figured that she was as ready as she ever would be.

She had no idea how to find them, but if the place responded to desire, she thought that it would be easy enough. First she thought of Kieran.

With black hair and the most blue eyes she had ever seen, Kieran was the man that she would always consider her first love. He was the one who had encouraged her to use her powers to their full extent, to stretch herself and to prove herself. He had never flinched from her, not even when her home coven had told him how dangerous she was. It was he, if anyone, who had given her the life she lived now. She was still stung from when he abandoned her in Wyoming, but then he had returned. The love that he shared with her and with Piers would steer her where otherwise she was blind.

Resolute, Hailey started to walk.

As she did, the landscape changed to become something a great deal more rocky and bare. The sky remained the same, but the ground beneath her feet became stony and rough. She almost tripped over something. When she looked down, she was shocked.

It was a broken doll, but it was not just any destroyed toy. It was a rag doll that her mother had made her, something that had been lost when she entered the foster care system.

For a moment, she held it, marveling at seeing it again, but then she felt the emotions that had gone with it. Instead of remembering her mother's love, she remembered the night she had been told her parents were dead. Instead of remembering her peaceful early childhood, she remembered what had come after. It was nothing but fear and pain and tears. She shook with the emotions that consumed her, but she didn't want to let go of the doll. It was all she had left of her mother, it was so important.

With a muffled groan, she forced herself to open her hands and to let the doll drop to the ground. To her disgust, the moment it hit the floor, it turned into a gleaming red scorpion. She watched as it scuttled away.

Out of nowhere a weasel-like creature sprang up from a rocky outcropping, pouncing on the scorpion and crunching it between its sharp teeth. It devoured the scorpion with every evidence of enjoyment before turning its beady eyes to Hailey.

"Well, then," it said with a faint British accent. "What are you all about?"

"I don't even know how surprised I should be that you can talk," Hailey said, shaking her head.

The small animal shrugged its bony shoulders.

"You'd be surprised how many things do talk out here. I figure that they're too afraid that they won't remember how if they stop."

Hailey shivered. She could well believe that that might be a risk in this barren place.

"My name's Hailey, and thank you for killing that… whatever it was."

"Baby demon."

"That…that was a baby demon?"

"I dunno. It was small, and basically it does what the big ones do. Maybe it'll grow up to be big enough to haunt cities, and maybe it'll just stay tiny, hoping to trap single souls that step wrong. I don't really trouble myself about the difference."

"You seem to know a lot about this place for a weasel."

"Hey now, I'm not a weasel. I'm a ferret, and I'll thank you not to use the W word around me."

He looked so puffed up and fierce that Hailey had to hide a smile.

"Well all right then, mister ferret, do you have a name?"

"Just Ferret will do until we find another one. Names are only good if you need to tell people apart, anyway. What are you doing out here, Miss Hailey? This is hardly a place for politely spoken folk such as yourself."

"I'm looking for two men, powerful warlocks. They were sent here by a dying demon's curse, and I've come to win them free."

If Ferret had been a human, she guessed that he would have whistled through his teeth. Instead, he chittered, a sound not unlike the clacking of small wooden marbles.

"Now that's a tall order and no mistake. Maybe I could convince you to come to my place instead, it's a nice little nook. It's a good place for new friends to get to know each other."

"Sorry, but I need to be on my way. Thank you for the offer though."

The ferret shook his head firmly. The more she looked at him, though, the more she thought he really was just a rather fluffy weasel. It amused her that a creature such as this would be so vain in such a place.

"Out of the question. I'm not about to let you go unescorted into the wilds of the Shadow Walk Prison, and that is that. I'll tag along, and then I'm sure we'll have better luck finding your men."

Hailey hesitated.

"Look, just because you ate a baby demon in front of me doesn't mean I know you, okay? No offense, but this place is creepy, and in my regular life, I'm not used to being around ferrets who talk. I mean, who are you really?"

To her surprise, he nearly flattened himself to the ground. She was no pro at reading ferret body language, but he looked heartbroken.

"That's a good question, isn't it?" he said, his formerly stentorian voice withered down to a squeak. "I don't remember who I used to be, but I get flashes sometimes, terrible flashes. There was a man and a woman, and they betrayed each other, and then I betrayed them. We were all here, and it was all terrible for us, but some fates are better than others, I guess."

Ferret turned liquid black eyes to her.

"It has been so long, and we've been punished enough, don't you think? Don't you think we've been punished enough?"

Hailey felt her heart go out to the animal.

"I couldn't say," she said honestly. "I've known very little of betrayal in my life and even less of demons. If you swear that you won't lead me astray, I'll let you come with me."

Ferret puffed up as if he had been re-inflated, sitting up tall on his hind legs

"On my honor and by my troth, I do so swear, Hailey my girl. I am your humble servant."

She grinned at what a martial picture he made.

"All right, that sounds splendid. Let's get going, the last thing that I want to do here is to put down roots."

She bent, offering him her hand. To her surprise, he took hold of her hoodie sleeve and scuttled up her sleeve with impressive speed. She squirmed, ticklish for a moment as he explored her hair and her hood. Finally, he curled around the back of her neck, his pert head poking out right beneath her left earlobe.

"All right, cry mercy for the good of St. George, let us off to find your warlocks!"

Hailey wished that she could feel as confident as Ferret did. Still, there was nothing to do but to walk forward, and so she did.

CHAPTER FIFTY

HAILEY WASN'T SURE how long she had walked, but the territory around her was shifting. Instead of being rocky and bare, grass began to grow up around her. With every step she took, the area took on new life. The grass grew tall around her boots, and here and there, she could see copses of trees. It would have been quite peaceful if the sky overhead had changed. Instead, it stayed the same sullen purple, rising up over everything like an acid storm ready to break.

"Where are we?" she asked softly.

Ferret made a soft thrumming noise that could almost be a purr. She thought he meant it to be comforting.

"Steady, lass, steady. The Shadow Walk Prison is a changeable place worked by many hands. Right now, I don't think this is shaped by yours. It could mean that it was shaped by a demon, but I don't think so."

"Oh? Why not?"

"I've been here long enough that I know a few tricks, and what I can see is that your desire leads you like an arrow. You know where you are going, and you know what you are going to find. I think we are where we need to be."

She smiled. Speaking of arrows made her think of the blessing that Liona had conferred upon her before she left Wyoming and the Castle. The witch had pricked Hailey's finger on an arrow before using a longbow to send it spinning off into the forest. The arrow's flight had been straight and true, even if they could not see where it was going to land. She knew that sooner or later, she too would strike her target.

She kept on walking, and after what felt like hours, she could hear sounds as well. There was the crashing of waves on a not-so-distant shore, there was the mewing of seagulls, and after a moment, she could hear the shrieks of children at play.

Hailey frowned. She had grown up rough, and she knew how terrible children's play could be. Without thinking about it, she started walking towards the cries. As they grew louder, her suspicions became certainties. Some of those children were shouting with glee, but there was at least one child whose voice was raised in terror and pain.

With a stifled curse, she started running towards the scene, and she was completely unsurprised at what she saw there. It was a pack of three boys roughing up a third, throwing his thin body from hand to hand. The smaller boy was cringing underneath the blows, his small body trembling and his face streaked with tears.

"What the *hell* is wrong with you?" Hailey snarled, grabbing one of the bigger boys and giving him a hard shove. "Get out of here. You're nothing more than a monster. Get out of here before I do something really nasty."

The boys looked like they were unimpressed, but then Hailey's temper peaked. She could hear a dry flashing sound. The boys' eyes widened, but no more than Hailey's did. Her rage had apparently mounted to the point where the ends of her hair lit aflame. It didn't hurt her; it never did when she was using fire, but it was an impressive display. As one, they took to their heels.

Her fire dimmed and then went out completely, much to the grumbling relief of Ferret who had taken refuge in the front pockets of her hoodie. Hailey ignored him in favor of the young boy who was still on the ground.

He lay flat on his face, his whole body wracked with sobs that he couldn't hide.

"Oh sweetheart, come here, I'm so sorry…"

She reached for him, but he flinched pulling away from her to sit with his back to her. He was dressed in archaic clothing, wearing only a poorly woven tunic belted at the waist with a cord. He looked like he was wearing bags of leather around his feet.

Hailey allowed him to sit farther away from her. She could remember being a hurt child all too well, and with that came an intense distrust of everyone, even the ones who did not mean any harm. Instead, she sat down on the ground beside him, gently coaxing Ferret out to play on her lap. She wiggled her fingers for the small animal to pounce.

It occurred to her to wonder if this little boy was a trap just as her old doll had been. He could have been just another demon looking to prey on her weakness. She decided that she didn't care. She wouldn't have been herself if she could look away from a child in need. If he turned out to be a demon, that was something that she could face when the time came. She didn't need to think about it just then.

Slowly, she saw the shaking of his shoulders subside, and he peeked over his shoulder to look at her. With his lank black hair in his eyes, he looked rather like an overgrown puppy. That made her smile until she thought of puppies that had been kicked once too often even in their short, little lives.

"Are you a woman of power, mistress?" he asked, his voice thick with an accent she could not name. "Are you going to eat me?"

She laughed.

"Do I look like I'm going to eat you?"

He looked her up and down carefully with such suspicion that she stifled another laugh.

"No, I suppose not. You don't look like a witch, more like a river woman, mayhap."

"What does a river woman do?'

"Oh they're pretty girls with red hair just like yourself. They sing, and they draw men down to the water, and when they come all the way down, they drown them."

"That doesn't sound very kind."

The boy shrugged.

"It's the way of things. You find the strength you can, and you use it as best you can. My master told me that."

Hailey blinked.

"Your master? Are you a slave?" It made her heart sick to think of this little boy being sold like a piece of chattel.

"No, mistress, I'm an apprentice to Tom Smith, who serves Dun Bellock. He's got the biggest smithy in the region."

"You're apprenticed to a blacksmith?"

She must not have been able to keep the incredulity out of her voice, because he winced, straightening up as best he could. She could see that he was a skinny child, nothing but long bones and skin. The thought of him working in a smithy was shocking to her.

"I can work the bellows," he said defiantly. "I can run and fetch and carry."

"It sounds like you do a great job," she said sincerely.

It broke her heart to see the emotions that spread over his face. First he checked her face for any sign of a lie. When he couldn't find any, he broke into the widest grin that she had seen.

"I'll be a fine smith someday with my own smithy," he said confidently. "And I won't make just horseshoes and bits, either, I'll make swords and spearheads for all the fine knights."

"That sounds like a good life," Hailey said with a smile. "I'm glad you have a plan."

Like clouds covering the sun, his expression darkened again.

"Jason and Richard say I can't, though. They say because I'm bastard born and so small besides that I'll never be more than a journeyman. I'll never be able to move up in the world, even though I've only been an apprentice a little less long than them."

Hailey reached out carefully to tousle his hair. When he didn't flinch, she patted his hand.

"Jason and Richard, were they two of the boys that were picking on you before?"

He nodded darkly.

"Them and Thomas too. They're not so much better than me. They're not half so clever. Everyone says so."

Hailey didn't quite know what to say. There was a kind of ugly rage on the boy's face, something that she was only used to seeing on people much older. If he had been bigger or older, she would have been frightened. Almost as if picking up on her thoughts, Ferret started chittering nervously in her pocket.

"I wish they were gone. I wish they would go back to the families that they have and make a living far away from me. I wish they would just leave me alone. I wish they were dead!"

On the last words, his voice rose up to a shout. Hailey reached out for him, but he pushed her hand away. There were tears in his eyes again, but they were bright and furious.

"Don't touch me, I'm not a baby who needs to be cosseted. I'll grow into a man who takes nothing from no one, and no one will be able to push me about again!"

"Of course you're not a baby, and I'm not cosseting you. But surely you can see that this rage will not serve you either? If you carry it around with you, if you keep it with you, you'll do yourself an evil."

"What do you know?" he snarled, glaring at her. "Do you go to sleep all emptied because they took your food? Does Tom Smith beat you bloody when they tip over the scrap slag and tell him it was you?"

Hailey flinched. From the way his tunic sagged off his shoulder, she could see old purple welts on his skin. That he had been beaten at so young an age made her stomach turn.

"I don't know any of that," she said, keeping her voice calm. "All I know is that hate has never served half as well as reason. Hate hurts you and blinds you. It makes you terrible to your enemies, but I know that it makes you terrible to those who would love you as well."

There was a brief moment where the boy looked like he would cry again, but that same anger swept over his face.

"No one loves me, mistress. No one loves bastards, and so I'm told over and over again. Leave me alone with your lies!"

He spun away from her, and it was only in that moment, when the angle was just right and when the hair flew out of his bright blue eyes that she knew who he was.

Kieran McCallen was a big man, tall and broad. It was hard to imagine him as a skinny, friendless child, but there it was. There was no uncertainty in her at all. That the man she loved had once been this abused and hurt child, made her want to cry.

"Kieran!"

He paused, but then he started to run. There was a moment where her finger touched the tip of his sleeve. She might have caught him, but he was too quick for her.

She knew that it was beyond a shadow of a doubt her lover. She couldn't let him go on with that hate, she knew it. It would bring him nothing but grief. It would make him suffer a man's burden before he was even big enough to swing a sword or a hammer.

The territory around her changed again. It grew colder and more rocky. She was so frantic about finding Kieran again that she nearly ran herself off a cliff. It was only Ferret's timely bite that made her pull back in shock.

The drop that she had almost run over was a steep one. There were sharp stones at the bottom and an impossible climb back up. She scanned the landscape around her anxiously. Far to her right was a lone figure standing on the edge. Whoever it was was far too tall to be the child Kieran, but she approached anyway.

"Sir? Sir, can I speak to you please?"

He turned around, and she gasped in shock. It was Kieran, but this time, he was a youth in his mid-teens. He had some of the height and some of the muscle that would characterize his adulthood, but his face was still so young it could have broken her heart.

"You were right," he said. His voice was recognizably Kieran's, but lighter, a boy's voice still in some ways. "You said that hate would carry me away like a river, and it did."

"What do you mean?" she asked, fear leaping up in her throat.

There was something glassy about Kieran's eyes, something that frightened her about the leaden way he moved.

In answer, he only pointed over the edge of the ravine.

Far below, there was a man lying dead. He had obviously met the same fate that she had barely avoided. Her stomach clenched. It was all she could do not to be sick. She forced herself to look away from the gory site, turning back to Kieran.

"Oh, Kieran, what have you done?"

"Jason and Thomas got better. They never liked me, but they left me alone. Richard was different. Sometimes it seemed like the only thing that gave Thomas life was making mine a living hell."

Kieran shook his head as if to clear it. She wondered if he was in shock.

"Kieran, what happened?"

"I grew angry, and I told him to come out here to the cliffs. We fought. We were always fighting. It was no different from what we usually did. Today...today was different. We were so close to the edge. We were going at it hammer and tongs."

"He fell."

"Aye, or I pushed him." The calm mask that was Kieran's face ripped apart, and it was replaced for a moment with pure agony. "Gods above, I do not know. Was it chance or my own hand that slew him? Am I to be damned for this?"

"Murder is intent," Hailey said, trying to keep her voice level. "I don't see a murderer in front of me."

"You are not the one who has to see me in the mirror," he said, his voice cracking. "Oh Hailey, I did not want you to see this at all."

Hailey looked up startled.

"You know who I am?"

Kieran's laugh was short and curt.

"I do now, and I know this is not truly the past. When this happened in my life, I nearly threw myself over the cliff after him, but Tom Smith stopped me. He gave me money and sent me away, for he knew that Richard was well-loved in town in the same way that I was not."

"He wouldn't speak for you?"

"For a bastard boy who would rather practice sword drills than pound a horseshoe? Why would he? I was lucky enough that he gave me money and sent me on to what came next."

"What did come next?" Hailey asked, her voice hollow.

Kieran shrugged, looking exhausted. He looked like a teenage boy who had not slept in a week. There were lavender circles under his vivid blue eyes. His hands shook.

"Life came next, I suppose. I went on the road, and I nearly starved to death before I found my feet. I got by on charity and sheer stubbornness. I smithied a little where I could. Eventually, I found a sword off of a dead man and set myself up as a soldier of fortune."

The smile that he gave her was ghastly, more like a skull's grimace than any kind of real merriment.

"How do you like me now, Hailey? There are so many things that I have never told you. There are so many men that I have been. Not all of them are as kind as the face that I have shown you until now."

"I love all of them," she whispered. "Kieran, I swear, I love all of them, they are all yours."

He started to reply, but then a look of sickened horror crossed his face.

"Ah gods, not you. Please, not you."

She turned in confusion. Kieran was looking behind her, his face as white as a sheet. His eyes were glassy and afraid. The man who lay at the bottom of the gorge was floating in the air behind her. He was whole, with none of the damage in his spectral form as was seen in his body, but there was something unmistakably dead about him. He was slightly transparent, and in a strange and gruesome detail, his feet faced backward, as if they had been screwed around.

His dead eyes looked only at Kieran. Slowly, he lifted his arm to point. Miserably, Kieran nodded.

"I see you, dead man," he said numbly. "I obey."

"No," Hailey said, her voice low and urgent. "You don't have to do any of that. You don't have to obey him. You don't have to do anything you don't want to. You would never allow me to be bullied in this way. I don't… You can't follow a specter simply because he orders you!"

Kieran's smile was ghastly on his face.

"The dead command me, Hailey. It is something that has always been with me. The dead haunt me. Do you think that I could have served so long in the Magus Corps without a trail of the dead behind me? Where they lead, I must follow. Where I think he is taking me now, I know it is something you need to see."

"Me?" asked Hailey in puzzlement. "What could you possibly have to show me?"

Kieran's voice was hollow and sad.

"You know me very little," he said softly. "You have seen a version of me that I have improved over time, and unlike those without powers, I have a very long time to fix the things that were wrong. What Thomas says to me here is that there are some things that will never be fixed. There are some things that will never be forgiven, no matter how long I live or how many lives I have saved."

"Kieran, I don't believe that at all. What are you saying?"

He turned away from her. The wraith of the man who had died floated forward to lead the way.

"Come with me and see," Kieran said over his shoulder. "I wish you would leave this place, wake up and find your own way. If you want to be with me, you will want to see what comes next. After that, you will leave, though with fewer good memories of me than bad ones."

Hailey fell into step behind Kieran. There was no question of her doing anything else. She knew that whatever came next, she would have to see it. She could feel her nervous energy shake her. Carefully, she reached up to stroke Ferret's head.

"What do you think he's going to show me?" she asked softly.

"Something to do with death," Ferret murmured. "It is only a loss of some kind or another that wears his shoulders down like this. Whatever he has lost will not be returned to him in this life or the next. Read his despair, lass, and you will see it."

Hailey shook her head.

"I believe in redemption," she said firmly. "Kieran is a good man."

Ferret's laugh was tinny. It was strangely unpleasant coming out of such a soft creature.

"Good men do many bad things. That is something that you best learn now. The goodness of a person does not tell you how many they've killed or how much innocent blood lies on their hands."

To that, Hailey could make no reply. She knew how terrible Kieran could be when he was roused. She knew exactly how deadly he was with his swords and the blades of ice that he commanded. There was a brief flash behind her eyes, strange and foreign, of Kieran bearing down on her, his hands full of ice-cold knives and every point directed at her face.

She shook the image away, focusing instead on Kieran's back. If he was going to follow the dead, she was going to follow him.

As he walked, she could see his form filling in. He already had his height, but now step by step, she could see his shoulders broaden, see his limbs thicken. He was becoming a man right before her eyes. In another place, she would have loved to see this happening. She loved Kieran with all her heart. She wanted to see every part of him. There were no photographs when he was born. He was a poor little smith's apprentice. No one would have painted a picture of him. She was seeing something that she could never have hoped to see.

She walked behind him, on and on. The ground changed again, becoming something forested and dark. There was a dampness to the air. She could smell smoke, and beneath that, there was something strange and unpleasant to it.

Kieran paused, looking at a pile of armor that lay by the side of their path. With a breath that bordered on being a sob, he picked it up, piece by piece and started to put it on. Clad in armor and in his full adult frame, there was no mistaking Kieran for anything but what he was. He was a machine made for war. The only human thing about him was his blue eyes.

"Are you ready?" Hailey asked softly.

Kieran laughed, his voice thready and sad.

"I never will be. But I am not such a fool to think that what happens next is under my control. Come along, Hailey. You deserve to see this."

He led her through the forest. His job done, the wraith disappeared, leaving a smell of bitter sulfur behind him. There were fires, small and shy, dotted through the trees. Hailey could make out men moving around them. She could tell it was meant to be night, but if she looked above, she could still make out openings in the foliage which told her the sky was that same demonic bruise.

Stepping into the scene as if he were an actor born to play a part, Kieran walked out of the dark and into a clearing that was well-lit by a larger fire. There was a man with silver hair sitting beside the fire, writing at a small traveling desk and pursing his lips over what he had inscribed.

"Commandant."

The man looked up briefly, waving a hand at Kieran.

"At ease, Captain. Or better yet, get out. There is no way that you are going to change my mind, and it is a waste of time to even try."

"Sir, I cannot do that."

The commandant returned to his writing, barely seeming to give Kieran another thought.

"And why is that, Captain?" he asked casually. "Do you have a lover in that village that you are so afraid for? Do you have a child down there?"

Kieran made a sharp motion with his hand.

"I don't, but that makes no difference. Those people are kin to someone. They are our kin in many ways. They deserve to be protected."

"And that is exactly what we are doing, Captain, or did you think we brought twenty Magus Corps members here for show?"

"All they are good for is show if you refuse to let them do anything."

In the blink of an eye, the commandant was up and backhanded Kieran. Kieran was a big man, but his commandant was hellishly fast. The blow struck so hard that Hailey flinched, shivering at the brutality.

"That is insubordination, Captain," said the commandant. "Another word, and I will have you flogged."

Rage and fury rose up in Kieran's face. For a moment, she thought he was going to murder the commandant. She almost wanted him to. Instead, he nodded curtly, licking the blood away from his split lip. He turned and walked back to where Hailey waited in the shadows. The rage was gone from his face, but the despair behind it was even worse.

"That was not a bad thing you did," she started, but he cut her off.

"No. Come with me. There is still another part to see."

He took her hand in his. Despite the terrible conditions that they were in, she found herself craving his warm touch. He was real, even if everything around them wasn't. He was solid. He was alive. No one had succeeded in taking him from her yet.

They climbed for what felt like hours. They emerged on a rise that looked down over a deep valley. The drop to the valley floor was sheer, but Kieran sat on the edge as if it were a bench, letting his feet dangle over the drop.

"Come sit with me?"

"I dislike the height," she said, but she came to sit with him gingerly anyway.

"Says the girl who can fly in her own form and that of an eagle."

There was a bit of teasing in his voice. Gratified to hear it, she snuggled up close to his solid side. Whatever happened, she resolved to herself that they were going to get through it. If there had been stars above, it would have been a perfect night. Instead, there was only that demon sky. She kept her eyes shut, instead relishing the feel of his warm body.

"Hailey, little fox, it is time to see."

She didn't want to. She did as he asked, however. Below them, she saw what she numbly first assumed was a flower opening. It was quite beautiful, a bloom of orange and red that opened up as prettily as a rose. Then a second one opened up next to it. She realized that they were not flowers, but instead were flames.

One after another, flames lifted up. The wind changed, allowing her to hear screams.

"What is this?" she asked, her voice soft and afraid.

"So falls Costain, and all afterward was silence," said Kieran, his voice heavy with grief. "The figures varied, but more than two hundred people died that night. Some guess that there were closer to three hundred people in town, that the Templars took the rest off to torture for information."

"It was Templars who did this?" she asked timidly.

"None other. They came toward this valley. We, that is, my unit and I, were meant to be ready for them. We were supposed to stop them. Our intelligence told us that they were still a week away, and so we held in readiness. The place where we were camped would have bottle-necked them if we were positioned correctly."

"Kieran, it was poor information and a poorer commander that cost those people their lives, not you."

He shook his head.

"It didn't have to be this way. There was a moment where Commandant McIntyre challenged me. In that moment, I could have mutinied. I could have walked away and turned at least half of the unit to walk with me. We could have gone into town. Trained fighters, experienced and deadly as we were, could have made all the difference."

Hailey's words stuck in her throat. She knew the question he needed to answer, but she didn't want to ask him. They sat in silence for a long moment until she got up the courage.

"Why didn't you?" she asked.

"Because I loved my rank. Because I had found something with the Magus Corps that I had never found anywhere else. That was a brotherhood that held me to exacting standards, who showed me how to excel, praised me when I did right and punished me when I did wrong."

He took a deep breath. Below them, the fires were flourishing brightly. There were people dying down there, but Hailey reminded herself that they had died a long time ago. She hadn't traveled through the years. This was nothing more than an illusion, an image projected on a flat white wall that was meant to pull her and Kieran in deeper and deeper.

"I am no good on my own," he said softly. "I have lived a long time. Most of that time was with the Magus Corps, but some of it was not. I am lost on my own. I am only as good as the master I follow. Once I followed a bad one, and many people died."

Hailey shook her head, pushing herself hard against his body. She needed to make him understand.

"You were not the one who put those people to fire and sword," she said desperately. "The sin here is that of the

Templars. It is not yours. You acted as you saw fit…"

"I did not. I failed to act because I loved my master better than I loved the idea of people living."

Hailey shook her head.

"That is the darkest way to see your actions. Those people are dead, but Kieran, I swear that you are not. You are better than this, you have grown and changed."

"Less than you think, less than I need."

He stood up, taking one last look at the valley on fire. All of the life had gone out of him. In that moment, he looked no more alive than the specter that had led him to this place.

"I want you to leave me now, Hailey."

Hailey's temper flared up bright and hot.

"If you think I came all this way to be sent home like a dog with my tail between my legs–"

"Don't you see how ashamed I am?" he asked her. His voice had a tone she had never heard before. There was grief there, but there was despair too. There was nothing left of him, and all he could do was ask her for mercy.

"I am *ashamed.* I have been for every day of my life since this happened. I have lived with the knowledge that I caused the deaths down there, and I will never be free of it. Leave me, Hailey. I can't stand your eyes on me anymore."

For a moment, Hailey was almost pulled down with his despair. Then a thought occurred. It was like a light in a dark room. Slowly, she shook her head.

"I don't think so. No, I really don't. You don't believe that."

Kieran glared down at her.

"What are you talking about?"

"You weren't thinking of Costain when we met in Italy. You weren't thinking of it when we fought demons in the Alps. You surely weren't thinking of it when you made love to me."

"Do you think that I had forgotten all of this? Do you actually believe that it was you that made me forget?"

There was a shade of contempt to his tone that could have made Hailey shrivel up and wither away. However, she knew she was right. She would forgive his caustic tone because she knew that she had the right of it.

"Frankly, I think you did."

"Hailey–"

"You were a whole man when we met. There were shadows in your past, just like there are shadows in mine. No one is pure, and no one goes through life blameless. The thing that keeps us going is the fact that we are human at the heart of it, no matter what our powers are. Even if we want to cling to the past versions of ourselves, time erases it slowly but surely."

"I will never forget these people."

"No. I'll never forget the foster home where they locked me outside on a winter night with no coat, either. Those things happened to us, but they do not define us, Kieran. You are not the same man who caved in to a superior officer. You would not do that again."

"You sound very sure of that."

"I am certain of that," she said, her tone firm and strong. "You don't need forgiveness here because in some ways you have already forgiven yourself. No, this is a fear that you have projected large and given the weight of an elephant. You are already beyond this–"

Hailey broke off with a startled gasp when a handful of ice splinters flew her way. They whizzed harmlessly by her head, but it was enough to distract her while Kieran took to his heels.

"Kieran, no!"

She tried to chase him through the forest, but this time, it was as if the land itself were working against her. Her feet seemed to find every tree root. Every other moment, she had to tear the end of her braid away from the grasping branches of a twig. Finally, she had to admit it to herself. Kieran was gone.

Breathing hard, she stumbled to her knees, leaning against a stump. All around her, she could hear the noise of the forest. The calls of the night birds, the howl of a lonely wolf, the bark of a fox, they all sounded like they were mocking her.

"That was a right chase," commented Ferret.

"You can say that again," said Hailey. "I don't know what to do next."

"Well, you find the man, if you want him."

"Of course I want him, why wouldn't I?" Hailey asked, indignant.

"You weren't wrong when you said that what he felt for those poor dead folks was made larger than life. That's true. On the other paw, he was right too when he said that that would always be something that lived with him. That man who caved to his commandant like a card house is who you are in love with as well."

Hailey thought about what Ferret said. He was right, after a fashion. There would always be a part of Kieran that needed structure and commands. However, she realized that was not so much of a bad thing as might be supposed.

"I don't mind giving orders from time to time," she said finally. "And if I can find him, I know someone who loves giving them more. I am going to find Kieran, and I will love him forever."

Ferret chuckled, twitching his whiskers so that they unpleasantly tickled her ear.

"That's a lovely idea."

Hailey was about to respond when she realized that there was something on the ground that hadn't been there before. It was too straight and regular to be a stick. When she looked at it, she realized to her shock it was a riding crop. Moreover, it was pointed towards a path that seemed to have opened up while she wasn't looking.

"This place has its own logic, doesn't it?"

"This place has its own traps is what you mean, lass," grumbled Ferret. "If you're not careful, you'll find out what I mean."

CHAPTER FIFTY-ONE

THE WAY WAS still tough. It wasn't much lighter than it had been before. Even though there was a path, it was mostly overgrown with roots and grass. Still, she managed to walk it without much trouble. She felt carefully ahead of herself with her hand, carrying the riding crop in the other.

The riding crop was a strange thing itself. It was made of old leather, supple and stiff at once. It had a peculiar weight to it, but it balanced well in her hand. She wasn't sure what it was for, but something in her prevented her from putting it down.

Finally, the woods thinned. She found herself in a little clearing. The only thing in it was a stone house that looked cheerful enough until she realized that the windows were small and barred.

"Do you think we should knock?" Ferret wondered.

"I'm not going to, but you're going to stay out here," Hailey said firmly. "I don't know exactly what is going to come next, but I think it is something that is absolutely not for weasel eyes."

"Ferret!" the animal replied angrily, but he leaped from her shoulder to begin nosing his way through the grass. When he pounced on something and began devouring it, licking his jaws all the while, she turned away.

The door was closed, but it swung open under her hand.

Inside, the little stone cottage was dim except for a single candle that stood by the door.

"Hailey? I thought I told you to leave."

"Well, I'm sure I would have listened if I thought that you were actually in charge."

There was a box of matches, a box of candles and a stack of candle holders by the first lit one, so she started lighting each one. She placed each lit candle on a different surface, expanding the amount she could see and bringing the place into sharper focus.

It was a barren little room. The walls were bare stone. There was a rickety table, where the candles were kept, a single chair, and a straw bed pushed against one wall. Kieran sat on the bed, his hands dangling between his knees. As she lit the candles, he squinted at her.

"Leave me be," he said, his voice dull. "This is where I am meant to be."

"This looks like a jail cell with an unlocked door," Hailey said, lighting another candle. "This is a place where the only person holding you is you, Kieran. You do not need to be here. This is not your place. The only reason you are here is because you think you must be."

"There must be punishment for what I did," he protested.

She wondered if there was a bit of weakness to that protest. Instead of sounding like he really believed what he was saying, he sounded like a man reading a part from a book. Hailey decided that it was an improvement of sorts.

"All right. If you believe there is a punishment, then there will be a punishment."

"What are you doing?"

The room was bright now, with candles set on the table and on the windowsills. It was enough light for what she had in mind, she reckoned.

"Here's the thing about punishment," she said pleasantly. "What does it mean if you decide it yourself?"

"I chose nothing…"

"I know that's not true. What I've learned about demons is that for the most part, they lack a certain creativity. They are masters of feeding us what we think we want and what frightens us, but they will never create something new on their own. The bars on the windows, the limited number of candles on the table? This place all came from you. This is your punishment, and you have smugly decided that you know what's fair."

Kieran started to speak, but then he stopped, frowning. She could see that he understood what she was saying, even if he hadn't internalized it yet.

"That's not the way punishment works," Hailey continued. "Not really. What you need to remember is that you have already repented, even if you don't understand that right now. You have made amends, you have saved lives, you have gone on to lead a productive life. What you need right now is punishment."

He still looked dubious. When she brandished the riding crop in front of him, his eyes went wide and his mouth opened. He closed his mouth, licking his lips a little nervously. A part of Hailey was watching all of this very anxiously, afraid to misstep because if she did so now it would only hurt him more. Another part of her relished the shine of his eyes, the way that his body seemed to straighten up to attention when he looked at her.

"Hailey…"

"You don't need to talk unless I ask you a question," she said softly. "I am going to beat you. It is going to hurt. Then it will be over. Then you'll be punished, and we can leave this place together. Do you understand?"

He started to speak, but then it was as if he was afraid that words would get the better of him. He only nodded.

Hailey felt the thrill of victory slide through her body. She had won, or at least she had her victory in sight. The thrill was real, though, sending a hot pulse through her body. She reminded herself that this was more for Kieran than it was for her. It would have been lying to state that she was unmoved, but if she allowed her feelings to run rampant in the Shadow Walk Prison, there was no telling what might manifest.

"All right. I want you to take off your clothes. Fold them up, and put them aside."

Silently, he did as she said, removing his archaic clothes mechanically and folding them before laying them on the floor. She realized with interest that his body was the version she had known and loved so well. He was a man in his prime, and though the scars were clustered thickly on his flesh, she was pleased with the fact that he was closer to what he was in truth.

"You're quite marked up," she said casually. She reached out with her riding crop to tap a slash on his calf. "Where did this come from?"

"I was helping a coven move their base across international borders. Templars caught up with us in Cappadocia."

"I see. And this mark on your arm?"

"Sword fight with a Templar in Paris."

Hailey didn't bother to hide her smile.

"And this little one here on your neck?"

"I was performing a search and rescue with another officer. A rope we were rigging slipped, and it burned against my neck."

"That is a lot of pain and a lot of blood simply to make sure that others don't suffer, Kieran. If there was a price to be paid, you began paying it a long time ago."

She walked around his body. This time, instead of looking at the scars, she was looking at the whole of him. He was densely muscled like a predatory wolf or lion. There was a kind of beauty in the harsh lines of his body, the way his black hair stood out in stark contrast against his face. Though he towered over her, his eyes still sought hers as if he desperately needed to know what she thought and what she wanted.

When Hailey reached out her hand to touch one pectoral muscle, he shivered. She ran her fingers over his flesh, pausing to tweak one nipple, then the other. She was rewarded by the goosebumps that rose up on his flesh and the way he shifted from foot to foot.

They had made love in many different ways, but never before had his body been so open to her. He was a storm in bed. He had that same power, but now it was leashed. She found that she very much liked that command. She walked around him again, this time tracing her fingers down the muscles of his back and the dip of his spine. She traced it from the back of his neck to the small of his back, hesitating before she cupped his buttock with her palm. The sound he made was nothing more than an inhalation of air, but it was enough to know that he was painfully aware of her.

"Are you ready to pay? To be punished?"

Kieran nodded without speaking. She decided that was fine. She hadn't commanded him to speak after all.

"Bring that chair over here."

He did as she said. She positioned him so that he was bent over the chair's high back with his hands hanging on to the seat. Even as tall as he was, the position stretched him out, held him taut for her. She realized that he was handsome like this, willing, open and vulnerable.

"This is going to hurt, and you are going to take it," she said softly.

For a moment, she thought of an incident that Liona had told her about, where she and Lucius had first learned about the pleasure of a gentle birching after a bath in an underground hot spring. This was a little akin to that, she thought, but it was going to have to be harder if Kieran was to understand it.

She walked around so that she was facing his rear and his legs. After a moment's thought, she pressed her booted foot to the inside of his foot, making him widen his stance. Now he looked incredibly open to her. She could see him, but he couldn't see her.

"Hailey…"

"You may call my name, you may thank me for punishing you. If you feel you are done, you may tell me and I will consider it. Otherwise, I will beat you as I see fit."

The sound that came out of him was nothing more than a whimper. On an impulse, Hailey reached down between his legs and realized that he was quite hard. She grinned. That was fine too, she decided.

She tapped the length of the riding crop against his buttocks, measuring the shaft and how it would fall. She reached back with her arm and pantomimed a full stroke, trying to see where it would land. She thought that if she worked slowly, she could lay the stroke on with a fair amount of accuracy.

"All right. I'm starting now."

She lifted the crop and brought it down with a whistling speed across his rear. The sound was like a gunshot in the quiet room, followed by an almost delayed pained grunt from Kieran. Hailey stopped to inspect her work. There was a clear red line right across the rise of his rear, though it was not raised at all. When Hailey curiously ran her thumbnail along its length, Kieran squirmed deliciously for her.

She took aim, drew back her arm, and landed another one just an inch above the first. This time, Kieran's grunt was heavier. There was another stripe almost precisely parallel to the first.

"Yes, this is what you need, isn't it darling?" she murmured.

She hadn't expected him to respond, but he nodded.

"Yes, Hailey."

There was a softness to his voice that she had never heard before. It made her want to hug him, but it also made her want to hit him harder. After all, she had a job to do here.

"You're doing very well, darling," she said sincerely. Then she struck him again.

She worked her way up and down his rear, paying special attention to the roundest part, where he sat. The marks turned a livid red, but she was careful. She never broke the skin.

Kieran took the strokes calmly and well, but by the end, he was biting back yelps with each stroke, shifting on his feet and jumping.

Final time pays for all, Hailey thought, moving slightly and taking careful aim.

The final blow ran a straight diagonal across his buttocks, crossing almost every welt she had laid on him. This was the hardest blow yet, and Kieran did yelp this time. He straightened up hard, his hands raising as if he wanted to clutch the abused skin. Then he regained control of himself, getting back into position. She marveled at the idea that he would get down for more pain.

"There," she said softly. "It's done, it's all over."

There was a sigh that was almost a sob in his voice, and slowly he rose and turned around to face her. He wasn't crying, exactly, but his eyes were wet. It was more than just the pain she had inflicted on him, she realized. It was the relief of having a heavy burden taken away. It was done, it was over, and Kieran could hardly believe it.

"Come here," she said, drawing him towards the bed.

To her surprise, it wasn't the simple straw cot that she had seen before. Instead it was a normal bed, though a fairly large one.

There was a plump white coverlet on it, and when she drew back the covers, she found crisp white sheets.

Now that she looked around, the entire room had changed. It was a fairly spacious, cozy bedroom, with a flat television hung on the wall facing the bed, and large windows that were currently curtained. It was a room for people to live, sleep and love. The candles that she had placed still burned, though they did so from a long mirrored dresser.

"Shh, here we are," she said, guiding Kieran to bed.

She lay him down on the clean white sheets, pausing only to strip off her boots and her clothes. Then she climbed in next to him, sitting with her back against the padded headboard.

Moving as if he had fought off an entire horde, Kieran crawled to her so that he was sprawled across her lap, his head pressed against her belly.

"Thank you," he whispered. "Gods above, thank you, Hailey."

"I will always give you what you need," she said quietly. "If I can, I will always try to offer you things that make you happy."

She rubbed his scalp with her fingertips, making him purr. With her free hand, she stroked his body, taking pleasure in the sheer feel of him. Curiously, she ran her hand over his hip, and then around to the curve of his buttocks. His flesh was almost shockingly warm. The welts were just a tiny bit raised. The feel of them aroused her, making her squirm.

Something about her posture must have alerted Kieran to her state, because he made a curious noise.

"What's the matter, Hailey?"

"I… when I started, you were hard," she said.

He chuckled a little, rolling over so that she could see him more easily.

"I never really stopped," he said.

She looked at his erection, licking her lips. He looked delicious, and if his ass was red because she had been beating it, it only made him more attractive to her. For a moment, she thought of condoms, but then she realized that they were in a dream world. She was a little disappointed that he wouldn't have those wonderful marks when they woke up, but that meant that other acts wouldn't have consequences either.

"Kieran, I want you to lie on your back."

Her firm and decisive tone brought a pink blush to his cheeks. He did as she said without a word, only flinching a little when his sensitive flesh made contact with the cool sheets below him.

He was laid out for her like a feast, and Hailey took full advantage. She rained small kisses over his face, teasing his mouth until he was begging for her. She slipped her tongue between his lips, thrusting it in aggressively and moaning in satisfaction as he started sucking.

I want to see you do this with Piers, she thought absently, but then she was too aware of her lover and his body to keep that thought in her mind.

When Kieran reached for her, she pinned his hands down to his sides.

"You can touch me when I tell you you can touch me," she said, and he nodded, though it looked as if it pained him.

She threw one leg over his thigh and straddled him, sitting just below his cock. She took it in her hands, touching the clear bead of liquid at the tip. She spread it all over the head of his cock, making him moan.

"I'm going to fuck you," she said.

From the desperate sounds he made, she could tell that that was what he wanted as well.

She gathered up the slick from his cock, and making sure that he was watching, she spread it between her own legs. His eyes widened as she spread herself wide, playing with her clit and dipping a finger into her own sweet depths. She moaned, letting him know in no uncertain terms how good it felt.

"You're going to feel so amazing inside me," she crooned. "You'll be so lovely when I'm on top of you."

"Please, please, please, Hailey, that's all I want…"

"Am I really what you want?" she mused quietly. "Am I truly something that you need with you?"

"With every fiber of my being, with every bit of my soul," he promised. "I love you. I need you with me, darling."

The pleasure she felt at those words was amazing. It was something that she had needed to hear for what felt like her entire life.

"I love you, Kieran," she said softly.

"I love you."

For a moment, she simply pressed herself against him. It was a strangely beautiful calm in the middle of their storm. It did not feel unnatural, however. It was simply a part of the way that they were made to be together.

Then her arousal reasserted itself. She wanted him, and she wasn't going to be denied a moment longer.

"Are you ready, love?" she whispered, her voice soft and sultry. "Are you ready to please me?"

"Forever," Kieran swore fervently. "I am ready to please you for the rest of my life and beyond."

With a soft pleased sound, Hailey slid her leg over Kieran's hip, mounting him the way she would a horse. For a moment, she straddled his thighs, gazing down at his dark erection. She ran her palm down its length, marveling at how hard and lovely it was.

When Kieran reached his hands up to touch her, she pushed them back.

"Hands behind your head," she whispered huskily. "I don't think I gave you permission to touch me."

Kieran groaned, his beautiful body shaking beneath hers. He wanted to touch her, she could tell. He wanted to bury his cock deep inside her, to make her cry out from pleasure. Right then, however, he wanted to please her more.

She squeezed his cock in her hand before palming his balls. The motion made him squirm, moaning a little. That moan became a startled cry when she squeezed them gently as well. She was careful; she didn't want to do him any real injury, but it was amazing to watch a dull flush redden his face. He squirmed beautifully.

When Hailey let up, he looked up at her with imploring eyes.

"I need you so much, darling," he whispered. "I need you, I love you, please, please…"

Hailey finally took pity on him, moving herself so that she sat directly over his cock. She let him feel the wetness of her slit and the light tangle of hair there. It aroused her as well that this powerful man was lying so open and vulnerable to her. It was amazing to see him squirm and twist, longing for her, needing her, all but begging for her.

She grew tired of teasing. She reached down between their bodies, giving herself a delicious shiver as she did so when her fingers brushed against her clit. She shifted his cock until it was at a comfortable angle.

Slowly, moving so that there was a light burn down her thighs, she started impaling herself on his cock. He was broad and hard, making it sting just a little, but she found that she loved that as well. They had all the time in the world. She knew it. She could feel it in her bones. There was no reason that she couldn't take her time. She inched down his cock, keeping her breathing slow and even. She could feel his body strain beneath her like a full-blooded stallion being held under rein.

"You want to bury yourself in me," she said, still a small space from being fully seated on his body. "You wish you could be making me scream right now."

The only response that Kieran could muster was a deep groan. Even then, however, he didn't thrust up into her. He didn't do anything that she didn't ask him to do, and that was wonderful in its own right. She knew that he wanted her badly enough to beg, but it was intoxicating that he was so still and so obedient.

Hailey took a deep breath, pushing herself full down on his cock, drawing a deep cry from both of them. Being able to feel the full length of his cock inside her made her gasp with pleasure. Biting her lower lip between her teeth, she started to ride him, her hands braced on his chest.

"Let me touch you, please," Kieran murmured.

"No, not yet," Hailey gasped. "I want to… to use you, I want you all for myself."

If anything, her cruel words made him harder inside her, made him moan wildly and with longing for her.

She loved riding him, adored how powerful he was beneath her. Her body was sleek with sweat, and she rolled over him more easily. Finally, she took pity on him, reaching down for his hand and placing it between her legs.

"Make me come," she whispered fiercely. "If you can't…"

She left the threat hanging in the air. It was all she needed to say, he rolled the pad of his thumb over her slick clit, making her movements faster and more erratic. She was still controlling their motion, but now he was controlling her as well. Now she was feeling the powerful chain of sensations that ran from where he filled her to his hand on her most intimate parts. The sensations were building up and building up in her. She tried to hold them off because the waiting was a pleasure too. She didn't need to hurry to her climax. She didn't need to rush to the payoff.

Instead, she simply reveled in the state of erotic tension that they had created. She could feel Kieran's body bucking underneath her. She incorporated that into her pleasure as well, letting it all create a tide inside her that would inevitably roll over her.

Soon, no matter how hard she tried, she couldn't fight the feelings off any longer. The pleasure started in her belly, sending waves of shocks throughout her frame. She reached down to dig her nails into Kieran's shoulders, holding herself steady as they tore through her. She held out for as long as she could, but then her own climax was too powerful. It started as a growl before becoming a roar. She was shouting with it, digging her nails hard into Kieran's flesh.

At some point during her climax, she felt him give up as well. His body tensed like a bow underneath hers, he arched up hard. She had never felt him spill inside her before, but now she knew how wonderful it was to feel that liquid heat shoot her full.

They both came to a shuddering calm, their breaths slowing and their bodies shaking.

For a long moment, Hailey rested on top of Kieran's form, her cheek snug against his chest. She felt a peace and wellness she had never known suffusing her being. She had never been safe before, not like this. There was nothing outside of this room, nothing beyond the circle of his arms.

After a while, Hailey pulled away before standing up. She stretched the kinks out of her legs and lower back for a moment before offering Kieran a hand.

"Come on," she said, a soft smile on her face.

"Where are we going?" he yawned, climbing to his feet.

"We're going to get a shower. Then I think we'll do something like that again."

CHAPTER FIFTY-TWO

THEIR HOUSE WAS beautiful. It was large and airy with plenty of rooms for the both of them to enjoy. There was an entertainment area with an enormous television and a media computer that held all of Kieran's music. To Hailey's surprise, he had a shy fondness for bluegrass that she would never have suspected.

There was a library for her, full of all of the books that she had ever read or wanted to read. Sometimes, she would find a reference that she needed to look up. She would despair of ever finding it, but then a quick search revealed that she must have purchased it on one bookstore trip or another. She could do all of the translating and all of the reading that she wanted to do, something she had never had the time for.

They would spend time on their own interests, but mostly, they simply were in each other's company. She would join Kieran for a movie in the entertainment center, or he would bring headphones to keep her company when she was on a particularly stubborn document. They would go to the large kitchen together, making simple meals of roasted meat, cheese and steamed vegetables.

Of course the room that they loved the most was the bedroom. In that room more than any other, they were connected to each other. Sometimes, Hailey would play the stern mistress, and other times, they would simply make love, falling into a sleep that was full of good dreams. Hailey had never in her life been free of nightmares, but in their house, she was.

Their cat, a small skinny, disgruntled thing, meowed angrily from time to time, but it was easy enough to ignore. It would twine around their ankles, but even when given food and treats, it obviously thought that there was something wrong.

Beyond that, however, Hailey's life was like a pool of warm salty water, lit by the day's last sunbeams. She could sink down into this sweet pleasure and never leave it.

She wondered why she didn't.

One night, lying in their bed, she turned to Kieran.

"What's missing?" she asked, her voice resonant in the darkness. Perhaps she wouldn't have been able to say it while they were making food or enjoying a movie, but in the dark, where she could see nothing, the question became important.

"What do you mean?"

"I don't think I know, exactly. Sometimes, I look around, and it's wonderful. I love our life together, and you make me more happy than I have ever been before. But then I get the feeling that there is something missing there. There's something that is always escaping me, like a mouse sneaking around a cat."

"You're becoming as bad as the cat," Kieran teased. "Next thing you know, I'll never be able to comfort you no matter how much I pet you."

She smiled briefly at his joke.

"No, it's not something I'm imagining. There's something missing. There's something wrong."

"Well, if you can think of what it is, let me know. Then we can fix it."

That night, Hailey didn't sleep at all. Kieran's breathing slowly evened out as he fell into a deeper slumber. She envied his ease, curled up against his back. They had a lovely life, an amazing one. There was nothing missing at all.

A few nights later, another thought occurred to her in the dark.

"Kieran, what's our cat's name?"

In the darkness, she could feel Kieran shift as he considered her question.

"What do you mean?"

"What is our cat's name? Surely we gave him a name at some point, right? Like normal people with a loving pet do?"

"We…we must have forgot," said Kieran, his voice uncertain. "Is that something that could happen?"

"Us forgetting to name him or us forgetting his name because we haven't used it enough? Neither sounds particularly likely."

She lay in the darkness, aware of the cat in question jumping up lightly on the bed. She reached down to pet it, but there was something a little odd about the way it felt. It was lighter and thinner than a cat should be, and a bit smaller as well.

In confusion, she turned on the light. It was just their cat, a tabby with green eyes and a rather surly expression. She turned off the light again. In the split second before the light shut down, she didn't see a cat at all. She saw a little weasel with a lean body and black oil droplet eyes. She cried out in surprise, making Kieran wrap his arms around her.

"Darling, what's the matter?"

"I…I think our cat is actually a weasel."

No, not a weasel. Was it a ferret?

The feelings were coming harder and faster now. She turned on the light, putting on her silk nightgown and walking out of the bedroom. It was hard to put her thoughts together somehow. Kieran followed her, putting his hand on her shoulder.

"Are you all right?"

"I don't know. There's just something wrong here. Something

is missing, and I don't know what."

The nameless cat mewed loudly, weaving in and out of their legs. It looked like it was trying to tell them something. She lifted it in her arms as much to comfort herself as to comfort it.

"What does the yard look like?" Kieran said suddenly.

"What?"

"The yard outside. What does it look like? Do we have a pool? Do we have a garden? Surely we have something."

There was something deeply unnatural about the gaps in their knowledge. Looking at each other, they nodded solemnly and approached a window. The airy curtains were still. To Hailey, there was something dead about them, something that made her skin crawl when she touched them.

She and Kieran pulled them aside together. For a long moment, they both stared dumbfounded at the brick wall that lay behind them. Moving as one, they moved through the house, ripping down curtains and finding the same thing.

"What is this place?" Hailey asked wildly. "What's going on?"

"This isn't where we're supposed to be," Kieran said slowly. "All of this…"

"It's all a lie," Hailey finished softly for him. "Everything here is just a lie."

It broke her heart to say it, but perhaps broken hearts were useful because they allowed things in that had been kept out. Suddenly she could remember the coven in Wyoming, the fact that she, Kieran and Piers—oh god, she had forgotten Piers—lay in a drugged stupor in the mountains. She could remember the demons that they had fought, she could remember everything.

Looking at Kieran, she could see that the same thing was happening to him. There was a sickened look on his face, fear and shame both.

As one they turned to the door, but Kieran took her hand

before they could walk through it.

"Hailey, be very sure that this is what you want to do."

"What do you mean?" she asked, her green eyes lighting up with anger. "Piers is out there, he is suffering just as you were suffering, and I need to go to him. This place isn't real, Kieran. It's… It's just a strange set piece where we can be held until our bodies die."

"Has it occurred to you that that might already have happened?"

At Hailey's startled look, Kieran waved his hand, encompassing everything about the house where they had been so happy.

"We have been here for what feels like months, if not years. We have been happy, and time has gone by for us. We have to accept the possibility that time might have passed for others. For our bodies."

Hailey's stomach dropped when she thought of what he was saying. She had read fairy tales when she was younger. As a young witch only allowed to translate and research in coven libraries, she had read darker reports of the faerie folk, very real, very dangerous and very present in some parts of the world. They would carry away a man or a woman to dance for a single night, only to return them a thousand years later. Something very similar could have happened while she and Kieran enjoyed their domestic idyll. She didn't know that it had, but the idea of leaving Piers alone, lost and frightened sickened her.

"I don't care," she said softly. "I don't care what might be on the other side of that door. All I know is this is a place without Piers. It's a place where I've run away and forgotten someone I love. I need to go through that door, Kieran."

There was such an expression of grief in Kieran's face that she almost relented. As he opened his mouth to speak, however, the bedroom door behind him opened.

Hailey gasped out loud. The woman who opened the door was her twin from the red hair to the green eyes to the diminutive stature.

"Piers, what's going on? Come back to bed, I miss you." Even the voice was a dead match for hers.

"A demon," Hailey whispered.

Kieran looked at the demon, a slightly glassy look in his eyes. She could see the desire in him, plain as day. This was the life that some part of him had always wanted. It was as safe for him as it had been for her, nothing to do but to love the person he wanted endlessly with no trouble in sight.

"Kieran, Kieran, that's not me," Hailey said, trying to keep her voice calm. "That's an impostor, that's not me at all."

"Kieran, who is that with you? Is…is it a demon?" The false-Hailey's face was suddenly a mask of fear. "Make it go away, please, Kieran. I need you here. Don't leave me."

"Kieran, please don't stay with her."

Hailey could feel terror rise up in the back of her throat. She could see the game that the demon was playing. If Kieran thought that someone needed him, he would never leave. Given the fact that the demon wore Hailey's face, that was bound to make it even harder.

"Stay with me. There's nothing beyond that door for you. There is no one who needs you like I do. There is no one who deserves you the way that I do. Please, I have been so sad. Please come to me?"

Kieran shook his head as if he had been aroused from a deep stupor. To Hailey's shock, he took a step closer to the false Hailey in the bedroom. She could barely stand to watch her man walk away from her.

She blinked when she realized that the temperature in the house was dropping quickly.

"You overplayed your hand, demon," he said, his voice cold and true. "Hailey would never tell me she was the only one who needed me. She would never say that."

The false Hailey stammered, but something about Kieran's cold tone seemed to throw her off. She was losing control of her own illusion. Her eyes flickered from Hailey's green to blue to something that looked like a slit cat's eye. She backed away slowly, still trying to use soothing words to calm Kieran, but there was no calming him.

Rage seemed to radiate from him like a heat wave. It even made Hailey a little afraid to approach her lover.

"She would never keep me from my duty. You have played your hand badly, demon, and now you are going to die for it."

The ice crystals spun from his hands faster than Hailey had ever seen them. They seemed to be forming even as they whipped through the air. The glittering blades of ice pierced the false Hailey's chest, but the resistance there was nothing at all like the blades entering flesh.

Instead they flew through her body as if she was nothing but mist and sugar floss, though she screamed as loudly as a human. The pain made her form shift, and for a moment, Hailey could see her true form.

The demon might have been a human once, but that was a long time ago. In that brief flicker, Hailey could see dry-dust skin stretched over a mostly complete skeleton, crooked bat wings that seemed to replace the demon's arms, and a face with a sucker of sorts instead of a mouth. She nearly gagged on her own fear and disgust, but in a moment, the false Hailey vanished in a foul puff of smoke and the house started collapsing.

Out of panic, Hailey tried to duck underneath a desk, but Kieran held her in place, quickly forming a disc of extremely cold, very clear, very thick ice over their heads. The entire house came down in a shower of broken shards, a muted roar that deafened both of them.

Hailey crowded against Kieran to stay away from the splinters, holding her hands over her ears until it was all over. When the last sounds of snapping wood and shattering glass had ceased, she carefully opened her eyes. All around them was the wreckage of the life that they had been living in comfort and ease. Above them was that same bruised, dark sky under which she had found Kieran.

"I can't believe I forgot it all," Hailey said, a terrible guilt and pain clenching her heart. "I forgot everyone except you. I forgot Piers, Julie, Beatrice, Liona, everyone. It didn't matter. I didn't care."

Kieran spun the ice away, taking her in his arms.

"It is this place. There are so many traps for the unwary. I believe that this is a place that is meant to prey on human thoughts and dreams of every stripe. The stronger a desire is, the more powerful the trap."

Hailey shook her head.

"Does that mean that I'm heartless?" she asked. "Does that mean that I simply don't have enough care for any of the other people in my life?"

Kieran thought for a moment, and then shook his head no.

"If you simply did not have enough love for others, I think we would still be living that life."

"Yeah, and I'd still be a goddamn cat," said a small voice.

"Ferret!"

The little animal squirmed his way out from under a pile of shingles, shaking his fur indignantly. Hailey knelt to scoop him up, squeaking with surprise when he simply swarmed up her reaching hand and arm, finding his accustomed place on her shoulder.

"That was a close one, girl," he said, stretching out. "They almost had you."

"What would have happened if we had been caught?" she asked.

Ferret shrugged, an odd thing on an animal so far from human.

"In my experience? Lived in stupid bliss until your spirits faded away to senseless wraiths. It's no heaven or hell or anything like that for those wraiths, they simply drift around the Shadow Walk Prison like a lot of idiot smoke. Outside of course, your bodies would have ceased to function and your guts gone to mush years ago, though, so there's nothing worth coming back to anyway."

Kieran raised an eyebrow at the little animal.

"Did you pick up a new friend while you were looking for us?"

"I did as a matter of fact," Hailey said. "Kieran, this is Ferret. Ferret, this is Major Kieran McCallen of the Magus Corps."

Both Kieran and Ferret sized each other up, looking over each other cautiously before shrugging and proceeding to cordially ignore each other. Hailey hid a smile.

"We need to get moving," she said. "We need to find Piers, and then we need to get out of here."

"Piers is in here too?" Kieran wondered. "Will…we find him as you found me?"

Hailey shrugged helplessly.

"You are both men of passion and you have pasts just like everyone else. I don't want to see these private places of yours until you show them to me, but right now, we might not have a choice."

"Hailey…"

"Yes, Kieran?"

"Living in a house entirely constrained to the two of us. Was that a trap for me or a trap for you?"

There were a dozen unasked questions in his voice. Hailey thought for a long moment before shaking her head.

"I don't know, love. I couldn't tell you."

They stood together for a moment. Finally, Kieran nodded and kissed her on the forehead.

"Let's go find Piers," he said, and she turned with relief.

She was still wearing a nightgown and Kieran was dressed in nothing at all. She showed him how to concentrate on the idea of clothes. She chose her usual uniform of jeans, hoodie and boots, and she waited as he experimented with the idea himself.

When he was done, Hailey raised her eyebrow. He was dressed not in the dark modern clothes that were the de facto uniform of the Magus Corps, but instead in the clothing of a Viking warrior prince. His clothing was mostly made of black wool, with tall boots that came up to his knees. Over his shoulders, he wore a massive black fur, something that made him look even larger. Across his back was a shield, and at his hip was a sword.

"I've not seen you in the clothing of your youth before."

"It seems fitting. If the past can harm me, it should also be able to turn those fangs outwards and heal me."

With Ferret on her shoulder and Kieran by her side, she took a deep breath. She summoned up Piers's face in her mind, the sardonic good humored twist of his mouth, his long blonde hair, the assured way he floated in the sky, and the feel of his sweet mouth across the back of her neck.

Oh darling, what will they have done with you? Hailey wondered.

She started walking, keeping the vision of Piers in front of her. She would find him. She had to.

CHAPTER FIFTY-THREE

THEY WALKED FOR a timeless distance, and slowly around them, the world changed. The sky was the same as it always was, but the ground turned hard and flinty, making them walk carefully. Soon they started seeing cairns, piles of blackened rocks that designated graves. There were small wooden staves around each cairn, each with a name. Hailey shivered when she realized that each grave marked the passing of at least eight people. Some marked as many as fifteen.

"What kind of place is this?" she murmured, keeping her voice deliberately low.

Kieran shook his head.

"It's a killing field," he said flatly. "These people died all at once. That doesn't happen in peace time. The only other thing it could be is a sickness."

Hailey felt her stomach churn at the suffering that Piers must have seen. She was prepared to find him as a crying child or a shattered man. She was not prepared for what came next.

The area that they were traveling through was misty. It was hard to see more than twenty feet in any one direction. The cairns rose up out of the mists like hulking beasts, making Hailey and Kieran walk a little closer together without thinking about it. They had stopped talking almost entirely.

The first thing she heard was a skitter of stone and the rush of feet. She heard voices, hushed and urgent, speaking, and then more running. She tugged on Kieran's arm to get him to wait. As she predicted, the people came right for them.

It was a man and a woman, and they skidded to a stop as soon as they saw Hailey and Kieran. Hailey stared. These people were completely recognizable as duplicates of Kieran and Hailey themselves, but they were so changed. The strange Kieran wore an eye patch, and his bare chest was latticed with scars. The strange Hailey was stick thin. Half of her head had been shaved. She stared around like a wild horse, the white completely visible around her eye.

"What new trickery is this?" the strange Kieran snarled. He didn't have a sword. Instead he shifted into a fighting stance, putting his body between his Hailey and the newcomers.

"We're not your enemies," Hailey said softly, showing the pair her empty hands. "I…I think we're you. Or you're us. But either way, I promise I won't bring you any harm. Please, stop and talk to us for a moment. We don't know what's going on."

The strange Kieran snorted.

"That sounds like a pretty pack of lies to me," he said.

"Are you phantasms that he conjured?" asked the other Hailey.

It hurt Hailey to look at her doppelgänger. There was something achingly young and vulnerable about the way that she held herself that made Hailey herself ill. She wondered if she had ever looked like that back in her hungry teen years, if she had been that wild-eyed, that frail. It was strange to be simultaneously repulsed by your double and to want to feed her a good meal.

"Who do you think sent us?" Hailey asked gently. "We swear, we are just travelers in this land looking for Piers Dayton."

At the mention of the name, the other Hailey whimpered, covering her head with her hands and shrinking away. The other

Kieran snarled, and he would have strode forward to do battle if her own Kieran hadn't unlimbered his shield, pushing him back.

"Calm down," Kieran snapped. "There's nothing we're going to do that will hurt you. Tell us what happened to you."

The other Kieran's laugh was slightly mad.

"You have the answer to your own question. Piers Dayton happened to us. We've escaped and we're not going back. We're leaving now. If you continue on your way, you'll find him, sure enough. If I had anything left to me, I would warn you away. Right now, though, all I can say is better you than us."

He tugged the other Hailey forward, pulling her along behind him as he strode off.

Hailey shuddered. She had seen her doppelgänger's back and legs through shredded clothing. The other woman's skin was striped with welts, some old and some very new.

"What's going on here?" Kieran wondered.

Hailey was afraid she knew.

"Piers's always been someone in charge. He feels his responsibilities and his powers very clearly, but I suppose that when you have that much control, there is a dark side to it. At the very least, perhaps you fear there is a dark side to it."

She turned to Kieran, making him look at her.

"Do you trust me?"

"With my life," he responded instantly.

"Do you trust Piers?"

Kieran hesitated.

"I trust him less than I trust you, but I do, yes."

Hailey bit her lip, and then she nodded.

"It'll have to be enough. I don't know what we're going to find. I don't know what's going to happen. All I have is a guess. I know Piers; in some ways, I know Piers better than I know you simply because Piers and I have spent more time together. I think I know what he fears, and I think I know how it needs to play out."

"What are you saying, Hailey?"

"I know Piers well enough to know that he will never really harm me. I know Piers well enough to know that he will never really harm you. Believe me. Trust me. If I tell you not to fight him, don't, okay?"

Kieran looked torn.

"If he harms you? If he tries to harm me? Hailey, did you not see the two who just went by? They were ripped to ribbons."

Hailey nodded.

"I did. But Kieran, everything we see here except for ourselves and for Ferret here are illusions or demons in disguise. Those two are imaginings from our minds or from Piers's. This place is meant to prey on the weakest parts of us. The worst parts, the parts that we don't want to look at."

"How do we defeat something like that?"

Hailey's smile was as brave as she could make it.

"With as much love as we can give. With enough faith and hope that it will drown all the rest out."

She leaned up to give him a soft kiss on the mouth.

"It'll be fine, I promise."

He opened his mouth, but whether he was going to agree with her or to fight with her, she never found out. A thunder of hoof beats came towards them, rapid as a rising storm. They were surrounded by men on horseback. For a moment, Hailey thought that they were all headless, like the demon that had cursed them, but then she realized that they were only suits of armor mounted on terrifying red eyed horses that clamped and champed at their bits.

The suits of armor wheeled around Kieran and Hailey. Though Kieran tried to keep them back, they were too many and too strong. As two kept Kieran occupied, a third scooped Hailey up around her waist. She reached for her power, but then reminded herself that this was the way things were meant to go. If she didn't fight, she might come to Piers sooner rather than later.

"Scoot off," she whispered to Ferret. "The last thing I want is for you to get stuck in a collapsing house again."

Ferret didn't respond, but he flung himself from her shoulder. She prayed the little animal wasn't trampled or hurt. A shout told her that they had subdued Kieran. As one, the suits of armor turned back the way they came, riding for a destination that she knew must involve Piers.

• • • • •

The suits took them to a place that first made Hailey's heart leap with joy. It was the Castle, the manse that contained Piers's coven. Tucked far up in the Wyoming mountains, it was nearly impregnable. It was the first place that she had ever felt safe. She felt some of the joy that she had experienced there wash over her, but then that joy was quickly washed away.

It would never be the Castle because the thing that made it essentially the Castle was missing. There were no people anywhere. There was no one to be found. The suits of armor marched her and Kieran through the echoing halls, bringing them to a wing that she was fairly sure didn't exist in the real version of the building.

The doors swung open to reveal a dark chamber that was lit only with torch light. At the far end there was a desk, and at the desk sat a man.

Hailey barely recognized Piers at first. Dressed in severe black clothes and with his hair pulled back from his face, he looked as strict and unyielding as a senior member of the Magus Corps. There was nothing of the laughing man she knew and loved in his face.

When she and Kieran were shoved in front of the desk, the suits stood back. Their iron presence behind Hailey made her nervous. When they went still, there was nothing at all that said that they could rise again, that they could suddenly grasp, grab and harm.

"Aren't you two tired of running yet?" Piers asked, his voice as cold as ice.

Hailey found her voice to speak.

"Piers, we wouldn't run from you–"

"Then you're very foolish," he said.

There was something dead about the way he spoke, as if he wasn't all there. It raised Hailey's fear, bringing a tremor to her voice that she strove to quell.

"Why would you say that, Piers?"

"Because I hurt you, Hailey," he said patiently, as if he was explaining to a little child. "You and Kieran both. You ran away, you were foolish enough to get caught. Now you're here again."

"I'm here with the two men I love. I fail to see a problem."

Piers stalked around his desk until he was facing her. Though he was not as tall or broad as Kieran, he was still an imposing man. Hailey had to crane her neck slightly to look up at him. The expression on his face was stern enough to make her tremble.

"You don't see a problem? Truly? Have you lost what little sense you have left?"

"That's not a very kind thing to say to me," she said, standing her ground.

She could feel Kieran tense, ready to come to her aid, but thankfully, he held steady. She was fairly sure that if it came down to a fight between the two of them that Kieran would win, but in a place that was ruled by Piers's fears, it would be a hard contest.

"I'm not a very kind man," Piers said. He tilted her chin up so that she had to look at him. "I thought you would have known that by now.

"I know nothing of the sort," Hailey said levelly. "I have known you for a little while now, and I hope to know you for years to come. All I have seen of you is that you are one of the kindest men I know, one of the most compassionate and most understanding."

"You really don't remember," Piers said, a bit of wonder in his voice. "You don't remember what I did to you."

"I remember very well," Hailey countered. "But I think I know what you are afraid you might do to us."

Hailey thought of those frightened and injured doppelgängers. She shivered a little when she thought of their scars and of the way that they cringed. They were desperate to get away from a Piers that had hurt them terribly.

It struck her in that moment that Piers was very different from Kieran. Kieran had been most ashamed and most afraid of the things that he had done. Piers was most afraid of what he could become.

"They weren't real though, Piers. They were projections of your mind, your deepest fears. There are so many things that we can have between us, so many things that I and Kieran both want. You don't scare me."

For a split second, there was a moment of doubt on Piers's face. She wondered if she had broken through the mask of cold cruelty that he believed he bore, but then it was back.

"I wonder. You sound so sure of yourself."

"I am. More than I am sure of myself, I am sure of you."

"And you?" Piers turned to Kieran, who had a wary look on his face. Hailey could see that he was still tensed to spring, but he nodded.

"I have not known you as long as Hailey has, but I saw Hailey before she met you and I see her now. She trusts you, so I trust you."

Hailey wondered if there had been such a change in her as that. She supposed it was true. She couldn't imagine doing half of what she had accomplished back when she was living on the charitable graces of the covens who had been forced to take her.

"It's almost as if you believe me incapable of cruelty."

To Hailey's surprise, Kieran's grin was as sharp as a knife.

"Not that. Never that. I think that no one who leads men the way that you do is incapable of it. At the very least, I would bet good money that your tongue is capable of stripping the hide off of a rhino. But cruelty is a tool, and you are a man who uses tools wisely."

Piers laughed a little, a dark thing.

"Are you willing to bet on it? Not one or the other of you taking me on yourself, but both of you?"

Hailey hesitated, and then she nodded. She prayed that she was right, because now she was betting Kieran's safety and sanity on it as well as her own.

"I will," she said, her voice thin. She turned pleading eyes to Kieran, who looked more cautious.

Finally, he nodded as well. "I think that you understand that Hailey is your soul. Kill her and you will kill it."

"I see."

Kieran cried out in surprise as the suit behind him closed its hands over his forearms. Hailey watched, wide-eyed, as he struggled. Even as large and strong as he was, the suit held him as immobile as a kitten.

"Hailey, stay right where you are. If you move from where you are, I'll make Kieran pay for it."

Hailey nodded, unable to process the rush of emotions that were pouring through her. She knew she should have been terrified. When Liona had told her her story, she hadn't used the term Wiccan. Instead she had used *people of power*, and that term suited Piers right then. He was a powerful man with two toys to play with.

Instead of terror, all she felt was a fluttery anticipation deep in her belly and a growing arousal. There was perhaps a little bit of fear there, but it only gave a savor to the warmth that was pooling between her legs and the tightness of her nipples.

Her mouth was dry as she watched Piers eye Kieran up and down. Kieran obviously was not used to this close scrutiny, and he tried to turn his face away.

Piers made a displeased sound, grabbing Kieran's jaw and forcing him to meet his eyes.

"I don't bed with men very often, but when I do, I like men like you."

"Bigger than you?"

Kieran's voice was slightly taunting, and it won a brief smile from Piers.

"Exactly so. There's something…pleasurable about seeing a man as big as you brought to his knees and begging."

Kieran started to say something, but then Piers squeezed him between the legs through his trousers. Kieran gasped, his hips bucking a little.

"You were already hard," Piers commented. "I don't think it would take that much before I got you to beg."

Kieran swore helplessly at Piers, who only laughed. Hailey felt a hot blush on her cheeks as Piers deftly unfastened Kieran's trouser, drawing his erection out fully. He pumped the other man's cock almost lazily, in absolutely no hurry at all.

When Piers stepped back, Kieran was fully hard and panting slightly. To Hailey's shock, Piers slapped the other man's hard flesh lightly, making Kieran groan.

"That's good for you right now. I have some other things I want to do."

Hailey realized that Piers was looking straight at her. She stood her ground as he walked over to her. The idea of being held and aroused helplessly made her want to whimper, but instead he only looked her over.

"Strip for me," he said finally. "Down to the skin. I've never thought that you should wear clothes."

Hailey gulped and nodded. Her boots and outer garments went quickly enough, but when she got down to her underthings, she paused. The hall was cold, and not only were Piers's avid eyes on her, but so were Kieran's. The suits of armor she knew were insensible, but they were a presence as well.

Taking a deep breath, she stripped the last of her clothing off to stand naked in front of Piers. She resisted the instinctive urge to cover herself. He had seen her naked before, but never in this cool and calculated way.

Piers examined her much as he had examined Kieran. When he reached for her, she expected a gentle caress or even a passionate one, but instead his hands ran down her shoulders and her arms, along her flanks and down her thighs. When he swept his fingers through the length of her red hair, she shivered at how close he was to her and everything that she could feel.

She felt like an object he was examining, perhaps deciding if he wished to purchase her or use her. When he tweaked first one nipple and then the other, she squeaked a little, making him smile.

"You're perfect for me," he said casually. "I've always thought so, but I love you like this."

She started to ask what he meant, but instead, she gasped when he lifted her in his arms as if she was as light as a feather. She clung to him for a moment, but they weren't going far. He was only depositing her on his desk, heedless of the papers that lay on it. She tried to close her legs, but he held them open, letting them dangle over the edge of the desk. She blinked when she realized that she was able to look straight at Kieran, who was still held by the suit.

He looked absolutely starved. His eyes were wide and glassy, and his gaze flickered between her naked body and the way Piers stood to one side, watching her closely.

Almost casually, much as he had done with Kieran, his hand closed over the space between her legs. She held her breath as he cupped that tender flesh before running his fingertip along her slit. Her lower lips were full and warm, but when he traced his finger along the seam between, she grew wet.

"Do you like being displayed, Hailey? Do you like me showing Kieran how wet you get for me? Would you like me to show you to an army of men, just like this?"

Hailey shook her head to clear it. She had to try twice before she could find her voice.

"I like being displayed," she said softly. "But I just want you and Kieran to see me. I…trust your eyes, I love you both."

She wondered if Piers would be displeased, but he only chuckled.

"My perfect, beautiful, little pet."

As if to reward her for speaking, he ghosted a fingertip over her clit, smearing some of the wetness from below over it. She purred, turning her face to rest it against his side, but he didn't do that for very long.

"Let's see how you like this."

She focused on a chain between his hands. She realized there were small clamps on either end, making her gasp.

"Do you know where these are going to go?"

Hailey gulped.

"I have an idea."

"Good. Let's see if that idea is right."

His hands were as calm and steady as a doctor's. She watched with a kind of fascinated dread as he plumped one small breast, making sure that the nipple stood up prominently. When it did, he opened one clamp to its full extension, showing her the rubber-padded tips.

She bit her lip, quivering a little. He brought the clamp to her nipple, closing the ends so slowly that her breath left her body almost completely on a long exhale. They were tight, oh they were so tight, and when he released them, Hailey cried out in a panic.

For a split second, she was sure she would have to take it off, that she would scream or cry or beg, but then the first tide of pain drew back, leaving behind a lush, throbbing ache.

"I can't… I can't…" she gasped, making Piers's hand hover over the clamp.

"Do you need it off?"

She finally shook her head, clinging to his sleeve tightly.

"I don't, it's… I think I can stand it."

"Good."

That was all the warning she got before he fastened the other one to her opposite nipple. With none of the warning that she got with the first one, Hailey shrieked out loud. The pain stung deeply, making her thrash, but like the first, it receded quickly as well.

She stared around her, eyes wide. The clamps attached to her nipples dulled down to a deep and sensuous pain, something she had never experienced before. When she glanced down to look, she was enchanted by how dark her small nipples were and how bright the silver chain running between them was.

"Those are beautiful on you," remarked Piers. "I think Kieran agrees."

She glanced over at Kieran, who was staring hard enough to make her burst into flames. His cock was fully hard, standing up proudly and with a drop of clear liquid at the tip.

"I think you should go show him how lovely they are."

Hailey started to ask Piers what he meant by that, but then he hooked his fingers through the chain between her nipples. When he gave a gentle tug, she gasped at the prickles of sensation that ran through her breasts. He gave a harder tug, and without thinking about it, she moved forward, hopping off of the desk to follow him. He led her the short distance to where Kieran was restrained. Kieran licked dry lips as she and Piers approached, longing and fear all at once.

"Down."

That was all the warning that Hailey got before Piers drew downwards on the chain. To avoid the painful pull, she dropped to the ground as gracefully as she could, staring up at the two men looming over her. Piers released the chain, but he cupped his hand over the back of her head.

"Show him how much you want him," Piers said softly.

She wasn't sure what he meant before he pressed her head forward, bringing her up so that she could nuzzle the length of Kieran's cock. She felt a thrill shiver her body at this act, at the idea that Piers was pressing her on Kieran. She opened her mouth willingly, running her tongue up and down his shaft. She stopped just short of the sensitive tip, making Kieran groan in frustration. She allowed Piers's hand to guide her, letting him press her up and down.

The small weight of the chain on her nipples made it impossible to forget that it was there, but instead she concentrated on giving Kieran all the pleasure she could, all the pleasure that Piers would allow her to give him.

Finally, Piers fed Kieran's cock into her mouth slowly, making her take him inch by inch until her mouth was full. She was briefly worried that he would push her on to it and gag her, but instead his hands were gentle. Kieran writhed as she drew her mouth back and forth on his cock. She could feel his entire body tense. He wanted to press further into her mouth, but Piers's grasp on her head and the suit of armor holding him steady prevented it.

"What do you want?" Piers asked.

"I want to come," Kieran murmured, trying to push into Hailey's mouth again.

"Not yet."

Piers's words were careless, as if he was declining a drink he didn't really want. He twisted his fist in Hailey's hair, drawing her up again. Having her hair pulled made her squirm, but she couldn't give herself to pleasure just yet because he was bringing her to face him.

"I want you completely full," he said softly. "I want to have every hole on you full when I fuck you. Do you understand?"

Swallowing hard, Hailey nodded.

"Are you willing?"

She didn't even hesitate. She nodded quickly, drawing a fresh blush to her cheeks. She was more than willing. Her legs were shaking with arousal. She stumbled a little as Piers guided her to his desk.

This time, he lifted her up so that she could crouch on all fours on the broad flat surface. Again, he positioned her so that she was facing Kieran. She could see the hungry look on his face, how hard his unsatisfied cock was. She met his eyes and was surprised to see a bright spark of humor there. He mouthed *I love you* to her, making her smile a little.

She tried to keep her knees close together, but a brisk slap on each thigh encouraged her to keep them spread apart. Piers's heavy hand between her shoulders pressed her down to her elbows. She gasped when the chain clattered on the desk. She had almost forgotten it was there. She heard him opening drawers in the desk behind, setting something on the desk by her knees.

"I think," Piers said considering, "that you are going to like this a lot. Tell me if you don't."

Hailey nodded, butterflies in her stomach. She felt his fingers, cool with lube, slide along her slit, swiping around her clit teasingly before drawing back to circle her rear hole. She sucked her breath in hard, trying to keep still and to be as obedient as he wanted her to be.

She had had daytime thoughts about that area before, about Piers or Kieran doing just that. She had thought about them doing more before wondering how she could take it, whether she could bear it at all. She was afraid of the pain, but there was no pain at all as Piers worked her open with patience and care.

Despite his careful preparations, she still squeaked with fright when she felt the rounded tip of what must have been a metal plug against her hole. It was slick, but there was something terribly unyielding about it. She braced herself, holding herself steady as he pressed it forward. He was being very slow with it, murmuring encouragement to her as he slid it inside her.

It already felt large inside when he paused.

"Just another little bit, sweetheart. Look up at Kieran now."

She was lightly covered with sweat and breathing a little hard, but she still managed to lift her chin so that she could look at her other lover. His mouth was partially open and his cock fully hard. If the suit of armor hadn't been holding him, she knew that he would have been on her in a heartbeat.

"I want to kiss him," she said, her voice strained.

Piers laughed, keeping the plug steady inside her.

"All right. Kieran, if I let you go, will you come kneel in front of the desk and kiss her as she wishes? No hands. Keep them behind your back."

"Yes…yes, I will."

The suit of armor let him go, and Kieran came to kneel in front of her. His eyes were so dilated that they were black. Hailey could see herself in them.

"Remember, keep your hands off her. If I see you touch so much as a hair on her head, I'll have you back up and restrained hand and foot while I use a paddle on her ass."

Hailey whimpered, but then Kieran's mouth was on hers, kissing her the precise way that she had wanted to be kissed. His mouth was soft and sweet, but there was a darker hunger underneath it, something that demanded everything that she had.

Piers pushed the rest of the plug home, stretching her and making her cry out into Kieran's mouth. He groaned with her, but he didn't stop kissing her. She could feel her body close around what she guessed was the narrow neck of the toy. It spread out behind the neck so that it was securely held in her body. She could neither push it out or allow it to slip further inside her.

"All right, now raise up for me, darling."

Under Piers's careful guidance, she rose up on her hands and knees, moving slowly and uncertainly as she did so. There was something terribly vulnerable about it. It made her whole body heat up and feel over-sensitized. She was more aware of the clamps on her nipples and of how cool the air felt against her naked body.

Still kneeling in front of the desk, Kieran watched her with wide eyes.

"Do you want to have her mouth again, Kieran?"

Kieran nodded, never taking his eyes off Hailey's body. He had told her that she was beautiful many times before, but he had never seen her like this before. She was strung out on sensation, every little piece of her craved more touch, more stimulation.

"Good. We're going to go to my bed chamber now and give you just that. Come on, Hailey."

She turned on the desk, ready to jump off, but Piers hooked his fingers around the chain again. It brought her to immediate attention, making her completely responsive to the chain's most gentle movement.

She followed him carefully as he got her off the desk and standing on the floor.

"I want you to crawl behind us, Kieran. There are no eyes here beyond mine and Hailey's. Can you do it?"

She honestly thought that Kieran would say no. She watched as he fought with himself. It wasn't a battle of whether he would do so because he loved her, she realized. He was fighting with his own pride for something that it looked like he wanted very much. To her pleasure, he nodded, even if his hands were shaking and his face was brick red. Before he got down on his hands and knees, she could see that his cock was still hard as stone.

"All right then."

They made a strange progression through the halls. There was no one there, but there was no doubt that they were halls that were made for people's use. At any moment, Hailey expected to be confronted by someone else, by an officiant, an ambassador, royalty or servants. Piers ruled here, but it looked like he ruled over nothing and no one.

He had mentioned before the idea of bringing her like this in front of people. Inadvertently, she imagined people filling the halls, stepping aside quietly to let them pass. Of course no one would question Piers, but their eyes would linger on her body, on the chain between her nipples. As she went past, they would see the gleam of the plug in her rear. What would they say about her later on? Would they think she was beautiful? Would they think she was a slut?

The thought of all those eyes on her made her whimper, and she straightened herself hastily. This was a place that responded to thoughts and to wishes, no matter how ill-advised. She kept her eyes on the ground as they walked to Piers's chamber. She was afraid to look because she might have seen shadowy figures watching them, their eyes on her naked body and on Kieran's crawl.

Piers's chamber was barren except for an enormous bed in the center of the room. A warm light from above suffused it, but there was something forbidding about it as well.

Not taking his hand from the chain between her breasts, Piers gestured to Kieran.

"Stand up. Take off the rest of your clothes."

Kieran did as he was told, standing unafraid in front of the other man. There was almost something challenging about his gaze. Hailey couldn't read it, but it made Piers smile.

"Lie down on the bed."

Kieran did as he was told, and Hailey and Piers came to join him. Piers stripped off his clothing quickly as well, and now all three of them were naked.

He positioned Hailey so that she was kneeling between Kieran's legs, his cock in the perfect place for her mouth. She licked her lips hungrily for him, but she glanced behind her at Piers, waiting for his command.

He grinned slightly at her. It struck her that he was more himself now, less deadened. There was a spark of good humor in his eyes, something that suited him far more than icy control.

I must remember this, she thought to herself. *He is made for command, but he is made for this very odd tenderness as well.*

He positioned himself behind her on his knees. She could feel his cock brushing against her thigh before it began nudging between her slick folds. She tried to push herself back on his cock, but his steadying hands on her hips prevented her from doing so.

"Take as much of his cock in your mouth as you can," Piers directed softly. "Be sweet with him."

She followed his directions, almost awed by how tender they were. Even though her mouth was gentle on him, he still moaned. Piers had kept him hard for quite some time. She was a little surprised he didn't spill at the first touch of her mouth, but she could tell that it wouldn't be too long for him. She lapped at his dark erect flesh, wetting it before sliding her mouth over the length of him. His thankful groan was deep, rumbling through his body.

She loved the taste and the feel of him in her mouth, craved more and more. She took him into her mouth by increments, slowly and sensually. She drew back when he threatened to gag her, but then she was pushing herself back, easing herself into a rhythm that made him groan.

She had almost forgotten Piers behind her, but then his blunt cock started to nudge at her opening, splitting her slowly but surely. The presence of the plug in her rear made his entry feel tight. There was a slight stretch there that made her moan deep in her throat.

Once the head of his cock had breached her, he didn't pause. Instead, he sunk himself deep into her body until he was lodged in her fully. Hailey shut her eyes tight, almost unable to cope with all of the emotions that were washing over her, turning her soft and liquid at her core.

"Please, please, Piers," panted Kieran. "Please I want to…"

"You want to what, hmm?" Piers asked, thrusting into Hailey's willing body with motions that were speeding up. "What do you want, handsome boy? Tell me what you want. Maybe then I will give it to you."

Despite how hard he was and how desperate he felt, Kieran stuttered for a moment. Hailey couldn't tell whether it was because he was shy or whether it was because he was so distracted with her mouth.

"I want to come," he said finally. "I want to come, please."

"Where?" Piers's tone was curt, almost brutal. "Hmm? Tell me where, Kieran."

"Down her throat. Please, please let me."

In response, Piers reached down, twisting his fist in Hailey's red hair again. With just a little bit of force, he lifted her head from Kieran's cock, drawing a deep groan from the other man.

"Well, darling? You heard him. Do you want him to spill down your throat? Do you want to swallow him?"

The whole time, he never stopped thrusting into her. Hailey had to breathe deeply a few times before she could respond. She nodded violently.

"Please, I want that, I do." Her voice was barely more than a squeak, making Piers laugh.

"Good. Swallow every drop, and I'll make sure that you come as well."

He pressed her head back down on Kieran's cock. This time he left it there, cupping his palm lightly on her head.

It only took a few more moments before Kieran's body tensed. Hailey watched fascinated as the muscles of his belly rippled. He was spilling. As Piers told her, she swallowed it. The taste was neither pleasant or unpleasant, but the act of doing so, of doing it because Piers had told her to, created a wave of sensation through her.

Just when Kieran's powerful body was going still, Piers's sped up. His strokes, formerly slow and steady, became more frantic, more demanding. Soon he was pulling her back on him with such force that she yowled with the intensity of it.

When he came, he buried himself in her as if he couldn't get close enough to her. As she had with Kieran, she thought of that heat inside her, how amazing it was, how much she wanted it.

For a long moment, he rested across her back. She bore his weight willingly, her mind in a blank pleasurable place. She was aware that she hadn't climaxed herself yet, but she cared very little. It was enough to be so close to the two men most important to her.

Piers withdrew from her. With gentle motions, he turned her until she was resting with her back against Kieran's chest. The shift reminded her of the plug in her rear. The thought sent another frisson of sensation through her.

"Here, this is what I want to do."

Piers took Kieran's hand and placed it between Hailey's wide-spread legs. He set Kieran's fingers in motion. Once he did so, Kieran kept the rhythm faithfully. He stroked her clit, making her clench and moan, occasionally reaching down to gather more wetness from below to smooth his way.

At first Hailey thought that Piers would just watch, but then his fingers found the base of the plug. Instead of removing it, he rocked it in her, making her arch and gasp. The sheer amount of sensation that she could feel was enveloping. It made her wonder what it would be like to have Piers or Kieran buried there instead of the plug.

Her orgasm was like the plucking of a harp string. It struck with unerring accuracy and then it reverberated through her body. It was pure pleasure, then it was relief. Piers had kept her dancing on the edge for so long that she could barely have taken another moment. She rested against Kieran's chest for an immeasurable time, drifting in the pleasure and marveling at how much her own simple body could do.

She murmured sleepily when both men moved, whispering about something over her head. She didn't protest as one or the other scooped her into the air and carried her. She could hear water running, but she was distracted by gentle fingers on the base of plug.

"Shh, darling, just relax."

Piers worked it out of her as easily as he had worked it in. She mewled when it was taken out, but then she was being lowered into a warm bath in a decadently deep tub. Kieran had climbed in with her. She found herself cuddled up next to him. He was smoothing wet hands over her shoulder, her neck, her torso, and her arms. He was comforting at first. Then he picked up a soapy washcloth, making her purr in pleasure as he began to wash her.

"Piers?"

"How are you?" he answered.

She thought before she answered.

"Good. I feel wonderful. I feel close with both of you. I feel so close with both of you. I love you."

"I… see."

There was something strange about the way Piers's voice sounded, but Kieran was doing such a good job bathing her that she couldn't think to figure it out. She was full of bliss and contentment in a way that she never knew she could be.

Peripherally, she was aware of Piers cleaning himself in the separate shower nearby. She waited, drowsy-eyed and pleased for him to come closer. She was not prepared to hear the door to the bathroom open and shut softly. It was so unexpected that she sat perfectly still for a moment, convinced that he was going to come back.

"Kieran," she said finally, lifting her head from his chest. "Where did Piers go?"

"I have no idea," he said, as baffled as she was.

"All right. I think it's time we went and had words with that man," she muttered.

Her concern about Piers robbed her of some of the pleasure of the bath. She stepped out of the tub quickly, reaching for one of the fluffy white towels nearby. As she dried herself, she wondered what became of all of this when they had moved on. Would anyone be out of sorts if she didn't hang it up? Did it simply disappear when she wasn't looking at it? She hung it up anyway.

Kieran followed her out of the bathroom. The bedroom was empty, and somehow, their clothes were folded on the chair nearby. Despite the presence of the clothing, Piers himself was nowhere to be seen.

Hailey felt her concern touch off an unexpected rage inside her. She reached for her clothes and put them on with jerky motions. Kieran did the same, watching her carefully.

"Hailey, what's going through your mind?" he asked.

"It occurs to me that simply because we let a man be in charge some times and in certain very intimate ways does not mean that he should be in charge all the time. Let's go find him."

• • • • •

Hailey was steaming as she walked through the halls of the false Castle. She understood what it represented, she knew some of the trauma that lay behind it. It was just that at that moment, she didn't quite care.

She relied on her senses to guide her to Piers. She didn't have to look into door after door to find him. Instead, she walked unerringly back to the door to his study, throwing it aside without even bothering to knock.

"You have some nerve," she snapped, walking in.

Piers was seated behind his desk, ostensibly working. However, Hailey noticed that he didn't have a pen in his hands. Instead, when she walked in, he was staring out the window, watching the bruised sky.

"Hailey? Kieran? I thought you had gone by now."

"Really? And where did you think we were gone to, hmm?"

"Away from me. Awakening. Leading the lives that you should have led if I weren't around."

Hailey felt her heart tug at how thoroughly he believed it. There was a real belief founded on a life of being different even for a Wiccan underneath it. She didn't let the sympathy restrain her; she thought that Piers needed to hear what she had to say. It felt in some ways as if he had needed to hear it for quite some time.

"All right, coven master. You are going to listen to me, and you are going to listen very well. What you did in that bedroom and in this office with us? That is not going to send us screaming into the night. I don't know what kind of weaklings you think we are, but we are made of far sterner stuff than that."

"Hailey?"

"Quiet, you are going to let me speak. What you did to us was nothing short of what we wanted and what we wanted from you. You did not do anything that hurt us or harmed us. Because we are strong, we would have stopped you. Do you know what I am?"

Piers looked at her. While she was talking she had come around the desk to face him. Now she stood inches away from him. Seated, he had to tilt his head back to look at her. He shook his head.

"I'm a vampire. That's what they always used to say about me. You helped me open myself to what I could truly do. Do you even understand what that means?"

"That you can pull power from anyone you touch…"

"Damn straight. What I was doing there with you involved a lot of touching, Piers. At any point, I could have taken enough power to fly away, to set you on fire, to turn into a wolf and bite your hand off. I didn't. I could have drained you dry, but I didn't. Do you know why?"

To her anger, he shook his head.

Growling, she reached out to grab the front of his shirt, dragging him close to her.

"Because I didn't want to!" she cried. "Everything that happened in that room was something I wanted. I want it still, and I want more of it."

"She's right," said Kieran quietly. "I wouldn't have done something like that unless I wanted it. I've always dreamed of things like that, and I am glad I got to experience them with you."

Piers still looked uncertain. Hailey sighed, her anger washing away as quickly as it had come. She leaned down and kissed his mouth sweetly. It was almost chaste except for the passion behind it. She felt some of the stiffness leave Piers's body. When his hand came up to tentatively touch her waist, she leaned into his body, draping her arms around his neck.

"What does it mean to you that we can still kiss like this?" she asked softly. "What does it mean to you that we can still touch like this?"

"That you're a very generous woman?"

Hailey made a displeased sound. She wound her fingers through his hair and tugged gently.

"It means that this is as much a part of us as what happened in your bedroom. It means that what we do gently and what we do roughly is all part of a whole. It is all a part of how we are, and we are like no one else in this world or out of it."

Kieran had moved to come stand behind Piers's chair, placing his hands on Piers's shoulders. In that moment, it startled Hailey a little to realize how much larger he was than Piers, both in height and in breadth. Piers was not a small man, but Kieran was a giant.

"She's right. Don't argue with her when she's right." Kieran paused. "I have seen monsters, Piers," he said finally. "I have seen the things that prey on the young and innocent. They do not make their victims strong. Instead, they make them weak. But what you have done for Hailey is to make her strong, and you have protected her. Monsters separate the weak from the herd and prey on them until there's nothing left of them. Then they do it again. You are no monster."

At Kieran's words, Piers's head dropped until it was resting on Hailey's shoulder. She wondered what was going on in his head, if his own monsters, the ones that lived in his head, were going to be stronger than her and Kieran.

Then his head came up, and he nodded.

"Thank you," he said softly. "I think I understand now. I believe… I believe you."

"Truly?" asked Hailey, making him meet her gaze. "Do you?"

He nodded with more decisiveness this time.

"I do."

He kissed her on the mouth, and then to her surprise, he stood turning to kiss Kieran as well. Kieran accepted the kiss as easily as he would from Hailey, drawing back to nod.

"Don't forget that again," Kieran said with a shrug. "We could grow tired of reminding you."

Piers grinned wryly, nodding.

That was it, Hailey thought. *It's only when he's defeated that he looks so much smaller than Kieran.*

"All right. Let's get out of here."

Hailey strode to the door with Piers and Kieran behind her. Before she opened the door. She thought *out* as clearly as she could. Then she opened the door.

CHAPTER FIFTY-FOUR

INSTEAD OF THE halls of the dead Castle or the barren rocky landscape she had walked through before, they were greeted with a dark forest. As they passed through the door, it ceased to exist behind them. Now they looked as if they had been dropped in this trackless forest with no path in sight. Even the bruised sky that Hailey had been braced for was invisible.

"I'm going up to see where we can go," Piers said, springing lightly into the air. He broke through the lower branches with a shower of leaves and twigs.

Hailey bit her lip nervously. The Shadow Walk Prison was a strange place with no logic to it, and the longer Piers stayed out of sight, the more worried she became. She was just suggesting that she could fly up after him when he returned, shaking twigs out of his hair and a befuddled look on his face.

"There's no sky," he said.

"What?"

"There's no sky, the trees go on as far as I can fly."

There was something horrible about it, that the thick trees that surrounded them were as dense and as enduring as the earth itself. The idea of it made Hailey dizzy. It was like being buried alive.

"All right, if we can't go over, we're committed to going

through," she said.

"What's going to keep us from going in circles?" Piers asked, eyes dark and concerned.

Hailey's smile was regretful.

"Our own minds. I'm learning more about the Shadow Walk Prison. The more time I've spent here, the more I think I can see how it works. It bends to our minds whether we want it to or not. It creates the world that we are expecting, even if it is not the world we want."

Both Piers and Kieran flinched at that. In both of their cases, it was altogether too true. Some fears could be magnified until they were their own prisons. The chains of the mind were far more powerful than chains of iron or steel.

"If we continue thinking that we are lost, if we panic, and if we fear, we will be lost and wandering around in circles forever. If we can keep our minds clear of pain and panic, we should be able to walk right out." She hesitated. "This place doesn't want to lose us, however. It feeds what it finds attractive, and it finds our fear and our sadness very wonderful indeed. We need to move forward without those thoughts."

Kieran frowned.

"Then I shouldn't be the one to lead us, and from what I know of Piers, he shouldn't be the one to lead either."

Hailey considered.

"I'm not someone without fear or sadness."

"You are someone who does not let them stop her, either," Piers pointed out.

Hailey wondered if she should protest again, but Piers took one hand and Kieran took the other. She stared for a moment, and then she smiled.

"You're right," she said softly. "I take my strength from myself, but I can also take it from you. With the two of you here, I can fight any pain or any sorrow."

Kieran's smile was slight but true.

"So lead us, little fox."

She smiled at him, kissing first Kieran's hand, then Piers's hand. She dropped them, and nodded, taking her first steps into the forest.

It looked like there was no path, but she quickly realized that wasn't true. When she started to move, she could see a deer track, a path so narrow and slight that she hadn't been able to see it in the forest's gloom. She wondered if there were deer in these forests or if the track was simply an aspect of her mind, something that she had conjured up when she started to walk.

It stayed dim for quite some time. She tried to keep her mind open while still concentrating on the idea of getting out, of finding a way to get home.

"I think it's getting a little lighter," Kieran muttered beside her.

She tried to take heart from what he said, but it wasn't easy. It made her think about the sheer force of will that Liona must have to simply enter this place when she pleased. She resolved to speak with Liona when she returned, to learn more about this half-world and what it meant. On one level, she, Kieran and Piers were safe in the fortress in the Alps, guarded by a warrior who had lived for more than a thousand years. In the most immediate sense, however, she and her lovers were traversing a dark and silent forest, uncertain if they would ever escape.

The forest was unnatural, she realized. There were no sounds, no running water and no birdsong. The silence made her think that it was just a set piece, something that was designed to keep them right where they were.

There was a rustle in the bushes nearby, drawing their attention and making her realize all over again how silent it was.

Piers and Kieran tensed, stepping forward almost as one, but then a familiar pointy nose popped out of the bushes.

"Ferret!" Hailey exclaimed. "You found us!"

"That I did," said the animal cheerfully. "And no easy task it was after what I have been through."

She leaned down to let the animal run up her arm. When he was seated on her shoulder again, he groomed himself for a moment before sitting up to speak.

"I've found you your way home," he said proudly. "There's a path through here that I can show you."

Piers was eying the little creature warily.

"Hailey?"

"Oh! I'm sorry. Piers, this is Ferret. He helped me when I first came here, and he's been helping me ever since."

Piers didn't lose his suspicious look.

"What are you really?" he asked Ferret, ignoring Hailey's startled look. "I've heard enough of the Shadow Walk Prison to know that what wears one face often possesses another."

Ferret chittered angrily at Piers, making Hailey stare at the little animal.

"Yeah, I guess not all of us are so lucky as you, mate. We don't all got brave girls to come looking when we're lost. Some of us make do, and some of us end up as ferrets."

Piers was unmoved.

"So what are you? Show us who you used to be."

Ferret cringed.

"Never ask a man what he once was," he muttered. "I don't know. I don't remember. I get flashes, like I told Hailey here. I don't have it anymore. I'd do anything to get it back, but I don't got it."

Even Piers looked a little taken aback by the small animal's despair.

"All right," he said, falling back. "I defer to your judgment on this, Hailey."

Ferret indicated a path that she had not seen before. Indeed, given the nature of the place, there was a chance it had not existed until Ferret had told her to look for it. It ran off to the left, pulling them into a darker part of the forest.

"Ferret, do you swear to us that you will show us the right way?"

If anything, Ferret shrunk even further into himself.

"I swear, I swear," he said softly. "Trust me, Hailey."

Hailey took a deep breath, and nodded.

After a few steps on Ferret's trail, the deer track behind them disappeared as if it had never been. Hailey understood what Piers meant. The path was dark, and there was something odd about Ferret. If she thought about how terrible the Shadow Walk Prison had been, however, she couldn't blame him for his mixed signals.

The way became more difficult than ever. There was still a track, but it was overgrown. They had to climb over dead falls and push their way through sickly-looking saplings that wanted to foul their every step. Still, though, it was growing lighter, just as the path they had been on before had been. Hailey tried to take heart from that. Sometimes, she reached up to her shoulder to stroke Ferret under the chin. Something about Piers's words had taken some of the spirit from the animal, making it cringe and shiver.

"When we get out of here, you could come with us, you know."

"Oh aye?" he whispered in return. "Don't you think I might just crumble down to dust whenever I set foot on proper ground again? Maybe I'd be nothing but a talking animal all my born days, a curiosity for them to stuff in a zoo."

"Or maybe you would be a man again," she said, her voice

warm. "There is hope for all of us, I believe that. You could be yourself again, or learn who that was."

Something about what she said made him laugh, a sad sound.

"Hailey, my love, on the road that I'm on, there is no looking back, and there is no version of myself from before that would make up for the man that I am now."

She started to ask what he meant, but then she saw a light up ahead, stronger than it had been before. It was almost piercing in the gloom of the forest, and she eagerly pointed ahead.

"I think it's the way out," she said in excitement. "I think we can go home!"

She started to walk forward, but Kieran reached forward to grab her hand.

"Let me go first," he said, unlimbering his sword. "I just want to make sure that…"

Almost as if his words had woken up the darkness of the forest, they were under attack.

Hailey's mind could barely understand it. One moment, there was nothing but the dimness and the silence of the forest, and the next moment, angry howls were filling the air around them. She saw flashes of tan and black, of bodies breaking from the bushes where they had been hiding, and the clash of steel weapons.

She saw Kieran engaged in battle with two enormous hulking men that simply looked as if they were shaped wrong, and she saw Piers being borne to the ground by something that had too many legs.

She started to run to help them, their names on her lips, but something thick and slimy twined around her ankles, tripping her so that she went sprawling on the floor. When she tried to struggle to her feet, the thing wrapped around her legs, binding her with an almost unimaginable strength. She cried out, but the thing only started drawing her backwards, pulling her towards the light that they had seen.

There was a flash of brown fur, and to her shock, Ferret bounded over her back, landing on the thing that had her trapped. For a horrible moment, she thought he was going to bite the thing that held her. He was going to be crushed in a matter of moments, she couldn't bear it. Then she heard what he was saying.

"I told you I'd bring them, didn't I? Isn't that what you wanted? Do I get what you promised me then?"

"You foul little monster!" cried Hailey furiously. "We *trusted* you!"

Ferret chittered at her, but she didn't get a response.

Hailey, Kieran and Piers were dragged towards the light. When they emerged from the trees, she could twist to see that what they had thought was a way out was in fact a huge bonfire, one that surged up and up into the twisting, roiling sky. Despite its monstrous size, it gave no heat. The three were dumped by the side of the fire. Now they could see their captors.

The demons that held them were a strange lot. The one that was still wrapped around Hailey was nothing more than a twist of roiling tentacles with what seemed to be an eye at the center of it. Its flesh was dry and rubbery. Where it touched her bare skin, it dragged and stuck.

Piers and Kieran were being held by a strangely identical set of men with the heads and tails of hyenas, their backs spotted black and tan. They seemed to have no language, but the strength they possessed was immense.

To Hailey's shock, she saw that both Piers and Kieran had been muzzled. Brutal leather and metal contraptions sat over their faces. It must have bound their powers as well, as Kieran had not created the ice blades that protected him and Piers had not lunged into the air. They had left her free, but she didn't even know what she could do in this place.

There was a tall demon with a brawny man's body and a pig's face, and it marched from Piers to Kieran and back again, inspecting them thoroughly before coming to investigate Hailey. She tried to shrink back from it when it thrust its bristled snout into her face, but the monster that held her refused to let her move back. The pig demon sniffed her twice, his lip curling back in disgust before standing erect again.

"You came through, little whiner. Here you go."

It tossed a small disk to where Ferret waited anxiously. The animal caught it deftly, flipping it to peer into the brightly reflective surface.

"That's what I looked like?" it asked in awe. "That was me? That was who I am?"

Hailey felt her stomach turn over. He had betrayed them for a simple chance to understand who he was. She was sickened and infuriated, but there was something there that she understood. She had seen first hand how the Shadow Walk Prison could twist everything that you wanted and needed. She had seen how it could turn good people into monsters.

"All right, they're the real thing. Do they suit you?"

She looked up to see the pig demon turning deferentially to a man in a blue suit. Between the pig demon and the demons that held her and her lovers, his normalcy made him almost more shocking.

"I suppose they do, though of course I will want to ask them some questions. Given the strangeness of this acquisition, they may not work at all."

The pig demon snarled at the man's indifferent tone, but the man raised his hand, his eyes as cold as ice.

"If you want your slop, you'll do as I say without the slobber, pig."

"Of course, Sir Knight. Anything you say, Sir Knight."

The pig demon bowed obsequiously, but when the man in the suit turned away, the pig demon's face contorted into a visage of hate. Hailey shivered, thinking about what that hate might look like if it were unleashed.

The man was of middle years with a slight limp to his step. In any other setting, he would have looked kind, though perhaps a bit odd. The hair on his head was dark, but the short beard on his face was almost pure white. He approached Kieran and Piers, staring at them intently. Something about him enraged Kieran. When the man got close, Kieran almost freed an arm from the demon that held it, lunging at the man. Though she couldn't see much of his face beyond the muzzle, his expression was one of sheer rage.

The man stepped back with a chuckle. Then he turned to Hailey. What she saw on his calm face chilled her more than the demons had. This was a man who had no understanding of her as a human, as a person. She was nothing more than dirt to him, and there was only one type of man who would think that of her. He was a Templar, and now he had all three of them bound. The Templars had spent centuries trying to eradicate all of Wiccan kind. The fact that he wasn't actually just killing them was alarming.

He stopped just a few feet away from her, looking at her curiously. He glanced down at a ring that he wore on his right hand. To her surprise, it sparked with green before going silent.

"Now you are a puzzle, little miss," he said, crouching down in front of her. "I can tell you are a witch, but I cannot tell anything about your powers. So far as I know, you have none."

"Is that a problem for you?" she spat, glaring at him.

"It puts me in a bit of a dilemma, that is true," he said, as if she had asked him a very logical question. "I am a Templar, you understand. I am not a monster. I do not kill humans–"

"Unless they get in your way. Unless they are inconvenient. Unless they are Wiccan."

"I do not kill humans, but you know that I cannot suffer a witch to live. Unfortunately, you are a witch, though you do seem to be a weak one. Is that why you've banded with these two monsters? Are you their whore?"

Hailey refused to say a word to him, making him shrug.

"It makes no difference, I suppose."

He stood up and began to walk away, but to Hailey's horror, the thing that held her spoke.

"Can I have her then, great lord? Can I? May I? I want her."

The Templar turned back to them, and the look of disgust on his face for the demon was almost equal to what he had for Kieran and Piers.

"And what would you do with her?"

"Walk," the thing crooned. "I would step out in her body and stretch my arms through her. I don't need to join the corps, I don't need to be part of the war, I just want to walk through her."

If anything, the look on the Templar's face only became more disgusted. He started to speak, but the pig demon interrupted him.

"There are many of us who want bodies. We have sworn and we have sacrificed, and we have licked your boots, Sir Knight. You will not grant the bodies of those who can receive us as you please. We have a rank and a hierarchy just as you do, and you will respect it."

Hailey shuddered at the thought. She thought of the Templar in Wyoming who had been infested with a demon. He had been dying when they found him, his body unable to cope with the changes that the demon had made. The Magus Corps officers that had been taken over by the demons, however corrupted and mangled they had become, were still living. Something about Wiccans made them more able to handle the possession of demons. They could be used as vessels, they could be used against other Wiccans like an unstoppable shock force. Whatever the Templar had been getting ready to say was erased by his contempt of the pig demon.

"You grow above yourself. You think that because we trade with you, because we deign to speak with you, you can dictate terms. Let me tell you here and now that you dictate nothing, no matter what you think. You will have one of the men. That was agreed upon. This woman, however, means nothing, and I will dispose of her as I please."

He turned to look at the thing that held Hailey.

"Have her, don't have her. It makes no difference to me."

The thing burbled with sick delight, clenching its arms even tighter around Hailey's body.

For a moment, her mind was nothing but a dark panic, but then she remembered where she was.

This is the Shadow Walk Prison, she thought. *This place bows to me when I am strong, and takes me captive when I am not. Gods above, I need strength!*

At the thought of strength, it was as if a door had opened in her mind. On one side was a turbulent dark sea with waves that rose up like skyscrapers. On the other was a field of light so bright it was nearly blinding. This was the power that she needed. It was always there waiting for her.

Thank you, Kieran. Thank you, Piers.

She opened herself to the power. She wasn't taking it this time. She was letting it flow through her. Like a dam collapsing after the weight of a decade, it came to her as if it belonged to her by right. She was full of it, it was hers, and she would use it.

There was a sudden shriek of pain as her body burst on fire. There was an eye-watering smell of burnt flesh as the thing holding her backed off. When the pig demon roared a battle challenge, she simply lifted her hand and summoned a bolt of lighting. She saw the demon lit up for a moment, its back arched and its face contorted with hate. Then it disappeared as if it had never been there, a drift of blackened ash and char drifting away.

Despite the carnage that she had just wreaked, she still felt completely calm. She felt as if she was floating, that there would never be anything that could get in her way again. Slowly, she turned to the hyena demons that were holding Piers and Kieran. For a moment, it looked like they wanted to run, and if they had, she would not pursue them.

Then one stepped forward, holding a short but evil looking knife to Kieran's throat. In that moment, any hope of pity or mercy fled her mind. She looked at them, her eyes fluttering closed. She imagined the red, living blood inside the demons, slowing down more and more. It grew sluggish, it almost stopped. She heard the howls of pain, piercing and loud, and then they cut off all together as their blood froze. Hailey watched in satisfaction as the hyena demons fell to the ground. The knife clattered away harmlessly.

She stepped closer to her lovers, reaching out to take the muzzles away from their faces. Both of them fell on her. For a long moment, she was overwhelmed by their arms around her, their mouths kissing her face. She did her best to return their affection, but it was a bit like being overwhelmed by two large dogs. When they finally threatened to knock her off her feet, she pushed them away with a laugh.

"I'm glad you're both all right," she said.

"All right and perhaps a little aroused," said Piers, looking around. "Hailey, what did you do?"

"Saved you?" she asked, slightly affronted. "What do you mean?"

"Do you have any idea how much you did?

He looked around the clearing. There was no sign of the many-armed thing that held her, but there was a scorch mark on the ground where she had lain. There was a pile of black char where the pig demon had been, and around them, she counted five hyena men that she had killed all at once.

"Oh," she whispered, eyes wide. Piers nodded.

"Those were acts that would tire three normal Wiccans."

Hailey shook her head.

"I didn't need to touch you, but I did draw it from you. I…I guess I needed you and you were there."

Piers smiled.

"It's a beautiful thought, but romance aside, you may have managed to do something that no one else has done before. This is entirely new."

"It might be an effect of the Shadow Walk Prison," Hailey argued. "It may simply be that we stand in a very strange place where the rules are not what we are used to."

Piers looked unwilling to concede the argument, but Hailey felt a snake of panic in her belly.

"Did I hurt you? When I drew from you, oh it was so much. I knew it was from you and Kieran, and I just… took."

Piers wrapped her in his arms comfortingly.

"I'm fine, I'm absolutely fine. I feel completely normal. Check if you like."

Hesitantly, Hailey touched his wrist, visualizing his power again. The light was still there, still bright, completely unchanged though perhaps it felt calmer now.

"It feels the way it always does," she said.

"Yes. I would have told you if there was something wrong, but there isn't. Seeing as how you have just saved our lives, I think we're doing well. All that, and you also killed a lot of demons."

"A lot but not all," said Kieran.

Hailey blinked to see him coming out of the forest.

"Where did you go, Kieran?"

"The Templar ducked out of the way as soon as you summoned lightning from the sky," he said, his voice grim. "I tracked him into the woods, but less than a hundred yards away, his tracks disappear as if he was vanished mid-stride. I think he left the Shadow Walk Prison right there."

Kieran had been hunting Templars for centuries. Hailey could see that to have one escape, especially one that communed with demons, was a sore spot for him.

"As long as he doesn't come back with reinforcements, I'm happy to let him go," said Piers with a shrug, but Kieran shook his head.

"There's more at stake now than one more Templar I didn't get to kill. He knows about Hailey, and he knows what she can do. That's going to make her a target. On top of that, it sounded like he knew what was going on with this alliance."

"Alliance?" Hailey blinked.

"Templars and demons leagued together? I would call it an alliance, but it might be more appropriate to say that it's the end of our world."

Kieran's words sent a shudder down Hailey's spine. She remembered how powerful the demons possessing the Magus Corps officers had been. She remembered how difficult that battle was and how much it had cost all of them.

"Kieran, could they have more Magus Corps officers?"

"They could. In the Magus Corps, we die and we disappear on a regular basis. There is no telling who might keep us. We had always assumed that the Templars killed us, but they might have kept some of the missing alive. Hell, they might not even need Magus Corps officers. It might be enough to use Wiccans recently awakened."

Kieran shook his head.

"We need to get out of here. The Magus Corps needs to know about this, as do all of the covens."

"Before that, what shall we do with him?"

Piers pointed at Ferret, who astonishingly seemed to have ignored the battle. He was in the same position that he had been in when he had caught the mirror. Standing practically in the curl of a hyena demon's arm, he smiled and chittered at the shape in the mirror.

Coming to crouch down beside him, Hailey could see what he saw. He had been a rather handsome young man dressed in Victorian clothing. With black hair and blue eyes, he bore a small resemblance to Kieran. The young man in the picture was joined by a tall willowy blond woman who kissed him and an amused black man who punched him lightly on the arm. She remembered what he had told her when they first met, of betrayals that had brought all three of them to the Shadow Walk Prison. Her heart twisted, and despite the way that Ferret had betrayed her, she couldn't find the anger that she'd once had.

"You're a sitting target right there," she said softly. "No good will come to you like this."

"Sounds fine to me," muttered Kieran, but she ignored him.

She put her hands to either side of the small animal who paid no attention to her. She closed her eyes, concentrating hard. She had no image in her mind. This time, she simply imagined peace, a place to be safe until something changed. She felt the earth move under her hands, felt it rise up and up. When she opened her eyes, she realized that she was kneeling next to a boulder that was almost waist high. When she put her ear to it, she could hear a chitter. With a soft sigh, she stroked the stone one last time and stood up.

"He'll be free when he gets over that grief," she said. "I don't know when that will be or if it will come at all, but he will be free."

"Better than he deserves," growled Kieran.

"It's time for us to go home," she said.

She felt tired suddenly, as if she was ready to wake up from this dream. She had been in the Shadow Walk Prison for what felt like a very long time. She wasn't certain whether people should be in it so long at all.

"Come here, take my hands."

Piers and Kieran obediently did so. It occurred to her what a precious gift they offered her, what beauty and what love. She had led them badly astray at least once already. Now they were trusting her to steer them right.

"Close your eyes. I have an idea."

She imagined a darkness that could tear a soul from its roots. She imagined a cold and windy place without anchor. It was strange and ugly, but underneath it all, despite the pleasures and temptations it offered, the Shadow Walk Prison was empty. It was nothing.

She imagined that darkness lightening. It had to end. It was not permanent. It was no place for her and her loved ones. They had a home to get back to, a home to build, a home to protect. It might take them years to make it what it needed to be, or it might take them no time at all. There was a world of change that needed them. She understood it as well as she understood her lovers. They needed to go home. They needed to be full of themselves, not just their desires or their fears.

The darkness was lightening. It was over. They were home.

CHAPTER FIFTY-FIVE

HAILEY REALIZED THAT she was lying flat on her back. Her hands were empty, but she did not fear that Piers and Kieran were lost. Beside her, she could hear them stirring in their narrow beds. With a smile, she sat up carefully.

"Oh hell…"

Hailey put her hand to her head, aware of a vicious pounding between her eyes.

"Hailey? Here, drink this."

Mindlessly, she drank the cup that was bumped against her lips. It was liquid fire. She coughed some of it up, but the rest of it went down her throat, making her cough violently.

"Why would you do that to me?"

Lucius looked unrepentant.

"Liona would always ask for a bit of something alcoholic to settle herself after a visit to the Shadow Walk Prison. She said it made her saner."

"Liona never felt that sane to begin with," Hailey groaned.

Despite the burning in her throat, she felt better. She could turn her head to look at Piers and Kieran. Kieran was rubbing his head as if it ached as well, but Piers was up and rummaging in the pile of their gear that Lucius had put in the corner.

"Are you already up?" she asked. "You've just spent hours–"

"Two days," muttered Lucius.

"Two days, thank you, in a place that I'm fairly sure inspired stories of Hell. You can take a break."

Piers spared her a fleeting smile.

"I'm afraid not, darling. People need to be told of the Templars and their nasty little project. I don't want anyone to be unprepared, and that means we need to take action now."

Kieran nodded, though he was moving more slowly.

"The Magus Corps needs to be made aware of this at once, and we can start getting the information out after. This feels big, and it feels like they're going to act soon. Especially now that they know we're on to them, they're going to start their strikes."

Hailey nodded soberly. The Templars had never made it a secret that their goal was the eradication of all Wiccans. With the demon-possessed officers that they had created, that goal might be far more of a reality than anyone wanted to admit.

She reached for the water on the stand by her bed, but Lucius brought her up short.

"What in the name of all the gods happened to your eyes?"

Lucius's voice was tight with control. She turned to look at him, startled.

"What do you mean? I can see just fine."

Now Kieran and Piers were crowding close. Their expressions flashed from concern to confusion and fear.

"Do you feel all right? Are you in any pain?" demanded Kieran.

She shook her head.

"Talk to me, what's happening?" she said, her voice quaking with nerves.

Instead, they guided her to a round mirror that hung on the wall. At first, she just saw her own face, pale from being in bed for two days and with red hair that was styled like a rat's nest. Then she saw her eyes, gasping in spite of herself.

Instead of the green that they had been her entire life, they were a livid, purple tinged with green. Instead of the color being confined to the iris, it flooded her entire eye. She had eyes the color of the Shadow Walk Prison's sky.

"What's happening to me?" she whispered.

• • • • •

Hailey's story concludes in SACRIFICED: Castle Coven Book Six, available now.

For a sneak peek, turn the page.

Excerpt:

SACRIFICED

Castle Coven Book Six

Her eyes still closed, Hailey smiled a little when she felt Liona's fingers trail down her face from brow to chin. The other woman's touch was light and sweet, making her think of the flutter of dove's wings against her skin.

"It is not so much," Hailey murmured softly. "I'm only tired."

Liona shifted so that she was a little closer to Hailey, so close that Hailey could feel Liona's sweet breath against her chin.

"Are you tired, dear one? Would you like to sleep for a little while?"

Hailey started to say yes, but something about Liona's tone, sincere but with an undercurrent of teasing to it, made her pause.

"I'd like to shower, I think," she said slowly.

"Of course, your long journey…"

"I might like it if you joined me."

Liona's laugh was soft and husky. When she spoke next, her lips brushed against Hailey's.

"What a good idea. I shouldn't want you to slip and fall because you are so tired after all."

Hailey was unused to the freedom that she, Kieran and

Piers had given each other to explore where they would. Some tiny part of her wondered if she was doing right. Then Liona was leading her to the bathroom where she ran the water and turned to Hailey with an expectant look.

"Come here, let's get you out of that."

Hailey mutely allowed Liona to strip her of her clothing and then guide her into the gentle spray. She watched in appreciation as Liona stripped herself. Liona's body was a great deal like hers, both slender and small breasted. When Liona stepped into the spray with her, Hailey couldn't help but embrace her, pulling her close for a kiss.

Liona kissed her for a moment before pulling away with a smile.

"I believe you're in here to get clean."

She picked up the washcloth, soaping it before running it all over Hailey's body. Under the warm spray, Hailey leaned against the tile wall, closing her eyes as Liona cleaned her all over. Whenever she tried to return the favor, Liona smacked her hand.

"Let me look after you, dear one," Liona murmured. "I'll get my turn in a bit."

Hailey wondered if she should be worried about it, but it simply felt too good. Liona's slow and gentle motions and the heat of the water made her fall into a sleepy languorous haze, something that struck her as amazingly luxurious after the days she had had.

Liona was so gentle that she almost didn't notice the other woman's clever hands stroking between her legs. Those slippery fingers were working between her folds and touching the tip of her clit before her eyes flew open.

"That feels good," she murmured, almost shy.

"Good, that's what it's supposed to feel like. Here, lean this way."

Liona positioned Hailey so that she was braced, both hands flat against the tiled wall. Liona's bare foot nudged Hailey's feet apart so that she had access to Hailey's most tender parts. For a brief moment, she simply pressed herself against Hailey's slick back, pressing her breasts and her hips firmly against Hailey's body. For a long moment, she rubbed herself against Hailey, purring with pleasure.

"Let's see how you feel like this."

Her hand slid against the curve of Hailey's buttocks, seeking low and between her legs. Hailey whimpered when Liona inserted two fingers inside her damp opening, prising her open with nothing more than pressure.

"Tight," Hailey murmured in surprise.

"Yes, and lovely as well. Tell me if it hurts."

"And if it doesn't?"

• • • • •

MORE BOOKS BY HAZEL HUNTER

THE HOLLOW CITY COVEN SERIES

A daring quest. A deadly enemy. A protector who won't quit. Although Wiccan Gillian Granger's life's work is finding a legendary city, her research in musty libraries hasn't prepared her for the field, let alone a gorgeous escort. Shayne Savatier knows he's on a milk run, especially after he meets his beautiful charge. But when enemies attack her, everything changes. Passion intertwines with protection, and duty bonds hard with desire.

Possessed (Hollow City Coven Book One)

Shadowed (Hollow City Coven Book Two)

Trapped (Hollow City Coven Book Three)

Sign up for my newsletter to be notified of new releases!

THE SILVER WOOD COVEN SERIES

Though she's taken the name given her by a kind stranger, Summer can no more explain waking up homeless and covered in blood, than she can the extreme attraction drawing people to her. Amnesiac, confused, and frightened, she's not even aware that she's a witch. But help arrives in two very different forms: the cool and restrained Templar Michael Charbon and his centuries-long friend Wiccan Major Troy Atwater.

Rescued (Silver Wood Coven Book One)

Stolen (Silver Wood Coven Book Two)

United (Silver Wood Coven Book Three)

Betrayed (Silver Wood Coven Book Four)

Revealed (Silver Wood Coven Book Five)

THE CASTLE COVEN SERIES

Novice witch Hailey Devereaux had resolved to live life as an outsider. Possessed of a unique Wiccan ability, her own people shun her. But that all ends when two very different men enter her life: the brooding Major Kieran McCallen and Coven Master Piers Dayton. But their training and tests are only the beginning. As she struggles to fulfill her destiny and find her place in the world, Hailey also discovers love.

Found (Castle Coven Book One)

Abandoned (Castle Coven Book Two)

Healed (Castle Coven Book Three)

Claimed (Castle Coven Book Four)

Imprisoned (Castle Coven Book Five)

Sacrificed (Castle Coven Book Six)

Castle Coven Box Set (Books 1 - 6)

THE MAGUS CORPS SERIES

Meet the warlocks of the Magus Corps, sworn to protect Wiccans at all costs. As they find and track fledgling witches, it's a race against an ancient enemy that would rather see all Wiccans dead. But where danger and intimacy come together, passion is never far behind.

Dominic (Her Warlock Protector Book 1)

Sebastian (Her Warlock Protector Book 2)

Logan (Her Warlock Protector Book 3)

Colin (Her Warlock Protector Book 4)

Vincent (Her Warlock Protector Book 5)

Jackson (Her Warlock Protector Book 6)

Trent (Her Warlock Protector Book 7)

Her Warlock Protector Box Set (Books 1 - 7)

THE SECOND SIGHT SERIES

Join psychic Isabelle de Grey and FBI profiler Mac MacMillan as they hunt a serial killer in the streets of Los Angeles. Even as their search closes in on the kidnapper, they discover not only clues, but a fiery passion that quickly consumes them.

Touched (Second Sight Book 1)

Torn (Second Sight Book 2)

Taken (Second Sight Book 3)

Chosen (Second Sight Book 4)

Charmed (Second Sight Book 5)

Changed (Second Sight Book 6)

Second Sight Box Set (Books 1 - 6)

THE EROTIC EXPEDITION SERIES

Travel the world in these breathless tales of erotic romance. Each features a different couple in fast-paced tales of fiery passion.

Arctic Exposure

A young couple is stranded in an Alaskan storm.

Desert Thirst

In the Sahara, a master tracker has the scent of his fiery client.

Jungle Fever

A forensic accountant blossoms under the care of a plantation owner in Thailand.

Mountain Wilds
A beautiful doctor on the rebound crashes with her pilot in British Columbia.

Island Magic
Two treasure-hunting scuba divers are kidnapped in the Caribbean.

THE ROMANCE IN THE RUINS NOVELS

Explore the ancient world and the new in these standalone novels of erotic romance. Each features a hero and heroine who come together against all odds, in exotic and remote settings where danger and love are found in equal measure.

Words of Love
Set in the heartland of the ancient Maya.

Labyrinth of Love
Set on the ancient Greek island of Crete.

Stars of Love
Set in the rugged Pueblo Southwest.

Sign up for my newsletter to be notified of new releases!

NOTE FROM THE AUTHOR

Dear Wonderful Reader,

Thank you so much for spending time with me. I can't tell you how much I appreciate it! My newsletter will let you know about new releases and *only* new releases. Don't miss the next sizzling, hot romance! Visit HazelHunter.com/books to find more great stories available *today*.

XOXO,
Hazel

Version 5.0

.....

SACRIFICED

Castle Coven Book Six

By Hazel Hunter

SACRIFICED
Castle Coven Book Six

Though Hailey, Kieran, and Piers have survived the Shadow Walk Prison, the news they bring with them is dire. Templars have allied with demons to eradicate all Wiccans. The horrifying and deadly combination has the covens and the Magus Corps scrambling, with no clear means to survive.

Nor has Hailey come through unscathed. Even Liona, the most ancient witch of them all, can't tell Hailey the meaning of her changed eyes. Though Hailey may have left the Shadow Walk Prison, it seems not to have left her.

Even in the midst of the turmoil, as the final battle draws nigh, she and her lovers forge a new relationship. For the first time in her life, Hailey knows love and true happiness. But as she struggles to fulfill her destiny and protect the people she loves, the Shadow Walk Prison beckons with an opportunity she can't refuse.

CHAPTER FIFTY-SIX

HAILEY COULD NOT escape the idea that she had done something wrong. Kieran and Piers stayed close to her the entire way back to Wyoming from the Alps. When they had been on the long commercial flight, she kept her head down, ensuring that her unnatural eyes were not noticed by the flight personnel that took care of them.

"But it doesn't hurt, right?" Kieran asked, an edge of anxiety in his voice.

He was a big man, big enough that his shoulders were a little cramped in the airline seats. In another situation, his anxious questions would have been amusing, but Hailey had never felt less like laughing.

"It doesn't. It doesn't at all. I'm fine if I just ignore how I look in the mirror."

It was true. When she looked in the mirror, most of her features were exactly where they were supposed to be. Her hair was still red and wavy, her skin was still fair, and she still had the same smatter of freckles over her nose. However, her eyes, which had been green since the day that she was born, were a deep and unsettling purple tinged with an ugly green. The color suffused them from the pupil through what used to be white. Though she could see just fine, the discoloration was a constant reminder of their journey in the Shadow Walk Prison, the hallucinatory dreamworld inhabited by demons.

Piers, her other lover, was uncharacteristically silent most of the way. He smiled comfortingly. He had handled the travel arrangements with competence and care. But when he wasn't on the phone with the Castle, he was often lost in his own thoughts.

It made a certain amount of sense, Hailey figured. He had only gone to the Alps in the first place because she was involved. Not only was she his lover, she was a member of his coven, the sanctuary for Wiccans known as the Castle. As the coven master, he took his responsibilities to his people very seriously.

Kieran had checked in with his own superiors at the Magus Corps as well. While on their rescue mission in the Alps, they had found that the Wiccans' ancestral enemy, the Templars, had found a way to control Wiccans infested with demons, creating supernatural powerhouses that were capable of immense destructive power. Those Templars were on the verge of launching an attack, and the Magus Corps had to be ready.

When they landed in Wyoming, Hailey was struck with a sense of déjà vu. It hadn't been all that long ago when Kieran had taken her from her home coven to Piers's. Just as she had then, Julie, a skilled pilot and witch, was there to greet them. They would make the last part of the journey in her small plane.

As they threw their luggage into the hold, Hailey quirked an eyebrow at Kieran.

"Not going to run off on me again?" she asked softly.

"That was not well done of me," he admitted. "Duty called, and I'm bad at resisting it."

"I understand that," she said, buckling herself in. "I just want to know if it is going to happen again."

His large hand closed over her small one.

"I wish I could tell you I would never leave you again," he said, his voice soft and regretful. "After this business with the Templars is over, I would swear to it. But right now? With what we know? I don't even know myself where I'm going to be in twenty-four hours."

Hailey felt her heart twist at his words. She knew that she couldn't expect him to stay when there might be a war in the works. She understood it, but she still couldn't stem the tide of sadness that overwhelmed her.

His hand on hers tightened and he leaned close to press his lips to hers in a soft kiss. No matter how she felt or what was going on, she could still take pleasure in this. She could still love the taste of him, the woodsy scent of his skin and the warmth of his body.

"I love you," he whispered. "I love you so much. The only thing I want more than to be at your side is to keep you safe. I can't promise you that I won't leave, but I promise that when I return, it'll be to stay for good."

Hailey nodded, trying to hold back her tears. It was enough. It would have to be.

She started to speak, but then Piers sat down on the seat across from theirs. Julie's plane was tiny. Hailey reached across the aisle to touch Piers, running her fingers over the angle of his jaw. He looked up at her surprised, then pleased.

"It's going to be all right," he said.

She quirked an eyebrow.

"Are you trying to convince me or yourself?" she asked.

He didn't respond, and she got the idea that he was holding something back from her. It was a feeling that nagged at the back of her mind, something that made her feel nervous and uneasy. She tried to tell herself that it was just a feeling, but she knew herself far too well for that. There was something going on. Whatever it was, she told herself that Piers would tell her when the time was right. After all, he was the master of the Castle. He had been away for quite some time. That meant that there were things that were on his mind, things that were running through his head.

The flight from the airport to the Castle's airstrip was not a terribly long one, but Hailey felt her eyelids droop. The last few days had been intense, taking her around the world and through an entirely alien one. She dozed off into a fitful slumber. Her dreams were fraught with things that she couldn't quite control, things she couldn't quite figure out. People were calling for her, she was needed, but she couldn't tell what was going on.

When Kieran gasped, she was happy to shed the vestiges of sleep, sitting up to see what had surprised him so. He was staring out the window, eyes wide. Hailey smiled.

"It's the Castle," she said. "It's home."

The Castle was nestled between two mountain peaks, a building which combined the grandeur of the castles of the old world with the modern luxuries of the new one. In the fading light of the day, the walls of the Castle were dyed a beautiful gold, giving it the radiance of a storybook palace. Hailey remembered her own reaction to the place, how she had both craved what it stood for while being wistfully certain that it wasn't for her.

"You've been here before," she murmured, taking Kieran's hand.

"I came overland up the mountain," he said with a shrug. "I knew it was a beautiful place, but I couldn't imagine something like this."

"You should be able to imagine it quite easily," Piers said firmly. "This is what the Magus Corps wants to protect. This is what you are defending from the people who would harm it."

Kieran flashed a smile that was almost shy at the other man.

"I understand that is the Magus Corps' mission. In all honesty, however, the Magus Corps is a great deal more about warring than it is about protection. I joined to protect things that I thought important, but I…I don't think I ever knew how grand those very things could be."

Hailey could see the battle on Piers's face. He and Kieran weren't lovers, not quite. They were linked by their love for her, and though at this point, they had a great deal of esteem for each other, they were still very much opposite sides of the same coin.

She knew that Piers's regard for the Magus Corps was historically indifferent at best. Like many coven masters who defended their covens on their own, he didn't care for the Magus Corps' interference with his affairs or the affairs of the people he considered under his protection. Kieran, on the other hand, was a man well-used to a wartime authority, where his word could change the course of battle in a heartbeat. He was used to demanding and receiving total obedience, something that he was more than willing to forfeit in bed with her and with Piers, but which made him bristle when in the field.

"Stay at the Castle as long as you wish," Piers said softly.

To Hailey's surprise, the voice he used was a shockingly intimate one. It was close to the same one that he used when he commanded them in bed, when he was making suggestions that should have made Hailey blush.

Kieran turned to him with a slightly regretful half-smile.

"That voice doesn't actually work on me when I'm not ready to get naked," he pointed out. "But thank you. I do appreciate the thought."

Piers shrugged, smiling a little in return.

"It was meant in good faith. The Castle is a shelter for all, and that includes you."

"We're entering in to some unusual times," Kieran responded.

"I don't know if I will be able to use the Castle the way that you intend, but thank you."

From the cockpit, Julie announced the landing. The plane, obedient to her controls, shifted as they lost altitude.

Returning to the Castle felt like returning home, but a certain part of Hailey wished that they had never landed, that they continued to soar above. In the sky, there was nothing that could hurt them. There was nothing that could change the peace and the love that existed between them. On the ground, Piers was the coven master, Kieran belonged to the Magus Corps, and she was always going to be somewhere in between. No matter how much she might wish it, however, there was nothing she could do to keep the plane in the air. The plane landed, and she stumbled off it.

All around them, people were waiting to welcome Piers back. Kieran was right behind her until a call on his phone pulled him away. He was frowning, talking in low and urgent tones to the person on the other end. In the midst of all of the hustle, Hailey felt oddly lost. She couldn't see the friends she had made in the crowd. She was thinking that she should slide back to her room for a shower to wash away the travel grime when a small hand looped through her arm and pulled her aside.

Liona di Orsini was a small woman with long silvery hair. Her eyes were as dark as obsidian, and even now, when her expression was kind, there was something about her that made Hailey just a little nervous. She was one of the oldest Wiccans known, and though she looked no older than Hailey herself, there was a sense of ancient power around her.

She seized Hailey and pulled her away from the crowd as neatly as a wolf separating a calf from the herd. Just inside the doorway to the main part of the Castle itself, she unexpectedly threw her arms around Hailey's neck, pulling the younger woman into a crushing embrace.

"Do you know what you have done for me?" she whispered fiercely. "Precious girl, do you even know?"

"You…you spoke with Lucius."

Lucius was a man who had proved instrumental to their success in the Alps. He had been captured and tortured by Templars for what must have been years, until he had all but forgotten what it meant to be a human being. Hailey had reminded him, and from there, he had remembered his love for his long lost Liona.

"He contacted me using Piers's phone. We spoke. He cried."

"He refused to come with us. He wanted to continue scouring the fortress where the Templars were," Hailey said apologetically. "Piers made arrangements for him to come in a few days though."

"What do you think a few days matter when I have kept one eye out for him for the past few centuries? You have brought him back to me, and that is all I care about."

Hailey smiled tremulously at her friend, meeting her eyes for the first time. Liona's eyes narrowed.

"I see you have had some adventures of your own."

"Yes. I spent time in the Shadow Walk Prison, and I think some of it has chosen to follow me home."

Liona's grin was hard, and if she was not totally convinced that Liona was on her side, Hailey would have shivered a little bit.

"Well, we shall see about that. Come with me."

• • • • •

Piers had given Liona her own rooms at the Castle. In many ways, it was a modern space with neutral though charming furniture and a state of the art computer that Liona had obviously been using. However, there were also signs that Liona had made the space her own. There was a vivid violet tapestry thrown over the back of the couch. On the coffee table in front of the couch was a small mirror set with candles. This was where Liona seated Hailey, lighting the candles as she did so.

Hailey breathed in the scents of sandalwood and copal, letting them cleanse her. They were strong scents, and perhaps in another environment, she would have been more sensitive. However, here with Liona, it felt just right.

Liona dimmed the lights throughout the apartment and shuttered the windows. Now the only light came from the candles. As Hailey watched them curiously, she could almost see them shimmer and swim.

"All right now. Let's see what is looking out of your eyes."

There was something uncomfortable about that phrase, something that made Hailey want to hide. Instead, she took a deep breath and sat as Liona positioned her. Liona's hand on her jaw was gentle, moving her face back and forth.

"Hmm. Let's see how well this goes."

Liona lifted one of the candles, a thick pillar that smelled strongly of fresh juniper. It was a bold and bracing scent, causing Hailey to breathe deep. Liona held the candle between them so that the flame danced just a foot from Hailey's nose.

"Look only into the flame," she said. "Don't look at my eyes, just look into the fire."

Hailey tried to do as she was told, but in many ways, it was difficult. The flame of the candle danced enticingly, but beyond were Liona's dark eyes, glittering and gorgeous. Hailey took a deep breath and concentrated on the flame.

She let her mind drift because there were no battles here, nothing that needed to be fought, nothing that needed to be resisted. She had almost fallen into a trance when Liona sighed, taking the candle away.

"Well, that's a relief."

She went to turn on the lights as Hailey looked after her in concern.

"What do you mean?"

"I've never seen eyes like the ones that you possess, but I have heard about it. People who spend too long in the Shadow Walk Prison often carry things out with them. In some cases, what they carry out is a demon, smuggled away in their mind and looking to do them harm."

Hailey shuddered.

"Something that would turn me into a monster."

Liona's laugh was dark.

"Something like that. In some cases, they will turn you into the twisted monsters that Lucius told me about. Not all demons crave blood, however. Some crave the small deaths that people can stretch out over the course of fifty or a hundred years. Some of them hide so well that you will never think they are there at all."

"Is such a thing possible?"

"More than possible. Some people simply become cruel. Perhaps they become cruel to themselves, or perhaps they become cruel to others. If you ask them if they are all right, they will tell you that they are, unaware that there is a demon hiding behind their eyes, telling them that person is weak or this person is a traitor. Over the years, they can do just as much evil as those intent on physical destruction."

Hailey thought of the sly traps set by some of the demons she had seen and the way the Shadow Walk Prison itself seemed to pull out the darkest bits of her personality and her soul. The idea of something like that hiding behind her eyes was enough to make her ill.

"But you saw nothing like that?"

"I sat in front of your eyes like the best kind of bait, another soul open to yours and willing to see what would happen. No demon came looking, and I think you are safe."

Hailey only breathed in relief for a moment before Liona started speaking again, her voice low and practical.

"That is the worst thing I have ever heard happening when people bring back the Shadow Walk Prison as you have done. The rest, well, we shall just have to see."

"See? See what?"

"You may find that your attraction to the Shadow Walk Prison grows. Don't look so disbelieving. A place like that, when you are in total control of your mind and the world around you? Some witches and warlocks have made themselves absolute rulers of the space for a while."

"Then what happened to them?"

"They collapsed underneath their own minds and souls, I imagine. No one should live in worlds entirely of their own making. Others see visions, and still others find that they can walk through the Shadow Walk Prison more easily without harm. Still others, well, it's just a strange look that they have."

Hailey closed her eyes. She didn't feel any different. She didn't feel linked to the Shadow Walk Prison, and she certainly didn't feel as if a demon was going to come out of her.

"So we just wait and see?"

"So much of life ends up telling us to wait and see, yes. It is not easy, but you can bear it. You have borne so much."

Her eyes still closed, Hailey smiled a little when she felt Liona's fingers trail down her face from brow to chin. The other woman's touch was light and sweet, making her think of the flutter of dove's wings against her skin.

"It is not so much," Hailey murmured softly. "I'm only tired."

Liona shifted so that she was a little closer to Hailey, so close that Hailey could feel Liona's sweet breath against her chin.

"Are you tired, dear one? Would you like to sleep for a little while?"

Hailey started to say yes, but something about Liona's tone, sincere but with an undercurrent of teasing to it, made her pause.

"I'd like to shower, I think," she said slowly.

"Of course, your long journey…"

"I might like it if you joined me."

Liona's laugh was soft and husky. When she spoke next, her lips brushed against Hailey's.

"What a good idea. I shouldn't want you to slip and fall because you are so tired after all."

Hailey was unused to the freedom that she, Kieran and Piers had given each other to explore where they would. Some tiny part of her wondered if she was doing right. Then Liona was leading her to the bathroom where she ran the water and turned to Hailey with an expectant look.

"Come here, let's get you out of that."

Hailey mutely allowed Liona to strip her of her clothing and then guide her into the gentle spray. She watched in appreciation as Liona stripped herself. Liona's body was a great deal like hers, both slender and small breasted. When Liona stepped into the spray with her, Hailey couldn't help but embrace her, pulling her close for a kiss.

Liona kissed her for a moment before pulling away with a smile.

"I believe you're in here to get clean."

She picked up the washcloth, soaping it before running it all over Hailey's body. Under the warm spray, Hailey leaned against the tile wall, closing her eyes as Liona cleaned her all over. Whenever she tried to return the favor, Liona smacked her hand.

"Let me look after you, dear one," Liona murmured. "I'll get my turn in a bit."

Hailey wondered if she should be worried about it, but it simply felt too good. Liona's slow and gentle motions and the heat of the water made her fall into a sleepy languorous haze, something that struck her as amazingly luxurious after the days she had had.

Liona was so gentle that she almost didn't notice the other woman's clever hands stroking between her legs. Those slippery fingers were working between her folds and touching the tip of her clit before her eyes flew open.

"That feels good," she murmured, almost shy.

"Good, that's what it's supposed to feel like. Here, lean this way."

Liona positioned Hailey so that she was braced, both hands flat against the tiled wall. Liona's bare foot nudged Hailey's feet apart so that she had access to Hailey's most tender parts. For a brief moment, she simply pressed herself against Hailey's slick back, pressing her breasts and her hips firmly against Hailey's body. For a long moment, she rubbed herself against Hailey, purring with pleasure.

"Let's see how you feel like this."

Her hand slid against the curve of Hailey's buttocks, seeking low and between her legs. Hailey whimpered when Liona inserted two fingers inside her damp opening, prising her open with nothing more than pressure.

"Tight," Hailey murmured in surprise.

"Yes, and lovely as well. Tell me if it hurts."

"And if it doesn't?"

"Well, if it doesn't, ride my fingers until you climax."

Hailey didn't think that she could climax without having her clit touched. She never had before. However there was something persistent about the way that Liona was touching her, something so perfect about the shape of Liona's fingers inside her. Obediently, she pressed herself down on Liona's hand, riding it just as Liona had told her to.

She could feel the pressure building up in her, powerful and remorseless. She thought for a moment it was an orgasm, but it rose and fell like the tide. Every time she thought she was getting close, it pulled back again, making her moan in frustration.

"It's right there, it's yours, take it," murmured Liona, breathless behind her.

When the pressure rose again, Hailey clamped down hard on Liona's hand, working her own muscles until they whimpered. The orgasm that swept over her was so powerful she screamed, pounding her hands against the tile. It was as if every muscle in her body had tightened and then released all at once. She couldn't bear it, so she let it go.

Behind her she could hear Liona laugh. In her head, it was only white noise, only the echoes of a pleasure so intense she could have cried. She was distantly aware of Liona pulling her hand away, of the water that continued to stream down around them.

Liona helped her out of the shower, drying her off in a caring way that made Hailey feel like she wanted to cry.

"Liona…do you like me?" The words were garbled, but they were painfully honest.

"Of course I do, dear one," said Liona firmly. "Come here, lie down. You can rest for a little while, poor thing, you deserve it."

"And then your turn?"

Liona's laugh was clear and lovely.

"Then my turn, dear one."

CHAPTER FIFTY-SEVEN

WHEN HAILEY HAD woken, Liona had been gone. As she'd dressed, she couldn't help but be a little disappointed. Even so, her exhaustion had finally won, and it had felt good to simply sleep. She returned to her room only to find an envelope slid under the door. Inside was a note.

Hailey–

The Castle provided you with these rooms, and of course they will always be yours alone. However, I want you to understand that you should consider my room yours as well, and if you wish to join me there tonight, I will always be pleased to see you. Kieran has received the same invitation. I love you so much, and I want to see you more than anything.

–Piers

If Hailey wondered how they were going to handle being three instead of two, she hadn't counted on Piers's attention to detail. With a smile, Hailey entered her room to pick up a toothbrush and a change of clothing. Trust Piers to think about logistics before they had to be an issue.

It was a little later than she thought it would be when she got to Piers's quarters. The clock was just chiming ten when she knocked on the door and received permission to enter. The scene that met her was a little startling to say the least.

Piers's quarters were a little stark, but they did not lack for comfort. Piers was seated on a couch that looked buttery soft to the touch. He had stripped out of the tactical gear that he had been wearing for the last few days, and changed into a paper-thin t-shirt and jeans that looked as if they might have been as old as Hailey.

He looked comfortable and casual, and if his expression was anything to go by, the man sleeping at his feet was no more unusual than the clothes he wore or the glass of wine on the table beside him.

Hailey looked down at Kieran, who seemed dead to the world. At some point, he had stripped down to a pair of sweatpants. He was an enormous length of man stretched on the floor in front of Piers. When he slept like this, he looked younger than she was used to him looking. Instead of being the war machine, he was simply someone who had finally found a place to rest.

Carefully, Hailey stepped over Kieran, coming to settle against Piers's side. He made a space for her next to him. For a long moment, they simply sat together. He gave her a sip of his wine, she pressed a gentle kiss to his hand.

"I don't want this to end," Hailey said, her voice soft and a little sad.

Piers grimaced. She could tell that he knew exactly what she was talking about. There was a great deal of trouble ahead of them. The Templars were on the move. The Castle had to be ready to defend itself, and Kieran would likely be whipped away in short order, called up by the Magus Corps to lend his formidable powers to their offensive strategies.

"All things end," Piers said finally. "What we won't always have is this moment."

He leaned over to kiss her, something strangely formal and almost chaste.

"Tonight, I was with Liona…"

Piers grinned easily.

"I suspected as much when I saw her pull you away. I'm glad you had time with her. There was enough that I had to deal with, and when I finished up, there was Kieran, still trying to arrange troop maneuvers while he was half a world away."

"You stopped him?"

"He was tired enough that he was on the verge of making what I thought might be some very unwise decisions. After a little while, he was even grateful for it."

"This is a very strange thing we are doing," Hailey mused. "This isn't exactly the fairytale romance that every little girl dreams of."

"I care less about whether it was every little girl's dream than I care about whether it was yours," Piers pointed out. "Was it?"

Hailey shook her head slowly.

"I never had dreams like this. When I was young, it was just a hustle to stay on top of things, to stay fed, to stay safe. Then I awakened. I learned about the Wiccan world, and just when I thought that things were going to be all right, I realized that I was even more of an outcast than I had been before."

All Wiccans had a power that they could wield, but Hailey's was stranger. She could pull energy from other Wiccans and use it to work whatever magic she wished. It frightened many Wiccans, leading them to call her a vampire. Piers and Kieran were among the very few who had never been frightened of her and what she could do. Instead, they had embraced her, given willingly to her. The result had been a bloom of strength that even now she didn't understand.

"And now?" Piers asked lowly.

"Now, all I know is that I am better loved than I have ever been in my life. It doesn't matter what I wanted before because this is what I want now. I want both of you, and it terrifies me that something might change that."

"All things change."

Hailey glanced down to see Kieran sit up and stretch out. Despite his rest, he still looked tired. When he leaned up to kiss her on the lips, she wrapped her arms around his shoulders.

"Everything will change from moment to moment, Hailey," Kieran said. "Everything. The fact that we have each other right now, in this moment, is amazing."

"We'll deal with the future when it arrives," Piers said firmly. "We will not falter, we will not fall. We will meet what comes next, and we will be together after it."

Hailey sighed softly, resting her forehead against Kieran's shoulder while holding Piers's hand tight in her own.

"I never looked for this kind of love and pleasure in my life," she said softly. "I never thought about the life I could share with one person, let alone two."

She squeaked with surprise when Kieran lifted her up in his arms, carrying her to the bedroom. Piers drained his glass of wine and followed behind.

Piers's bed was enormous. When Kieran lay her down on it, she sighed with pleasure. He came to rest on one side of her while Piers came to rest on the other. For a long moment, they simply lay together, holding hands and breathing softly in the dim light.

Hailey was on the verge of falling asleep, but she could feel a little tickle in her hands where she touched her lovers. It felt like what happened when she pulled power from them to fuel her own strength, but this was something a little different. There was no taking or giving. Instead there was something open and loving.

Their energies were mingling, she realized sleepily. On one hand was the vast and tumultuous sea that was the core of Kieran's power. On her other hand was a feeling of light and warmth, the core of Piers's.

She could feel their different energies, one in each hand as she drifted in the dimness. She wanted to rest. It was a deep and soul-healing pleasure to be joined with them in this way. She could feel the tickle of their energies flow through her. It surprised her not at all when they met each other and mingled.

Liona had told her something before the three of them had left for the Alps. She had said that in certain circumstances, there was no taking of power. Instead, it could mingle and become more than what it was.

Hailey was exhausted. On one side, she could tell that Kieran was already asleep. On the other was Piers. He was resting and drifting off. She could sense it as much through the power that flowed through him as she could through the way his breath evened and soothed. They were so close to drifting off. She herself was on the border between sleep and wakefulness.

It seemed like the most natural thing in the world to let those energies mix, to feel how they came together in a place that seemed to be located just beneath her heart. All she knew was that she was a little warmer than she was before, a little safer than she had been.

When she drifted off to sleep, finally, she did not think about battles that could not be won; she did not even think of her eyes, tempestuous and unreliable. Instead, she rested cradled between the two people she loved best in the world, and she was happy.

CHAPTER FIFTY-EIGHT

THE TIME AFTER that was strange. Although she still had her own chambers, for the most part she slept in Piers's large bed with him and Kieran. It seemed Kieran had given up his guest quarters entirely, content to turn Piers's living space into a control room for speaking with other members of the Magus Corps.

One day, Hailey came in to see him poring over a map and speaking in what sounded like Spanish over his phone. She waited quietly until he was done. Then she came to wrap her arms around him.

"Things are getting serious," she observed, but he shook his head.

"Things are getting strange," he said instead. "Templars have withdrawn from almost every place we thought they were hiding. It seems as if they've disappeared from view."

"That's not a good thing?"

His smile was sharp and wintry.

"If there is a snake in my garden, I prefer to know where it is and where it makes its nest. No, when they pull back like this, it is usually for some kind of enormous push. Our job is to try to find where that push might be taking place and to meet them as best we can."

Hailey glanced at the maps he had spread out on the table.

"You are afraid," she said softly. "You are afraid that it will be Costain all over again."

Kieran flinched at her words, but he couldn't deny them. Costain, the Wiccan settlement destroyed by Templars long ago, was the ghost that would follow him for the rest of his life. Sometimes, the ghost was larger, and sometimes it was smaller, but some scars never went away.

"I need to keep it from being another Costain," he said grimly.

"And in doing so, you've turned Piers's chamber into a war room."

"I'd worry more about that if the man himself were ever here to see."

Piers still came home to sleep, but he often crawled into the large bed long after dark. Most mornings, he was up long before dawn, and Hailey and Kieran were lucky if they saw him between morning and night. The Castle had its own preparations to make if there was going to be a war with the Templars.

"In many ways, the Castle's a child," Piers said one night. "It's never really been tested in battle against something like the Templars before." He laughed a little. "Is it strange that I am afraid that it will all end up in ashes no matter what?"

"It won't," Hailey said, squeezing his hand in hers. "It won't."

He had smiled at her, but she had no idea what kind of reassurance he took from her.

For her own part, Hailey was learning more about her abilities. There was a time not all that long ago when she needed someone to pull energy from there right before she was able to use her power at all. Now, under her own study and under Liona's careful tutelage, she could pull energy from someone and hold it, keeping it in reserve until she could use it later.

In the morning, she would pull her power from Kieran or Piers or, on the rare and very special occasion when all three lay abed together, from both of them. She would go and practice with Liona in the training field, seeing how far the power could take her and what the limits of her own skill might be.

Most modern Wiccans she knew were limited to one skill, whether it was flight, like Piers, or mastery over an element, like Kieran. She found that there was no such limiting factor on her, and she noted that Liona was very much the same.

"It stands to reason," Liona said with a shrug. "Power is power after all."

Hailey wasn't sure how sanguine she should feel about being able to change the way that Wiccans had looked at their skills for centuries. Liona had no problem breaking rules, but Hailey had always wanted her borders to be clear and decisive.

Her training with Liona came to a halt in a few days, however, because Lucius arrived at the Castle. For a man out of time, Hailey had to admit that he looked good. Dressed fashionably in black, Hailey initially mistook him for a Magus Corps officer. He was not a terribly tall man, but he was muscular, and with his curly black hair cut into a modern style, he wouldn't have looked out of place on a photo shoot.

"Well you clean up nicely," she said.

Lucius smiled and started to answer her, but then there was a streak of white that shot towards him. Liona threw herself into his arms, kissing him with a ferocity that spoke of a wait of more than a hundred years.

Hailey felt tears prickle her eyes as the two spoke low in a melodic language that she guessed might actually be Latin. Without putting her down, without another word, Lucius strode off, and neither of them were seen for a full day.

When she emerged, Liona looked tired, but her smirk was unmistakeable.

"You look well," Hailey commented. Liona's smile only got

wider.

"I feel well," Liona replied. "I left him snoring like a pig, so I thought I'd sneak out to get some food."

Hailey made her friend a sandwich before broaching something that had been on her mind for some time.

"You never speak of Gaius," said Hailey carefully. Liona and Lucius had had another lover as well, a Gaelic sorcerer who had stayed with Liona to form the coven system while Lucius went on to form what would become the Magus Corps.

"Do I not? I suppose there is not much to say about those who are a part of you."

"So…he did not leave?"

"That is an interesting question when you live as long as we do, Hailey. The first hundred years or so, no, we never left each other's sides. Then the relationship wore at me for a bit, so he remained in Alexandria with the coven while I went exploring down the Nile. After that, we lost track of each other for a long while, and then spent a full two hundred years together building the coven in Rome."

Hailey's head spun at the stretch of history that Liona described. The other woman had lived such a long time, with so much seen and known and learned. If she were lucky, her own life would stretch as long, but right now, she couldn't imagine it.

"Are you together now?'

Liona's smile was a little wistful.

"Over more than a thousand years, I would say that we have spent more of it together than apart. He felt the need for solitude a few years ago, and went into the human world. I believe he's studying in Beijing these days."

"And you'll see him again?"

"If he lives and I live. If we wish it."

Hailey chewed her lip, unable to voice the agitation that was welling up in her. As if sensing her disquiet, Liona pulled her into her arms for a warm hug.

"You have two men who love you. The more I live in this world, the more I learn that you should control the things that you can control, and everything else will happen as it happens. You have them today. Love them today. Let tomorrow take care of itself."

Hailey understood the wisdom of Liona's words, but it was hard. It made her think of her immortality, or the potential for it. As of yet, she was uninitiated. Wiccans only became immortal after an act of unprotected sex with another Wiccan. Piers and Kieran had lived for centuries, but for herself, she had not yet decided whether she wanted the extended lifetime at all.

When she thought of a long life with Piers and Kieran, however, the decision seemed clear. She would do whatever she could to have more time with them, to be with them as long as fate and chance allowed.

She wished that she could talk with both of them about it, but it was becoming increasingly hard to find them. Piers was closeted away and working on something, while Kieran was increasingly frustrated with the lack of action he was seeing from the Magus Corps. He had been told to hold his position for the moment. Hailey could see it wearing at him.

When he wasn't pacing, he was training, spending time honing his skills and staying sharp. She was beginning to worry that he would be so sharp he became brittle, but she could think of nothing that she could do to help him.

One morning, not long after Lucius reappeared, she came across the man himself at one of the tables in the cafeteria of the Castle, using a tablet with intense interest.

"Fantastic little devices," he said, showing her the video he was watching. To her amusement, it was a television show about

Rome. “I could have used these at just about any point throughout the last millennium or so.”

“I’m not sure the tenth century had that many good shows or good wifi, but I see your point.”

She came to sit beside him, offering him one of the apples she had taken from the kitchen.

“You look troubled,” he observed.

Hailey bit her lip before nodding.

“Things are getting ready to change. I wish that they would just do it already.”

“Waiting for action is always the worst part of it,” Lucius agreed. “I’d say try to take your mind off it, but that has never worked when Liona said it to me.”

Hailey grinned and was about to respond when she felt a stabbing pain shoot through her mind. Distantly, she was aware that Lucius was next to her, cradling her body as she slumped over on her side. Her vision flickered, swimming in and out of focus, but then her eyes opened wide. She was not looking at the friendly walls of the Castle. Instead, she was in the Shadow Walk Prison again.

The sky above was painfully familiar, a bruised and sullen purple streaked with green lightning. She stood on ground that was sharp and cracked, and all around her, she could hear the groaning of what sounded like a horde of people in pain. In this dream, she had form but no weight. She drifted over the ground, cresting over a rise, and what she saw made her cover her mouth in horror.

Ranged below her were at least a hundred people melded with demons. There was a curious solidity to them, and with a sickening turn of her belly, she realized that their physical forms had somehow been brought into the Shadow Walk Prison. She, Piers and Kieran had only ever ventured into that dark place with their spirits. This was far worse. The Shadow Walk Prison was no place for physical bodies. At the very least, it seemed to make those bodies suffer and twist.

Walking through the ranks were men that she knew instinctively to be Templars. They pushed the possessed Wiccans into place, disgust and fear on their faces as well. They might have made these monsters, but it was clear that they had no deep love for them at all.

"A fine shock troop."

The voice was a deep growl, and it was uttered so close to where Hailey stood that she nearly stumbled down the hill in surprise. Behind her were two figures that must have walked up the hill behind her. To her great relief, neither of them seemed able to see her despite the fact that she stood just a few feet away. The speaker was enormous. His body was that of a strong man, though his muscles were attached at odd angles to his bones, something that gave him a strange and misshapen profile. He was covered with short, sleek black fur, and in place of a human head, he had a horse's skull. Two hellish pricks of light filled his eye sockets, giving him a strangely knowing look.

Despite the monstrosity of the demon, it was the man next to him that made Hailey shiver with fear. He was a man of middle years. His face was kind, framed between his dark hair and a snow white, cropped beard. She knew this man. He was the one who had spoken so calmly about infesting Piers and Kieran while passing her seemingly powerless body over to a minor demon for its own use. He looked more like a friendly banker than a warrior bent on the annihilation of all of her kind, but she knew that he was a Templar.

"They are ready," the Templar said with easy confidence. "They will be magnificent."

The demon snorted, the sound oddly horse-like.

"So you say, son of man. They are abominations in my sight and the sight of my kind."

The Templar shrugged as if it worried him very little.

"Your kind deal in abominations. Be grateful you are getting this chance to walk the world. For now, our enemies are one and the same."

The demon moved as if he would very much like to kick the Templar, but then he calmed.

"When shall we move?"

"You told me that travel through the Shadow Walk Prison operates on a different time span than travel through the real world. We should move soon. The place in the Shadow Walk Prison corresponding to the mountains of Wyoming should be easy enough to get to, but it is a long trek, especially for an army such as this one."

Hailey's gasp was so loud that she was convinced that the Templar and the demon must have heard her. Instead, she felt herself be pulled backwards, powerfully as if by an unseen hand. She flailed hard, trying to prevent the crash that was imminent.

Instead, she nearly smashed Lucius in the face with a flailing hand before sitting up straight. She was surrounded by a group of concerned faces. She was confused for a moment, but then Lucius was pushing them back, telling them to give her air.

"Are you well?" he asked.

She started to say yes, but then she shook her head.

"Nothing is well at all," she said. "I need to speak with Kieran and Piers."

CHAPTER FIFTY-NINE

CLOSETED IN PIERS'S office, she outlined what she had seen to Kieran and Piers. She could tell from the alarmed looks on their faces that they understood the importance of her vision immediately.

Kieran looked ill.

"That means that they at least think that they can strike anywhere and at anytime. They could travel through the Shadow Walk Prison and attack when a community is not expecting it."

"And they're aimed in our general direction," Piers agreed.

He had gone paler and paler when Hailey had been talking about the vision.

"Surely they would be targeting the Castle with a force like that?" asked Hailey.

Piers shook his head.

"Wyoming's a very popular place with Wiccans," he explained to her. "We're far from the only coven located in the state. We're not even the biggest one. The biggest one is located to the west, and it's quite old."

"So all we know is that they can travel in a way that we cannot track, and that they are aimed in our general direction." Hailey shook her head with disgust.

"We know more than we did," said Kieran, dropping a kiss on

her head. "That's something."

Both Kieran and Piers swung into action, and Hailey was once again left to her own devices. She spent the rest of the day training in the courtyard with the other adults of the Castle. There were children who lived at the Castle as well, but she saw that they were being kept at home and at the small school more often than not. There was a sense of danger all around, of a tension that might snap at any moment. It hurt her heart to see the place she thought of as home looking like this, but there was something right about it as well. She understood that the people who lived in the Castle were getting ready to defend it.

She was just finishing up her shower that evening when she heard a soft knock at her door. Wrapping herself in her soft robe, she wrung out her hair as best she could. When she opened the door, Kieran smiled at her. He didn't mince words.

"I'm leaving in the morning," he said softly. "I've received my orders."

Her eyes wide, Hailey threw herself into his arms. All of the good advice that she had received about letting things come as they would, about realizing that there was nothing she could do to control the world, flew right out of her head. Instead, all she knew was that she wasn't ready.

She tugged Kieran into the room with her, closing the door behind him.

"I don't want you to leave," she said miserably.

With a soft sigh, he gathered her up into his arms, cradling her on his lap as they sat on the couch.

"I don't want to leave. I swear to you, I will come back to you. There isn't a force on earth that could keep me from your side."

Hailey throttled her misery as much as she could. There would be time later to address it, to worry and to mull things over. Right now, she had the man she loved in her arms. That was all that the moment promised, and she swore that she would make the most of it.

Twisting in his arms, she turned around so that she could kiss his mouth fully. He was at first startled at her passionate embrace, but then he fell into it, holding her just as tightly. He was still dressed casually in a jeans and a black T-shirt. She could feel his muscular body easily through the thin fabric.

She turned around to straddle his lap as she continued kissing him. She could tell from his brief gasp that he had seen her robe gape open. The fabric of his jeans was rough against the tenderness of her inner thighs, something that made her press even more closely against his body.

"So beautiful to me," she whispered. "So lovely."

He laughed a little.

"I could say the same about you," he whispered.

She could feel him grow hard underneath her. His body was like a well-tuned machine, made for war. She relished the fact that she could evoke this powerful response in him, that she could bring him the kind of release that he wanted and that his body craved. Deliberately, she reached down between them and squeezed him gently through his jeans, wringing a soft moan from him.

"I love you both," she murmured, "but I loved you first. And I do love you, so, so much, Kieran."

He stirred under her touch. When he looked at her, his eyes were dark and unfocused.

"You have opened up more in me than I ever expected existed," he said, his voice a soft rumble. "I have never wanted another woman more. The life we have chosen is a strange one, but it is ours, and I would never turn my back on it."

"I want you," she murmured, kissing him deeply. "May I have you?"

Kieran nodded, cupping the back of her head with his large hand. Though she could feel his strength in every motion that he made, she knew that he would never harm her. He would never hurt her or cause her pain.

"I need you," he whispered. "Right now, I need you so much."

His blue eyes were brilliant as she stepped back and dropped the robe that she had been wearing. She knew how she looked. Her fair skin was warm and wet, aching for touch. She reached out to take his hand, laying it on her small breast.

"Give me all of you right now," she whispered. "I can see the beast in you, did you know that? You want me, so have me."

That was all the signal that Kieran needed. In a split second, he was off the couch and on top of her. He didn't bother taking her to her bed or even the couch behind them. Instead, he bore her to the carpeted floor, pushing her down on her back so that she looked up at him.

Some part of her thrilled at the power of his frame, the way he kissed her throat and her shoulder so roughly. She knew that he was powerful enough to take what he wanted, but she also knew his heart. He would never offer her harm, never take what she didn't want to give.

His hot mouth trailed from her shoulder down to her breast. His skilled pink tongue lapped her nipple until it was hard and aching. Then he turned his attention to the other, making her wiggle against him in impatience.

"I want you now," she whispered, and the only response was a soft laugh.

She started to ask him what he thought was so funny when he trailed his fingers down her belly to stroke between her legs. She whimpered as his body shifted to one side, giving him all the access to her form he needed.

"Let me touch you, let me look at you," he whispered urgently.

"I love you, and where I am going, I will be out of my mind with missing you."

Hailey swallowed hard and nodded. It was the most blissful kind of torture to have him move over her, to feel his powerful hands touching her with so much gentleness and care. He stroked her thighs open, exposing the very core of her to his mouth. She tensed when he lowered his mouth to her, but then she closed her eyes, pressing herself upwards towards his skilled touch and tongue.

She felt the waves of pleasure that threatened to suffuse her, drown her. She knew that if she gave him an inch, she would be borne away on those waves. She would find her own thunderous satisfaction, and she couldn't deal with that at the moment, not when it might leave him wanting.

As if he could read her thoughts, he drew back and reached into his pocket for a condom. For one wild moment, Hailey thought about telling him to leave it off. If she had to wait for him, she would be willing to wait forever. However, there was something that made her hold her tongue. Instead, she watched with hungry eyes as he smoothed the condom over his straining flesh. She reached down to squeeze his cock in her hand firmly, making him groan.

"I want all of you," he murmured intimately.

With a soft sigh of surrender, she lay back, spreading her legs wide. He took her narrow hips in his hands, lifting her up to him. She felt the tip of his cock at her entrance. She whimpered. She couldn't stand it if he teased her. A hoarse laugh from her lover told him that he had no intention of doing that.

Instead, he slid deep inside her, filling her up in one long and sensual stroke. There was nothing that she wanted more than him. There was nothing better than the way he felt inside her. When he was fully seated inside her, she opened her eyes and looked at him.

"You're so beautiful," she whispered, making him chuckle.

"I'm nothing but scars and anger," Kieran murmured. "You're the beautiful one."

Before she could argue with him longer, he took a firmer grip on her hips and started to thrust deep inside her. He drew almost all the way out before surging in again. His motions were slow and steady, letting her lose herself in the sensations that he was creating inside her. There was so much he could make her feel, so much that she wanted.

"More, I want more," she whispered brokenly.

His motions quickened, pushing inside her and driving her higher and higher. When he moved one hand to her clit, though, she pushed his hand away.

"I want to watch you," she said softly. "I want to see you spill first."

Kieran groaned at her words, and his motions became even more rough. In a matter of moments, he went from slow and measured thrusts to something much more rapid, something much more desperate. She felt him drive into her over and over again, lost in his own fury.

She could feel the way her body responded to him. She couldn't take her hands off of his chest and his shoulders. She needed him, and in that moment, he was more important than her own pleasure. She wondered at how strong he was.

When his motions sped up, she tightened her legs around his waist, pulling him even deeper inside her.

"I want you to spill," she whispered. "I need you, I want you, Kieran my love."

He stiffened and shuddered, his climax shaking violently. In the Shadow Walk Prison, a land of spirits and not bodies, she had felt how it would be if he spilled all hot and wet inside her. She shivered at the memory, clinging to him as his breathing slowed.

He withdrew after a moment, removing the condom before turning back to her with a stern look in his eye.

"I want to see you come."

"It's not necessary."

"I would disagree with that," he said. "Come here."

He seated himself on the edge of the couch. When she wobbled to her feet to approach him, he picked her up as if she weighed nothing. She had no time to mount a protest before she found herself straddling his knee. She could feel the rough fabric against her most sensitive parts. She knew that she was dampening the fabric with her own juices. The thought made her blush, but Kieran smiled at her.

"If you got to see me come, I think it's only fair that I get to see you, isn't it?"

She barely murmured a response when he started to press his knee up hard against her mound. Her legs were sprawled on the ground. Most of the weight of her body rested squarely on her most tender parts.

Reflexively, she clung to Kieran. The pressure on her sensitive clit and mound were alarming at first, but now she could feel them start to overtake her. It was exciting being mounted on Kieran's leg like this. It was amazing having those brilliant blue eyes on her, watching her every desperate move with a glowing love.

"Come on, love, you know how to ride me."

She did. She rocked her body back and forth against his. He was as solid as rock, as stable as the world she walked in. She felt the low pressure of a climax come up through her belly, swelling and unstoppable. She ground herself down on him even harder, wanting more and more. Her orgasm shook her from her toes to the crown of her head. She didn't realize that she was crying out until her face was buried in Kieran's chest. She whimpered through it, unable to resist the way her body was shaking.

"I love you," she said when she was at last able to do so. "I'll wait as long as I must to have you by my side again."

Kieran chuckled as he eased her off of his knee and onto the couch.

"Perhaps you can do some reading as you wait."

Hailey wasn't sure she had heard him correctly at first. She frowned at him, trying to make his words make more sense.

"What do you mean?"

He laughed, pulling a small volume from the couch where he had earlier set it. He must have been carrying it when he came in.

"Do you recognize this?"

For a moment, she didn't, but then her eyes widened.

"This is the book that you took from me!"

"It's the book that I bought at a ridiculous cost because I didn't realize you were bidding to drive the price higher."

"You should not have picked a fight with me to get to know me. There are other ways of getting to know me, after all."

The feel of the small leather-bound volume in her hands took her right back to that day in Italy. She had been living with her previous coven at the time. He had come to test her for her capabilities and her skills, and the best way he had thought to do that was to apparently bully her. She had lost the book she wanted, he had paid an exorbitant rate for it, and after that, she had forgotten all about it.

Now with the book in her hands, she felt a rush of emotions for the people they had been before. Everything had changed that morning, whether she and Kieran knew it or not.

"Do you regret it?" Kieran asked softly.

She shook her head.

"I never could. This is a strange world, but sometimes, we find the things that we need. Sometimes, we survive and thrive."

And sometimes we don't.

Neither of them said the words unspoken. Hailey sat with her hands stroking the leather of the book. It was one that Liona had written centuries ago, a rare little volume that she had been eager to get her hands on. How shocked that younger Hailey would have been to know that Liona di Orsini was still alive and so lovely in bed.

She laughed a little, setting the book aside.

"That feels like a lifetime ago when we fought over it."

"And now?" Kieran's eyes were a brilliant blue. Sometimes, she thought that she could lie with him forever, looking into those gorgeous eyes.

"Now all I want is a lifetime with you."

He smiled.

"We can have it. I want it with you. I will return. I have no interest in a life without you."

She leaned over to kiss him. Her hand wound up tangled in his shirt, tugging a little.

"It is time for these to come off, and for us to sleep," she said softly.

"I have to leave first thing in the morning. I don't want to waste a moment of our time with sleep, but I think I must."

Hailey bit her lip.

"Do you want Piers?"

Kieran made a face.

"I do, actually. I told him I was leaving, and he just turned and walked away."

"What?" Hailey stared.

There was no hint of lie in Kieran's face, but she couldn't imagine Piers being so cruel.

"He looked…I don't know. I think he had somehow forgotten

that I was in the Magus Corps."

"He can't do that," Hailey said, her temper beginning to rise. "He cares for you just as I do, he can't treat you like this."

She was ready to go storming after the coven master, demanding why he had treated Kieran like that, but Kieran shook his head.

"He's a man with his own thoughts and his own counsel to keep. If that was his goodbye, so be it. Some people cannot deal with it. Thank you for being so brave."

Hailey allowed herself to be coaxed back to bed, but her temper kept her awake long after Kieran had faded off to a deep snore.

Piers, what are you doing?

• • • • •

The next morning, Kieran roused her when he was dressed. Blinking sleepily, she noted with some sadness that he was dressed in black again, the uniform of the Magus Corps. His sigil indicating his rank glittered on the pin on his lapel. It took a bit of will to make sure that she was not simply blindly angry at it.

"Do you want to walk me out to the plane? You can sleep if you like–"

"No, I want to come with you as long as I can."

She stumbled into her clothes, dressing by feel as much as anything. It was barely dawn yet. The light that came into her room was a dull and lifeless gray. She took Kieran's hand. They walked silently towards the field together. She wondered if Piers would catch them, but their lover was nowhere to be seen. Anger mixed with the grief of leaving Kieran. She couldn't believe that Piers had left Kieran behind so abruptly, that he wouldn't be there to see him off.

Julie was giving Kieran a lift back to a major airport. Waiting for him as well was his enormous wolf, Cavanaugh. The wolf allowed Hailey a gentle stroke on his broad head, but his yellow eyes were trained on Kieran.

When she saw him like this, it was hard to see her gentle lover in the military man. To her dismay, it felt like an ending. It felt like they were leaving behind a dream that she had cherished. Now it was over, and they both needed to get back to real life.

"Be well," she said finally. "I will think of you every day."

"Hailey," he began, and then he frowned glancing up at the sky. "Hmm. He decided to show up after all."

Hailey looked up just in time to see Piers fall out of the sky. He was a flyer, a skill that saw him crossing long distances as quickly as a bird. He landed heavily on the ground beside them, something that startled Hailey because usually he was grace incarnate.

"Piers?" Hailey started, but she was taken aback by the wild look in his eyes.

"You're not leaving," he said bluntly to Kieran.

Kieran looked confused and wary.

"I most definitely am. What are you talking about?"

"Do you care about the cause of the Magus Corps?" Piers demanded.

Hailey was startled to see lavender circles under his eyes. He looked like he hadn't slept in a week. Given what she knew about his habits, that might have been true.

"You're treading on dangerous ground, Piers," Kieran said, his voice just short of a growl.

"Tell me the mission of the Magus Corps."

"To protect Wiccans and to defend them from all harm whether from within or without."

Piers nodded triumphantly.

"Yes. What I have—what I know I have—is the ability to protect us forever. The three of us can do it. If you want to truly fulfill your mission, if you truly believe what the Magus Corps says its cause is, you need to stay with us."

"Piers, what are you talking about?" Hailey finally managed to say.

Her lover was always a bit like a firecracker, ready to go off and chase down the next idea, but there was something desperate about him now.

"The three of us together. I've been talking with Liona. I've been studying and researching, and now I think we can do it. The three of us, with the power we bring to bear, we can work a kind of magic the Wiccan world has never seen."

"And all that I need to do is to give up my post." Kieran's voice was dry.

"I'm not asking this of you lightly," Piers said, his voice solemn. "I can't ask it of any of us lightly. Hailey, what we are doing is dangerous, but it will be especially dangerous to you. I've told you about my ideas before, and they require you taking on more power than perhaps any witch ever has. The consequences of what that might be are not known at this time. It could hurt you. It could harm you in a permanent way."

"I'm ready for that," Hailey said as resolutely as she could.

She had been brought to the Castle in the first place for just that purpose. She knew that others might think that she was a fool, a sacrificial lamb, but the Castle had been her first real home. She couldn't turn her back on it, not now.

Piers turned to Kieran.

"I didn't stop you until I was sure," he said, and now there was a hint of a plea in his voice. "I wouldn't have kept you from your post for anything short of my being sure."

For a terrible moment, Hailey thought that Kieran was just

going to shake his head and get on the plane. Piers's dislike for the Magus Corps was well-known. If she were completely honest, Kieran often acted independently and against the wishes of other coven masters.

They stared at each other for a long moment, but finally Kieran sighed, setting his bag down.

"All right. Because I know you, and I know you wouldn't say something like that if you weren't sure." He turned to Julie. "I'm sorry, but it looks like I won't be needing the flight to Casper today."

Kieran's eyes when he turned to Hailey were gentle, if rueful.

"You get to keep me a little longer then, little fox. Maybe by the time I need to go again, you'll be tired and willing to see me out the door."

"Never," she said, finally giving in to the temptation to hug him tightly. He held her as well, but she could tell that his attention was directed at Piers.

"If you give me cause to doubt you, if you have kept me from a place where I could do what I was trained and raised to do, you will regret it."

Piers nodded.

"I would, and not simply because of the harm I know you could bring to me. I wouldn't have stopped you if I wasn't sure."

Hailey felt a chill run down her spine at their words. They cared for each other. She would even bet that they loved each other. However, sometimes that love came at a great cost. She needed to remember that in many ways, they were polar opposites. The tension between them was real, and not all of the love and care in the world could banish it.

"It'll be fine," she said softly. "I have faith in the three of us."

• • • • •

Kieran spent the morning calling his commandant and the other officers that had been counting on his arrival. Hailey sat with him, tight-lipped and nervous. Cavanaugh sat at his feet, occasionally whimpering in sympathy and nosing his knee.

The conversations began as shouting matches, and then they grew tense. Hailey had hated it when Kieran was shouting. She liked it even less when his voice dropped down to clipped single words that revealed the conflict within him. There were never enough members of the Magus Corps to go around. They were a small organization, and even if their reach was global, their resources were often scanty. There were not many warriors as old and as skilled as Kieran. If he was absenting himself from the battle to come, there could very well be people who would die because he was not there to watch their backs.

Once Kieran committed to something, however, he committed with everything he had. He stayed firm and calm in the face of men who were demanding his presence, reminding him of the most serious oath of his life and all but threatening him. Finally, he hung up the phone, shaking his head. They were in Piers's office. Hailey and Piers had been going over what they could do to improve their strength and to consider what their goals could be. Hailey looked up, concerned.

"All done?" she asked.

"As done as I will be. Some of the Magus Corps are convinced that I've gone mad, and the others are calling me a Templar spy. I've always been told that you don't really understand an organization until you do something they don't like. I'm beginning to see the truth of that."

He looked up, and though there was something lost on his face, he still smiled gamely at Piers and Hailey.

"I guess what that means is that I'm all yours."

Hailey had never heard sweeter words, but she could wish that it hadn't come with a cost. However, there was little time to go into that. Kieran was holding himself back from the Magus Corps for a reason. She had to make his sacrifice count for something.

She and Piers had quickly realized that she needed to be the one to take the lead on the work they were doing.

"As much as I love running the show, this is one place where I can't," he admitted. "At this point, Kieran and I are like power sources for you. We can give you strength, and we can support you, but you're the only one who can figure out what we can do with it."

Hailey nodded, thinking of what she had learned of her own abilities.

"I want to try something big," she said finally. "I don't want Kieran's sacrifice to be for something he regrets."

Kieran raised an eyebrow at her.

"It won't be. And that's not your decision to make, though I appreciate the thought."

She smiled at him briefly.

"All right, then let's get started."

• • • • •

Instead of working in the training field inside the walls of the Castle, Hailey led them into the forest instead. If there were any ill-effects from their work, she wanted the people of the Castle shielded from it.

In a clearing, she took several deep breaths. She wanted to be as clear and cool as a mountain stream for what came next, but there was a part of her that whispered that it was all foolishness, that she would bend and break at the worst possible time. She tried to shut the voice down as completely as she could. Kieran and Piers, and indeed everyone who was counting on her deserved better.

"What I want to start with is hiding," she explained to the two listening men. "I want to see if I can camouflage things. I want to see if I can make them entirely free from notice.

Piers looked thoughtful.

"There are some Wiccans who can do that to themselves and to the things that they are holding. What you are proposing is something entirely new."

"Well, like I said, there's no point in starting small," Hailey said with a shrug.

Kieran nodded.

"I would rather go for something offensive rather than defensive, but it sounds like a good idea. How do we start?"

Hailey offered the two men her hands. They each took one as she closed her eyes. For a moment, she simply relished the feel of them together, the way the air was just a little chilled and the sounds of birdsong all around them.

She reached for their power simultaneously. She found Kieran's tempestuous sea and Piers's ocean of light. They were not so different, she realized now. They were immense reserves of strength and passion, and they were both being offered lovingly to her.

When she had taken strength from them in the past, it had always been something that she was careful about. She didn't want to drain them. She didn't want to leave them thinking she had stolen something from them.

Now, with the threat of war breathing down her neck, she had to take what she needed. She had to take it without fear. Taking a deep breath, she started to pull the power from them. No matter how much she held, she found she could hold more. She started to feel a warm tingle through her body as the power mingled, became greater, became hers.

When she let go of their hands, there was a smile on her face. She felt a little lightheaded. If she spoke, she didn't think she could do so without slurring.

"Hailey?"

That was Kieran, reaching for her, but she waved him off. She felt like an over-full bowl that might tip at any second. She glanced around her. There was an ancient spruce not ten yards away, enormous and tattered with age. Hailey directed her thoughts and her powers towards it. The tree shimmered as if it was at the center of a mirage. It faded slowly, and then at the last, it disappeared entirely.

"There," she said softly.

Piers whistled while Kieran laughed with delight.

The three of them approached the place where they knew the tree to be. From any angle they could approach it, it was invisible. When Hailey touched it with her hand, she could feel the bark and the low hanging branches, but when she climbed up into the tree, she disappeared as well.

"That's amazing," Piers said, gazing at what was properly a lack of a tree. "I've never even heard of someone doing something like that."

"There are no limits that I can find yet," said Hailey soberly. "We need to learn more about it, to test it."

She found that she could remove the enchantment simply by willing it gone, but making it stay was another matter. At first the illusion held for just fifteen minutes before allowing the tree to flicker back into visibility. It was like an old-fashioned television coming back into focus.

When she tried again, she made the illusion last for an hour, and after that, it lasted most of the afternoon. Hailey's frustration was growing.

"If I can't make it last, what's the point of it?" she asked finally.

The sun was approaching the horizon, and Piers had forced them to stop to eat some food that he had packed. The sandwich sat forgotten in Hailey's hand until Piers tapped it meaningfully.

"This is far more than anyone could expect," said Kieran thoughtfully. "What we are doing here has never been done before."

"But it's not good enough," Hailey retorted, finally eating her sandwich. "If this is going to be worth the cost of taking us all away–"

"Nothing is accomplished without risk," Piers said firmly. "Sometimes that risk is personal, which seems to be something that you'll take on without thought. Sometimes that risk is to a number of people, and you must be willing to let them bear it as they can."

Hailey made a face, but she allowed it to pass. She understood what they were saying, but there was a kind of pressure hanging over her that she had never felt before. Between the arrival of the Templars and the unspoken menace of her own eyes and what that might mean, she had no idea how long they really had.

She did her best to take their advice to heart though. After they ate, they went back to it. She could hide things and reveal them. But she could not make the spell last for any meaningful length of time. The more frustrated she got, the more fragile the spell seemed to become.

Finally, Kieran put his hand on her shoulder. She was nearly fuming with frustration, and she turned towards him ready to snap.

"What?"

"You're done," he said calmly.

"Really? I am?"

He nodded, a bit of steel in his gaze.

"You are. You are in a place where you no longer do yourself or anyone around you any good. Even if we were in a real battle, I would send you away because the chances of you hurting yourself or one of your allies is simply too great to risk."

Hailey started to reply angrily to his words, but then she caught herself. If she was ready to snap, then it made sense that she needed a break. She took a deep breath, and then another. She nodded.

"You're right," she said reluctantly. "I'm exhausted, and you two can't be any better."

Piers looked surprised.

"I'm not so sure about that. I don't feel all that different from when we started."

Hailey stared at him.

"What do you mean?"

"I feel a little worn. I feel like perhaps I will sleep very soundly tonight. I'm not sure I feel as tired as I should after what we've been doing."

"Or I," agreed Kieran with a frown.

The three of them made their way back to the Castle. They spoke about how they felt and what they had observed, but it seemed like there was nothing that could account for it. Hailey was shaking with exhaustion, but Kieran and Piers were merely a little tired.

They ate in a nearly empty dining hall, quiet and confused. Hailey didn't feel defeated exactly, but she could feel that same panic scrabbling at the back of her brain, telling her that there was no time. She was just getting ready to suggest that they call it a night when Liona came in. The other witch went to take an apple from the basket on a nearby table, and came to sit with them.

"How goes your crusade to change the world?" she asked, her voice light and teasing.

Hailey shook her head.

"Strangely, let's put it that way. I think we can do the spells that we had in mind, but we can't make them stick. On top of that, I'm feeling worn down to a nub, but Kieran and Piers don't feel the drain at all."

Kieran and Piers looked a little guilty at the last. Liona eyed them curiously.

"How long have all three of you been lovers?"

"Liona!" Hailey cried. "What in the world does that have to do with anything?"

Liona's smile was amused.

"More than you might think it does, dear one. I have never attempted to do what you are doing now. However, when I have bedded with two instead of one, there was an increase in the power that was available to all of us. At least, there was if there was a complete and open understanding between all parties together."

Piers frowned.

"You think that there's a connection here that is weaker."

Liona nodded, taking a bite of her apple thoughtfully.

"I don't always know exactly what is going on in the world, but this time I feel as if I'm right. Life is very strange sometimes, and magic sometimes moves up mountains and flies out of gorges. It has its own rhythm, and its own logic. When three wish to act as one, it does them no good if there is uneasiness between two."

Kieran was nodding.

"That makes sense. Both of us love and care for Hailey. I'm certain we would give our lives for her."

"But she cannot always be the bridge between us," Piers

realized. "It's like a three legged stool with only two strong legs. It'll never work."

Liona started to say something, but then she turned to Hailey.

Hailey's face was white, and everything felt very far away.

"Hailey?" Liona took her hand. "Are you all right? Whatever's the matter?"

"Secrets," Hailey said finally. "Could secrets be keeping the two apart?"

"It is one of the possibilities. You look like you've seen a ghost."

Hailey laughed a little, her voice high and strained. Her friend understood more than she knew.

"That is a very interesting thing for you to say, Liona. Thank you very much. I'm not sure I would have figured this out without you."

Liona didn't look reassured. Piers and Kieran looked worried. They still had no idea what she had realized. For a moment, she wondered if they could work around it. Some things should stay secrets. Some wounds didn't need to be opened anew. Then she remembered what was at stake and shook her head.

"Are you done with your food?" she asked. When they both nodded, she stood.

"Thank you again, Liona. You'll have to excuse us now. There's something we need to do."

Instead of heading for her quarters or Piers's, she instead led her lovers to an empty room. She had once hidden in it when she was trying to understand why Kieran would turn away from her. Now it felt only right that she was there with both of them.

It was an empty space, but someone had stuck a few old chairs in it. Hailey took her place on the window seat. Behind her, night had fallen. There was just the sliver of a white moon lighting up the forest. As she watched, a snowy owl winged its way from the trees, flashing its bright wings and golden eyes at her once before fluttering away.

"Good hunting, Merit," she whispered.

Her familiar was a wild thing, but it comforted her to know that she was always there, always listening and watching for Hailey in the long reaches of the night. She could use all the comfort that she could get right now.

"Please sit down," she said.

Puzzled, Piers and Kieran drew their chairs up close to her.

"Hailey, no matter what this is, we don't have to deal with it right now while you're exhausted," Piers started, but she shook her head.

"You both need this," she said, trying to keep her voice as firm as she could. "If I kept this from you for a single night, I don't know if you would forgive me."

Hailey had heard once that every major revelation was a risk. If you kept on as you were, without ever asking for change or revealing new information, things would continue as they always had. That could be a blessing or a curse, but right now, Hailey understood that she did not have that luxury.

She took a deep breath. Without thinking about it. She had taken their hands in hers. They were warm and living. Without even looking for it, she could feel the pulse of their power beneath their skin. It was beautiful, and it was waiting for her.

"We need to talk about Costain."

CHAPTER SIXTY

SOME THREE HUNDRED years ago, the village of Costain had been one of the largest communities of Wiccans in Europe. It was an older coven, hidden deep in the mountains of Scotland. It was a place of refuge and scholarship. Perhaps most importantly, it was a place where so many who had been shunned by the greater world could find rest.

For more than a century, it had stood as a haven for those born with powers. The people who lived there must have thought it so well hidden that attack was unthinkable. Then the Templars came.

When she mentioned the name of the Wiccan village, both Piers and Kieran flinched. Piers's eyes lit up with an immediate rage that three hundred years had not quelled. Kieran simply looked ill.

"Will you both allow me to speak?" she said softly. "This history belongs to you both, but I cannot allow one or the other of you to set the story for us all."

Piers nodded curtly, Kieran only a moment or so behind.

"Costain was a great tragedy. Many people were killed. When I first entered the Shadow Walk Prison, I saw that Piers was there, part of a group that was trying to salvage what was left. When I next entered the Shadow Walk Prison, I saw Kieran there, part of the group of Magus Corps officers that were protecting it."

Piers's eyes narrowed.

"What do you mean?" he asked, his voice soft and threatening as distant thunder. "There were no Magus Corps officers present."

"There were." Kieran looked like he was forcing himself to speak. "There were. We were camped on the ridge, a full force of us. We knew that the Templars were on the move. We bottle-necked the wrong entrance to the glen. Because of our mistake, people died."

"Two-hundred and eighty-nine people died," Piers spat. "What were you doing on that ridge? Why the hell didn't you come down to aid?"

"My commanding officer refused to allow us to move in. When we realized what was happening, it was too late. The entire town was being razed."

Piers's face was white with rage. He started to stand up, but Hailey's hand on his kept him down.

"Piers, this was not Kieran's fault. He was there to perform a job, and he did it as best he could."

Piers turned to her. The pain in his eyes was fresh, as if he had turned the bodies of the slain over the day before, not three hundred years ago.

"You can't truly believe that, Hailey. You were with me in the Shadow Walk Prison. You know what happened to those people."

"I was with Kieran in the Shadow Walk Prison as well. I saw him ask his commanding officer to change position. I saw his commanding officer refuse. Piers, there was nothing he could do."

"That's wrong."

Both Hailey and Piers turned to look at Kieran in surprise. He had not moved from his place. He could have been cut from stone.

"That's wrong," he repeated. "I could have risked a mutiny. I could have risked being punished. Others thought as I did. We weren't many, but we may have been enough. I think about it sometimes. I wonder what I could have done differently, what I might have said that might have saved all of those lives."

"You are not to blame, Kieran," Hailey said gently. "This is not your burden. It is the burden of the Templars who killed so many innocents. You cannot carry that crime for them, and you should not even try."

"Who will remember them, then?" Kieran asked.

She could sense that this was a question he had asked himself many times over the past three hundred years. She could tell that if she didn't stop it, he would go on asking himself.

"It is right for things to be forgotten," she said softly. "I want you both to understand that. Things happened long ago, and we cannot change them. The dead would not want to be remembered in a way that caused such pain to the living. It would not comfort them, and it certainly will not allow them to live again."

She held both of their hands tightly. She wondered if she could feel some of the pain and hurt drain out of them. It was still there, but they were both listening to her at least.

"We need to be together," she said softly. "I know that you love me. I can feel that to the very bottom of my heart. It is the most wonderful thing that I have ever experienced in my life, and all I know is that I never want it to end. I don't know if you feel that way towards each other. I don't know if you need to. But please, for this to work, I need you to be open to each other."

To her surprise, Kieran spoke first.

"That is the very darkest part of me," he said softly. "The memory of Costain and what I could have done. What I should have done. It follows me to bed at night sometimes, and I dream of those fires, and of waiting in the cold forest, knowing that nothing I could do would change the world I had created."

For a moment, Piers was silent. Hailey squeezed his hand, trying to will some of the love that she had for him through their skin. He had such a capacity for joy and for generosity. She prayed that he would find it.

"It is the darkest day that I can remember in my life," he said finally. "There have been greater abominations, worse battles. But that one stands very tall in my mind."

"Will you forgive me?"

"No."

Both Kieran and Hailey flinched from his word. It was uttered quietly, but the force behind it was profound.

"There is nothing that I can forgive there," he continued. "It is not for me to say whether you have suffered enough. But…I think you have. Before the Shadow Walk Prison brought me back to that place, the ghosts of Costain were muted. They haunt me like they haunt you, but the Shadow Walk Prison found that weak spot in my armor and would have used it to keep me forever."

"Neither of you did wrong," Hailey said quietly. "Neither of you deserve to be punished."

Piers nodded, but Kieran looked less sure. Hailey's heart ached for him. Despite the fellowship of the other Magus Corps officers, he had stood alone in many ways. In that, she was closer to him than she was to Piers.

"I don't want to punish you," Piers said. "Nothing in me wants to see you broken for Costain."

Kieran started to speak, but Piers acted first. With his free hand, he wrapped his palm around the back of Kieran's neck, pulling him in for a long, deep kiss. Hailey's eyes widened when it went on, rich and slow and tender.

When Piers broke the kiss, his mouth was red, and there was a slight smile on his face.

"I suppose that's one way to open ourselves to each other."

Kieran looked a little breathless from the kiss, but he frowned.

"That is not the answer to everything."

Piers shrugged.

"It's the answer that I have the energy for. It's late, and I can't think of anything else I want to try. What do you think, Hailey?"

Hailey worried at her lower lip. The demons were still out there, and their fledgling connection was still so untested. Despite those things, she could feel the tug of weariness that Piers mentioned.

"I want to see you two together," she whispered. "Please."

Piers's grin was slow and sensuous. Kieran looked down for a long moment before nodding.

They found their way back to Piers's quarters. Piers, with a natural gift for command that had served him well throughout his long life, told Hailey to strip, seating her at the head of the bed with her back against the wall.

As Hailey watched, wide-eyed and fascinated, Piers undressed Kieran himself. Kieran kept himself brutally still as Piers's clever hands did their work. In a matter of moments, Kieran was stripped to the skin, clad only in his scars.

"Gorgeous man," Piers muttered, almost to himself. "Do you want me?"

"Yes."

"Have you lain with a man before me?"

Kieran nodded.

"A few. None were like you."

Piers's grin was more than a little smug.

"I've been told that a time or two. I think I know what you like, but you must be willing to guide me, all right? The instant I do something you don't like, I need to hear about it."

"Or what?"

"Or I'll stop entirely, and I'll make you watch for weeks while I bring Hailey to orgasm over and over again."

Hailey shivered at the image of Piers making love to her while Kieran watched them with starving eyes. She had never thought of what it might look like to watch quietly as two beautiful men touched each other. She felt the heat between her legs, making her rock a little. They aroused her when they touched her; now she knew that they aroused her when they touched each other as well.

Piers drew Kieran down for a long and lingering kiss. Kieran was larger than he was, but there was absolutely no question about who was in charge.

"Lie down on the bed, put your head in Hailey's lap."

Silently, Kieran did as he was told, glancing up at Hailey for a moment. She smiled encouragingly at him, stroking his dark hair.

"You're so beautiful," she murmured.

Kieran started to speak, but then he gasped instead when Piers wrapped his hand around Kieran's dark erection. Both Hailey and Kieran watched wide eyed as Piers drew his hand up and down Kieran's length.

"You're very right, Hailey. He is beautiful." Piers glanced at Kieran. "I want you to put your hands on my head. If you shove or try to gag me, I'll bite you."

Kieran's hands threaded through Piers's loose golden hair. He gasped when Piers started lapping at his cock, twisting and moaning at the sensations that were being pressed on him.

Hailey found her own fingers clenched in Kieran's hair. She couldn't figure out if she wanted to watch his face or if she wanted to watch the way Piers was devouring the meal in front of him. She saw him swallow Kieran's cock until she was certain he would gag. The sight made her whimper, squirming a little.

"Are you going to last long?" she whispered to Kieran. "Do you think you can?"

Kieran groaned with frustration, shaking his head. Hailey dropped her voice even further.

"I want to see him swallow."

Those words were all it took for Kieran to spill over the edge. She saw his finger's tighten on Piers's hair, but he didn't shove or try to gag the other man. Hailey had always thought there must be something at least a little submissive about loving someone in this fashion, but there was nothing controlling about Kieran's motions. He was laid out and exhausted by pleasure. He shook so hard she wrapped her arms around him until he stopped.

Piers sat up, wiping his mouth with the back of his hand. The expression on his face was, if anything, even hungrier than it had been when he was just looking at the pair of them. He stroked Kieran's chest gently.

"Are you well?" he asked.

Kieran nodded, still getting his breath back. He grunted with surprise when Piers landed a light slap on his hip.

"On your hands and knees now. Hailey and I haven't had ours yet. Hailey, spread your legs for Kieran."

His words brought a fresh rush of heat through her body. Hailey hastened to do as Piers said. In a matter of seconds, Kieran was positioned over her, his mouth bare inches from her tender flesh.

"Not yet," Piers was saying. He came back from his nightstand and settled behind Kieran.

"You can have her when I'm in you, and not a moment before."

Hailey couldn't take her eyes off Kieran's face as Piers prepared him. She knew he was using his fingers just as he had used a toy on her when they made love in the Shadow Walk

Prison. She knew how open and vulnerable it must feel.

Kieran's expression was a cross between fascination and discomfort. She could see it when he relaxed, opening fully for Piers. Hailey stroked his face, sliding down to kiss him for a moment before returning to her position.

"All right, that's open enough, I think. Isn't it, Kieran?"

For a moment, Hailey didn't think Kieran would be able to say anything. Finally, however, he managed to nod.

"Yes, Piers."

"Good."

She saw Piers rise up on his knees behind Kieran. She could see Kieran bite his lip as Piers slid inside him. For a long moment, Piers was utterly still. The only sound that Hailey could hear in the room was Kieran's rough breath.

Finally, Piers twined his fingers in Kieran's hair, pushing him down to Hailey's waiting flesh.

"Pleasure her," he said.

Hailey cried out when Kieran's mouth laved at her most sensitive flesh. She had been aroused when Piers had done this for Kieran. Now it felt as if her nerves were turned all the way up. The pleasure sizzled through her, making her buck up against Kieran's mouth. Her fingers landed in his hair, where they twined with Piers's.

She opened her eyes to look up at Piers, who was moving against Kieran with a rough stroke. His eyes were closed with pleasure, and he was so beautiful she could have cried.

Kieran's mouth had absolutely no mercy on her. She could feel her nerves wind tighter and tighter. She couldn't get enough, but it was too much, all at the same time. She didn't want her climax, not yet. She wanted more of these sensations. She kept it off as long as she could, but then she couldn't help herself.

With a loud cry, she tipped over the edge. It felt like she was going to shake to pieces, but the sensations drew out longer and longer, sweeping over her with the force of a hurricane. She could hear Piers shouting as well. She was aware that he was thrusting into Kieran harder and harder, pushing Kieran harder against her.

For a single moment, she could feel both of them, the bonds between them and the energy that they had given to her and now to each other.

Her climax faded slowly. She wrapped her arms around Kieran's shoulders as Piers gently pulled out and disposed of the condom he had put on. With gentle words, Piers directed all three of them into his enormous shower.

The stream of warm water was pure pleasure, and Hailey giggled at the feel of being surrounded by naked slippery limbs.

"Everyone feeling all right?" Piers asked.

There was a hint of vulnerability in his voice. Hailey remembered that one of his darkest dreams was of taking his command too far, of hurting those he cared about.

She started to reassure him, but to her surprise, Kieran landed a heavy hand on Piers's shoulder.

"Better than all right," he said softly. "You did well by me."

Piers's smile was shy but brilliant. Hailey felt her heart swell with love for the both of them. They were so different, but the places where they came together and loved each other were beautiful. She didn't know whether they would last as long as Liona and her lovers. She couldn't see the future. All she knew was that she had them right now. That was all that mattered.

CHAPTER SIXTY-ONE

THE KNOCKING ON the door was loud and unwelcome. Hailey roused from under Piers's heavy arm, disentangling her legs from Kieran's.

They were both awake, but she urged them back to bed while she stomped to the door, dressed only in Piers's shirt. It came down to her knees, and she reckoned it was enough for anyone who cared to bother them at six in the morning.

"What in the world is it?"

To her surprise, it was Liona at the door, her face grim.

"Sorry to interrupt, but the Castle has visitors from the Magus Corps, and they seem to have brought a demon with them."

Liona's bald words felt like buckets of ice water had been dumped down Hailey's spine.

"They can't have!"

"They most certainly can. Get your men up. I figured it was better me coming for you than the Magus Corps themselves."

Hailey thanked her friend hastily. Kieran and Piers, aware of her distress, were up, and she explained what Liona had said. Kieran in particular looked a little pale, but Piers looked positively thunderous.

"The Castle is not a Magus Corps holding. They have no right to bring danger within these walls."

All three of them dressed hurriedly, and in less than a quarter of an hour, they were down in the training field where two Magus Corps officers and a man looped in chains were waiting.

Hailey couldn't take her eyes off of the man who was chained. He wore nothing but a tattered loincloth. She could see the way his muscles bulged unnaturally, and how spurs of bone jutted from his elbows and his knees. The skin of his feet was thickened until it resembled horn. Every few moments, he let out a great gust of air, as if he could not breathe. He kept his face down, his hair running down around it, but she could occasionally see a maddened glimpse of a reddened eye. She could tell that he had been beaten badly. He crouched on the ground, and though he would growl if anyone came close, she could see that he ached with violence.

There were two Magus Corps officers with him. To Hailey's surprise, she recognized one of them.

"Stephan?"

She had met Stephan when she first came to the Castle. During time off, he had come to take advantage of the Castle's workshop resources. Though he was a major, the same rank as Kieran, he was as skinny as a rail with a mop of brown hair. His rank came from his skills at creating magical devices, things that could turn the tide of a battle or detect a hint of magical talent in a recently awakened witch. With his slender frame, Stephan made an unlikely warrior, and he looked unhappy to be there.

"Hey, Hailey. Wish we could be meeting under better circumstances."

The man standing next to Stephan made a sound that was remarkably like a growl. He was a bear of a man, only a hair smaller than Kieran. His hair and cropped beard were iron gray, and his gaze wandered over the group contemptuously.

"Our business is with Major McCallen," he snapped. "We've

got nothing to say to the vampire."

The word stung, but it stung less than it would have even a few months ago. She knew her worth and her value now, and not even a member of the vaunted Magus Corps was going to take it away from her. Piers looked like he was going to boil over, but Kieran stepped forward.

"General Vancleave. What brings you to the Castle?"

"We were the officers closest to Wyoming when we got the call. We were meant to rendezvous with you in Casper when we realized that you wouldn't be meeting up with us." Vancleave didn't bother to hide the disgust in his voice. "Still we're doing our job. We caught this one wandering the snow line, and we knew that you were here. We thought you might like to have a crack at it."

Piers couldn't take any more. He strode towards Vancleave, his eyes full of fire.

"You have no authority here. You have brought a danger within these walls, and you have shown yourself to be every inch the–"

"Piers."

Stephan's voice was curt, but there was enough force in it to turn Piers towards him. Hailey thought that it would only have taken a very slight twist of fate to make Stephan into a loyal coven member at the Castle instead of a major with the Magus Corps. She thought that Piers knew it too.

"The General has questions. If you answer them, we can get out of here faster. Get this guy out of here too."

"You're not here to bargain," Piers said coldly.

"We don't really want to be here at all," Stephan replied. "Look, just…just hear us out, okay?"

Piers's eyes narrowed at that, but he turned back to the general. If anything, his calmer voice was actually more frightening.

"What do you want here?"

"Major McCallen has seen fit to abandon his post and his brothers. I wasn't the one who gave him permission to stay, but I heard why it was permitted. I was told it was because he was working on something powerful, something that would win this fight for us."

Kieran was silent. She knew that the events of Costain were fresh in his mind. She didn't know what he would do right now. She only knew that whatever he did, she would love him.

"Major McCallen has offered us his help in creating something that might protect people when the Templars come," said Piers sharply. "We are not looking for help from the Magus Corps when that inevitably happens."

"And yet here he stands," Vancleave said sourly. "I want to see what he's doing out here with my own eyes. I want you to prove to me that what you are doing is so very worth it."

Kieran, to his credit, didn't flinch.

"I don't answer to you," he said. "General Aroqua gave me the leave I requested. If you are so intent on seeing what we have, however, I can show you."

Vancleave's gaze landed on her, making Hailey feel as exposed as if she were naked. She could see what he thought of her, what he thought of perhaps every witch or warlock who wasn't in the Magus Corps. She tried to put his distaste out of her mind when she turned to Piers and Kieran.

"There is something I very much do not like about this," Kieran muttered softly. "I want to show him what we can do, but directly after that, he needs to leave."

"We don't owe him anything," Piers spat. "The only reason that man is still standing here is because of your patience. When that wears out, he will be leaving."

Hailey reached for both their hands, as much to calm them as to draw power from them. She could feel the difference right away. The power that the three of them generated was fuller and smoother. She could pull it into herself without thinking of it, and when she had it, it was fluid in her control. She hadn't realized how much they were fighting each other before, even if they had no intention of fighting her. It came with an ease that made her smile.

"You want to see what I can do, general?" she called. "Here, I'll show you."

She stepped away from Piers and Kieran, looking up into the sky above. It was just coming on dawn. She had always loved the beauty of the Castle and the mountain peaks that surrounded it. Right now, she was struck with a wonder for it all over again. She thought of the colors of the dawn, and the way sunlight bent to cradle the world.

Hailey took a deep breath and opened her hands, sending the power up. She wasn't trying to hide a simple tree. This time, she was hiding the Castle. She could feel the power flowing through her. A small part of her cried that it was not enough, that it would never be enough. She would burn herself to nothing but ash to do this. Another part of her laughed at the idea.

What I have touched goes on forever. There is no end to it, and there will be no end to us.

Distantly, she was aware of shouting. Through half-closed eyes, she could see a golden glow that lit the sky. She imagined power pouring out of her and arching into the sky, creating a dome that surrounded the Castle in its embrace. The powers that she used threatened to overwhelm her more than once, but she reminded herself that this was power that loved her. It was a part of her, just as Piers and Kieran were.

Above her, the dome closed, and she closed her hands, shutting off the power like a tap. She was light-headed and shaky, falling to her knees on the ground. In the space of a second, Kieran and Piers were by her side.

"Are you all right?" Kieran asked anxiously. "Was it too much?"

"Never," she whispered. "What have I done?"

"Look up," Piers suggested.

When she could focus again, she looked up at the sky. It was still the dawn sky, indigo with streaks of pink and purple. However, now overlaid with it all was a shimmer of gold. Through it, she could see the dark trees beyond the Castle's wall. When she looked at the gold shield, she felt protected.

As if on cue, Piers's smartphone rang. He picked it up, and to Hailey's surprise, he grinned.

"No, no I know what's going on. Get on the road coming up to the gate. It is still there even if you can't see it."

He glanced at Hailey and Kieran.

"That was Jasper and Kittridge. They were out on patrol, and while they were heading back, they saw the Castle disappear."

Vancleave was staring up at the golden shield, his mouth slightly open. Stephan, for his part, was openly in awe. When he glanced at Hailey, he gave her a thumbs-up gesture, a wide grin on his face.

"How long will this last?" Vancleave demanded. "How strong is it?

"It will last until I take it down, I think," Hailey offered. "I don't know how strong it is. People should be able to walk right through it, but since they're seeing a gorge, I think they will be very disinclined to do so." At her lovers' stunned looks, she grinned. "I didn't want to just hide, I also wanted to misdirect. I think we've done it."

She felt a deep exhaustion take over her body. It felt as if she had been running for a week. Despite her weariness, she was exultant. Here finally was proof that she wasn't just something that took from others. She leaned against Kieran's bulk, feeling his comforting arm come around her.

"That has to be worth it," she whispered to him. "That must be enough for them."

Vancleave was nodding slowly, looking up at the shield with calculating eyes.

"You need both the major and the coven master to do this?"

Vancleave's question shocked Hailey out of her pleasant haze.

"I do," she said. "Theoretically I could do it with others, but it might harm them in ways that we don't even understand yet."

Vancleave was silent for another long moment. Then it was as if he had come to a conclusion.

"Major McCallen, you are now under orders from a superior officer. You will take both the coven master and the witch, secure them, and bring them with us. That is an order."

Piers immediately strode up to the man, furious enough that he was utterly silent, but it was Kieran's growl that filled the pre-dawn air.

"I will not do that," he snarled.

Suddenly, he looked bigger than he ever had. Hailey realized that the temperature was dropping suddenly and there was ice forming on the tips of his fingers.

Vancleave's face was red. He ignored Piers, looking instead at Kieran.

"That is a direct order, Major. In case you have forgotten the oaths that you took, there are orders that cannot be disobeyed, not and have you keep your place. These two are undeniable assets in the war that we are fighting, and you *will* secure them for us."

"I will not," Kieran said, his voice even more furious. "They are not members of the Magus Corps, they have taken no vows, and they are not going anywhere that they do not wish to go."

Vancleave's eyes glittered with a cruel light. Kieran was a terrifying man when he was roused, but Hailey knew that you did not attain a high rank in the Magus Corps by being a coward.

"We are the Magus Corps, and we do what must be done. These two can save far more lives, kill far more Templars where we are going than they can hiding in this little mountain fairyland. You should understand that. We do what it takes to win our wars, Major."

"We do what we must do to protect Wiccans as a whole," snapped Kieran. "What I see now isn't going to protect anyone. What I see is a man hungry for a slaughter."

Vancleave started towards Kieran, but Piers got in his way, shoving him back with a strength borne of fury.

"You are no longer welcome within these walls, if you ever were to begin with," he snapped. "Now get the hell out before I haul you over the wall and drop you down a gorge."

Vancleave's temper seemed to snap then, because his hand dropped to the sword by his side. Whether he meant to use it or he only meant to threaten Piers with it, Hailey wasn't sure. Kieran on the other hand, who had been fighting for centuries, only knew one way to take a weapon that was being drawn on someone he cared about.

With a low roar that reminded Hailey more of a wolf than a man, he lunged towards Vancleave, ice forming around his hand and shaping it into a blade of ice.

Everything felt as if it was moving in slow motion. Hailey saw Piers throwing himself up into the air to get out of the reach of the general's weapon. She saw Kieran lunging forward. Then out of the corner of her eye, she saw something that made her heart stop.

The demon in chains roared hoarsely, and it took advantage of the distraction to throw itself into the fray. Somehow, it had worked an arm loose, and she saw four diamond sharp, twisted nails flash through the air. Hailey's breath caught in her lungs as it slashed towards Kieran's unprotected back. She saw that brutal hand come down, she saw it made contact.

All she could think was *no.*

Hailey reached out for the power that she knew was there. It was waiting for her, both Kieran's and Piers's. Without touching them, she had to pull harder, but she did it. The power pulsed inside her, all hers. What she wanted to do most right then was to protect the men dear to her.

Instead of freezing the demon in its tracks or setting it alight, she reached forward with invisible hands and found the thing's mind. What she discovered shocked her. There was an alien consciousness there, one that was made of nothing but heat and anger and fury. Connected to it, however, was a fibrous silvery strand, and on the other end was a human voice chanting something over and over again.

Hailey made out the words "let me go let me go let me go."

Without thinking, she reached out and took the silvery connecting cord in her grasp. She pulled as hard as she could. For a moment, there was absolutely no give at all. She was convinced that she couldn't do it, but with her last bit of strength, she tore it apart.

There was a brilliant flash of light that felt like it wanted to burn out everything she was. She screamed. She could hear it echo off the walls. She thought she was falling forever, but when she struck the pounded dirt of the training field, she realized that she had only fallen to her knees.

She could taste blood in her mouth. Then she was being turned over. Hailey smiled hazily when she recognized Piers's worried face over her.

"What happened?" she asked fuzzily.

"We could ask you the same thing," he retorted. "Look."

He turned her so that she could see the tableau just a short distance away. Vancleave, Kieran and Stephan all stood over the twisting demon on the ground. Vancleave had his sword drawn, Kieran spun razor sharp ice shards around his hands, and Stephan had a small silvery box that Hailey knew was at least as dangerous as the weapons carried by the other men.

The demon was no longer trying to capture or kill anyone. Instead, it writhed and moaned, clawing at its own face. As Hailey watched, however, she could see that its monstrous features were changing. They were twisting and shrinking. The process was a slow and painful one. None of the people watching it moved.

It soon became clear that it was changing what the demon was. After a few minutes, Hailey saw a face underneath the folds of flesh and what looked like protrusions of horn. The man's mouth was constantly stretched open in a howl of agony, but slowly, so slowly, the man was winning.

"Gods above," Piers whispered. "What did you do?"

The demonic features melted away from him. His body shrunk down. Soon, a man with brown hair lay stretched on the ground, panting hard and staring up at the sky. His eyes were a pale blue. Even Hailey could see them from where she sat. They were round with panic and fear.

It was Stephan who spoke first.

"Easy soldier. We're your friends here. We're with the Magus Corps. We want to help you."

The man struggled to a sitting position. Stephan had put away his weapon, but Vancleave and Kieran still held theirs warily.

"I'm Captain Jude Warwick of the Magus Corps," he said, panting softly.

It reminded Hailey eerily of the men they had found in the Alps. For a brief moment, they had been able to break free of the demons that held them, and when they did, they told Kieran their name and their rank before asking for death.

"I'm Major Stephan Martel of the Magus Corps," Stephan said quietly. "You're safe here."

The man looked up at him, clearly disbelieving. As Hailey watched, his face crumpled into tears. She could see the moment when he truly believed it. Unashamed, he wept into his hands.

"What have you done?" Piers repeated, dazed.

Hailey wished she could answer him.

• • • • •

They took the formerly possessed man to the infirmary where the infirmary keeper immediately put him on a liquid diet and shooed everyone else out of the room.

The lot of them milled in the corridor for a moment. Vancleave looked like he was ready to speak, but Kieran interrupted him.

"It is time for you to leave now, General," he said.

He was calm but there was a real menace in his voice.

"You do not command me, Major."

"I don't, but I have my own reports to make. What you are doing here verges dangerously close to sabotage."

Vancleave's face went brick-red. He looked like he was going to start bellowing, infirmary be damned, but then another voice cut through the air.

"He's right, General."

They all turned to Stephan, who was perfectly calm and self-possessed. Hailey knew that he must have been as shaken as the rest of them, but though he was a bit pale, he forged onward.

"What we have seen here is exactly what General Aroqua told us we would see. Major McCallen is working on developing a resource that we may very well need in the months to come. In my professional opinion as a weapons developer, to pull him away from his work would be disastrous. In addition to that, to try to force him to come along with us would be tantamount to destroying all of the work that he has put in."

"You don't know that," Vancleave began, but Stephan smiled, a narrow white thing.

Hailey realized that he was enraged.

"It doesn't matter," he said, his voice low. "What matters is what General Aroqua will think of it. What matters is how it will look when the others hear that you might have lost the war right here."

Vancleave stared at Stephan for a very long moment. Hailey could hear the tension in the air crackle. Kieran was quiet, watching the interplay warily, while Piers simply looked furious at not being able to run Vancleave out of his Castle.

Finally Vancleave cursed, spun around and walked out.

"I don't think he'll give you any more problems after this," Stephan said with a sigh. He shook his head. "What you are doing here is important. I truly believe that. You deserve the best chance you have, and that doesn't necessarily mean that the Magus Corps is on your side."

His words made Kieran flinch, but he nodded.

"Thank you. That could have gone very differently if you weren't there to step in."

Stephan smiled a little.

"There may be a very long war ahead of us, Major. I'd like to see you back to it sooner rather than later, but if you can come back with some real firepower, I'd like that even more. We can hold the line until you return."

After that, Stephan had to leave with Vancleave. Hailey wondered what was going to happen to him. He was the only

Magus Corps officer that she had ever had much contact with beyond Kieran.

"Hailey, are you quite well?"

She turned her curious gaze to Piers.

"I am, why do you ask?"

"Your eyes."

In her bathroom mirror, she gasped to see that her eyes were darker than they ever had been before. The purple looked even darker, the green even more vivid. It had its own sort of beauty, but the sight of it made her stomach turn.

"I think you need to tell us exactly what happened," said Kieran.

She came and sat between Piers and Kieran on her couch, taking a deep breath.

"He was going to hurt you," she remembered. "I didn't know what to do. I remember thinking that if I used fire or ice that I would hurt someone. I couldn't bear that. I…I guess I reached into his brain instead. It was like when I froze that Templar's blood, a little. I reached into his brain, and I found a…a cord…or something. It stretched from his mind to someone who just kept saying *let me out* over and over again. I didn't think about it. I acted completely on instinct. I broke the cord with my hands. Then you saw what happened. I was lucky. If it had turned out differently, I would have killed that man."

"The way I killed those men in the Alps," Kieran said, and she could hear the guilt thick in his voice.

"We could never have known that there was a way to heal them," she said. "At that point, there literally wasn't. The only reason that I could do this today was because of what happened between the three of us last night. Let that grief go, Kieran, it doesn't belong to you either."

Kieran nodded. She knew that at least he would try.

"But this does change things," said Piers slowly. "Those demons that the Magus Corps are going to go fight. They're not just demons any more."

"No," Hailey agreed. "They're people. They are people who have a chance of coming back, and of being healed."

"Could we do it?" Piers asked. "Would you have the power to do so?"

Hailey wanted to be able to say yes with everything that she had inside her. She wanted to be able to tell him that there was a way back for every demon-possessed man or woman. She thought of the intense will and power that it had taken her to do so, and she hesitated.

"It took so much," she said softly. "Not only from me, but from both of you."

"Not to mention what it did to her connection to the Shadow Walk Prison," Kieran growled. "You may not remember what happened, Hailey, but I do. It only took you a few seconds to sever the shackle between the demon and the man, but if you tried that with a horde? With fifty demons? With a hundred? You might win a handful free, but after that, they would overwhelm you."

"She wouldn't be alone," Piers pointed out. "The ones she healed would be there as well."

"They're not fit for duty," Kieran retorted. "Captain Warwick hasn't been missing all that long. I don't know the man, but I know of him. He wasn't fit for combat when Hailey brought him back."

Hailey laid her hands on theirs, bringing a halt to their discussion.

"I want to find a way," she said firmly. "This is my power and my choice. You can tell me that you will not help me, and I will understand, but I need to see this through to the end."

"I would never hold anything back from you," said Kieran, and Piers nodded as well.

"The Castle is protected," Hailey said. "Or at least, we believe it to be so. We should test it. We should learn more about what I can do. However, when we're not doing that, I need to find a way to help those people."

Piers looked concerned.

"Do you remember what you told Kieran?" he asked gently. "It is not your fault that they are trapped. It is only the demons that are to blame."

Hailey shivered.

"You didn't hear him," she murmured. "You didn't hear him saying *let me out* over and over and over again. If it had gone on long enough, if the demon had stayed seated in his body and kept him from it, it would have been all that he was able to say. He would have been a ghost haunting his own body with only those words left to guide him." She straightened up. "I will find out how to help those people.

CHAPTER SIXTY-TWO

HAILEY WANTED TO help the demon-possessed men and women that the Templars were using as a shock force more than anything. However, even she knew that it was easier said than done. In the days that followed, she was busy enough herself. The spell she had cast over the Castle seemed to be stable. It took them a few days to get the word out that the Castle itself was shielded, and some returning patrols still had problems.

She still worked with Piers and with Kieran on fine-tuning the powers that she possessed, but she spent an increasing amount of time with Liona as well. Some things she had to learn on her own, but there were other topics where Liona simply had years of knowledge.

Finally though, Liona had to shake her head.

"I want to give you the answers that you are looking for, but at the bottom of all of it, I just don't have them."

"Well, who does?" Hailey exclaimed in frustration. "Who do I need to talk to find out more about the Shadow Walk Prison?"

Liona's smile was rueful.

"If you wish me to be perfectly, brutally honest with you? No one. Witches and warlocks have never liked spending time in the Shadow Walk Prison. Some rare ones fall into it, and only a few fall out. Some go in seeking it, and you can imagine how few of those come back."

"Surely there are some people who can find their way in and out. Surely some have explored it."

Liona shook her head.

"As far as I can tell and as far as I know, you are the witch who has spent the most time in the Shadow Walk Prison in the last two hundred years. I wandered it a little, but then I realized that I very much preferred my heart and soul as mine rather than as demon food."

Hailey's frustration must have shown on her face, because Liona took her hand.

"Take heart, dear one," she said softly. "After all, I'm still here. I'm still waiting to see how it all turns out."

Hailey had almost forgotten how Liona's own gift had brought her away from her beloved Rome. Liona was a seer, a witch skilled in the art of seeing the future. For the first time in hundreds of years, she had found her vision clouded. After time and study, she realized that the source of the disruption lay with Hailey in Wyoming. Something that Hailey did or was about to do could change the future in an enormous way. The fact that it hadn't been the creation of the shield spell was troubling.

"I don't want any part in prophecies," Hailey muttered. "I just want to help those people."

Liona was quiet for a long time.

"I'm not Piers or Kieran," she said finally. "You're lovely, and perhaps one day we will love each other, but right now, I am at least capable of some objectivity. If you want to learn more about the Shadow Walk Prison, I think we both know that there is only one way that you are going to be able to do that."

Hailey was silent for a long time.

"You mean that I'll have to go back in again," she whispered.

"Yes. There are some things that can only be experienced.

There are reasons why witches and warlocks have steered clear of that realm for long centuries. The risk to you is very real. Right now, there are three choices available to you. You can ignore those possessed by the demons and allow the dice to fall where they may–"

"I can't do that."

"You can keep on searching for a solution in the books and in the experiences of those who have come before you."

"You just told me that there was no hope of that."

"Nevertheless, there may be some profit in it. There may be some forgotten tome or obscure witch who knows more than we ever dreamed. Or…"

"Or I can go back into the Shadow Walk Prison," Hailey said.

She felt a peculiar weight in her belly. She wasn't sure what she was feeling right then. Dread, certainly, and definitely fear, but she wondered if there was some kind of complicated longing there as well. The Shadow Walk Prison was a terrible place, but it had brought her, Piers and Kieran closer together than she had ever dreamed possible.

In many ways, she had learned to control that realm, to make it do the thing that she had needed. It was terrifying to think that it could be a place where she felt at home, but still she couldn't shake the feeling.

Liona leaned over to give her a hug.

"Your fate is your own," Liona said. "At the end of the day, it is always your choice. No one is going to force you or to take your choice away from you. No one is going to fault you. But Hailey? Right now I will tell you a secret, one that has kept me going for a very long time."

Hailey looked up, surprised. Liona leaned close to whisper in her ear.

"No one is going to be able to stop you either, brilliant girl."

Liona's words stayed with Hailey for the rest of the day. After dinner, she came to Piers's quarters, where she practically lived now. Kieran was often up and about, training when he wasn't working with her or Piers, but he had given up his own guest quarters as well.

She found them going over a map when she got in.

"What's this all about."

Piers spun the map towards her so that she could see that it was a map of the western United States. Locations marked in blue ink indicated the locations of the other large covens. Someone had traced a path that connected all of them.

"If you are willing, we thought that we could offer the protection of the camouflage spell to the other covens," said Piers. "It would be a thing that allowed the covens to be more independent and much safer."

Hailey traced her finger along the path, thoughtful.

"I do want to do that, but there are the Templars to consider. The demon-possessed are on the move."

"All the more reason to get started as soon as we can," said Kieran seriously. "The best offense is a good defense sometimes. This will save lives."

Hailey looked at him curiously.

"I had thought that you would be more invested in stopping the Templars in their tracks."

"I am, but I also know what battles need to be fought. The Magus Corps will engage with the demons directly. Our place should be one of defense."

Hailey smiled crookedly at her lover.

"I am glad that you are playing it safe. It just figures that right now, I don't want to agree with you."

Piers and Kieran regarded her warily.

"I want to take on the demon-possessed," she said quietly.

"Liona seems to think that means entering the Shadow Walk Prison again. I…am beginning to agree with her."

"Absolutely not," Piers said immediately. "That place almost cost us everything."

"You're not the one who gets to make that decision for me," she said firmly. "I would never force either of you back into that place. Your personal demons can grow very large there, and you're right, it almost cost us everything. The answers that I have been looking for live in that place, however. If there is no other way to get them, then I have no other choice."

"Think on it longer," Kieran said.

It surprised her in some ways that he had ended up the peacekeeper, the one who balanced out her views and Piers's.

"There have been no attacks yet," he continued. "We know very little of what is going on. I am in constant communication with other officers. When they know something, so will we. Acting without proper intelligence is suicide, and right now, we have very little."

Hailey reluctantly agreed. That was part of what was frustrating her. She had so little information, and there was simply so much she needed to know. For now, though, what she had would have to be enough.

Kieran and Piers pulled her into the shower with them. It was a pleasure all its own, and it didn't have anything to do with sex. They were establishing a fragile kind of domesticity in the middle of a very frightening time. It always felt as if the Templars were on the doorstep, but right now, sandwiched between her two naked slippery lovers, she felt as if nothing cruel or cold would ever touch them.

She closed her eyes blissfully as Piers sudsed her hair. She and Kieran tackled Piers with a towel, drying him vigorously until he cried for mercy.

It was home. It was more than she had ever expected. Sometimes she still thought that it was only a dream.

As she drifted off to sleep that night, she wondered if she should call off her search. Anything she found would be more than likely dangerous. She had a life that she would fight to keep. Endangering it seemed not only foolish but disrespectful.

Hailey's eyes drifted closed. Perhaps it was best to halt her search.

• • • • •

This time, Hailey knew that she was not truly in the Shadow Walk Prison. She was a wraith again, invisible and without form or substance. It should have disturbed her that she was becoming oddly comfortable with this place. Instead, she only looked around, wondering what it was she could find this time.

She emerged from a thicket of groaning trees, shivering when she felt their twigs brushing at her skin and the human voices that came from them. When she had first truly visited the Shadow Walk Prison on her own, she had almost become one of them herself. They were what became of people who had given in to despair. They took root, and ever after, they were left to mourn what they had become.

Directly outside of the grove, she found herself in what looked like a fortress courtyard. For a moment, she thought it was a dark reflection of her Castle, but when she looked more closely, she found that this was a place that was far more ancient, and far more grim. It was made of nothing but gray stone, with no comfort or joy in it. After a moment, she became aware of a number of voices whispering in a chorus of misery.

Something about it was different from the grove, however. She knew that there was something that needed to be found here. She knew that there was something she needed to see.

Bracing herself, she walked from the courtyard through the main gates. The great hall was empty and echoing. When she looked upwards, she could see tattered banners. Once she thought they must have represented royal houses with beautiful queens and brave kings. Now they were nothing but rags, the people that they represented long gone. She was wondering which hallway to explore when she heard two voices.

"I hate this place."

"Everyone does. You're not special."

They were two utterly human voices, and she responded to the fear that she heard in them. She followed them as best she could. Her path led her down a dark tunnel, one that started slanting deep underground. In a matter of moments, she could feel the chill of the place and the way it soaked through her clothes to make her skin rise up in goosebumps.

The voices faded and rose again as the tunnel twisted and turned. She knew that the two men were frightened and scared. She knew that they were guarding something. She had a tickle of a hope at the back of her mind for what it could be, but she ignored it.

Finally, she came to a place where she could see a light up ahead. She slowed her steps because she did not know how visible she truly was. She could see that the tunnel opened into a room, one that was lit with the flicker of torches.

She stayed in the shadows as best she could, but she soon realized that there was no need. The two men had no idea she was there. She could walk close to them if she wished. When she did, she felt a brief chill when she saw the insignia that they wore.

She didn't know what two Templars were doing in the Shadow Walk Prison, but whatever they were doing there, she could tell that they didn't like it. Occasionally they glanced behind them and around them. They both flinched when a low angry roar came out of the darkened room behind them.

"We have to go in there again," one of them said flatly.

The other nodded, reluctantly taking a torch from the wall. Even though they were part of an organization that had hunted her and people like her for hundreds, if not thousands of years, she felt a kind of pity for them.

Following them closely, she stepped into the darkened room right behind them.

The darkness seemed absolute. When she stepped into it, she immediately felt as if it was engulfing her, that she was drowning in sorrow. The torchlight was an island of sanity. She realized that they were surrounded by people, men and women both, and they were in chains. The light glinted flatly off their eyes, and they watched the two men with hate.

"All right," one man said. "Show us your chains."

Slowly, each of the people in the darkness held their chains up in their hands, showing the guards the unbroken length. One of the guards took a deep breath, and he began counting. Hailey felt the bottom drop out of her belly as the count grew to be more than fifty. Then it was more than seventy. Finally, it hit an even one hundred.

As he counted, she looked deep in the eyes of the chained people. They were mostly men, but there were some women. There were some who looked like they were barely out of their teens.

The Templars turned, relieved to go. As Hailey watched, however, a dark-eyed girl looped her chain around one upraised foot. The Templar, cursed, pinwheeling his arms in a panic before falling into the mass of chained bodies. The scream that he made tore right through Hailey's soul, making her scream as well.

She sat up straight in bed, the scream still on her lips. Piers and

Kieran jerked up out of their own sleep, Piers immediately touching Hailey to see what was wrong and Kieran scanning the room for some sign of threat.

"A nightmare?" asked Piers.

Hailey shook her head.

"No," she said softly, "but I think I know what we need to do.

• • • • •

"Are you absolutely insane? No."

Hailey bristled.

"Do you really think that you are going to get very far by taking that tone with me?" she asked angrily. "Do you think that you can order me around like I was a teenager getting your burger?"

"I think that you should listen to common sense," Piers snapped. "Hailey, you're not talking about a hike in the woods. You're talking about a journey into a place that left us all with scars and that nearly succeeding in keeping us more than once."

"I'm talking about a place where people are being held," she said. "Those people being guarded by Templars, those have to be the spirits that the demons have replaced. They weren't destroyed, and if Captain Warwick is any indication, they can be rehabilitated. They can be saved."

"At what cost? Hailey, we don't know what is really going on. They could be a trap. They could be something completely unrelated to the attack that we are facing now. There are too many variables to assume that going in is worth the risk."

"That is not a decision you get to make for me," Hailey cried, exasperated. "Liona, tell him!"

They were seated in Piers's office. Liona was perched on a window seat peeling an apple as if it mattered not a bit to her.

"Tell him what?" she asked. "You already have. What I will tell *you,* Hailey, is that you need to consider the risks as well. There is of course the risk of you being killed in the Shadow Walk Prison, or captured or enslaved forever."

"Oh yes, just that," Kieran murmured sarcastically.

"But more than that, there is the risk that you will simply be unable to leave."

Hailey frowned.

"My eyes."

"I see you have my meaning. Every time you step into the Shadow Walk Prison, it sinks its claws deeper and deeper into you. It turns into something that is more a part of you. Your eyes show us that."

"It doesn't mean that that place will defeat us," Hailey said.

Liona shrugged.

"Of course. Put it this way. If there were bets being taken, I would say that I believe in you more than I believe in the Shadow Walk Prison. However, that would be a very close thing."

Hailey sighed.

"Thank you for your honesty," she said.

She meant it though. Liona cared for her, but the other witch was deeply pragmatic.

Liona hopped off of the window seat.

"I have told you everything that I can tell you. At this point, Hailey at least knows more about the Shadow Walk Prison than I do. Kieran and Piers, you know more than most others. All I can tell you is that I have the utmost faith in all three of you. The future that I see is still murky, but I can tell that it is coming closer."

She closed the door behind her softly.

"So whatever we do, it's going to have vast and world-changing consequences," said Kieran drily. "That makes this ever so much easier."

Piers scowled.

"It shouldn't be easy. Hailey, there are so many risks to this. The worst part is that they are risks that we don't need to take. We may never need to take them."

"But we won," Hailey said.

Piers frowned at her while Kieran raised an eyebrow. She thought that in this matter she was closer to Kieran than she was to Piers. Piers liked things in certainties, and he placed the lives of his people at the highest priority. Kieran was used to weighing his options, taking risks and understanding that some sacrifices needed to be made.

"What are you talking about, Hailey?"

"The last time we fought the Shadow Walk Prison, we won," she replied. "Don't you remember that, at least, Piers? It tried to take us, and it couldn't. We defeated it."

"We got out with our skins," Piers sighed, but at least he looked a little more open to the idea.

They resolved to speak more on it later. Hailey was a little disappointed, but she knew that there was no leaving right away, not when Piers had so many responsibilities as coven master.

She assumed that there would still be time to figure out the intricacies of the trip, to learn what needed to be done and to make it easier.

She was wrong.

CHAPTER SIXTY-THREE

THE NEXT MORNING, she and Piers were trying to figure out where they could go to deploy their camouflage spell next. Some covens would benefit from it greatly, but their very obscurity would mean that it was difficult to get to them.

A knock on the door made Hailey look up in surprise, and she was even more shocked when the door opened before Piers even called out.

Julie appeared in the doorway, her face grim. Hailey was shocked to smell smoke on the other woman. Julie was a firecracker, what the Wiccan world called a witch who controlled fire. In the months that she had known Julie, however, Hailey had always seen a level-headed woman who loved her plane more than she cared about her more esoteric affinity with fire. Now, though, there was murder in Julie's eyes. She made the air crackle.

"Piers, there's Templars at our perimeter."

Piers immediately stepped away from the map, heading towards the window.

"Where? How far out?"

Julie's laugh was nasty.

"At our perimeter. Right by our wall. They're definitely looking for something. They've not tested the gorge yet, but they will."

Piers nodded, opening the window.

"Get all of the children and people who can't fight down to the cellars. After that, come looking for me."

He spared a glance at Hailey. She could tell that he was torn on where she should be, so she made the choice for him. She laid her hand on his elbow, pulling the energy from him as quickly as possible. Before he could say anything, she pushed herself out the window, flying towards the wall. She could hear him curse behind her as he did the same.

When they landed in the ramparts, there were already several people there. They were unaccountably quiet, staring over the edge. When she looked too, Hailey could see why.

There was a score of Templars just a hundred yards or so away from the base of the wall. They looked like men who were on business. They were armed, and she could tell that they were searching.

The illusion that she had created was one that stretched out beyond the walls. To the Templars, it looked as if they were standing close to the edge of a gorge. Though her illusion was sound, she felt sick to her stomach. It would only take one moment, one step to reveal that there was no gorge there but solid ground.

Kieran climbed up on the ramparts, his face grim.

"There are demons in the woods. The full hundred that Hailey saw in her dream unless I miss my guess. They're lying down with some Templars watching them, but they look ready for battle."

"Can we fight them?" Hailey asked, her voice hushed.

"We can defend against them, certainly," Piers said. "They didn't call in a helicopter strike after all. The Castle was designed to maintain defensive capabilities against Templars. If it was just those below? I'd bet on us on a heartbeat."

"But the demons..." Hailey said.

Piers nodded. "The demons are a game changer. We always

knew they would be."

Julie approached them, her face still tense.

"The kids and those who can't fight are below, boss. Got any orders for us?"

Piers thought for a moment.

"It looks like everyone's already at their watch stations. If they actually seem to figure out we're here, rain hell down on them. Until then…"

Hailey turned just in time to see one of the Templars wander a little closer to the space that she knew marked the edge of her illusion. He looked out over what he thought was a gorge, unaware that a dozen tense people were looking back from an invisible manor wall.

Hailey didn't realize that she was holding her breath until another Templar called. He turned away, making her breathe a silent sigh of relief.

"The Castle was never made to defend against demons," she said softly.

Piers looked torn, and then he nodded reluctantly.

"Every time we've faced a demon, we've barely survived it. Kieran, could the Magus Corps do any better?"

To Kieran's credit, he said nothing about Piers's asking after Magus Corps aid.

"No," he said flatly. "We're ready for combat, but the demons are something else again."

"All right," Piers said.

There was something final in his voice. Hailey knew what he meant even before he said it. Even though it was something that she wanted, it still made her ache to see him capitulate.

"I need an hour to make sure that the people of the Castle know what to do. Kieran, give the Magus Corps a full report of what is happening here. Let them know, however, that our role at the moment is purely defensive. Hailey…get Liona."

"We're going back into the Shadow Walk Prison," she said softly. He nodded.

"Gods above help us, but we are."

• • • • •

Hailey helped Liona get her supplies ready, and then she, Liona and Lucius brought them to the bedroom that she, Piers and Kieran shared.

"What do you see?" she asked as Liona set up her supplies. Liona glanced at her.

"I see greatness," she said softly. "I don't know how this will turn out for you or your men, dear one. Whatever you do is going to change the way our world works, however. If it is any comfort, all I know for sure is that I have complete faith in you."

Hailey smiled. Her stomach was churning with nerves, but in many ways, she felt ready. There was a kind of freedom in knowing that there were no other choices. She knew what she had to do. She was going to do it.

Lucius took her aside as Liona busied herself. In some ways, it was hard to remember that this man had been living in the forest for years, unaware of the woman who missed him so fiercely. Hailey supposed that when you had more than a thousand years to learn about yourself and who you were, you took transitions a little more easily. His curly hair was professionally dressed, and there was very little of the wolf in him, until you looked deeply into his eyes.

"Liona has faith in you, but do you have faith in yourself?"

Hailey shrugged uneasily.

"I know what needs to be done, and I know that I am going to do it. Does that count?"

Lucius's smile was rueful.

"It serves for most things. I am a veteran of many battles, Hailey. All of mine have been fought in the real world, but if you would listen, I have advice for you." When Hailey nodded, he continued. "Battles are won and lost by very small factors sometimes. Some battles will never be won no matter how much you fight, but others can turn on a missing horseshoe or a mislaid message. Sometimes faith in yourself and in the soldiers who fight with you are what it takes to turn a battle. Sometimes it's enough."

"Thank you," Hailey said. She would have said more, but at that moment, Piers came through the door, Kieran just a few steps behind him.

"How are things?" she asked, meeting them and accepting a kiss from both.

"Strained, as you may imagine," said Piers with a shrug. "People know what they can do. They know what Templars are capable of. If the Castle falls, there are ways out that will take them through the mountains."

Hailey had some idea how much it must have cost Piers to speak of the fall of his precious cathedral. She squeezed his hand tight, wishing that she could take away some of the fear in his voice.

"The Magus Corps is aware of what is happening here. The closest troops are close to a full day away. We can't risk tipping our hand and alerting the Templars to our presence by flying in, so the ones who can get here have a long hike in front of them."

Liona indicated that the three should lie down on the bed. Hailey lay in the middle, holding hands with both of them.

"I love you both so much," she whispered.

She tilted her head to kiss Kieran, and then Piers. They looked determined, and she felt a fresh surge of hope. They could do this. She knew that they could.

She felt a brief prick on her arm as Liona injected her with the drugs that could send them to the Shadow Walk Prison. Her vision immediately started to dim, and she was overcome with a sense of intense weariness.

"Gods go with you, beautiful ones," Liona murmured, and then Hailey felt nothing at all.

CHAPTER SIXTY-FOUR

WHEN HAILEY OPENED her eyes to see the Shadow Walk Prison's sullen sky, she was momentarily disturbed to realize that it didn't feel foreign to her any longer. Instead there was something intensely familiar about it, even a sense of comfort. Liona's words about getting lost in the strange realm ringing in her ears, she sat up.

To her surprise, instead of being in a field or in a forest grove, she was in a city. The buildings around her were blackened with soot, and the only cars that she could see were dismantled for their parts and sat like strewn, dead bodies on the broken streets. It reminded her of a few of the places that she lived. She swallowed hard before beginning to walk. More than once, she was convinced that there were eyes watching her from the broken windows, but whenever she focused on them, they disappeared.

Piers and Kieran, she thought fiercely. *If I can just focus on them, I can find them.*

She continued walking, ignoring the skitters of things that moved just beyond her sight. She knew who she was looking for, and she didn't want any distractions.

She turned a corner, and found Kieran waiting for her patiently underneath a shattered streetlight. He was dressed in a tunic and leggings bound up to his legs with straps. Over all of it, he wore a wolf fur thrown over his shoulders, which failed to hide the sword at his side. He looked every inch the mercenary he had been for his early life. Something about it did not look strange at all in this place.

Hailey embraced him for a moment because it was simply so good to feel him in her arms. Then with him by her side, they continued.

They found Piers just a few moments later. Of all things, he was in one of the shopfronts, intent on a pinball game.

"Piers?"

He looked up, faintly embarrassed.

"I probably shouldn't have underestimated how addictive these things are."

Hailey smiled. It was a relief, in some ways. They were still themselves. They were together. She had just learned that Piers liked pinball.

They made their way through the city. Sometimes they could feel eyes on their back. Once Kieran thought that he heard his name being called. Hailey fell into the lead, and she wondered if she should have been worried that she was so comfortable in this strange and dark place. Navigating it was becoming second nature to her.

She remembered the fortress that she had found in her dream, and she concentrated on it. The Shadow Walk Prison wasn't a real place, not like the Castle or a real country. It was a realm bounded by desires and dreams. She only had to remember how strong she was and how much she wanted what she did.

The buildings gave way to a grassy plain. When she looked back, the city was gone as if it had sunk beneath the rolling hills. They kept walking and soon enough, they saw the spires of the fortress.

"I don't know what we are going to find here," she said softly.

"I only know that we have to free the people inside."

Kieran unsheathed his sword, while Piers made one appear from nowhere. It occurred to her that her men were getting comfortable in the Shadow Walk Prison as well.

As it had been when she was last there, Hailey found the fortress deserted. She could hear the faint groan of desperate voices from the basement. Unerringly, she led them down the tunnels and the stairs. She realized that she didn't know the way precisely. With a certain kind of dream logic, she only understood that she wanted to know the way, so she did.

When they heard voices, Kieran and Piers took the lead. They were no branchings in the tunnel, and when they came to the lit area again, they immediately confronted the pair of Templars that they found there.

The Templars shouted with surprise, but they immediately fell back into the room, to Hailey's surprise.

"Kieran, Piers, stop!"

Hailey's shout came just in the nick of time. They halted in their tracks just short of falling into the darkened room where the prisoners were held. She came to join them, and together they looked in.

The two Templars were holding something in their hands that glowed bright blue. They were an island of light surrounded by chained people, a human defense wall. Those people in chains stared balefully at the Templars and at Piers, Hailey and Kieran as well.

"I don't think they know us," she whispered. "I think they have been so hurt and enraged that they might tear us to pieces as they would the Templars."

Kieran paced, a great tide of anger emanating from his body. "They're right there," he growled. "Cowards."

Cowards they might have been, but they were safe and

protected even in the midst of the possessed. Hailey realized uncomfortably that the longer they were allowed to shelter there, the more likely it was that they would summon reinforcements.

"Perhaps they won't harm us?" wondered Piers.

He reached tentatively in the room, but the hand that clawed at his answered that.

"They aren't animals," Hailey said suddenly. She wasn't sure if what she was thinking was going to work, but she had to try.

Clearing her throat, she stepped right up to the doorway. Suddenly, it felt as if every eye was on hers.

"My name is Hailey Devereaux," she said as loudly as she could. "I'm from the Castle, and I am here to help you. Please, let me try to break your chains. It will send you back to your bodies. It can take you back to where you were."

A moaning came up from the crowd of chained people. At first she wasn't sure if it was rage or even if they understood what she was trying to say. After a moment, an enormous man came to the front. He was easily as big as Kieran, perhaps even bigger. He stood impassively in front of her before kneeling down to show her his collar and chain.

Hailey bit her lip. The way the doorway was set up, she couldn't get to the man's chain unless she was willing to step into the room. She could feel the Templars' eyes on her. Piers was saying something, Kieran was already reaching for her.

Taking a quick breath, she stepped into the room.

She could feel the presence of the possessed all around her, but though they watched her closely, they did not reach for her. Carefully, she took the man's chain in her hands. Just as she had with Captain Warwick, she started to pull.

For a moment, she thought that it wouldn't work, that it was mere luck or chance she had freed Warwick. It was like pulling on steel cord. Then abruptly, the cord burst, and the man sprang to his feet. She could see light and life in his eyes now. He grinned fiercely at her, mouthing *thank you* before fading away.

Now the possessed were stirring, crowding close to her. She was weary from breaking that first chain, but she was exultant at her success as well.

"One at a time," she said. "I promise I will get to all of you, but in the meantime, Piers and Kieran must reach those men."

A path immediately opened up between the doorway and the Templars. The Templars turned to run, but a dozen hands caught them. Kieran walked along the path, followed by Piers, both their faces grim.

As Hailey turned to free a woman, she saw Piers pluck the blue device out of one of the Templar's frozen hands.

"I don't think you are going to need that again," he said.

• • • • •

Hailey worked for what felt like hours breaking the chains of the possessed. It was tiring and difficult work, but whenever she needed power or energy, she simply reached for Kieran or Piers, and they gave it to her.

A small eternity later, she had freed the last of the possessed, and the room was empty. She turned exultant eyes to her lovers.

"Let's go home," she said. "I want to see whether we've done well."

The first time she had been in the Shadow Walk Prison, she had dreamed their way home. This time, Hailey simply concentrated. As Piers and Kieran watched, she sketched the shape of a door in the air. As she worked, it took a solid form, becoming a door frame and a normal wooden door standing in the middle of the empty room.

Piers walked in a circle all the way around it, raising an eyebrow at Hailey.

"Go on, open it," she said.

When the door was opened, it led down a deep tunnel. At the very end of it, she could see a glint of light. It was so small, but she recognized it right away as the lamp from Piers's bedroom. Suddenly, she was so homesick she could barely breathe.

"Let's go home," she said exultantly.

They walked together through the door, or at least Piers and Kieran did. Hailey realized that she was stuck. No matter what she did, she couldn't make her feet cross the threshold. She couldn't move herself over the step.

Piers and Kieran, already in the tunnel turned to look at her.

"I can't move," she said, her voice choked with fear.

It was true. Piers and Kieran together couldn't pull her into the tunnel with them. Kieran couldn't pick her up and carry her. She couldn't run over it or jump over it.

Hailey sank to her knees in the room, looking at the door dumbly.

"Liona said it would happen," she whispered. "She said that I might go wandering and never come back."

"Liona says a lot of things," Piers said impatiently. "You are not stuck here."

It seemed to be true, though. No matter what she tried, Hailey couldn't pass through the door. When it threatened to waver out of existence, she panicked, slamming her hands down on it. It killed the last bit of hope in her.

"You both need to go through," she said finally. "I don't know how long I can keep the door open, and I don't know what might happen if you stay here. You've been in the Shadow Walk Prison almost as much as I have. You can't stay here."

Kieran was examining the door for what felt like the millionth time.

"We can keep trying," he started, but Hailey cut him off.

"No. No, Kieran. There is no time." Hailey did what she could to keep the sob out of her voice. "Don't you see? There's just no time."

She tried to pull Kieran towards the door, but it was like pushing on stone. He only looked at her steadily.

"It doesn't matter," he said softly. "There's all the time in the world. If you are not going through, then we continue looking until we find a way for you to get through as well."

She stared up at him.

"Don't you understand?" she said. "This isn't a matter of finding the right door. I'm not going to suddenly open a door that I can walk through. The Shadow Walk Prison doesn't work like that."

"I think the Shadow Walk Prison reflects our own thoughts and desires," said Piers gamely. "I think that we can find a way back. You were right. We beat this place before, we can do it again."

It seemed somehow particularly cruel to have her own words thrown at her like this. Why couldn't they understand?

"Go through the damn door!" she cried. "Don't you get it? I can't go through with you. I've stayed here too long."

To her shock, Kieran carefully and gently closed the door. Then, resting his hand over it, he caused it to disappear. He looked a bit self-satisfied for a moment and then he turned to her.

"You're the one who doesn't understand, Hailey," he said quietly. "If that isn't a way home for you, it's not one for us, either."

Hailey stared at him, her heart beating a hundred times too fast.

"You can't mean it." She turned desperately to Piers. "You can't agree with him. You have the Castle to get back to."

"That was something I settled before I came to meet you in the bedroom," he said. "I told Julie she was in charge in the event that I didn't return. If I didn't return in a month, she was to do what she saw fit."

"I spoke with my commandant," added Kieran. "He's not pleased, but he's not surprised, either. When old soldiers become unpredictable, well, usually it's best to let them have their way."

Hailey looked from one to the other, horror dawning on her.

"You have lives," she whispered.

Kieran nodded.

"We do. And our lives are with you."

She couldn't take it any longer. She fell down into a heap and cried. After a moment, Kieran and Piers crouched down with her.

"We can have a life here," Kieran said softly. "We are all of us stronger than this place, and we can shape it."

"Speak for yourself," Piers said with a snort. "I'm still certain we can find a way out."

Having their hands on her helped. She wasn't pulling power from them at the moment, but sensing it, Piers's light and Kieran's sea, helped keep her stable. Even then, though, she was exhausted. She had broken a hundred chains that day. She had found out that she wasn't going home. She had nothing left. Hailey started to fall.

I just want to go home, she thought miserably, as their hands grabbed at her suddenly limp body. *I'm with Kieran and Piers,* she realized as they caught her. Her vision was dimming. They were shouting her name, but more than that, they both held her. It was precisely where she needed to be. *I am home.*

• • • • •

Hailey awoke to the sound of shouting. At first she wanted to bury her head under the pillow, because surely it was too early for that. But then it struck her that she wasn't in a bed when last she remembered. She was in a broken fortress in the Shadow Walk Prison.

She sat bolt upright, ignoring the pain that shot through her skull. She was in bed, her bed, and beside her, Kieran and Piers were rousing as well.

Liona's smile was wide, but Hailey only had eyes for her lovers. In a moment, they were in each other's arms, holding each other, kissing each other, never wanting to let go.

"I thought we would be there forever," she whispered over and over again. "I thought we were lost."

"Never lost when I'm with you," Kieran said, spitting out a lock of her hair.

"Once again, I do think we would have found a way out of there," Piers said. "Even so, I am glad it happened sooner rather than later."

Hailey only slowly became aware of a pounding on the door. She looked up just in time to see the door blow open and an enormous man push his way in.

"Where is she? Where is the little redhead?"

Liona started forward, fire in her eye, but Kieran and Piers were quicker. Piers pulled a sword from who knew where, and the temperature of the room dropped substantially.

"Who wants to know?" demanded Piers.

The enormous man looked down on Piers from his great height, chewing on his mustache furiously. He was the first man whose chain she had broken, Hailey realized. In close quarters, he was even bigger, with long, blond hair and a braided beard that made him look like a Viking raider.

"I'm Asger Olafsson, warlord of the Solari, and I'm the one

who wants to know."

"Asger? Gods above, how extraordinary."

As if there were not men armed all around her, Liona stepped forward looking closely up into Asger's face. To Hailey's surprise, the man backed off almost immediately, putting some distance between himself and the small witch.

"Liona," he rumbled. "I should have known you would have had a hand in this."

"The things that you should know would just barely fill an ocean, I think," responded Liona tartly. She turned to the others in the room.

"Coven Master Piers Dayton, Major Kieran McCallen, Hailey Deveraux, this shaved bear is Asger Olafsson, the leader of what you would call the Magus Corps throughout most of the thirteenth century."

Kieran's jaw dropped.

"I've heard of you," he said unsteadily. "You disappeared."

Asger made a sour face.

"That I did, but now here I am, and I have that lass to thank."

Hailey found herself swept up into Asger's arms, hugged so tightly that she could barely breathe.

"Thank you," he whispered in her ear. "From the bottom of my soul, thank you."

When he put her down, Hailey turned to Liona.

"Liona, what do you see when you look ahead?"

Liona's gaze went blank for a moment, and then she smiled.

"Oh, well then." And she would say no more.

Hailey would have pressed her, but Liona handed her a mirror. For a moment, Hailey was confused, but when she looked, she grinned.

Her eyes were green again.

CHAPTER SIXTY-FIVE

THE WHOLE STORY was pieced together easily enough. After Hailey freed the demon possessed Wiccans, they turned on their Templars with an utter lack of mercy. One of the casualties of the attack was the Templar man with the black hair and the white beard who had almost killed Hailey. She was unsurprised to discover that he was someone that the Magus Corps had been after for some time. The actual hierarchy of the Templars remained a mystery, but he was a man who ranked close to the top.

The people who were rescued from the Templar's rule were being helped and healed at the Castle, though some of the closer covens had offered to take people as well. There were requests coming in from covens all over the world. People were looking for their friends, their children and their lovers.

Hailey had to talk to some of them. She had to tell some heartbroken people that their loved ones were not among those rescued, but often she could deliver joyful news as well. She still smiled when she heard a woman's sobs of joy from hearing that her lover was recovered.

Some days later, she finally managed to find the time to go looking for Liona. She felt her heart squeeze a little when she realized that Liona was packing up to return to Rome.

"I have a great deal of work to do after all," she said. "I've been away from Rome for quite some time, and Lucius should be home for at least a while. Perhaps we can convince Asger to come with us."

"Are you ever going to tell us what you see now that your vision is clear?" asked Hailey plaintively.

Liona turned to her with a smile.

"You have your ending. You, Kieran and Piers walked out of the Shadow Walk Prison whole of heart and soul after freeing a hundred people from the bondage of the Templars."

"Did we change anything at all?" Hailey wondered.

"The Templars have been dealt a heavy blow. They know that tactic will no longer work. There are now a hundred people in the world who would have been lost to it without you. Some of them are exceedingly powerful witches and warlocks. Others might have an untapped potential in them we cannot see. You have changed the world, dear one, and that is all I will say."

With that, Hailey had to be content.

She could see a little of it already. Asger had many questions for Kieran about what had happened to the organization he had ruled for almost a century, and the answers did not please him. Hailey wasn't sure, but she thought it would be very unpleasant to be in the high command of the Magus Corps for a little while.

For herself, she had come to a decision on a very important matter. She didn't know if it would change the world the same way that Liona said she had done in the Shadow Walk Prison, but she knew that it would change her life forever.

She spoke with Kieran and with Piers about it, and finally, on a full moon just six weeks after their return from the Shadow Walk Prison, Hailey bathed herself thoroughly, dabbing just a touch of musk behind her ears and at her pulse points.

In the dimness of the shower that now belonged to all of

them, she asked herself if she was ready. She found the answer was yes.

Stripped to the skin, she entered the bedroom where Piers and Kieran waited for her naked on the bed. There were no power games that night. There was no speech at all. Instead, it was only touch and mouths, moans and sighs.

She thought she would never get enough of them. She would always love the feel of Piers's hair in her fingers. She would always adore the press of Kieran's muscled thigh between her legs. Their mouths traveled all over her body, making her gasp and moan. She wasn't sure whose fingers brought her to her first climax. Her second, she was reasonably certain came from Piers. They loved the taste and feel of her as much as she loved the taste and feel of them.

She was a woman drowning in love and pleasure. She could think of fewer promising beginnings. When she was nearly wrung out from ecstasy, Kieran held up the white silk blindfold.

"Are you sure?" he asked, the first words he had spoken in hours.

Hailey smiled, nodding shyly.

"Completely," she replied.

The blindfold was knotted over her eyes with tenderness and care. Now she could feel their hands and their mouths and their bodies, but she couldn't see them at all. In short order, she lost track of who was kissing her and who was lapping at her neck. It was exactly as she had wished.

She reached for them, bringing them so close that they were almost one being. She knew she was ready for what came next.

Hailey felt one man pull her to his chest, holding her so that her back was pillowed against him. As his mouth toyed with her ear, the other man knelt between her legs, spreading her slick folds with his fingers. When she felt the tip of his blunt, bare cock, she whimpered.

The first thrust was so smooth and so sweet her nerves immediately sang. She had climaxed so many times already. She wasn't sure if she could do more, but here was her body insisting that she could.

"I want you," she whispered, reaching back to bury her fingers in one of her lovers' hair.

"I want you," she whispered, laying her hand on her other lover's hip.

It was a perfect rhythm that rocked her now. He thrust into her with gentleness and care, his breath roughening as they sped up.

She felt the other man's hand slide between their sleek bodies, seeking and finding her clit. She could have tried to guess who was who. She didn't.

The waves of pleasure rolled over her, rising higher and higher with every swell. Her climax broke over her like a spring rain. As she trembled, the man above her groaned, spilling inside her as well. She reveled in the heat and the wetness inside her. The meaning of it, the fact that she was now immortal, was lost to the pleasure and the sweetness of the moment.

Still blindfolded, she was lifted and carried to the shower. Only when all three of them were under the streaming water was the blindfold removed.

"I love you," she said softly. "I love you."

Piers and Kieran kissed her softly, murmuring love words in her ear.

We're home, she thought, joy rising to fill her like an infinite tide. *Forever.*

THE END

I hope you enjoyed getting to know Hailey, Kieran, and Piers. I'm a little sad to leave them! Though their story has concluded, more romance is available in RESCUED: Silver Wood Coven Book One.

RESCUED
Silver Wood Coven Book One

Templar Michael Charbon has been watching the young witch for months. Homeless, beautiful, and living in Central Park, she seems to charm everyone she meets. They shower her with kindness, and yet he never witnesses magic. Only when he rescues her from a rapist, does he understand why: Summer has no memory, not even of her real name. Though he barely resists her inexplicable pull on him, he would gladly break his vows to make her his own.

Magus Corps Major Troy Atwater is surprised to hear from Michael. But their long past together puts Michael's word beyond doubt. Troy collects the beautiful, young witch from the Templar, before her strange attraction drives half of New York wild. A powerful warlock in his own right, Troy manages to veil her seductive appeal, so that he and the coven can help her. But a passionate bond quickly envelopes them that goes far beyond her charms.

For her part, Summer's head is swimming. With barely a memory, she can hardly comprehend the ancient world of Wiccans and Templars. More than that she finds herself torn between two very different men. But as the extent of her powers reveal themselves and her deadly past returns in painful snippets, she finds that she isn't meant to be with Michael *or* Troy. She must have them both.

Excerpt:

RESCUED

Silver Wood Coven Book One

Warmth and the scent of wood smoke surrounded Summer as she opened her eyes and saw a crackling fire. Beneath her was a sinfully soft down comforter spread over a mattress, although she wasn't in a bed. She was curled on her side, her back pressed into against a broad, hard chest, and a heavy arm circled her waist.

"This is nice," she murmured, watching the flames through half-closed eyes. "How did I get here?"

"I carried you," Troy said softly in her ear. "You fainted in my arms, and I couldn't let you go." He paused. "You look beautiful in the firelight."

Summer shifted onto her back so she could see his face. The fire loved him, too, and streaked his thick black hair with glowing gold.

"Is this the curse talking, or you?"

"Me." His gaze moved all over her face. "Do you remember anything?"

"Floating. Pain. More pain." She watched him prop himself up on one elbow. "And weirdly-behaving water. That's all. Did I say anything this time?"

"Nothing that made any sense." He rested his hand on her belly and rubbed his thumb across the dent of her navel. "Except that I would make a fine mate."

She'd said that? She felt her cheeks flush. But his hand on her belly was moving insistently, and it made her bold.

"You'd make a fine anything," she said lowly. Warmth flickered to life beneath his broad palm, as she covered his hand with hers. "I know it's only been a week, but it's time to find out now, isn't it? About us, and how it could be."

"I already know." He lifted her hand to his mouth, and pressed his lips to her palm. "Let me show you."

Troy rolled on top of her, bracing himself with his hands to keep the bulk of his weight off her as he settled his lower body between her thighs. As soon as he dipped his head she met his mouth halfway, her lips parting as she accepted his hungry kiss. He used his wicked tongue to stroke hers, and worked an arm under her to lift her up in a sitting position before his hands got busy unbuttoning her blouse and sliding it down her arms.

"Oh." She broke their kiss with a gasp as he unclipped her bra and covered her bare breasts with his hands. "You're fast."

"I've been thinking about this every night since we got here. Believe me, this is slow." As he stroked his fingers over her nipples he watched her eyes. "It's a good thing that couch can't talk, either."

"Really." She smiled as she pulled his shirt over his head and dropped it before she ran her hands over his tightly-muscled chest. "If it could, what would it say?"

He leaned forward to whisper against her ear.

"Stop rubbing your cock, and go give it to that beautiful lady in the next room." He drew her hand down to the thick bulge in his crotch. "She'll know how to play with it."

"I can't really remember." Summer cupped the heavy length of his erection, squeezing it a little before she reached for the button of his jeans. "Maybe I should do a little hands-on research."

"Now who's fast?" Troy teased as he took her hand away and lifted her up to stand with him so he could strip off her jeans and panties.

He hissed in a breath when she leaned closer to rub her curves across his ripped abs. He lowered his head to touch his brow to hers as he cradled her breasts and massaged them. She pressed herself against his erection and slowly gyrated. He hissed again.

"You have a hundred years to stop doing that."

• • • • •

MORE BOOKS BY HAZEL HUNTER

THE HOLLOW CITY COVEN SERIES

A daring quest. A deadly enemy. A protector who won't quit. Although Wiccan Gillian Granger's life's work is finding a legendary city, her research in musty libraries hasn't prepared her for the field, let alone a gorgeous escort. Shayne Savatier knows he's on a milk run, especially after he meets his beautiful charge. But when enemies attack her, everything changes. Passion intertwines with protection, and duty bonds hard with desire.

Possessed (Hollow City Coven Book One)

Shadowed (Hollow City Coven Book Two)

Trapped (Hollow City Coven Book Three)

Sign up for my newsletter to be notified of new releases!

THE SILVER WOOD COVEN SERIES

Though she's taken the name given her by a kind stranger, Summer can no more explain waking up homeless and covered in blood, than she can the extreme attraction drawing people to her. Amnesiac, confused, and frightened, she's not even aware that she's a witch. But help arrives in two very different forms: the cool and restrained Templar Michael Charbon and his centuries-long friend Wiccan Major Troy Atwater.

Rescued (Silver Wood Coven Book One)

Stolen (Silver Wood Coven Book Two)

United (Silver Wood Coven Book Three)

Betrayed (Silver Wood Coven Book Four)

Revealed (Silver Wood Coven Book Five)

THE CASTLE COVEN SERIES

Novice witch Hailey Devereaux had resolved to live life as an outsider. Possessed of a unique Wiccan ability, her own people shun her. But that all ends when two very different men enter her life: the brooding Major Kieran McCallen and Coven Master Piers Dayton. But their training and tests are only the beginning. As she struggles to fulfill her destiny and find her place in the world, Hailey also discovers love.

Found (Castle Coven Book One)

Abandoned (Castle Coven Book Two)

Healed (Castle Coven Book Three)

Claimed (Castle Coven Book Four)

Imprisoned (Castle Coven Book Five)

Sacrificed (Castle Coven Book Six)

Castle Coven Box Set (Books 1 - 6)

THE MAGUS CORPS SERIES

Meet the warlocks of the Magus Corps, sworn to protect Wiccans at all costs. As they find and track fledgling witches, it's a race against an ancient enemy that would rather see all Wiccans dead. But where danger and intimacy come together, passion is never far behind.

Dominic (Her Warlock Protector Book 1)

Sebastian (Her Warlock Protector Book 2)

Logan (Her Warlock Protector Book 3)

Colin (Her Warlock Protector Book 4)

Vincent (Her Warlock Protector Book 5)

Jackson (Her Warlock Protector Book 6)

Trent (Her Warlock Protector Book 7)

Her Warlock Protector Box Set (Books 1 - 7)

THE SECOND SIGHT SERIES

Join psychic Isabelle de Grey and FBI profiler Mac MacMillan as they hunt a serial killer in the streets of Los Angeles. Even as their search closes in on the kidnapper, they discover not only clues, but a fiery passion that quickly consumes them.

Touched (Second Sight Book 1)

Torn (Second Sight Book 2)

Taken (Second Sight Book 3)

Chosen (Second Sight Book 4)

Charmed (Second Sight Book 5)

Changed (Second Sight Book 6)

Second Sight Box Set (Books 1 - 6)

THE EROTIC EXPEDITION SERIES

Travel the world in these breathless tales of erotic romance. Each features a different couple in fast-paced tales of fiery passion.

Arctic Exposure

A young couple is stranded in an Alaskan storm.

Desert Thirst

In the Sahara, a master tracker has the scent of his fiery client.

Jungle Fever

A forensic accountant blossoms under the care of a plantation owner in Thailand.

Mountain Wilds
A beautiful doctor on the rebound crashes with her pilot in British Columbia.

Island Magic
Two treasure-hunting scuba divers are kidnapped in the Caribbean.

THE ROMANCE IN THE RUINS NOVELS

Explore the ancient world and the new in these standalone novels of erotic romance. Each features a hero and heroine who come together against all odds, in exotic and remote settings where danger and love are found in equal measure.

Words of Love
Set in the heartland of the ancient Maya.

Labyrinth of Love
Set on the ancient Greek island of Crete.

Stars of Love
Set in the rugged Pueblo Southwest.

Sign up for my newsletter to be notified of new releases!

NOTE FROM THE AUTHOR

Dear Wonderful Reader,

Thank you so much for spending time with me. I can't tell you how much I appreciate it! My newsletter will let you know about new releases and *only* new releases. Don't miss the next sizzling, hot romance! Visit HazelHunter.com/books to find more great stories available *today*.

XOXO,
Hazel

Version 5.0

Made in the USA
Coppell, TX
26 March 2024

30582398R00415